GUY MANNERING

WALTER SCOTT was born in Edinburgh in 1771, educated at the High School and University there, and admitted to the Scottish Bar in 1792. From 1799 until his death he was Sheriff-Depute of Selkirkshire, and from 1806 to 1830 he held a well-paid office as a principal clerk to the Court of Session in Edinburgh, the supreme Scottish civil court. From 1805, too, Scott was secretly an investor in, and increasingly controller of, the printing and publishing businesses of his associates, the Ballantyne brothers.

Despite suffering crippling polio in infancy, conflict with his Calvinist lawyer father in adolescence, rejection by the woman he loved in his twenties, and financial ruin in his fifties, Scott displayed an amazingly productive energy and his personal warmth was attested by almost everybody he met. His first literary efforts, in the late 1790s, were translations of romantic and historical German poems and plays. In 1805 Scott's first considerable original work, *The Lay of the Last Minstrel*, began a series of narrative poems that popularised key incidents and settings of early Scottish history, and brought him fame and fortune.

In 1813 Scott, having declined the poet-laureateship and recommended Southey instead, moved towards fiction and devised a new form that was to dominate the early-nineteenth-century novel. *Waverley* (1814) and its successors draw on the social and cultural contrasts and the religious and political conflicts of recent Scottish history to illustrate the nature and cost of political and cultural change and the relationship between the historical process and the individual. *Waverley* was published anonymously and, although many people guessed, Scott did not acknowledge authorship of the Waverley Novels until 1827. Many of the novels from *Ivanhoe* (1819) on extended their range to the England and Europe of the Middle Ages and Renaissance. Across the English-speaking world, and by means of innumerable translations throughout Europe, the Waverley Novels changed forever the way people constructed their personal and national identities.

Scott was created a baronet in 1820. During the financial crisis of 1825–6 Scott, his printer Ballantyne, and his publishers Constable and their London partner became insolvent. Scott chose not to be declared bankrupt, determining instead to work to generate funds to pay his creditors. Despite his failing health he continued to write new novels, to revise and annotate the earlier ones for a new edition, and to write a nine-volume *Life of Napoleon* and a history of Scotland under the title *Tales of a Grandfather*. His private thoughts during and after his financial crash are set down in a revealing and moving *Journal*. Scott died in September 1832; his creditors were finally paid in full in 1833 from the proceeds of his writing.

PETER GARSIDE, born 1942, was educated at Cambridge and Harvard universities, and works at Cardiff University, where he is a Professor in English Literature and Chair of the Centre for Editorial and Intertextual Research. He is a member of the editorial boards of the Edinburgh Edition of the Waverley Novels and the Stirling/South Carolina Research Edition of the Collected Works of James Hogg, and is also one of the general editors of *The English Novel, 1770–1829: A Bibliographical Survey of Prose Fiction Published in the British Isles* (2 vols., 2000). He has also written widely on aspects of Romantic fiction, Scottish literature and publishing history.

JANE MILLGATE is Emeritus Professor of English at the University of Toronto. She is the author of *Macaulay* (1973), *Walter Scott: The Making of the Novelist* (1984), *Scott's Last Edition: A Study in Publishing History* (1987), and of numerous articles on nineteenth-century literature and the History of the Book. Her *Union Catalogue of the Correspondence of Sir Walter Scott*, comprising approximately 14,000 records for letters from and to Scott, is available on the National Library of Scotland website.

DAVID HEWITT, born in 1942, was brought up in the Borders, and studied English at the University of Edinburgh. Since 1994 he has been Professor in Scottish Literature at the University of Aberdeen. He has published widely on Scottish and Romantic literature, and is editor-in-chief of the Edinburgh Edition of the Waverley Novels.

CLAIRE LAMONT is Professor of English Romantic Literature at the University of Newcastle upon Tyne, specialising in the study of English and Scottish poets and novelists of the late eighteenth and early nineteenth centuries. She has published editions of *Waverley* (1981) and *The Heart of Midlothian* (1982), and is Advisory Editor for the Waverley Novels in Penguin and the Textual Adviser for the new Penguin edition of the novels of Jane Austen.

WALTER SCOTT

GUY MANNERING

Edited by
P. D. GARSIDE
with an introduction by
JANE MILLGATE

PENGUIN BOOKS

PENGUIN BOOKS

Published by the Penguin Group
Penguin Books Ltd, 80 Strand, London WC2R 0RL, England
Penguin Putnam Inc., 375 Hudson Street, New York, New York 10014, USA
Penguin Books Australia Ltd, 250 Camberwell Road, Camberwell, Victoria 3124, Australia
Penguin Books Canada Ltd, 10 Alcorn Avenue, Toronto, Ontario, Canada M4V 3B2
Penguin Books India (P) Ltd, 11, Community Centre, Panchsheel Park, New Delhi – 110 017, India
Penguin Books (NZ) Ltd, Cnr Rosedale and Airborne Roads, Albany, Auckland, New Zealand
Penguin Books (South Africa) (Pty) Ltd, 24 Sturdee Avenue, Rosebank 2196, South Africa

Penguin Books Ltd, Registered Offices: 80 Strand, London WC2R 0RL, England

www.penguin.com

First published 1815
Published in the Edinburgh Edition of the Waverley Novels by
the Edinburgh University Press 1999
Published with revised critical apparatus in Penguin Classics 2003
026

Typeset in Linotype Ehrhardt

Printed and bound in Great Britain by Clays Ltd, Elcograf S.p.A.

CONTENTS

ACKNOWLEDGEMENTS

The editors of a critical edition incur many debts, and the indebtedness of the editors of the Edinburgh Edition of the Waverley Novels and of its paperback progeny in the Penguin Scott is particularly heavy. The universities which employ the editors (in this case Cardiff University) have, in practice, provided the most substantial assistance; but in addition the Universities of Edinburgh and of Aberdeen have been particularly generous with their grants towards the costs of editorial preparation, and it has been the support of the Humanities Research Board of the British Academy that has allowed the Edition to employ a research fellow.

The Edinburgh Edition of the Waverley Novels has been most fortunate in having as its principal financial sponsor the Bank of Scotland, which has continued its long and fruitful involvement with the affairs of Walter Scott. The P. F. Charitable Trust and the Robertson Trust have also given generous grants.

Scott's manuscripts are widely distributed, but the greatest concentrations are in the National Library of Scotland in Edinburgh and the Pierpont Morgan Library in New York, the latter of which owns the manuscript of *Guy Mannering*. Without their preparedness to make manuscripts readily accessible, and to provide support beyond the ordinary, this edition would not have been feasible.

The editors have, perforce, had to seek specialist advice on many matters, and they are most grateful to their consultants, Professor John Cairns, Professor Thomas Craik, Caroline Jackson-Houlston, Professor David Nordloh, Roy Pinkerton, and Professor David Stevenson. They owe much to their research fellows, Mairi Robinson, Dr Alison Lumsden, and Gerard Carruthers. They have asked many colleagues far and wide for information. They have continuously sought advice from the members of the Scott Advisory Board, and are particularly grateful for the support of the late Sir Kenneth Alexander, Professor David Daiches, Professor Douglas Mack, Professor Jane Millgate, and Dr Archie Turnbull.

Additionally, the editor of *Guy Mannering* would like to thank the following for specific advice, information, or assistance: Dr Ian Clark, Professor Rainer Emig, Professor Hans de Groot, Dr Gillian Hughes, Tony Inglis, the late Robin Moffet, Dr Sharon Ragaz, Dr Michael

J. H. Robson, the late William Ruddick, the late Margaret Tait and Professor Rainer Schöwerling.

To all of these the editors express their thanks, and acknowledge that the production of the Edinburgh Edition of the Waverley Novels and the Penguin Scott has involved a collective effort to which all those mentioned by name, and very many others, have contributed generously and with enthusiasm.

David Hewitt
Editor-in-chief and general editor for this title

Claire Lamont
Advisory editor, the Penguin Scott and general editor for this title

J. H. Alexander,
P. D. Garside,
G. A. M. Wood
General editors

THE WAVERLEY NOVELS IN PENGUIN

The novels of Walter Scott published in Penguin are based on the volumes of the Edinburgh Edition of the Waverley Novels (EEWN). This series, which started publication in 1993 and which when complete will run to thirty volumes, is published in hardback by Edinburgh University Press. The Penguin edition of *Guy Mannering* reproduces the text of the novel, Historical Note, Explanatory Notes and Glossary unaltered from the EEWN volume. It does not reproduce the substantial amount of textual information in the Edinburgh Edition but instead provides, in the following paragraphs, a summary of general issues common to all Scott's novels and, in the Note on the Text, a succinct statement of the textual history of *Guy Mannering*. A new critical introduction has been written specifically for the paperback, as well as a Chronology of Scott's life and a list of recommended further reading.

The most important aspect of the EEWN is that the text of the novels is based on the first editions, corrected so as to present what may be termed an 'ideal first edition'. Normally Scott's novels gestated over a long period: for instance, the historical works on which he drew for *The Tale of Old Mortality* (1816) had all been read by 1800. By contrast the process of committing a novel to paper, and of converting the manuscript into print, was in most cases extremely rapid. Scott wrote on only one side of his paper, and he used the blank back of the preceding leaf for additions and corrections, made both as he wrote and as he read over what he had written the previous day. Scott's novels were published anonymously—hence the title 'the Waverley Novels', named after the first of them—which meant that only a few people could be allowed to see his handwritten manuscript. Before delivery to the printing-house, therefore, the manuscript was copied and it was the copy that went to the compositor. The person who oversaw the printing of Scott's novels was his friend and business partner James Ballantyne, with whom he jointly owned the printing firm of James Ballantyne & Co. from 1805 (except for the period 1816–22 when Scott was sole partner) until they both became insolvent in 1826.

The compositors in the printing-house set the novels as copy arrived, and while doing so they inserted the great majority of the punctuation marks, normalised and regularised the spelling without standardising it, and corrected many small errors. It was in the printing-house that the presentation of the texts of the novels was changed from the conventions appropriate to manuscript to those of a printed novel of the early nineteenth century. Proofs were corrected in-house, and then a new set of proofs was given to Ballantyne, who annotated them prior to sending them to the author. Scott did not read his proofs against his manuscript or against the printer's copy; he read for sense and, making full use of the prerogatives of ownership, he took the opportunity of revising, amplifying, and even introducing new ideas. Thus for Scott reading proofs was a creative rather than just a corrective engagement with his texts. The proofs went back to Ballantyne, who oversaw the copying of Scott's new material on to a clean set of proofs and its incorporation into the printed text. Only occasionally did Scott see revised proofs. Two points in particular might be noted about the above procedures. First, Scott delivered his manuscript in batches as he wrote it, and the result was that the first part of a novel was set in type, and proofs corrected, before the end was written. And secondly, in the business of turning a rapidly written text from manuscript to print Scott was indebted to a series of people, copyist, printer, proof-reader, whom Scott editors have come to refer to as 'the intermediaries'.

The business of producing a Waverley novel was so pressurised that mistakes were inevitable. The manuscript was sometimes misread or misunderstood (Scott's handwriting is neat but his letters poorly differentiated); punctuation was often inserted in a mechanical way and the implication of Scott's light manuscript punctuation lost; period words were sometimes not recognised and more obvious, modern terms were substituted for them. The EEWN has examined every aspect of the first-edition texts in the light of the manuscript and the full textual history of the novel. This has enabled the editors to correct the text where Scott's intentions were clearly not fulfilled in the first edition. The EEWN corrects errors, but it does so conservatively bearing in mind that the production of the printed text was a collective effort to which Scott had given his sanction.

Most of the Waverley Novels went through many editions in Scott's lifetime; Scott was not normally involved in the later editions although very occasionally he did see proofs. But in 1827, after his insolvency the previous year, it was decided to issue the first full collected edition of the Waverley Novels, and much of Scott's time in the last years of his life was committed to writing introductions and notes, and to reviewing his text for what he called his 'Magnum Opus' ('Great Work'), or Magnum for short. Scott had acknowledged his authorship of the novels in 1827, and this enabled him to describe the origins of his novels in the introductions to the Magnum edition in a way which was impossible to an author seeking anonymity. The Magnum (48 vols, Edinburgh, 1829–33) has formed the basis of every edition of the Waverley Novels published from Scott's death in 1832 until the EEWN chose the first editions as its base-text. In the EEWN the additions made for the Magnum will be published in two volumes at the end of the series. In the volumes published in Penguin, passages from the Magnum Introduction relating to the genesis of the novel are included in the new original material produced for the paperback edition.

This edition of Scott in Penguin offers the reader a text which is not only closer to what the author actually wrote and intended but is also new in that it uses for the first time material recovered from manuscripts and proof-sheets, revealing to fuller view the flair and precision of Scott's writing. In addition it supplies the editorial assistance necessary for a modern reader to interpret and enjoy the novel.

David Hewitt
Editor-in-chief
The Edinburgh Edition of the Waverley Novels

INTRODUCTION

THE 'AUTHOR OF WAVERLEY' AND WALTER SCOTT

Waverley, published in 1814, was the earliest of Scott's novels. The second, *Guy Mannering*, was the first to carry on its title-page the ascription 'By the Author of Waverley', and when *Mannering* proved as popular as its predecessor the new authorial persona rapidly became the best-selling novelist of the age. At the time of *Mannering*'s publication at the end of February 1815, its readers could either accept the unknown author as a new arrival or attempt to find a likely candidate among existing literary figures. The latter response was much the more common, and far and away the most popular choice was the poet Walter Scott, already famous worldwide as the author of *The Lay of the Last Minstrel* (1805), *Marmion* (1808), *The Lady of the Lake* (1810), *Rokeby* (1813), and *The Lord of the Isles* (published only weeks before *Mannering* at the beginning of January 1815).

These six-canto verse romances, all but one set in Scotland or the Borders and involving figures from Scottish history as well as fictional protagonists, had become hugely famous. Not only were the songs they contained set to music and sung in every drawing room, but dramatisations of entire narratives were quickly mounted, to be followed almost immediately by operas, so that *The Lady of the Lake* in the guise of *La Donna del Lago* became as well known in Europe and America as throughout the British Isles.[1] *Mannering*'s teasing of the reader with the possibility that the 'Author of Waverley' might be one and the same with the poet Walter Scott marked in fact the beginning of the anonymity game that Scott thereafter played with the readers of his novels—a game whose bravura complexities were ratcheted up with the appearance of each successive title and the emergence over time of a whole series of subordinate narrative personæ.

The question of why Scott moved from poetry to fiction remains vexed. His own explanation, as enshrined and amplified after his death in the seven-volume biography published by his son-in-law John Gibson Lockhart in 1837–38, was that Byron beat him, the immense and instant popularity of the younger poet's exotic Eastern tales having displaced their Scottish predecessors in the public favour. But Scott always preferred simple narrative to complex self-analysis, and the actual situation was much less straightforward. In *Rokeby* (1813), the least successful of his poems, and the only one with a purely English setting, Scott had found himself pushing against the limitations of the flat patterning that characterised the narrative strategies of his poems. Their conventions—involving fixed characters, limited time-frames, and actions composed of a continuous series of high points with no free scenes—precluded psychological complexity or a realistic depiction of historical and regional particularity. *Rokeby*, in particular, has restricted temporal and moral dimensions and an excessively literary apparatus: its pirates, outlaws, and burning castles remain too obviously pasteboard. For all the local colour Scott is so careful to include,[2] the poem's setting presents an unreal world, and his struggles to psychologise the portraits of the paired protagonists, Wilfred and Redmond, similarly end in failure.

Scott, one of whose favourite mottoes was, 'If it is na weel bobbit we'll bobb it again,'[3] had not forgotten the lessons of *Rokeby*, and *Mannering* displays in some respects a curiously antiphonal relationship to that poem, exploiting as it does the narrative possibilities of the double hero and providing melodramatic smugglers to match *Rokeby*'s pirates. At the same time the temporal and geographical dimensions of *Mannering* are significantly broader, its scope extends to the domestic as well as to the heroic side of life, and it shifts, above all, from a detached to an engaged form of presentation, one in which the narrative is no longer external to the characters but sees with them and dramatises their lives in process. The transition from verse to prose narrative thus enabled Scott to make of the journey into the other world of romance not simply a transition to *there* rather than *here*, *then* rather than *now*, but an encounter with an actual place with a geography, history, and culture of its own, and with established connections in time and space to the ordinary world inhabited by author and reader.

WAVERLEY AND ITS SUCCESSORS AS HISTORICAL NOVELS

Where early readers searched diligently for connections among *Mannering*, *Waverley*, and the immensely popular poems that preceded them, later readers, blissfully unaware of the detail of the poems, have too often concentrated simply on Scott's novels and succumbed to an uncritical assumption that one narrative set in eighteenth-century Scotland is much like another, and that little significance attaches either to the shift from the 1740s of *Waverley* to the 1780s of *Mannering* or to the change of setting from the east of Scotland to Dumfries and Galloway in the south-west. Because the words 'By the Author of Waverley' became very quickly the sign of a text's inclusion in a long series of historical novels with (for the most part) Scottish settings and plots that commingled private narratives with well-known historical events, *Mannering*'s status as the second of the series has profoundly affected subsequent critical responses to this novel. Particularly in recent years there have been many lamentations about the paucity of historical detail, the difficulty of precisely dating the main events, and, more comprehensively, *Mannering*'s failure to square with the Georg Lukács view of Scott's role in historicising the nineteenth-century novelistic imagination.[4]

It seems clear, however, that by withholding his name from the title-page of *Mannering* Scott was challenging his readers to find differences as well as similarities when making comparisons either with *Waverley* or with the poetry of Walter Scott. To place too much stress on the affinities between *Mannering* and its predecessor and successors among the Waverley Novels is to risk missing the originality of this second work of fiction: not only do its historical and geographical settings differ substantially from those of *Waverley*, but its narrative strategies are distinct, original, and deliberately experimental. Though both novels clearly exemplified what came increasingly to be known as the 'Scotch novel', much of the action of *Waverley* took place in the officially 'romantic' Highlands and dealt with the historically dramatic events of Bonny Prince Charlie's attempt to win the British throne back for the Stewarts in 1745–46. *Mannering*, on the other hand, was located in a part of Scotland with literary associations that were far less well developed and of relatively recent date. After all, when Scott sat down to write *Mannering* in the Christmas vacation of 1814–15, the time gap separating him from the moment of the novel's main action amounted to a mere thirty years or so, well within the memory of many in his audience.

ORIGINS OF THE NARRATIVE MATERIAL

Where *Waverley* had been written in at least three tranches several years apart, *Mannering* was the product of a single outpouring from December 1814 to February 1815, impelled forward by the enormous relief Scott felt at escaping the 'peine forte et dure' of composing *The Lord of the Isles*.[5] But if *Mannering* marks the point at which the novelist unequivocally supplanted the poet, the problem of tracing the novel's genesis and origins is complicated by Scott's adoption, apparently before composition had even begun, of a subtitle harking back to a type of Gothic fiction that by 1815 had already become very stale novelistic goods. Having allowed the subtitle 'The Astrologer' to appear in advertisements for the new work, Scott was obliged to retain it. In Chapter 11 of the published novel, however, after the youthful Guy Mannering of the opening has been replaced by the much more complex middle-aged figure of Colonel Mannering, Scott mischievously arranges for the Colonel to overhear what local storytelling has made of his student-of-astrology younger self: 'an ancient man, strangely habited', with 'a grey beard three quarters lang', who, after casting the horoscope of the newborn heir of Ellangowan, had 'vanished away, and no man of this country ever saw mair o' him' (64). The astrologer's horoscope is indeed reinvoked later as one of many markers confirming the inevitability of the plot's denouement, but the troublesome subtitle has been effectively disposed of.

What still remains, however, is the question of Scott's sources for the novel's setting and narrative materials. In *Waverley* the interweaving of the private action with the most famous sequence of historical events in Scotland's recent past meant that its locations came ready imbued with an almost legendary fame, so that no reader needed to ask: why then, why there? But *Mannering*, in the words Scott used to his friend Morritt in a letter of 19 January 1815, is specifically 'a tale of private life,'[16] set in the recent past and in parts of Scotland about which history—and Scott the poet—had been relatively silent. Lockhart's biographical amplification of Scott's own 1829 discussion of the novel's genesis in the introduction to the Magnum Opus edition of the novel has created the impression that the material of the novel had to be deliberately got up, and that Joseph Train, a Galloway Customs officer and amateur antiquarian, was a major source. It is true that Train had introduced himself to Scott in July 1814 by sending a small volume of his own poems, *Strains of the Mountain Muse*, and offering further information on local legends, and that he remained for the rest of Scott's life both an eager supplier of Galloway anecdotes and legends and a persistent petitioner for letters supportive of his own advancement in the Excise service. But when sending Lockhart biographical information following Scott's death, Train not only overstated the importance of the documentary materials supplied for *Mannering* but implied that they had been sent at an earlier date than was actually the case.

Peter Garside, in his account of the genesis of *Mannering* in the Edinburgh Edition of the Waverley Novels edition of the novel, argues far more convincingly that Scott's indebtedness was primarily to sources within his own family and specifically to his sister-in-law Elizabeth McCulloch Scott, who was married to his brother Thomas. Garside offers persuasive evidence of similarities between the family history of the McCullochs and that of the Bertrams of Ellangowan. James Murray McCulloch, Elizabeth's elder brother, lived at Ardwall close to Gatehouse of Fleet, right in the heart of *Mannering* country, and although Scott himself in his 1829 introduction lent support to the tradition that Caerlaverock Castle, on the coast to the south of Dumfries, was a possible original for Ellangowan Old Place, a stronger case can in fact be made for Barholm Castle, closer to Gatehouse, the home of another branch of the McCulloch family.

James Murray McCulloch was also the likeliest source of Scott's information about the gypsies of Galloway. Scott had long been familiar with the gypsies of Kirk Yetholm in Roxburghshire, close to one of his childhood homes at Kelso, and contributed information about them to an article on gypsies in the first issue of *Blackwood's Edinburgh Magazine* in April 1817, but McCulloch was probably the author of an article on the Galloway gypsies that followed in the August 1817 issue of the same magazine. The McCulloch family had in any case tolerated for nearly a century the presence on their lands of the family of the famous Galloway gypsy William Marshall (d. 1792), and Scott seems to have combined information about the Marshall clan with what he already knew about the Yetholm gypsy family of Gordon. The identification of Meg Merrilies with Jean Gordon, the most notable of the Yetholm gypsies, first made in the April 1817 *Blackwood's* article, was later confirmed by Scott in his own correspondence and in the 1829 Magnum introduction.[7]

Such combining of what he learned from others with what he knew from personal experience was typical of Scott's handling of sources in *Mannering*, and if McCulloch family talk provided a good deal of the background material for the novel it was certainly supplemented by memories from the outset of Scott's own career. As a young lawyer, in 1793, he had unsuccessfully defended before the General Assembly of the Church of Scotland the Rev. M'Naught, minister in the parish of Girthon near Gatehouse, who was charged with a range of scandalous clerical conduct as well as with abuse of his office of Justice of the Peace. M'Naught's failings may or may not have been deliberately echoed within the novel in the delinquencies of Godfrey Bertram, but Scott's still-surviving law papers for the case certainly reveal a detailed knowledge of the lower aspects of Galloway life at a time only ten years removed from that of the main action of *Mannering*. And though 'lost heir' plots were the stuff of many traditional tales in Galloway and elsewhere, convincing evidence can also be adduced that Scott may have had in mind some of the famous cases he heard about during his legal training—in particular the case of the Annesley claimant from the 1740s. Closer to home was the case of Routledge against Carruthers, which involved legitimacy issues and which was heard repeatedly by the Court of Session in the years just before the composition of *Mannering*. Scott himself, in his role as Clerk to the Court of Session, wrote the interlocutor or summary of the judgment in this case.[8]

As far as personal acquaintance with Galloway went, Scott had to rely on what he had learned in 1793 and during a short visit in 1807, but for Dandie Dinmont's Liddesdale and the legal world of Pleydell's Edinburgh he had far larger funds of direct experience available. For seven years, from 1792 onwards, Scott had devoted substantial portions of his summer vacations to a series of 'Border raids' in search of traditional ballad material, and Liddesdale's remote fastnesses drew him repeatedly back even after 1797, when marriage had somewhat limited his summer rambles.[9] On such occasions he would often sleep the night in farmhouses much like the novel's Charlieshope, and Robert Shortreed, his frequent companion in these expeditions, later provided Lockhart with a number of candidates for the original of Dandie Dinmont. For Pleydell Scott could draw upon several representatives of the old school of Edinburgh lawyers whom he had encountered when pursuing his own legal studies in the late 1780s, as well as upon still older figures who, though deceased, had remained within the profession the subjects of legend and anecdote. The identification of actual figures who had served, at least in part, as the 'originals' for Dinmont, Pleydell, or Meg Merrilies became a favourite nineteenth-century pastime, and the relevant evidence is set out in the Historical Note to the present edition. But Scott, of course, modified, adapted, combined and in any case transcended such sources, creating through the power of his novelistic imagination vivid and idiosyncratic figures who seemed to take on such independent lives of their own that readers were apt to speak of Dandie and Meg as though they had known them personally.

GUY MANNERING AND INDIA

Like many Scots of his generation and class, Scott had a large network of Indian connections. Accounts of the Scottish diaspora during the eighteenth and nineteenth centuries frequently quote his reference to India as 'the Corn Chest for Scotland where we poor gentry must send our younger sons as we send out black cattle to the South,'[10] and readers of his correspondence will know how often he found himself interceding on behalf of young fellow countrymen anxious to find employment in India. The most obvious target for such intercessions was Scott's old schoolfriend Robert Dundas, second Viscount Melville, who for many years oversaw affairs in British India as Chairman of the Board of Control, but Scott was also well acquainted with Lord Minto, Governor General from 1807–14, and with several other persons of position or influence in the sub-continent, among them his brother-in-law Charles Carpenter, Commercial Resident in Salem, Madras, from the late 1790s till his death in 1814, and his distant relation Colonel William Russell of Ashestiel, whose military career paralleled in many respects that assigned to Guy Mannering.[11] When, in late 1810, there was talk of Robert Dundas going out to India himself as Governor General, Scott, troubled by the shaky financial state of the publishing firm of John Ballantyne and Co. (in which he was the main partner), even considered going there himself in the hope of ensuring the financial future of his growing family.

Iain Gordon Brown has recently pointed out Scott's familiarity from earliest childhood with the clutch of 'returned Indians' living near his father's house in George Square.[12] Having amassed large commercial fortunes in India, such men represented the Scottish form of the nabob stereotype, already familiar in both the literary and popular discourses of the late eighteenth century. The inhabitants of Kippletringan are quick to characterise Mannering himself as a nabob, and even the astute Mac-Morlan blames Mannering's failure to appear at the sale of the Ellangowan estate on 'the fickleness and caprice of these Indian Nabobs' (81). Tara Ghoshal Wallace, however, has alerted us to the care with which Scott in fact distanced Mannering from the curry-eating, free-spending, vulgar, and sometimes corrupt image then often conjured up by the term nabob.[13] Mannering's career has been military not commercial; he has served with the British Army, not the forces of the East India Company; his fortune comes by inheritance from his London merchant uncle; and his sternly upright character is free of any hint of wrongdoing.[14]

Mannering's Englishness also separates him from the Indian returnees familiar in so many parts of Scotland in the late eighteenth century and contributes to a sense of his 'apartness' that is further enhanced by his being a man of books as well as of action, a poet and an artist, one whose knowledge of India and of things Indian comes from immersion in the history and culture of the sub-continent as well as from direct personal experience. Importantly, Mannering's special appreciation for Indian history and for India's aesthetic appeal as a locus of romance proves to be something that he has in common both with his daughter Julia and with Harry Bertram, the novel's young hero. Bertram in particular not only shares Mannering's taste for drawing both Indian subjects and the romantic scenery of the Lake District, but has frequent recourse to Indian analogies when seeking to articulate his own romantic response to the hills and picturesque ruins of southern Scotland.

One of Scott's favourite books as a boy had been Robert Orme's *History of the Military Transactions of the British Nation in Indostan*, and during a childhood illness he had consoled himself by fighting his way in imagination through the battles recorded in that work, whose 'copious plans', as he later recalled, 'aided by the clear and luminous explanations of the author, rendered my imitative amusement peculiarly easy."[15] This early enthusiasm for Indian history and for Eastern tales endured into manhood, and as late as 1807–8 he was actively involved in proposing a multi-volume edition of Eastern tales to a number of London publishers. There is a wealth of references to such materials throughout the novel, most notably in scenes involving Mannering or Julia, and although there are elements of humorous self-dramatisation in Julia's fondness for Indian legends—having been born 'in the land of talisman and spell' she has heard these magic narratives as they 'flowed, half poetry, half prose, from the lips of the tale-teller' (92)—the motif of India as land of romance has continuing power throughout the novel. Even the presentation of Meg Merrilies draws some of its aura of mystery from an eastern connection, invoking the belief, widely held at the end of the eighteenth century, that the origins of the gypsies could be traced back to India.

MANNERING, A TALE OF PRIVATE LIFE

The discussion which follows refers to the outcome of the story. New readers may wish to wait until finishing the actual novel before reading the remainder of this introduction.

Guy Mannering; or, The Astrologer is indeed 'a tale of private life'. Though the blank for the date in its opening sentence—'It was in the beginning of the month of November, 17—' (3)—might seem to hark back to the *Sixty Years Since* subtitle of *Waverley*, this turns out to be a way of teasing the reader in order to establish the distinctiveness of this new novel from its predecessor. The references to India and to the American War do approximately locate the text in historical time—so that Mannering's first arrival can be placed at the end of the 1750s, the child's disappearance in the mid-1760s, and the main action at the beginning of the 1780s—but it is with the workings of personal time and the consequences of private actions that this novel is essentially concerned.

Structurally, the most striking features of *Mannering* are its use of two heroes and of a two-generation plot with an almost seventeen-year time gap at its centre. The doubling of the hero and the break in continuity are at once exploited and resolved in terms of a series of echoing relationships between apparently disparate situations and characters. Mannering is counterpointed against both the Bertrams, father and son; Mannering's return to Ellangowan is set off against both his own first visit more than twenty years earlier and the entry of Harry Bertram into the lost place of his childhood; Pleydell's inconclusive first investigation of the murder and abduction prepares the way for the success of his second attempt; the actual and the potential father figures are mutually defining; Mannering as astrologer is linked to Meg as sibyl; Glossin the bad lawyer contrasts with Pleydell the good; and so it goes on. It becomes at once necessary and natural to read minor as well as major features of the novel in terms of the responsive echoes, contrasts, and variations to be found elsewhere in its pages.

As in many Scott novels, the motif of the journey connects episodes together, while the traveller himself also functions as perspective device. But *Mannering* addresses in a more fundamental fashion the condition of strangeness, isolation, and exile, and the introductory sequence in which the young Mannering attempts to find his way along difficult roads in the twilight, with little assistance from a suspicious peasantry, reverberates throughout the remainder of the text. The figure of Mannering as the wanderer for whom no simple resolution or homecoming to happiness is possible continues to haunt the narrative and modify its final effect, even after the second narrative strand has culminated in the re-establishment of the novel's younger hero, Harry Bertram, in his proper home and place as returned heir.

ROMANTIC TESTING

Scott was from his childhood a passionate reader of Renaissance romance—not just Malory and Spenser, but Ariosto and Tasso and even the long French prose romances of the seventeenth century. In *Guy Mannering* he deftly employs key narrative components of such romances in the service of a realistic tale set against a landscape articulated in all its geographical and temporal particularity. In Bertram's case the wanderer motif is easily translatable into the pattern of the quest. He has, after all, returned from India in pursuit of Julia Mannering. But he gradually realises that he is also engaged in a second and more important quest, not forward in search of his beloved but backward in search of his own origins and identity. The physical goal of both journeys is Scotland, and only by confirming that Ellangowan is his rightful place can he in fact be sure of securing the lady. The dynamic of the novel involves not merely the question of whether Bertram will win Julia but how his identity is to be established and his worthiness proved.

When he sets out northwards from the Lake District towards Scotland Bertram is leaving the false world of modern literary romance—a world in which a taste for picturesque scenery and Eastern lore allows him to function both as an appropriate protagonist in the fictions Julia creates in letters to her bosom friend Matilda, and as the self-consciously stylised wanderer figure of his own correspondence with his artist friend Delaserre. The entire Lakes episode is handled with a humour and lightness that render it entirely delightful but also fundamentally non-serious. Julia is well aware that the extravagance of her own enthusiasm for picturesque scenery adds piquancy to the tale of her love affair with Bertram, and by choosing the epistolary mode for her novelising she deliberately places a premium on sentiment and sensation. All her perceptions are coloured by art or literature: the mountains and lakes are seen as if through the eyes of Claude or Salvator Rosa; the balcony scene with her lover is preceded by a reading of Lorenzo and Jessica's moonlight scene from *The Merchant of Venice*. This making of fictions is an inherited trait. Mrs Mannering is said to have reworked her reading of romances into 'a little family novel of her own', with Julia as 'the principal heroine', while Colonel Mannering has fashioned a much darker drama in which he casts himself in the role of Othello. Bertram, for his part, shrewdly recognises that if Julia is thinking of 'love and a farm, it is a *ferme ornée*, such as is only to be found in poetic description, or in the park of a gentleman of twelve thousand a-year' (113).

As he moves northwards Bertram ceases to be one of those 'walking gentlemen of all descriptions, poets, players, painters, musicians, who come to rave, and recite, and madden, about this picturesque land of ours' (90). The novel's second volume opens with a literal breath of fresh air: the mountains are no longer generalised scenery but have names—Skiddaw and Saddleback—and a meditation on the Roman Wall and the fall of ancient civilisations quickly gives way to the promptings of hunger that lead Bertram into a 'small public-house' (118). He has adopted the simplest of dress and carries the minimum of belongings; the only tribute to his literary tastes is a small pocket Shakespeare. He whistles as he walks along, his scampering terrier Wasp at his side, and he has 'a kind greeting or a good-humoured jest' for everyone he meets, eliciting in response: '"That's a koind heart, God bless un!"' (118). The contrast between this and the twilight journey of Mannering that opened the novel could not be more marked—though Bertram has in fact ahead of him an even more dangerous journey over the very terrain traversed by Mannering on that occasion.

What at first seems paramount in this particular transition is the emergence of the young hero from self-absorbed contemplativeness into a more active encounter with nature. But in terms of literary convention, signalled by his change of dress and scene, his association with simpler folk, and the recognition he receives, Bertram is entering into a pastoral world, embarking upon the ritual of 'proving' traditionally dramatised in the pastoral interludes of Renaissance romance.

Scott's combination of the realistic with the emblematic is carried off with tact and wit, not least in his invocation of the classic debate about nature and nurture in Dinmont's breeding of generations of terriers all called Pepper or Mustard—'a fancy of my ain to mark the breed' (120)—and the farmer's lament over Bertram's failure to train his own terrier to go after vermin: 'beast or body, education should aye be minded' (119). Again, the crossing of Bewcastle Moss and the defence of Dandie from the robbers who attack him clearly constitute a version of the perilous journey of romance, but simultaneously present to the reader are the sharply drawn physical features of an actual landscape, the reminders of the region's past history in the scattered remnants of Border fortresses, and the highly individualised figure and speech of Dinmont himself. Scott's conquest for the novel of this special combination of the regional and the pastoral would make possible some of the finest things in his own later fiction as well as that of such successors as George Eliot and Thomas Hardy.[16]

The description of Charlieshope as Bertram and Dinmont approach it after their journey across the barren waste is both pastoral and biblical—'a land which a patriarch would have chosen to feed his flocks and herds' (127). Its associated values are human and moral rather than aesthetic, and Bertram is welcomed as one who has already fought in defence of his host. But while he participates in the hunting, feasting, and dancing that are the familiar rituals of Charlieshope, he remains, like the traditional hero in pastoral interludes, only a temporary member of this world, never losing his separateness. The testing, reductive processes embodied in such sequences may involve the shedding of certain superficial attributes, the reordering of personal values, but they do not require a change of identity. Just as the traditional hero does not become a simple shepherd, so Bertram remains the Captain, his otherness never lost sight of or glossed over. He thus places a little aesthetic distance between himself and the gorier aspects of the salmon-spearing; it is at his suggestion that a particularly resolute old badger is spared; and he declines to have Wasp entered against the vermin after all.

What, however, most profoundly distinguishes Dinmont's world from Mannering's India, or from Bertram's childhood experience after his kidnapping from Ellangowan, is the full love and trust openly expressed between husband and wife, parents and children, hosts and guest. The young man's acceptance by this world is complete—'"Captain, come back,"' urges the six-year-old as she kisses him goodbye, '"and I'll be your wife my ain sell"' (140)—and Dandie's last and finest gesture of trust is to offer money to help him in that other world where the Captain actually belongs: '"I have heard that you army gentlemen can sometimes buy yoursells up a step, and if a hundred or twa would help ye on such an occasion, the bit scrape o' your pen would be as good to me as the siller, and ye might just take ye're ain time of settling it—it wad be a great convenience to me"' (141). The delicacy matches that which Bertram had himself exhibited in asking Ailie for a plaid like Dandie's, and though he declines Dandie's offer, the bond of mutual trust is sealed by his leaving Wasp behind, safe despite the whole tribe of Peppers and Mustards.

Bertram's ability to function harmoniously with nature in the simpler society of Charlieshope has confirmed his worth and endorsed the earlier recognition of his kind heart. Scott's tact again ensures, however, that Charlieshope's pastorality does not belong to some fantasised 'golden world' but is, on the contrary, fully historicised, with a prehistory memorialised in ballads and attested to by ruined peel towers. Time moves on in Liddesdale as elsewhere, its presence marked not so much by the customary pastoral acknowledgement of death—*et in arcadia ego*—as by the developmental changes that constitute history. The narrator-as-historian makes the point explicitly when identifying the differences between the farmers of the region in Dinmont's day and in his own. But the point is no less effectively made by Dandie's turning outwards to the legal world of Edinburgh for redress in his dispute with Jock o' Dawstone Cleugh after the repeated failure of the traditional process of resolution, combat by single-stick.

CITY PASTORAL

In the analogical structure of *Guy Mannering* Mannering's visit to Edinburgh counterbalances Bertram's stay at Charlieshope, though distinctly urban experiences replace the rural pursuits of badger-hunting and salmon-spearing. As Mannering hears the Rev. John Erskine preach in Greyfriars Church, attends an old-fashioned funeral and will reading, enjoys a venison dinner with Pleydell and other Edinburgh figures, and makes good use of his introductions to David Hume, Adam Smith, Adam Ferguson, Lord Kames, John Clerk of Eldin and other literati of the Athens of the North, he displays all the adaptive powers Bertram had displayed in Liddesdale, finding easy admission to 'a circle never closed against strangers of sense and information' (226). In Scott's original manuscript these Edinburgh episodes received full treatment through the inclusion of a series of excerpts from Mannering's letters to his friend Mervyn. The unidentified portraits in those excerpts invited the reader's active engagement in the game of providing the requisite names, while driving home the point about Mannering's acceptance as an intellectual equal by this distinguished company. As the Note on the Text points out, the present edition follows the EEWN edition in restoring these passages to Chapter 18 of Volume 2, and thereby helps to re-establish a narrative balance between Charlieshope and Edinburgh that is absent from other printed texts of the novel.

Dinmont's reappearance serves to confirm the parallels between the two episodes, and it is indeed in Dinmont's sturdy company that Mannering makes his own comically perilous journey through Edinburgh's dark streets and noisome alleys to that inner world within the urban pastoral realm where the game of High Jinks is in full swing, with Pleydell as leading participant. The lawyer, whose normal dress is 'a well-brushed black suit, with very clean shoes and gold buckles', and whose customary manner is 'rather reserved and formal than intrusive' (211), is now found coatless, his wig on one side, 'his head crowned with a bottle-slider' (204), as he acts out the part of a medieval Scottish monarch surrounded by a boisterous court. Like the 'second world' of Renaissance literature, High Jinks is a recurrent ritual of serious game-playing that offers an artificial withdrawal from the world of daily realities.

In the daytime world of the law Pleydell does not allow himself the luxury of role-playing; his old man's flirtation with Julia at the supper table in a later episode constitutes merely a brief excursion into High Jinks in a toned-down and domesticated form. At the same time, the flirtation ritual, like the rituals of power in the monarchy game in the Edinburgh tavern, hints at aspects of the self deliberately suppressed—in this case a yearning for a fuller expression of the life of the affections. In this portrait of a divided personality, the distinction drawn by Scott between *homo ludens* and *homo laborans* points forward to such Dickensian figures as Wemmick in *Great Expectations*, and the point is underlined by the setting off of the complexity of Pleydell against the simple wholeness of Dandie Dinmont, whose response to High Jinks is, '"Deil hae me, if they are na a' mad thegither!"' (205).

Like Mannering, the man of arms, the man of law suffers from a restriction of part of his personality. He is by no means inhumane—he well knows what burdens the slow workings of the law place upon individual men and women—but he also knows that to allow such awareness too loud a voice would inhibit his ability to function in the daytime world of the law. Significantly, neither Pleydell nor Mannering can share Dinmont's direct involvement in the final rescue of Bertram. Though Pleydell tells Bertram, '"[S]ince you have wanted a father so long, I wish from my heart I could claim the paternity myself"' (309), this cannot be—and the tragedy is Pleydell's rather than Bertram's. In the absence of his real father, Bertram can draw on the strengths of the various surrogate fathers who stand in the wings at his rebirth, but the existence of an available heir does not necessarily transform into genuine fathers those with wealth or wisdom to bestow.

THE TWO PROTAGONISTS

In *Waverley* there is never any doubt about the centrality of the young hero. The older father figures—such as Baron Bradwardine or Colonel Talbot—who aid in his education and ensure his survival remain narratively subordinate to Edward himself. But in *Guy Mannering* the satisfyingly complete romance plot of the lost heir Harry Bertram is set directly against the incompleteness of the Mannering plot. The ritual over which Meg Merrilies presides in the final stages of the novel serves not only to connect the separated parts of Bertram's life but to affirm his links both with his ancestors and his community. He is recognised as the abducted child—through the survival of the astrological prediction round his neck—and as his father's son: 'the resemblance was too striking to be denied' (337). His power to bring about a future very different from the disaster his father has made of his inheritance is affirmed by the absence of his actual father and the presence instead of so many wiser surrogates.

The time-shift which initially looks so disruptive of the Harry Bertram story thus provides the central dynamic of the novel's final stages. Any suspense about the identity of Captain Brown is dissipated very early in the tale, and the impulse towards connecting past and present becomes the strongest force in the narrative—embodied as it is in Bertram's need to establish his legitimacy, in Pleydell's anxiety to find the solution that eluded his original inquiry, and in Meg's insistence on a re-enactment that will carry Harry Bertram back over the ground of his childhood abduction until he is face to face in the cave with the man who broke his life into separate fragments.

But this very drive towards completion underlines the poignancy of Mannering's situation as witness rather than protagonist. Whereas the young Captain Vanbeest Brown can be transformed into Harry Bertram and the connection re-established with the child he once was, no such rebonding is possible for the broken halves of Mannering's own life. The young tourist with a taste for the picturesque who figures in the novel's opening sequence is very far removed from the stern victor of numerous Indian battles who returns to Ellangowan two decades later. In youth he dreamed of retirement with his beloved Sophia in a place like Ellangowan, but in fact he transported her to the alien world of India and left her very much to her own devices, with tragic consequences that might even have destroyed the happiness of their daughter. Mannering has devoted himself to his profession rather than to domestic affection, as if in an attempt to reincarnate one of his medieval ancestors famed for his skill in arms, and in this pursuit of military glory he has lost touch with his wife and almost made a stranger of his daughter. When Julia laments, only half humorously, to her friend, 'O Matilda, I hope none of your ancestors ever fought at Poictiers or Agincourt' (97), something more is at issue than comic satire of family pride. While the reader is aware of the anguish Mannering suffers at the loss of his wife and the probable death of Bertram, it is one of the novel's saddest ironies that Julia believes that her father is quite comfortable with the idea of death. The fundamental source of Mannering's unhappiness and estrangement is that he has subsumed the man of feeling within the man of arms. His isolation continues up to and beyond the end of the novel, and it is by means of this dark figure of the returned stranger who carries with him the condition of exile that Scott effectively weaves into the main plot of the lost heir the theme of the severed life.

What emerges, indeed, is that the two heroes, though comprising the second apparent awkwardness in the novel's plotting, are in fact as essential as the seventeen-year time gap itself to the work's overall structure and meaning. The epigraph from Time as Chorus in *The Winter's Tale* that signals the break in the action invites the reader to compare the cases of Bertram and Mannering with the lost children and lonely father figures of Shakespeare's late romances. For Mannering the magical resolutions and rebindings of the world of Shakespearian romance are not available in their most complete form. He never really 'finds' his daughter; the scene that should mark a new confidence and openness between them is only partially achieved; the relationship remains one of felt vacancy rather than the strong bond of Prospero and Miranda or Leontes' magical recovery of Perdita. Mannering's inability to speak fully and openly to Julia creates an undertow of unexpressed emotion throughout the later scenes. He can do more for Godfrey Bertram's daughter than for his own, while Julia, for her part, is more at ease with Pleydell than with her father.

At the end of the novel Mannering can contribute only his wealth to the restoration process, not enjoy it in his own right, and when the young people go off to plan the rebuilding of Meg's cottage at Derncleugh, he is left alone to plan a retreat for himself identified by the deliberately alien word, 'Bungalow'.[17] Realistic fiction is in the end very different from Shakespearian romance and Mannering must live in the time-bound world of consequences where the happy endings available to the children cannot obliterate the unrecoverable losses of the fathers. This is a story about mistakes and their sometimes irreparable consequences, and Mannering never for one moment shares Dominie Sampson's illusion that the seventeen-year time gap can be obliterated.

For a novelist who did not publish his first novel until his mid-forties this emphasis on the middle-aged hero may strike modern readers as not altogether surprising, and the novels that were to follow *Mannering* included other middle-aged figures—Jonathan Oldbuck in *The Antiquary* (1816) or Baillie Nicol Jarvie and Rob Roy in *Rob Roy* (1818)—who were among the most memorable in his fiction. But the plot conventions of the day insisted on the primacy of a love story involving a young hero and heroine with marriage as the narrative goal, so that Scott had to find his own way, through the deployment of the two-generation plot of consequences, to accommodate his fascination with what Henry James was to describe much later as the 'thickened motive and accumulated character'[18] of an older protagonist. *Guy Mannering* with its two heroes was in many ways as innovative as *Waverley* itself, but it was not until the end of the nineteenth century that a novelist such as James was ready to take up the challenge constituted by Scott's complex representation of his middle-aged hero.

NOTES

1 The derivatives (plays, operas, settings of individual songs, etc.) from *The Lady of the Lake* alone take up over thirty-four large pages in the standard bibliography of Scott's works (William B. Todd and Ann Bowden, *Sir Walter Scott: A Bibliographical History* (New Castle, DE, 1998), 192–237). They began to appear as soon as the poem was published and included by 1815 the setting of 'Hail to the Chief' that subsequently became the American presidential anthem. Schubert's setting of 'Ave Maria' did not appear till 1826, but the immensely popular Rossini opera, *La Donna del Lago*, based on the dramatisation by Andrea Leone Tottola, was first performed in Naples in 1819. Many of the novels of the 'Author of Waverley' were to follow their poetic predecessors as the basis of immensely successful operas: see Jerome Mitchell, *The Walter Scott Operas* (Tuscaloosa, AL, 1977) and *More Scott Operas* (Lanham, NY, 1996).

2 Scott set *Rokeby* in the area surrounding the north Yorkshire home of his close friend J. B. S. Morritt and used remembered details from earlier visits, supplemented by a special trip there in 1812 and a whole series of subsequent letters requesting exact details of scenery, local names, etc. See *The Letters of Sir Walter Scott*, ed. H. J. C. Grierson and others, 12 vols (London, 1932–37), 3.40–41, 88, 202. (Hereafter *Letters*.)

3 *Letters*, 6.160.

4 Georg Lukács, *The Historical Novel* (London, 1962), 19–88.

5 Scott to Daniel Terry, 10 November 1814 (*Letters*, 3.514). Writing to Morritt on 19 January 1815, after the poem had been published, Scott insisted, 'It closes my poetic labour on an extended scale' (*Letters*, 4.12), but a few days later he was still wincing at the memory of his 'literary tormenter . . . a certain Lord of the Isles' (*Letters*, 4.18).

6 *Letters*, 4.13.

7 *Letters*, 9.474. For detailed discussion of the sources and locations see the Genesis section of the Essay on the Text, *Guy Mannering*, EEWN 2, ed.

P. D. Garside (Edinburgh, 1999), and the Historical Note in the present edition.

8 For the M'Naught affair and Court of Session cases involving lost heirs, see the Garside Essay on the Text (EEWN 2, 364–67) and Jane Millgate, 'Scott and the Law: *The Heart of Midlothian*' in *Rough Justice: Essays on Crime in Literature*, ed. Martin L. Friedland (Toronto, 1991), 95–113.

9 Scott returned to Liddesdale in the summers of 1800 and 1801, and as late as 1808 the Liddesdale fascination left its emblematic mark on the most famous of the many portraits of Scott, the large picture, painted by Raeburn for Scott's publisher Archibald Constable, and made familiar all over the world in innumerable engravings. The portrait depicts the poet and ballad collector, pencil and notebook in hand, seated against the ruins of Hermitage Castle in Liddesdale. The painting is now in the collection of the Duke of Buccleuch.

10 *Letters*, 6.489.

11 For a full discussion of the possible links between Mannering and Russell, see Richard D. Jackson, 'The Indian Colonel: Colonel William Russell of Ashestiel and Scott's Guy Mannering', *Scott Newsletter*, 38 (Spring 2001), 8–14.

12 Iain Gordon Brown, 'Griffiths, Nabobs and a Seasoning of Curry Powder' in *The Tiger and the Thistle: Tipu Sultan and the Scots in India, 1760–1800*, ed. Anne Buddle (Edinburgh, 1999), 71–79. This essay provides extensive evidence of Scott's familiarity with things Indian.

13 Tara Ghoshal Wallace, 'The Elephant's Foot and the British Mouth: Walter Scott on Imperial Rhetoric', *European Romantic Review*, 13 (September 2002), 311–24. Wallace offers the most sophisticated discussion to date of the Indian element in both *Guy Mannering* and Scott's later novel *The Surgeon's Daughter*.

14 Public exposure to the theme of Indian corruption reached its apogee during the efforts to impeach Warren Hastings in the late 1780s. Though ultimately acquitted, Hastings retired from public life and it is one of those serendipitous connections that he proved to be a great admirer of Scott's *Lay of the Last Minstrel* and communicated to Scott, through David Anderson of St Germains, information about parallels between the story of the *Lay* and certain eastern legends (*Letters*, 12.382, and National Library of Scotland, MS 3880, ff.194–97).

15 J. G. Lockhart, *Memoirs of the Life of Sir Walter Scott, Bart.*, 7 vols (Edinburgh, 1837–38), 1.48. Scott owned the three-volume second edition of Orme's history, published 1775–78; see J. G. Cochrane, *Catalogue of the Library at Abbotsford* (Edinburgh, 1838), 253.

16 Ian Duncan in *Modern Romance and the Transformations of the Novel* (Cambridge, 1992) offers a complex analysis of *Mannerings*'s many variations on romance strategies and particularly emphasises its influence on later novelists, not least by its deployment of a range of narrative modes that anticipate 'the great polyphonic narratives of Victorian fiction' (119).

17 This word of Hindustani origin (meaning 'belonging to Bengal') was initially adopted into English to denote a type of one-storeyed summerhouse specific to India. It seems to have been only at the beginning of the twentieth century that it began to be applied to one-storeyed houses in general, and especially to those of modest scale.

18 Henry James, 'Preface', *The Ambassadors*, New York Edition (New York, 1909), 1. viii.

CHRONOLOGY OF WALTER SCOTT

1771	*15 August*. Born in College Wynd, Edinburgh. His father, Walter (1729–99), son of a sheep-farmer at Sandyknowe, near Smailholm Tower, Roxburghshire, was a lawyer. His mother, Anne Rutherford (1732–1819), was daughter of Dr John Rutherford, Professor of Medicine at the University of Edinburgh. His parents married in April 1758; Walter was their ninth child. The siblings who survived were Robert (1767–87), John (1769–1816), Anne (1772–1801), Thomas (1774–1823), and Daniel (?1776–1806).
1772–73	*Winter*. Contracted what is now termed poliomyelitis, and became permanently lame in his right leg. His grandfather Rutherford advised that he be sent to Sandyknowe to benefit from country air, and, apart from a period of 'about a year' in 1775 spent in Bath, a spell in 1776 with his family in their new home on the west side of George Square, Edinburgh, and a time in 1777 at Prestonpans, near Edinburgh, he lived there until 1778. From his grandmother and his aunt Janet he heard many ballads and stories of the Border past, and these narratives were crucial to his intellectual and imaginative development.
1779–83	Attended the High School of Edinburgh; he was particularly influenced by the Rector, Dr Alexander Adam, and his teaching of literature in Latin. After the High School, he spent 'half a year' with his aunt Janet in Kelso, where he attended the grammar school, and read for the first time Thomas Percy's *Reliques of Ancient English Poetry*.
1783–86	Attended classes in Edinburgh University, including Humanity (Latin), Greek, Logic and Metaphysics, and Moral Philosophy.
1786	Studies terminated by serious illness; convalescence in Kelso. Apprenticed as a lawyer to his father.
1787	Met Robert Burns at the house of the historian and philosopher, Adam Ferguson.
1789	Decided to prepare for the Bar.
1789–92	Attended classes at Edinburgh University, including History, Moral Philosophy, Scots Law, and Civil Law.
1792	*11 July*. Admitted to the Faculty of Advocates.

Autumn. First visit to Liddesdale, in the extreme south of Scotland, with Robert Shortreed, in search of ballads and ballad-singers. Seven such 'raids' followed over seven years. Shortreed later commented: 'He was makin' himsell a' the time'. His tours took him into many parts of Scotland and the north of England: e.g. in 1793 to Perthshire and the Trossachs; in 1796 to the north-east of Scotland; and in 1797 to Cumberland and the Lake District.

1794 In April involved in a brawl with some political radicals and bound to keep the peace. In September attended the trials of the radicals Watt and Downie, and in November Watt's execution.

c.1794–96 In love with Williamina Belsches, culminating in April 1796 with an invitation to her home, Fettercairn House, Kincardineshire.

1796 Anonymous publication of *The Chase and William and Helen*, Scott's translations of two of Bürger's poems.
October. Announcement of the engagement of Williamina Belsches to William Forbes.

1797 Volunteered for the new volunteer cavalry regiment, the Royal Edinburgh Light Dragoons, and appointed quartermaster.
September. Met Charlotte Carpenter (1770–1826), at Gilsland, Cumberland, and within three weeks proposed marriage. Charlotte's parents were Jean François Charpentier and Margaret Charlotte Volère (d. 1788), of Lyons. Sometime after the break-up of the marriage around 1780, her mother brought Charlotte and her brother Charles (1772–1818) to England; Charlotte and Charles later became the wards of the 2nd Marquess of Downshire, and changed their name to Carpenter.
24 December. Married Charlotte in Carlisle, and set up house at 50 George Street, Edinburgh.

1798 Met Matthew Gregory ('Monk') Lewis, and agreed to contribute to *Tales of Wonder* (published 1801).
Rented cottage in Lasswade near Edinburgh for the summer, and made many political and literary contacts, including Lady Louisa Stuart, who proved to be one of the most acute and trusted of his friends and critics.
Moved to 19 Castle Street, Edinburgh.
October. Birth and death of first son.

1799 Publication of *Goetz of Berlichingen*, Scott's translation of Goethe's tragedy.

	April. Death of Scott's father.
	Met John Leyden and the publisher Archibald Constable, and had his first discussion with the printer James Ballantyne about undertaking book-printing: Ballantyne brought out Scott's anthology *An Apology for Tales of Terror* in 1800.
	October. Birth of daughter, Charlotte Sophia Scott.
	December. Appointed Sheriff-Depute of Selkirkshire.
1801	*October.* Birth of son, Walter Scott.
	Moved to 39 Castle Street, Edinburgh.
1802	Publication of *Minstrelsy of the Scottish Border*, Vols 1 and 2. The *Minstrelsy* was the first publication in a lifetime of scholarly editing, and it shows both the strengths and weaknesses of Scott as editor. He found new texts (of the 72 ballads he published, 38 had not appeared in print before), and his literary, historical, and anthropological essays and notes are always illuminating; but, following the editorial practice of the time, he had no settled methods or principles for choosing or establishing a text.
	Met James Hogg.
1803	*February.* Birth of daughter, Anne Scott.
	Second edition of *Minstrelsy of the Scottish Border*, Vols 1 and 2, and first edition of Vol. 3.
	Began to contribute reviews to the *Edinburgh Review.* Scott was an acute reviewer, in the expansive manner characteristic of heavyweight reviews in the early nineteenth century, and was particularly perceptive about such contemporaries as Jane Austen, Byron, and Mary Shelley.
	September. Visit from William and Dorothy Wordsworth.
1804	Took the lease of Ashestiel near Selkirk as his country house in place of the cottage in Lasswade.
	Publication of Scott's edition of the medieval metrical romance, *Sir Tristrem.*
1805	Publication of *The Lay of the Last Minstrel*, the first of a series of verse romances which established his fame as a poet.
	Entered into partnership with James Ballantyne in the printing business of James Ballantyne & Co. Until the financial crash in 1826, the partnership was not just a financial arrangement, but a unique collaboration: Ballantyne managed the business, but also acted as Scott's editor; Scott seems to have been responsible for much of the financial planning, and it was a standard part of his

contracts with publishers that his works should be printed by James Ballantyne & Co.

December. Birth of son, Charles Scott.

1806 Hurried to London to secure his appointment as one of the Principal Clerks to the Court of Session, a position which had been under negotiation for much of the previous year but which was imperilled by the advent of a new government after the death of William Pitt on 23 January. The appointment was announced on 8 March. Scott took the place of an elderly Clerk, but, as there was no retirement and pension scheme, allowed his predecessor to keep the salary of £800 per annum for life. While in London Scott was 'taken up' by high society.

1807 Brother Tom bankrupt. It also emerged that Tom, a lawyer who had inherited his father's practice, and who had been retained as agent for the Duddingston estate of the Marquess of Abercorn, had misappropriated some of his client's money. Scott felt financially and morally endangered by his brother's breach of trust, and extended efforts were required over several years to protect his own financial credit and provide for his brother and his family.

1808 Publication of poem *Marmion* (the rights of which the publisher Archibald Constable had bought for £1050 in 1807).

Appointed secretary to the Parliamentary Commission to Inquire into the Administration of Justice in Scotland. The Commission ended its work in 1810.

Publication of *The Works of John Dryden . . . with Notes . . . and a Life of the Author*, 18 vols.

Cancelled his subscription to the *Edinburgh Review* because of its 'defeatist' view of the war in Spain, and began (with others) planning the *Quarterly Review* and the *Edinburgh Annual Register*, both launched in 1810. The political disagreement developed into a quarrel with Archibald Constable & Co., and Scott and the Ballantyne brothers, James and John, set up and became the partners in a rival publishing business, John Ballantyne & Co. Scott entrusted his own works to the new business and whenever possible directed other writers and new ventures to it, but Constable withdrew printing work from James Ballantyne & Co., and the printing firm stopped making significant profits.

1809 Publication of *A Collection of Scarce and Valuable Tracts*

(Somers' Tracts), Vols 1–3; completed in 13 vols 1812.

1810 Publication of *The Lady of the Lake*, his most commercially successful poem.

1811 Scott's predecessor as Clerk of Session agreed to apply for a pension, and from 1812 Scott was paid a salary of £1300 per annum.

Publication of poem *The Vision of Don Roderick*.

Purchase of Cartley Hole, the nucleus of the Abbotsford Estate, between Galashiels and Melrose.

1812 Byron began correspondence with Scott.

Removal from Ashestiel to Abbotsford, and plans for rebuilding the small farmhouse there.

1813 Publication of poems *Rokeby* and *The Bridal of Triermain*.

First financial crisis. It became apparent in 1812 that the publishing firm of John Ballantyne & Co. was making losses on every publication except Scott's poetry, and that the *Edinburgh Annual Register* was losing £1000 per issue. The firm was undercapitalised, and depended overmuch on bank credit. The national financial crisis of 1812–14 led to reduced orders for books from retailers, late payments, and to the bankruptcy of many companies whose debts to John Ballantyne & Co. were either not paid or paid in part. John Ballantyne & Co. found itself unable to pay its own bills and repay the banks on time, and *Rokeby*, greatly profitable though it was, failed to generate enough ready money to meet obligations. Protracted negotiations with Constable over much of 1813 led to the purchase of Ballantyne stock, on the condition that John Ballantyne & Co. ceased to be an active publisher, to the sale of a share in *Rokeby*, and later to the advance sale to Constable of rights for the publication of the long poem *The Lord of the Isles*. Scott had to ask the Duke of Buccleuch to guarantee a bank loan of £4000, and many friends gave small loans. All the personal loans were repaid in 1814, and the publishing business was eventually wound up profitably in 1817, largely through Scott's efforts. As part of the reconciliation Constable commissioned essays on Chivalry and the Drama for the Supplement to the *Encyclopaedia Britannica* (published 1818 and 1819 respectively).

Offered and declined the poet-laureateship.

1814 Publication of his first novel, *Waverley*. The novel was probably begun in 1808 (the date '1st November, 1805' in the first chapter is part of the fiction), continued in

1810, and completed 1813–14; it was first advertised in 1810, and again in January 1814. The early parts (up to the beginning of Chapter 5, and Chapters 5–7) were probably written in parallel with Scott's autobiography (first published at the beginning of Lockhart's *Life of Scott* in 1837).

Publication of *The Works of Jonathan Swift . . . with Notes and a Life of the Author*, 19 vols.

Toured the northern and western isles of Scotland with the Lighthouse Commissioners. His diary of the voyage is published in Lockhart's *Life of Scott* (1837).

1815 Publication of poem *The Lord of the Isles* and *Guy Mannering*, his second novel.

First visit to the Continent, including Waterloo and Paris, where he was lionised.

1816 Publication of *Paul's Letters to his Kinsfolk*, *The Antiquary*, and *Tales of my Landlord* (*The Black Dwarf* and *The Tale of Old Mortality*).

1817 Publication of *Harold the Dauntless* (Scott's last long poem) and *Rob Roy* (1818 on title page).

1817–19 First phase of the building of Abbotsford.

1818 Publication of *Tales of my Landlord*, second series (*The Heart of Mid-Lothian*).

Offered and accepted a baronetcy (announced March 1820).

1819 Seriously ill, probably from gallstones. From 1817 Scott had been suffering stomach cramps, but in the spring and early summer of 1819 he was thought to be dying. Nonetheless he continued to work, dictating to an amanuensis when he was too ill to write. He completed *The Bride of Lammermoor* in April (the greater part of the manuscript is in his own hand) but the latter part of the novel and most of *A Legend of the Wars of Montrose* must have been dictated. The two tales constitute *Tales of my Landlord*, third series, and were published in June 1819.

Purchase by Constable of the copyrights of the 'Scotch novels' and publication of the first collection of Scott's fiction as *Novels and Tales of the Author of Waverley*, 16 vols. All the novels eventually appeared in collected editions in three formats: 8vo, 12mo and 18mo. Publication of three articles in the *Edinburgh Weekly Journal*, later issued as a pamphlet entitled *The Visionary*, which was in essence political propaganda for the constitutional status

	quo in the period after Peterloo, when there was a real possibility of a radical rising in the west of Scotland.
	December. Death of Scott's mother.
	Publication of *Ivanhoe* (1820 on title-page).
1820	Publication of *The Monastery* and *The Abbot*.
	Marriage of daughter Sophia to John Gibson Lockhart.
	Elected president of the Royal Society of Edinburgh.
1821	Publication of *Kenilworth* and *The Pirate* (1822 on title-page).
1821–24	Publication of *Ballantyne's Novelist's Library*, for which Scott wrote the lives of the novelists.
1822	Publication of *The Fortunes of Nigel* and *Peveril of the Peak* (1823 on title-page).
	Visit of King George IV to Edinburgh.
1822–25	Demolition of the original house and second phase of the building of Abbotsford.
1823	Bannatyne Club founded and Scott made first president.
	Publication of *Quentin Durward* and *St Ronan's Well* (1824 on title-page).
1824	Publication of *Redgauntlet*.
1825	Marriage of son Walter to Jane Jobson.
	Publication of *Tales of the Crusaders* (*The Betrothed* and *The Talisman*).
	Began his journal.
1826	*January*. Scott insolvent. There was a severe economic recession in the winter of 1825–26 and many companies and individuals became bankrupt. Scott's principal publishers, Archibald Constable & Co., and the printers James Ballantyne & Co., in which he was co-partner, had always been undercapitalised, and relied on bank borrowings for working capital. In paying for goods and services, including such things as paper, printing, and publication rights, all parties used promissory bills, a system in which the drawer promised to pay stated sums on stated dates, and which the acceptor 'discounted' at the banks, i.e. got the money in advance of the date less the amount the banks charged in interest for what was in fact a loan. Both Constable's and Ballantyne's hoped that the money coming in from the sale of books when they were published would be sufficient to pay off the money due to the banks, but in practice both firms too often borrowed more money to pay off debts when they were due, and acted as guarantors for each other's loans. In December 1825 it was realised

that they were unable to get further credit from the banks; and in January the bankruptcy of the London publishers of Scott's works, Hurst, Robinson & Co., precipitated the collapse of Constable's, then Ballantyne's, and the ruin of all the partners. Scott, the only one of those involved with a capacity to generate a large income, signed a trust deed undertaking to repay his own private debts (£35,000), all the debts of the printing business for which he and James Ballantyne were jointly liable (£41,000), the debts of Archibald Constable & Co. for which he was legally liable (£40,000), and a mortgage on Abbotsford (£10,000), amounting in all to over £126,000. Such were the profits from works like *Woodstock*, *The Life of Napoleon Buonaparte*, and above all the Magnum Opus, the collected edition of the Waverley Novels with introductions and notes specially written by Scott, and issued in monthly parts from 1829–33, that by Scott's death in 1832 more than £53,000 had been repaid, and the remaining debts were paid in 1833.

Publication of three letters in the *Edinburgh Weekly Journal*, later issued as *The Letters of Malachi Malagrowther*, in which Scott attacked a government proposal to restrict the rights of the Scottish banks to issue their own banknotes; Scott was so effective that the government withdrew its proposal.

Sale of 39 Castle Street, Edinburgh, on behalf of creditors.

15 May. Death of wife, Charlotte Scott.

Publication of *Woodstock*.

Autumn. Visit to Paris.

1827 Public acknowledgement of the authorship of the Waverley Novels.

Publication of *The Life of Napoleon Buonaparte*, 9 vols, *Chronicles of the Canongate* (Chrystal Croftangry's Narrative, 'The Highland Widow', 'The Two Drovers' and 'The Surgeon's Daughter'), and *Tales of a Grandfather* (Scotland to 1603).

1828 Publication of *Chronicles of the Canongate*, second series (*The Fair Maid of Perth*), and *Tales of a Grandfather*, second series (Scotland 1603–1707).

1829 Publication of *Anne of Geierstein*, *History of Scotland*, Vol. 1, and *Tales of a Grandfather*, third series (Scotland 1707–45). The first volume of the Magnum Opus, completed in 48 vols in 1833, appeared on 1 June.

1830 *February*. First stroke.
November. Retired as Clerk to the Court of Session with pension of £864 per annum. Second stroke.
Publication of *Letters on Demonology and Witchcraft*, *Tales of a Grandfather* (France), and *History of Scotland*, Vol. 2.

1831 *April*. Third stroke.
Publication of *Tales of my Landlord*, fourth series (*Count Robert of Paris* and *Castle Dangerous*).
October. Departure on HMS *Barham* to the Mediterranean, Malta and Naples.

1832 Overland journey home, via Rome, Florence, Venice, Verona, the Brenner Pass, Augsburg, Mainz, and down the Rhine, but had his fourth stroke at Nijmegen. Travelling by sea to London and then Edinburgh, he reached Abbotsford on 11 July.
21 September. Death at Abbotsford.

FURTHER READING

THE WORKS OF SCOTT

The Journal of Sir Walter Scott, ed. W. E. K. Anderson (Oxford, 1972).
The Letters of Sir Walter Scott, ed. H. J. C. Grierson and others, 12 vols (London, 1932–37). The index to this edition is by James C. Corson, *Notes and Index to Sir Herbert Grierson's Edition of the Letters of Sir Walter Scott* (Oxford, 1979).
'Memoirs', in *Scott on Himself: A Selection of the Autobiographical Writings of Sir Walter Scott*, ed. David Hewitt (Edinburgh, 1981).
The Poetical Works of Sir Walter Scott, ed. J. Logie Robertson (Oxford, 1904; frequently reprinted).
The Poetical Works of Sir Walter Scott, Bart. [ed. J. G. Lockhart], 12 vols (Edinburgh, 1833–34).
The Prose Works of Sir Walter Scott, Bart., 28 vols (Edinburgh, 1834–36).
Waverley Novels, 48 vols (Edinburgh, 1829–33), known as the 'Magnum Opus'.

The Waverley Novels were among the most frequently reprinted works of the nineteenth century, and all editions after Scott's death were based upon the edition of 1829–33. Of these, the best are the Centenary Edition, 25 vols (London, 1871), the Dryburgh Edition, 25 vols (London, 1892–94), and the Border Edition, ed. Andrew Lang, 24 vols (London, 1892–94). The first critical edition is the Edinburgh Edition of the Waverley Novels (1993–), on which the volumes of the new Penguin Scott are based.

The most complete listing of the works of Scott is in:
William B. Todd and Ann Bowden, *Sir Walter Scott: A Bibliographical History 1796–1832* (New Castle, DE, 1998).

There are two simpler listings:
J. G. Lockhart, 'Chronological List of the Publications of Sir Walter Scott', in *Memoirs of the Life of Sir Walter Scott, Bart.*, 7 vols (Edinburgh, 1837–38; many times republished), 7, 433–39.
J. H. Alexander, 'Sir Walter Scott', in *The Cambridge Bibliography of English Literature, Volume 4: 1800–1900*, 3rd edn, ed. Joanne Shattock (Cambridge, 1999), 992–1063.

BIOGRAPHY

There are very many biographies of Scott. The most important still is by J. G. Lockhart for although it is unreliable in some of its detail, it is the work of someone who knew Scott and his circle intimately. The most comprehensive of the modern works is by Edgar Johnson; it is generally reliable. John Buchan's one-volume life is the most sympathetic of all the studies of Scott, while John Sutherland takes a harsher view of the way in which Scott used those in his circle for his own advantage.

James Hogg, *Anecdotes of Scott*, ed. Jill Rubinstein (Edinburgh, 1999).

J. G. Lockhart, *Memoirs of the Life of Sir Walter Scott, Bart.*, 7 vols (Edinburgh, 1837–38; many times republished).

John Buchan, *Sir Walter Scott* (London, 1932).

Sir Herbert Grierson, *Sir Walter Scott, Bart.: A New Life supplementary to, and corrective of, Lockhart's Biography* (London, 1938).

Arthur Melville Clark, *Sir Walter Scott: The Formative Years* (Edinburgh, 1969).

Edgar Johnson, *Sir Walter Scott: The Great Unknown*, 2 vols (London, 1970).

John Sutherland, *The Life of Walter Scott* (Oxford, 1995).

CRITICISM

Complete listings of critical works on Scott are to be found in:

James C. Corson, *A Bibliography of Sir Walter Scott: A Classified and Annotated List of Books and Articles relating to his Life and Works 1797–1940* (Edinburgh, 1943).

Jill Rubenstein, *Sir Walter Scott: A Reference Guide* (Boston, MA, 1978) [covers the period 1932–77].

Jill Rubenstein, *Sir Walter Scott: An Annotated Bibliography of Scholarship and Criticism 1975–1990* (Aberdeen, 1994).

THE FOLLOWING ARE USEFUL FOR THE STUDY OF *GUY MANNERING*:

Alexander Welsh, *The Hero of the Waverley Novels* (New Haven, 1963; new edn, with essays on Scott, Princeton, 1992).

Coleman O. Parsons, *Witchcraft and Demonology in Scott's Fiction* (Edinburgh, 1964).

Francis R. Hart, *Scott's Novels: The Plotting of Historic Survival* (Charlottesville, 1966), Section 4, Chapter 2.

David Brown, *Walter Scott and the Historical Imagination* (London, 1979), Chapter 2.

Graham McMaster, *Scott and Society* (Cambridge, 1981).

Jana Davis, 'Landscape Images and Epistemology in *Guy Mannering*' in *Scott and his Influence: The Papers of the Aberdeen Scott Conference 1982*, ed. J. H. Alexander and David Hewitt (Aberdeen, 1983), 119–28.

Jane Millgate, *Walter Scott: The Making of the Novelist* (Edinburgh, 1984), Chapter 4.

Elaine Jordan, 'The Management of Scott's Novels' in *Europe and Its Others, Volume Two: Proceedings of the Essex Conference on the Sociology of Literature*, ed. Francis Barker, Peter Hulme, Margaret Iversen, and Diana Loxley (Colchester, 1985), 146–61.

Claire Lamont, 'Meg the Gipsy in Scott and Keats', *English*, 36 (Summer 1987), 137–45.

Ian Duncan, *Modern Romance and Transformations of the Novel: The Gothic, Scott, Dickens* (Cambridge, 1992), Chapter 3.

Peter Garside, 'Meg Merrilies and India', in *Scott in Carnival: Selected Papers from the Fourth International Scott Conference, Edinburgh 1991*, ed. J. H. Alexander and David Hewitt (Aberdeen, 1993), 154–71.

Peter Garside, 'Picturesque Figure and Landscape: Meg Merrilies and the Gypsies' in *The Politics of the Picturesque: Literature, Landscape and Aesthetics since 1770*, ed. Stephen Copley and Peter Garside (Cambridge, 1994), 145–74.

Nicola J. Watson, *Revolution and the Form of the British Novel 1790–1825: Intercepted Letters, Interrupted Seductions* (Oxford, 1994), Chapter 3.

Katie Trumpener, *Bardic Nationalism: The Romantic Novel and the British Empire* (Princeton, 1997).

Megan Perigoe Stitt, *Metaphors of Change in the Language of Nineteenth-Century Fiction: Scott, Gaskell and Kingsley* (Oxford, 1998).

Andrew Lincoln, 'Scott's *Guy Mannering*: The Limits and Limitations of Anglo-British Identity', *Scottish Literary Journal*, 26: 1 (June 1999), 48–61.

Richard D. Jackson, 'The Indian Colonel: William Russell of Ashestiel and Scott's *Guy Mannering*', *The Scott Newsletter*, 38 (Spring 2001), 8–14.

Tara Ghoshal Wallace, 'The Elephant's Foot and the British Mouth: Walter Scott on Imperial Rhetoric,' *European Romantic Review*, 13 (September 2002), 311–24.

A NOTE ON THE TEXT

This present text is based on the first edition of *Guy Mannering*, published in three volumes in late February 1815, but incorporates readings from Scott's original manuscript which were lost through accident, error, or misunderstanding. It also includes a number of readings from later printed editions in Scott's lifetime which correct manifest errors.

The remark attributed to Scott by his biographer, J. G. Lockhart, that *Guy Mannering* was 'the work of six weeks at a Christmas', has been treated with scepticism by some commentators,[1] but surviving evidence tends to corroborate the broad outline of this report, with Scott starting to write late in December 1814 and completing his novel virtually by mid-February 1815. The decision to engage in a second novel was probably taken shortly after his return early in September 1814 from a sea tour of the northern and western isles of Scotland, when the runaway success of his first novel, the anonymous *Waverley* (1814), had become fully apparent. Negotiations over publication were entered into during October, and involved Scott's two close associates James Ballantyne, the printer, and his brother, John, who effectively acted as Scott's literary agent, the novel being finally offered to the London firm of Longman & Co., with the Edinburgh-based Archibald Constable & Co. also taking a share. The work, under the full title of *Guy Mannering; or, The Astrologer*, was first advertised as forthcoming ('in the course of the month') early in December, but there is no evidence that Scott actually commenced writing until Christmas or Boxing Day, the first batch of material not being in James Ballantyne's hands until early in the New Year. The final stages of production were conducted at great pace, partly in an effort to release much-needed funds that would follow from completion. The novel first went on sale in Edinburgh on Friday, 24 February, with Constable's quarter share selling rapidly, and with Longmans distraught at having to delay commencement of their sales until copies shipped to them arrived.

The manuscript, now owned by the Pierpont Morgan Library, survives in its entirety, and several physical characteristics support the idea of a fairly uninterrupted composition, with Scott sending off batches to the printer as he proceeded. One noteworthy feature is the presence there of four areas of text missing from the first edition (and from all subsequent editions until the Edinburgh Edition text of 1999, the text used for this Penguin edition). Most significant of these is the sequence of 'Fragments' describing Colonel Mannering's meetings with literati of the Edinburgh Enlightenment, which is now restored to Volume 2, Chapter 18. Also absent in all previous editions, but present in the manuscript without signs of deletion are: 1) a longish discourse on the merits and demerits of the military and legal professions, positioned immediately after Mannering's first meeting Pleydell (see 210.23–211.3); 2) a concluding exchange in the debate between Sir Robert Hazelwood and his son, concerning the troops stationed at Hazelwood-house (see 289.12–20); and 3) a significant part of the gypsy Gabriel's testimony relating to the kidnapping of the young Bertram (see 347.11–18). There is no evidence as to why any of the above were omitted, and a concern for space seems to be the most likely common determining factor. Another possibility that has been mooted in the case of the Edinburgh 'Fragments' is that the inaccessibility of these materials for English readers combined with their all too great transparency for Scottish ones (risking exposure of the author) influenced the omission.[2] Yet there is little sense of such inhibitions in James Ballantyne's glowing commendation to Archibald Constable, likening the account to naturalist painting, shortly after having received copy from Scott: 'The scenes in *Edinburgh* beat the Dutch. I promise you a pro-di-gi-ous roar.'[3] Along with the three other omissions mentioned, all of which thematically enhance the narrative, the manuscript text is restored in full with the addition of a punctuation system and other standardisations in keeping with those normally applied by the intermediaries (Ballantyne and his employees) in processing Scott's texts.

No evidence has been found to identify the transcriber of *Guy Mannering* (employed to preserve Scott's anonymity in the printing house), though John Ballantyne is one possibility; nor have any proofs of the novel apparently survived. There can be little doubt though that the process of turning the text into its public form was hectic in the extreme, and it is clear from internal evidence that Scott was already coping with proofs well before having reached the halfway point in his novel. During the preparation of the first edition, a new punctuation system was added, with a much larger use of conventional points; Scott's older or personally idiosyncratic spellings were generally ironed out (though the first edition is far from achieving standardisation); and over 450 words were changed from English to Scottish forms in the mouths of Scots speakers. The first edition achieves consistency in the case of several proper names, where the manuscript appears irregular, though variants also remain in other instances. Additionally nearly 3000 verbal changes took place in single words or groups of words, these varying between embellishments and adjustments which are almost certainly authorial, routine corrections which could be either by Scott or by an intermediary, and palpable misreadings or misinterpretations of the manuscript. At least one sizeable adjustment was made at a very late stage, evidently as a result of a realisation that the roup (auction) of Ellangowan cannot take place 'tomorrow', as Mrs Mac-Candlish states in the manuscript, since this would place it on the Sabbath, the landlady's utterance being adjusted to the present reading as at 67.36–39, effectively postponing the sale to Monday ('the first free day'). The change had a knock-on effect, however, since the next chapter (13), commencing with Colonel Mannerings's departure for the event, begins 'Early next morning'. This problem was dealt with by the insertion of a cancel (replacement leaf) in the first edition, incorporating the additional paragraph at the end of Chapter 12 which describes Mannering's attendance at church on 'the Sunday following'.

The overall aim of the present text is to provide a version of *Guy Mannering* comparable to the first edition that might have been produced if conditions had been less pressured and if the intermediaries had carried out all their functions correctly. In all more than 2000 emendations have been made to the first-edition base text, a large majority of these involving restoration of the manuscript reading where it has been lost through error or misunderstanding. The first edition's punctuation has largely been accepted, with the exception of cases such as those in which intermediaries failed to unravel Scott's syntactical structure, or where an invasive comma significantly disrupts sense or stress; additionally in some 100 cases the present text endeavours to re-establish the force of Scott's original dashes within speech. Orthography likewise is largely untouched, interventions mainly being limited to cases where the manuscript incorrectly spells a technical term, where a significant phonetic difference is involved, or where the first edition is clearly in error. The present text nevertheless restores more than ninety Scots forms that were either deliberately or inadvertently anglicised by the first edition, in the process reintroducing elements of Scots to three characters, Sampson, Glossin, and Pleydell, whose speech is normally rendered in English orthography. While the large majority of words Scoticised by the first edition have been retained, in some twenty cases the present text reverts to the manuscript's original 'English' form, mostly on the grounds that the Scots replacement has been used unintelligently or is a form not found at any point in the manuscript. The following proper names have been standardised throughout on the authority of Scott's preferred usage as deduced from the manuscript: Charlieshope, Dandie (as opposed to Dandy), Dawstone, Ellangowan, Gordon Arms, Hattaraick, Hazelwood, Jansen,

Skreigh, and Verbruggen. In three of these instances this reverses the first edition, whose choice of Hatt*e*raick, Haz*le*wood, and a hyphenated Charlies-hope are all deemed to represent the wrong option.

Verbal changes made on the authority of the manuscript range from single-word substitutions to more substantial alterations and rearrangements. Amongst smaller changes, the most common category of error is misreading or misunderstanding. As a result of emendations made on the grounds of misreading, Sampson's 'iron' not 'own' countenance now remains unshifting at 16.18; astrologers consult 'astral' not 'abstract' influences (19.39); the dismounted dragoons guarding Hazelwood House stump rather than stamp about (see 287.9); and Sir Robert is apprehensive that the family pictures will be 'damaged' not 'deranged' (289.42). In cases of misunderstanding, errors often occurred when Scott's technical knowledge, especially in law, exceeded that of the intermediaries. Glossin, an ex-land agent, is quite correct when referring at 191.33 to a division of the estate 'rig-about' (rather than, as in the first edition, 'ridge about'); Protocol, a precisian as his name suggests, correctly refers to 'deducing' (not simply 'deducting') a fee for himself (221.12); and a projected new road threatens the 'Mains inclosures' (not 'main inclosures') at Hazelwood (see 284.35 and note). Unfamiliarity as much as simple misreading also probably led to the transmutation of Meg Merrilies's 'fremit giberish', now restored at 278.23, to an implausible-seeming 'French gibberish'. In more general terms, a considerable number of emendations have been made in areas of dialogue, where the intermediaries appear to have insensitively applied grammatical and stylistic conventions more appropriate to formal narrative. Indicative instances are the removal of 'an' from the first edition's '"I have been in an error,"' at 50.8, releasing the manuscript's fuller sense of Sampson's biblical rhetoric, and the restoration of 'can' (as opposed to the first edition's 'could') in Dinmonts's spontaneous '"I can guess that be your Southland tongue"' at 120.18. Equally Pleydell is more regally in character at High Jinks with '"then will we [not 'we will'] give no offence to the Assembly of the Kirk"' (205.8). As the examples given above indicate, many of these changes are local in nature, but the cumulative effect is telling, and the narrative now has a sharper, more direct feel, not least in areas of rapid dialogic exchange, where the interventions of the printing house served to flatten the diverse patterns originally created by Scott.

Relatively few emendations have been introduced from subsequent printed editions, which in all amounted to ten in Scott's lifetime (including reprintings in collected sets), and more than half of these originate from the second edition, which was published only a month after the first. Verbal changes from printed editions include substitutions to prevent close repetition and the correction of grammar in formal narrative – emendations of a kind that ideally should have been made by the first edition. Close examination of these editions in sequence points to a generally accretive process, owing to the common practice of using the immediately previous edition as copy text, with Scott's text becoming more densely punctuated, heavily Scoticised, and 'logically' explicit, largely as a result of changes introduced by hands other than his own. By the time of the Magnum Opus edition, in which *Guy Mannering* appeared as Volumes 3 and 4 in August and September 1829, over 4000 textual variants had built up. Of these some 750 can be identified as stemming from the Interleaved Set (ISet), which had been presented to Scott by Constable in the mid-1820s, and in which he made textual alterations and annotations for the collected set that was eventually to emerge as the Magnum. Scott here, however, was working not only at a considerable distance from the initial creative process but also with a base text (the 1822 octavo edition of *Novels and Tales of the Author of Waverley*) irretrievably altered through the accretions of different printings; and while, in some instances, a creative re-engagement with the original narrative can be sensed (as in a delightful insertion describing how Dinmont took Wasp with him to Portanferry), other interventions have a routine feel to them, as in the introduction of no fewer than 320 dialogic signposts ('he said', etc.) explicitly identifying speakers. The bulk of Scott's effort in the production of the Magnum appears to have been focused on the new Introduction and Notes, which he definitely saw in proof, and which in the case of *Guy Mannering* can arguably be seen at points to further distance the novel from its original genesis. An exception of sorts is found in an Additional Note on 'Galwegian Localities and Personages which have been supposed to be alluded to in the Novel', appended to Volume 4, and based largely on communications from the antiquary Joseph Train; though the possibility of any connection is heavily qualified by Scott, who himself may not have wished to revive old associations.

Compared with the Magnum Opus version, which has formed the basis of all printed editions since Scott's death until the Edinburgh and Penguin editions, the present text reflects the period of Scott's original and most intense involvement with a novel conceived at the height of his powers and launched at a crucial stage in his literary career. A more extensive explanation of emendations and a full list are to be found in the Edinburgh Edition: *Guy Mannering*, EEWN 2, ed. P. D. Garside (Edinburgh, 1999), 410–93.

NOTES

1 J. G. Lockhart, *Memoirs of the Life of Sir Walter Scott, Bart.*, 7 vols (Edinburgh, 1837–38), 3.321. Doubt is cast on the claim in Sir Herbert Grierson, *Sir Walter Scott, Bart.* (London, 1938), 125; and in John Sutherland's more mixed discussion of 'the improbable "six weeks at Christmas" claim', in *The Life of Walter Scott: A Critical Biography* (Oxford, 1995), 180–81.

2 For an earlier discussion of the possibilities, see Jane Millgate's article, '*Guy Mannering* in Edinburgh: The Evidence of the Manuscript', *The Library*, 32 (1977), 238–45, which also provided the first transcript of the 'Fragments' from the manuscript.

3 National Library of Scotland, MS 23230, f. 59r (letter of 30 January, 1815).

GUY MANNERING;

OR,

THE ASTROLOGER.

BY THE AUTHOR OF "WAVERLEY."

'Tis said that words and signs have power
O'er sprites in planetary hour;
But scarce I praise their venturous part,
Who tamper with such dangerous art.
Lay of the Last Minstrel.

IN THREE VOLUMES.

VOL. I.

EDINBURGH:
Printed by James Ballantyne and Co.
FOR LONGMAN, HURST, REES, ORME, AND BROWN,
LONDON; AND ARCHIBALD CONSTABLE AND CO.
EDINBURGH.

1815.

GUY MANNERING

OR

THE ASTROLOGER

VOLUME I

Chapter One

"He cannot deny, that, looking round upon the dreary region, and seeing nothing but bleak fields, and naked trees, hills obscured by fogs, and flats covered with inundations, he did for some time suffer melancholy to prevail upon him, and wished himself again safe at home."

Travels of Will. Marvel, Idler, No. 49

IT WAS in the beginning of the month of November, 17—, when a young English gentleman, who had just left the university of Oxford, made use of the liberty afforded him to visit some parts of the north of England; and curiosity extended his tour into the adjacent frontier of the sister country. He had visited, upon the day that opens our history, some monastic ruins in the county of Dumfries, spent much of the day in making drawings of them from different points, and, upon mounting his horse to resume his journey, the brief and gloomy twilight of the season had already commenced. His way lay through a wide tract of black morass, extending for miles on each side and before him. Little eminences arose like islands on its surface, bearing here and there patches of corn, which even at this season was green, and sometimes a hut, or farm-house, shaded by a willow or two, and surrounded by large elder-bushes. These insulated dwellings communicated with each other by winding passages through the moss, impassable by any but the natives themselves. The public road, however, was tolerably well-made and safe, so that the prospect of being benighted brought with it no real danger. Still it is uncomfortable to travel, alone and in the dark, through an unknown country, and there are few ordinary occasions upon which Fancy frets herself so much as in a situation like that of Mannering.

As the light grew faint and more faint, and the morass appeared blacker and blacker, our traveller questioned more closely each chance passenger upon his distance from the village of Kippletringan, where he proposed to quarter for the night. His queries were usually answered by a counter-challenge as to the place from whence he came. While sufficient day-light remained to shew the dress and appearance of a gentleman, these cross interrogatories were usually put in the form of a case supposed, as, "Ye'll hae been at the auld Abbey o' Halycross, sir? there's mony English gentlemen gang to see that."—Or, "Your honour will be come frae the house o' Pouderloupat?" But when the voice of the querist alone was distinguishable, the response usually was, "Where are ye coming frae at sick a time o' night as the like o' this?"—or, "Ye'll no be of this country, freend?" The answers, when obtained, were neither very reconcileable to each other, nor accurate in the information which they afforded. Kippletringan was distant at first "*a gay bit.*" Then the "*gay bit*" was more accurately described, as "*aiblins three miles;*" then the "*three miles*" diminished into "*like a mile and a bittock*;" then extended themselves into "*four miles or there awa;*" and, lastly, a female voice having hushed a wailing infant which she carried in her arms, assured Guy Mannering, "It was a weary lang gait yet to Kippletringan, and unco heavy road for foot passengers." The poor hack upon which Mannering was mounted was probably of opinion that it suited him as ill as the female respondent; he began to flag very much, answered each application of the spur with a groan, and stumbled at every stone (and they were not few) which lay in his road.

Mannering now grew impatient. He was occasionally betrayed into a deceitful hope that the end of his journey was near, by the apparition of a twinkling light or two; but, as he came up, he was disappointed to find the gleams proceeded from some of those farm-houses which occasionally ornamented the surface of this extensive bog. At length, to compleat his perplexity, he arrived at a place where the road divided itself into two. If there had been light to consult the reliques of a finger-post which stood there, it would have been of little avail, as, according to the good custom of North-Britain, the inscription had been defaced shortly after its erection. Our adventurer was therefore compelled, like a knight-errant of old, to trust to the sagacity of his horse, which, without any demur, chose the left-hand path, and seemed to proceed at somewhat a livelier pace than formerly, affording thereby a hope that he knew he was drawing near to his quarters for the evening. This hope was not speedily accomplished, and Mannering, whose impatience made every furlong seem three, began to think that Kippletringan was actually retreating before him in proportion to his advance.

It was now very cloudy, although the stars, from time to time, shed a twinkling and uncertain light. Hitherto nothing had broken the silence around him, but the deep cry of the bog-blitter, or bull-of-the-bog, a large species of bittern; and the sighs of the wind as it passed along the weary morass. To these was now joined the distant roar of the ocean, towards which the traveller seemed to be fast approaching. This was no circumstance to make his mind easy. Many of the roads in that county then lay along the sea-beach, and were liable to be flooded by the tides, which rise with great height, and advance with extreme rapidity. Others were intersected with creeks and small inlets, which it was only safe to pass at particular times of the tide. Neither circumstance would have suited a dark night, a fatigued horse, and a traveller ignorant of his road. Mannering resolved, therefore, definitively, to halt for the night at the first inhabited place, however poor, which he might chance to reach, unless he could procure a guide to this unlucky village of Kippletringan.

A miserable hut gave him an opportunity to execute his purpose. He found out the door with no small difficulty, and for some time knocked without producing any other answer than a duett between a female and a cur-dog, the latter yelping as if he would have barked his heart out, the other screaming in chorus. By degrees the human tones predominated; but the angry bark of the cur being at the instant changed into a howl, it is probable something more than fair strength of lungs had contributed to the ascendancy.

"Sorrow be in your thrapple than!" these were the first articulate words, "will ye no let me hear what the man wants, wi' your yaffing?"

"Am I far from Kippletringan, good dame?"

"Frae Kippletringan!!!" in an exalted tone of wonder, which we can but faintly express by three points of admiration. "Ow, man! ye should hae hadden *easel* to Kippletringan—ye maun gae back as far as the Whaap, and haud the Whaap till ye come to Ballenloan, and than"——

"This will never do, good dame! my horse is almost quite set up—can you not give me a night's lodging?"

"Troth and can I no—I am a lone woman, for James he's awa to Drumshourloch fair with the year-aulds, and I darena for my life open the door to ony of your gang-there-out sort o' bodies."

"But what must I do then, good dame? for I can't sleep here upon the road all night?"

"Troth, I ken na, unless ye like to gae doun and speer for quarters at the Place. I'se warrant they'll take ye, whether ye be gentle or semple."

"Simple enough, to be wandering here at such a time of night," thought Mannering, who was ignorant of the meaning of the phrase, "but how shall I get to the *place*, as you call it?"

"Ye maun haud *wessel* by the end o' the loan, and take tent o' the jaw-hole."

"O, if you get to *easel* and *wessel* again, I am undone!—Is there no boy that could guide me to this *place?* I will pay him handsomely."

The word *pay* operated like magic. "Jock, ye villain," exclaimed the voice from the interior, "are ye lying routing there, and a young gentleman seeking the way to the Place? Get up, ye fause loon, and shew him the way down the meikle loaning.—He'll shew you the way, sir, and I'se warrant ye'll be weel put up; for they never turn awa' naebody frae the door; and ye'll be come in the canny moment I'm thinking, for the laird's servant—that's no to say his body-servant, but the helper like—rade express by this e'en to fetch the houdie, and he just staid the drinking o' twa pints o' tippeny, to tell us how my leddy was ta'en wi' her pains."

"Perhaps," said Mannering, "at such a time a stranger's arrival might be inconvenient?"

"Hout na, ye needna be blate about that; their house is muckle eneugh, and clecking time's aye canty time."

By this time Jock had found his way into all the intricacies of a tattered doublet, and more tattered pair of breeches, and sallied forth a great white-headed, bare-legged, lubberly boy of twelve years old, so exhibited by the glimpse of a rush-light, which his half-naked mother held in such a manner as to get a peep at the stranger, without greatly exposing herself to view in return. Jock moved on westward, by the end of the house, leading Mannering's horse by the bridle, and piloting, with some dexterity, along the little firm path which bordered the formidable jaw-hole, whose vicinity the stranger was made sensible of by means of more organs than one. His guide then dragged the weary hack along a broken and stony cart-track, next over a ploughed field, then broke down a *slap*, as he called it, in a dry stone fence, and lugged the unresisting animal through the breach, about a rood of the simple masonry giving way in the sputter with which he passed. Finally, he led the way, through a wicket, into something which had still the air of an avenue, though many of the trees were felled. The roar of the ocean was now near and full, and the moon, which began to make her appearance, gleamed on a turreted and apparently a ruined mansion of considerable extent. Mannering fixed his eyes upon it with a disconsolate sensation.

"Why, my little fellow, this is a ruin, not a house."

"Ah, but the lairds lived there langsyne—that's Ellangowan Auld Place; there's a hantle bogles about it—but ye needna be feared—I never saw ony mysell, and we're just at the door of the New Place."

Accordingly, leaving the ruins on the right, a few steps brought the traveller in front of a small modern house, at which his guide rapped with great importance. Mannering told his circumstances to the servant; and the gentleman of the house, who heard his tale from the parlour, stepped forward, and welcomed the stranger hospitably to Ellangowan. The boy, made happy with half-a-crown, was dismissed to his cottage, the weary horse was inducted into a stall, and Mannering found himself in a few minutes seated by a comfortable supper, to which his cold ride gave him a hearty appetite.

Chapter Two

——Comes me cranking in,
And cuts me from the best of all my land,
A huge half-moon, a monstrous cantle out.
Henry Fourth, Part I

THE COMPANY in the parlour at Ellangowan consisted of the Laird himself, and a sort of person who might be the village schoolmaster, or perhaps the minister's assistant; his appearance was too shabby to indicate the minister, considering he was on a visit to the Laird.

The Laird himself was one of those second-rate sort of persons, that are to be found frequently in rural situations. Fielding has described one class as *feras consumere nati;* but the love of field-sports indicates a certain activity of mind, which had forsaken Mr Bertram, if he ever possessed it. A good-humoured listlessness of countenance formed the only remarkable expression of his features, although they were rather handsome than otherwise. In fact, his physiognomy indicated the inanity of character which pervaded his life. I will give the reader some insight into his state and conversation, before he has finished a long lecture to Mannering, upon the propriety and comfort of wrapping his stirrup-irons round with a wisp of straw, when he had occasion to ride in a chill evening.

Godfrey Bertram of Ellangowan succeeded to a long pedigree and a short rent-roll, like many lairds of that period. His list of forefathers ascended so high, that they were lost in the barbarous ages of Galwegian independence; so that his genealogical-tree, besides the christian and crusading names of Godfreys, and Gilberts, and Dennis's, and Rolands, without end, bore heathen fruit of yet darker ages,—Arths, and Knarths, and Donagilds, and Hanlons. In truth, they had been formerly the stormy chiefs of a desart, but extensive domain, and the heads of a numerous tribe, called Mac-Dingawaie, though they afterwards adopted the Norman surname of Bertram. They had made war, raised rebellions, been defeated, beheaded, and hanged, as became a family of importance, for many centuries. But they had gradually lost ground in the world, and, from being themselves the heads of treason and traitorous conspiracies, the Bertrams, or Mac-Dingawaies of Ellangowan, had sunk into subordinate accomplices. Their most fatal exhibitions in this capacity took place in the seventeenth century, when the foul fiend possessed them with a spirit of contradiction which uniformly involved them in controversy with the ruling powers. They reversed the conduct of the celebrated Vicar of Bray, and adhered as tenaciously to the weaker side, as that worthy divine to the stronger. And truly, like him, they had their reward.

Allan Bertram of Ellangowan, who flourished *tempore Caroli primi*, was, says my authority, Sir Robert Douglas, in his Scottish Baronage, (see the title Ellangowan,) "a steady loyalist, and full of zeal for the cause of his sacred majesty, in which he united with the great Marquis of Montrose, and other truly zealous and honourable patriots, and sustained great losses in that behalf. He had the honour of knighthood conferred upon him by his most sacred majesty, and was sequestrated as a malignant by the parliament, 1642, and afterward as a resolutioner, in the year 1648."—These two cross-grained epithets of malignant and resolutioner cost poor Sir Allan one half of the family estate. His son Dennis Bertram married a daughter of an eminent fanatic, who had a seat in the council of state, and saved by that union the remainder of the family property. But, as the devil would have it, he became enamoured of the lady's principles as well as her charms, and my author gives him this character: "He was a man of eminent parts and resolution, for which reason he was chosen by the western counties one of the committee of noblemen and gentlemen, to report their griefs to the privy council of Charles II. anent the coming in of the Highland host in 1678." For undertaking this patriotic task he underwent a fine, to pay which he was obliged to mortgage half of the remaining moiety of his paternal property. This loss he might have recovered by dint of severe economy, but upon the breaking out of Argyle's rebellion, Dennis Bertram was again suspected by government, apprehended, sent to Dunnottar Castle, on the coast of the Mearns, and there broke his neck in an attempt to escape from a subterranean habitation, called the Whigs' Vault, in which he was confined with some eighty of the same persuasion. The appriser, therefore, (as the holder of a mortgage was then called,) entered upon possession, and, in the language of Hotspur, "came me cranking in," and cut the family out of another monstrous cantle of their remaining property.

Donohoe Bertram, with somewhat of an Irish name, and somewhat of an Irish temper, succeeded to the diminished property of Ellangowan. He turned out of doors the Rev. Aaron Macbriar, his mother's chaplain, (it is said they quarrelled about the good graces of a milk-maid,) drank himself daily drunk with brimming healths to the King, Council, and Bishops; held orgies with the Laird of Lagg, Theophilus Oglethorpe, and Sir James Turner; and lastly took his grey gelding, and joined Clavers at Killie-krankie. At the skirmish of Dunkeld, 1689, he was shot dead by a Cameronian with a silver button (it is said he had proof from the Evil One against lead and steel,) and his grave is still called the "Wicked Laird's Lair."

His son, Lewis, had more prudence than seems usually to have belonged to the family. He nursed what property was yet left to him; for Donohoe's excesses, as well as fines and forfeitures, had made another inroad upon the estate. And although even he did not escape the fatality which induced the Lairds of Ellangowan to interfere in politics, he had yet the prudence, ere he went *out* with Lord Kenmore in 1715, to convey his estate to trustees, in order to parry pains and penalties, in case the Earl of Mar could not put down the protestant succession. But Scylla and Charybdis—a word to the wise—he only saved his estate at expence of a law-suit, which again subdivided the family property. He was, however, a man of resolution. He sold part of the lands, evacuated the old castle, where the family lived in their decadence, as a mouse (said an old farmer) lives under a firlot. Pulling down part of these venerable ruins, he built a narrow house of three stories height, with a front like a grenadier's cap, two windows on each side, and a door in the midst, full of all manner of cross lights. This was the New Place of Ellangowan, in which we left our hero, better amused, perhaps, than our readers, and to this Lewis Bertram retreated, full of projects for re-establishing the prosperity of his family. He took some land into his own hand, rented some from neighbouring proprietors, bought and sold Highland cattle and Cheviot sheep, rode to fairs and trysts, fought hard bargains, and held necessity at the staff's end as well as he might. But what he gained in purse he lost in honour, for such agricultural and commercial negociations were very ill looked upon by his brother lairds, who minded nothing but cock-fighting, hunting, coursing, and horse-racing. These occupations encroached, in their opinion, upon the article of Ellangowan's gentry, and he found it necessary gradually to estrange himself from their society, and sink into what was then a very ambiguous character, the gentleman farmer. In the midst of his schemes death claimed his tribute, and the scanty remains of a large property descended upon Godfrey Bertram, the present possessor, his only son.

The danger of the father's speculations was soon seen. Deprived of his personal and active superintendance, all his undertakings miscarried, and became either abortive or perilous. Without a single spark of energy to meet or repel these misfortunes, Godfrey put his faith in the activity of another. He kept neither hunters, nor hounds, nor any other southern preliminaries to ruin; but, as has been observed of his countrymen, he kept *a man of business*, who answered the purpose equally well. Under this gentleman's supervision small debts grew into large, interests were accumulated upon capitals, moveable bonds became heritable, and law charges were heaped upon all; though Ellangowan possessed so little the spirit of a litigant, that he was upon two occasions *charged* to make payment of the expences of a long litigation, although he had never before heard that he had such a case in court.

Meanwhile his neighbours predicted his final ruin, those of the higher rank, with some malignity, accounting him already a degraded brother. The lower classes, seeing nothing enviable in his situation, marked his embarrassments with more compassion. He was even a kind of favourite with them, and upon the division of a common, or the holding of a black-fishing, or poaching court, or any similar occasion, when they conceived themselves oppressed by the gentry, they were in the habit of saying to each other, "Ah, if Ellangowan, honest man, had his ain that his forebears had afore him, he wad na see the puir folk trodden down this gait." Meanwhile, this general good opinion never prevented their taking the advantage of him on all possible occasions, turning their cattle into his parks, stealing his wood, shooting his game, and so forth, "for the laird, honest man, he'll never find it,—he never minds what a puir body does."—Pedlars, gypsies, tinkers, vagrants of all descriptions, roosted about his outhouses, or harboured in his kitchen, and the laird, who was "nae nice body," but a thorough gossip, as most weak men, found recompence for his hospitality in the pleasure of questioning them on the news of the country side.

A circumstance arrested Ellangowan's progress upon the high road to ruin. This was his marriage with a lady who had a portion of about four thousand pounds. Nobody in the neighbourhood could conceive why she married him, and endowed him with her wealth, unless because he had a tall handsome figure, a good set of features, a genteel address, and the most perfect good humour. It might be some additional consideration, that she was herself at the reflecting age of twenty-eight, and had no near relations to controul her actions or choice.

It was in this lady's behalf (confined for the first time after her marriage) that the speedy and active express, mentioned by the old dame of the cottage, had been dispatched to Kippletringan on the night of Mannering's arrival.

Though we have said so much of the Laird himself, it still remains that we make the reader in some degree acquainted with his companion. This was Abel Sampson, commonly called, from his occupation as a pedagogue, Dominie Sampson. He was of low birth, but evincing, even from his cradle, an uncommon seriousness of disposition, the poor parents were encouraged to hope that their *bairn*, as they expressed it, "might wag his pow in a pu'pit yet." With an ambitious view to such a consummation, they pinched and pared, rose early and lay down late, eat dry bread and drank cold water, to secure to Abel the means of learning. Meantime, his tall ungainly figure, his taciturn and grave manners, and some grotesque habits of swinging his limbs, and screwing his visage while reciting his task, made poor Sampson the ridicule of all his school-companions. The same qualities secured him at college a plentiful share of the same sort of notice. Half the youthful mob "of the yards" used to assemble regularly to see Dominie Sampson, (for he had already attained that honoured title,) descend the stairs from the Greek class, with his Lexicon under his arm, his long mis-shapen legs sprawling abroad, and keeping awkward time to the play of his immense shoulder-blades, as they raised and depressed the loose and threadbare black coat which seemed his constant and only wear. When he spoke, the efforts of the professor were totally inadequate to restrain the inextinguishable laughter of the students, and sometimes unequal to repress his own. The long sallow visage, the goggle eyes, the huge under-jaw, which appeared not to open and shut by an act of volition, but to be dropped and hoisted up again by some complicated machinery within the inner man, the harsh and dissonant voice, and the screech-owl notes to which it was exalted when he was exhorted to pronounce more distinctly, all added fresh subject for mirth to the torn cloak and tattered shoe, which have afforded legitimate subjects of raillery against a poor scholar from Juvenal's time downward. It was never known that Sampson either exhibited irritability at this ill usage, or made the least attempt to retort upon his tormentors. He slunk from college by the most secret paths he could discover, and plunged himself into his miserable lodgings, where, for eighteen-pence a-week, he was allowed the benefit of a straw mattress, and, if his landlady was in good humour, permission to study his task by her fire. Under all these disadvantages, he attained a competent knowledge of Greek and Latin, and some acquaintance with the sciences.

In process of time, Abel Sampson, probationer of divinity, was admitted to the privileges of a preacher. But, alas! betwixt his own bashfulness, and a strong disposition to risibility which pervaded the congregation upon his first attempt, he became totally incapable of proceeding in his intended discourse, gasped, grinned hideously, rolled his eyes till the congregation thought them flying out of his head, shut the Bible, stumbled down the pulpit-stairs, trampling upon the old women who generally take their station there, and was ever afterward designated as a "stickit minister." And thus he wandered back to his own country, with blighted hopes and prospects, to share the poverty of his parents. As he had neither friend nor confidant, hardly even an acquaintance, no one had the means of observing closely, how Dominie Sampson bore a disappointment which supplied the whole town where it happened with a week's sport. It would be endless even to mention the numerous jokes to which it gave birth, from a ballad, called "Sampson's Riddle," written upon the subject by a smart young student of humanity, to the sly hope of the principal, that the fugitive had not taken the college gates along with him in his retreat.

To all appearance the equanimity of Sampson was unshaken. He sought to assist his parents by teaching a school, and soon had plenty of scholars, but very few fees. In fact, he taught the sons of farmers for what they chose to give him, and the poor for nothing; and, to the shame of the former be it spoken, the pedagogue's gains never equalled those of a skilful ploughman. He wrote, however, a good hand, and added something to his pittance by copying accounts and writing letters for Ellangowan. By degrees, the Laird, who was much estranged from general society, became partial to that of Dominie Sampson. Conversation, it is true, was out of the question, but the Dominie was a good listener, and stirred the fire with some address. He attempted also to snuff candles, but was unsuccessful, and relinquished that ambitious post of courtesy after having twice reduced the parlour to total darkness. So his civilities, in future, were confined to taking off his glass of ale in exactly the same time and measure with the Laird, and in uttering certain indistinct murmurs of acquiescence at the conclusion of the long prosing stories of Ellangowan.

Upon one of these occasions, he presented for the first time to Mannering his tall, gaunt, awkward, boney figure, attired in a threadbare suit of black, with a coloured handkerchief, not over clean, about his long sinewy, scraggy neck, and his nether person arrayed in grey breeches, deep-blue stockings, clouted shoes, and small copper buckles.

Such is the brief outline of the lives and fortunes of those two persons, in whose society Mannering now found himself comfortably seated.

Chapter Three

Do not the hist'ries of all ages
Relate miraculous presages,
Of strange turns in the world's affairs,
Foreseen by astrologers, sooth-sayers,
Chaldeans, learned Genethliacs,
And some that have writ almanacks?
Hudibras

THE CIRCUMSTANCES of the landlady were pleaded to Mannering, first, as an apology for her not appearing to welcome her guest, and for those deficiencies in his entertainment which her attention might have supplied, and then as an excuse for pressing an extra bottle of good wine.

"I cannot well sleep," said the Laird, with all the anxious feelings of a father in such a predicament, "till I hear she's gotten ower with it—and if you, sir, are not very sleepry, and would do me and the Dominie the honour to sit up wi' us, I am sure we will not detain you very late. Luckie Howatson is very expeditious;—there was anes a lass that was in that way—she did not live far from hereabouts—ye need na shake your head and groan, Dominie—I am sure the kirk dues were all well paid, and what can a man do more?—it was put till her ere she had a sark ower her head; and the man that she since wadded does not think her a pin the worse for the misfortune. —They live, Mr Mannering, by the shore-side, at Annan, and a more decent orderly couple, with six as fine bairns as you would wish to see plash in a salt-water dub; and little curlie Godfrey—that's the eldest, the come-o'-will, as I may say—he's on board an excise yacht—I hae a cousin at the Board of Excise, that's Commissioner Bertram; he got his commissionership in the great contest for the county, that ye must have heard of, for it was appealed to the House of Commons—now I should have voted there for the Laird of Balruddery; but ye see my father was a jacobite, and *out* with Kenmore, so he never took the oaths; and I ken not well how it was, but all that I could do and say they keepit me off the roll, though my agent, that had a vote upon my estate, ranked as a good vote for auld Sir Thomas Kittlecourt. But, to return to what I was saying, Luckie Howatson is very expeditious, for this lass"——

Here the desultory and long narrative of the Laird of Ellangowan was interrupted by the voice of some one ascending the stairs from the kitchen story, and singing at full pitch of voice. The high notes were too shrill for a man, the low seemed too deep for a woman. The words, as far as Mannering could distinguish them, seemed to run thus:

> Canny moment, lucky fit;
> Is the lady lighter yet?
> Be it lad, or be it lass,
> Sign wi' cross, and sain wi' mass.

"It's Meg Merrilies, the gypsie, as sure as I am a sinner," said Mr Bertram. The Dominie groaned deeply, uncrossed his legs, drew in the huge splay foot which his former position had extended, placed it perpendicular, and stretched the other limb over it instead, puffing out between whiles huge volumes of tobacco smoke. "What needs ye groan, Dominie? I am sure Meg's sangs do nae harm."

"Nor good neither," answered Dominie Sampson, in a voice whose untuneable harshness corresponded with the awkwardness of his figure. They were the first words which Mannering had heard him speak; and as he had been watching, with some curiosity, when this eating, drinking, moving, and smoking automaton would perform the part of speaking, he was a good deal diverted with the harsh timber tones which issued from it. But at this moment the door opened, and Meg Merrilies entered.

Her appearance made Mannering start. She was full six feet high, wore a man's great-coat over the rest of her dress, had in her hand a goodly sloe-thorn cudgel, and in all points of equipment, except her petticoats, seemed rather masculine than feminine. Her dark elf-locks shot out like the snakes of the gorgon, between an old-fashioned bonnet called a Bongrace, heightening the singular effect of her strong and weather-beaten features, which they partly shadowed, while her eye had a wild roll that indicated something like real or affected insanity.

"Aweel, Ellangowan," she said, "wad it no hae been a bonnie thing, an the leddy had been brought a-bed, and me at the fair o' Drumshourloch, no kenning nor dreaming a word about it? Wha was to hae keepit awa the worriecows, I trow? Aye, and the elves and gyre carlings frae the bonny bairn, grace be wi' it? Aye, or said Saint Colme's charm for its sake, the dear?" And without waiting an answer she began to sing—

> "Trefoil, vervain, John's-wort, dill,
> Hinder witches of their will;
> Weel is them, that weel may
> Fast upon St Andrew's day.

"Saint Bride and her brat,
Saint Colme and his hat,
Saint Michael and his spear,
Keep the house frae reif and weir."

This charm she sung to a wild tune, in a high and shrill voice, and, cutting three capers with such strength and agility as almost to touch the roof of the room, concluded, "And now, Laird, will ye no order me a tass o' brandy?"

"That you shall have, Meg—Sit down yont there at the door, and tell us what news ye have heard at the fair o' Drumshourloch."

"Troth, Laird, and there was mickle want o' you, and the like o' you; for there was a whin bonnie lasses there, forbye mysell, and deil ane to gie them hansels."

"Weel, Meg, and how mony gypsies were sent to the tolbooth?"

"Troth, but three, Laird, for there were nae mair in the fair, bye mysell as I said before, and I e'en gae them leg-bail—there's nae ease in dealing with quarrelsome folk.—And there's Dunbog has warned the Red Rotten and John Young aff his grounds—black be his cast! he's nae gentleman, nor drap's bluid o' gentleman, wad grudge twa gangrel puir bodies the shelter o' a waste house, and the thristles by the road side for the bit cuddy, and the bits o' rotten birk to boil their drap parridge wi'. Weel, there's ane abune a'—but we'll see if the red cock craw not in his bonnie barn-yard ae morning before day-dawing."

"Hush! Meg, hush! hush! that's nae safe talk."

"What does she mean?" said Mannering to Sampson in an under tone.

"Fire-raising," answered the laconic Dominie.

"Who, or what is she, in the name of wonder?"

"Harlot, thief, witch, and gypsey," answered Sampson again.

"O troth, Laird," continued Meg, during this bye-talk, "it's but to the like o' you ane can open their heart; ye see, they say Dunbog's nae mair a gentleman than the blunker that's biggit the bonnie house doun in the howm. But the like o' you, Laird, that's a real gentleman for sae mony hundred years, and never hounds puir folk off your ground as if they were mad tykes, nane o' our fowk wad steer your gear if ye had as mony capons as there's leaves on the trysting-tree.—And now some o' ye maun lay down your watch, and tell me the very minute o' the hour the wean's born, and I'll spae its fortune."

"Aye, but, Meg, we shall not want your assistance, for here's a student from Oxford that knows much better than you how to spae his fortune—he does it by the stars."

"Certainly, sir," said Mannering, entering into the simple humour of his landlord, "I will calculate his nativity according to the rule of the Triplicities, as recommended by Pythagoras, Hippocrates, Diocles, and Avicenna. Or I will begin *ab hora questionis*, as Haly, Messahala, Ganivetus, and Guido Bonatus, have recommended."

One of Sampson's great recommendations to the favour of Mr Bertram was, that he never suspected the most gross imposition, so that the Laird, whose humble attempts at jocularity were chiefly confined to what were then called *bites* and *bams*, since denominated *hoaxes* and *quizzes*, had the fairest possible subject of wit in the unsuspecting Dominie. It is true, he never laughed, or joined in the laugh which his own simplicity afforded—nay it is said, he never laughed but once in his life, and upon that memorable occasion his landlady miscarried, betwixt surprise at the event itself, and terror at the hideous grimaces which attended this unusual cachinnation. The only effect which the discovery of such impositions produced upon this saturnine personage was, to extort an ejaculation of "Prodigious!" or "Very facetious!" pronounced syllabically, but without moving a muscle of his iron countenance.

Upon this occasion, he turned a gaunt and ghastly stare upon the youthful astrologer, and seemed to doubt if he had rightly understood his answer to his patron.

"I am afraid, sir," said Mannering, turning towards him, "you may be one of those unhappy persons, whose dim eyes being unable to penetrate the starry spheres, and to discern therein the decrees of heaven at a distance, have their hearts barred against conviction by prejudice and misprision."

"Truly," said Sampson, "I opine with Sir Isaac Newton, Knight, and umwhile master of his majesty's mint, that the (pretended) science of astrology is altogether vain, frivolous, and unsatisfactory." And here he reposed his oracular jaws.

"Really," resumed the traveller, "I am sorry to see a gentleman of your learning and gravity labouring under such strange blindness and delusion. Will you place the brief, the modern, and, as I may say, the vernacular name of Isaac Newton in opposition to the grave and sonorous authorities of Dariot, Bonatus, Ptolemy, Haly, Etzler, Dieterick, Naibod, Hasfurt, Zael, Tanstettor, Agrippa, Duretus, Maginus, Origan, and Argol? Do not Christians and Heathens, and Jews and Gentiles, and poets and philosophers, unite in allowing the starry influences?"

"*Communis error*—it is a general mistake," answered the inflexible Dominie Sampson.

"Not so," replied the young Englishman, "it is a general and well-grounded belief."

"It is the resource of cheaters, knaves, and cozeners," said Sampson.

"*Abusus non tollit usum.* The abuse of any thing doth not abrogate the lawful use thereof."

During this discussion, Ellangowan was somewhat like a woodcock caught in his own springe. He turned his face alternately from the one spokesman to the other, and began, from the gravity with which Mannering plied his adversary, and the learning which he displayed in the controversy, to give him credit for being half serious. As for Meg, she fixed her bewildered eyes upon the astrologer, overpowered by a jargon more mysterious than her own.

Mannering pressed his advantage, and ran over all the hard terms of art which a tenacious memory supplied, and which, from circumstances hereafter to be noticed, had been familiar to him in early youth.

Signs and planets, in aspects sextile, quartile, trine, conjoined or opposite; houses of heaven, with their cusps, hours, and minutes; Almuten, Almochoden, Anahibazon, Catahibazon; a thousand terms of equal sound and significance, poured thick and threefold upon the unshrinking Dominie, whose stubborn incredulity bore him out against the pelting of this pitiless storm.

At length, the joyful annunciation that the lady had presented her husband with a fine boy, and was (of course) as well as could be expected, broke off this interview. Mr Bertram hastened to the lady's apartment, Meg Merrilies descended to the kitchen to secure her share of the "groaning malt," and Mannering, after looking his watch, and noting, with great minuteness, the hour and minute of the birth, requested, with becoming gravity, that the Dominie would conduct him to some place where he might have a view of the heavenly bodies.

The schoolmaster, without further answer, rose and threw open a door half sashed with glass, which led to an old-fashioned terrace-walk behind the modern house, communicating with the platform on which the ruins of the ancient castle were situated. The wind had arisen, and swept before it the clouds which had formerly obscured the sky. The moon was high, and at full, and all the lesser satellites of heaven shone forth in cloudless effulgence. The scene which their light presented to Mannering was in the highest degree unexpected and striking.

We have observed, that in the latter part of his journey our traveller approached the sea-shore, without being aware how nearly. He now perceived that the ruins of Ellangowan castle were situated upon a promontory, or projection of rock, which formed one side of a small and placid bay on the sea-shore. The modern mansion was situated lower, though closely adjoining, and the ground behind it descended to the sea by a smooth swelling green bank, divided into levels by natural terraces, on which grew some old trees, and terminating upon the white sand. The other side of the bay, opposite to the old castle, was a sloping and varied promontory, covered chiefly with copsewood, which on that favoured coast grows almost within water-mark. A fisherman's cottage peeped from among the trees. Even at this dead hour of night there were lights moving upon the shore, probably occasioned by the unloading a smuggling lugger from the Isle of Man, which was lying in the bay. On the light being observed from the sashed door of the house, a halloo from the vessel of "Ware hawk! Douse the glim!" alarmed those who were on shore, and the lights instantly disappeared.

It was now one hour after midnight, and the prospect around was lovely. The grey old towers of the ruin, partly entire, partly broken, here bearing the rusty weather-stains of ages, and there partially mantled with ivy, stretched along the verge of the dark rock which rose on Mannering's right hand. In his front was the quiet placid bay, whose little waves, crisping and sparkling to the moon-beams, rolled successively along its surface, and dashed with a soft and murmuring ripple against the silvery beach. To the left the woods advanced into the ocean, waving in the moonlight along ground of an undulating and varied form, and presented those varieties of light and shade, and that interesting combination of glade and thicket, upon which the eye delights to rest, charmed with what it sees, yet curious to pierce still deeper into the intricacies of the woodland scenery. Above rolled the planets, each, by its own liquid orbit of light, distinguished from the inferior or more distant stars. So strangely can imagination deceive even those by whose volition it has been excited, that Mannering, while gazing upon these brilliant bodies, was half inclined to believe in the influence superstition ascribed to them over human events. But Mannering was a youthful lover, and might perhaps be influenced by the feelings so exquisitely expressed by a modern poet:

For fable is Love's world, his home, his birth-place:
Delightedly dwells he 'mong fays and talismans,
And spirits, and delightedly believes
Divinities, being himself divine.
The intelligible forms of ancient poets,
The fair humanities of old religion,
The power, the beauty, and the majesty,
That had their haunts in dale, or piny mountain,
Or forest by slow stream, or pebbly spring,
Or chasms and wat'ry depths; all these have vanish'd.
They live no longer in the faith of reason!
But still the heart doth need a language, still

Doth the old instinct bring back the old names.
And to yon starry world they now are gone,
Spirits or gods, that used to share this earth
With man as with their friend, and to the lover
Yonder they move, from yonder visible sky
Shoot influence down: and even at this day
'Tis Jupiter who brings whate'er is great,
And Venus who brings every thing that's fair.

Such musings soon gave way to others. "Alas!" he thought, "my good old tutor, who used to enter so deep into the controversy between Heydon and Chambers on the subject of astrology, he would have looked upon this scene with other eyes, and would have seriously endeavoured to discover from the respective position of these luminaries their probable effects upon the destiny of the new-born infant, as if the courses or emanations of the stars superseded, or, at least, were co-ordinate with Divine Providence. Well, rest be with him! he instilled into me enough of knowledge for erecting a scheme of nativity, and therefore will I presently go about it." So saying, and having noted the position of the principal planetary bodies, Guy Mannering returned to the house. The Laird met him in the parlour, and, acquainting him, with great glee, that he was the father of a healthy boy, seemed rather disposed to press further conviviality. He admitted, however, Mannering's plea of weariness, and conducting him to his sleeping apartment, left him at repose.

Chapter Four

Come and see! trust thine own eyes,
A fearful sign stands in the house of life,
An enemy; a fiend lurks close behind
The radiance of thy planet—O be warned.
COLERIDGE, from SCHILLER

THE BELIEF in astrology was almost universal in the middle of the seventeenth century; it began to waver and become fickle towards the close of that period, and in the beginning of the eighteenth the art fell into general disrepute, and even under general ridicule. Yet it still had its partizans even in the seats of learning. Grave and studious men were loth to relinquish the calculations which had become the principal objects of their studies, and reluctant to descend from the predominating height to which an insight into futurity, by the power of consulting astral influences and conjunctions, afforded them over the rest of mankind.

Among those who cherished this imaginary privilege with undoubting faith, was an old clergyman, with whom Mannering was placed during his youth. He wasted his eyes in observing the stars, and his brains in calculations upon their various combinations. His pupil, in early youth, naturally caught some portion of his enthusiasm, and laboured for a time to make himself master of the technical process of astrological research; and, before he became convinced of its absurdity, William Lilly himself would have allowed him "a curious fancy and piercing judgment upon resolving a question of nativity."

Upon the present occasion, he arose as early in the morning as the shortness of the day permitted, and proceeded to calculate the nativity of the young heir of Ellangowan *secundum artem*, as well to keep up appearances, as from a sort of curiosity to know whether he yet remembered, and could practise, the imaginary science. He accordingly erected his scheme, or figure of heaven, divided into its twelve houses, placed the planets therein according to the Ephemeris, and rectified their position to the hour and moment of the nativity. Without troubling our readers with the general prognostications which judicial astrology would have inferred from other circumstances in this diagram, there was one significator which pressed remarkably upon our astrologer's attention. Mars having dignity in the cusp of the twelfth house, threatened captivity, or sudden and violent death, to the native; and Mannering, having recourse to those further rules by which diviners pretended to ascertain the vehemency of this evil direction, observed, from the result, that three periods would be particularly hazardous—his *fifth*—his *tenth*—his *twenty-first* year. It was somewhat remarkable, that Mannering had once before tried a similar piece of foolery, at the instance of Sophia Wellwood, the young lady to whom he was attached, and that a similar conjunction of planetary influence threatened her with death, or imprisonment, in her thirty-ninth year. She was at this time eighteen; so that, according to the result of the scheme in both cases, the same year threatened her with the same misfortune that was presaged to the native or infant whom that night had introduced into the world. Struck with this coincidence, Mannering repeated his calculations; and the result approximated the events predicted, until, at length, the same month, and day of the month, seemed assigned as the period of peril to both.

It will be readily believed, that, in mentioning this circumstance, we lay no weight whatever upon the pretended information thus conveyed. But it often happens, such is our natural love for the marvellous, that we willingly contribute our own efforts to beguile our better judgments. Whether the coincidence I have mentioned was really one of those singular chances, which sometimes happen against all ordinary calculation; or whether Mannering, bewildered amid the arithmetical labyrinth and technical jargon of astrology, had insensibly twice followed the same clue to guide him out of the maze; or whether his imagination, seduced by some point of apparent resemblance, lent its aid to make the similitude between the two operations more exactly accurate than it might otherwise have been, it is impossible to guess; but the impression upon his mind, that the results exactly corresponded, was vividly and indelibly strong.

He could not help feeling surprise at a coincidence so singular and unexpected. "Does the devil mingle in the dance, to avenge himself for our trifling with an art said to be of magical origin? Or is it possible, as Bacon and Sir Thomas Browne admit, that there is some truth in a sober and regulated astrology, and that the influence of the stars is not to be denied, though the due application of it, by the knaves who pretend to practise the art, is greatly to be suspected?"—A moment's consideration of the subject induced him to dismiss this opinion as fantastical, and only retained by these learned men, either because they durst not at once shock the universal prejudices of their age, or because they themselves were not altogether freed from the contagious influence of a prevailing superstition. Yet the result of his calculations in these two instances left so unpleasing an impression upon his mind, that, like Prospero, he mentally relinquished his art, and resolved, neither in jest nor earnest, ever again to practise judicial astrology.

He hesitated a good deal what he should say to the Laird of Ellangowan, concerning the horoscope of his first-born; and, at length, resolved plainly to tell him the judgment which he had formed, at the same time acquainting him with the futility of the rules of art on which he had proceeded. With this resolution he walked out upon the terrace.

If the view of the scene around Ellangowan had been pleasing by moonlight, it lost none of its beauty by the light of the morning sun. The land, even in the month of November, smiled under its influence. A steep, but regular ascent, led from the terrace to the neighbouring eminence, and conducted Mannering to the front of the old castle. It consisted of two massive round towers, projecting, deeply and darkly, before a curtain, or flat wall, which united them, and thus protecting the main entrance that opened through a lofty arch into the inner court of the castle. The arms of the family, carved in freestone, frowned over the gateway, and the portal shewed the spaces arranged by the architect for lowering the port-cullis, and raising the drawbridge. A rude farm-gate, made of young fir-trees nailed together, now formed the only safeguard of this once formidable entrance. The esplanade in front of the castle commanded a noble prospect.

The dreary scene of desolation through which Mannering's road had lain on the preceding evening was excluded from the view by some rising grounds, and the landscape shewed a pleasing alternation of hill and dale, intersected by a river, which was in some places visible, and hidden in others as it rolled betwixt deep and wooded banks. The spire of a church, and the appearance of some houses, indicated the situation of a village at the place where it had its junction with the ocean. The vales seemed well cultivated, the little enclosures into which they were divided skirting the bottom of the hills, and sometimes carrying their lines of straggling hedge-rows a little way up the ascent. Above these were green pastures, tenanted chiefly by herds of black cattle, then the staple commodity of the county, whose distant low gave no unpleasing animation to the landscape. The remoter hills were of a sterner character; and, at still greater distance, swelled into mountains of dark heath, bordering the horizon with a screen which gave a defined and limited boundary to the cultivated, and added, at the same time, the pleasing idea, that it was sequestered and solitary. The sea-coast, which Mannering now saw in its extent, corresponded in variety and beauty with the inland view. In some places it rose into tall rocks, frequently crowned with the ruins of old buildings, towers, or beacons, which, according to tradition, were placed within sight of each other, and, in times of invasion or civil war, communicated by signal for mutual defence and protection. Ellangowan castle was by far the most extensive and important of these ruins, and asserted from size and situation the superiority which its founders were said once to have possessed among the chiefs and nobles of the district. In other places, the shore was of a more gentle description, indented with small bays, where the land sloped smoothly down, or sent into the sea promontories covered with wood.

A scene so different from what last night's journey had presaged, produced a proportional effect upon Mannering. Beneath his eye lay the modern house; an awkward mansion, indeed, in point of architecture, but well situated, and with a warm and pleasant exposure. "How happily," thought our hero, "would life glide on in such a retirement! On the one hand the striking remnants of ancient grandeur, with the secret consciousness of family pride which they inspire; on the other, enough of modern elegance and comfort to satisfy every moderate desire. Here then, and with thee, Sophia!"—

We will not pursue a lover's day-dream any farther. Mannering stood a minute with his arms folded, and then turned to the ruined castle.

Upon entering the gateway, he found that the rude magnificence of the inner court amply corresponded with the grandeur of the exterior. On the one side ran a range of windows lofty and large, divided by carved mullions of stone, which had once lighted the great hall of the castle; on the other were various buildings of different heights and dates, yet so united as to present to the eye a certain general effect of uniformity of front. The doors and windows were ornamented with projections exhibiting rude specimens of sculpture and tracery, partly entire and partly broken down, partly covered by ivy and trailing plants, which grew luxuriantly among the ruins. That end of the court which faced the entrance had also been formerly closed by a range of buildings; but owing, it was said, to its having been battered by the ships of the Parliament under Deane, during the long civil war, this part of the castle was much more ruinous than the rest, and exhibited a great chasm, through which Mannering could observe the sea, and the little vessel (an armed lugger) which retained her station in the centre of the bay.

While Mannering was gazing round the ruins, he heard from the interior of an apartment on the left hand the voice of the gypsey he had seen on the preceding evening. He soon found an aperture, through which he could observe her without being himself visible; and could not help feeling, that her figure, her employment, and her situation, conveyed the exact impression of an ancient sybil.

She sat upon a broken corner-stone in the angle of a paved apartment, part of which she had swept clean to afford a smooth space for the evolutions of her spindle. A strong sunbeam, through a lofty and narrow window, fell upon her wild dress and features, and afforded her light for her occupation; the rest of the apartment was very gloomy. Equipt in a habit which mixed the national dress of the Scottish common people with something of an eastern costume, she spun a thread, drawn from wool of three different colours, black, white, and grey, by assistance of those ancient implements of housewifery now almost banished from the land, the distaff and spindle. As she spun, she sung what seemed to be a charm. Mannering, after in vain attempting to make himself master of the exact words of her song, afterwards attempted the following paraphrase of what, from a few intelligible phrases, he concluded was its purport:

Twist ye, twine ye! even so
Mingle shades of joy and woe,
Hope and fear, and peace and strife,
In the thread of human life.

While the mystic twist is spinning,
And the infant's life beginning,
Dimly seen through twilight bending,
Lo, what varied shapes attending!

Passions wild, and follies vain,
Pleasures soon exchanged for pain;
Doubt, and jealousy, and fear,
In the magic dance appear.

Now they wax, and now they dwindle,
Whirling with the whirling spindle.
Twist ye, twine ye! even so,
Mingle human bliss and woe.

Ere our translator, or rather our free imitator, had arranged these stanzas in his head, and while he was yet hunting out a rhyme for *spindle*, the task of the sybil was accomplished, or her wool was expended. She took the spindle, now charged with her labours, and, undoing the thread gradually, measured it, by casting it over her elbow, and bringing each loop round between her forefinger and thumb. When she had measured it out, she muttered to herself—"A hank, but not a haill ane—the full years o' the three score and ten, but thrice broken, and thrice to *oop*, (i.e. unite); he'll be a lucky lad an he win through wi't."

Our hero was just going to speak to the prophetess, when a voice, hoarse as the waves with which it mingled, halloo'd twice, and with increasing impatience—"Meg, Meg Merrilies!—Gypsey—hag—tausend deyvils!"

"I am coming, I am coming, captain," answered Meg, and in a moment or two the impatient commander whom she addressed made his appearance from the broken part of the ruins.

He was apparently a seafaring man, rather under the middle size, and with a countenance bronzed by a thousand conflicts with the north-east wind. His frame was prodigiously muscular, strong, and thick-set; so that it seemed as if a man of much greater height would have been an inadequate match in any close personal conflict. He was hard-favoured, and, what was worse, his face bore nothing of the *insouciance*, the careless frolicsome jollity and vacant curiosity of a sailor on shore. These qualities, perhaps, as much as any others, contribute to the high popularity of our seamen, and the general good inclination which our society expresses towards them. Their gallantry, courage, and hardihood are qualities which excite reverence, and perhaps rather humble pacific landsmen in their presence; and neither respect, nor a sense of humiliation, are feelings easily combined with familiar fondness towards those who inspire them. But the boyish frolics, the exulting high spirits, the unreflecting mirth of a sailor when enjoying himself on shore, temper the more formidable points of his character. There was nothing like these in this man's face. On the contrary, a surly and even savage scowl appeared to darken features which would have been harsh and unpleasant under any expression or modification. "Where are you, Mother Deyvilson?" said he, with somewhat of a foreign accent, though speaking perfectly good English. "Donner and blitzen! we have been staying this half hour—Come, bless the good ship and the voyage, and be cursed to ye for a hag of Satan!"

At this moment he noticed Mannering, who, from the position which he had taken to watch Meg Merrilies's incantation, had the appearance of some one who was concealing himself, being half hidden by a buttress behind which he stood. The captain, for such he stiled himself, made a sudden and startled pause, and thrust his right hand into his bosom between his jacket and waistcoat, as if to draw some weapon. "What cheer, brother? you seem on the outlook—eh?"

Ere Mannering, somewhat struck by the man's gesture and insolent tone of voice, had made any answer, the gypsey emerged from her vault and joined the stranger. He questioned her in an under tone, looking at Mannering—"A shark alongside; eh?"

She answered in the same tone of under dialogue, using the canting language of her tribe—"Cut ben whids, and stow them—a gentry cove of the ken."

The fellow's cloudy visage cleared up. "The top of the morning to you, sir; I find you're a visitor of my friend Mr Bertram—I beg pardon, but I took you for another sort of a person."

Mannering replied, "And you, sir, I presume, are the master of that vessel in the bay?"

"Aye, aye, sir; I am Captain Dirk Hattaraick, of the Yungfrau Haagenslaapen, well known on this coast; I am not ashamed of my name, nor of my vessel,—nor of my cargo neither for that matter."

"I dare say you have no reason, sir."

"Tausend donner—no; I'm all in the way of fair trade—Just loaded yonder at Douglas, in the Isle of Man—neat coniac—real hyson and souchong—Mechlin lace, if you want any—We bumped ashore a hundred kegs last night."

"Really, sir, I am only a traveller, and have no sort of occasion for any thing of the kind at present."

"Why, then, good morning to you, for business must be minded—unless ye'll go aboard and take schnaps—you shall have a pouch-full of tea ashore—Dirk Hattaraick knows how to be civil."

There was a mixture of impudence, hardihood, and suspicious fear about this man, which was inexpressibly disgusting. His manners were those of a ruffian, conscious of the suspicion attending his character, yet wishing to bear it down by the affectation of a careless and hardy familiarity. Mannering briefly rejected his proffered civilities;

and, after a surly good morning, he retired with the gypsey to that part of the ruins from which he had first made his appearance. A very narrow staircase here descended to the beach, intended probably for the convenience of the garrison during a siege. By this stair, the couple, equally amiable in appearance, and respectable by profession, descended to the sea-side. The soi-disant captain embarked in a small boat with two men who appeared to wait for him, and the gypsey remained on the shore, reciting or singing, and gesticulating with great vehemence.

Chapter Five

> Whilst they have fed upon my seignories,
> Disparked my parks, and felled my forest woods,
> From mine own windows torn my household coat,
> Razed out my impress, leaving me no sign,
> Save men's opinions and my living blood,
> To show the world I am a gentleman.
>
> *Richard II*

WHEN THE BOAT which carried the worthy Captain on board his vessel had accomplished that task, the sails began to ascend, and the ship was got under way. She fired three guns as a salute to the house of Ellangowan, and then shot away rapidly before the wind, which blew off shore, under all the sail she could crowd.

"Aye, aye," said the Laird, who had sought Mannering for some time, and now joined him, "there they go—there go the free-traders —there goes Captain Dirk Hattaraick, and the Yungfrow Hagenslaapen, half Manks, half Dutchman, half devil! run out the boltsprit, up main-sail, top and top-gallant sails, royals, and skyscrapers, and away—follow who can! That fellow, Mr Mannering, is the terror of all the excise and customs cruisers; they can make nothing of him; he drubs them or distances them;—and, speaking of excise, I come to bring you to breakfast; and you shall have some tea, that"——

Mannering, by this time, was aware that one thought linked strangely on to another in the concatenation of worthy Mr Bertram's ideas,

> Like orient pearls at random strung;

and, therefore, before the current of his associations had drifted farther from the point he had left, he brought him back by some enquiry about Dirk Hattaraick.

"O he's a—a—good sort of blackguard fellow enough—no one cares to trouble him—smuggler, when his guns are in ballast—privateer, or pirate, faith, when he gets them mounted. He has done more mischief to the revenue folk than any rogue that ever came out of Ramsay."

"But, my good sir, such being his character, I wonder he has any protection and encouragement on this coast."

"Why, Mr Mannering, people must have brandy and tea, and there's none in this country but what comes this way—and then there's short accounts, and maybe a keg or two, or a dozen pounds left at your stable door at Christmas, instead of a d—d lang account from Duncan Robb, the grocer at Kippletringan, who has aye a sum to make up, and either wants ready money, or a short-dated bill. Now, Hattaraick will take wood, or he'll take barley, or he'll take just what's convenient at the time. I'll tell you a good story about that. There was ance a laird—that's Macfie of Gudgeonford,—he had a great number of kain hens—that's hens that the tenants pay to the landlord—like a sort of rent in kind—They aye feed mine very ill; Luckie Finniston sent up three that were a shame to be seen only last week, and yet she has twelve bows sowing of victual; indeed her goodman, Duncan Finniston—that's him that's gone—(we must all die, Mr Mannering; that's ower true)—and, speaking of that, let us live in the meanwhile, for here's breakfast on the table, and the Dominie ready to say grace."

The Dominie did accordingly pronounce a benediction, that exceeded in length any speech which Mannering had yet heard him utter. The tea, which of course belonged to the noble Captain Hattaraick's trade, was pronounced excellent. Still Mannering hinted, though with due delicacy, at the risk of encouraging such desperate characters: "Was it but in justice to the revenue, I should have supposed"——

"Ah, the revenue-lads"—for Mr Bertram never embraced a general or abstract idea, and his notion of the revenue was personified in the commissioners, surveyors, comptrollers, and riding officers, whom he happened to know—"the revenue-lads can look sharp enough out for themselves—no one needs to help them—and they have all the soldiers to assist them besides—And as to justice—you'll be surprised to hear it, Mr Mannering;—but I am not a justice of peace."

Mannering assumed the expected look of surprise, but thought within himself that the worshipful bench suffered no great deprivation from wanting the assistance of his good-humoured landlord. Mr Bertram had now hit upon one of the few subjects on which he felt sore, and went on with some energy.

"No, sir,—the name of Godfrey Bertram of Ellangowan is *not* in the last commission, though there's scarce a carle in the country that has a plough-gate of land, but what he must ride to quarter sessions, and write J. P. after his name. I ken full well who I am obliged to—Sir Thomas Kittlecourt as good as told me he would sit in my skirts, if he had not my interest at the last election, and because I chose to go with my own blood and third cousin, the Laird of Balruddery, they keepit me off the roll of freeholders, and now there comes a new nomination of justices, and I am left out—And whereas they pretend it was because I let David Mac-Guffog, the constable, draw the warrants, and manage the business his own gate, as if I had been a nose o' wax, it's a main untruth; for I never granted but seven warrants in my life, and the Dominie wrote every ane of them—and if it had not been that unlucky business of Sandy Mac-Gruthar's, that the constables should have keepit for two or three days up yonder at the auld castle, just till they could get conveniency to send him to the county jail—and that cost me aneugh of siller—But I ken what Sir Thomas wants very well —it was just sick and sicklike about the seat in the Kirk of Kilmagirdle —was I not entitled to have the front gallery facing the minister, rather than Mac-Crosskie of Creochstone, the son of Deacon Mac-Crosskie the Dumfries weaver?"

Mannering expressed his acquiescence in the justice of these various complaints.

"And then, Mr Mannering, there was the story about the road, and the fauld dike—I ken Sir Thomas was behind the curtain there, and I said plainly to the clerk to the trustees that I saw the cloven foot, let them take that as they like—Would any gentleman, or set of gentlemen, go and drive a road right through the corner of a fauld-dike, and take away, as my agent observed to them, like two roods of good moorland pasture?—And there was the story about chusing the collector of the cess"——

"Certainly, sir, it is hard you should meet with any neglect in a country, where, to judge from the extent of their residence, your ancestors must have made a very important figure."

"Very true, Mr Mannering—I am a plain man, and do not dwell on these things; and I must needs say, I have little memory for them; but I wish you could have heard my father's stories about the old fights of the Mac-Dingawaies—that's the Bertrams that now is—wi' the Irish, and wi' the Highlanders, that came here in their berlings from Ilay and Cantire—and how they went to the Holy Land—that is, to Jerusalem and Jericho, wi' a' their clan at their heels—they had better have gaen to Jamaica, like Sir Thomas Kittlecourt's uncle—and brought home reliques, like what catholics have, and a flag that's up yonder in the garret—if they had been casks of Muscovado, and puncheons of rum, it would have been better for the estate at this day—But there's little comparison between the auld keep at Kittlecourt and the castle of

Ellangowan—I doubt if the keep's forty feet of front—But ye make no breakfast, Mr Mannering; ye're no eating your meat; allow me to recommend some of the kipper—It was John Hay that catched it Saturday was three weeks down at the stream below Hempseed ford," &c. &c. &c.

The Laird, whose indignation had for some time kept him pretty steady to one topic, now launched forth into his usual roving stile of conversation, which gave Mannering ample time to reflect upon the disadvantage attending the situation, which, an hour before, he had thought worthy of so much envy. Here was a country gentleman, whose most estimable quality seemed his perfect good nature, secretly fretting himself and murmuring against others for causes which, compared with any real evil in life, must weigh like dust in the balance. But such is the equal distribution of Providence. To those who lie out of the road of great afflictions, are assigned petty vexations, which answer all the purpose of disturbing their serenity; and every reader must have observed, that neither natural apathy nor acquired philosophy can render country gentlemen insensible to the grievances which occur at elections, quarter sessions, and meetings of trustees.

Curious to investigate the manners of the country, Mannering took the advantage of a pause in good Mr Bertram's string of stories, to enquire what Captain Hattaraick so earnestly wanted with the gypsey woman.

"O to bless his ship, I suppose—you must know, Mr Mannering, that these free-traders, whom the law calls smugglers, having no religion, make it all up in superstition, and they have as many spells, and charms, and nonsense"——

"Vanity and waur," said the Dominie, "it is a trafficking with the Evil One. Spells, periapts, and charms, are of his device—choice arrows out of Apollyon's quiver."

"Hold your peace, Dominie—you're speaking for ever—(by the way it was the first words the poor man had uttered that morning, excepting that he said grace, and returned thanks) Mr Mannering cannot get in a word for you—And so, Mr Mannering, talking of astronomy, and spells, and these matters, have you been so kind as to consider what we were speaking about last night?"

"I begin to think, Mr Bertram, with your worthy friend here, that I have been rather jesting with edge-tools; and although neither you nor I, nor any sensible man, can put faith in the predictions of astrology, yet, as it has sometimes happened that enquiries into futurity undertaken in jest, have in their results produced serious and unpleasant effects both upon actions and characters, I wish you would dispense with my replying to your question."

It was easy to see that this evasive answer only rendered the Laird's curiosity more uncontroulable. Mannering was, however, determined in his own mind not to expose the infant to the inconveniences which might have arisen from his being supposed the object of evil prediction. He therefore delivered the paper into Mr Bertram's hand, and requested him to keep it for five years with the seal unbroken. When the month of November was expired, after that date had intervened, he left him at liberty to examine the writing, trusting that the first fatal period being then safely over-passed, no credit would be paid to its further contents. This Mr Bertram was content to promise, and Mannering, to ensure his fidelity, hinted at misfortunes which would certainly take place if his injunctions were neglected.

The rest of the day, which Mannering by Mr Bertram's invitation spent at Ellangowan, past over without any thing remarkable; and on the morning of that which followed, the traveller mounted his palfrey, bade a courteous adieu to his hospitable landlord, and to his clerical attendant, repeated his good wishes for the prosperity of the family, then, turning his horse's head towards England, disappeared from the sight of the inmates of Ellangowan. He must also disappear from that of our readers, for it is to another and later period of his life that the present narrative relates.

Chapter Six

—Next the Justice,
In fair round belly, with good capon lined,
With eyes severe, and beard of formal cut,
Full of wise saws, and modern instances:
And so he plays his part.—

WHEN MRS BERTRAM of Ellangowan was able to hear the news of what had passed during her confinement, her apartment rung with all manner of gossiping respecting the handsome young student from Oxford, who had told such a fortune by the stars to the young Laird, "blessings on his dainty face." The form, face, accent, and manners, of the stranger, were expatiated upon. His horse, bridle, saddle, and stirrups, did not remain unnoticed. All this made a great impression upon the mind of Mrs Bertram, for the good lady had no small store of superstition.

Her first employment, when she became capable of a little work, was to make a small velvet bag for the scheme of nativity which she had obtained from her husband. Her fingers itched to break the seal, but credulity proved stronger than curiosity, and she had the firmness to inclose it, in all its integrity, within two slips of parchment, which she sowed round it, to prevent its being chafed. The whole was then enclosed in the velvet bag aforesaid, and hung as a charm round the neck of the infant, where his mother resolved it should remain until the period for the legitimate satisfaction of her curiosity should arise.

The father also resolved to do his part by the child, in securing him a good education; and with the view that should commence with the first dawnings of reason, Dominie Sampson was easily induced to renounce his public profession of parish schoolmaster, make his constant residence at the Place, and, in consideration of a sum not quite equal to the wages of a footman even at that time, undertake to communicate to the future Laird of Ellangowan all the erudition which he had, and all the graces and accomplishments which he had not indeed, but which he had never discovered that he wanted. In this arrangement, also, the Laird found his private advantage; securing the constant benefit of a patient auditor to whom he told his stories when they were alone, and at whose expence he could break a sly jest when he had company.

About four years after this time, a great commotion took place in the county where Ellangowan is situated.

Those who watched the signs of the times, had long been of opinion that a change of ministry was about to take place; and, at length, after a due proportion of hopes, fears, and delays, rumours from good authority, and bad authority, and no authority at all—after some clubs had drank Up with this statesman, and others Down with him—after riding, and running, and posting, and addressing, and counter addressing, and proffers of lives and fortunes, the blow was at length struck, the administration of the day was dissolved, and parliament, as a natural consequence, was dissolved also.

Sir Thomas Kittlecourt, like other members in the same situation, posted down to his county, and met but an indifferent reception. He was a partizan of the old administration; and the friends of the new had already set about an active canvass in behalf of John Featherhead, Esq. who kept the best hounds and hunters in the shire. Among others who joined the standard of revolt was Gilbert Glossin, writer in Kippletringan, agent for the Laird of Ellangowan. This honest gentleman had either been refused some favour by the old member, or, what is equally likely, he had got all that he had the most distant pretension to ask, and could only look to the other side for fresh advancement. Mr Glossin had a vote upon Ellangowan's property, as has been before observed; and he was now determined that his patron should have one also, as there was no doubt of which side Mr Bertram would embrace in the contest. He easily persuaded Ellangowan, that it would be creditable to him to take the field at the head of as strong a party as possible; and immediately went to work, making voters, as every Scottish lawyer knows how, by splitting and subdividing the superiorities upon this ancient and once powerful barony. These were so extensive, that, by dint of clipping and paring here, adding and eiking there, and creating over-lords upon all the estate which Bertram held of the crown, they advanced, upon the day of contest, at the head of nine as good men of parchment as ever took the oath of trust and possession. This strong reinforcement turned the dubious day of battle. The principal and his agent divided the honour; the reward fell to the latter exclusively. Mr Gilbert Glossin was made clerk of the peace, and Godfrey Bertram had his name inserted in a new commission of justices, issued immediately upon the sitting of the parliament.

This had been the summit of Mr Bertram's ambition. Not that he liked either the trouble or the responsibility of the office, but he thought it was a dignity to which he was well entitled, and that it had been withheld from him by malice prepense. But there is an old and true Scotch proverb, "Fools should not have chapping sticks;" that is, weapons of offence. Mr Bertram was no sooner possessed of the judicial authority which he had so much longed for, than he began to exercise it with more severity than mercy, and totally belied all the opinions which had hitherto been formed of his inert good-nature. We have read somewhere of a justice of peace, who, upon being nominated in the commission, wrote a letter to a bookseller for the statutes respecting his official duty, in the following orthography,—"Please send the Ax relating to A gustus pease." No doubt, when this learned gentleman had possessed himself of the axe, he hewed the laws with it to some purpose. Mr Bertram was not quite so ignorant of English grammar as his worshipful predecessor; but Augustus Pease himself could not have used more indiscriminately the weapon unwarily put into his hand.

In good earnest, he considered the commission with which he had been entrusted as a personal mark of favour from his sovereign; forgetting that he had formerly thought his being deprived of a privilege, or honour, common to those of his rank, was the result of a mere party cabal. He commanded his trusty aid-de-camp, Dominie Sampson, to read aloud the commission; and at the first words, "The king has been pleased to appoint"—"*Pleased!*" exclaimed he, in a transport of gratitude; "Honest gentleman! he cannot be mair pleased than I am."

Accordingly, unwilling to confine his gratitude to mere feelings, or verbal expressions, he gave full current to the new-born zeal of office, and endeavoured to express his sense of the honour conferred upon him, by an unmitigated activity in the discharge of his duty. New brooms, it is said, sweep clean; and I myself can bear witness, that, upon the arrival of a new housemaid, the ancient, hereditary, and domestic spiders, who have spun their webs over the lower division of my book-shelves, (consisting chiefly of law and divinity,) during the peaceful reign of her predecessor, fly at full speed before the unexpected inroads of the new mercenary. Even so the Laird of Ellangowan ruthlessly commenced his magisterial reform, at the expence of various established and superannuated pickers and stealers, who had been his neighbours for half a century. He wrought his miracles like a second Duke Humphrey; and, by the influence of the beadle's rod, caused the lame to walk, the blind to see, and the palsied to labour. He detected poachers, black-fishers, orchard-breakers, and pigeon-shooters; had the applause of the bench for his reward, and the public credit of an active magistrate.

All this good had its rateable proportion of evil. Even an admitted nuisance, of ancient standing, should not be abated without some caution. The zeal of our worthy friend now involved in great distress sundry personages, whose idle and mendicant habits his own *lachesse* had contributed to foster until these habits became irreclaimable, or whose real incapacity of exertion rendered them fit objects, in their own phrase, for the charity of all well-disposed Christians. The "long-remembered beggar," who for twenty years had made his regular round within the neighbourhood, received rather as an humble friend than as an object of charity, was sent to the neighbouring workhouse. The decrepid dame, who travelled round the parish upon a hand-barrow, circulating from house to house like a bad shilling, which every one is in haste to pass upon her neighbour; she, who used to call for her bearers as loud, or louder, than a traveller demands post-horses, even she shared the same disastrous fate. The "daft Jock," who, half knave, half idiot, had been the sport of each succeeding race of village children for a good part of a century, was remitted to the county bridewell, where, secluded from free air and sunshine, the only advantages he was capable of enjoying, he pined and died in the course of six months. The old sailor, who had so long rejoiced the smoky rafters of every kitchen in the country, by singing *Captain Ward*, and *Bold Admiral Benbow*, was banished from the county for no better reason, than that he was supposed to speak with a strong Irish accent. Even the annual rounds of the pedlar were abolished by the Justice, in his hasty zeal for the administration of rural police.

These things did not pass without notice and censure. We are not made of wood or stone, and the things which connect themselves with our hearts and habits cannot, like bark or lichen, be rent away without our missing them. The farmer's dame lacked her usual share of intelligence, perhaps also the self-applause which she had felt while distributing the *awmous* (alms,) in shape of a *gowpen* (handful) of oatmeal, to the mendicant who brought it. The cottages felt inconvenience from interruption of the paltry trade carried on by the itinerant dealers. The children had not their sugar-plums and toys; the young women wanted pins, ribbons, combs, and ballads; and the old women could no longer barter their eggs for salt, snuff, and tobacco. All these circumstances brought the busy Laird of Ellangowan into discredit, which was more general on account of his former popularity. Even his lineage was brought up in judgment against him. They thought "naething of what the like of Greenside, or Burnville, or Viewfirth, might do, that were strangers in the country; but Ellangowan! that had been a name amang them since the mirk Monanday, and lang before—*he* to be grinding the poor at that rate!—They ca'd his grandfather the Wicked Laird; but, though he was whiles fractious aneuch, when he got into roving company, and had ta'en the drap drink, he would have scorned to go on at this gate. Na, na, the muckle chimney in the auld Place reeked like a killogie in his time, and there were as mony puir folk riving at the banes in the court, and about the door, as there were gentles in the ha'. And the lady, on ilka Christmas night as it came round, gae twelve siller pennies to ilka puir body about, in honour of the twelve apostles like. They were fond to ca' it papistrie; but I think our great folk might take a lesson frae the papists whiles. They gie another sort o' help to the puir folk than just dinging down a saxpence in the broad on the sabbath, and kilting, and scourging, and drumming them a' the six days o' the week besides."

Such was the gossip over the good two-penny in every ale-house within three or four miles of Ellangowan, that being about the diameter of the orbit in which our friend Godfrey Bertram, Esq. J. P. must be considered as the principal luminary. Still greater scope was given to evil tongues by the removal of a colony of gypsies, with one of whom our reader is somewhat acquainted, and who had for a great many years enjoyed their chief settlement upon the estate of Ellangowan.

Chapter Seven

Come, princes of the ragged regiment,
You of the blood! *Prigg*, my most upright lord,
And these, what name or title e'er they bear,
Jarkman, or *Patrico*, *Cranke* or *Clapper-dudgeon*,
Frater or *Abram-man*—I speak of all.—

Beggar's Bush

ALTHOUGH THE ORIGIN of those gypsy tribes, which formerly inundated most of the nations of Europe, and which in some degree subsist among them as a different people, is generally known, the reader will pardon my saying a few words respecting their situation in Scotland.

It is well known that the gypsies were, at an early period, acknowledged as a distinct and independent people by one of the Scottish monarchs, and that they were less favourably distinguished by a subsequent law, which rendered the character of gypsy equal, in the judicial balance, to that of common and habitual thief, and prescribed his punishment accordingly. Notwithstanding the severity of this and other statutes, the fraternity prospered amid the distresses of the country, and received large accessions from those whom famine, oppression, or the sword of war, had deprived of ordinary means of subsistence. They lost in a great measure, by this intermixture, the national character of Egyptians, and became a mingled race, having all the idleness and predatory habits of their eastern ancestors, with a ferocity which they probably borrowed from the men of the north who joined their society. They travelled in different bands, and had rules among themselves, by which each was confined to its own district. The least invasion of the precincts which had been assigned to another tribe produced desperate skirmishes, in which there was much bloodshed.

The patriotic Fletcher of Saltoun drew a picture of these banditti about a century ago, which my readers will peruse with astonishment.

"There are at this day in Scotland (besides a great many poor families very meanly provided for by the church boxes, with others, who, by living upon bad food, fall into various diseases) two hundred thousand people begging from door to door. These are not only no way advantageous, but a very grievous burden to so poor a country. And though the number of them be perhaps double to what it was formerly, by reason of this present great distress, yet in all times there have been about one hundred thousand of those vagabonds, who have lived without any regard or subjection either to the laws of the land, or even those of God and nature; fathers incestuously accompanying with their own daughters, the son with the mother, and the brother with the sister. No magistrate could ever discover, or be informed, which way one in a hundred of these wretches died, or that ever they were baptized. Many murders have been discovered among them; and they are not only a most unspeakable oppression to poor tenants, (who, if they give not bread, or some kind of provision to perhaps forty such villains in one day, are sure to be insulted by them,) but they rob many poor people who live in houses distant from any neighbourhood. In years of plenty many thousands of them meet together in the mountains, where they feast and riot for many days; and at country weddings, markets, burials, and other the like public occasions, they are to be seen, both men and women, perpetually drunk, cursing, blaspheming, and fighting together."

Notwithstanding the deplorable picture presented in this extract, and which Fletcher himself, (the energetic and eloquent friend of freedom,) saw no better mode of correcting than by introducing a system of domestic slavery, the progress of time, and increase both of the means of life and of the power of the laws, gradually reduced this dreadful evil within more narrow bounds. The tribes of gypsies, jockies, or cairds,—for by all these denominations such banditti were known,—became few in number, and many were entirely rooted out. Still, however, enough remained to give occasional alarm and constant vexation. Some rude handicrafts were entirely resigned to these itinerants, particularly those of trencher-making, of manufacturing horn-spoons, and the whole mystery of the tinker. To these they added a petty trade in the coarser sorts of earthen-ware. Such were their ostensible means of livelihood. Each tribe had usually some fixed place of rendezvous, which they occasionally occupied and considered as their standing camp, in the vicinity of which they usually abstained from depredation. They had even their talents and accomplishments, which made them occasionally useful or entertaining. Many cultivated music with success, and the favourite fiddler or piper of a district was often to be found in a gypsy town. They understood all out-of-door sports, especially otter-hunting, fishing, or finding game. In winter, the women told fortunes, the men shewed tricks of legerdemain; and these accomplishments often helped away a weary or stormy evening in the circle of the "farmer's ha'." The wildness of their character, and the indomitable pride with which they despised all regular labour, commanded a certain awe, which was not diminished by the consideration, that these strollers were a vindictive race, and were restrained by no checks, either of fear or conscience, from taking desperate vengeance upon those who had offended them.

These tribes were, in short, the *Parias* of Scotland, living like wild Indians among European settlers, and, like them, judged of rather by their own customs, habits, and opinions, than as if they had been members of the civilized part of the community. Some hordes of them yet remain, chiefly in such situations as afford a ready escape either into a waste country, or into another jurisdiction; nor are the features of their character much softened. Their numbers, however, are so greatly diminished, that, instead of one hundred thousand, as calculated by Fletcher, it would now be impossible to collect above five hundred through all Scotland.

A tribe of these itinerants, to whom Meg Merrilies appertained, had long been as stationary as their habits permitted, in a glen upon the estate of Ellangowan. They had erected a few huts, which they denominated their "city of refuge," and where they harboured unmolested as the crows that roosted in the old ash-trees around them. They had been such long occupants, that they were considered in some degree as proprietors of the wretched sheelings which they inhabited. This protection they were said anciently to have repaid, by service to the laird in war, and, more frequently, by infesting and plundering the lands of those neighbouring barons with whom he chanced to be at feud. Latterly, their services were of a more pacific nature. The women spun mittens for the lady and boot-hose for the laird, which were annually presented at Christmas with great form. The aged sybils blessed the bridal bed of the laird when he married, and the cradle of the heir when born. The men repaired her ladyship's cracked china, and assisted the laird on his sporting parties, wormed his dogs, and cut the ears of his terrier puppies. The children gathered nuts in the wood, and crane-berries in the moss, and mushrooms upon the pastures, for tribute to the Place. These acts of voluntary service, and acknowledgments of dependence, were rewarded by protection on some occasions, connivance upon others, and broken victuals, ale, and brandy, when circumstances called for a display of generosity; and this mutual intercourse of good offices, which had taken place for at least two centuries, rendered the inhabitants of Derncleugh a kind of privileged banditti upon the estate of Ellangowan. "The knaves" were the Laird's "exceeding good friends;" and he would have deemed himself very ill used, if his countenance could not now and then have borne them out against the law of the country and the local magistrate. But this friendly union was soon to be dissolved.

The community of Derncleugh, who cared for no rogues but their own, took no alarm at the severity of the justice's proceedings towards other itinerants. They had no doubt that he intended, according to their rude proverb, to "keep his own fish-guts for his own sea-mews," and to suffer no mendicants or strollers in the country, but what resided on his own property, and practised their trade by his immediate permission, implied or expressed. Nor was Mr Bertram in a hurry to exert his newly-acquired authority at the expence of these old settlers. But he was driven on by circumstances.

At a quarter sessions, our new justice was publicly upbraided by a gentleman of the opposite party in county politics, that, while he affected a great zeal for the public police, and seemed ambitious of the fame of an active magistrate, he fostered a tribe of the greatest rogues in the country, and permitted them to harbour within a mile of the house of Ellangowan. To this there was no reply, for the fact was too evident and well-known. The Laird digested the taunt as he best could, and in his way home amused himself with speculations on the easiest method of ridding himself of those vagrants, who brought a stain upon his fair fame as a magistrate. Just as he had resolved to take the first opportunity of quarrelling with the Parias of Derncleugh, a cause of provocation presented itself.

Since our friend's advancement to be a conservator of the peace, he had caused the gate at the head of his avenue, which formerly, having only one hinge, remained at all times hospitably open—he had caused this gate, I say, to be newly hung and handsomely painted. He had also shut up with paling, curiously twisted with furze, certain holes in the fences adjoining, through which the boys used to scramble into the plantations to gather birds' nests, the seniors of the village to make a short cut from one point to another, and the lads and lasses for evening rendezvous—all without offence taken, or leave asked. But these halcyon days were now to have end, and a minatory inscription upon one side of the gate intimated "prosecution according to law" (the painter had spelt it *persecution*—l'un vaut bien l'autre) to all who should be found trespassing on these enclosures. Upon the other side, for uniformity's sake, was a kind precautionary annunciation of spring-guns, stamps, and man-traps of such formidable powers, that, said the rubrick, with an emphatic *nota bene*—"If a man goes in, they will break a horse's leg."

In defiance of these threats, six well-grown gypsy boys and girls were riding cock-horse upon the new gate, and plaiting may-flower, which it was but too evident had been gathered within the forbidden precincts. With as much anger as he was capable of feeling, or perhaps of assuming, the Laird commanded them to descend;—they paid no attention to his mandate: he then began to pull them down one after another;—they resisted, passively at least, each sturdy bronzed varlet making himself as heavy as he could, or climbing up as fast as he was dismounted.

The Laird then called in the assistance of his servant, a surly fellow, who had immediate recourse to his horse-whip. A few lashes sent the party a-scampering; and thus commenced the first breach of peace between the house of Ellangowan and the gypsies of Derncleugh.

The latter could not for some time imagine that the war was real, until they found that their children were horse-whipped by the grieve when found trespassing; that their asses were poinded by the ground-officer when left in the plantations, or even when turned to graze by the road side against the provisions of the turnpike acts; that the constable began to make curious enquiries into their mode of gaining a livelihood, and expressed his surprise that the men should sleep in the hovels all day, and be abroad the greater part of the night.

When matters came to this point, the gypsies adopted with scruple measures of retaliation. Ellangowan's hen-roosts were plundered, his linen stolen from the lines or bleaching ground, his fishings poached, his dogs kidnapped, his growing trees cut or barked. Much petty mischief was done, and some evidently for the mischief's sake. On the other hand, warrants went forth without mercy, to pursue, search for, take, and apprehend; and, notwithstanding their dexterity, one or two of the depredators were unable to avoid conviction. One, a stout young fellow who sometimes had gone to sea a-fishing, was handed over to the captain of the impress service at D——; two children were soundly flogged, and one Egyptian matron sent to the house of correction.

Still, however, the gypsies made no motion to leave the spot which they had so long inhabited, and Mr Bertram felt an unwillingness to deprive them of their ancient "city of refuge;" so that the petty warfare we have noticed continued for several months, without abatement of hostility upon either side.

Chapter Eight

So the red Indian, by Ontario's side,
Nursed hardy on the brindled panther's hide,
As fades his swarthy race, with anguish sees
The white man's cottage rise beneath the trees;
He leaves the shelter of his native wood,
He leaves the murmur of Ohio's flood,
And forward rushing in indignant grief,
Where never foot has trode the fallen leaf,
He bends his course where twilight reigns sublime,
O'er forests silent since the birth of time.

Scenes of Infancy

IN TRACING the rise and progress of the Scottish Maroon war, we must not omit to mention that years had now rolled on, and that little Harry Bertram, one of the hardiest and most lively children that ever made a sword and grenadier's cap of rushes, now approached his fifth revolving birth-day. A hardihood of disposition, which early developed itself, made him already a little wanderer; he was well acquainted with every patch of lea ground and dingle around Ellangowan, and could tell in his broken language upon what *baulks* grew the bonniest flowers, and what copse had the ripest nuts. He repeatedly terrified his attendants by clambering about the ruins of the old castle, and had more than once made a voluntary excursion as far as the gypsy hamlet.

Upon these occasions he was brought back by Meg Merrilies, who, though she could not be prevailed upon to enter the Place of Ellangowan after her nephew had been given up to the press-gang, did not apparently extend her resentment to the child. On the contrary, she often contrived to way-lay him in his walks, sing him a gypsy song, give him a ride upon her jack-ass, and thrust into his pocket a piece of gingerbread or a red-cheeked apple. This woman's ancient attachment to the family, repelled and checked in every other direction, seemed to rejoice in having some object on which it could yet repose and expand itself. She prophesied an hundred times, "that young Mr Henry would be the pride o' the family, and there had nae been sick a sprout frae the auld aik, since the death of Arth Mac-Dingawaie, that was killed in the battle o' the Bloody Bay; as for the present stick, it was good for naething but fire-wood." Upon one occasion, when the child was ill, she lay all night below the window, chaunting a rhyme which she believed sovereign as a febrifuge, and could neither be prevailed upon to enter the house, nor to leave the station she had chosen, till she was informed that the crisis was over.

The affection of this woman became matter of suspicion, not indeed to the Laird, who was never hasty in suspecting evil, but to his wife, who had indifferent health and poor spirits. She was now far advanced in a second pregnancy, she could not walk abroad herself, the woman who attended upon Harry was young and thoughtless, and she prayed Dominie Sampson to undertake the task of watching the boy in his rambles, when he should not be otherwise accompanied. The Dominie loved his young charge, and was enraptured with his own success, in having already brought him so far in his learning as to spell words of three syllables. The idea of this early prodigy of erudition being carried off by the gypsies, like a second Adam Smith, was not to be tolerated; and accordingly, though the charge was contrary to all his habits of life, he readily undertook it, and might be seen stalking about with a mathematical problem in his head, and his eye upon a child of five years old, whose rambles led him into an hundred awkward situations. Twice was the Dominie chased by a cross-grained cow, once he fell into the brook crossing at the stepping-stones, and another time was bogged up to the middle in the slough of Lochend, in attempting to gather a water-lily for the young Laird. It was the opinion of the village matrons who relieved Sampson on the latter occasion, that the Laird might as well trust the care of his child to a "potatoe-bogle;" but the good Dominie bore all his disasters with gravity and serenity equally imperturbable. "Prodi-gi-ous!" was the only ejaculation they ever extorted from the much-enduring man.

The Laird had, by this time, determined to make root-and-branch work with the Maroons of Derncleugh. The old servants shook their heads at his proposal, and even Dominie Sampson ventured upon an indirect remonstrance. As, however, it was couched in the oracular phrase, "*Ne moveas Camerinam,*" neither the allusion, nor the language in which it was expressed, were calculated for Mr Bertram's edification, and matters proceeded against the gypsies in form of law. Every door in the hamlet was chalked by the ground-officer, in token of a formal warning to remove at next term. Still, however, they showed no symptoms either of submission or of compliance. At length the term-day, the fatal Martinmas, arrived, and violent measures of ejection were resorted to. A strong posse of peace-officers, sufficient to render all resistance vain, charged the inhabitants to depart by noon; and, as they did not obey, the officers, in terms of their warrant, proceeded to unroof the cottages, and pull down the wretched doors and windows,—a summary and effectual mode of ejection still practised in some remote parts of Scotland, where a tenant proves refractory. The gypsies, for a time, beheld the work of destruction in sullen silence and inactivity; then set about saddling and loading their asses, and making preparations for their departure. These were soon accomplished, where all had the habits of wandering Tartars, and they set forth on their journey to seek new settlements, where their patron should neither be of the quorum, nor custos rotulorum.

Certain qualms of feeling had deterred Ellangowan from attending in person to see his tenants expelled. He left the executive part of the business to the officers of the law, under the immediate direction of Frank Kennedy, a supervisor, or riding-officer belonging to the customs, who had of late become intimate at the Place, and of whom we shall have more to say in the next chapter. Mr Bertram himself chose that day to make a visit to a friend at some distance. But it so happened, notwithstanding his precautions, that he could not avoid meeting his late tenants during their retreat from his property.

It was in a hollow way, near the top of a steep ascent upon the verge of the Ellangowan estate, that Mr Bertram met the gypsy procession. Four or five men formed the advanced guard, wrapped in long loose great coats, that hid their tall slender figures, as the large slouched hats, drawn over their brows, concealed their wild features, dark eyes, and swarthy faces. Two of them carried long fowling-pieces, one wore a broad sword without a sheath, and all had the Highland dirk, though they did not wear that weapon openly or ostentatiously. Behind them followed the train of laden asses, and small carts, or *tumblers*, as they are called in that country, on which were laid the decrepid and the helpless, the aged and infant part of the exiled community. The women in their red cloaks and straw hats, the elder children with bare heads, and bare feet, and almost naked bodies, had the immediate care of the little caravan. The road was narrow, running between two broken banks of sand, and Mr Bertram's servant rode forward, smacking his whip with an air of authority, and motioning to the drivers to allow free passage to their betters. His signal was unattended to. He then called to the men who lounged idly on before, "Stand to your beasts' heads, and make room for the Laird to pass."

"He shall have his share of the road," answered a male gypsy from under his slouched and large brimmed hat, and without raising his face, "and he shall have no more; the highway is as free to our cuddies as to his gelding."

The tone of the man being sulky, and even menacing, Mr Bertram thought it best to put his dignity in his pocket, and pass by the procession quietly, upon such space as they chose to leave for his accommodation, which was narrow enough. To cover with an appearance of indifference his feeling of the want of respect with which he was treated, he asked one of the men, as he passed him without any show of greeting, salute, or recognition,—"Giles Baillie," he said, "have you heard that your son Gabriel is well?" (The question respected the young man who had been pressed.)

"If I had heard otherwise," said the old man, looking up with a stern and menacing countenance, "*you* should have heard of it too." And he plodded on his way, tarrying no farther question. When the Laird had pressed onward with difficulty among a crowd of familiar faces, in which he now only read hatred and contempt, but which had on all former occasions marked his approach with the reverence due to that of a superior being, and had got clear of the throng, he could not help turning his horse, and looking back to mark the progress of their march. The group would have been an excellent subject for the pencil of Calotte. The van had already reached a small and stunted thicket, which was at the bottom of the hill, and which gradually hid the line of march until the last stragglers disappeared.

His sensations were bitter enough. The race, it is true, which he had thus summarily dismissed from their ancient place of refuge, was idle and vicious; but had he endeavoured to render them otherwise? They were not more irregular characters now, than they had been while they were admitted to consider themselves as a sort of subordinate dependants of his family; and ought the circumstance of his becoming a magistrate to have made at once such a change in his conduct towards them? Some means of reformation ought at least to have been tried, before sending seven families at once upon the wide world, and depriving them of a degree of countenance, which withheld them at least from atrocious guilt. There was also a natural yearning of heart upon parting with so many known and familiar faces; and to this feeling Godfrey Bertram was peculiarly accessible, from the limited qualities of his mind, which sought its principal amusement among the petty objects around him. As he was about to turn his horse's head to pursue his journey, Meg Merrilies, who had lagged behind the troop, unexpectedly presented herself.

She was standing upon one of those high banks, which, as we before noticed, overhung the road; so that she was placed considerably higher than Ellangowan, even though he was on horseback; and her tall figure, relieved against the clear blue sky, seemed almost of supernatural stature. We have noticed, that there was in her general attire, or rather in her mode of adjusting it, somewhat of a foreign costume, artfully adopted perhaps for the purpose of adding to the effect of her spells and predictions, or perhaps from some traditional notions respecting the dress of her ancestors. On this occasion, she had a large piece of red cotton cloth rolled about her head in the form of a turban, from beneath which her dark eyes flashed with uncommon lustre. Her long and tangled black hair fell in elf-locks from the folds of this singular head-gear. Her attitude was that of a sybil in frenzy, and she stretched out, in her right hand, a sapling bough which seemed just pulled.

"I'll be d—d," said the groom, "if she has not been cutting the young ashes in the Dukit Park."—The Laird made no answer, but continued to look at the figure which was thus perched above his path.

"Ride your ways," said the gypsy, "ride your ways, Laird of Ellangowan—ride your ways, Godfrey Bertram!—This day have ye quenched seven smoking hearths—see if the fire in your ain parlour burn the blyther for that.—Ye have riven the thack off seven cottar houses—look that your ain roof-tree stand the faster.—Ye may stable your stirks in the shealings at Derncleugh—see that the hare does not couch on the hearthstane at Ellangowan.—Ride your ways, Godfrey Bertram—what do ye glowr after our folk for?—There's thirty hearts there, that wad hae wanted bread ere ye had wanted sunkets, and spent their life-blood ere ye had scratched your finger—Yes—there's thirty yonder, from the auld wife of an hundred to the babe that was born last week, that ye have turned out o' their bits o' bields, to sleep with the tod and the black-cock in the moors!—Ride your ways, Ellangowan.—Our bairns are hinging at our weary backs—look that your braw cradle at hame be the fairer spread up—not that I am wishing ill to little Harry, or to the babe that's yet to be born—God forbid—and make them kind to the poor, and better folk than their father.—And now, ride e'en your ways, for these are the last words ye'll ever hear Meg Merrilies speak, and this is the last reise that I'll ever cut in the bonny woods of Ellangowan."

So saying, she broke the sapling she held in her hand, and flung it into the road. Margaret of Anjou, bestowing on her triumphant foes her keen-edged malediction, could not have turned from them with a gesture more proudly contemptuous. The Laird was clearing his voice to speak, and thrusting his hand in his pocket to find half-a-crown; the gypsy waited neither for his reply nor his donation, but strode down the hill to overtake the caravan.

Ellangowan rode pensively home; and it was remarkable that he did not mention this interview to any of his family. The groom was not so reserved: he told the story at great length to a full audience in the kitchen, and concluded by swearing, that "if ever the devil spoke by the mouth of a woman, he had spoken by Meg Merrilies that blessed day."

Chapter Nine

Paint Scotland greeting ower her thrissle,
Her mutchkin stoup as toom's a whistle,
An' d—mn'd excisemen in a bustle,
Seizing a stell;
Triumphant crushing't like a mussell,
Or lampit shell.

BURNS

DURING THE PERIOD of Mr Bertram's active magistracy, he did not forget the affairs of the revenue. Smuggling, for which the Isle of Man then afforded peculiar facilities, was general, or rather universal, all along the south-western coast of Scotland. Almost all the common people were engaged in these practices, the gentry connived at them, and the officers of the revenue were frequently discountenanced in the exercise of their duty, by those who should have protected them.

There was, at this period, employed as a riding officer or supervisor, in that part of the country, a certain Francis Kennedy, already named in our narrative; a stout, resolute, and active man, who had made several seizures to a great amount, and was proportionally hated by those who had an interest in the *fair-trade*, as they called their contraband adventures. This person was natural son to a gentleman of good family, owing to which circumstance, and to his being of a jovial convivial disposition, and singing a good song, he was admitted to the occasional society of the gentlemen of the country, and was a member of several of their clubs for practising athletic games, at which he was particularly expert.

At Ellangowan, Kennedy was a frequent and always an acceptable guest. His vivacity relieved Mr Bertram of the trouble of thought, and the labour which it cost him to support a detailed communication of ideas; while the daring and dangerous exploits which he had undertaken in the discharge of his office, formed excellent conversation. To all these revenue adventures did the Laird of Ellangowan seriously incline, and the amusement which he derived from his society formed an excellent reason for countenancing and assisting the narrator in the execution of his invidious and hazardous duty.

"Frank Kennedy," he said, "was a gentleman, though on the wrong side of the blanket—he was connected with the family of Ellangowan through the house of Glengabble. The last Laird of Glengabble would have brought the estate into the Ellangowan line, but happening to go to Harrigate, he there met with Miss Jean Hadaway—by the bye, the Green Dragon at Harrigate is the best house of the two—but for Frank Kennedy, he's in one sense a gentleman born, and it's a shame not to support him against these blackguard smugglers."

After this league had taken place between judgement and execution, it chanced that Captain Dirk Hattaraick had landed a cargo of spirits, and other contraband goods, upon the beach not far from Ellangowan, and, confiding in the indifference with which the Laird had formerly regarded similar infractions of the law, he was neither very anxious to conceal nor to expedite the transaction. The consequence was, that Mr Frank Kennedy, armed with a warrant from Ellangowan, and supported by some of the Laird's people who knew the country, and by a party of military, pounced down upon the kegs, bales, and bags, and, after a desperate affray, in which severe wounds were given and received, succeeded in clapping the broad arrow upon the articles, and bearing them off in triumph to the next custom-house. Dirk Hattaraick vowed, in Dutch, German, and English, a deep and full revenge, both against the gauger and his abettors; and all who knew him thought it likely he would keep his word.

A few days after the departure of the gypsy tribe, Mr Bertram asked his lady one morning at breakfast, whether this was not little Harry's birth-day?

"Five years old exactly, this blessed day," answered the lady; "so we may look into the English gentleman's paper."

Mr Bertram liked to show his authority in trifles. "No, my dear, not till to-morrow. The last time I was at quarter sessions the sheriff told us, that *dies*—that *dies inceptus*—in short, you don't understand Latin, but it means that a term day is not begun till it's ended."

"That sounds like nonsense, my dear."

"May be so, my dear; but it may be very good law for all that. I am sure, speaking of term days, I wish, as Frank Kennedy says, that Whitsunday would kill Martinmas, and be hanged for the murder—for there I have got a letter about that interest of Jenny Cairnes's, and deil a tenant's been at the Place yet wi' a boddle of rent,—nor will not till Candlemas—but, speaking of Frank Kennedy, I dare say he'll be here the day, for he was away round to Wigton to warn a king's ship that's lying in the bay about Dirk Hattaraick's lugger being on the coast again, and he'll be back this day; so we'll have a bottle of claret, and drink little Harry's health."

"I wish," replied the lady, "Frank Kennedy would let Dirk Hattaraick alane—what needs he make himself more busy than other folk? —cannot he sing his sang, and take his drink, and draw his salary like Collector Snail, honest man, that never fashes ony body? And I wonder at you, Laird, for meddling and making—Did we ever want to send for tea or brandy frae the Borough-town, when Dirk Hattaraick used to come quietly into the bay?"

"Mrs Bertram, you know nothing of these matters. Do ye think it becomes a magistrate to let his own house be made a receptacle for smuggled goods? Frank Kennedy will shew you the penalties in the act, and ye ken yoursell they used to put their run goods into the auld Place of Ellangowan up bye there."

"Ow dear! Mr Bertram, and what the waur were the wa's and the vault o' the auld castle for having a whin kegs o' brandy in them at an orra time? I am sure ye were not obliged to ken ony thing about it; or what the waur was the King that the lairds here got a soup o' drink, and the ladies their drap o' tea at a reasonable rate?—it's a shame to them to pit such taxes on them!—and was na I much the better of these Flanders head and pinners, that Dirk Hattaraick sent me all the way frae Antwerp? It will be lang or the King sends me ony thing, or Frank Kennedy either. And then ye would quarrel wi' these gypsies too. I expect every day to hear the barn yard's in a low."

"I tell you once more, my dear, you don't understand these things—and there's Frank Kennedy coming galloping up the avenue."

"A weel! a weel! Ellangowan," said the lady, raising her voice as the Laird left the room, "I wish ye may understand them yoursell, that's a'."

From this nuptial dialogue the Laird joyfully escaped to meet his feal friend, Mr Kennedy, who arrived in high spirits. "For the love of life, Ellangowan," he said, "get up to the castle! you'll see that old fox Dirk Hattaraick, and his majesty's hounds in full cry after him." So saying, he flung his horse's bridle to a boy, and ran up the ascent to the old castle, followed by the Laird, and indeed by several others of the family, alarmed by the sound of guns from the sea, now distinctly heard.

On gaining that part of the ruins which commanded the most extensive outlook, they saw a lugger, with all her canvass crowded, standing across the bay, and closely pursued by a sloop of war, that kept firing upon the chase from her bows, which the lugger returned with her stern-chasers. "They're but at long bowls yet," cried Kennedy in great exultation, "but they will be closer bye and bye.——D—n him, he's starting his cargo! I see the good Nantz pitching overboard, keg after keg!—that's a d—d ungenteel thing of Mr Hattaraick, as I shall let him know bye and bye.—Now, now! they've got the wind of him!—that's it, that's it!—hark to him! hark to him!—now, my dogs! now, my dogs!—hark to Ranger, hark!"

"I think," said the old gardener to one of the maids, "the gauger's *fie;*" by which word the common people express those violent spirits which they think a presage of death.

Meantime the chase continued. The lugger, being pilotted with great ability, and using every nautical shift to make her escape, had now reached, and was about to double, the head-land which formed the extreme point of land on the left side of the bay, when a ball having hit the yard in the slings, the main-sail fell upon the deck. The consequences of this accident appeared inevitable, but could not be seen by the spectators; for the vessel, which had just doubled the head-land, lost steerage, and fell out of their sight behind the promontory. The sloop of war crowded all sail to pursue, but she had stood too close upon the cape, so that they were obliged to wear the vessel for fear of going ashore, and to make a large tack back into the bay, in order to recover sea-room enough to double the head-land.

"They'll lose her by ——, cargo and lugger, one or both," said Kennedy; "I must gallop away to the Point of Warroch (this was the head-land so often mentioned,) and make them a signal where she has drifted to on the other side. Good bye for an hour, Ellangowan—get out the gallon punch-bowl, and plenty of lemons. I'll stand for the French article by the time I come back, and we'll drink the young Laird's health in a bowl that would swim the collector's yawl." So saying, he mounted his horse, and cantered away.

About a mile from the house, and upon the verge of the woods, which, as we have said, covered a promontory terminating in the cape called the Point of Warroch, Kennedy met young Harry Bertram, attended by his tutor, Dominie Sampson. He had often promised the child a ride upon his galloway; and, from singing, dancing, and playing Punch for his amusement, was a particular favourite. He no sooner came scampering up the path, than the boy loudly claimed the promise; and Kennedy, who saw no risque in indulging him, and wished to tease the Dominie, in whose visage he read a remonstrance, caught up Harry from the ground, placed him before him, and continued his route; Sampson's "Peradventure, Master Kennedy"—— being lost in the clatter of his horse's feet, and in the tune of "the deil's awa wi' the exciseman," which he whistled with great spirit. The pedagogue hesitated a moment whether he should go after them; but Kennedy being a person in full confidence of the family, and with whom he himself had no delight in associating, "being that he was addicted unto profane and scurrilous jests," he continued his own walk at his own pace, till he reached the Place of Ellangowan.

The spectators from the ruined walls of the castle were still watching the sloop of war, which at length, but not without the loss of considerable time, recovered sea-room enough to weather the Point of Warroch, and was lost to their sight behind that wooded promontory. Some time afterwards the discharges of several cannon were heard at a distance, and, after an interval, a still louder explosion, as of a vessel blown up, and a cloud of smoke rose above the trees, and mingled with the blue sky. All then separated upon their different occasions, auguring variously upon the fate of the smuggler, but most insisting that her capture was inevitable, if she had not already gone to the bottom.

"It is near our dinner-time, my dear," said Mrs Bertram to her husband, "will it be long before Mr Kennedy comes back?"

"I expect him every moment, my dear," said the Laird; "perhaps he is bringing some of the officers of the sloop with him."

"My stars, Mr Bertram! why did not ye say so, that we might have had the large round table?—and then, they're a' tired o' salt-meat, and, to tell you the plain truth, a rump of beef is the best part of your dinner—and then I wad have put on another gown, and ye wad na have been the waur o' a clean neck-cloth—But ye delight in surprising and hurrying one—I am sure I am no to haud out for ever against that sort of going on—But when folk are missed, then they are moaned."

"Pshaw, pshaw, deuce take the beef, and the gown, and the table, and the neck-cloth!—we shall do all very well.—Where's the Dominie, John?—(to a servant who was busy about the table) where's the Dominie and little Harry?"

"Mr Sampson's been at home these twa hours and mair, but I dinna think Mr Harry came home wi' him."

"Not come home wi' him?" said the lady, "beg Mr Sampson to step this way directly."

"Mr Sampson," said she, upon his entrance, "is it not the most extraordinary thing in this world, that you, who have your free up-putting—bed—board—and washing—and twelve pounds sterling a-year, just to look after that boy, should let him out of your sight for twa or three hours?"

Sampson made a bow of humble acknowledgment at each pause which the angry lady made in her enumeration of the advantages of his situation, in order to give more weight to her remonstrance, and then, in words which we will not do him the injustice to imitate, told how Master Francis Kennedy had assumed "spontaneously the charge of Master Henry, in spite of his remonstrances in the contrary."

"I am very little obliged to Mr Francis Kennedy for his pains," said the lady peevishly; "suppose he lets the boy drop from his horse, and lames him?—or suppose one of the cannons comes ashore and kills him?—or suppose"——

"Or suppose, my dear," said Ellangowan, "what is much more likely than any thing else, that they have gone aboard the sloop, or the prize, and are to come round the Point with the tide?"

"And then they may be drowned," said the lady.

"Verily," said Sampson, "I thought Mr Kennedy had returned an hour since—Of a surety I deemed I heard his horse's feet."

"That," said John with a broad grin, "was Grizel chasing the humbled cow out of the close."

Sampson coloured up to the eyes—not at the implied taunt, which he would never have discovered, or resented if he had, but at some idea which crossed his own mind. "I have been in error," he said, "of a surety I should have tarried for the babe." So saying, he snatched his cane and hat, and hurried away towards Warroch-wood, faster than he was ever known to walk before, or after.

The Laird lingered some time, debating the point with the lady. At length, he saw the sloop of war again make her appearance; but, without approaching the shore, she stood away to the westward with all her sails set, and was soon out of sight. The lady's state of timorous and fretful apprehension was so habitual, that her fears went for nothing with her lord and master; but an appearance of disturbance and anxiety among the servants now excited his alarm, especially when he was called out of the room, and told in private, that Mr Kennedy's horse had come to the stable door alone, with the saddle turned round below his belly, and the reins of the bridle broken; and that a farmer had informed them in passing, that there was a smuggling lugger burning like a killogie on the other side of the Point of Warroch, and that, though he had come through the wood, he had seen or heard nothing of Kennedy and the young Laird, "only there was Dominie Sampson, gaun rampaging about, like mad, seeking for them."

All was now bustle at Ellangowan. The Laird and his servants, male and female, hastened to the wood of Warroch. The tenants and cottagers in the neighbourhood lent their assistance, partly out of zeal, partly from curiosity. Boats were manned to search the sea-shore, which, on the other side of the Point, rose into high and indented rocks. A vague suspicion was entertained, though too horrible to be expressed, that the child might have fallen from one of these cliffs.

The evening had begun to close when the parties entered the wood, and dispersed different ways in quest of the boy and his companion. The darkening of the atmosphere, and the hoarse sigh of the November wind through the naked trees, the rustling of the withered leaves which strewed the glades, the repeated halloos of the different parties, which often drew them together in expectation of meeting the object of their search, gave a cast of dismal sublimity to the scene.

At length, after a minute and fruitless investigation through the wood, the searchers began to draw together into one body and to confer notes. The agony of the father grew beyond concealment, yet it scarcely equalled the anguish of the tutor. "Would to God I had died for him!" the affectionate creature repeated in notes of the deepest distress. Those who were less interested, rushed into a tumultuary discussion of chances and possibilities. Each gave his opinion, and each was alternately swayed by that of the others. Some thought they had gone aboard the sloop; some that they had gone to a village at three miles distance; some whispered they might have been on board the lugger, a few planks and beams of which the tide now drifted ashore.

At this instant, a shout was heard from the beach, so loud, so shrill, so piercing, so different from every sound which the woods had that day rung to, that nobody hesitated a moment to believe that it conveyed tidings, and tidings of dreadful import. All hurried to the place, and, venturing without scruple upon paths, which, at another time, they would have shuddered to look at, descended towards a cleft of the rock, where one boat's crew was already landed. "Here, sirs!—this way, for God's sake!—this way!" was the reiterated cry. Ellangowan broke through the throng which had already assembled at the fatal spot, and beheld the object of their terror. It was the dead body of Kennedy. At first sight he seemed to have perished by a fall from the rocks, which rose in a precipice of a hundred feet above the beach. He was lying half in, half out of the water; the advancing tide, raising his arm and stirring his clothes, had given him at some distance the appearance of motion, so that those who first discovered the body thought that life remained. But every spark had been long extinguished.

"My bairn! my bairn!" cried the distracted father, "where can he be?"—A dozen mouths were opened to communicate hopes which no one felt. Some one at length mentioned the gypsies. In a moment Ellangowan had reascended the cliffs, flung himself upon the first horse he met, and rode furiously to the huts at Derncleugh. All was there dark and desolate; and, as he dismounted to make more minute search, he stumbled over fragments of furniture which had been thrown out of the cottages, and the broken wood and thatch which had been pulled down by his orders. At that moment the prophecy, or anathema, of Meg Merrilies fell heavy on his mind. "You have stripped the thatch off seven cottages,—see that the roof-tree of your own house stand the surer!"

"Restore," he cried, "restore my bairn! restore my son, and all shall be forgot and forgiven!" As he uttered these words in a sort of frenzy, his eye caught a glimmering of light in one of the dismantled cottages —it was that in which Meg Merrilies formerly resided. The light seemed to proceed from fire, which glimmered not only through the window, but also through the rafters of the hut where the thatch had been torn off.

He flew to the place; the door was bolted; despair gave the miserable father the strength of ten men; he rushed against the door with such violence that it gave way before the *momentum* of his weight and force. The cottage was empty, but bore marks of recent habitation—there was fire on the hearth, a kettle, and some preparation for food. As he looked eagerly round for something that might confirm his hope that his child yet lived, though in the power of those strange people, a man entered the hut.

It was his old gardener. "O sir!" said the old man, "such a night as this I trusted never to live to see!—ye maun come to the Place directly!"

"Is my boy found? is he alive? have ye found Harry Bertram?"

"No"——

"Then he is kidnapped! I am sure of it, Andrew! as sure as that I tread upon earth!—She has stolen him—and I will never stir from this place till I have tidings of him!"

"O, but ye maun come hame, sir! ye maun come hame!—We have sent for the sheriff, and we'll set a watch here a' night, in case the gypsies return; but *you*—ye maun come hame, sir,——for my lady's in the dead-thraw."

Bertram turned a stupified and unmeaning eye on the messenger who uttered this calamitous news; and, repeating the words "in the dead-thraw?" as if he could not comprehend the meaning, suffered the old man drag him towards his horse. During the ride home, he only said, "Wife and bairn, baith—mother and son, baith—Sair, sair to abide!"

It is needless to dwell upon the new scene of agony which awaited him. The news of Kennedy's fate had been eagerly and incautiously communicated at Ellangowan, with the gratuitous addition, that, doubtless, "he had drawn the young Laird ower the craig wi' him, though the tide had swept away the child's body—he was light, puir thing, and would flee farther into the surf."

Mrs Bertram heard the tidings; she was far advanced in her pregnancy; she fell into the pains of premature labour, and, ere Ellangowan had recovered his agitated faculties, so as to comprehend the full distress of his situation, he was the father of a female infant, and a widower.

Chapter Ten

But see, his face is black, and full of blood;
His eye-balls farther out than when he lived,
Staring full ghastly like a strangled man;
His hair uprear'd, his nostrils stretch'd with struggling,
His hands abroad display'd, as one that grasp'd
And tugg'd for life, and was by strength subdued.
Henry VI. Part II

THE SHERIFF-DEPUTE of the county arrived at Ellangowan next morning by day-break. To this provincial magistrate the law of Scotland assigns judicial powers of considerable extent, and the task of enquiring into all crimes committed within his jurisdiction, apprehension and commitment of suspected persons, and so forth.

The gentleman who held the office in the shire of —— at the time of this catastrophe, was well born and well educated; and, though somewhat pedantic and professional in his habits, he enjoyed general respect as an active and intelligent magistrate. His first employment was to examine all witnesses whose evidence could throw light upon this mysterious event, and make up the written report, *procès verbal*, or precognition, as it is technically called, which the practice of Scotland has substituted for a coroner's inquest. Under the sheriff's minute and skilful enquiry, many circumstances appeared, which were incompatible with the original opinion, that Kennedy had accidentally fallen from the cliffs. We shall briefly detail some of those circumstances.

The body had been deposited in a neighbouring fisher-hut, but without altering the condition in which it was found. This was the first object of the Sheriff's examination. Though fearfully crushed and mangled by the fall from such a height, it was found to exhibit a deep cut in the head, which, in the opinion of a skilful surgeon, must have been inflicted by a broad-sword, or cutlass. The experience of this gentleman discovered other suspicious indications. The face was much blackened, the eyes distorted, and the veins of the neck swelled. A black handkerchief, which the unfortunate man had worn around his neck, did not present the usual appearance, but was much loosened, and the knot displaced and dragged extremely tight: the folds were also compressed, as if it had been used as a mode of grappling the deceased, and dragging him perhaps to the precipice.

On the other hand, poor Kennedy's purse was found untouched; and, what seemed yet more extraordinary, the pistols which he usually carried when about to encounter any hazardous adventure, were found in his pockets loaded. This appeared particularly strange, for he was known and dreaded by the contraband traders as a man equally fearless and dexterous in the use of his weapons, of which he had given many signal proofs. The Sheriff enquired, whether Kennedy was not in the practice of carrying any other arms. Most of Mr Bertram's servants recollected that he generally had a *couteau de chasse*, or short hanger, but no such was found upon the dead body; nor could those who had seen him on the morning of the fatal day, take it upon them to assert whether he then carried that weapon or not.

The corpse afforded no other *indicia* respecting the fate of Kennedy; for, though the clothes were much displaced, and the limbs dreadfully fractured, the one seemed the probable, the other the certain, consequence of such a fall. The hands of the deceased were clenched fast, and full of turf and earth; but this also seemed equivocal.

The magistrate then proceeded to the place where the corpse was first discovered, and made those who had found it give, upon the spot, a particular and detailed account of the manner in which it was lying. A large fragment of the rock appeared to have accompanied, or followed, his fall from the cliff above. It was of so solid and compact a substance, that it had fallen without any great diminution by splintering, so that the Sheriff was enabled, first, to estimate the weight by measurement, and then to calculate, from the appearance of the fragment, what proportion of it had been bedded into the cliff from which it had fallen. This was easily detected, by the raw appearance of the stone where it had not been exposed to the atmosphere. They then ascended the cliff, and surveyed the place from whence the stony fragment had descended. It seemed plain, from the appearance of the bed, that the mere weight of one man standing upon the projecting part of the fragment, supposing it in its original situation, could not have destroyed its bias, and precipitated it, with himself, from the cliff. At the same time, it seemed to have lain so loose, that the use of a lever, or the combined strength of three or four men, might easily have hurled it from its position. The short turf about the brink of the precipice was much trampled, as if stamped by the heels of men in a mortal struggle, or in the act of some violent exertion. Traces of the same kind, less visibly marked, guided the sagacious investigator to the verge of the copsewood, which, in that place, crept high up the bank towards the top of the precipice.

With patience and perseverance, they traced these marks into the thickest part of the copse, a route which no person would have voluntarily adopted, unless for the purpose of concealment. Here they found plain vestiges of violence and struggling, from space to space.

Small boughs were torn down, as if grasped by some resisting wretch who was dragged forcibly along; the ground, where in the least degree soft or marshy, shewed the print of many feet; there were vestiges also, which might be those of human blood. At any rate, it was certain that several persons must have forced their passage among the oaks, hazels, and underwood, with which they were mingled; and in some places appeared traces, as if a sack full of grain, a dead body, or something of that heavy and solid description, had been dragged along the ground. In one place of the thicket there was a small swamp, the clay of which was whitish, being probably mixed with marl. The back of Kennedy's coat appeared besmeared with stains of the same colour.

At length, about a quarter of a mile from the brink of the fatal precipice, the traces conducted them to a small open space of ground, very much trampled, and plainly stained with blood, although withered leaves had been strewed upon the spot, and other means hastily taken to efface the marks, which seemed obviously to have been derived from a desperate affray. On one side of this patch of open ground was found the sufferer's naked hanger, which seemed to have been thrown into the thicket; on the other, the belt and sheath, which appeared to have been hidden with more leisurely care and precaution.

The magistrate caused the foot-prints which marked this spot to be carefully measured and examined. Some corresponded to the foot of the unhappy victim; some were larger, some less; indicating, that at least four or five men had been busy around him. Above all, here, and here only, were observed the vestiges of a child's foot; and as it could be seen no where else, and the hard horse-track which traversed the wood of Warroch was contiguous to the spot, it was natural to think that the boy had escaped in that direction during the confusion. The Sheriff made a careful entry of all these memoranda, and did not suppress his opinion, that the deceased had met with foul play, and that the murderers, whoever they were, had possessed themselves of the person of the child Harry Bertram.

Every exertion was now made to discover the criminals. Suspicion hesitated between the smugglers and the gypsies. The fate of Dirk Hattaraick's vessel was certain. Two men from the opposite side of Warroch Bay (so the inlet on the southern side of the Point of Warroch is called) had seen, though at a great distance, the lugger drive eastward, after doubling the head-land, and, as they judged from her manœuvre, in a disabled state. Shortly after, they perceived that she grounded, smoked, and, finally, took fire. She was, as one of them expressed himself, *in a light low*, (bright flame,) when they observed a king's ship, with her colours up, heave in sight from behind the cape.

The guns of the burning vessel discharged themselves as the fire reached them; and they saw her, at length, blow up with a great explosion. The sloop of war kept aloof for her own safety; and, after hovering till the other ship exploded, stood away southward under a press of sail. The Sheriff anxiously interrogated these men whether any boats had left the vessel. They could not say—they had seen none—but they might have put off in such a direction as to keep the burning vessel between their course and the witnesses.

That the ship destroyed was Dirk Hattaraick's no one doubted. His lugger was well known on the coast, and had been expected just at this time. A letter from the commander of the king's sloop, to whom the Sheriff made application, left the matter beyond doubt; he sent also an extract from his log-book of the transactions of the day, which intimated their being on the outlook for a smuggling lugger, Dirk Hattaraick master, upon the information and requisition of Francis Kennedy, of his majesty's excise service; and that Kennedy was to be upon the outlook on the shore, in case Hattaraick, who was known to be a desperate fellow, and had been outlawed repeatedly, should attempt to run his ship aground. About nine o'clock A.M. they discovered a sail, which answered the description of Hattaraick's vessel, chased her, and, after repeated signals to her to show colours or bring-to, fired upon her. The chase then showed Hamburgh colours, and returned the fire; and a running fight was maintained for three hours, when, just as the lugger was doubling the Point of Warroch, they observed her main-yard was shot in the slings, and that the vessel was disabled. It was not in their power for some time to profit by this circumstance, owing to their having kept too much in-shore for doubling the headland. After two tacks they accomplished this, and observed the chase on fire, and apparently deserted. The fire having reached some casks of spirits, which were placed on the deck, with other combustibles, probably on purpose, burned with such fury, that no boats durst approach the vessel, especially as her shotted guns were discharging, one after another, by the heat. The captain had no doubt whatever that the crew had set the vessel on fire, and escaped in their boats. After watching the conflagration till the ship blew up, his majesty's sloop, the Shark, stood towards the Isle of Man, with the purpose of intercepting the retreat of the smugglers, who, though they might conceal themselves in the woods for a day or two, would probably take the first opportunity of endeavouring to make for this asylum. But they never saw more of them than is above narrated.

Such was the account given by William Pritchard, master and commander of his majesty's sloop of war, Shark, who concluded by regretting deeply, that he had not had the happiness to fall in with the scoundrels who had had the impudence to fire on his majesty's flag, and with an assurance, that, should he meet Mr Dirk Hattaraick in any future cruise, he would not fail to bring him into port under his stern, to answer whatever might be alleged against him.

As, therefore, it seemed tolerably certain that the men on board the lugger had escaped, the death of Kennedy, if he fell in with them in the woods, when irritated by the loss of their vessel, and by the share he had had in it, was easily to be accounted for. And it was not improbable, that to such brutal tempers, rendered desperate by their own circumstances, even the murder of the child, against whose father Hattaraick was known to have uttered deep threats, would not appear a very heinous crime.

Against this hypothesis it was urged, that a crew of fifteen or twenty men could not have lain hidden upon the coast, where so close a search took place immediately after the destruction of their vessel; or, at least, that if they had hid themselves in the woods their boats must have been seen on the beach;—that in such precarious circumstances, and when all retreat must have seemed difficult, if not impossible, it was not to be thought that they would have all united to commit an useless murder, for the mere sake of revenge. Those who held this opinion, supposed, either that the boats of the lugger had stood out to sea without being observed by those who were intent upon gazing at the burning vessel, and so gained safe distance before the sloop got round the headland, or else, that the boats being staved or destroyed by the fire of the Shark during the chase, the crew had obstinately determined to perish with the vessel. What gave some countenance to this supposed act of desperation was, that neither Dirk Hattaraick nor any of his sailors, all well-known men in the fair-trade, were again seen upon that coast, or heard of in the Isle of Man, where strict enquiry was made. On the other hand, only one dead body, apparently that of a seaman killed by a cannon shot, drifted ashore. So all that could be done was, to register the names, description, and appearance of the individuals belonging to the ship's company, and offer a reward for the apprehension of them, or any one of them; extending also to any person, not the actual murtherer, who should give evidence tending to convict those who had murthered Francis Kennedy.

Another opinion, which was also plausibly supported, went to charge this horrid crime upon the late tenants of Derncleugh. They were known to have resented highly the conduct of the Laird of Ellangowan towards them, and to have used threatening expressions, which every one supposed them capable of carrying into effect. The kidnapping the child was a crime much more consistent with their habits than with those of smugglers, and his temporary guardian might have fallen in an attempt to protect him. Besides it was remembered, that Kennedy had been an active agent, two or three days before, in the forcible expulsion of these people from Derncleugh, and that harsh and menacing language had been exchanged between him and some of the Egyptian patriarchs upon that memorable occasion.

The Sheriff received also the depositions of the unfortunate father and his servant, concerning what passed at their meeting the caravan of gypsies as they left the estate of Ellangowan. The speech of Meg Merrilies seemed particularly suspicious. There was, as the magistrate observed in his law language, *damnum minatum*, a damage or evil turn threatened, and *malum secutum*—an evil of the very kind predicted shortly afterwards following. A young woman, who had been gathering nuts in Warroch wood upon the fatal day, was also strongly of opinion, though she declined to make oath, that she had seen Meg Merrilies, at least a woman of her remarkable size and appearance, start suddenly out of a thicket—she said she had called to her by name, but, as the figure turned from her, and made no answer, she was uncertain if it were the gypsy, or her wraith, and was afraid to go nearer to one who was reckoned, in the vulgar phrase, *no canny*. This vague story received some corroboration from the circumstance of a fire being that evening found in the gypsy's deserted cottage. To this fact Ellangowan and his gardener bore evidence. Yet it seemed extravagant to suppose, that, had this woman been accessory to such a dreadful crime, she would have returned that very evening on which it was committed, to the place, of all others, where she was most likely to be sought after.

Meg Merrilies was, however, apprehended and examined. She denied strongly having been either at Derncleugh or in the wood of Warroch upon the day of Kennedy's death; and several of her tribe made oath in her behalf, that she had never quitted their encampment, which was in a glen about ten miles distant from Ellangowan. Their oaths were indeed little to be trusted to; but what other evidence could be heard in the circumstances? There was one remarkable fact, and only one, which arose from her examination. Her arm appeared to be slightly wounded by the cut of a sharp weapon, and was tied up with a handkerchief of Harry Bertram's. But the chief of the horde acknowledged he had "corrected her" that day with his whinger—she herself, and others, gave the same account of her hurt; and, for the handkerchief, the quantity of linen stolen from Ellangowan during the last months of their residence on the estate easily accounted for it, without charging Meg with a more heinous crime.

It was observed upon her examination, that she treated the questions respecting the death of Kennedy, or "the gauger," as she called him, with indifference; but expressed great and emphatic scorn and indignation at being supposed capable of injuring little Harry Bertram. She was long confined in jail, under the hope that something might yet be discovered to throw light upon this dark and bloody transaction. Nothing, however, occurred; and Meg was at length liberated, but under sentence of banishment from the county, as a vagrant, common thief, and disorderly person. No traces of the boy could ever be discovered; and, at length, the story, after making much noise, was gradually given up as altogether inexplicable, and only perpetuated by the name of "The Gauger's Loup," which was generally bestowed on the cliff from which the unfortunate man had fallen or been precipitated.

Chapter Eleven

Enter Time, as Chorus.

I—that please some, try all; both joy and terror
Of good and bad; that make and unfold error—
Now take upon me, in the name of Time,
To use my wings. Impute it not a crime
To me, or my swift passage, that I slide
O'er sixteen years, and leave the growth untried
Of that wide gap.———

Winter's Tale

OUR NARRATIVE is now about to make a large stride, and omit a space of nearly seventeen years. The gap is a wide one; yet if the reader's experience in life enables him to look back on so many years, the space will scarce appear longer in his recollection, than the time consumed in turning these pages.

It was, then, in the month of November, about seventeen years after the catastrophe narrated in the last chapter, that, during a cold and stormy night, a social group had closed around the kitchen fire of the Gordon Arms at Kippletringan, a small but comfortable inn, kept by Mrs Mac-Candlish in that village. The conversation which passed among them will save me the trouble of telling the few events occurring during this chasm in our history, with which it is necessary that the reader should be acquainted.

Mrs Mac-Candlish, throned in a comfortable easy chair lined with black leather, was regaling herself, and a neighbourly gossip or two, with a cup of comfortable tea, and at the same time keeping a sharp eye upon her domestics, as they went and came in prosecution of their various duties and commissions. The clerk and precentor of the parish enjoyed at a little distance his Saturday night's pipe, and aided its bland fumigation by an occasional sip of brandy and water. Deacon Bearcliff, a man of great importance in the village, combined the indulgences of both parties—he had his pipe and his tea-cup, the latter being laced with a little brandy. One or two clowns sat at some distance, drinking their two-penny ale.

"Are ye sure the parlour's ready for them, and the fire burning clear, and the chimney no smoking?" said the hostess to a chamber-maid.

She was answered in the affirmative.—"Ane wadna be uncivil to them, especially in their distress," said she, turning to the Deacon.

"Assuredly not, Mrs Mac-Candlish; assuredly not. I am sure ony small thing they might want frae my shop, under seven, or eight, or ten pounds, I would book them as readily for it as the first in the country. —Do they come in the auld chaise?"

"I dare say no," said the precentor; "for Miss Bertram comes on the white poney ilka day to the kirk—and a constant kirk-keeper she is—and it's a pleasure to hear her sing the psalms, winsome young thing."

"Aye, and the young Laird of Hazelwood rides hame half the road wi' her after sermon," said one of the gossips in company; "I wonder how auld Hazelwood likes that."

"I kenna how he may like it now," answered another of the tea-drinkers; "but the day has been Ellangowan wad hae liked as little to see his daughter taking up with their son."

"Aye, *has been*," answered the first with emphasis.

"I am sure, neighbour Ovens," said the hostess, "the Hazelwoods of Hazelwood, though they're a very gude auld family in the county, never thought, till within this twascore o' years, of evening themselves till the Ellangowans—Wow, woman, the Bertrams of Ellangowan are the auld Dingawaies lang syne—there is a sang about ane o' them marrying a daughter of the King of Man; it begins,

> Blithe Bertram's ta'en him ower the faem,
> To wed a wife, and bring her hame——

I dare say Mr Skreigh can sing us the ballad."

"Good-wife," said Skreigh, gathering up his mouth, and sipping his tiff of brandy punch with great solemnity, "our talents were given us to other use than to sing daft auld sangs sae near the Sabbath-day."

"Hout fie, Mr Skreigh, I'se warrant I hae heard ye sing a blythe sang on Saturday at e'en—But as for the family carriage, Deacon, it has na been out o' the coach-house since Mrs Bertram died, that's sixteen or seventeen years syne—Jock Jabos is away wi' a chaise of mine for them;—I wonder he's no come back. It's pit mirk—but there's no an ill turn in the road but twa, and the brigg ower Warroch burn is safe eneugh, if he haud to the right side. But than there's Heaveside-brae, that's just a murder for post-cattle—but Jock kens the road brawly."

A loud rapping was heard at the door.

"That's no them. I dinna hear the wheels.—Grizel, ye limmer, gang to the door."

"It's a single gentleman," whined out Grizel; "maun I take him into the parlour?"

"Foul be in your feet than;—it will be some English rider; coming without a servant at this time o' night!—Has the ostler ta'en his horse? —Ye may light a spunk o' fire in the red room."

"I wish, ma'am," said the traveller, entering the kitchen, "you would give me leave to warm myself here, for the night is very chill."

His appearance, voice, and manner, produced an instantaneous effect in his favour. He was a handsome tall thin figure, dressed in black, as appeared when he laid aside his riding coat; his age might be between forty and fifty; his cast of features grave and interesting, and his air somewhat military. Every point of his appearance and address bespoke the gentleman. Long habit had given Mrs Mac-Candlish an acute tact in ascertaining the quality of her visitors, and proportioning her reception accordingly:—

> To every guest the appropriate speech was made,
> And every duty with distinction paid;
> Respectful, easy, pleasant, or polite——
> "Your Honour's servant!—Mister Smith, good night."

On the present occasion, she was low in her curtsey, and profuse in her apologies. The stranger begged his horse might be attended to—she went out herself to school the ostler.

"There was never a prettier bit o' horse-flesh in the stable o' the Gordon Arms," said the man; which information increased the landlady's respect for the rider. Upon the stranger declining to go into another apartment, (which indeed, she allowed, would be but cold and smoky till the fire burned up,) she installed her guest comfortably by the fire-side, and offered what refreshments her house afforded.

"A cup of your tea, ma'am, if you will favour me."

Mrs Mac-Candlish bustled about, reinforced her teapot with hyson, and proceeded in her duties with her best grace. "We have a very nice parlour, sir, and every thing very agreeable for gentlefolks; but it's bespoke the-night for a gentleman and his daughter that are going to leave this part of the country—ane of my chaises is gone for them, and will be back forthwith—they're not sae weel in the world as they have been; but we're a' subject to ups and downs in this life, as your honour must needs ken—but is not the tobacco-reek disagreeable to your honour?"

"By no means, ma'am; I am an old campaigner, and perfectly used to it.—Will you permit me to make some enquiries about a family in this neighbourhood?"

The sound of wheels was now heard, and the landlady hurried to the door to receive her expected guests; but returned in an instant, followed by the postillion—"No, they canna come at no rate, the Laird's sae ill."

"But God help them," said the landlady, "the morn's the term—the very last day they can bide in the house—a' thing's to be roupit."

"Weel, but they can come at no rate I tell ye—Mr Bertram canna be moved."

"What Mr Bertram?" said the stranger; "not Mr Bertram of Ellangowan, I hope?"

"Just e'en that same, sir; and if ye be a friend o' his, you have come at a time he's sair bestad."

"I have been abroad for many years—is his health so much deranged?"

"Aye, and his affairs an' a'," said the Deacon; "the creditors have entered into possession o' the estate, and it's for sale; and some that made the maist by him—I name nae names, but Mrs Mac-Candlish kens wha I mean—(the landlady shook her head significantly) they're sairest on him e'en now—I have a sma' matter due mysell, but I wad rather have lost it than gane to turn the auld man out of his house, and him just dying."

"Aye but," said the clerk, "Mr Glossin wants to get rid of the auld Laird, and drive on the sale for fear the heir-male should cast up upon them—for I have heard, if there was an heir-male, they could not sell the estate for auld Ellangowan's debt."

"He had a son born a good many years ago," said the stranger; "he is dead, I suppose?"

"Nae man can say for that," said the clerk mysteriously.

"Dead!" said the Deacon, "I'se warrant him dead lang syne; he has na been heard of these twenty years or therebye."

"I wot weel it's no twenty years," said the landlady; "it's no abune seventeen at the outside in this very month; it made an unco noise ower a' this country—the bairn disappeared the very day that Supervisor Kennedy came by his end.—If ye kend this country lang syne, your honour wad maybe ken Frank Kennedy the Supervisor. He was a heartsome pleasant man, and company for the best gentleman in the county, and mickle mirth he's made in this house. I was young then, sir, and newly married to Baillie Mac-Candlish, that's dead and gone —(a sigh)—and muckle fun I've had with the Supervisor. He was a daft dog—O an' he could have hadden aff the smugglers a bit! but he was aye venturesome.—And so ye see, sir, there was a king's sloop down in Wigton bay, and Frank Kennedy, he behoved to have her up to chace Dirk Hattaraick's lugger—ye'll mind Dirk Hattaraick, Deacon? I dare say ye may have dealt wi' him—(the Deacon gave a sort of acquiescent nod and *umph.*) He was a daring chield, and he fought his ship till she blew up like the peelings of onions; and Frank Kennedy he had been the first man to board, and he was flung like a quarter of a mile off, and fell into the water below the rock at Warroch Point, that they ca' the Gauger's Loup to this day."

"And Mr Bertram's child," said the stranger, "what is all this to him?"

"Ow, sir,—the bairn aye held an unco wark wi' the Supervisor; and it was generally thought he went on board the vessel alang wi' him, as bairns are aye forward to be in mischief."

"No, no," said the Deacon, "ye're clean out there, Luckie—for the young Laird was stown away by a randy gypsy woman they ca'd Meg Merrilies,—I mind her looks weel,—in revenge for Ellangowan having gar'd her be drum'd through Kippletringan for stealing a silver spoon."

"If ye'll forgie me, Deacon," said the precentor, "ye're e'en as far wrang as the gudewife."

"And what is your edition of the story, sir?" said the stranger, turning to him with interest.

"That's maybe no sae canny to tell," said the precentor, with solemnity.

Upon being urged, however, to speak out, he preluded with two or three large puffs of tobacco-smoke, and out of the cloudy sanctuary which these whiffs formed around him, delivered the following legend, having cleared his voice with one or two hems, and imitating, as nearly as he could, the eloquence which weekly thundered over his head from the pulpit.

"What we are now to deliver, my brethren,—hem,—I mean, my good friends,—was not done in a corner, and may serve as an answer to witch-advocates, atheists, and misbelievers of all kinds.—Ye must know that the worshipful Laird of Ellangowan was not so preceese as he might have been in clearing his land of witches, (concerning whom it is said, 'Thou shalt not suffer a witch to live,') nor of those who had familiar spirits, and consulted with divination and sorcery, and lots, which is the fashion with the Egyptians, as they call themselves, and other unhappy bodies, in this our country. And the Laird was three years married without having a family—and he was so left to himsell, and it was thought he held ower mickle trocking and communing wi' that Meg Merrilies, wha was the most notorious witch in all Galloway and Dumfries-shire baith."

"Aweel I wot there's something in that," said Mrs Mac-Candlish; "I've kend him order her twa glasses o' brandy in this very house."

"Aweel, gudewife, the less I lee—Sae the lady was wi' bairn at last, and on the night when she should have been delivered, there comes to the door of the ha' house—the Place of Ellangowan as they ca'd it—an ancient man, strangely habited, and asked for quarters. His head, and his legs, and his arms, were bare, although it was winter time o' the year, and he had a grey beard three quarters lang. Weel, he was admitted; and when the lady was delivered, he craved to know the very moment of the hour of the birth, and he went out and consulted the stars. And when he came back, he tell'd the Laird, that the Evil One wad have power over the knave-bairn that was that night born, and he charged him that the babe should be bred up in the ways of piety, and that he should aye hae a godly minister at his elbow, to pray *wi'* the bairn and *for* him. And the aged man vanished away, and no man of this country ever saw mair o' him."

"Now, that will not pass," said the postillion, who, at a respectful distance, was listening to the conversation, "begging Mr Skreigh's and the company's pardon,—there was no sae mony hairs on the warlock's face as there's on his at this moment; and he had as gude a pair o' boots as a man need striek on his legs, and gloves too;—and I should understand boots by this time."

"Whisht, Jock," said the landlady.

"What do ye ken of the matter, friend Jabos?" said the Precentor contemptuously.

"No mickle, to be sure, Mr Skreigh—only that I lived within a penny-stane cast o' the head o' the avenue at Ellangowan, when a man came jingling to our door that night the young Laird was born, and my mother sent me, that was a hafflin callant, to shew the stranger the gate to the Place, which, if he had been such a warlock, he might hae kend himsell, ane wad think—and he was a young, weel-faur'd, weel-dressed man, like an Englishman. And I tell ye he had as gude a hat, and boots, and gloves, as ony gentleman need to have. To be sure he *did* gie an awesome glance up at the auld castle—and there was some spae-wark gaed on—I aye heard that; but as for his vanishing, I held the stirrup mysell when he gaed away, and he gied me a round half-crown—he was riding on a haik (hack) they ca'd Souple Sam—it belanged to the George at Dumfries—it was a blood-bay beast, very ill o' the spavin—I hae seen the beast baith before and since."

"Aweel, aweel, Jock," answered Mr Skreigh, with mild solemnity, "our accounts differ in no material particulars; but I had no knowledge that ye had seen the man—So ye see, my friends, that this soothsayer having prognosticated evil to the boy, his father engaged a godly minister to be with him morn and night."

"Aye, that was him they ca'd Dominie Sampson," said the postillion.

"He's but a dumb dog, that," observed the Deacon; "I have heard that he never could preach five words of a sermon endlang, for as lang as he has been licensed."

"Weel, but," said the Precentor, waving his hand, as if eager to recover the command of the discourse, "he waited on the young Laird by night and day. Now, it chanced, when the bairn was near five years auld, that the Laird had a sight of his errors, and determined to put these Egyptians aff his ground. And he caused them to remove; and that Frank Kennedy, that was a rough swearing fellow, he was sent to turn them aff. And he cursed and damned at them, and they swore at him, and that Meg Merrilies, that was the maist powerful with the Enemy of Mankind, she as gude as said she would have him body and soul before three days were ower his head. And I have from a sure hand, and that's ane wha saw it, and that's John Wilson that was the Laird's groom, that Meg appeared to the Laird as he was riding hame from Singleside over Gibbie's-know, and threatened him wi' what she wad do to his family—but whether it was Meg, or something warse in her likeness, for it seemed bigger than ony mortal creature—John could not say."

"Aweel," said the postillion, "it might be sae—I canna say against it, for I was not in the country at the time—but John Wilson was a blustering kind of fellow, without the heart of a sprug."

"And what was the end of all this?" said the stranger, with some impatience.

"Ow, the event and upshot of it was, sir," said the Precentor, "that while they were all looking on, beholding a king's ship chase a smuggler, this Kennedy suddenly brake away frae them without ony reason that could be descried—rapes nor tows wad not hae held him—and made for the wood of Warroch as fast as his beast could carry him; and by the way he met the young Laird and his governor, and he snatched up the bairn, and swore, if *he* was bewitched, the bairn should hae the same luck as him—and the minister followed as fast as he could, and almaist as fast as them, for he was wonderfully swift of foot—and he saw Meg the witch, or her master in her similitude, rise suddenly out of the ground, and claught the bairn suddenly out of the gauger's arms—and then he rampauged and drew his sword—for ye ken a fie man and a cusser fears na the deil."

"I believe that's very true," said the postillion.

"So, sir, she grippit him, and clodded him like a stane from the sling ower the craigs of Warroch-head, where he was found that evening—but what became of the babe, frankly I cannot say. But he that was minister here than, that's now in a better place, had an opinion that the bairn was only conveyed to Fairy-land for a season."

The stranger had smiled slightly at some parts of this recital, but ere he could answer, the clatter of a horse's hoofs was heard, and a smart servant, handsomely dressed, with a cockade in his hat, bustled into the kitchen, with "make a little room, good people;" when, observing the stranger, he descended at once into the modest and civil domestic, his hat sunk down by his side, and he put a letter into his master's hands. "The family at Ellangowan, sir, are in great distress, and unable to receive any visits."

"I know it," replied his master: "And now, madam, if you will have the goodness to allow me to occupy the parlour you mentioned, as you are disappointed of your guests"——

"Certainly, sir;" and Mrs Mac-Candlish lighted the way with all the imperative bustle which an active landlady loves to display upon such an occasion.

"Young man," said the Deacon to the servant, filling a glass, "ye'll no be the warse of this after your ride."

"Not a feather, sir—your very good health."

"And wha may your master be, friend?"

"What, the gentleman that was here?—that's the famous Colonel Mannering, from the East Indies."

"What, him we read of in the newspapers?"

"Aye, aye, just the same. It was he relieved Cuddiebum, and defended Chingalore, and defeated the great Mahratta chief, Ram Jolli Bundleman—I was with him in most of his campaigns."

"Lord safe us," said the landlady, "I must go see what he would have for supper—that I should have set him down here!"

"O, he likes that all the better, mother;—you never saw a plainer creature in your life than the Colonel; and yet he has a spice of the devil in him too."

The rest of the evening conversation below stairs tending little to edification, we shall, with the reader's leave, step up to the parlour.

Chapter Twelve

——Reputation?—that's man's idol
Set up against God, the Maker of all laws,
Who hath commanded us we should not kill,
And yet we say we must, for Reputation!
What honest man can either fear his own,
Or else will hurt another's reputation?
Fear to do base and unworthy things is valour;
If they be done to us, to suffer them
Is valour too.—

BEN JONSON

THE COLONEL was walking pensively up and down the parlour, when the officious landlady re-entered to take his commands. Having given them in the manner he thought would be most acceptable "for the good of the house," he begged to detain her a moment.

"I think," he said, "madam, if I understood these good people right, Mr Bertram lost his son in his fifth year?"

"O aye, sir, there's nae doubt of that, though there are mony idle clashes about the way and manner; for it's an auld story now, and every body tells it, as we were doing, their ain way by the ingle-side. But lost the bairn was in his fifth year, as your honour says, Colonel; and the news being rashly told to the lady, then great with child, cost her her life that samyn night—and the Laird never throve after that day, but was just careless of every thing—though, when his daughter Miss Lucy got up, she tried to keep order within doors—but what could she do, poor thing?—so now they're out of house and hauld."

"Can you recollect, madam, about what time of the year the child was lost?" The landlady, after a pause, and some recollection, answered, "she was positive it was about this season;" and added some local recollections that fixed the date in her memory, as occurring in the middle of November, 17—.

The stranger took two or three turns round the room in silence, but signed to Mrs Mac-Candlish not to leave it.

"Did I rightly apprehend," he said, "that the estate of Ellangowan is in the market?"

"In the market?—it will be sold the morn to the highest bidder—that's no the morn, Lord help me! which is the Sabbath, but on Monday, the first free day; and the furniture and stocking is to be roupit at the same time on the ground—it's the opinion of the haill country, that the sale has been shamefully forced on at this time, when there's sae little money stirring in Scotland wi' this weary American war, that somebody may get the land a bargain—Deil be in them, that I should say sae!"—the good lady's wrath rising at the supposed injustice.

"And where will the sale take place?"

"On the premises, as the advertisement says—that's at the house of Ellangowan, as I understand it."

"And who exhibits the title-deeds, rent-roll, and plan?"

"A very decent man, sir; the sheriff substitute of the county, who has authority from the Court of Session. He's in the town just now, if your honour would like to see him; and he can tell you mair about the loss of the bairn than ony body, for the sheriff depute (that's his principal like,) took much pains to come at the truth o' that matter, as I have heard."

"And this gentleman's name is?——"

"Mac-Morlan, sir—he's a man of character, and weel spoken of."

"Send my compliments—Colonel Mannering's compliments—to him, and I would be glad he would do me the pleasure of supping with me, and bring these papers with him—and I beg, good madam, you will say nothing of this to any one else."

"Me, sir? deil a word shall I say—I wish your honour, (a curtsey) or ony honourable gentleman that's fought for his country, (another curtsey) had the land, since the auld family maun quit, (a sigh) rather than that wily scoundrel, Glossin, that's risen on the ruin of the best friend he ever had—and now I think on't, I'll slip on my hood and pattens, and gang to Mr Mac-Morlan mysell—he's at hame e'en now —it's hardly a step."

"Do so, my good landlady, and many thanks—and bid my servant step here with my portfolio in the mean time."

In a minute or two, Colonel Mannering was quietly seated with his writing materials before him. We have the privilege of looking over his shoulder as he writes, and we willingly communicate its substance to our readers. The letter was addressed to Arthur Mervyn, Esq. of Mervyn-Hall, Llanbraithwaite, Westmoreland. It contained some account of the writer's previous journey since parting with him, and then proceeded as follows:

"And now, why will you still upbraid me with my melancholy, Mervyn?—Do you think, after the lapse of twenty-five years, battles, wounds, imprisonment, misfortunes of every description, I can be still the same lively unbroken Guy Mannering, who climbed Skiddaw with you, or shot grouse upon Crossfell? That you, who have remained in the bosom of domestic happiness, experience little change; that your step is as light, and your fancy as full of sunshine, is a blessed effect of health and temperament, co-operating with content and a smooth current down the course of life. But *my* career has been one of difficulties, and doubts, and errors. From my infancy I have been the sport of accident, and though the wind has often borne me into harbour, it has seldom been into that which the pilot destined. Let me recall to you in two sentences the odd and wayward fates of my youth, and the misfortunes of my manhood.

"The former, you will say, had nothing very appalling. All was not for the best; but all was tolerable. My father, the eldest son of an ancient but reduced family, left me with little, save the name of the head of the house, to the protection of his more fortunate brothers. They were so fond of me that they almost quarrelled about me. My uncle, the bishop, would have had me in orders, and offered me a living—my uncle, the merchant, would have put me into a counting-house, and proposed to give me a share in the thriving concern of Mannering and Moregold, in Lombard Street—So, between these two stools, or rather these two soft, easy, well-stuffed chairs of divinity and commerce, my unfortunate person slipped down and pitched upon a dragoon saddle. Again, the bishop wished me to marry the niece and heiress of the Dean of Lincoln; and my uncle, the alderman, proposed to me the only daughter of old Sloethorn, the great wine-merchant, rich enough to play at span-counter with moidores, and make thread-papers of bank-notes—and somehow I slipped my neck out of both nooses, and married—poor—poor Sophia Wellwood.

"You will say, my military career in India, when I followed my regiment there, should have given me some satisfaction, and so it assuredly has. You will remind me also, that if I disappointed the hopes of my guardians, I did not incur their displeasure—that the bishop, at his death, bequeathed me his blessing, his manuscript sermons, and a curious portfolio, containing the heads of eminent divines of the Church of England; and that my uncle, Sir Paul Mannering, left me sole heir and executor to his large fortune. Yet all this availeth me nothing—I told you I had that upon my mind which I should carry to my grave with me, a perpetual aloes in the draught of existence. I will tell you the cause more in detail than I had the heart to do while under your hospitable roof. You will often hear it mentioned, and perhaps with different and unfounded circumstances. I will, therefore, speak it out, and let the event itself, and the sentiments of melancholy with which it has impressed me, never again be subject of discussion between us.

"Sophia, as you well know, followed me to India. She was as innocent as gay; but, unfortunately for us both, as gay as innocent. My own manners were partly formed by studies I had forsaken, and habits of seclusion, not quite consistent with my situation as commandant of a regiment, in a country where universal hospitality is offered and expected by every settler claiming the rank of a gentleman. In a moment of peculiar pressure, (you know how hard we were sometimes run to obtain white faces to countenance our line of battle) a young man, named Brown, joined our regiment as a volunteer, and, finding the military duty more to his fancy than commerce, in which he had been engaged, remained with us as a cadet.—Let me do my unhappy victim justice—he behaved with such gallantry on every occasion that offered, that the first vacant commission was considered as his due. I was absent for some weeks upon a distant expedition;—when I returned, I found this young fellow established quite as the friend of the house, and habitual attendant of my wife and daughter. It was an arrangement which displeased me in many particulars, though no objection could be made to his manners or character—Yet I might have been reconciled to his familiarity in my family, but for the suggestions of another. If you read over—what I never dare open—the play of Othello, you will have some idea of what followed—I mean of my motives—my actions, thank God! were less reprehensible. There was another cadet ambitious of the vacant situation. He called my attention to what he led me to term coquetry between my wife and this Brown. Sophia was virtuous, but proud of her virtue, and irritated by my jealousy. She was so imprudent as to press and encourage the intimacy which she saw I disapproved and regarded with suspicion. Between Brown and me therefore subsisted a sort of internal dislike. He made one effort or two to overcome my prejudice; but, prepossessed as I was, I placed them to a wrong motive. Feeling himself repulsed, and with scorn, he desisted; and as he was without family and friends, he was naturally more watchful of the deportment of one who had both.

"It is odd with what torture I write this letter. I feel inclined, nevertheless, to protract the narrative, just as if my doing so could put off the catastrophe which has long embittered my life. But it must be told, and it shall be told briefly.

"My wife, though no longer young, was still eminently handsome, and—let me say thus far in my own justification—she was fond of being thought so. I am repeating what I said before—In a word, of her virtue I never entertained a doubt; but, pushed on by the artful suggestions of Archer, I thought she cared little for my peace of mind, and that this young fellow, Brown, paid his attentions in my despite, and in defiance of me. He perhaps considered me, on his part, as an oppressive aristocratic man, who made my rank in society, and in the army, the means of galling those whom circumstances placed beneath me. And if he discovered my silly jealousy, he probably considered the fretting me in that sore point of my character, as one means of avenging the petty indignities to which I had it in my power to subject him. Yet an acute friend of mine gave a more harmless, or at least a less offensive, construction to his attentions, which he conceived to be meant for my daughter Julia, though immediately addressed to propitiate the influence of her mother. This might have been no very flattering or pleasing enterprise on the part of an obscure and nameless youngster; but I could not have been offended at such folly as I was at the higher degree of presumption I suspected. Offended, however, I was, and in a mortal degree.

"A very slight spark will kindle a flame where every thing lies open to catch it. I have absolutely forgot the proximate cause of quarrel, but it was some trifle which occurred at the card-table, which occasioned high words and a challenge. We met in the morning beyond the walls and esplanade of the fortress which I then commanded, on the frontiers of the settlement. This was arranged for Brown's safety had he escaped. I almost wish he had, though at my own expence; but he fell by the first fire. We strove to assist him, but some of these *Looties*, a species of native banditti, who are always on the watch for prey, poured in upon us. Archer and I gained our horses with difficulty, and cut our way through them after a hard conflict, in the course of which he received some desperate wounds. To complete the misfortunes of this miserable day, my wife, who suspected the design with which I left the fortress, had ordered her palanquin to follow me, and was surprised by a party of the plunderers. She was quickly released by a patrole of our cavalry; but I cannot disguise from myself, that the incidents of this fatal morning gave a severe shock to health already delicate. The confession of Archer, who thought himself dying, that he had invented some circumstances, and, for his purposes, put the worst construction upon others; and the full explanation and exchange of forgiveness which this produced, could not check the progress of her disorder. She died within about eight months after this incident, bequeathing me only the girl, of whom Mrs Mervyn is so good as to undertake the temporary charge. Julia was also extremely ill, so much so, that I was induced to throw up my command and return to Europe, where her native air, time, and the novelty of the scenes around her, have contributed to dissipate her dejection, and to restore her health.

"Now that you know my story, you will no longer ask me the reason of my melancholy, but permit me to brood upon it as I may. There is, surely, in the above narrative, enough to embitter, though not to poison, the chalice, which the fortune and fame you so often mention had prepared to regale my years of retirement.

"I could add circumstances which our old tutor would have quoted as instances of *day fatality*—you would laugh were I to mention such particulars, especially as you know I put no faith in them. Yet, since I have come to the very house from which I now write, I have learned a singular coincidence, which, if I find it truly established by tolerable evidence, will serve us hereafter for subject of curious discussion. But I will spare you at present, as I expect a person to speak about a purchase of property now open in this part of the country. It is a place to which I have a foolish partiality, and I hope my purchasing may be convenient to those who are parting with it, as there is a plan for buying it under the value. My respectful compliments to Mrs Mervyn, and I will trust you, though you boast to be such a lively young gentleman, to kiss Julia for me.—Adieu, dear Mervyn.—Thine ever,

"GUY MANNERING."

Mr Mac-Morlan now entered the room. The well-known character of Colonel Mannering at once disposed this gentleman, who was a man of intelligence and probity, to be free and confidential. He explained the advantages and disadvantages of the property. "It was settled," he said, "the greater part of it at least, upon heirs-male, and the purchaser would have the privilege of retaining in his hands a large proportion of the price, in case of the re-appearance, within a certain limited term, of the child who had disappeared."

"To what purpose, then, force forward a sale?" said Mannering.

Mac-Morlan smiled. "Ostensibly," he said, "to substitute the interest of money, instead of the ill-paid and precarious rents of an unimproved estate; but chiefly, it was supposed, to suit the wishes and views of a certain intended purchaser, who had become a principal creditor, and forced himself into the management of the affairs, by means best known to himself, and who, it was thought, would find it very convenient to purchase the estate without paying down the price."

Mannering consulted with Mr Mac-Morlan upon the proper steps for thwarting this unprincipled attempt. They then conversed long upon the singular disappearance of Harry Bertram upon his fifth birth-day, verifying thus the random prediction of Mannering, of which, however, it will readily be supposed he made no boast. Mr Mac-Morlan was not himself in office when that incident took place; but he was well acquainted with all the circumstances, and promised that our hero should have them detailed by the sheriff-depute himself, if, as he proposed, he should become a settler in that part of Scotland.

With this assurance, they parted well satisfied with each other, and with the evening's conference.

On the Sunday following, Colonel Mannering attended the parish church with great decorum. None of the Ellangowan family were present; and it was understood that the old Laird was rather worse than better. Jock Jabos, once more dispatched for him, returned once more without his errand. Next day Miss Bertram hoped he might be removed.

Chapter Thirteen

> They told me, by the sentence of the law,
> They had commission to seize all thy fortune.—
> Here stood a ruffian with a horrid face,
> Lording it o'er a pile of massy plate,
> Tumbled into a heap for public sale;—
> There was another, making villainous jests
> At thy undoing; he had ta'en possession
> Of all thy ancient most domestic ornaments.
>
> OTWAY

EARLY NEXT MORNING, Mannering mounted his horse, and, accompanied by his servant, took the road to Ellangowan. He had no need to enquire the way. A sale in the country is a place of public resort and amusement, and people of various descriptions streamed to it from all quarters.

After a pleasant ride of about an hour, the old towers of the ruin presented themselves in the landscape. The thoughts with what different feelings he had lost sight of them so many years before, thronged upon the mind of the traveller. The landscape was the same; but how changed the feelings, hopes, and views, of the spectator! Then, life and love were new, and all the prospect was gilded by their rays. And now, disappointed in affection, sated with fame, and what the world calls success, his mind goaded by bitter and repentant recollections, his best hope was to find a retirement in which he might nurse the melancholy that was to accompany him to his grave. "Yet why should an individual mourn over the instability of our hopes, and the vanity of our prospects? The ancient chiefs, who erected these enormous and massive towers to be the fortress of their race, and the seat of their power, could they have dreamed the day was to come, when the last of their descendants should be expelled, a ruined wanderer, from his possessions! But Nature's bounties are unaltered. The sun will shine as fair on these ruins, whether the property of a stranger, or of a sordid and obscure trickster of the abused law, as when the banners of the founder first waved upon their battlements."

These reflections brought Mannering to the door of the house, which was that day open to all. He entered among others, who traversed the apartments, some to select articles for purchase, others to gratify their curiosity. There is something melancholy in such a scene, even under the most favourable circumstances. The confused state of the furniture, displaced for the convenience of being easily viewed and carried off by the purchasers, is disagreeable to the eye. Those articles which, properly and decently arranged, looked creditable and well-assorted, have then a paltry and wretched appearance; and the apartments, stripped of all that rendered them commodious and handsome, have an aspect of ruin and dilapidation. It is disgusting also, to see the scenes of domestic society and seclusion thrown open to the gaze of the curious and the vulgar; to hear their coarse speculations and jests upon the fashions and furniture to which they are unaccustomed,—a frolicksome humour much cherished by the whiskey which in Scotland is always put in circulation upon such occasions. All these are ordinary effects of such a scene as Ellangowan now presented; but the moral feeling, that, in this case, they indicated the total ruin of an ancient and honourable family, gave them treble weight and poignancy.

It was some time before Colonel Mannering could find any one disposed to answer his reiterated questions concerning Ellangowan himself. At length, an old maid-servant, who held her apron to her eyes as she spoke, told him, "the Laird was something better, and they hoped he would be able to leave the house that day. Miss Lucy expected the chaise every moment, and, as the day was fine for the time o' year, they had carried him in his easy chair up to the green before the auld castle, to be out of the way of this unco spectacle." Thither Colonel Mannering went in quest of him, and soon came in sight of the little group, which consisted of four persons. The ascent was steep, so that he had time to reconnoitre them as he advanced, and to consider in what mode he should make his address.

Mr Bertram, paralytick, and almost incapable of moving, occupied his easy chair, attired in his night-cap, and a loose camlet coat, his feet wrapped in blankets. Behind him, with his hands crossed on the cane on which he rested, stood Dominie Sampson, whom Mannering recognised at once. Time had made no change upon him, unless that his black coat seemed more brown, and his gaunt cheeks more lank, than when Mannering last saw him. On one side of the old man was a sylph-like form—a young woman of about seventeen, whom the Colonel accounted to be his daughter. She was looking, from time to time, anxiously towards the avenue, as if expecting the post-chaise; and between whiles busied herself in adjusting the blankets, so as to protect her father from the cold, and in answering enquiries, which he seemed to make with a captious and querulous manner. She did not trust herself to look towards the Place, as it was called, although the hum of the assembled crowd must have drawn her attention in that direction. The fourth person of the group was a handsome and genteel young man, who seemed to share Miss Bertram's anxiety, and her solicitude to sooth and accommodate her patient.

This young man was the first who observed Colonel Mannering, and immediately stepped forward to meet him, as if politely to prevent his drawing nearer to the distressed group. Mannering instantly paused and explained. "He was," he said, "a stranger, to whom Mr Bertram had formerly shewn kindness and hospitality; he would not have intruded himself upon him at a period of distress, did it not seem to be in some degree a moment also of desertion; he wished merely to offer such services as might be in his power to Mr Bertram and the young lady."

He then paused a little distance from the chair. His old acquaintance gazed at him with lack-lustre eye, that intimated no tokens of recognition—the Dominie seemed too deeply sunk in distress even to observe his presence. The young man spoke aside with Miss Bertram, who advanced timidly, and thanked Mr Mannering for his goodness; "but," she said, the tears gushing fast into her eyes—"her father, she feared, was not so much himself as to be able to remember him."

She then retreated towards the chair, accompanied by the Colonel. —"Father," she said, "this is Mr Mannering, an old friend, come to enquire after you."

"He's very heartily welcome,"—said the old man, raising himself in his chair, and attempting a gesture of courtesy, while a gleam of hospitable satisfaction seemed to pass over his faded features; "but, Lucy, my dear, let us go down to the house, you should not keep the gentleman here in the cold;—Dominie, take the key of the wine-cooler. Mr a—a—the gentleman will take something after his ride."

Mannering was unspeakably affected by the contrast which memory made between this reception and that with which he had been greeted by the same individual when in full possession of his faculties. He could not restrain his tears, and his evident emotion at once attained him the confidence of the friendless young lady.

"Alas!" said she, "this is distressing even to a stranger;—but it is maybe better for my poor father to be in this way, than if he knew and could feel all."

A servant in livery now came up the path, and spoke in an under tone to the young gentleman—"Mr Charles, my lady's wanting you yonder sadly, to bid for her for the black ebony cabinet; and Lady Jean

Devorgoil is wi' her an a'—ye maun come away directly."

"Tell them you could not find me, Tom, or, stay—say I am looking at the horses."

"No—no—no—" said Lucy Bertram earnestly; "if you would not add to the misery of this miserable moment, go to the company directly.—This gentleman, I am sure, will see us to the carriage."

"Unquestionably, madam," said Mannering, "your young friend may rely on my attention."

"Farewell, then," said Mr Charles, and whispered a word in her ear—then ran down the steep hastily, as if not trusting his resolution at a slower pace.

"Where's Charles Hazelwood running," said the invalid, who apparently was accustomed to his presence and attentions; "where's Charles Hazelwood running—what takes him away now?"

"He'll return in a little while," said Lucy gently.

The sound of voices was now heard from the ruins. The reader may remember there was a communication between the castle and the beach, up which the speakers had ascended.

"Yes—there's plenty of shells and sea-ware, as you observe—and if one inclined to build a new house, which might indeed be necessary, there's a great deal of good hewn stone about this old dungeon for the devil here"——

"Good God!" said Miss Bertram hastily to Sampson, "'tis that wretch Glossin's voice—if my father sees him, it will kill him outright!"

Sampson wheeled perpendicularly round, and moved with long strides to confront the attorney, as he issued from beneath the portal arch of the ruin. "Avoid ye!" he said—"Avoid ye! would'st thou kill and take possession?"

"Come, come, Master Dominie Sampson," answered Glossin insolently, "if ye cannot preach in the pulpit, we'll have no preaching here. We go by the law, my good friend—we leave the gospel to you."

The very mention of this man's name had been of late a subject of the most violent irritation to the unfortunate patient. The sound of his voice now produced an instantaneous effect. Mr Bertram started up without assistance, and turned round towards him; the ghastliness of his features forming a strange contrast with the violence of his exclamation.

"Out of my sight, ye viper!—ye frozen viper, that I warmed till he stung me!—Art thou not afraid that the walls of my fathers should fall and crush thee limb and bone?—Are ye not afraid the very lintel of the door of Ellangowan castle should break open and swallow you up!—Were ye not friendless, houseless, pennyless, when I took ye by the hand—and are ye not expelling me—me, and that innocent girl—friendless, houseless, and pennyless, from the home that has sheltered us and ours for a thousand years?"

Had Glossin been alone, he would probably have slunk off; but the consciousness that a stranger was present, besides the person who came with him (a sort of land-surveyor,) determined him to resort to impudence. The task, however, was almost too hard, even for his effrontery—"Sir—Sir—Mr Bertram—Sir, you should not blame me, but your own imprudence, sir"——

The indignation of Mannering was mounting very high. "Sir," he said to Glossin, "without entering into the merits of this controversy, I must inform you, that you have chosen a very improper place, time, and presence for it. And you will oblige me by withdrawing without more words."

Glossin was a tall, strong, muscular man, and not unwilling to turn upon a stranger whom he hoped to bully, rather than maintain his wretched cause against his injured patron—"I do not know who you are, sir, and I shall permit no man to use such d—d freedom with me."

Mannering was naturally hot-tempered—his eyes flashed a dark light—he compressed his nether lip so closely that the blood sprung, and, approaching Glossin—"Look you, sir," he said, "that you do not know me is of no consequence. *I know you;* and, if you do not instantly descend that bank, without uttering a single syllable, by the Heaven that is above us, you shall make but one step from the top to the bottom."

The commanding tone of rightful anger silenced at once the ferocity of the bully. He hesitated, turned on his heel, and, muttering something between his teeth about unwillingness to alarm the lady, relieved them of his hateful company.

Mrs Mac-Candlish's postillion, who had come up in time to hear what passed, said aloud, "If he had stuck by the way, I would have lent him a heezie, the dirty scoundrel, as willingly as ever I pitched a boddle."

He then stepped forward to announce that his horses were in readiness for the invalid and his daughter.

But they were no longer necessary. The debilitated frame of Mr Bertram was exhausted by this last effort of indignant anger, and when he sunk again upon his chair, he expired almost without a struggle or groan. So little alteration did the extinction of the vital spark make upon his external appearance, that the screams of his daughter, as she saw his eye fix and felt his pulse stop, first announced his death to the spectators.

Chapter Fourteen

The bell strikes one,—we take no note of time
But from its loss. To give it then a tongue
Is wise in man. As if an angel spoke,
I feel the solemn sound——

YOUNG

THE MORAL, which the poet has rather quaintly deduced from the necessary mode of measuring time, may be well applied to our feelings respecting that portion of it which constitutes human life. We observe the aged, the infirm, and those engaged in occupations of immediate hazard, trembling as it were upon the very brink of existence, but we draw no lesson from the precariousness of their tenure until it has altogether failed. Then, for a moment at least,

Our hopes and fears
Start up alarmed, and o'er life's narrow verge
Look down—On what?—a fathomless abyss,
A dark eternity, how surely ours!——

The crowd of assembled gazers and idlers at Ellangowan had followed the views of amusement, or what they called business, which brought them there, with little regard to the feelings of those who were suffering upon that occasion. Few, indeed, knew any thing of the family. The father, betwixt seclusion, misfortune, and imbecillity, had drifted, as it were, for many years, out of the notice of his contemporaries—the daughter had never been known to them. But when the general murmur announced that the unfortunate Mr Bertram had broken his heart in the effort to leave the mansion of his forefathers, there poured forth a torrent of sympathy, like the waters from the rock when stricken by the wand of the prophet. The ancient descent and unblemished integrity of the family were respectfully remembered; above all, the sacred veneration due to misfortune, which in Scotland seldom demands its tribute in vain, then claimed and received it.

Mr Mac-Morlan hastily announced, that he would suspend all further proceedings in the sale of the estate and other property, and relinquish the possession of the premises to the young lady, until she could consult with her friends, and provide for the burial of her father.

Glossin had cowered for a few minutes under the general expression of sympathy, till, hardened by observing that the popular indignation was not directed his way, he had the audacity to require that the sale should proceed.

"I will take it upon my own authority to adjourn it," said the Sheriff-substitute, "and will be responsible for the consequences. I will also give due notice when it is again to go forward. It is for the benefit of all concerned that the lands should bring the highest price the state of the market will admit, and this is surely no time to expect it—I will take the responsibility upon myself."

Glossin left the room and the house with secrecy and dispatch; and it was probably well for him that he did so, since our friend Jock Jabos was already haranguing a numerous tribe of bare-legged boys on the propriety of pelting him off the estate.

Some of the rooms were hastily put in order for the reception of the young lady, and of her father's dead body. Mannering now found his farther interference would be unnecessary, and might be misconstrued. He observed, too, that several families connected with that of Ellangowan, and who indeed derived their principal claim of gentility from the alliance, were now disposed to pay to their trees of genealogy a tribute, which the adversity of their supposed relatives had been inadequate to call forth; and that the honour of superintending the funeral rites of the dead Godfrey Bertram (as in the memorable case of Homer's birth-place) was likely to be debated by seven gentlemen of rank and fortune, none of whom had offered him an asylum while living. He therefore resolved, as his presence was altogether useless, to make a short tour of a fortnight, at the end of which period the adjourned sale of the estate of Ellangowan was again to proceed.

But before he departed, he solicited an interview with the Dominie. The poor man appeared, upon being informed a gentleman wanted to speak to him, with some expression of surprise in his gaunt features, to which recent sorrow had given an expression yet more grisly. He made two or three profound reverences to Mannering, and then, standing erect, patiently waited an explanation of his commands.

"You are probably at a loss to guess, Mr Sampson," said Mannering, "what a stranger may have to say to you?"

"Unless it were to request, that I would undertake to train up some youth in polite letters, and humane learning—but I cannot—I cannot —I have yet a task to perform."

"No, Mr Sampson, my wishes are not so ambitious. I have no son, and my only daughter, I presume, you would not consider as a fit pupil."

"Of a surety, no! Nathless, it was I who did educate Miss Lucy in all useful learning,—albeit it was the housekeeper who did teach her those unprofitable exercises of hemming and shaping."

"Well, sir, it is of Miss Lucy I meant to speak—you have, I presume, no recollection of me?"

Sampson, always sufficiently absent in mind, neither remembered the astrologer of past years, nor even the stranger who took his patron's part against Glossin, so much had his friend's sudden death embroiled his ideas.

"Well, that does not signify—I am an old acquaintance of the late Mr Bertram, able and willing to assist his daughter in her present circumstances. Besides, I have thoughts of making this purchase, and I should wish things kept in order about the place; will you have the goodness to apply this small sum in the usual family expences?"—He put into the Dominie's passive hand a purse containing some gold.

"Pro-di-gi-ous!" exclaimed Dominie Sampson. "But if your honour would tarry"——

"Impossible, sir—impossible," said Mannering, making his escape from him.

"Pro-di-gi-ous!" again exclaimed Sampson, following to the head of the stairs, still holding out the purse. "But as touching this coined money"——

Mannering escaped down stairs as fast as possible.

"Pro-di-gi-ous!" exclaimed Dominie Sampson, yet the third time, now standing at the front door. "But as touching this coin"——

But Mannering was now on horseback, and out of hearing. The Dominie, who had never, either in his own right, or as trustee for another, been possessed of a quarter part of this sum, though it was not above twenty guineas, "took counsel," as he expressed himself, "how he should demean himself with respect unto the fine gold" thus left in his charge. Fortunately he found a disinterested adviser in Mac-Morlan, who pointed out the most proper means of disposing of it for contributing to Miss Bertram's convenience, being no doubt the purpose to which it was destined.

Many of the neighbouring gentry were now sincerely eager in pressing offers of hospitality and kindness upon Miss Bertram. But she felt a natural reluctance to enter any family, for the first time, as an object rather of benevolence than hospitality, and determined to wait the opinion and advice of her father's nearest female relation, Mrs Margaret Bertram of Singleside, an old unmarried lady, to whom she wrote an account of her present distressful situation.

The funeral of the late Mr Bertram was performed with decent privacy, and the unfortunate young lady was now to consider herself as but the temporary tenant of the house in which she had been born, and where her patience and soothing attentions had so long "rocked the cradle of declining age." Her communication with Mr Mac-Morlan encouraged her to hope, that she would not be suddenly or unkindly deprived of this asylum; but fortune had ordered otherwise.

For two days before the appointed day for the sale of the lands and estate of Ellangowan, Mac-Morlan daily expected the appearance of

Colonel Mannering, or at least a letter containing powers to act for him. But none such arrived. Mr Mac-Morlan waked early in the morning,—walked over to the Post-office,—there were no letters for him. He endeavoured to persuade himself he should see Colonel Mannering to breakfast, and ordered his wife to place her best china, and prepare herself accordingly. But the preparations were in vain. "Could I have foreseen this," he said, "I would have travelled Scotland over, but I would have found some one to bid against Glossin." Alas! such reflections were all too late. The appointed hour arrived; and the parties met in the Masons' Lodge at Kippletringan, being the place fixed for the adjourned sale. Mac-Morlan spent as much time in preliminaries as decency would permit, and read over the articles of sale as slowly as if he had been reading his own death-warrant. He turned his eye every time the door of the room opened, with hopes which grew fainter and fainter. He listened to every noise in the street of the village, and endeavoured to distinguish in it the sound of hoofs or wheels. It was all in vain. A bright idea then occurred, that Colonel Mannering might have employed some other person in the transaction—he would not have wasted a moment's thought upon the want of confidence in himself, which such a manœuvre would have evinced. But this hope also was groundless. After a solemn pause, Mr Glossin offered the upset price for the lands and barony of Ellangowan. No reply was made, and no competitor appeared; so, after a lapse of the usual interval by the running of a sand-glass, upon the intended purchaser entering the proper sureties, Mr Mac-Morlan was obliged, in technical terms, to "find and declare the sale lawfully completed, and to prefer the said Gilbert Glossin as the purchaser of the said lands and estate." The honest writer refused to partake of a splendid entertainment with which Gilbert Glossin, Esquire, now of Ellangowan, treated the rest of the company, and returned home in huge bitterness of spirit, which he vented in complaints against the fickleness and caprice of these Indian Nabobs, who never knew what they would be at for ten days together. Fortune generously determined to take the blame upon herself, and cut off even this vent of Mr Mac-Morlan's resentment.

An express arrived about six o'clock at night, "very particularly drunk," the maid-servant said, with a packet from Colonel Mannering, dated four days back, at a town about a hundred miles distance from Kippletringan, containing full powers to Mr Mac-Morlan, or any one whom he might employ, to make the intended purchase, and stating, that some family business of consequence called the Colonel himself to Westmoreland, where a letter would find him, addressed to the care of Arthur Mervyn, Esq. of Mervyn Hall.

Mac-Morlan, in the transport of his wrath, flung the power of attorney at the head of the innocent maid-servant, and was only forcibly withheld from horse-whipping the truant messenger, by whose sloth and drunkenness the disappointment had taken place.

Chapter Fifteen

My gold is gone, my money is spent,
 My land now take it unto thee.
Give me the gold, good John o' the Scales,
 And thine for aye my land shall be.

Then John he did him to record draw,
 And John he caste him a gods pennie;
But for every pounde that John agreed,
 The land, I wis, was well worth three.

Heir of Linne

THE GALWEGIAN John o' the Scales was a more clever fellow than his prototype. He contrived to make himself heir of Linne without the disagreeable ceremony of "telling down the good red gold." Miss Bertram no sooner heard this painful, and of late unexpected intelligence, than she proceeded on the preparations she had already made for leaving the mansion-house instantly. Mr Mac-Morlan assisted her in these arrangements, and pressed upon her so kindly the hospitality and protection of his roof, until she should receive an answer from her cousin, or be enabled to adopt some settled plan of life, that she felt there would be unkindness in refusing an invitation urged with such earnestness. Mrs Mac-Morlan was a lady-like person, and well qualified by birth and manners to receive the visit, and to make her house agreeable to Miss Bertram. A home, therefore, and an hospitable reception, were secured to her, and she went on, with better heart, to pay the wages and receive the adieus of the few domestics of her father's family.

Where there are estimable qualities on either side, this task is always affecting—the present circumstances rendered it doubly so. All received their due, and even a trifle more, and with thanks and good wishes, to which some added tears, took farewell of their young mistress. There remained in the parlour only Mr Mac-Morlan, who came to attend his guest to his house, Dominie Sampson, and Miss Bertram. "And now," said the poor girl, "I must bid farewell to one of my oldest and kindest friends.—God bless you, Mr Sampson, and requite to you all the kindness of your instructions to your poor pupil, and your friendship to him that is gone—I hope I shall often hear from you." She slid into his hand a paper containing some pieces of gold, and rose, as if to leave the room.

Dominie Sampson also rose; but it was to stand aghast with utter astonishment. The idea of parting from Miss Lucy, go where she might, had never once occurred to the simplicity of his understanding. —He laid the money on the table. "It's certainly inadequate," said Mac-Morlan, mistaking his meaning, "but the circumstances"——

Mr Sampson waved his hand impatiently—"It is not the lucre—it is not the lucre—but I, that have eat of her father's loaf, and drunk of his cup, for twenty years and more—to think that I am going to leave her —and to leave her in distress and dolour—No, Miss Lucy, you need never think it! You would not consent to put forth your father's puir dog, and would you use me warse than a messan?—No, Miss Lucy Bertram, while I live I will not separate from you—I'll be no burthen —I have thought how to prevent that. But, as Ruth said unto Naomi, 'Intreat me not to leave thee, nor to depart from thee; for whither thou goest I will go, and where thou dwellest I will dwell; thy people shall be my people, and thy God shall be my God. Where thou diest will I die, and there will I be buried—The Lord do so to me, and more also, if aught but death do part thee and me.'"

During this speech, the longest ever Dominie Sampson was known to utter, the affectionate creature's eyes streamed with tears, and neither Lucy nor Mac-Morlan could refrain from sympathizing with this unexpected burst of feeling and attachment. "Mr Sampson," said Mac-Morlan, after having had recourse to his snuff-box and handkerchief alternately, "my house is large enough, and if you will accept of a bed there, while Miss Bertram honours us with her residence, I shall think myself very happy, and my roof much favoured by receiving a man of your worth and fidelity."

And then, with a delicacy which was meant to remove any objections on Miss Bertram's part to bringing with her this unexpected satellite, he added, "My business requires my frequently having occasion for a better accountant than any of my present clerks, and I should be glad to have recourse to your assistance in that way now and then."

"Of a surety—of a surety," said Sampson eagerly, "I understand book-keeping by double entry and the Italian method."

Our postillion had thrust himself into the room to announce his chaise and horses; he tarried, unobserved, this extraordinary scene, and assured Mrs Mac-Candlish it was the most moving thing he ever saw; "the death of the grey mare, puir hizzie, was naething till't." This trifling circumstance afterwards had consequences of greater importance.

The visitors were hospitably welcomed by Mrs Mac-Morlan, to whom, as well as to others, her husband intimated that he had engaged Dominie Sampson's assistance to disentangle some perplexed accompts; during which occupation, he would, for convenience sake, reside with the family. Mr Mac-Morlan's knowledge of the world induced him to put this colour upon the matter, aware, that however honourable the fidelity of the Dominie's attachment might be, both to his own heart and to the family of Ellangowan, his exterior ill qualified him to be a "squire of dames," and rendered him, upon the whole, rather a ridiculous appendage to a beautiful young woman of seventeen.

Dominie Sampson achieved with great zeal such tasks as Mr Mac-Morlan chose to entrust him with: but it was speedily observed, that, at a certain hour after breakfast, he regularly disappeared, and returned again about dinner time. The evening he occupied in the labour of the office. Upon the Saturday he appeared before Mac-Morlan with a look of great triumph, and laid on the table two pieces of gold.

"What is this for, Dominie?" said Mac-Morlan.

"First to indemnify you of your charges in my behalf, worthy sir—and the balance for the use of Miss Lucy Bertram."

"But, Mr Sampson, your labour in the office much more than recompenses me—I am your debtor, my good friend."

"Then be it all," said the Dominie, waving his hand, "for Miss Lucy Bertram's behoof."

"Well, but Dominie, this money"——

"It is honestly come by, Mr Mac-Morlan—it is the bountiful reward of a young gentleman to whom I am teaching the tongues—reading with him three hours daily."

A few more questions extracted from the Dominie that this pupil was young Hazelwood, and that he met his preceptor daily at the house of Mrs Mac-Candlish, whose proclamation of Sampson's disinterested attachment to the young lady had procured him the indefatigable and liberal pupil.

Mac-Morlan was much struck with what he heard. Dominie Sampson was a very good scholar, and an excellent man, and the classics were unquestionably very well worth reading; yet that a youngster of twenty should ride seven miles and back again each day in the week, to hold this sort of *tête-à-tête* of three hours, was a zeal for literature to which he was not prepared to give entire credit. Little art was necessary to sift the Dominie, for the honest man's head never admitted any but the most direct and simple ideas. "Does Miss Bertram know how his time is engaged, my good friend?"

"Surely not as yet—Mr Charles recommended it should be concealed from her, lest she should scruple to accept of the small assistance arising from it; but," he added, "it would not be possible to conceal it long, since Mr Charles proposed taking his lessons occasionally in this house."

"O, he does!" said Mac-Morlan: "Yes, yes, I can understand that better.—And pray, Mr Sampson, are these three hours entirely spent in construing and translating?"

"Doubtless, no—we have also colloquial intercourse to sweeten study—*neque semper arcum tendit Apollo.*"

The querist proceeded to elicit from this Galloway Phœbus, what their discourse chiefly turned upon.

"Upon our past meetings at Ellangowan—and, truly, I think very often we discourse concerning Miss Lucy—for Master Charles Hazelwood, in that particular, resembleth me, Mr Mac-Morlan. When I begin to speak of her I never know when to stop—and, as I say jocularly, she cheats us out of half our lesson."

"O ho!" thought Mac-Morlan, "sits the wind in that quarter? I've heard something like this before."

He then began to consider what conduct was safest for his *protegée*, and even for himself; for old Mr Hazelwood was powerful, wealthy, ambitious, and vindictive, and looked for both fortune and title in any connection which his son might form. At length, having the highest opinion of his guest's good sense and penetration, he determined to take an opportunity, when they should happen to be alone, to communicate the matter to her as a simple piece of intelligence. He did so in as natural a manner as he could;—"I wish you joy of your friend Mr Sampson's good fortune, Miss Bertram; he has got a pupil who pays him two guineas for twelve lessons of Greek and Latin."

"Indeed!—I am equally happy and surprised—who can be so liberal?—is Colonel Mannering returned?"

"No, no, not Colonel Mannering; but what do you think of it?—your acquaintance, Mr Charles Hazelwood—he talks of taking his lessons here—I wish we may have accommodation."

Lucy blushed deeply. "For Heaven's sake, no, Mr Mac-Morlan—do not let that be—Charles Hazelwood has had enough of mischief about that already."

"About the classics, my dear young lady?—most young gentlemen have so at one period or another, sure enough; but his present studies are voluntary."

Miss Bertram let the conversation drop, and her host made no effort to renew it, as she seemed to pause upon the intelligence in order to form some internal resolution.

The next day she took an opportunity of conversing with Mr Sampson. Expressing in the kindest manner her grateful thanks for his disinterested attachment, and her joy that he had got such a provision, she hinted to him that his present mode of superintending Charles Hazelwood's studies must be inconvenient to his pupil,—that while that engagement lasted, he had better consent to a temporary separation, and reside either with his scholar, or as near him as might be. Sampson refused, as indeed she had expected, to listen a moment to this proposition—he would not quit her to be made preceptor to the Prince of Wales. "But I see," he added, "you are too proud to share my pittance; and, peradventure, I grow wearisome unto you."

"No indeed—you were my father's ancient, almost his only friend—I am not proud—God knows, I have no reason to be so—you shall do what you judge best in other matters; but oblige me by telling Mr Charles Hazelwood, that you had some conversation with me concerning his studies, and that I was of opinion, that his carrying them on in this house was altogether impracticable, and not to be thought of."

Dominie Sampson left her presence altogether crest-fallen, and as he shut the door, could not help muttering the "*varium et mutabile*" of Virgil. Next day he appeared with a very rueful visage, and tendered Miss Bertram a letter.—"Mr Hazelwood," he said, "was to discontinue his lessons, though he had generously made up the pecuniary loss—But how will he make up the loss to himself of the knowledge he might have acquired under my instruction? Even in that one article of writing, he was an hour before he could write that brief note, and destroyed many scrolls, four quills, and some good white paper—I would have taught him in three weeks a firm, current, clear, and legible hand—he should have been a calligrapher—but God's will be done."

The letter contained but a few lines, deeply regretting and murmuring against Miss Bertram's cruelty, who not only refused to see him, but to permit him in the most indirect manner to hear of her health and contribute to her service. But it concluded with assurances that her severity was vain, and that nothing could shake the attachment of Charles Hazelwood.

Under the active patronage of Mrs Mac-Candlish, Sampson picked up some other scholars—very different indeed from Charles Hazelwood in rank—and whose lessons were proportionally unproductive. Still, however, he gained something, and it was the glory of his heart to carry it to Mr Mac-Morlan weekly, a slight peculium only subtracted, to supply his snuff-box and tobacco-pouch.

And here we must leave Kippletringan to look after our hero, lest our readers should fear they have lost sight of him for another quarter of a century.

Chapter Sixteen

Our Polly is a sad slut, nor heeds what we have taught her;
I wonder any man alive will ever rear a daughter;
For when she's drest with care and cost, all tempting fine and gay,
As men should serve a cucumber, she flings herself away.

Beggar's Opera

AFTER THE DEATH of Mr Bertram, Mannering had set out upon a short tour, proposing to return to the neighbourhood of Ellangowan before the sale of that property should take place. He went, accordingly, to Edinburgh and elsewhere, and it was in his return toward the south-western district of Scotland, in which our scene lies, that, at a post-town about a hundred miles from Kippletringan, to which he had requested his friend, Mr Mervyn, to address his letters, he received one from that gentleman, which contained rather unpleasing intelligence. We have assumed already the privilege of acting *a secretis* to this gentleman, and therefore shall present the reader with an extract of this letter.

"I beg your pardon, my dearest friend, for the pain I have given you, in forcing you to open wounds so festering as those your letter referred to. I have always heard, though erroneously perhaps, that the attentions of Mr Brown were intended for Miss Mannering. But, in any case, it could not be supposed that in your situation his boldness should escape notice and chastisement. Wise men say, that we resign to civil society our natural rights of self-defence, only on condition that the ordinances of law should protect us. Where the price cannot be paid, the resignation takes no place. For instance, no one supposes I am not entitled to defend my purse and person against a highwayman, as much as if I were a wild Indian, who owns neither law nor magistracy. The question of resistance, or submission, must be determined by my means and situation. But if, armed and equal in force, I submit to injustice and violence from any man, high or low, I presume it will hardly be attributed to religious or moral feeling in me, or in any one but a quaker. An aggression on my honour seems to me much the same. The insult, however trifling in itself, is one of much deeper consequence to all views of life than any wrong which can be inflicted by a depredator on the highway, and redress is much less in the power of public jurisprudence, or rather it is entirely beyond its reach. If any man chuses to rob Arthur Mervyn of the contents of his purse, if he has not means of defence, or skill and courage to use them, the assizes at Lancaster or Carlisle will do him justice by tucking up the robber:—Yet who will say I am bound to wait for this justice, and submit to being plundered in the first instance, if I have myself the means and spirit to protect my own property? But if an affront is offered to me, submission to which is to tarnish my character for ever with men of honour, and for which the twelve judges of England, with the chancellor to boot, can afford me no redress, by what rule of law or reason am I to be deterred from protecting what ought to be, and is, so infinitely dearer to every man of honour than his whole fortune? Of the religious view of the matter I shall say nothing, until I find a reverend divine who shall condemn self-defence in the article of life and property. If its propriety in that case be generally admitted, I suppose little distinction can be drawn between defence of person and goods, and defence of reputation. That the latter is liable to be assailed by persons of a different rank in life, untainted perhaps in morals, and fair in character, cannot affect my legal right of self-defence. I may be sorry that circumstances have engaged me in personal strife with such an individual; but I should feel the same sorrow for a generous enemy who fell under my sword in a national quarrel. I will leave the question with the casuists, however, only observing, that what I have written will not avail either the professed duellist, or he who is the aggressor in a dispute of honour. I only presume to exculpate him who is dragged into the field by such an offence, as, submitted to in patience, would forfeit for ever his rank and estimation in society.

"I am sorry you have thoughts of settling in Scotland, and yet glad that you will still be at no immeasurable distance, and that the latitude is all in our favour. To move from Devonshire to Westmoreland might make an East Indian shudder; but to come to us from Galloway or Dumfries-shire, is a step, though a short one, nearer the sun. Besides, if, as I suspect, the estate in view be connected with the old haunted castle in which you played the astrologer in your northern tour some four or five-and-twenty years since, I have heard you too often describe the scene with comic unction, to hope you will be deterred from making the purchase. I trust, however, the hospitable gossiping old Laird has not run himself upon the shallows, and that his chaplain, whom you so often made us laugh at, is still in *rerum natura*.

"And here, dear Mannering, I wish I could stop, for I have incredible pain in telling the rest of my story, although I am sure I can warrant you against any intentional impropriety on the part of my temporary ward, Julia Mannering. But I must still earn my college nickname of 'Downright Dunstable.' In one word then, here is the matter.

"Your daughter has much of the romantic turn of your disposition, with a little of that love of admiration which all pretty women share less or more. She will besides, apparently, be your heiress; a trifling circumstance to those who view Julia with my eyes, but a prevailing bait to the specious, artful, and worthless. You know how I have jested with her about her soft melancholy, and lonely walks at morning before any one is up, and in the moon-light when all should be gone to bed, or set down to cards, which is the same thing. The incident which follows may not be beyond the bounds of a joke, but I had rather it came from you than me.

"Two or three times during the last fortnight, I heard, at a late hour in the night, or very early in the morning, a flageolet play the little Hindu tune to which your daughter is so partial. I thought for some time that some tuneful domestic, whose taste for music was laid under constraint during the day, chose that silent hour to imitate the strains which he had caught up by the ear during his attendance in the drawing-room. But last night I sat late in my study, which is immediately under Miss Mannering's apartment, and, to my surprise, I not only heard the flageolet distinctly, but satisfied myself that it came from the lake under the windows. Curious to know who serenaded us at that unusual hour, I stole softly to the window of my apartment. But there were other watchers than I. You may remember, Miss Mannering preferred that apartment on account of a balcony which opened from her window upon the lake. Well, sir, I heard the sash of her window thrown up, the shutters opened, and her own voice in conversation with some person who answered from below. This is no 'Much ado about nothing;' I could not be mistaken in her voice, and such tones, so soft, so insinuating—And, to say the truth, the accents from below were in passion's tenderest cadence too—But of the sense I can say nothing. I raised the sash of my own window that I might hear something more than the mere murmur of this Spanish rendezvous, but, though I used every precaution, the noise alarmed the speakers; down slid the young lady's casement, and the shutters were barred in an instant. The dash of a pair of oars in the water announced the retreat of the male person of the dialogue. Indeed, I saw his boat, which he sculled with great swiftness and dexterity, fly across the lake like a twelve-oared barge. Next morning I examined some of my domestics, as if by accident, and I found the game-keeper, when making his rounds, had twice seen that boat beneath the house, with a single person, and had heard the flageolet. I did not care to press any farther questions, for fear of implicating Julia in the opinions of those at whom they might be asked. Next morning I dropped at breakfast a casual hint about the serenade of the evening before, and I promise you, Miss Mannering looked red and pale alternately. I immediately gave the circumstance such a turn as might lead her to suppose that my observation was merely casual. I have since caused a watch-light be burned in my library, and have left the shutters open, to deter the approach of our nocturnal guest; and I have stated the severity of approaching winter, and the rawness of the fogs, as an objection to solitary walks. Miss Mannering acquiesced with a passiveness which is no part of her character, and which, to tell you the plain truth, is a feature about the business which I like least of all. Julia has too much of her own dear papa's disposition to be curbed in any of her humours, were there not some little lurking consciousness that it may be as prudent to avoid debate.

"Now my story is told, and you will judge what you ought to do. I have not mentioned the matter to my good woman, who, a faithful secretary to her sex's foibles, would certainly remonstrate against your being made acquainted with these particulars, and might, instead, take it into her head to exercise her eloquence on Miss Mannering; a faculty, which, however powerful when directed against me, its legitimate object, might, I fear, do more harm than good in the case supposed. Perhaps even you yourself will find it most prudent to act without remonstrating, or appearing to be aware of this little anecdote. Julia is very like a certain friend of mine; she has a quick and lively imagination, and keen feelings, which can make both the good and evil they find in life. She is a charming girl however, as generous and spirited as she is lovely. I paid her the kiss you sent her with all my heart, and she rapped my fingers for my reward with all hers. Pray return as soon as you can. Meantime rely upon the care of yours faithfully,

"ARTHUR MERVYN.

"P. S. You will naturally wish to know if I have the least guess concerning the person of the serenader. In truth, I have none. There is no young gentleman of these parts, who might be in rank or fortune a match for Miss Julia, that I think at all likely to play such a character. But on the other side of the lake, nearly opposite to Mervyn-Hall, is a d—d cake-house, the resort of walking gentlemen of all descriptions, poets, players, painters, musicians, who come to rave, and recite, and madden, about this picturesque land of ours. It is paying some penalty for its beauties, that they are the means of drawing this swarm of coxcombs together. But were Julia my daughter, it is one of these sort of fellows that I should fear on her account. She is generous and romantic, and writes six sheets a-week to a female correspondent; and it's a sad thing to lack a subject in such a case, either for exercise of the feelings or of the pen. Adieu once more—were I to treat this matter more seriously than I have done, I should do injustice to your feelings;

were I altogether to overlook it, I should discredit my own."

The consequence of this letter was, that, having first dispatched the faithless messenger with the necessary powers to Mr Mac-Morlan for purchasing the estate of Ellangowan, Colonel Mannering turned his horse's head in a more southerly direction, and neither "stinted nor staid" until he arrived at the mansion of his friend Mr Mervyn, upon the banks of one of the lakes of Westmoreland.

Chapter Seventeen

"Heaven first, in its mercy, taught mortals their letters,
For ladies in limbo, and lovers in fetters,
Or some author, who, placing his persons before ye,
Ungallantly leaves them to write their own story."

WHEN MANNERING returned to England, his first object had been to place his daughter in a seminary for female education of established character. Not, however, finding her progress in the accomplishments which he wished her to acquire so rapid as his impatience expected, he had withdrawn Miss Mannering from the school at the end of the first quarter. So she had only time to form an eternal friendship with Miss Matilda Marchmont, a young lady about her own age, which was nearly eighteen. To her faithful eye were addressed those formidable quires which issued forth from Mervyn Hall, on the wings of the post, while Miss Mannering was a guest there. The perusal of a few extracts from these may be necessary to render our story intelligible.

FIRST EXTRACT.

"Alas! my dearest Matilda, what a tale is mine to tell! Misfortune from the cradle has set her seal upon your unhappy friend. That we should be severed for so slight a cause—an ungrammatical phrase in my Italian exercise, and three false notes in one of Paesiello's sonatas! But it is a part of my father's character—of whom it is impossible to say, whether I love, admire, or fear him the most. His success in life and in war—his habit of making every obstacle yield before the energy of his exertions, even where they seemed unsurmountable—All these have given a hasty and peremptory cast to his character, which can neither endure contradiction, nor make allowance for deficiencies. Then he is himself so very accomplished. Do you know there was a murmur, half confirmed too by some mysterious words which dropped from my poor mother, that he possesses other sciences, now lost to the world, which enable the possessor to summon up before him the dark and shadowy forms of future events! Does not the very idea of such a power, or even of the high talent and commanding intellect which the world may mistake for it—does it not, dear Matilda, throw a mysterious grandeur about its possessor?—You will call this romantic—but consider I was born in the land of talisman and spell, and my childhood lulled by tales which you can only enjoy through the gauzy frippery of a French translation. O Matilda, I wish you could have seen the dusky visages of my Indian attendants, bending in passive attention round the magic narrative, that flowed, half poetry, half prose, from the lips of the tale-teller. No wonder that European fiction sounds cold and meagre, after the wonderful effects which I have seen the romances of the East produce upon the hearers."

SECOND EXTRACT.

"You are possessed, my dear Matilda, of my bosom-secret in those sentiments with which I regard Brown—I will not say his memory—I am convinced he lives, and is faithful. His addresses to me were countenanced by my deceased parent—imprudently countenanced perhaps, considering the prejudices of my father in favour of birth and rank. But I, then almost a girl, could not be expected surely to be wiser than her under whose charge nature had placed me. My father, constantly engaged in military duty, I saw but at rare intervals, and was taught to look up to him with more awe than confidence. Would to Heaven it had been otherwise! it would have been better for us all at this day!"

THIRD EXTRACT.

"You ask me why I do not make known to my father that Brown yet lives, at least that he survived the wound he received in that unhappy duel; and wrote to my mother, expressing his entire convalescence, and his hope of speedily escaping from captivity. A soldier, that 'in the trade of war has oft slain men,' feels probably no uneasiness at reflecting upon the supposed catastrophe, which almost turned me into stone. And should I shew him that letter, does it not follow, that Brown, alive and maintaining with pertinacity the pretensions for which my father formerly sought his life, would be a more formidable disturber of his peace of mind than in his supposed grave? If he escapes from the hands of these marauders, I am convinced he will soon be in England, and it will be then time to consider how his existence is to be disclosed to my father—But if, alas! my earnest and confident hope should betray me, what would it avail to tear open a mystery fraught with so many painful recollections?—My dear mother had such dread of its being known, that I think she even suffered my father to suspect that Brown's attentions were directed towards herself, than permit him to discover the real object; and O, Matilda, whatever respect I owe to the memory of a deceased parent, let me do justice to a living one.—I cannot but condemn the dubious policy which she adopted, as unjust to my father, and highly perilous to herself and me.—But peace be with her ashes—her actions were guided by the heart rather than the head; and shall her daughter, who inherits all her weakness, be the first to withdraw the veil from her defects?"

Fourth Extract.

"*Mervyn-Hall.*

"If India be the land of magic, this, my dearest Matilda, is the country of romance. The scenery is such as nature brings together in her sublimest moods—sounding cataracts—hills which rear their scathed heads to the sky—lakes, that, winding up the shadowy valleys, lead at every turn to yet more romantic recesses—rocks which catch the clouds of heaven. All the wildness of Salvator here, and there the fairy scenes of Claude. I am happy too, in finding at least one subject upon which my father can share my enthusiasm. An admirer of nature, both as an artist and a poet, I have experienced the utmost pleasure from the observation by which he explains the character and the effect of these brilliant specimens of her power. I wish he would settle in this enchanting land. But his views lie still farther north, and he is at present absent on a tour in Scotland, looking, I believe, for some purchase of land which may suit him as a residence. He is partial, from early recollections, to that country. So, my dearest Matilda, I must be yet farther removed from you before I am established in a home—And O how delighted shall I be when I can say, come, Matilda, and be the guest of your faithful Julia!

"I am at present the inmate of Mrs and Mr Mervyn, old friends of my father. The first is precisely a good sort of woman—lady-like and housewifely—but for accomplishment or fancy—good lack, my dearest Matilda, your friend might as well seek sympathy from Mrs Teach'em,—you see I have not forgot school nicknames. Mr Mervyn is a different—quite a different being from my father, yet he amuses me and endures me—He is fat and good-humoured, gifted with strong shrewd sense, and some powers of humour—I delight to make him scramble to the top of eminences and the foot of water-falls, and am obliged in return to admire his turnips, his lucerne, and his timothy grass. He thinks me, I fancy, a simple romantic Miss, with some —(the word will be out) beauty, and some good nature; and I hold that the gentleman has good taste for the female outside, and do not expect he should comprehend my sentiments farther. So he rallies, and hands, and hobbles, (for the dear creature has got the gout too,) and tells old stories of high life, of which he has seen a great deal, and I listen, and smile, and look as pretty and as pleasant as I can, and we do very well.

"But, alas! my dearest Matilda, how would time pass away, even in this paradise of romance, tenanted as it is by a pair assorting so ill with the scenes around them, were it not for your fidelity in replying to my uninteresting details? Pray do not fail to write three times a-week at least—you can be at no loss what to say."

Fifth Extract.

"How shall I communicate what I have now to tell!—My hand and heart still flutter so much that the task of writing is almost impossible.—Did I not say that he lived? did I not say that he was faithful? did I not say I would not despair? How could you suggest, my dear Matilda, that my feelings, considering I had parted from him so young, rather rose from the warmth of my imagination than of my heart?—O I was sure that they were genuine, deceitful as the dictates of our bosom so frequently are—But to my tale—let it be, my friend, the most sacred, as it is the most sincere pledge of our friendship.

"Our hours here are early—earlier than my heart, with its load of care, can compose itself to rest. I, therefore, usually take a book for an hour or two after retiring to my own room, which I think I have told you opens to a small balcony, looking down upon that beautiful lake, of which I attempted to give you a slight sketch. Mervyn Hall, being partly an ancient building, and constructed with a view to defence, is situated on the verge of the lake. A stone dropped from the projecting balcony plunges into water deep enough to float a skiff. I had left my window partly unbarred, that, before I went to bed, I might, according to my custom, look out and see the moon-light shining upon the lake. I was deeply engaged with that beautiful scene in the Merchant of Venice, where two lovers, describing the stillness of a summer night, enhance upon each other its charms, and was lost in the associations of story and of feeling which it awakens, when I heard upon the lake the sound of a flageolet. I have told you it was Brown's favourite instrument. What could wake it in a night which, though still and serene, was too cold, and too late in the year, to invite forth any wanderer for mere pleasure? I drew yet nearer the window, and hearkened with breathless attention—the sounds paused a space, were then resumed—paused again—and again reached my ear, ever coming nearer and nearer—at length, I distinguished plainly that little Hindu air which you called my favourite—I have told you by whom it was taught me—The instrument, the tones were his own—was it earthly music, or notes passing on the wind to warn me of his death?

"It was some time ere I could summon courage to step on the balcony—nothing could have emboldened me to do so but the strong conviction of my mind, that he was still alive, and that we should again meet—But that conviction emboldened me and I did venture, though with a throbbing heart. There was a small skiff with a single person—O Matilda, it was himself!—I knew his appearance after so long an absence, and through the shadow of the night, as perfectly as if we had parted yesterday, and met again in the broad sun-shine! He guided his boat under the balcony, and spoke to me—I hardly know what he said, or what I replied. Indeed I could scarcely speak for weeping, but they were joyful tears. We were disturbed by the barking of a dog at some distance, and parted, but not before he had conjured me to prepare to meet him at the same place and hour this evening. But where and to what is all this tending?—can I answer this question?—I cannot—Heaven, that saved him from death and delivered him from captivity, that saved my father, too, from the guilt of shedding the blood of one who would not have blemished one hair upon his head—that heaven must guide me out of this labyrinth. Enough for me the firm resolution, that Matilda shall not blush for her friend, my father for his daughter, or my lover for her on whom he has fixed his affection."

Chapter Eighteen

Talk with a man out a window!—a proper saying.
Much Ado about Nothing

WE MUST PROCEED with our extracts of Miss Mannering's letters, which throw light upon natural good sense, principle, and feelings, blemished by an imperfect education, and the folly of a misjudging mother, who called her husband in her heart a tyrant until she feared him as such, and read romances until she became so enamoured of the complicated intrigues which they contain, as to assume the management of a little family novel of her own, and constitute her daughter, a girl of sixteen, the principal heroine. She delighted in petty mystery, and intrigue, and secrets, and yet trembled at the indignation which these paltry manœuvres excited in her husband's mind. Thus she frequently entered upon a scheme merely for pleasure, or perhaps for the love of contradiction, plunged deeper into it than she was aware, endeavoured to extricate herself by new arts, or to cover her error by dissimulation, became involved in meshes of her own weaving, and was forced to carry on, from fear of discovery, machinations which she had formerly resorted to in mere wantonness.

Fortunately the young man whom she so imprudently introduced into her intimate society, and encouraged to look up to her daughter, had a fund of principle and honest pride, which rendered him a safer inmate than Mrs Mannering ought to have dared to hope or expect. The obscurity of his birth could alone be objected to him—in every other respect,

With prospects bright upon the world he came,
Pure love of virtue, strong desire of fame;
Men watched the way his lofty mind would take,
And all foretold the progress he would make.

But it could not be expected that he should resist the snare which Mrs Mannering's imprudence threw in his way, or avoid becoming attached to a young lady whose beauty and manners might have justified his passion, even in scenes where these are more generally met with, than in a remote fortress in our Indian settlements. The scenes which followed have been partly detailed in Mannering's letter to Mr Mervyn; and to expand what is there stated into further explanations would be to abuse the patience of our readers.

We shall therefore proceed with our promised extracts from Miss Mannering's letters to her friend.

Sixth Extract.

"I have seen him again, Matilda,—seen him twice. I have used every argument to convince him that this secret intercourse is dangerous to us both—I even pressed him to pursue his views of fortune without farther regard to me, and to consider my peace of mind as sufficiently secured by the knowledge that he had not fallen under my father's sword. He answers—but how can I detail all he has to answer? he claims those hopes as his due which my mother permitted him to entertain, and would persuade me to the madness of a union without my father's sanction. But to this, Matilda, I will not be persuaded. I have resisted; I have subdued the rebellious feeling which arose to aid his plea; yet how to extricate myself from this unhappy labyrinth, in which fate and folly have entangled us!

"I have thought upon it, Matilda, till my head is almost giddy—nor can I conceive a better plan than to make a full confession to my father. He deserves it, for his kindness is unceasing; and I think I have observed in his character, since I have studied it more nearly, that his harsher feelings are chiefly excited where he suspects deceit or imposition; and in that respect, perhaps, his character was formerly misunderstood by one who was dear to him. He has, too, a tinge of romance in his disposition; and I have seen the narrative of a generous action, a trait of heroism, or virtuous self-denial, extract tears from him, which refused to flow at a mere tale of distress. But then, Brown urges, that he is personally hostile to him—And the obscurity of his birth—that would be indeed a stumbling-block.—O Matilda, I hope none of your ancestors ever fought at Poictiers or Agincourt. If it were not for the esteem which my father attaches to the memory of old Sir Miles Mannering, I should make out my explanation with half the tremor which must now attend it."

SEVENTH EXTRACT.

"I have this instant received your letter—your most welcome letter!—Thanks, my dearest friend, for your sympathy and your counsels—I can only repay them with unreserved confidence.

"You ask me, what Brown is by origin, that his descent should be so unpleasing to my father. His story is shortly told. He is of Scottish extraction, but, being left an orphan, his education was undertaken by a family of relations settled in Holland. He was bred to commerce, and sent very early to one of our settlements in the East, where his guardian had a correspondent—But this correspondent was dead when he arrived in India, and he had no other resource than to offer himself as a clerk to a counting-house. The breaking out of the war, and the straits to which we were at first reduced, threw the army open to all young men who were disposed to embrace that mode of life; and Brown, whose genius had a strong military tendency, was the first to leave what might have been the road to wealth, and to chuse that of fame. The rest of his history is well known to you; but conceive the irritation of my father, who despises commerce, (though, by the way, the best part of his property was made in that honourable profession by my great uncle,) and has a particular antipathy to the Dutch; think with what ear he was likely to receive proposals for his only child from Van-beest Brown, educated for charity by the house of Vanbeest and Verbruggen! O, Matilda, it will never do—nay, so childish am I, I hardly can help sympathizing with his aristocratic feelings.—Mrs Vanbeest Brown?—the name has little to recommend it.—What children we are!"

EIGHTH EXTRACT.

"It is all over now, Matilda!—I shall never have courage to tell my father—nay, most deeply do I fear he has already learned my secret from another quarter, which will entirely remove the grace of my communication, and ruin whatever gleam of hope I had ventured to connect with it. Yesternight, Brown came as usual, and his flageolet on the lake announced his approach. We had agreed that he should continue to use this signal. These romantic lakes attract numerous visitors, who indulge their enthusiasm by visiting the scenery at all hours; and we hoped, that if Brown were noticed from the house, he might pass for one of those admirers of nature, who gave vent to his feelings through the medium of music. The sounds might also be my apology should I be observed in the balcony. But last night, while I was eagerly enforcing my plan of a full confession to my father, which he as earnestly deprecated, we heard the window of Mr Mervyn's library, which is under my room, open softly. I signed to Brown to make his retreat, and immediately re-entered, with some faint hopes that our interview had not been observed.

"But, alas! Matilda, these hopes vanished the instant I beheld Mr Mervyn's countenance at breakfast the next morning. He looked so provokingly intelligent and confidential, that, had I dared, I could have been more angry than ever I was in my life—But I must be on good behaviour, and my walks are limited within his farm precincts, where the good gentleman can amble along by my side without inconvenience. I have detected him once or twice in attempting to sound my thoughts, and watch the expressions of my countenance. He has talked of the flageolet more than once; and has, at different times, made eulogium upon the watchfulness and ferocity of his dogs, and the severity with which his keeper makes his round with a loaded fowling-piece. He mentioned even men-traps and spring-guns. I should be loth to affront my father's old friend in his own house, but I do long to show him that I am my father's daughter, a fact of which Mr Mervyn will certainly be convinced, if ever I trusted my voice and temper with a reply to these indirect hints. Of one thing I am certain, and I am grateful to him on that account—he has not told Mrs Mervyn. Lord help me, I should have had such lectures about the danger of love and the night air on the lake, the risk arising from colds and fortune-hunters, the comforts and convenience of sack-whey and closed windows!—I cannot help trifling, Matilda, though my heart be sad enough. What Brown will do I cannot guess. I presume, however, the fear of detection prevents his resuming his nocturnal visit. He lodges at an inn on the opposite shore of the lake, under the name, he tells me, of Dawson,—he has a bad choice in names, that must be allowed. He has left the army, I believe, but says nothing of his present views.

"To complete my anxiety, my father is returned suddenly, and in high displeasure. Our good hostess, as I learned from a bustling conversation between her housekeeper and her, had no expectation of seeing him for a week, but I rather suspect his arrival was no surprise to his friend Mr Mervyn. His manner to me was singularly cold and constrained—sufficiently so to have damped all the courage with which I once resolved to throw myself on his generosity. He lays the blame of his being discomposed and out of humour upon the loss of a purchase in the south-west of Scotland, on which he had set his heart; but I do not suspect his equanimity of being so easily thrown off its balance. His first excursion was with Mr Mervyn's barge across the lake to the inn I have mentioned. You may imagine the agony with which I awaited his return—Had he recognized Brown, who can guess the consequence? He returned, however, apparently without having made any discovery. I understand, that, in consequence of his late disappointment, he means now to hire a house in the neighbourhood of this same Ellangowan, of which I am doomed to hear so much —he seems to think it probable that the estate which he wishes for may soon be again in the market. I will not send away this letter until I hear more distinctly what are his intentions."

"I have now had an interview with my father, as confidential, as, I presume, he means to allow me. He requested me to-day after breakfast to walk with him into the library; my knees, Matilda, shook under me, and, it is no exaggeration to say, I could scarce follow him into the room. I feared I knew not what—From my childhood I had seen all around him tremble at his frown—He motioned me to seat myself, and I never obeyed a command so readily, for, in truth, I could hardly stand. He himself continued to walk up and down the room. You have seen my father, and noticed, I recollect, the remarkably expressive cast of his features. His eyes are naturally rather light in colour, but agitation or anger gives them a darker and more fiery glance; he has a custom also of drawing in his lips, when much moved, which implies a combat between native ardour of temper and the habitual power of self-command. This was the first time we had been alone together since his return from Scotland, and, as he betrayed these tokens of agitation, I had little doubt that he was about to enter upon the subject I most dreaded.

"To my unutterable relief, I found I was mistaken, and that whatever he knew of Mr Mervyn's suspicions or discoveries, he did not intend to converse with me on the topic. Coward as I was, I was inexpressibly relieved, though if he had really investigated the reports which may have come to his ear, the reality could have been nothing to what his suspicions might have conceived. But, although my spirits rose high at my unexpected escape, I had not courage myself to provoke the discussion, and remained silent to receive his commands.

"'Julia,' he said, 'my agent writes me from Scotland, that he has been able to hire a house for me, decently furnished, and with the necessary accommodation for my family—it is within three miles of that I had designed to purchase.'——Then he made a pause, and seemed to expect an answer.

"'Whatever place of residence suits you, sir, must be perfectly agreeable to me.'

"'Umh!—I do not propose, however, Julia, that you shall reside quite alone in this house during the winter.'

"Mr and Mrs Mervyn, thought I to myself. 'Whatever company is agreeable to you, sir.'

"'O, there is a little too much of this universal spirit of submission; an excellent disposition in action, but your constantly repeating the jargon of it puts me in mind of the eternal salams of our black dependants in the East. In short, Julia, I know you have a relish for society, and I intend to invite a young person, the daughter of a deceased friend, to spend a few months with us.'

"'Not a governess, for the love of Heaven, papa!' exclaimed poor I, my fears at that moment surpassing my prudence.

"'No, not a governess, Miss Mannering,' replied the Colonel, somewhat sternly, 'but a young lady from whose excellent example, tried as it has been in the school of adversity, I trust you may learn the art to govern yourself.'

"To answer this was trenching on too dangerous ground, so there was a pause.

"'Is the young lady a Scotchwoman, papa?'

"'Yes,—' dryly enough.

"'Has she much of the accent, sir?'

"'Of the devil!' answered my father hastily; 'do you think I care about *a*'s and *aa*'s, and *i*'s and *ee*'s—I tell you, Julia, I am serious in this matter. You have a genius for friendship, that is, for running up intimacies which you call such—(was not this very harshly said, Matilda?)—Now I wish to give you an opportunity at least to make one deserving friend, and therefore I have resolved that this young lady shall be a member of my family for some months, and I expect you will pay to her that attention which is due to misfortune and virtue.'

"'Certainly, sir—is my future friend red-haired?'

"He gave me one of his stern glances; you will say, perhaps, I deserved it, but I think the deuce prompts me with teasing questions on these occasions.

"'She is as superior to you, my love, in personal appearance, as in prudence and affection for her friends.'

"'Lord, papa, do you think that superiority a recommendation?—

Well, sir, but I see you are going to take all this too seriously—Whatever the young lady may be, I am sure, being recommended by you, she shall have no reason to complain of my want of attention.—(After a pause)—Has she any attendant, that I may provide for her proper accommodation, if she is without one?'

"'N—no—no—not properly an attendant—the chaplain who lived with her father is a very good sort of man, and I believe I shall make room for him in the house.'

"'Chaplain, papa? Lord bless us!'

"'Yes, Miss, chaplain; is there any thing very new in that word? had we not a chaplain at the Residence, when we were in India?'

"'Yes, papa, but you were a commandant then.'

"'So I will be now, Miss Mannering,—in my own family at least.'

"'Certainly, sir,—but will he read the Church of England service?'

"The apparent simplicity with which I asked this question got the better of his gravity. 'Come, Julia,' he said, 'you are a sad girl, but I gain nothing by scolding you—of these two strangers, the young lady is one whom you cannot fail, I think, to love—the person whom, for want of a better term, I called chaplain, is a very worthy and somewhat ridiculous personage, who will never find out you laugh at him, if you don't laugh very loud indeed.'

"'Dear papa, I am delighted with that point of his character—but pray, is the house we are going to as pleasantly situated as this?'

"'Not perhaps so much to your taste—there is no lake under the windows, and you will be under the necessity of having all your music within doors.'

"This last *coup de main* ended the keen encounter of our wits, for you may believe, Matilda, it quelled all my courage to reply.

"Yet my spirits, as perhaps will appear too manifest from this dialogue, have risen insensibly, and, as it were, in spite of myself. Brown alive, and free, and in England!—embarrassment and anxiety I can and must endure. We leave this in two days for our new residence. I will not fail to let you know what I think of these Scotch inmates, whom I have but too much reason to believe my father means to quarter in his house as a brace of honourable spies—a sort of Rosencrantz and Guildenstern, one in a cassock, the other in tartan petticoats. What a contrast to the society I would willingly have secured to myself! I will write instantly on my arriving at our new place of abode, and acquaint my dearest Matilda with the farther fates of—her Julia Mannering."

Chapter Nineteen

> Which sloping hills around enclose,
> Where many a beech and brown oak grows,
> Beneath whose dark and branching bowers,
> Its tides a far-famed river pours.
> By nature's beauties taught to please,
> Sweet Tusculane of rural ease!—
>
> WARTON

WOODBOURNE, the habitation which Mannering, by Mr Mac-Morlan's mediation, had hired for a season, was a large comfortable mansion, snugly situated beneath a hill covered with wood, which shrouded the house upon the north and east; the front looked upon a little lawn bordered by a grove of old trees—beyond were some arable fields, extending down to the river, which was seen from the windows of the house. A tolerable, though old-fashioned garden, a well-stocked dove-cot, and the possession of any quantity of ground which the convenience of the family might require, rendered the place in every respect suitable, as the advertisements have it, for the accommodation of a genteel family.

Here, then, Mannering resolved, for some time at least, to set up the staff of his rest. Though an East-Indian, he was not partial to an ostentatious display of wealth. In fact, he was too proud a man to be a vain one. He resolved, therefore, to place himself upon the footing of a country gentleman of easy fortune, without assuming, or permitting his household to assume, any of the *faste* which then was considered as characteristic of a nabob. He had still his eye upon the purchase of Ellangowan, which Mac-Morlan conceived Mr Glossin would be compelled to part with, as some of the creditors disputed his title to retain so large a part of the purchase-money in his own hands, and his power to pay it was much questioned. In that case, Mac-Morlan was assured he would readily give up his bargain, if tempted with something above the price which he had stipulated to pay. It may seem strange, that Mannering was so much attached to a spot which he had seen only once, and that for a short time, in early life. But the circumstances which passed there had laid strong hold on his imagination. There seemed to be a fate which conjoined the remarkable passages of his own family history with those of the inhabitants of Ellangowan, and he felt a mysterious desire to call the terrace his own, from which he had read in the book of heaven a fortune strangely accomplished in the person of the infant heir of that family, and corresponding so closely with one which was as strikingly fulfilled in his own. Besides, when once this thought had got possession of his imagination, he could not, without great reluctance, brook the idea of his plan being defeated, and by a fellow like Glossin. So Pride came to the aid of Fancy, and both combined to fortify his resolution to buy the estate if possible.

Let us do Mannering justice. A desire to serve the distressed had also its share in determining him. He had considered the advantages which Julia might receive from the company of Lucy Bertram, whose genuine prudence and good sense could so surely be relied upon. This idea had become much stronger since Mac-Morlan had confided to him, under the solemn seal of secrecy, the whole of her conduct towards young Hazelwood. To propose to her to become an inmate in his family, if distant from the scenes of youth and the few whom she called friends, would have been less delicate; but at Woodbourne she might without difficulty be induced to become the visitor of a season, without being depressed into the situation of an humble companion. Lucy Bertram, with some hesitation, accepted the invitation to reside a few weeks with Miss Mannering. She felt too well, that, however the colonel's delicacy might disguise the truth, his principal motive was a generous desire to afford her countenance and protection. About the same time she received a letter from Mrs Margaret Bertram, the relation to whom she had written, as cold and comfortless as could well be imagined. It inclosed, indeed, a small sum of money, but strongly recommended economy, and that Miss Bertram should board herself in some quiet family, either at Kippletringan or in the neighbourhood, assuring her, that though her own income was very scanty, she would not see her kinswoman want. Miss Bertram shed some natural tears over this cold-hearted epistle, for in her mother's time, this good lady had been a guest at Ellangowan for nearly three years, and it was only upon succeeding to a property of about 400*l.* a-year that she had taken farewell of that hospitable mansion, which, otherwise, might have had the honour of maintaining her until the death of the owner. Lucy was strongly inclined to return the paltry donation, which, after some struggles with avarice, pride had extorted from the old lady. But upon consideration, she contented herself with writing, that she accepted it as a loan, which she hoped in a short time to repay, and consulted her relative upon the invitation she had received from Colonel and Miss Mannering. This time the answer came in course of post, so fearful was Mrs Bertram, that some frivolous delicacy or nonsense, as she termed it, might induce her cousin to reject such a promising offer, and thereby at the same time leave her still a burthen upon her hands. Lucy, therefore, had no alternative, unless she preferred continuing a burthen upon the worthy Mac-Morlans, who were too liberal to be rich. Those who had formerly requested the favour of her company, either silently, or with some expressions of resentment that she should have preferred Mac-Morlan's invitation to theirs, had gradually withdrawn their notice.

The fate of Dominie Sampson would have been deplorable had it depended upon any one except Mannering, who was an admirer of originality. Mac-Morlan had given a full account of his proceedings towards the daughter of his patron. The answer was a request from Mannering to know whether the Dominie possessed upon all occasions that admirable virtue of taciturnity by which he was so notably distinguished at Ellangowan? Mac-Morlan replied in the affirmative. "Let Mr Sampson know," said the colonel's next letter, "that I shall want his assistance to catalogue and put in order the library of my uncle, the bishop, which I have ordered to be sent down by sea. I shall also want him to copy and arrange some papers—fix his salary at what you think befitting—let the poor man be properly dressed, and accompany his young lady to Woodbourne."

Honest Mac-Morlan received this mandate with great joy, but pondered much upon executing that part of it which related to newly attiring the worthy Dominie. He looked at him with a scrutinizing eye, and it was but too plain that his present garments were daily waxing more deplorable. To give him money, and bid him go and furnish himself, would be only giving him the means of making himself ridiculous; for when such a rare event arrived to Mr Sampson, as the purchase of new garments, the additions which he made to his wardrobe by the guidance of his own taste usually brought all the boys of the village after him for many days. On the other hand, to bring a tailor to measure him, and send home his clothes as for a school-boy, would probably give great offence. At length he resolved to consult Miss Bertram, and request her interference. She assured him, that she could not pretend to superintend a gentleman's wardrobe, but that nothing was more easy than to arrange the Dominie's—

"At Ellangowan," she said, "whenever my poor father thought any part of the Dominie's dress wanted renewal, a servant was directed to enter his room by night, for he sleeps as fast as a dor-mouse, carry off the old vestment, and leave the new one; nor could we ever observe that the Dominie exhibited the least consciousness of the change put upon him."

Mac-Morlan, therefore, procured a skilful artist, who, on looking at the Dominie attentively, undertook to make for him two suits of clothes, one black, and one raven-grey, and that they should fit him as well at least, (so the tailor qualified his enterprise,) as a man of such an out-of-the-way build could be fitted by merely human needles and shears. When he had accomplished his task, and the dresses were brought home, Mac-Morlan, judiciously resolving to accomplish his purpose by degrees, withdrew that evening an important part of his dress, and substituted the new article of raiment in its stead. Perceiving that this passed totally without notice, he next ventured on the waistcoat, and last upon the coat. When fully metamorphosed, and arrayed for the first time in his life in a decent dress, they did observe, that the Dominie seemed to have some indistinct and embarrassing consciousness that a change had taken place upon his outward man. Whenever they observed this dubious expression gather upon his countenance, accompanied with a glance, that fixed now upon the sleeve of his coat, now upon the knees of his breeches, where he probably missed some antique patching and darning, which, being executed with blue thread upon a black ground, had somewhat the effect of embroidery, they always took care to turn his attention into some other channel, until his garments, "by the aid of use, cleaved to their mould." The only remark he was ever known to make upon the subject, was, "the air of a town, like Kippletringan, seemed favourable unto wearing apparel, for he thought his coat looked as new as the first day he put it on, which was when he went to stand trials for his licence as a preacher."

When he heard the liberal proposal of Colonel Mannering, he first turned a jealous and doubtful glance towards Miss Bertram, as if he suspected that the project involved their separation; but when Mr Mac-Morlan hastened to explain that she would be a guest at Woodbourne for some time, he rubbed his huge hands together, and burst into a portentous sort of chuckle, like that of the Afrite in the tale of the Caliph Vathek. After this unusual explosion of satisfaction, he remained quite passive in all the rest of the transaction.

It had been settled that Mrs and Mr Mac-Morlan should take possession of the house a few days before Mannering's arrival, both to put every thing in perfect order, and to make the transference of Miss Bertram's residence from their family to his as easy and delicate as possible. Accordingly, in the beginning of the month of December, the party were settled at Woodbourne.

Chapter Twenty

A gigantic genius, fit to grapple with whole libraries.
BOSWELL'S *Life of Johnson*

THE APPOINTED DAY arrived, when the Colonel and Miss Mannering were expected at Woodbourne. The hour was fast approaching, and the little circle within doors had each their separate subjects of anxiety. Mac-Morlan naturally desired to attach to himself the patronage and countenance of a person of Mannering's wealth and consequence. He was aware, from his knowledge of mankind, that Mannering, though generous and benevolent, had the foible of expecting and exacting a minute compliance with his directions. He was therefore racking his recollection to discover if every thing had been arranged to meet the Colonel's wishes and instructions, and, under this uncertainty of mind, he traversed the house more than once from the garret to the stables. Mrs Mac-Morlan revolved in a lesser orbit, comprehending the dining parlour, housekeeper's room, and kitchen. She was only afraid that the dinner might be spoiled, to the discredit of her housewifely accomplishments. Even the usual passiveness of the Dominie was so far disturbed, that he twice went to the window, which looked out upon the avenue, and twice exclaimed, "Why tarry the wheels of their chariot?" Lucy, the most quiet of the expectants, had her own melancholy thoughts. She was now about to be consigned to the charge, almost to the benevolence, of strangers, with whose character, though hitherto very amiably displayed, she was but imperfectly acquainted. The moments, therefore, of suspense passed anxiously and heavily.

At length the trampling of horses, and the sound of wheels, were heard. The servants, who had already arrived, drew up in the hall to receive their master and mistress, with an importance and *empressement*, which, to Lucy, who had never been accustomed to society, or witnessed what is called the manners of the great, had something alarming. Mac-Morlan went to the door to receive the master and mistress of the family, and in a few moments they were in the drawing-room.

Mannering, who had travelled as usual on horseback, entered with his daughter hanging upon his arm. She was of the middle size, or rather less, but formed with much elegance; piercing dark eyes, and jet-black hair of great length, corresponded with the vivacity and intelligence of features, in which were blended a little haughtiness, and a little bashfulness, a great deal of shrewdness, and some power of humorous sarcasm. "I shall not like her," was the result of Lucy Bertram's first glance; "and yet I rather think I shall," was the thought excited by the second.

Miss Mannering was furred and mantled up to the throat against the severity of the weather; the Colonel in his military great coat. He bowed to Mrs Mac-Morlan, whom his daughter also acknowledged with a fashionable courtesy, not dropped so low as at all to incommode her person. The Colonel then led his daughter up to Miss Bertram, and, taking the hand of the latter, with an air of great kindness, and almost paternal affection, he said, "Julia, this is the young lady whom I hope our good friends have prevailed on to honour our house with a long visit. I shall be much gratified indeed if you can render Woodbourne as pleasant to Miss Bertram, as Ellangowan was to me when I first came as a wanderer into this country."

The young lady curtsied acquiescence, and took her new friend's hand. Mannering now turned his eye upon the Dominie, who had made bows since his entrance into the room, sprawling out his legs, and bending his back like an automaton, which continues to repeat the same movement until the motion is stopped by the artist. "My good friend, Mr Sampson,"—said Mannering, introducing him to his daughter, and darting at the same time a reproving glance at the damsel, notwithstanding he had himself some disposition to join her too obvious inclination to risibility: "This gentleman, Julia, is to put my books in order when they arrive, and I expect to derive great advantage from his extensive learning."

"I am sure we are obliged to the gentleman, papa, and, to borrow a ministerial mode of giving thanks, I shall never forget the extraordinary countenance he has been pleased to shew us.—But, Miss Bertram," continued she hastily, for her father's brow began to darken, "we have travelled a good way,—will you permit us to retire before dinner?"

This intimation dispersed all the company, save the Dominie, who, having no idea of dressing but when he was to rise, or of undressing but when he meant to go to bed, remained by himself, chewing the cud of mathematical demonstration, until the company again assembled in the drawing-room, and from thence adjourned to the dining-parlour.

When the day was concluded, Mannering took an opportunity to hold a minute's conversation with his daughter in private.

"How do you like your guests, Julia?"

"O, Miss Bertram of all things—but this is a most original parson—why, dear sir, no human being will be able to look at him without laughing."

"While he is under my roof, Julia, every one must learn to do so."

"Lord, papa, the very footmen could not keep their gravity!"

"Then let them strip off my livery, and laugh at their leisure. Mr Sampson is a person whom I esteem for his simplicity and benevolence of character."

"O I am convinced of his generosity too," said this lively lady, "he cannot lift a spoonful of soup to his mouth without bestowing a share on every thing round."

"Julia, you are incorrigible;—but remember I expect your mirth on this subject is to be under such restraint, that it shall neither offend this worthy man's feelings, nor those of Miss Bertram, who may be more apt to feel upon his account than he on his own. And so, good night, my dear, and remember, that though Mr Sampson has not sacrificed to the graces, there are many things in this world more truly deserving of ridicule than either awkwardness of manners or simplicity of character."

In a day or two Mr and Mrs Mac-Morlan left Woodbourne, after taking an affectionate farewell of their late guest. The household were now settled in their new quarters. The young ladies followed their studies and amusements together. Colonel Mannering was agreeably surprised to find that Miss Bertram was well skilled in French and Italian, thanks to the assiduity of Dominie Sampson, whose labour had silently possessed him of most modern as well as ancient languages. Of music she knew little or nothing, but her new friend undertook to give her lessons; in exchange for which, she learned from Lucy the habit of walking, and the art of riding, and the courage necessary to defy the season. Mannering was careful to substitute for their amusement in the evenings such books as might convey some solid instruction with entertainment, and, as he read aloud with great skill and taste, the winter nights passed pleasantly away.

Society was quickly formed where there were so many inducements. Most of the families of the neighbourhood visited Colonel Mannering, and he was soon able to select from among them such as best suited his taste and habits. Charles Hazelwood held a distinguished place in his favour, and was a frequent visitor, not without the consent and approbation of his parents; for there was no knowing, they thought, what assiduous attention might produce, and the beautiful Miss Mannering, with an Indian fortune, was a prize worth looking after. Dazzled with such a prospect, they never considered the risk which had once been some object of their apprehension, that his boyish and inconsiderate fancy might form an attachment to the pennyless Lucy Bertram, who had nothing on earth to recommend her, but a pretty face, good birth, and a most amiable disposition. Mannering was more prudent. He considered himself acting as Miss

Bertram's guardian, and, while he did not think it incumbent upon him altogether to check her intercourse with a young gentleman for whom, excepting in wealth, she was a match in every respect, he laid it under such insensible restraints as might prevent any engagement or eclaircissement taking place until the young man should have seen a little more of life and of the world, and have attained that age when he might be considered as entitled to judge for himself in the matter in which his happiness was chiefly interested.

While these matters engaged the attention of the other members of the Woodbourne family, Dominie Sampson was engaged, body and soul, in the arrangement of the bishop's library, which had been sent from Liverpool by sea, and conveyed by thirty or forty carts from the sea-port at which it was landed. Sampson's joy at beholding the ponderous contents of these chests arranged upon the floor of the apartment, from whence he was to transfer them to the shelves, baffled all description. He grinned like an ogre, swung his arms like the sails of a wind-mill, shouted "prodigious" till the roof rung to his raptures. "He had never," he said, "seen so many books together, except in the College Library;" and now his dignity and delight in being superintendant of the collection, raised him, in his own opinion, almost to the rank of the academical librarian, whom he had always regarded as the greatest and happiest man on earth. Neither were his transports diminished upon a hasty examination of the contents of these volumes. Some, indeed, of belles lettres, poems, plays, or memoirs, he tossed indignantly aside, with the implied censure of "psha," or "frivolous;" but the greater and bulkier part of the collection bore a very different character. The deceased prelate, a divine of the old and deeply-learned cast, had loaded his shelves with volumes which displayed the antique and venerable attributes so happily described by a modern poet,

> That weight of wood, with leathern coat o'erlaid,
> Those ample clasps of solid metal made,
> The close-press'd leaves unclosed for many an age,
> The dull red edging of the well-fill'd page,
> On the broad back the stubborn ridges roll'd,
> Where yet the title stands in tarnish'd gold.

Books of theology and controversial divinity, commentaries and polyglots, sets of the fathers, and sermons, which might each furnish forth ten brief discourses of modern date, books of science ancient and modern, classical authors in their best and rarest forms; such formed the late bishop's venerable library, and over such the eye of Dominie Sampson gloated with rapture. He entered them in the catalogue with his best running hand, forming each letter with the accuracy of a lover writing a valentine, and placed each individually on the destined shelf with all the reverence which I have seen a lady pay to a jar of old china. With all this zeal his labours advanced slowly. He often opened a volume when half way up the library steps, fell upon some interesting passage, and, without shifting his inconvenient posture, continued immersed in the fascinating perusal until the servant pulled him by the skirts to assure him that dinner waited. He then repaired to the parlour, and shovelled his meat down his capacious throat in squares of three inches, answered aye and no at random to whatever question was asked at him, and again hurried back to the library so soon as his napkin was removed.

How happily the days
Of Thalaba went bye!

And having thus left the principal characters of our tale in a situation, which, being sufficiently comfortable to themselves, is, of course, utterly uninteresting to the reader, we take up a person who has as yet only been named, and who has all the interest that uncertainty and misfortune can give.

Chapter Twenty-One

What say'st thou, Wise-One? "—that all powerful Love
Can fortune's strong impediments remove.
Nor is it strange that worth should wed to worth,
The pride of genius with the pride of birth."

CRABBE

V. BROWN—I will not give at full length his thrice unhappy name —had been from infancy a ball for fortune to spurn at; but nature had given him that elasticity of mind, which rises higher from the rebound. His form was tall, manly, and active, and his features corresponded with his person; for, although far from regular, they had an expression of intelligence and good humour, and when he spoke or was particularly animated, might be decidedly pronounced interesting. His manner indicated a good deal the military profession which had been his choice, and in which he had now attained the rank of captain, the person who succeeded Colonel Mannering in his command having laboured to repair the injustice which Brown had sustained by that gentleman's prejudice against him. But this, as well as his liberation from captivity, had taken place after Mannering had left India. Brown followed at no distant period, his regiment being recalled home. His first enquiry was after the family of Mannering, and, easily learning their route northward, he followed it with the purpose of resuming his addresses to Julia. With her father he deemed he had no measures to keep; for, ignorant of the more venomous belief which had been instilled into the colonel's mind, he regarded him as an oppressive aristocrat, who had used his power as a commanding officer to deprive him of the preferment due to his behaviour, and had forced upon him a personal quarrel without any better reason than his attentions to a pretty young woman, agreeable to herself, and permitted and countenanced by her mother. He was determined, therefore, to take no rejection unless from the young lady herself, believing that the heavy misfortunes of his painful wound and imprisonment were direct injuries received from the father, which might dispense with his using much ceremony towards him. How far his scheme had succeeded when his nocturnal visit was discovered by Mr Mervyn, our readers are already informed.

Upon this unpleasant occurrence, Captain Brown absented himself from the inn in which he had resided under the name of Dawson, so that Colonel Mannering's attempts to discover and trace him were unavailing. He resolved, however, that no difficulties should prevent his continuing his enterprise, while Julia left him a ray of hope. The interest he had secured in her bosom was such as she had been unable to conceal from him, and with all the courage of romantic gallantry he determined upon perseverance. But we believe the reader will be as well pleased to learn his mode of thinking and intentions from his own communication to his special friend and confidant, Captain Delaserre, a Swiss gentleman, who had a company in his regiment.

Extract.

"Let me hear from you soon, dear Delaserre—Remember I can learn nothing about regimental affairs but through your friendly medium, and I long to know what has become of Ayre's court-martial, and whether Elliot gets the majority—also how recruiting comes on, and how the young officers like the mess. Of our kind friend, the Lieutenant-Colonel, I need ask nothing; I saw him as I passed through Nottingham, happy in the bosom of his family. What a happiness it is, Philip, for us poor devils, that we have a little resting-place between the camp and the grave, if we can manage to escape disease, and steel, and lead, and the effects of hard living. A retired old soldier is always a graceful and respected character—he grumbles a little now and then, but then his is licensed murmuring—were a lawyer, or a physician, or a clergyman, to breathe a complaint of hard luck or want of preferment, a hundred tongues would blame his own incapacity as the cause. But the most stupid veteran that ever faultered out the thrice-told tale of a siege and a battle, and a cock and a bottle, is listened to with sympathy and reverence when he shakes his thin locks, and talks with indignation of the boys that are put over his head.

And you and I, Delaserre, foreigners both,—for what am I the better that I was originally a Scotchman, since, could I prove my descent, the English would hardly acknowledge me a countryman?—we may boast that we have fought out our preferment, and gained that by the sword which we had not money to compass otherwise. The English are a wise people—while they praise themselves and affect to undervalue all other nations, they leave us, luckily, trap-doors and back-doors open, by which we strangers, less favoured by nature, may arrive at a share of their advantages. And thus they are, in some respects, like a boastful landlord, who exalts the value and flavour of his six-years-old mutton, while he is delighted to dispense a share of it to all the company. In short, you, whose proud family, and I, whose hard fate, made us soldiers of fortune, have the pleasant recollection, in the British service, that stop where we may upon our career, it is only for want of money to pay the turnpike, and not from our being prohibited to travel the road. If, therefore, you can persuade little Weischel to come into *ours*, for God's sake let him buy the ensigncy, live prudently, mind his duty, and trust to the fates for promotion.

"And now, I hope you are expiring with curiosity to learn the end of my romance. I told you I had deemed it convenient to make a few days tour on foot among the mountains of Westmoreland, with Dudley, a young English artist, with whom I have formed some acquaintance. A fine fellow this, you must know, Delaserre—he paints tolerably, draws beautifully, converses well, and plays charmingly on the flute; and, though thus well entitled to be a coxcomb of talent, is, in fact, a modest unpretending young man. Upon our return from our little tour, I learned that the enemy had been reconnoitring. Mr Mervyn's barge had crossed the lake, I was informed by my landlord, with the squire himself and a visitor.

"'What sort of person, landlord?'

"'Whoy, ho was a dark officer-looking mon, at they called colonel —Squoire Mervyn questioned me as close as had I been at sizes—I had a guess, Mr Dawson' (I told you that was my feigned name)— 'But I tould him nought of your vagaries, and going a-laking on the mere a-noights—not I—an I can make no sport I'se spoil none—And Squoire Mervyn's as cross as poy-crust too, mon—he's aye maundering an my guests but land beneath his house, though it be marked for the fourth Station on the Survey. Noa, noa, e'en let un smell things out o' themsells, for Joe Hodge is——'

"You will allow there was nothing for it after this, but paying honest Joe Hodge's bill, unless I had preferred making him my confidant, for which I felt in no shape inclined. Besides, I learned abroad that our *ci-devant* colonel was on full retreat for Scotland, carrying off poor Julia along with him. I understand from those who conduct the heavy baggage, that he takes his winter quarters at a place called Woodbourne, in —— shire in Scotland. He will be all on the alert just now, so I must let him enter his entrenchments without any new alarm. And then, my good colonel, to whom I owe so many grateful thanks, pray look to your defence.

"I protest to you, Delaserre, I often think there is a little contradiction enters into the ardour of my pursuit. I think I would rather bring this haughty insulting man to the necessity of calling his daughter Mrs Brown, than I would wed her with his full consent, and with the king's permission to change my name for the stile and arms of Mannering, though his whole fortune went with them. There is only one circumstance that chills me a little—Julia is young and romantic. I would not willingly hurry her into a step which her riper years might disapprove —no;—nor would I like to have her upbraid me, were it but with a glance of her eye, with having ruined her fortunes—far less give her reason to say, as some ladies have not been slow to tell their lords, that, had I left her time for consideration, she would have been wiser and done better. No, Delaserre—this must not be. The picture presses closer upon me, because I am aware a girl in Julia's situation has no distinct and precise idea of the value of the sacrifices she makes. She knows difficulties only by name, and if she thinks of love and a farm, it is a *ferme ornée*, such as is only to be found in poetic description, or in the park of a gentleman of twelve thousand a-year. She would be ill prepared for the privations of that real Swiss cottage we have so often talked of, and for the difficulties which must necessarily surround us even before we obtained that haven. This must be a point clearly ascertained. Although Julia's beauty and playful tenderness have made an impression on my heart never to be erased, I will be satisfied that she perfectly understands the advantages she foregoes, before she sacrifices them for my sake.

"Am I too proud, Delaserre, when I trust that even this trial may terminate favourably to my wishes?—Am I too vain when I suppose, that the few personal qualities which I possess, with means of competence however moderate, and the determination of consecrating my life to her happiness, may make some amends for all I must call upon her to forego? Or will a difference of dress, of attendance, of stile, as it is called, of the power of shifting at pleasure the scenes in which she seeks amusement,—will these outweigh, in her estimation, the prospect of domestic happiness, and the interchange of unabating affection? I say nothing of her father;—his good and evil qualities are so strangely mingled, that the former are neutralized by the latter, and that which she must regret as a daughter is so much blended with what she would gladly escape from, that I place the separation of the father and child as a circumstance which weighs little in her remarkable case. Meantime I keep up my spirits as I may. I have incurred too many hardships and difficulties to be presumptuous or confident in success, and I have been too often and too wonderfully extricated from them to be despondent.

"I wish you saw this country. I think the scenery would delight you. At least it often brings to my remembrance your glowing descriptions of your native canton. To me it has in a great measure the charm of novelty. Of the Scottish hills, though born among them, as I have always been assured, I have but an indistinct recollection. Indeed my memory rather dwells upon the blank which my youthful mind experienced in gazing on the levels of the isle of Zealand than on any thing which preceded that feeling. But I am confident, from that sensation, that hills and rocks had been familiar to me at an early period, and that though now only remembered by contrast, and by the blank which I felt while gazing round for them in vain, they must have made an indelible impression on my infant imagination. I remember when we first mounted that celebrated pass in the Mysore country, while most of the others felt only awe and astonishment at the height and grandeur of the scenery, I rather shared your feelings and those of Cameron, whose admiration of these wild rocks was blended with familiar love, derived from early association. Despite my Dutch education, a blue hill to me is as a friend, and a roaring torrent like the sound of a domestic song that has soothed my infancy. I never felt the impulse so strongly as in this land of lakes and mountains, and nothing grieves me so much as that the duty prevents your being with me in my numerous excursions among its recesses. Some drawings I have attempted, but I succeed vilely—Dudley, on the contrary, draws delightfully, with that rapid touch which seems like magic, while I labour and botch, and make this too heavy, and that too light, and produce at last a base caricature. I must stick to the flageolet, for music is the only one of the fine arts which deigns to acknowledge me.

"Did you know that Colonel Mannering was a draughtsman?—I believe not, for he scorned to display his accomplishments to the view of a subaltern. He draws beautifully however. Since he and Julia left Mervyn Hall, Dudley was sent for there. The squire, it seems, wanted a set of drawings made up, of which Mannering had done the first four, but was interrupted, by his hasty departure, in his purpose of completing them. Dudley says he has seldom seen any thing so masterly, though slight, and each had attached to it a short poetical description. Is Saul, you will say, among the prophets?—Colonel Mannering write poetry?—Why surely this man must have taken all the pains to conceal his accomplishments that others do to display theirs—Yet how proud and unsociable he appeared among us—how little disposed to enter into any conversation which could become generally interesting?—And then his attachment to that unworthy Archer, so much below him in every respect; and all this, because he was the brother of Viscount Archerfield, a poor Scottish peer! I think if Archer had longer survived his wounds in the affair of Cuddyboram, he would have said something that might have thrown light upon the inconsistencies of this singular man's character. He repeated to me more than once, 'I have that to say which will alter your hard opinion of our late colonel.' But death pressed him too hard; and if he owed me any atonement, which some of his expressions seemed to imply, he died before it could be made.

"I propose to make a farther excursion through this country while this fine frosty weather serves, and Dudley, almost as good a walker as myself, goes with me for some part of the way. We part on the borders of Cumberland, when he must return to his lodging in Marybone, up three pair of stairs, and labour at what he calls the commercial part of his profession. There cannot, he says, be such a difference betwixt any two portions of existence, as between that in which the artist, if an enthusiast, collects the subjects of his drawings, and that which must necessarily be dedicated to turning over his portfolio, and exhibiting them to the provoking indifference, or more provoking criticism, of fashionable amateurs. 'During the summer of my year,' says Dudley, 'I am as free as a wild Indian, enjoying myself at liberty amid the grandest scenes of nature; while, during my winters and springs, I am not only cabbined, cribbed, and confined in a miserable garret, but condemned to as intolerable subservience to the humour of others, and to as indifferent company, as if I were a literal galley-slave.' I have promised him your acquaintance, Delaserre; you will be delighted with his sketches, and he with your Swiss fanaticism for mountains and torrents.

"When I lose Dudley's company, I am informed that I can easily enter Scotland by stretching across a wild country in the upper part of Cumberland; and that route I shall follow, to give the colonel time to pitch his camp ere I reconnoitre his position.—Adieu! Delaserre—I shall hardly find another opportunity of writing till I reach Scotland."

END OF VOLUME FIRST

GUY MANNERING

OR

THE ASTROLOGER

VOLUME II

Chapter One

Jog on, jog on, the footpath way,
And merrily bend the stile a;
A merry heart goes all the day,
A sad one tires in a mile a.
Winter's Tale

LET THE READER conceive to himself a clear frosty November morning, the scene an open heath, having for the back-ground that huge chain of mountains in which Skiddaw and Saddleback are pre-eminent; let him then look along that *blind road*, by which I mean a tract so slightly marked by the passengers' footsteps, that it can but be traced by a slight shade of verdure from the darker heath around it, and, being only visible to the eye when at some distance, ceases to be distinguished while the foot is actually treading it. Along this faintly-traced path advances the object of our present narrative. His firm step, his erect and free carriage, give him a military air, which corresponds well with his well-proportioned limbs and his stature of six feet high. His dress is so plain and simple that it indicates nothing as to rank—it might be that of a gentleman who travels in this manner for his pleasure, or of an inferior person of whom it is the proper and usual garb. Nothing can be on a more reduced scale than his travelling equipment. A volume of Shakespeare in one pocket, a small bundle with a change of linen in the other, an oaken cudgel in his hand, complete our pedestrian's accommodations, and in this equipage we present him to our reader.

Brown had parted that morning from his friend Dudley, and begun his solitary walk towards Scotland.

The first two or three miles were rather melancholy, from want of the society to which he had of late been accustomed. But this unusual mood of his mind soon gave way to the influence of his natural good spirits, excited by the exercise and the bracing effects of the frosty air. He whistled as he went along, not "from want of thought," but to give vent to those buoyant feelings which he had no other mode of expressing. For each peasant whom he chanced to meet, he had a kind greeting or a good-humoured jest; the hardy Cumbrians grinned as they passed, and said, "That's a koind heart, God bless un!" and the market-girl looked more than once over her shoulder at the athletic form, which corresponded so well with the frank and blithe address of the stranger. A rough terrier dog, his constant companion, rivalled his master in glee, scampered at large in a thousand wheels round the heath, and came back to jump up on him, and assure him he participated in the pleasures of his journey. Dr Johnson thought life had few things better than the excitation produced by being whirled rapidly along in a post-chaise; but he who has in youth experienced the confident and independent feeling of a stout pedestrian in an interesting country, and during fine weather, will hold the taste of the great moralist cheap in comparison.

Part of Brown's view in chusing that unusual track which leads through the eastern wilds of Cumberland into Scotland, had been a desire to view the remains of the celebrated Roman Wall, which are more visible in that direction than in any other part of its extent. His education had been imperfect and desultory; but neither the busy scenes in which he had been engaged, nor the pleasures of youth, nor the precarious state of his own circumstances, had diverted him from the task of mental improvement.—"And this then is the Roman Wall," said he, scrambling up to a height which commanded the course of that celebrated work of antiquity: "What a people! whose labours, even at this extremity of their empire, comprehended such space, and were executed upon such a scale of grandeur! In future ages, when the science of war shall have changed, how few traces will exist of the labours of Vauban and Coehorn, while this wonderful people's remains will even then continue to interest and astonish posterity! Their fortifications, their aqueducts, their theatres, their fountains, all their public works, bear the grave, solid, and majestic character of their language; and our modern labours, like our modern tongues, seem but constructed out of their fragments." Having thus moralized, he remembered he was hungry, and pursued his walk to a small public-house, at which he proposed to get some refreshment.

The ale-house, for it was no better, was situated in the bottom of a little dell, through which trilled a small rivulet. It was shaded by a large ash tree, against which the clay-built shade, that served the purpose of a stable, was erected, and upon which it seemed partly to recline. In this shade stood a saddled horse, employed in eating his corn. The cottages in this part of Cumberland partake of the rudeness which characterizes those in Scotland. The outside of the house promised little for the interior, notwithstanding the vaunt of a sign, where a tankard of ale voluntarily decanted itself into a tumbler, and a hieroglyphical scrawl below attempted to express a promise of "good entertainment for men and horse." Brown was no fastidious traveller—he stooped and entered the cabaret.

The first object which caught his eye in the kitchen, was a tall, stout, country-looking man, in a large jockey great-coat, the owner of the horse which stood in the shade, who was busy discussing huge slices of cold boiled beef, and casting from time to time an eye through the window, to see how his steed sped with his provender. A large tankard of ale flanked his plate of victuals, to which he applied himself by intervals. The good woman of the house was employed in baking. The fire, as is usual in that country, was made on a stone hearth in the midst of an immensely large chimney, which had two seats extending beneath the vent. On one of these sat a remarkably tall woman, in a red cloak and slouched bonnet, with the appearance of a tinker or beggar. She was busily engaged with a short black tobacco-pipe.

At the request of Brown for some food, the landlady wiped with her mealy apron one corner of the deal table, placed a wooden trencher and knife and fork before the traveller, pointed to the round of beef, recommended Mr Dinmont's good example, and, finally, filled a brown pitcher with her home-brewed. Brown lost no time in doing ample credit to both. For some time his opposite neighbour and he were too busy to take much notice of each other, except by a good-humoured nod as each in turn raised the tankard to his head. At length, when our pedestrian began to supply the wants of little Wasp, the Scotch store-farmer, for such was Mr Dinmont, found himself at leisure to enter into conversation.

"A bonnie terrier that, sir—and a fell chield at the vermin, I warrant him—that is, if he's been weel entered, for it a' lies in that."

"Really, sir, his education has been somewhat neglected, and his chief profession is being a pleasant companion."

"Ay, sir? that's a pity, begging your pardon—it's a great pity that—beast or body, education should aye be minded. I have six terriers at hame, forbye other dogs. There's auld Pepper and auld Mustard, and young Pepper and young Mustard, and little Pepper and little

Mustard—I had them a' regularly entered, first wi' rottens—then wi' stots or weazles—and then wi' the brocks—and they fear naething that ever came wi' a hair skin upon it."

"I have no doubt, sir, they are thorough bred—but, to have so many dogs, you have a very limited variety of names for them?"

"O, that's a fancy of my ain to mark the breed, sir—the Deuke himsell has sent as far as Charlieshope to get ane o' Dandie Dinmont's Pepper and Mustard terriers—Lord, man—he sent Jamie Grieve the keeper, and sicken a day as we had wi' the foumarts and the tods, and sicken a blithe gae-down as we had again e'en! Faith, that was a night!"

"I suppose game is very plenty with you?"

"Plenty, man!—I believe there's mair hares nor sheep on my farm; and for the moor-fowl, or the grey-fowl, they lie as thick as doo's in a dooket—Did ye ever shoot a black-cock, man?"

"Really I had never even the pleasure to see one, except in the museum at Keswick."

"There now—I can guess that be your Southland tongue. It's very odd of these English folk that come here, how few of them has seen a black-cock—I'll tell you what—ye seem to be an honest lad, and if you'll call on me—on Dandie Dinmont—at Charlieshope—ye shall see a black-cock, and shoot a black-cock, and eat a black-cock too, man."

"Why, the proof of the matter is the eating to be sure, sir; and I shall be happy if I can find time to accept your invitation."

"Time, man? what ails ye to gae hame wi' me e'en now? how do you travel?"

"On foot, sir; and if that handsome poney be yours, I should find it impossible to keep up with you."

"No unless ye can walk up to fourteen miles an hour—But ye can come on the night as far as Riccarton, where there is a public—or if ye like to stop at Jock Grieve's at the Rone, they wald be blithe to see ye, and I am just gaun to stop and drink a dram at the door wi' him, and I would tell him you're coming up—or stay—gudewife, could ye lend this gentleman the gudeman's gallaway, and I'll send it ower the Waste in the morning wi' the callant?"

The galloway was turned out upon the fell, and was swear to catch —"Aweel, aweel, there's nae help for't, but come up the morn at ony rate.—And now, gudewife, I maun ride, to get to the Liddel or it be dark, for your Waste has but a kittle character, ye ken yoursell."

"Fie, fie, Mr Dinmont, that's no like you to gie the country an ill name—I wot, there has been nane stirred in the Waste since Sawney Culloch, the travelling merchant, that Rowley Overdees and Jock

Penny suffered for at Carlisle twa year since. There's no ane in Bewcastle would do the like o' that now—we'll be a' true folk now."

"Aye, Tib, that will be when the deil's blind,—and his e'en are no sair yet. But hear ye, gudewife, I've been through maist feck o' Galloway and Dumfries-shire, and I have been round by Carlisle, and I was at the Staneshiebank fair the day, and I would like ill to be rubbit sae near hame, so I'll take the nag."

"Hae ye been in Dumfries and Galloway?" said the old dame, who sate smoking by the fire-side, and who had not yet spoke a word.

"Troth have I, gudewife, and a weary round I've had o't."

"Then ye'll maybe ken a place they ca' Ellangowan?"

"Ellangowan, that was Mr Bertram's?—I ken the place weel eneugh. The Laird died about a fortnight since, as I heard."

"Dead!"—said the old woman, dropping her pipe, rising and coming forward upon the floor—"dead!—are ye sure of that?"

"Troth am I," said Dinmont, "for it made nae sma' noise in the country-side. He died just at the roup of the stocking and furniture; it stoppit the roup, and mony folk were disappointed. They said he was the last of an auld family too, and mony were sorry—for gude blude's scarcer in Scotland than it has been."

"Dead!" repeated the old woman, whom our readers have already recognised as their acquaintance Meg Merrilies—"dead! that quits a' scores. And did ye say he died without an heir?"

"Aye, did he, gudewife, and the estate's selled by the same token; for they said, they could na have selled it, if there had been an heir-male."

"Sold!" echoed the gypsy, with something like a scream, "and wha durst buy Ellangowan that was not of Bertram's blude?—and wha could tell whether the bonny knave-bairn may not come back to claim his ain?—wha durst buy the estate and the castle of Ellangowan?"

"Troth, gudewife, just ane o' thae writer chields that buy a' thing—they ca' him Glossin, I think."

"Glossin?—Gibbie Glossin!—that I have carried in my creels a hundred times, for his mother was na mickle better than mysell—he to presume to buy the barony of Ellangowan!—Gude be wi' us—it is an awfu' warld!—I wished him ill—but no sick a downfall as a' that neither—waesome! waesome to think o't!"—She remained a moment silent, but still opposing with her hand the farmer's retreat, who, betwixt every question, was about to turn his back, but good-humouredly stopped on observing the deep interest his answers appeared to excite.

"It will be seen and heard of," she said, "it will be seen and heard of—earth and sea will not hold their peace langer!—Can ye say if the same man be now Sheriff of the county, that has been sae for some years past?"

"Na, he's got some other berth in Edinburgh, they say—but gude-day, gudewife, I maun ride."—She followed him to his horse, and, while he drew the girths of his saddle, adjusted the walise, and put on the bridle, still plied him with questions concerning Mr Bertram's death, and the fate of his daughter; on which, however, she could obtain little information from the honest farmer.

"Did ye ever see a place they ca' Derncleugh, about a mile frae the Place of Ellangowan?"

"I wot weel have I, gudewife,—a wild-looking den it is, wi' a whin auld wa's o' shealings yonder—I saw it when I gaed ower the ground wi' ane that wanted to take the farm."

"It was a blithe bit ance!" said Meg, speaking to herself—"Did ye notice if there was an auld saugh tree that's maist blawn down, but yet its roots are in the earth, and it hings ower the bit burn—mony a day hae I wrought my stocking, and sat on my sunkie under that saugh."

"Hout, deil's in the wife, wi' her saughs, and her sunkies, and Bertrams and Ellangowans—Godsake woman, let me away—there's saxpence t'ye to buy half a mutchkin, instead o' clavering about thae auld warld stories."

"Thanks to ye, good-man—and now ye hae answered a' my questions, and never speired wherefore I asked them, I'll gie a bit canny advice, and ye manna speir what for neither. Tib Mumps will be out wi' the stirrup-dram in a gliffing—She'll ask ye whether ye gang ower Willie's brae, or through Conscouthart-moss—tell her ony ane ye like, but be sure (speaking low and emphatically) to take the ane ye dinna tell her." The farmer laughed and promised, and the gypsy retreated.

"Will you take her advice?" said Brown, who had been an attentive listener to this conversation.

"That will I no—the randy quean!—I had far rather Tib Mumps kend which way I was gaun than her—though Tib's no mickle to lippen to neither, and I would wish ye on no account to stay in the house a' night."

In a moment after, Tib, the landlady, appeared with her stirrup-cup, which was taken off. She then, as Meg had predicted, enquired whether he went the hill or the moss road. He answered, the latter; and, having bid Brown good-bye, and again told him, "he depended on seeing him at Charlieshope, the morn at latest," he rode off at a round pace.

Chapter Two

Gallows and knock are too powerful on the highway.

Winter's Tale

THE HINT of the hospitable farmer was not lost on Brown. But, while he paid his reckoning, he could not avoid repeatedly fixing his eyes on Meg Merrilies. She was, in all respects, the same witch-like figure as when we first introduced her at Ellangowan-Place. Time had grizzled her raven locks, and added wrinkles to her wild features, but her height remained erect, and her activity was unimpaired. It was remarked of this woman, as of others of the same description, that a life of activity, though not of labour, gave her the perfect command of her limbs and figure, so that attitudes into which she most naturally threw herself, were free, unconstrained, and picturesque. At present, she stood by the window of the cottage, her person drawn up so as to shew to full advantage her masculine stature, and her head somewhat thrown back, that the large bonnet, with which her face was shrouded, might not interrupt her steady gaze at Brown. At every gesture he made, and every tone he uttered, she seemed to give an almost imperceptible start. On his part, he was surprised to find that he could not look upon this singular figure without some emotion. "Have I dreamed of such a figure?" he said to himself, "or does this wild and singular-looking woman recal to my recollection some of the strange figures I have seen in an Indian pagoda?"

While he embarrassed himself with these discussions, and the hostess was engaged in rummaging out silver in change of half-a-guinea, the gypsy suddenly made two strides, and seized Brown's hand. He expected, of course, a display of her skill in palmistry, but she seemed agitated by other feelings.

"Tell me," she said, "in the name of God, young man, what is your name, and whence you came?"

"My name is Brown, mother, and I come from the East Indies."

"From the East Indies!" dropping his hand with a sigh, "it cannot be then—I am such an auld fool, that every thing I look on seems the thing I want maist to see. But the East Indies!—that cannot be—Weel, be what ye will, ye hae a face and a tongue that puts me in mind of auld times. Good day—make haste on your road, and if ye see ony of our folk, meddle not and make not, and they'll do you nae harm."

Brown, who had by this time received his change, put a shilling into her hand, bade his hostess farewell, and, taking the route which the farmer had gone before, walked briskly on, with the advantage of being guided by the fresh hoof-prints of his horse. Meg Merrilies looked after him for some time, and then muttered to herself, "I maun see that lad again—and I maun gang back to Ellangowan too.—The Laird's dead—a weel, death pays a' scores—he was a kind man ance. —The Sheriff's flitted, and I can keep canny in the bush—so there's no mickle hazard o' scouring the cramp-ring.—I would like to see bonny Ellangowan again or I die."

Brown, meanwhile, proceeded at a round pace along the moorish tract called the Waste of Cumberland. He passed a solitary house, towards which the horseman who preceded him had apparently turned up, for his horse's tread was evident in that direction. A little farther, he seemed to have returned again into the road. Mr Dinmont had probably made a visit there either of business or pleasure. "I wish," thought Brown, "the good farmer had staid till I came up; I should not have been sorry to ask him a few questions about the road, which seems to grow wilder and wilder."

In truth, nature, as if she had designed this tract of country to be the barrier between two hostile nations, has stamped upon it a character of wildness and desolation. The hills are neither high nor rocky, but the land is all heath and morass; the huts poor and mean, and at a great distance from each other. Around them there is generally some little attempt at cultivation; but a half-bred foal or two, straggling about with shackles on their hind-legs, to save the trouble of inclosures, intimate the farmer's chief resource to be the breeding of horses. The people, too, are of a ruder and more inhospitable class than are elsewhere to be found in Cumberland, arising partly from their own habits, partly from their intermixture with vagrants and criminals, who make this wild country a refuge from justice. So much were the men of these districts in early times the objects of suspicion and dislike to their more polished neighbours, that there was, and perhaps still exists, a bye-law of the corporation of Newcastle, prohibiting any freeman of that city to take for apprentice a native of certain of these dales. It is pithily said, "Give a dog an ill name and hang him;" and it may be added, if you give a man, or race of men, an ill name, they are very likely to do something that deserves hanging. Of this Brown had heard something, and suspected more, from the discourse between the landlady, Dinmont, and the gypsy; but he was naturally of a fearless disposition, had nothing visible about him that might tempt the spoiler, and trusted to get through the *waste* with day-light. In this last particular he was likely to be disappointed. The way proved longer than he had anticipated, and the horizon began to grow gloomy, just as he entered upon an extensive morass.

Chusing his steps with care and deliberation, he proceeded along a path that sometimes sunk between two broken black banks of moss earth, sometimes crossed narrow but deep ravines, filled with a consistence between mud and water, and sometimes along heaps of gravel and stones, which had been swept together when some torrent or water-spout from the neighbouring hills overflowed the marshy ground below. He began to ponder how a horseman could make his way through such broken ground; the traces of hoofs, however, were still visible; he even thought he heard their sound at some distance, and, convinced Mr Dinmont's progress through the morass must be even slower than his own, he resolved to push on, in hopes to overtake him, and have the benefit of his knowledge of the country. At this moment his little terrier sprang forward, barking most furiously.

Brown quickened his pace, and, attaining the summit of a small rising ground, saw the subject of the dog's alarm. In a hollow, about a gun-shot below him, a man, whom he easily recognised to be Dinmont, was engaged with two others in a desperate struggle. He was dismounted, and defending himself as he best could with the butt of his heavy whip. Our traveller hastened on to his assistance; but, ere he could get up, a stroke had levelled the farmer with the earth, and one of the robbers, improving his victory, struck him some merciless blows on the head. The other villain, hastening to meet Brown, called to his companion to come along, "for that one's *content*," meaning, probably, past resistance or complaint. One ruffian was armed with a cutlass, the other with a bludgeon; but as the road was pretty narrow, "bar firearms," thought Brown, "and I may manage them well enough." They met accordingly, with the most murderous threats on the part of the ruffians. They soon found, however, that their new opponent was equally stout and resolute; and, after exchanging two or three blows, one of them told him to "follow his nose over the heath, in the devil's name, for they had nothing to say to him."

Brown rejected this composition, as leaving to their mercy the unfortunate man whom they were about to pillage, if not to murder outright; and the skirmish had just recommenced, when Dinmont unexpectedly recovered his senses, his feet, and his weapon, and hasted to the scene of action. As he had been no easy antagonist, even when surprised and alone, the villains did not chuse to wait his joining forces with a man who had singly proved a match for them both, but fled across the bog as fast as their feet could carry them, pursued by Wasp, who had acted gloriously during the skirmish, annoying the heels of the enemy, and repeatedly effecting a moment's diversion in his master's favour.

"Deil, but your dog's weel entered wi' the vermin now," were the first words uttered by the jolly farmer, as he came up, his head streaming with blood, and recognised his deliverer and his attendant.

"I hope, sir, you are not hurt dangerously?"

"O, deil a bit—my head can stand a gay clour—nae thanks to them though, and mony to you. But now, hinney, you maun help me to catch the beast, and ye maun get on behind me, for we maun aff like whittrets before the whole clanjamfray be down upon us—the rest of them will no be far off." The galloway was, by good fortune, easily caught, and Brown made some apology for overloading the palfrey.

"Deil a fear, man," answered the proprietor, "Dumple could carry six folk, if his back was lang aneugh—But God's sake haste ye, get on, for I see some folk coming through the slack yonder, that it may be just as weel no to wait for."

Brown was of opinion, that this apparition of five or six men coming across the moss towards them should abridge ceremony; he therefore mounted Dumple *en croupe*, and the little spirited nag cantered away with two men of great size and strength, as if they had been children of six years old. The rider, to whom the paths of these wilds seemed intimately known, pushed on at a rapid pace, managing, with much dexterity, to chuse the safest route, in which he was aided by the sagacity of the galloway, who never failed to take the difficult passes exactly at the particular spot, and in the special manner, by which they could be most safely crossed. Yet, even with these advantages, the road was so broken, and they were so often thrown out of the direct course by various impediments, that they did not gain much on their pursuers. "Never mind," said the undaunted Scotchman to his companion, "if we were ance by Withershins-latch, the road's no near sae *saft*, and we'll show them fair play for't."

They soon came to the place he named, a narrow channel, through which soaked, rather than flowed, a small stagnant stream, mantled over with bright green mosses. Dinmont directed his steed towards a pass where the water appeared to flow with more freedom over a harder bottom; but Dumple backed from the proposed crossing place, put his head down as if to reconnoitre the swamp more nearly, stretched forward his fore-feet, and stood as fast as if he had been cut out of stone.

"Had we not better," said Brown, "dismount and leave him to his fate—or can you not urge him through the swamp?"

"No, no," said his pilot, "we maun cross Dumple at no rate—he has mair sense than mony a Christian." So saying, he relaxed the reins, and shook them loosely. "Come now, lad, take your ain way o't—let's see where ye'll take us through."

Dumple, left to the freedom of his own will, trotted briskly to another part of the *latch*, less promising, as Brown thought, in appearance, but which the animal's sagacity or experience recommended as the safer of the two, and, plunging in, attained the other side with little difficulty.

"I am glad we're out o' that moss," said Dinmont, "where there's mair stables for horses than change-houses for men—we have the *Maiden-way* to help us now at ony rate." Accordingly, they speedily gained a sort of rugged causeway so called, being the remains of an old Roman road, which traverses these wild regions in a due northerly direction. Here they got on at the rate of nine or ten miles an hour, Dumple seeking no other respite than what arose from changing his going from canter to trot. "I could gar him show mair action," said his master, "but we are twa lang-legged chields after a', and it would be a pity to stress Dumple—there was na the like o' him at Staneshiebank fair the day."

Brown readily assented to the propriety of sparing the horse, and added, that, as they were now far out of reach of the rogues, he thought Mr Dinmont had better tie a handkerchief round his head, for fear of the cold frosty air aggravating the wound.

"What would I do that for?" answered the hardy farmer, "the best way's to let the blood barken upon the cut—that saves plaisters, hinney."

Brown, who in his military profession had seen a great many hard blows pass, could not help remarking, "he had never known such severe strokes received with so much apparent indifference."

"Hout tout, man—I would never be making a hum-dudgeon about a scart on the pow—but we'll be in Scotland in five minutes now, and ye maun gang up to Charlieshope wi' me, that's a clear case."

Brown readily accepted the offered hospitality. Night was now falling, when they came in sight of a pretty little river winding its way through a pastoral country. The hills were more green and more abrupt than those Brown had lately passed, sinking their grassy sides at once upon the river. They had no pretensions to magnificence of height or to romantic shapes, nor did their smooth swelling slopes exhibit either rocks or woods. Yet the view was wild, solitary, and pleasingly rural. No inclosures, no roads, almost no tillage—it seemed a land which a patriarch would have chosen to feed his flocks and herds. The remains of here and there a dismantled and ruined tower, showed that it had once harboured beings of a very different description from its present inhabitants; those freebooters, namely, to whose exploits the wars between England and Scotland bear witness.

Descending by a path towards a well-known ford, Dumple crossed the small river, and then, quickening his pace, trotted about a mile briskly up its banks, and approached two or three low thatched houses, placed with their angles to each other, with a great contempt of regularity. This was the farm-steading of Charlieshope, or, in the language of the country, "the town." A most furious barking was up at their approach, by the whole three generations of Mustard and Pepper, and a number of allies, names unknown. The farmer made his well-known voice lustily heard to restore order—the door opened, and a half-dressed ewe-milker, who had done that good office, shut it in their faces, in order that she might run *ben the house*, to cry "Mistress, mistress, it's the master, and another man wi' him." Dumple, turned loose, walked to his own stable-door, and there pawed and whinnied for admission, in strains which were answered by his acquaintances from the interior. Amid this bustle, Brown was fain to secure Wasp from the other dogs, who, with ardour corresponding more to their own names than to the hospitable temper of their owner, were much disposed to use the intruder roughly.

In about a minute a stout labourer was patting Dumple, and introducing him into the stable, while Mrs Dinmont, a well-looked buxom dame, welcomed her husband with unfeigned rapture. "Eh, sirs! goodman, ye hae been a weary while away!"

Chapter Three

Liddell till now, except in Doric lays
Tuned to her murmurs by her love-sick swains,
Unknown in song—though not a purer stream
Rolls towards the western main.
Art of Preserving Health

THE PRESENT STORE-FARMERS of the south of Scotland are a much more refined race than their fathers, and the manners I am now to describe have either altogether disappeared, or are greatly modified. Without losing their rural simplicity of manners, they now cultivate arts unknown to the former generation, not only in the progressive improvement of their possessions, but in all the comforts of life. Their houses are more commodious, their habits of life regulated so as better to keep pace with those of the civilized world, and the best of luxuries, the luxury of knowledge, has gained much ground among their hills during the last thirty years. Deep drinking, formerly their greatest failing, is now fast losing ground; and, while the frankness of their extensive hospitality continues the same, it is, generally speaking, refined in its character, and restrained in its excesses.

"Deil's in the wife," said Dandie Dinmont, shaking off his spouse's embrace, but gently and with a look of great affection; "deil's in ye, Ailie—d'ye no see the stranger gentleman?"

Ailie turned to make her apology—"Troth I was sae weel pleased to see the gudeman, that—But, good gracious, what's the matter wi' ye baith!"—for they were now in her little parlour, and the candle showed the streaks of blood which Dinmont's wounded head had plentifully imparted to the clothes of his companion as well as to his own. "Ye've been fighting again, Dandie, wi' some of the Bewcastle horse-coupers—Wow, man, a married man, wi' a bonny bairn-time like yours, should ken better what a father's life's worth."—The tears stood in the good woman's eyes as she spoke.

"Whisht! whisht! gudewife," said her husband, with a smack that had much more affection than ceremony in it, "Never mind—never mind—I have not been roving this time. There's a gentleman that will tell you, that just when I had ga'en up to Lowrie Lowther's, and had biddin the drinking of twa cheerers, and gotten just in again upon the moss, and was whigging cannily awa hame, twa land-loupers jumpit out of a peat-hag on me or I was aware, and got me down, and knevelled me sair aneuch, or I could gar my whip walk about their lugs—and troth, guid wife, if this honest gentleman had na come up, I would have gotten mair licks than I like, and lost mair siller than I could weel spare; so you maun be thankful to him for it, under God." With that he drew from his side-pocket a large greasy leather pocket-book, and bade the gudewife lock it up in the kist.

"God bless the gentleman, and e'en God bless him wi' a' my heart—but what can we do for him, but to give him the meat and quarters we wadna refuse to the poorest body on earth—unless (her eye directed to the pocket-book, but with a feeling of natural propriety which made the inference the most delicate possible,) unless there was ony other way"——Brown saw, and estimated at its due rate, the mixture of simplicity and grateful generosity which took the downright way of expressing itself, yet qualified with so much delicacy; he was aware his own appearance, plain at best, and now torn and spattered with blood, made him an object of pity at least, and perhaps of charity. He hastened to say his name was Brown, a captain in the —— regiment of cavalry, travelling for pleasure, and upon foot, both from motives of independence and economy; and he begged his kind landlady would look at her husband's wounds, the state of which he had refused to permit him to examine. Mrs Dinmont was used to her husband's broken heads more than to the presence of a captain of dragoons. She therefore glanced at a table cloth, not quite clean, and conned over her proposed supper about two moments, before, patting her husband on the shoulder, she bade him sit down for "a hard-headed loon, that was aye bringing himsell and other folks into collie-shangies."

When Dandie Dinmont, after executing two or three caprioles, and cutting the Highland-fling, by way of ridicule of his wife's anxiety, at last deigned to sit down, and commit his round, black, shaggy bullet of a head to her inspection, Brown thought he had seen the regimental surgeon look grave upon a more trifling case. The goodwife, however, showed some knowledge of chirurgery—she cut away with her scissars the gory locks, whose stiffened and coagulated clusters interfered with her operations, and clapped on the wound some lint, besmeared with a vulnerary salve, esteemed sovereign by the whole dale, (which afforded upon Fair nights considerable experience of such cases)—she then fixed her plaister with a bandage, and, spite of her patient's resistance, pulled over all a night-cap, to keep every thing in its right place. Some contusions on the brow and shoulders she fomented with a little brandy, which the patient did not permit till the medicine had paid a heavy toll to his mouth. Mrs Dinmont then simply, but cordially, offered her assistance to Brown.

He assured her he had no occasion for any thing but the accommodation of a bason and towel.

"And that's what I should have thought of sooner," she said, "but I durst na open the door, for there's a' the bairns, poor things, sae keen to see their father."

This explained a great drumming and whining at the door of the little parlour, which had somewhat surprised Brown, though his kind landlady had only noticed it by drawing the bolt as soon as she heard it begin. But on her opening the door to seek the bason and towel, (for she did not think of showing the guest a separate room), a whole tide of white-headed urchins streamed in, some from the stable, where they had been seeing Dumple, and giving him a welcome home with part of their four-hours scones; others from the kitchen, where they had been listening to auld Elspeth's tales and ballads; and the youngest half-naked, out of bed, all roaring to see daddy, and to enquire what he had brought home for them from the various fairs he had visited in his peregrinations. Our knight of the broken head first kissed and hugged them all round, then distributed whistles, penny-trumpets, and gingerbread, and, lastly, when the tumult of their joy and welcome got beyond bearing, exclaimed to his guest—"This is a' the gudewife's fault, captain—she will gie the bairns a' their ain way."

"Me! God help me," said Ailie, who at that instant entered with the bason and ewer, "how can I help it?—I have naething else to gie them, poor things!"

Dinmont then exerted himself, and, between coaxing, threats, and shoving, cleared the room of all the intruders, excepting a boy and girl, the two eldest of the family, who could, as he observed, behave themselves "distinctly." For the same reason, but with less ceremony, all the dogs were kicked out, excepting the venerable patriarchs, old Pepper and Mustard, whom frequent castigation and the advance of years had inspired with such a share of passive hospitality, that, after mutual explanation in the shape of some growling, they admitted Wasp, who had hitherto judged it safe to keep beneath his master's chair, to a share of a dried wedder's skin, which, with the wool uppermost and unshorn, served all the purposes of a Bristol hearth-rug.

The active bustle of the mistress (so she was called in the kitchen, and the gudewife in the parlour) had already signed the fate of a couple of fowls, which, for want of time to dress them otherwise, soon appeared reeking from the gridiron—or brander, as Mrs Dinmont denominated it. A huge piece of cold beef-ham, eggs, butter, cakes, and barley-meal bannocks in plenty, made up the entertainment, which was to be diluted with home-brewed ale of excellent quality, and a case-bottle of brandy. Few soldiers would find fault with such cheer after a day's hard exercise, and a skirmish to boot; accordingly Brown did great honour to the edibles. While the goodwife partly aided, partly instructed, a great stout servant girl, with cheeks as red as her topknot, to remove the supper matters, and supply sugar and hot water, (which, in her anxiety to gaze on an actual live captain, she was in some danger of forgetting,) Brown took an opportunity to ask his host, whether he did not repent of having neglected the gypsy's hint.

"Wha kens?" answered he; "they're queer devils;—maybe I might just have 'scaped ae gang to meet the other. And yet I'll no say that neither; for if that randy wife was coming to Charlieshope, she should have a pint bottle o' brandy and a pound o' tobacco to wear through her winter. They're queer devils, as my auld father used to say—they are warst where they are warst guided—there's baith gude and ill about the gypsies."

This, and some other desultory conversation, served as a "shoeing-horn" to draw on another cup of ale and another *cheerer*, as Dinmont termed it in his country phrase, of brandy and water. Brown then resolutely declined all farther conviviality for that evening, pleading his own weariness and the effects of the skirmish,—being well aware that it would have availed nothing to have remonstrated with his host on the danger that excess might have occasioned to his "raw wound and his bloody coxcomb." A very small bed-room, but a very clean bed, received the traveller, and the sheets made good the courteous vaunt of the hostess, "that they would be as pleasant as he could find ony gate, for they were washed wi' the fairy-well water, and bleached on the bonnie white gowans, and beetled by Nelly and hersell, and what could woman, if she was a queen, do mair for them?"

They indeed rivalled snow in whiteness, and had, besides, a

pleasant fragrance from the manner in which they had been bleached. Little Wasp, after licking his master's hand to ask leave, couched himself on the coverlet at his feet; and the traveller's senses were soon lost in grateful oblivion.

Chapter Four

> ——Give, ye Britons, then
> Your sportive fury, pitiless, to pour
> Loose on the nightly robber of the fold.
> Him, from his craggy winding haunts unearthed,
> Let all the thunder of the chace pursue.
>
> THOMSON'S *Seasons*

BROWN ROSE EARLY in the morning, and walked out to look at the establishment of his new friend. All was rough and neglected in the neighbourhood of the house;—a paltry garden, no pains taken to make the vicinity dry or comfortable, and all those little neatnesses which give the eye so much pleasure in looking at an English farm-house totally wanting. There were, notwithstanding, evident signs that this arose only from want of taste or ignorance, not from poverty, or the negligence which attends it. On the contrary, a noble cow-house, well filled with good milch-cows, a feeding-house, with ten bullocks of the most approved breed, a stable with two good teams of horses, the appearance of domestics active, industrious, and apparently contented with their lot; in a word, an air of liberal though sluttish plenty indicated the wealthy farmer. The situation of the house above the river formed a gentle declivity, which relieved the inhabitants of the nuisances which might otherwise have stagnated around them. At a little distance was the whole band of children, playing and building houses with peats around a huge doddered oak tree, which was called Charlie's-Bush, from some tradition respecting an old freebooter who had once inhabited the spot. Between the farm-house and the hill pasture was a deep morass, termed in that country a slack—it had once been the defence of a fortalice, of which no vestiges now remained, but which was said to have been inhabited by the same doughty hero we have above alluded to. Brown endeavoured to make some acquaintance with the children, but "the rogues fled from him like quicksilver"—though the two eldest stood peeping when they had got to some distance. The traveller then turned his course towards the hill, crossing the aforesaid swamp by a range of stepping-stones, neither the surest nor steadiest that could be imagined. He had not climbed far up the hill when he met a man descending.

He soon recognised his worthy host, though a *maud*, as it is called, or grey shepherd's plaid, supplied his travelling jockey coat, and a cap, faced with wild-cat's fur, more commodiously covered his bandaged head than a hat would have done. As he appeared through the morning's mist, Brown, accustomed to judge of men by their thewes and sinews, could not help admiring his height, the breadth of his shoulders, and the steady firmness of his step. Dinmont internally paid the same compliment to Brown, whose athletic form he now perused somewhat more at leisure than he had done formerly. After the usual greetings of the morning, the guest enquired whether his host found any inconvenient consequences from the last night's affray.

"I had almost forgot," said the hardy Borderer, "but I think this morning, now that I am fresh and sober, if you and I were at the Withershins-latch, wi' ilk ane a gude oak souple in his hand, we wald not turn back, no for half a dozen o' yon scaff-raff."

"But are you prudent, my good sir, not to take an hour or two's repose after receiving such severe contusions?"

"Confusions! L—d, Captain, naething confuses my head—I anes jumped up and laid the dogs on the fox after I had tumbled from the tap o' Christenbury Craig, and that might have confused me to purpose. Na, na, naething confuses me, unless it be a screed o' drink at an orra time. Besides, I behooved to be round the hirsel this morning, and see how the herds were coming on—they're apt to be negligent wi' their foot-balls, and fairs, and trysts, when ane's away. And there I met wi' Tam o' Todshaw, and a whin of the rest of the billies on the water side; they're a' for a fox-hunt this morning,—ye'll gang? I'll gie you Dumple, and take the brood mare mysell."

"But I fear I must leave you, Mr Dinmont."

"The fiend a bit o' that—I'll no part wi' you at ony rate for a fortnight, man—we dinna meet sic friends as you on a Bewcastle moss every night."

Brown had not designed his journey should be a speedy one; he therefore readily compounded with this hearty invitation, by agreeing to pass a week at Charlieshope.

On their return to the house, where the goodwife presided over an ample breakfast, she heard news of the proposed fox-hunt, not indeed with approbation, but without alarm or surprise. "Ah Dand! ye're the auld man yet—naething will make you take warning till you're brought hame some day with your feet foremost."

"Tut, lass! ye ken yoursell I am never a prin the waur o' my rambles."

So saying, he exhorted Brown to be hasty in dispatching his

breakfast, as, "the frost having given way, the scent would lie this morning prime."

Out they sallied accordingly for Otterscope-scaurs, the farmer leading the way. They soon quitted the little valley, and involved themselves among hills as steep as they could be without being precipitous. The sides often presented gullies, down which, in winter season, or after heavy rain, the torrents descended with great fury. Some dappled mists still floated along the hills, the remnants of the morning clouds, for the frost had broken up with a smart shower. Through these fleecy screens were seen a hundred little temporary streamlets, or rills, descending from the sides of the mountains like silver threads. By small sheep-tracks along these steeps, over which Dinmont trotted with the most fearless confidence, they at length drew near the scene of sport, and began to see other men, both on horse and foot, making towards the place of rendezvous. Brown was puzzling himself to conceive how a fox-chase could take place among hills, where it was barely possible for a poney, accustomed to the ground, to trot along, but where, quitting the track for half a yard's breadth, the rider might be either bogged, or precipitated down the bank. His wonder was not diminished when he came to the place of action.

They had gradually ascended very high, and now found themselves on a mountain-ridge, overhanging a glen of great depth, but extremely narrow. Here the sportsmen had collected, with an apparatus which would have shocked a member of the Pychely Hunt; for, the object being the removal of a noxious and destructive animal, as well as the pleasures of the chase, poor Reynard was allowed much less fair play than when pursued in form through an open country. The strength of his habitation, however, and the nature of the ground by which it was surrounded on all sides, supplied what was wanting in the courtesy of his pursuers. The sides of the glen were broken banks of earth, and rocks of rotten stone, which sunk sheer down to the little winding stream below, affording here and there a tuft of scathed brush-wood, or a patch of furze. Along the edges of this ravine, which, as we have said, was very narrow, but of profound depth, the hunters on horse and foot ranked themselves; almost every farmer had with him at least a brace of large and fierce greyhounds, of the race of those deer-dogs which were formerly used in that country, but are now greatly lessened in size from being crossed with the common breed. The huntsman, a sort of provincial officer of the district, who receives a certain supply of meal, and a reward for every fox he destroys, was already at the bottom of the dell, whose echoes thundered to the chiding of two or three brace of fox-hounds. Terriers, including the whole generation of Pepper and Mustard, were also in attendance, having been sent forward under the care of a shepherd. Mongrel, whelp, and cur of low degree, filled up the burthen of the chorus. The spectators on the brink of the ravine, or glen, held their greyhounds in leash, in readiness to slip them at the fox, as soon as the activity of the party below should force him to abandon his cover.

The scene, though uncouth to the eye of a professed sportsman, had something in it wildly captivating. The shifting figures on the mountain ridge, having the sky for their back-ground, appeared to move in air. The dogs, impatient of their restraint, and maddened with the baying beneath, sprung here and there, and strained at the slips, which prevented them from joining their companions. Looking down, the view was equally striking. The thin mists were not totally dispersed in the glen, so that it was often through their gauzy medium that the eye strove to discover the motions of the hunters below. Sometimes a breath of wind made the scene visible, the blue rill glittering as it twined itself through its solitary and rude dell. They then could see the shepherds springing with fearless activity from one dangerous step to another, and cheering the dogs upon the scent, the whole so diminished by depth and distance, that they looked like pigmies. Again the mists close over them, and the only signs of their continued exertion are the halloos of the men, and the clamour of the hounds, ascending, as it were, out of the bowels of the earth. When the fox, thus persecuted from one strong-hold to another, was at length obliged to abandon his valley, and to break away for a more distant retreat, those who watched his motions from the top slipped their greyhounds, which, excelling the fox in swiftness, and equalling him in ferocity and spirit, soon brought the plunderer to his life's end.

In this way, without any attention to the ordinary rules and decorums of sport, but apparently as much to the gratification both of bipeds and quadrupeds as if all had been followed, four foxes were killed on this memorable morning; and even Brown himself, though he had seen the princely sports of India, and ridden an elephant a-hunting with the Nabob of Arcot, professed to have received a day's excellent amusement. When the sport was given up for the day, most of the sportsmen, according to the established hospitality of the country, went to dine at Charlieshope.

During their return homeward, Brown rode a little way beside the huntsman, and asked him some questions concerning the mode in which he exercised his profession. The man showed an unwillingness to meet his eye, and a disposition to be rid of his company and conversation, for which he could not easily account. He was a thin, dark, active fellow, well framed for the hardy profession which he exercised. But his face had not the frankness of the jolly hunter; he was down-looked, embarrassed, and avoided the eyes of those who looked hard at him. After some unimportant observations on the success of the day, Brown gave him a trifling gratuity, and rode on with his landlord. They found the goodwife prepared for their reception—the fold and the poultry-yard furnished the entertainment, and the kind and hearty welcome made amends for all deficiencies in elegance and fashion.

Chapter Five

The Elliots and Armstrongs did convene,
They were a gallant company!
Ballad of Johnnie Armstrong

WITHOUT NOTICING the occupations of an intervening day or two, which, as they consisted of the ordinary sylvan amusements of shooting and coursing, have nothing sufficiently interesting to detain the reader, we pass to one in some degree peculiar to Scotland, which may be called a sort of salmon-hunting. This chase, in which the fish is pursued and struck with barbed spears, or a sort of long-shafted trident, called a *waster*, is much practised at the mouth of the Esk, and in the other salmon rivers of Scotland. The sport is followed by day and night, most commonly in the latter, when the fish are discovered by means of torches, or fire-grates, filled with blazing fragments of tar-barrels, which shed a strong, though partial light upon the water. Upon the present occasion, the principal party were embarked in a crazy boat upon a part of the river which was enlarged and deepened by the restraint of a mill-wear, while others, like the ancient Bacchanals in their gambols, ran along the banks, brandishing their torches and spears, and pursuing the salmon, some of which endeavoured to escape up the stream, while others, shrouding themselves under roots of trees, fragments of stones, and large rocks, attempted to elude the researches of the fishermen. These the party in the boat detected by the slightest indication; the twinkling of a fin, or the rising of an air-bell, was sufficient to point out to these adroit spearmen in what direction to use their weapon.

The scene was inexpressibly animating to those accustomed to it; but as Brown was not practised to use the spear, he soon tired of making efforts, which were attended with no other consequences than jarring his arms against the rocks at the bottom of the river, upon which, instead of the devoted salmon, he often bestowed his blow. Nor did he relish, though he concealed feelings which would not have been understood, being quite so near the agonies of the expiring salmon, which lay flapping about in the boat, which they moistened with their blood. He therefore requested to be put ashore, and, from the top of a *heugh*, or broken bank, enjoyed the scene much more to his own satisfaction. Often he thought of his friend Dudley the artist, as he observed the effect produced by the strong red glare on the romantic banks under which the boat glided. Now the light diminished to a distant star that seemed to twinkle on the waters, like those which, according to the legends of the country, the water-kelpy sends for the purpose of indicating the watery grave of his victims. Then it advanced nearer, brightening and enlarging as it again approached, till the broad flickering flame rendered bank, and rock, and tree, visible as it passed, tinging them with its own red glare of dusky light, and resigning them gradually to darkness, or to pale moonlight, as it receded. By this light also were seen the figures in the boat, now holding high their weapons, now stooping to strike, now standing upright, bronzed by the same red glare, into a colour which might have befitted the regions of Pandæmonium.

Having amused himself for some time with these effects of light and shadow, Brown strolled homeward towards the farm-house, gazing in his way at the other persons engaged in the sport, two or three of whom generally kept together, one holding the torch, the others with their spears, ready to avail themselves of the light it afforded to strike their prey. As he observed one man struggling with a very weighty salmon which he had speared, but was unable completely to raise from the water, Brown advanced close to the bank to see the issue of his exertions. The man who held the torch in this instance was the huntsman, whose sulky demeanour Brown had already noticed with surprise—"Come here, sir! come here, sir! look at this ane! look at this ane! He turns up a side like a sow."—Such was the cry from the assistants when some of them observed Brown advancing.

"Ground the waster weel, man! ground the waster weel!—haud him down—you hae nae the pith of a cat!"—Such were the cries of advice and encouragement from those who were on the bank to the sportsman engaged with the salmon, who stood up to his middle in water, jingling among broken ice, struggling against the force of the fish and the strength of the current, and dubious in what manner he should attempt to secure his booty. As Brown came to the edge of the bank, he called out—"Hold up your torch, friend huntsman," for he had already distinguished his dusky features by the strong light cast upon it by the blaze—But the fellow no sooner heard his voice, and saw, or rather concluded it was Brown who approached him, than, instead of advancing his light, he let it drop, as if accidentally, in the water.

"The deil's in Gabriel"—said the spearman, as the fragments of glowing wood floated half-blazing, half-sparkling, but soon extinguished, down the stream—"the deil's in the man—I'll never master him without the light—and a braver kipper, could I but land him, never reisted abune a pair o' cleeks."—Some dashed into the water to lend their assistance, and the fish, which was afterwards found to weigh nearly thirty pounds, was landed in safety.

The behaviour of the huntsman struck Brown, although he had no recollection of his face, nor could conceive why he should, as it appeared he evidently did, shun his observation—Could he be one of the footpads he had encountered a few days before?—the supposition was not altogether improbable, although unwarranted by any observation he was able to make upon the man's figure and face. To be sure the villains wore their hats much slouched, had loose coats, and their size was not in any way so peculiarly discriminated as to enable him to resort to that criterion. He resolved to speak to his host Dinmont on the subject, but for obvious reasons concluded it were best defer the explanation until a cool hour in the morning.

The sportsmen returned loaded with fish, upwards of one hundred salmon having been killed within the range of their sport. The best were selected for the use of the principal farmers, the others divided among their shepherds, cottars, dependants, and others of the inferior rank who attended. These fish, dried in the turf smoke of their cabins, or shealings, formed a savoury addition to the mess of potatoes, mixed with onions, which were the principal part of their winter food. In the meanwhile there was a liberal distribution of ale and whiskey among them, besides what was called a kettle of fish,—two or three large salmon, namely, plunged into a cauldron, and boiled for their supper. Brown accompanied his jolly landlord and the rest of his friends into the large and smoky kitchen, where this savoury mess reeked on an oaken table, massy enough to have dined Johnnie Armstrong and his merry-men. All was hearty cheer and huzza, and jest and clamorous laughter, and bragging alternately, and raillery between whiles. Our traveller looked earnestly around for the dark countenance of the fox-hunter, but it was no where to be seen.

At length he hazarded a question concerning him. "That was an awkward accident, my lads, of one of you, who dropped his torch in the water when his companion was struggling with the large fish."

"Awkward!" returned a shepherd looking up, (the same stout young fellow had speared the salmon) he deserved his paiks for't—to put out the light when the fish was on ane's witters!—I'm weel convinced Gabriel dropped the *roughies* in the water on purpose—he does na like to see ony body do a thing better than himsell."

"Aye," said another, "he's sair shamed o' himsell, else he would have been up here the night—Gabriel likes a little o' the gude thing as weel as ony o' us."

"Is he of this country?" said Brown.

"Na, na, he's been but shortly in office, but he's a fell hunter—he's frae down the country, some gate on the Dumfries side."

"And what's his name, pray?"

"Gabriel."

"But Gabriel what?"

"Oh, Lord kens that; we dinna mind folks after-names mickle here, they run sae much into clans."

"Ye see, sir," said an old shepherd, rising, and speaking very slow—"the folks hereabout are a' Armstrongs and Elliots, and sick like—twa or three given names—and so, for distinction's sake, the lairds and farmers have the names of their places that they live at—as for example, Tam o' Todshaw, Will o' the Flat, Hobbie o' Sorbietrees, and our good master here o' the Charlieshope—Aweel, sir, and than the inferior sort o' people, ye'll observe, are kend by sorts o' bye-names some o' them, as Glaikit Christie, and the Dewke's Gibbie, or may be, like this lad Gabriel, by his employment, as for example, Tod Gabbie, or Hunter Gabbie. He's no been lang here, sir, and I dinna think ony body kens him by ony other name—But it's no right to rin him down ahint his back, for he's a fell fox-hunter, though he's may be no sae clever as some o' the folk here awa wi' the waster."

After some further desultory conversation, the superior sportsmen retired to conclude the evening after their own manner, leaving the others to enjoy their mirth unawed by their presence. That evening, like all those which Brown had passed at Charlieshope, was spent in much innocent mirth and conviviality. The latter might have approached to the verge of riot but for the good women; for several of the neighbouring *mistresses* (a phrase of a signification how different from what it bears in more fashionable life!) had assembled at Charlieshope to witness the event of this memorable evening. Finding the punch-bowl was so often replenished, that there was some danger of their gracious presence being forgotten, they rushed in valorously upon the recreant revellers, headed by our good mistress Ailie, so that Venus speedily routed Bacchus. The fiddler and piper next made their appearance, and the best part of the night was gallantly consumed in dancing to their music.

An otter-hunt the next day, and a badger-baiting the day after, consumed the time merrily.—I hope our traveller will not sink in the reader's estimation, sportsman though he may be, when I inform him, that upon this last occasion, after young Pepper had lost a fore-foot, and Mustard the second had been nearly throttled, he begged as a particular and personal favour of Mr Dinmont, that the poor badger, who had made so gallant a defence, should be permitted to retire to his earth without farther molestation. The farmer, who would probably have treated this request with supreme contempt, had it come from any other person, was contented, in Brown's case, to express the utter extremity of his wonder.—"Weel," he said, "that's queer aneugh!—But since ye take his part, deil a tyke shall meddle wi' him mair in my day—we'll e'en mark him, and ca' him the Captain's Brock—and I am glad I can do ony thing to oblige you—but, Lord safe us, to care about a brock!"

After a week spent in rural sport, and distinguished by the most frank attentions on the part of his honest landlord, Brown bade adieu to the banks of the Liddel, and the hospitality of Charlieshope. The children, with all of whom he had now become an intimate and a favourite, roared manfully in full chorus at his departure, and he was obliged to promise twenty times that he would soon return and play over all their favourite tunes upon the flageolet till they had got them by heart—"Come back, captain," said one little sturdy fellow, "and Jenny will be your wife."—Jenny was about eleven years old—she ran and hid herself behind her mammy.

"Captain, come back," said a little fat roll-about girl of six, holding her mouth to be kissed, "and I'll be your wife my ain sell."

They must be of harder mould than I who could part from so many kind hearts with indifference. The good dame too, with matron modesty, and an affectionate simplicity that marked the olden time, offered her cheek to the departing guest—"It's little the like of us can do," she said, "little indeed—but yet—if there were but ony thing——"

"Now, my dear Mrs Dinmont, you embolden me to make a request—would you but have the kindness to give me, or work me, just such a grey plaid as the goodman wears?"—He had learned the language and feelings of the country even during the short time of his residence, and was aware of the pleasure the request would confer.

"A tait o' woo' would be scarce amang us," said the goodwife brightening, "if you should nae hae that, and as good a tweel as ever came aff a pirn. I'll speak to Johnnie Goodsire, the weaver at the Castletown, the morn.—Fare ye weel, sir;—and may ye be just as happy yoursell as ye like to see a' body else—and that would be a sair wish to some folk."

I must not omit to mention, that our traveller left his trusty attendant Wasp to be a guest at Charlieshope for a season. He foresaw that he might prove a troublesome attendant in the event of his being in any situation where secrecy and concealment might be necessary. He was therefore consigned to the care of the eldest boy, who promised, in the words of the old song, that he should have

> A bit of his supper, a bit of his bed,

and that he should be engaged in none of those perilous pastimes in which the race of Mustard and Pepper had suffered frequent mutilation. Brown now prepared for his journey, having taken a temporary farewell of his trusty little companion.

There is an odd prejudice in these hills in favour of riding. Every farmer rides well, and rides the whole day. Probably the extent of their large pasture farms, and the necessity of surveying them rapidly, first introduced this custom; or a very zealous antiquary might derive it from the times of the Lay of the Last Minstrel, when twenty thousand assembled at the light of the beacon-fires. But the truth is undeniable; they like to be on horseback, and can be with difficulty convinced, that any one chuses walking from other motives than those of convenience or necessity. Accordingly Dinmont insisted upon mounting his guest, and accompanying him upon horseback as far as the nearest town in Dumfries-shire, where he had directed his baggage to be sent, and from which he proposed to pursue his intended journey towards Woodbourne, the residence of Julia Mannering.

Upon the way he questioned his companion concerning the character of the fox-hunter; but gained little information, as he had been called to that office while Dinmont was making the rounds of the Highland fairs. "He was a shake-rag like fellow," he said, "and he dared to say, had gypsy blood in his veins—but at ony rate he was na ane of the smaiks that had been on their quarters in the moss—he wad ken them weel if he saw them again.—There were some no bad folk amang the gypsies too, to be such a gang—if ever I see that auld randle-tree of a wife again, I'll gie her something to buy tobacco—I have a great notion she meant me very fair after a'."

When they were about finally to part, the good farmer held Brown long by the hand, and at length said, "Captain, the woo's sae weel up the year, that it's paid a' the rent, and we have naething to do wi' the rest o' the siller, when Ailie has had her new gown, and the bairns their bits o' duds—now I was thinking of some safe hand to put it into, for it's ower muckle to ware on brandy and sugar—now I have heard that you army gentlemen can sometimes buy yoursells up a step, and if a hundred or twa would help ye on such an occasion, the bit scrape o' your pen would be as good to me as the siller, and ye might just take ye're ain time of settling it—it wad be a great convenience to me."

Brown, who felt the full delicacy that wished to disguise the conferring an obligation under the show of asking a favour, thanked his grateful friend most heartily, and assured him he would have recourse to his purse, without scruple, should circumstances ever render it convenient for him. And thus they parted with many expressions of mutual regard.

Chapter Six

If thou hast any love of mercy in thee,
Turn me upon my face that I may die.
JOANNA BAILLIE

OUR TRAVELLER hired a post-chaise at the town where he separated from Dinmont, with the purpose of proceeding to Kippletringan, there to enquire into the state of the family at Woodbourne, before he should venture to make his presence in the country known to Miss Mannering. The stage was a long one of eighteen or twenty miles, and the road lay across the country. To add to the inconveniences of the journey, the snow began to fall pretty quickly. The postillion, however, proceeded upon his journey for a good many miles, without expressing doubt or hesitation. It was not until the night was completely set in that he intimated his doubts whether he were in the right road. The increasing snow rendered this intimation trebly alarming, for as it drove full in the lad's face, and lay whitening all around him, it served in two different ways to confuse his knowledge of the country, and to diminish the chance of his recovering the right track. Brown then himself got out and looked round, not, it may be well imagined, from any better hope than that of seeing some house at which he might make enquiry. But none appeared—he could therefore only tell the lad to drive steadily on. The road on which they were, run through plantations of considerable extent and depth, and the traveller therefore conjectured that there must be a gentleman's house at no great distance. At length, after struggling wearily on for about a mile, the post-boy stopped, and protested his horses would not budge a foot farther; "but he saw," he said, "a light among the trees, which must proceed from a house; the only way was to enquire the road there." Accordingly he dismounted, heavily encumbered with a long great coat, and a pair of boots which might have rivalled in thickness the sevenfold shield of Ajax. As in this guise he was plodding forth upon his voyage of discovery, Brown's impatience prevailed, and, jumping out of the carriage, he desired the lad to stop where he was, by the horses, and he would himself go to the house—a command which the driver joyfully obeyed.

He groped along the side of the inclosure from which the light glimmered, in order to find some mode of approaching in that direction, and after proceeding for some space, at length found a stile in the hedge, and a pathway leading into the plantation, which in that place was of great extent. This promised to lead to the light which was the object of his search, and accordingly Brown proceeded in that direction, but soon totally lost sight of it among the trees. The path, which at first seemed broad, and well marked by the opening of the wood through which it winded, was now less easily distinguishable, although the whiteness of the snow afforded some reflected light to assist his search. Directing himself as much as possible through the more open parts of the plantation, he proceeded almost a mile without either recovering a view of the light, or seeing any thing resembling a habitation. Still, however, he thought it best to persevere in that direction. It must surely have been a light in the hut of a forester, for it shone too steadily to be the glimmer of an *ignis fatuus*. The ground at length became broken, and declined rapidly, and although Brown conceived he still moved along what had once at least been a path-way, it was now very unequal, and the snow concealing those breaches and inequalities, the traveller had one or two falls in consequence. He began now to think of turning back, especially as the falling snow, which his impatience had hitherto prevented his attending to, was coming on thicker and thicker.

Willing, however, to make a last effort, he still advanced a little way, when, to his great delight, he beheld the light opposite at no great distance, and apparently upon a level with him. He quickly found that this last appearance was deception, for the ground continued so rapidly to sink, as made it obvious there was a deep dell, or ravine of some kind, between him and the object of his search. Taking every precaution to preserve his footing, he continued to descend until he reached the bottom of a very steep and narrow glen, through which winded a small rivulet, whose course was then almost choked with snow. He next found himself embarrassed among the ruins of cottages, whose black gables, rendered more distinguishable by the contrast with the whitened surface from which they rose, were still standing; the side-walls had long since given way to time, and, piled in shapeless heaps, and covered with snow, offered frequent and embarrassing obstacles to our traveller's progress. Still, however, he persevered, crossed the rivulet, not without some trouble, and, by exertions which became at length both painful and perilous, ascended its opposite and very rugged bank, until he came on a level with the building from which the gleam proceeded.

It was difficult, especially by so imperfect light, to discover the nature of this edifice; but it seemed a square building of small size, the upper part of which was totally ruinous. It had, perhaps, been the abode, in former times, of some lesser proprietor, or a place of strength and concealment, in case of need, for one of greater importance. But only the lower vault remained, the arch of which formed the roof in the present state of the building. Brown first approached the place from whence the light proceeded, which proved to be a long narrow slit or loop-hole, such as are usually found in old castles. Impelled by curiosity to reconnoitre the interior of this strange place before he entered, Brown gazed in at this aperture. A scene of greater desolation could not well be imagined. There was a fire upon the floor, the smoke of which, after circling through the apartment, escaped by a hole broken in the arch above. The walls, seen by this smoky light, had the rude and waste appearance of a ruin of three centuries at least. A cask or two, with some broken boxes and packages, lay about the place in confusion. But the inmates chiefly occupied Brown's attention. Upon a lair composed of straw, with a blanket stretched over it, lay a figure, so still, that, except that it was not dressed in the ordinary habiliments of the grave, Brown would have concluded it to be a corpse. On a steadier view he was satisfied it was only on the point of becoming so, for he heard one or two of those low, deep, and hard-drawn sighs, that precede dissolution when the frame is tenacious of life. A female figure, dressed in a long cloak, sat on a stone by this miserable couch; her elbows rested upon her knees, and her face, averted from the light of an iron lamp placed beside her, was bent upon that of the dying person. She moistened his mouth from time to time with some liquid, and between whiles sung, in a low monotonous cadence, one of those prayers, or rather spells, which, in some parts of Scotland, and the north of England, are used by the vulgar and ignorant to speed the passage of a parting spirit, like the tolling of the bell in catholic days. She accompanied this dismal sound with a slow rocking motion of her body to and fro, as if to keep time with her song. The words ran nearly thus:—

Wasted, weary, wherefore stay,
Wrestling thus with earth and clay?
From the body pass away;—
Hark! the mass is singing.

From thee doff thy mortal weed,
Mary Mother be thy speed,
Saints to help thee at thy need;—
Hark! the knell is ringing.

Fear not snow-drift driving fast,
Sleet, or hail, or levin blast;

Soon the shroud shall lap thee fast,
And the sleep be on thee cast
That shall ne'er know waking.

Haste thee, haste thee, to be gone,
Earth flits fast, and time draws on,—
Gasp thy gasp, and groan thy groan,
Day is near the breaking.

The songstress paused, and was answered by one or two deep and hollow groans, that seemed to proceed from the very agony of the mortal strife—"It will not be," she muttered to herself—"He cannot pass away with that on his mind—it tethers him here—

Heaven cannot abide it,
Earth refuses to hide it.

"I must open the door;" and, rising, she paced towards the door of the apartment, observing heedfully not to turn back her head, and, withdrawing a bolt or two, (for, notwithstanding the miserable appearance of the place, the door was cautiously secured) she lifted the latch,

"Open lock—end strife,
Come death, and pass life."

Brown, who had by this time moved from his post, stood before her as she opened the door. She stepped back a pace, and he entered, instantly recognising, but with no comfortable sensation, the same gypsy woman whom he had met in Bewcastle. She also knew him at once, and her attitude, figure, and the anxiety of her countenance, assumed the appearance of the well-disposed ogress of a fairy tale, warning a stranger not to enter the dangerous castle of her husband. The first words she spoke (holding up her hand in a reproving manner,) were, "Said I not to ye, Make not, meddle not?—Beware of the redding strake! you are come to no house o' fair-strae death."

So saying, she raised the lamp, and turned its light on the dying man, whose rude and harsh features were now convulsed with the last agony. A roll of linen about his head was stained with blood, which had soaked also through the blanket and the straw. It was, indeed, under no natural disease that the wretch was suffering. Brown started back from this horrible object, and, turning to the gypsy, exclaimed, "Wretched woman, who has done this?"

"They that were permitted," answered Meg Merrilies, while she scanned with a close and keen glance the features of the expiring man, —"He has had a sair struggle—but it's passing—I knew he would pass when you came in.—That was the death ruckle—he's dead."—Sounds were now heard at a distance as of voices.—"They are coming," said she to Brown, "you are a dead man if you had as mony lives as hairs." Brown eagerly looked round for some weapon of defence. There was none near. He then rushed to the door, with the intention of plunging among the trees, and making his escape by flight, from what he now esteemed a den of murderers, but Meg Merrilies held him by a masculine grasp. "Here," she said, "here—be still and you are safe—Stir not, whatever you see or hear, and nothing shall befall you."

Brown, in these desperate circumstances, remembered this woman's intimation formerly, and thought he had no chance of safety but in obeying her. She caused him to couch down among a parcel of straw on the opposite side of the apartment from the corpse, covered him carefully, and flung over him two or three old sacks which lay about the place. Anxious to observe what was to happen, Brown arranged as softly as he could the means of peeping from under the coverings by which he was hidden, and awaited with a throbbing heart the issue of this strange and most unpleasant adventure. The old gypsy, in the mean time, set about arranging the dead body, composing its limbs, and straiting the arms by its side. "Best to do this," she muttered, "ere he stiffen." She placed on the dead man's breast a trencher, with salt sprinkled upon it, set one candle at the head, and another at the feet of the body, and lighted both. Then she resumed her song, and awaited the approach of those whose voices had been heard without.

Brown was a soldier, and a brave one, but he was also a man, and at this moment his fears mastered his courage so completely, that the cold drops burst out from every pore. The idea of being dragged out of his miserable concealment by wretches, whose trade was that of midnight murder, without weapons or the slightest means of defence, except entreaties, which would be only their sport, and cries for help, which could never reach other ear than their own—his safety entrusted to the precarious compassion of a being associated with those felons, and whose trade of rapine and imposture must have hardened her against every human feeling——the bitterness of his emotions almost choaked him. He endeavoured to read in her withered and dark countenance, as the lamp threw its light upon her features, something that promised those feelings of compassion, which women, even in their most degraded state, can seldom altogether smother. There was no such touch of humanity about this woman. The interest, whatever it was, that determined her in his favour, arose not from the impulse of compassion, but from some internal, and probably capricious, association of feelings, to which he had no clew. It rested, perhaps, on a fancied likeness, such as Lady Macbeth found to her father in the sleeping monarch. Such were the reflections that passed in rapid succession through Brown's mind, as he gazed from his hiding-place upon this extraordinary personage. Meantime the gang did not yet approach, and he was almost prompted to resume his original intention of attempting an escape from the hut, and cursed internally his own irresolution, which had consented to his being cooped up where he had neither room for resistance or flight.

Meg Merrilies seemed equally on the watch. She bent her ear to every sound that whistled round the old walls. Then she turned again to the dead body, and found something new to arrange or alter in its position. "He's a bonny corpse," she muttered to herself, "and weel worth the streaking."—And in this dismal occupation she appeared to feel a sort of professional pleasure, entering slowly into all the sad minutiæ, as if with the skill and feelings of a connoisseur. A long dark-coloured sea-cloak, which she dragged out of a corner, was disposed for a pall. The face she left bare, after closing the mouth and eyes, and arranged the capes of the cloak so as to hide the bloody bandages, and give the body, as she muttered, "a mair decent appearance."

At once three or four men, equally ruffians in appearance and dress, rushed into the hut. "Meg, ye limb of Satan, how dare you leave the door open?" was the first salutation of the party.

"And wha ever heard of a door being barred when a man was in the dead-thraw?—how d'ye think the spirit was to get awa' through bolts and bars like thae?"

"Is he dead then," said one who went to the side of the couch to look at the body.

"Eye, eye—dead enough," said another—"but here's what shall give him a rousing like-wake." So saying, he fetched a keg of spirits from a corner, while Meg hastened to display pipes and tobacco. From the activity with which she undertook the task, Brown conceived good hope of her fidelity towards her guest. It was obvious that she wished to engage the ruffians in their debauch, to prevent the discovery which might take place, if, by accident, any one of them should approach too nearly the place of Brown's concealment.

Chapter Seven

Nor board nor garner own we now,
 Nor roof nor latched door,
Nor kind mate, bound, by holy vow,
 To bless a good man's store.
Noon lulls us in a gloomy den,
 And night is grown our day;
Uprouse ye then, my merry men!
 And use it as ye may.
JOANNA BAILLIE

BROWN COULD NOW reckon his foes—they were five in number; two of them were very powerful men, who appeared to be either real seamen, or mendicant strollers who assumed that character; the other three, an old man and two lads, were slighter made, and, from their black hair and dark complexions, seemed to belong to Meg's tribe. They passed from one to another the cup out of which they drank their spirits. "Here's to his good voyage!" said one of the seamen, drinking; "a squally night he's got, however, to drift through the sky in."

We omit here various execrations with which these honest gentlemen garnished their discourse, retaining only such of their expletives as are least offensive.

"'A does not mind wind and weather—'A has had many a north-easter in his day."

"He had his last yesterday," said the other gruffly, "and now old Meg may pray for his last fair wind, as she's often done before."

"I'll pray for nane o' him," said Meg, "nor for you neither, you randy dog. The times are sair altered since I was a kinchin-mort. Men were men then, and fought other in the open field, and there was nae milling in the darkmans. And the gentry had kind hearts, and would have given both lap and pannel to ony poor gypsy; and there was not one, from Johnnie Faa the upright man, to little Christie that was in the panniers, would cloyed a dud from them. But ye are a' altered from the good auld rules, and no wonder that you scour the cramp-ring, and trine to the cheat so ofter. Yes, you are a' altered—you'll eat the goodman's meat, drink his drink, sleep on the strammel in his barn, and break his house and cut his throat for his pains! There's blood on your hands too, ye dogs—more than ever came there by fair fighting. See how ye'll die then—lang it was ere he died—he strove, and strove sair, and could neither die nor live;—but you—half the country will see how ye'll grace the woodie."

The party set up a hoarse laugh at Meg's prophecy.

"What made you come back here?" said one of the gypsies, "you old beldam? could ye not have staid where you were, and spaed fortunes to the Cumberland flats?—Bing out and tour, ye old devil, and see nobody has scented; that's all you're good for now."

"Is that all I am good for now? I was good for mair than that in the great fight between our folk and Patrico Salmon's; if I had not helped you with these very fambles, (holding up her hands) Jean Baillie would have frummagem'd you, ye feckless do-little."

There was here another laugh at the expence of the hero who had received this amazonian assistance.

"Here, mother," said one of the sailors, "here's a cup of the right for you, and never mind that bully-huff."

Meg drank the spirits, and, withdrawing herself from further conversation, sate down before the spot where Brown lay hid, in such a posture that it would have been difficult for any one to have approached it without her rising. The men, however, shewed no disposition to disturb her.

They closed around the fire, and held deep consultation together; but the low tone in which they spoke, and the canting language which they used, prevented Brown understanding much of their conversation. He gathered in general, that they expressed great indignation against some individual. "He shall have his gruel," said one, and then whispered something very low into the ear of his comrade.

"I'll have nothing to do with that," said the other.

"Are you turned hen-hearted, Jack?"

"No, by G—, no more than yourself—but I won't—it was something like that stopped all the trade fifteen or twenty years ago—You have heard of the Loup!"

"I heard *him* (indicating the corpse by a jerk of his head) tell about that job—G—d, how he used to laugh when he shewed us how he fetched him off the perch!"

"But it did up the trade for one while."

"How should that be?"

"Why, the people got rusty about it, and would not deal, and they had bought so many brooms that"——

"Well, for all that, I think we should be down upon the fellow one of these darkmans, and let him get it well."

"But old Meg's asleep now," said another; "she grows a driveller, and is afraid of her shadow. She'll sing out, one of these odd-come-shortlies, if you don't look sharp."

"Never fear," said the old gypsy man; "Meg's true-bred; she's the last in the gang that will start—but she has some queer ways, and often cuts queer words."

With more of this gibberish, they continued the conversation, rendering it thus, even to each other, a dark obscure dialect, eked out by significant nods and signs, but never expressing distinctly, or in plain language, the subject on which it turned. At length one of them observing Meg was still fast asleep, or appeared to be so, desired one of the lads "to hand in the black Peter, that they might flick it open." The lad stepped to the door, and brought in a portmanteau, which Brown instantly recognised for his own. His thoughts immediately turned to the unfortunate lad he had left with the carriage. Had the ruffians murdered him? was the horrible idea that crossed his mind. The agony of his attention grew yet keener, and while the villains pulled out and admired the different articles of his clothes and linen, he eagerly listened for some indication that might intimate the fate of the postillion. But the ruffians were too much delighted with the prize, and too much busied in examining its contents, to enter into any details concerning the manner in which they had acquired it. The portmanteau contained various articles of apparel, a pair of pistols, a leathern case with a few papers and some money, &c. &c. At any other time it would have provoked Brown excessively to see the unceremonious manner in which the thieves shared his property, and made themselves merry at the expence of the owner. But the moment was too perilous to admit any thoughts but what had immediate reference to self-preservation.

After a sufficient scrutiny into the portmanteau, and an equitable division of its contents, the ruffians applied themselves more closely to the serious occupation of drinking, in which they spent the greater part of the night. Brown was for some time in great hopes that they would drink so deep as to render themselves insensible, when his escape would have been an easy matter. But their dangerous trade required precautions inconsistent with such unlimited indulgence, and they stopped short on this side of absolute intoxication. Three of them at length composed themselves to rest, while the fourth watched. He was relieved in this duty by one of the others, after a vigil of two hours. When the second watch had elapsed, the sentinel awaked the whole, who, to Brown's inexpressible relief, began to make some preparations as if for departure, bundling up the various articles which each had appropriated. Still, however, there remained something to be done. Two of them, after some rummaging, which not a little alarmed Brown, produced a mattock and shovel, another took a pick-axe from behind the straw on which the dead body was extended. With these implements they left the hut, but three, (and two of these were the seamen, both very strong men,) still remained in garrison.

After the space of about half an hour, one of those who had departed again returned, and whispered the others. They wrapped up the dead body in the sea-cloak which had served as a pall, and went out, bearing it along with them. The aged sybil then arose from her real or feigned slumbers. She first went to the door, as if for the purpose of watching the departure of her late inmates, then returned, and commanded Brown, in a low and stifled voice, to follow her instantly. He obeyed; but, on leaving the hut, he would willingly have repossessed himself of his money and papers at least, but this she prohibited in the most peremptory manner. It immediately occurred to him that the suspicion of having removed any thing, of which he might repossess himself, would fall upon this woman, by whom, in all probability, his life had been saved. He therefore immediately desisted from his attempt, contenting himself with seizing a cutlass, which one of the ruffians had flung aside among the straw. On his feet, and possessed with this weapon, he already found himself half delivered from the dangers which beset him. Still, however, he felt stiffened and cramped, both with the cold, and by the constrained and unaltered position which he had occupied all night. But as he followed the gypsy from the door of the hut, the fresh air of the morning, and the action of walking, restored circulation and activity to his benumbed limbs.

The pale light of a winter's morning was rendered more clear by the snow, which was lying all around, crisped by the influence of a severe frost. Brown cast a hasty glance at the landscape around him, that he might be able again to know the spot. The little tower, of which only a single vault remained, forming the dismal apartment in which he had spent this remarkable night, was perched on the very point of a projecting rock overhanging the rivulet. It was accessible only on one side, and that by a very difficult and rude path ascending from the ravine or glen below. On the other three sides the bank was precipitous, so that Brown had on the preceding evening escaped more dangers than one; for, if he had attempted to go round the building, which was once his purpose, he must have been dashed to pieces. The dell was so narrow that the trees met in some places from the opposite sides. They were now loaded with snow instead of leaves, and thus formed a sort of frozen canopy over the rivulet beneath, which was marked by its darker colour, as it soaked its way obscurely through wreaths of snow. In one place, where the glen was a little wider, leaving a small piece of flat ground between the rivulet and the bank, were situated the ruins of the hamlet in which Brown had been involved on the preceding evening. The ruined gables, the insides of which were japanned with turf smoke, looked yet blacker, contrasted with the patches of snow which had been driven against them by the wind, and with the drifts which lay around them.

Upon this wintry and dismal scene, Brown could only at present cast a very hasty glance; for his guide, after pausing an instant, as if to permit him to indulge his curiosity, strode hastily before him down the path which led into the glen. He observed, with some feelings of suspicion, that she chose a track already marked by several feet, which he could only suppose were those of the depredators who had spent the night in the vault. A moment's recollection, however, put his suspicions to rest. It was not to be thought that the woman, who might have delivered him up to her gang when in a state totally defenceless, would have suspended her supposed treachery until he was armed, and in the open air, and had so many better chances of defence or escape. He therefore followed his guide in confidence and silence. They crossed the small brook at the same place where it previously had been passed by those who had gone before. The foot-marks then proceeded through the ruined village, and from thence down the glen, which again narrowed to a ravine, after the small opening in which they were situated. But the gypsy no longer followed the same track; she turned aside, and led the way by a very rugged and uneven path up the bank which overhung the village. Although the snow in many places hid the pathway, and rendered the footing uncertain and unsafe, Meg proceeded with that firm and determined step which indicated an intimate knowledge of the ground she traversed. At length they gained the top of the bank, though by a passage so steep and intricate, that Brown, though convinced it was the same by which he had descended on the night before, was not a little surprised how he had accomplished the task without breaking his neck. Above the bank, the country opened wide and uninclosed for about a mile or two on the one hand, and on the other were thick plantations of considerable extent.

Meg, however, still led the way along the brink of the ravine out of which they had ascended, until she heard beneath the murmur of voices. She then pointed to a deep plantation of trees at some distance, —"The road to Kippletringan," she said, "is on the other side of these inclosures—Make the speed ye can; there's mair rests on your life than on other folk's.—But you hae lost all—Stay"——She fumbled in an immense pocket, from which she produced a greasy purse. "Many's the *awmous* your house has gi'en Meg and hers—and she has lived to pay it back in a small degree;"—and she placed the purse in his hand.

"The woman is insane," thought Brown; but it was no time to debate the point, for the sounds he heard in the ravine below probably proceeded from the banditti. "How shall I repay this money," he said, "or how acknowledge the kindness you have done me?"

"I hae twa boons to crave," answered the sybil, speaking low and hastily; "one, that you will never speak of what you have seen this night; the other, that you will not leave this country till you see me again, and that you leave word at the Gordon Arms where you are to be heard of; and when I next call for you, be it in church or market, at wedding or at burial, Sunday or Saturday, meal-time or fasting, that ye leave every thing else and come with me."

"Why, that will do you little good, mother."

"But 'twill do yoursell mickle, and that's what I'm thinking of.—I am not mad, although I have had enough to make me sae—I am not mad, nor doating, nor drunken—I know what I am asking, and I know it has been the will of God to preserve you in strange dangers, and that I shall be the instrument to set ye in your father's seat again.—Sae give me your promise, and mind that you owe your life to me this blessed night."

There's wildness in her manner, certainly, thought Brown, and yet it is more like the wildness of energy than of madness.

"Well, mother, since you do ask so useless and trifling a favour, you have my promise. It will at least give me an opportunity to repay your money with additions. You are an uncommon kind of a creditor, no doubt, but"——

"Away, away, then!" said she, waving her hand. "Think not about the gowd—it's a' your ain—but remember your promise, and do not dare to follow me or to look after me." So saying, she plunged again into the dell, and descended it with great agility, the icicles and snow-wreaths showering down after her as she disappeared.

Notwithstanding her prohibition, Brown endeavoured to gain some point of the bank, from which he could, unseen, gaze down into the glen; and with some difficulty, (for it must be conceived that the utmost caution was necessary,) he succeeded. The spot which he attained for this purpose was the point of a projecting rock, which rose precipitously from among the trees. By kneeling down among the snow, and stretching his head cautiously forward, he could observe what was going on in the bottom of the dell. He saw, as he expected, his companions of the last night, now joined by two or three others. They had cleared away the snow from the foot of the rock, and dug a deep pit, which was designed to serve the purpose of a grave. Around this they now stood, and lowered into it something wrapped in a naval cloak, which Brown instantly concluded to be the dead body of the man he had seen expire. They then stood silent for half a moment, as if under some touch of feeling for the loss of their companion. But if they experienced such, they did not long remain under its influence, for all hands went presently to work to fill up the grave; and Brown, perceiving that task would be soon ended, thought it best to take the gypsy woman's hint, and walk as fast as possible until he gained the shelter of the plantation.

Having arrived under cover of the trees, his first thought was on the gypsy's purse. He had accepted it without hesitation, though with something like a feeling of degradation, arising from the character of the person by whom he was thus accommodated. But it relieved him from a serious though temporary embarrassment. His money, excepting a very few shillings, was in his portfolio, and that was in possession of Meg's friends. Some time was necessary to write to his agent, or even to apply to his good host at Charlieshope, who would gladly have supplied him. In the mean time, he resolved to avail himself of Meg's subsidy, confident he would have a speedy opportunity of replacing it with a handsome reward. "It can be but a trifling sum," said he to himself, "and I dare say the good lady may have a share of my bank-notes to make amends."

With these reflections he opened the leathern-purse, expecting to find at most three or four guineas. But how much was he surprised to discover that it contained, besides a considerable quantity of gold pieces, of different coinages and various countries, the joint amount of which could not be short of a hundred pounds, several valuable rings and ornaments set with jewels, and, as appeared from the slight inspection he had time to give them, of very considerable value.

Brown was equally astonished and embarrassed by the circumstances in which he found himself, possessed, as he now seemed to be, of property to a much greater amount than his own, but which had been obtained in all probability by the same nefarious means through which he had himself been plundered. His first thought was to enquire out the nearest justice of peace, and to place in his hands the treasure of which he had thus unexpectedly become the depositary, telling, at the same time, his own remarkable story. But a moment's consideration brought several objections to this mode of procedure. In the first place, he should break his promise of silence, and was certain by that means to involve the safety, perhaps the life, of this woman, who had risked her own to preserve his, and who had voluntarily endowed him with this treasure,—a generosity which might thus become the means of her ruin. This was not to be thought of. Besides he was a stranger, and, for a time at least, disprovided of all means of establishing his own character and credit to the satisfaction of a stupid or obstinate country magistrate. "I will think over the matter more maturely," he said; "perhaps there may be a regiment quartered at the county-town, in which case my knowledge of the service, and acquaintance with many officers of the army, cannot fail to establish my situation and character by evidence, which a civil judge could not sufficiently estimate. And then I shall have the commanding officer's assistance in managing matters so as to screen this unhappy madwoman, whose mistake or prejudice has been so fortunate for me. A civil magistrate might think himself obliged to send out warrants for her at once, and the consequence in case of her being taken is pretty evident —No, she has been on honour with me if she were the devil, and I will be equally on honour with her—She shall have the privilege of a court-martial, where the point of honour can qualify strict law. Besides I may see her at this place, Kipple—Couple—what did she call it?—and then I can make restitution to her, and even let the law claim its own when it can secure her. In the meanwhile, however, I cut rather an awkward figure for one who has the honour to bear his majesty's commission, being little better than the receiver of stolen goods."

With these reflections, Brown took from the gypsy's treasure three or four guineas, for the purpose of his immediate expences, and tying up the rest in the purse which contained them, resolved not again to open it, until he could either restore it to her by whom it was given, or put it into the hands of some public functionary. He next thought of the cutlass, and his first impulse was to leave it in the plantation. But when he considered the risk of meeting with these ruffians, he could not resolve upon parting with his arms. His walking-dress, though plain, had so much of a military character as suited not amiss with his having such a weapon. Besides, though the custom of wearing swords by persons out of uniform had been gradually becoming antiquated, it was not yet so totally forgotten as to occasion any particular remark towards those who chose to adhere to it. Retaining, therefore, his weapon of defence, and placing the purse of the gypsy in a private pocket, our traveller strode gallantly on through the wood in search of the promised high-road.

Chapter Eight

All school day's friendship, childhood innocence,
We, Hermia, like two artificial gods,
Have with our needles created both one flower,
Both on one sampler, sitting on one cushion,
Both warbling of one song, both in one key,
As if our hands, our sides, voices, and minds,
Had been incorporate.

A Midsummer Night's Dream

Julia Mannering to Matilda Marchmont.

"HOW CAN YOU upbraid me, my dearest Matilda, with abatement in friendship or fluctuation in affection? Is it possible for me to forget that you are the chosen of my heart, in whose faithful bosom I have deposited every feeling which your poor Julia dares to acknowledge to herself? And you do me equal injustice in upbraiding me with exchanging your friendship for that of Lucy Bertram. I assure you she has not the materials I must seek for in a bosom confidante. She is a charming girl, to be sure, and I like her very much, and I confess our forenoon and evening engagements have left me less time for the exercise of my pen than our proposed regularity of correspondence demands. But she is totally devoid of elegant accomplishment, excepting the knowledge of French and Italian, which she acquired from the most grotesque monster you ever beheld, whom my father has engaged as a kind of librarian, and whom he patronizes, I believe, to show his defiance of the world's opinion. Colonel Mannering seems to have formed a determination, that nothing shall be considered as ridiculous, so long as it appertains to or is connected with him. I remember in India he had picked up somewhere a little mongrel cur, with bandy legs, a long back, and huge flapping ears. Of this uncouth creature he chose to make a favourite, in despite of all taste and opinion; and I remember one instance which he alleged, of what he called Brown's petulance, was, that he had criticized severely the crooked legs and drooping ears of Bingo. On my word, Matilda, I believe he nurses his high opinion of this most awkward of all pedants upon a similar principle. He seats the creature at table, where he pronounces a grace that sounds like the scream of the man in the square that used to cry mackarel, flings his meat down his throat by shovelsfull, like a person loading a cart, and without apparently the most distant perception of what he is swallowing,—then bleats forth another set of unnatural tones, by way of returning thanks, stalks from the room, and immerses himself among a parcel of huge worm-eaten folios that are as unfashionable as himself! I could endure the creature well enough, had I any body to laugh with; but Lucy Bertram, if I but verge on the border of a jest affecting this same Mr Sampson, (such is the horrid man's horrid name) looks so piteous, that it deprives me of all spirit to proceed, and my father knits his brow, flashes fire from his eye, bites his lip, and says something that is extremely rude and uncomfortable to my feelings.

"It was not of this creature, however, that I meant to speak to you—only that, being a good scholar in the modern, as well as the ancient languages, he has contrived to make Lucy Bertram mistress of the former, and she has only, I believe, to thank her own good sense or obstinacy, that the Greek, Latin, (and Hebrew, for aught I know,) were not added to her acquisitions. And thus she really has a great fund of information, and I assure you I am daily surprised at the power which she seems to possess of amusing herself by recalling and arranging the subjects of her former reading. We read together every morning, and I assure you I begin to like the Italian much better than when we were teased by that conceited animal *Cicipici*;—this is the way to spell his name, and not Chichipichi—you see I grow a connoisseur.

"But perhaps I like Miss Bertram more for the accomplishments she wants, than for the knowledge she possesses. She knows nothing of music whatever, and no more of dancing than is here common to the meanest peasants, who, by the way, dance with great zeal and spirit. So I am instructor in my turn, and she takes with great gratitude lessons from me upon the harpsichord, and I have even taught her some of La Pique's steps, and you know he thought me a promising scholar.

"In the evening papa often reads, and I assure you he is the best reader of poetry you ever heard—not like that actor, who made a kind of jumble between reading and acting, staring and bending his brow, and twisting his face, and gesticulating as if he were on the stage, and dressed out in all his costume. My father's manner is quite different—it is the reading of a gentleman who produces effect by feeling, taste, and inflection of voice, not by action or mummery. Lucy Bertram rides remarkably well, and I can now accompany her on horseback, having become emboldened by example. We walk also a good deal in spite of the cold—So upon the whole I have not quite so much time for writing as I used to have.

"Besides, my love, I must really use the apology of all stupid correspondents, that I have nothing to say. My hopes, my fears, my anxieties about Brown are of a less interesting cast, since I know that he is at liberty, and in health. Besides, I must own, I think that by this time the gentleman might have given me some intimation what he was doing. Our intercourse may be an imprudent one, but it is not very complimentary to me, that Mr Vanbeest Brown should be the first to discover that, and to break off in consequence. I can promise him that we would not differ much in opinion should that happen to be his, for I have sometimes thought I have behaved extremely foolishly in that matter. Yet I have so good an opinion of poor Brown, that I cannot but think there is something extraordinary in his silence.

"To return to Lucy Bertram—No, my dearest Matilda, she can never, never rival you in my regard, so that all your affectionate jealousy on that account is without foundation. She is, to be sure, a very pretty, a very sensible, a very affectionate girl, and I think there are few persons to whose consolatory friendship I could have recourse more freely in what are called the *real evils* of life. But then these so seldom come in one's way, and one wants a friend who will sympathize with distresses of sentiment, as well as with actual misfortunes. Heaven knows, and you know, my dear Matilda, that these diseases of the heart require the balm of sympathy and affection as much as those evils of a more obvious and determinate character. Now Lucy Bertram has nothing of this kindly sympathy—nothing at all, my dearest Matilda. Were I sick of a fever, she would sit up night after night to nurse me with the most unrepining patience; but with the fever of the heart, which my Matilda has soothed so often, she has no more sympathy than her old tutor. And yet what provokes me is, that the demure monkey actually has a lover of her own, and that their mutual affection (for mutual I take it to be) has a great deal of complicated and romantic interest. She was once, you must know, a great heiress, but was ruined by the prodigality of her father, and the villainy of a horrid man in whom he confided. And one of the prettiest young gentlemen in the country is attached to her, but as he is heir to a great estate, she discourages his addresses on account of the disproportion of their fortune.

"But with all these, moderation, and self-denial, and modesty, and so forth, Lucy is a sly girl—I am sure she loves young Hazelwood, and I am sure he has some guess of that, and would probably bring her to acknowledge it too, if my father or she would allow him an opportunity. But you must know the Colonel is always himself in the way to pay Miss Bertram those attentions which afford the best direct opportunities for a young gentleman in Hazelwood's situation. I would have my good papa take care that he does not himself pay the usual penalty of meddling folks. I assure you, if I were Hazelwood, I should look on his compliments, his bowings, his cloakings, his shawlings, and his handings, with some little suspicion; and truly I think Hazelwood does so too at some odd times. Then imagine what a silly figure your poor Julia makes upon such occasions! Here is my father making the agreeable to my friend; there is young Hazelwood watching every word of her lips, and every motion of her eye; and I have not the poor satisfaction of interesting a human being—not even the uncouth monster of a parson, for he also sits with his mouth open, and his huge goggling eyes fixed like those of a statue, admiring Mess Baartraam!

"All this makes me sometimes a little nervous, and sometimes a little mischievous. I was so provoked at my father and the lovers the other day for turning me completely out of their thoughts and society, that I began an attack upon Hazelwood, from which it was impossible for him, in common civility, to escape. He insensibly became warm in his defence—I assure you, Matilda, he is a very clever, as well as a very handsome young man, and I don't think I ever remember having seen him to the same advantage—when, behold, in the midst of our lively conversation, a very soft sigh from Miss Lucy reached my not ungratified ears. I was greatly too generous to prosecute my victory any farther, even if I had not been afraid of papa. Luckily for me he had at that moment got into a long description of the peculiar notions and manners of a certain tribe of Indians, who live far up the country, and was illustrating them by making drawings on Miss Bertram's work-patterns, three of which he utterly damaged, by introducing among the intricacies of the pattern his specimens of oriental costume. But I believe she thought as little of her own gown at the moment as of the India turbands and cummerbands. However, it was quite as well for me that he did not see all the merit of my little manœuvre, for he is as sharp-sighted as a hawk, and a sworn enemy to the slightest shade of coquetry.

"Well, Matilda, Hazelwood heard this same half-audible sigh, and instantly repented his temporary attentions to such an unworthy object as your Julia, and, with a very comical expression of consciousness, drew near to Lucy's work-table. He made some trifling observation, and her reply was one in which nothing but an ear as acute as that of a lover, or a curious observer, like myself, could have distinguished any thing more cold and dry than usual. But it conveyed reproof to the self-accusing hero, and he stood abashed accordingly. You will admit that I was called upon in generosity to act as mediator.—So I mingled in the conversation, in the quiet tone of an unobserving and uninterested third party, led them into their former habits of easy chat, and, after having served awhile as the channel of communication through which they chose to address each other, set them down to a pensive game at chess, and very dutifully went to teaze papa, who was still busied with his drawing. The chess-players, you must observe, were placed near the chimney beside a little work-table, which held the board and men, the Colonel, at some distance, with lights upon a library table,—for it is a large old-fashioned room, with several recesses, and hung with grim tapestry, representing what it might have puzzled the artist himself to explain.

"'Is chess a very interesting game, papa?'

"'I am told so,' without honouring me with his attention.

"'I should think so, from the attention Mr Hazelwood and Lucy are bestowing on it.'

"He raised his head hastily, and held his pencil suspended for an instant. Apparently he saw nothing that excited his suspicions, for he was resuming the folds of a Mahratta's turban in tranquillity, when I interrupted him with—'How old is Miss Bertram, papa?'

"'How should I know, Miss?—about your own age, I suppose.'

"'Older, I should think, papa. You are always telling me how much more gravely she goes through all the little honours of the tea-table—Lord, papa, what if you should give her a right to preside once and for ever!'

"'Julia, my dear, you are either a fool outright, or you are more disposed to make mischief than I have yet believed you.'

"'Oh, papa! put your best construction upon it—I would not be thought a fool for all the world.'

"'Then why do you talk like one?'

"'Lord, sir, I am sure there is nothing so foolish in what I said just now—every body knows you are a very handsome man,' (a smile was just visible) 'that is, for your time of life,' (the dawn was over-cast) 'which is far from being advanced, and I am sure I don't know why you should not please yourself if you have a mind—I am sure I am but a thoughtless girl, and if a graver companion could render you more happy'——

"There was a mixture of displeasure and grave affection in the manner in which my father took my hand, that was a severe reproof to me for trifling with his feelings. 'Julia,' he said, 'I bear with much of your petulance, because I think I have in some degree deserved it by neglecting to superintend your education sufficiently closely. Yet I would not have you give it the reins upon a subject so delicate. If you do not respect the feelings of your surviving parent towards the memory of her whom you have lost, attend at least to the sacred claims of misfortune; and observe, that the slightest hint of such a jest reaching Miss Bertram's ear, would at once induce her to renounce her present asylum, and go forth, without a protector, into a world she has already felt so unfriendly.'

"What could I say to this, Matilda?—I only cried heartily, begged pardon, and promised to be a good girl in future. And so here am I neutralized again, for I cannot, in honour, or common good nature, teaze poor Lucy by interfering with Hazelwood, although she has so little confidence in me; and neither can I, after this grave appeal, venture again upon such delicate ground with papa. So I burn little rolls of paper, and sketch Turks' heads upon visiting cards with the blackened end—I assure you I succeeded in making a superb Hyder-Ally last night—and I jingle on my unfortunate harpsichord, and begin at the end of a grave book and read it backward.—After all I begin to be very much vexed about Brown's silence. Had he been obliged to leave the country, I am sure he would at least have written to me—Can it be possible that my father can have intercepted his letters?—But no—that is contrary to all his principles—I don't think he would open a letter addressed to me to-night, to prevent my jumping out of window to-morrow—What an expression I have suffered to escape my pen! I should be ashamed of it, even to you, Matilda, and used in jest. But I need not take much merit for acting as I ought to do —This same Mr Vanbeest Brown is by no means so very ardent a lover as to hurry the object of his attachment into such inconsiderate steps. He gives one full time to reflect, that must be admitted. However, I will not blame him unheard, nor permit myself to doubt the manly firmness of his character which I have so often extolled to you. Were he capable of doubt, of fear, of the shadow of change, I should have little to regret.

"And why, you will say, when I expect such steady and unalterable constancy from a lover, why should I be anxious about what Hazelwood does, or to whom he offers his attentions?—I ask myself the question a hundred times a-day, and it only receives the very silly answer, that one don't like to be neglected altogether, though one would not encourage a serious infidelity.

"I write all these trifles, because you say that they amuse you, and yet I wonder how they should. I remember in our stolen voyages to the world of fiction, you always admired the grand and the romantic tales of knights, dwarfs, giants, and distressed damsels, soothsayers, visions, beckoning ghosts, and bloody hands,—whereas I was partial to the involved intrigues of private life, or at farthest, to so much only of the supernatural as is conferred by the agency of an eastern genie or a beneficent fairy. You would have loved to shape your course of life over the broad ocean with its dead calms and howling tempests, its tornadoes, and its billows mountain high, whereas I should like to trim my little pinnace to a brisk breeze in some inland lake or tranquil bay, when there was just difficulty of navigation sufficient to give interest and to require skill, without any great degree of danger. So that, upon the whole, Matilda, I think you should have had my father, with his pride of arms and of ancestry, his chivalrous point of honour, his high talents, and his abstruse and mystic studies—You should have had Lucy Bertram too for your friend, whose fathers, with names which alike defy memory and orthography, ruled over this romantic country, and whose birth took place, as I have been indistinctly informed, under circumstances of deep and peculiar interest—You should have, too, our residence surrounded by mountains, and our lonely walks to haunted ruins—And I should have, in exchange, the lawns and shrubs, and green-houses, and conservatories of Pine-park, with your good quiet indulgent aunt, her chapel in the morning, her nap after dinner, her hand at whist in the evening, not forgetting her fat coach-horses and fatter coachman. Take notice, however, that Brown is not included in this proposed barter of mine—his good humour, lively conversation, and open gallantry, suit my plan of life, as well as his athletic form, handsome features, and high spirit, would accord with a character of chivalry. So as we cannot change altogether out and out, I think we must e'en abide as we are."

Chapter Nine

> I renounce your defiance; if you parley so roughly I'll
> barricado my gates against you—Do you see yon bay
> window? Storm,—I care not, serving the good Duke
> of Norfolk.
>
> *Merry Devil of Edmonton*

Julia Mannering to Matilda Marchmont.

"I RISE from a sick-bed, my dearest Matilda, to communicate the strange and frightful scenes which have just passed. Alas! how little we ought to jest with futurity! I closed my letter to you in high spirits, with some flippant remarks on your taste for the romantic and the extraordinary in fictitious narrative. How little I expected to have had such events to record in the course of a few days! And to witness scenes of terror, or to contemplate them in description, is as different, my dearest Matilda, as to bend over the brink of a precipice holding by the frail tenure of a half-rooted shrub, or to admire the same precipice in the landscape of Salvator. But I will not anticipate my narrative.

"The first part of my story is frightful enough, though it had nothing to interest my feelings. You must know that this country is particularly favourable to the commerce of a set of desperate men from the Isle of Man, which is nearly opposite. These smugglers are numerous, resolute, and formidable, and have at different times become the dread of the neighbourhood, when any one has interfered with their contraband trade. The local magistrates, from timidity or worse motives, are become shy of acting against them, and impunity has rendered them equally daring and desperate. With all this, my father, a stranger in the land, and invested with no official authority, had, one would think, nothing to do. But it must be owned, that, as he himself expresses it, he was born when Mars was lord of his ascendant, and that strife and bloodshed find him out in circumstances and situations the most retired and pacific.

"About eleven o'clock on last Tuesday morning, while Hazelwood and my father were proposing to walk to a little lake about three miles distance, for the purpose of shooting wild-ducks, and while Lucy and I were busied with arranging our plan of work and study for the day, we were alarmed by the sound of horses' feet, advancing very fast up the avenue. The ground was hardened by a severe frost, which made the clatter of the hoofs sound yet louder and sharper. In a moment two or three armed men, mounted and each leading a spare horse loaded with packages, appeared on the lawn, and without keeping upon the road, which there makes a small sweep, they pushed right across the lawn for the door of the house. Their appearance was in the utmost degree hurried and disordered, and they frequently looked back like men who apprehended a close and deadly pursuit. My father and Hazelwood hurried to the front door to demand who they were, and what was their business. They were revenue officers, they stated, who had seized these horses, loaded with contraband articles, at a place about three miles off. But the smugglers had been reinforced, and were now pursuing them with the avowed purpose of recovering the goods, and putting to death the officers who had presumed to do their duty. The men said, that their horses being tired, and the pursuers gaining ground upon them, they had fled to Woodbourne, conceiving, that as my father had served the king, he would not refuse to protect the servants of government, when threatened to be murdered in the discharge of their duty.

"My father, to whom, in his enthusiastic feelings of military loyalty, even a dog would be of importance if he came in the king's name, gave prompt orders for securing the goods in the hall, arming the servants, and defending the house in case it should be necessary. Hazelwood seconded him with great spirit, and even the strange animal they call Sampson stalked out of his den and seized upon a fowling-piece, which my father had laid aside, to take what they call a rifle-gun, with which they shoot tygers, &c. in the East. The piece went off in the awkward hands of the poor parson, and very nearly shot one of the excisemen. At this unexpected and voluntary explosion of his weapon, the Dominie (such is his nickname) exclaimed 'prodigious!' which is his usual ejaculation when astonished. But no power could force the fright of a man to part with his discharged piece, so they were contented to let him retain it, with the precaution of trusting him with no ammunition. This (excepting the alarm occasioned by the report) escaped my notice at the time, you may easily believe; but in talking over the scene afterwards, Hazelwood made us very merry with the Dominie's ignorant but zealous valour.

"When my father had got every thing into proper order for defence, and his people stationed at the windows with their fire-arms, he wanted to order us out of danger—into the cellar, I believe—but we could not be prevailed upon to stir. Though terrified to death, I have so much of his own spirit, that I would look upon the danger which threatens us rather than hear it rage around me without knowing its nature or its progress. Lucy, looking as pale as a marble statue, and keeping her eyes fixed on Hazelwood, seemed not even to hear the prayers with which he conjured her to leave the front of the house. But, in truth, unless the hall-door should be forced, we were in little danger—the windows were almost blocked up with cushions and pillows, and, what the Dominie most lamented, with folio volumes, brought hastily from the library, leaving only spaces through which the defenders might fire upon the assailants.

"My father had now made his dispositions, and we sat in breathless expectation in the darkened apartment, the men remaining all silent upon their posts, in anxious contemplation probably of the approaching danger. My father, who was quite at home in such a scene, walked from one to another, and reiterated his orders, that no one should presume to fire until he gave the word. Hazelwood, who seemed to catch courage from his eye, acted as his aid-de-camp, and displayed the utmost alertness in bearing his directions from one place to another, and seeing them properly carried into execution. Our force, with the strangers included, might amount to about twelve men.

"At length the silence of this awful period of expectation was broken by a sound, which, at a distance, was like the rushing of a stream of water, but as it approached, we distinguished the thick-beating clang of a number of horses advancing very fast. I had arranged a loop-hole for myself, from which I could see the approach of our enemy. The noise increased and came nearer, and at length thirty horsemen and more rushed at once upon the lawn. You never saw such horrid wretches! Notwithstanding the severity of the season, they were most of them stripped to their shirts and trowsers, with silk handkerchiefs knotted about their heads, and all well armed with carbines, pistols, and cutlasses. I, who am a soldier's daughter, and accustomed to see war from my infancy, was never so terrified in my life as by the savage appearance of these ruffians, their horses reeking with the speed at which they had moved, and their furious exclamations of rage and disappointment when they saw themselves baulked of their prey. They paused, however, when they saw the preparations made to receive them, and appeared to hold a moment's consultation among themselves. At length, one of the party, his face blackened with gunpowder by way of disguise, came forward with a white handkerchief on the end of his carbine, and asked to speak with Colonel Mannering. My father, to my infinite terror, threw open a window near which he was posted, and demanded what he wanted. 'We want our goods which we have been robbed of by these sharks,' said the fellow; 'and our lieutenant bids me say, that if they are delivered, we'll go off for this bout without clearing scores with the rascals who took them; but if not, we'll burn the house, and have the heart's blood of every one in it;'—a threat which he repeated more than once, only graced by a fresh variety of imprecations, and the most horrid denunciations that cruelty could suggest.

"'And which is your lieutenant?' said my father in reply.

"'That gentleman upon the grey horse,' said the miscreant, 'with the red handkerchief bound about his brows.'

"'Then be pleased to tell that gentleman, that if he, and the scoundrels who are with him, do not ride off the lawn this instant, I will fire upon them without ceremony.' So saying, my father shut the window, and broke short the conference.

"The fellow no sooner regained his troop, than, with a loud hurra, or rather a savage yell, they fired a volley against our garrison. The glass of our windows was shattered in every direction, but the precautions already noticed saved the party within from suffering. Three such volleys were fired without a shot being returned from within. My father then observed them getting hatchets and crows, probably to assail the hall door, and called aloud, 'Let none fire but Hazelwood and I—Hazelwood, mark the ambassador.' He himself aimed at the man on the grey horse, who fell on receiving his shot. Hazelwood was equally successful. He shot the spokesman, who had dismounted, and was advanced with an axe in his hand. Their fall discouraged the rest, who began to turn round their horses; and a few shots fired at them soon sent them off, bearing along with them their slain or wounded companions, although we could not observe that they suffered any farther loss. Shortly after their retreat a party of soldiers made their appearance, to my infinite relief. These men were quartered at a village some miles distant, and had marched upon the first rumour of the skirmish. A part of them escorted the terrified revenue officers and their seizure to a neighbouring sea-port as a place of safety, and at my earnest request two or three files remained with us for this and the following day, for the security of the house from the vengeance of these banditti.

"Such, dearest Matilda, was my first alarm. I must not forget to add, that the ruffians left, at a cottage on the road-side, the man whose face was blackened with powder, apparently because he was unable to bear transportation. He died in about half an hour after. Upon examining the corpse, it proved to be that of a boor in the neighbourhood, a person notorious as a poacher and smuggler. We received many messages of congratulation from the neighbouring families, and it was generally allowed that a few such instances of spirited resistance would greatly check the presumption of these lawless men. My father distributed rewards among his servants, and praised Hazelwood's courage and coolness to the skies. Lucy and I came in for a share of applause, because we had stood fire with firmness, and had not disturbed him with screams or expostulations. As for the Dominie, my father took an opportunity of begging to exchange snuff-boxes with him. The honest gentleman was much flattered with the proposal, and extolled the beauty of his new box excessively. 'It looked,' he said, 'as weel as if it were real gold from Ophir'—Indeed it would be odd if it should not, being formed in fact of that very metal; but, to do this honest creature justice, I believe the knowledge of its real value would not enhance his sense of my father's kindness, supposing it, as he does, to be pinchbeck gilt. He has had a hard task replacing the folios which were used in the barricade, smoothing out the creases and dogs-ears, and repairing the other disasters they have sustained during their service in the fortification. He brought us some pieces of lead and bullets which these ponderous tomes had intercepted during the action, and which he had extracted with great care; and, were I in spirits, I could give you a comic account of his astonishment at the apathy with which we heard of the wounds and mutilation suffered by Thomas Aquinas, or the venerable Chrysostom. But I am not in spirits, and I have yet another and a more interesting incident to communicate. I feel, however, so much fatigued with my present exertion, that I cannot resume the pen till to-morrow. I will detain this letter, notwithstanding that you may feel any anxiety upon account of your own

"JULIA MANNERING."

Chapter Ten

Here's a good world! Knew you of this fair work?
King John

Julia Mannering to Matilda Marchmont.

"I MUST TAKE UP the thread of my story, my dearest Matilda, where I broke off yesterday.

"For two or three days we talked of nothing but our siege and its probable consequences, and dinned into my father's unwilling ears a proposal to go to Edinburgh, or at least to Dumfries, where there is remarkably good society, until the resentment of these outlaws should blow over. He answered with great composure, that he had no mind to have his landlord's house and his own property at Woodbourne destroyed; that, with our good leave, he had usually been esteemed competent to taking measures for the safety or protection of his family—that if he remained quiet at home, he conceived the welcome the villains had received was not of a nature to invite a second visit, but should he shew any signs of alarm, it would be the sure way to incur the very risk which we were afraid of. Heartened by his arguments, and by the extreme indifference with which he treated the supposed danger, we began to grow a little bolder, and to walk about as usual. Only the gentlemen were sometimes invited to take their guns when they attended us, and I observed that my father for several nights paid particular attention to having the house properly secured, and required his domestics to keep their arms in readiness in case of necessity.

"But three days ago chanced an occurrence, of a nature which alarmed me more by far than the attack of the smugglers.

"I told you there was a small lake at some distance from Woodbourne, where the gentlemen sometimes go to shoot wild-fowl. I happened at breakfast to say I should like to see this place in its present frozen state, occupied by skaters and curlers, as they call those who play a particular sort of game upon the ice. There is snow on the ground, but frozen so hard that I thought Lucy and I might venture to that distance, as the footpath leading there was well beaten by the repair of those who frequented it for pastime. Hazelwood instantly offered to attend us, and we stipulated that he should take his fowling-piece. He laughed a good deal at the idea of going a-shooting in the snow, but, to relieve our tremors, desired that a groom, who acts as game-keeper occasionally, should follow us with his gun. As for Colonel Mannering, he does not like crowds or sights of any kind where human figures make up the show, unless indeed it were a military review—So he declined the party.

"We set out unusually early, upon a fine frosty exhilarating morning, and we felt our minds, as well as our nerves, braced by the elasticity of the pure air. Our walk to the lake was delightful, or at least the difficulties were only such as diverted us, a slippery descent for instance, or a frozen ditch to cross, which made Hazelwood's assistance absolutely necessary. I don't think Lucy liked her walk the less for these occasional embarrassments—but what have I to do with her affairs?

"The scene upon the lake was beautiful. One side of it is bordered by a steep crag, from which hung a thousand enormous icicles all glittering in the sun; on the other side was a little wood, now exhibiting that fantastic appearance which the pine-trees present when their branches are loaded with snow. On the frozen bosom of the lake itself were a multitude of moving figures, some flitting along with the velocity of swallows, some sweeping in the most graceful circles, and others deeply interested in a less active pastime, crowding round the spot where the inhabitants of two rival parishes contended for the prize at curling,—an honour of no small importance, if we were to judge from the anxiety expressed both by the players and bye-standers. We walked round the little lake, supported by Hazelwood, who lent us each an arm. He spoke, poor fellow, with great kindness to old and young, and seemed deservingly popular among the assembled crowd. At length we thought of retiring.—

"Why do I mention these trivial occurrences?—not, heaven knows, from the interest I can now attach to them—but because, like a drowning man who catches at a brittle twig, I seize every apology for delaying the subsequent and dreadful part of my narrative. But it must be communicated—I must have the sympathy of at least one friend under this heart-rending calamity.—

"We were returning home by a foot-path, which led through a plantation of firs. Lucy had quitted Hazelwood's arm—it is only the plea of absolute necessity which reconciles her to accept his assistance. I still leaned upon his other arm. Lucy followed us close, and the servant was two or three paces behind us. Such was our position, when at once, and as if he had started out of the earth, Brown stood before us at a short turn of the road! He was very plainly, I might say, coarsely dressed, and his whole appearance had something in it wild and agitated. I screamed between surprise and terror—Hazelwood mistook the nature of my alarm, and, when Brown advanced towards me as if to speak, commanded him haughtily to stand back, and not to alarm the lady. Brown replied, with equal asperity, he had no occasion to take lessons from him how to behave to that or any other lady. I rather believe that Hazelwood, impressed with the idea that he belonged to the band of smugglers, and had some bad purpose in view, heard and understood him imperfectly. He snatched the gun from the servant, who had come up on a line with us, and pointing the muzzle at Brown, commanded him to stand off at his peril. My screams, for my terror prevented my finding articulate language, only hastened the catastrophe. Brown, thus menaced, sprung upon Hazelwood, grappled with him, and had nearly succeeded in wrenching the fowling-piece from his grasp, when the gun went off in the struggle, and the contents were lodged in Hazelwood's shoulder, who instantly fell. I saw no more, for the whole scene reeled before my eyes, and I fainted away. But, by Lucy's report, the unhappy perpetrator of this action gazed a moment on the scene before him, until her screams began to alarm the people upon the lake, several of whom now came in sight. He then bounded over a hedge, which divided the foot-path from the plantation, and has not since been heard of. The servant made no attempt to stop or secure him, and the report he made of the matter to those who came up to us, induced them rather to exercise their humanity in recalling me to life, than shew their courage by pursuing a desperado, described by the groom as a man of tremendous personal strength, and completely armed.

"Hazelwood was conveyed home, that is to Woodbourne, in safety —I trust his wound will prove in no respect dangerous, though he suffers much. But to Brown the consequences must be most disastrous. He is already the object of my father's resentment, and he has now incurred danger from the law of the country, as well as from the clamorous vengeance of the father of Hazelwood, who threatens to move heaven and earth against the author of his son's wound. How will he be able to shroud himself from the vindictive activity of the pursuit? how to defend himself, if taken, against the severity of laws which I am told may even affect his life? and how can I find means to warn him of his danger? Then poor Lucy's ill-concealed distress, occasioned by her lover's wound, is another source of remorse to me, and every thing round me appears to bear witness against that indiscretion which has occasioned this calamity.

"For two days I was very ill indeed. The news that Hazelwood was doing well, and that the person who had shot him was no where to be traced, only that for certain he was one of the leaders of the gang of smugglers, gave me some comfort. The suspicion and pursuit being directed towards those people, must naturally facilitate Brown's escape, and, I trust, has ensured it. But patroles of horse and foot traverse the country in all directions, and I am tortured by a thousand confused and unauthenticated rumours of arrests and discoveries.

"Meanwhile, my greatest source of comfort is the generous candour of Hazelwood, who persists in declaring, that with whatever intentions the person by whom he was wounded approached our party, he is convinced that the gun went off in the struggle by accident, and that the injury he received was undesigned. The groom, on the other hand, maintains that the piece was wrenched out of Hazelwood's hands, and deliberately pointed at his body, and Lucy inclines to the same opinion —I do not suspect them of intentional exaggeration, yet such is the fallacy of human testimony, for the unhappy shot was most unquestionably discharged unintentionally. Perhaps it would be the best way to confide the whole secret to Hazelwood—but he is very young, and I feel the utmost repugnance to communicate to him my folly. I once thought of disclosing the mystery to Lucy, and began by asking what she recollected of the person and features of the man whom we had so unfortunately met—but she ran out into such a horrid description of a hedge-ruffian, that I was deprived of all courage and disposition to own my attachment to him. I must say Miss Bertram is strangely biassed by her prepossessions, for there are few handsomer men than poor Brown. I had not seen him for a long time, and even in his strange and sudden apparition on this unhappy occasion, and under every disadvantage, his form seems to me, on reflection, improved in grace, and his features in expressive dignity.—Shall we ever meet again? —who can answer that question?—Write to me kindly, my dearest Matilda—but when did you otherwise?—yet, again, write to me soon, and write to me kindly. I am not in a situation to profit by advice or reproof, nor have I my usual spirits to parry them by raillery. I feel the terrors of a child, who has, in heedless sport, put in motion some powerful piece of machinery; and, while he beholds wheels revolving, chains clashing, and cylinders rolling around him, is equally astonished at the tremendous powers which his weak agency has called into action, and terrified for the consequences which he is compelled to await without the possibility of averting them.

"I must not omit to say that my father is very kind and affectionate. The alarm which we received forms a sufficient apology for my nervous complaints. My hopes are, that Brown has made his escape into the sister kingdom of England, or perhaps to Ireland, or the Isle of Man. In either case he may wait the issue of Hazelwood's wound in safety and with patience, for the communication of these countries with Scotland, for the purpose of justice, is not (thank Heaven) of an intimate nature. The consequences of his being apprehended would be terrible at this moment. I endeavour to strengthen my mind by arguing against the possibility of such a calamity. Alas! how soon have sorrows and fears, real as well as severe, followed the dull and tranquil state of existence at which so lately I was disposed to repine! But I will not oppress you any longer with my complaints. Adieu, my dearest Matilda!

"JULIA MANNERING."

Chapter Eleven

> A man may see how this world goes with no eyes.—
> Look with thine ears: See how yon justice rails upon
> yon simple thief. Hark in thine ear—Change places;
> and, handy-dandy, which is the justice, which is the
> thief?
>
> *King Lear*

AMONG THOSE who took the most lively interest in endeavouring to discover the person by whom young Charles Hazelwood had been way-laid and wounded, was Gilbert Glossin, Esquire, late writer in Kippletringan, now Laird of Ellangowan, and one of the worshipful commission of justices of the peace for the county of ——. His motives for exertion upon this occasion were manifold; but we presume our readers, from what they already know of this gentleman, will acquit him from being actuated by any zealous or intemperate love of abstract justice.

The truth was, that this respectable gentleman felt himself less at ease than he had expected, when his machinations put him into possession of his benefactor's estate. His reflections within doors, where so much occurred to remind him of former times, were not always the self-congratulations of successful stratagem. And when he looked abroad, he could not but be sensible that he was excluded from the society of the gentry of the country, to whose rank he conceived he had raised himself. He was not admitted to their clubs, and at meetings of a public nature found himself thwarted and looked upon with coldness and contempt. Both principle and prejudice co-operated in creating this dislike; for the gentlemen of the country despised him for the lowness of his birth, while they hated him for the means by which he had raised his fortune. With the common people his reputation stood still worse. They would neither yield him the territorial appellation of Ellangowan, nor the usual compliment of *Mr* Glossin;—with them he was bare Glossin, and so incredibly was his vanity interested by this trifling circumstance, that he was known to give half-a-crown to a beggar, because he had thrice called him Ellangowan, in beseeching him for a penny. He therefore felt acutely the general want of respect, and particularly when he contrasted his own character and reception in society with that of Mr Mac-Morlan, who, in far inferior worldly circumstances, was beloved and respected both by rich and poor, and was slowly but securely laying the foundation of a moderate fortune, with the general good-will and esteem of all who knew him.

Glossin, while he repined internally at what he would fain have called the prejudices and prepossessions of the country, was too wise to make any open complaint. He was sensible his elevation was too recent to be immediately forgiven, and the means by which he had attained it too odious to be soon forgotten. But time, thought he, diminishes wonder and palliates misconduct. With the dexterity, therefore, of one who had made his fortune by studying the weak points of human nature, he determined to lie bye for opportunities to make himself useful even to those who most disliked him; confiding that his own abilities, the disposition of country gentlemen to fall into quarrels where a lawyer's advice becomes precious, and a thousand other contingencies, of which, with patience and address, he doubted not to be able to avail himself, would soon place him in a more important and respectable light to his neighbours.

The attack upon Colonel Mannering's house, followed by the accident of Hazelwood's wound, appeared to Glossin a proper opportunity to impress upon the country at large the service which could be rendered by an active magistrate, (for he had been in the commission for some time) well acquainted with the law, and no less so with the haunts and habits of the illicit traders. He had acquired the latter kind of experience by a former close alliance with some of the most desperate smugglers, in consequence of which he had occasionally acted, sometimes as partner, sometimes as legal adviser, with these persons. But the connection had been dropped many years; nor, considering how short is the race of eminent characters of this description, and the frequent circumstances which occur to make them retire from particular scenes of action, had he the least reason to think that his present researches could possibly compromise any old friend who might possess means of retaliation. The having been concerned in these practices abstractedly, was a circumstance which, according to his opinion, ought in no respect to interfere with his now using his experience in behalf of the public, or rather to further his own private views. To acquire the good opinion and countenance of Colonel Mannering would be no small object to a gentleman who was much disposed to escape from Coventry; and to gain the favour of old Hazelwood, who was a leading man in the county, was of more importance still. Lastly, if he should succeed in discovering, apprehending, and convicting the culprits, he would have the satisfaction of mortifying, and in some degree disparaging, Mac-Morlan, to whom, as sheriff-substitute of the county, this sort of investigation properly belonged, and who would certainly suffer in public opinion, should the voluntary exertions of Glossin be more successful than his own.

Actuated by motives so stimulating, and well acquainted with the lower retainers of the law, Glossin set every spring in motion to detect and apprehend, if possible, some of the gang who had attacked Woodbourne, and more particularly the individual who had wounded Charles Hazelwood. He promised high rewards, he suggested various schemes, and used his personal interest among his old acquaintances who favoured the trade, urging that they had better make sacrifice of an understrapper or two than incur the odium of having favoured such atrocious proceedings. But for some time these exertions were all in vain. The common people of the country either favoured or feared the smugglers too much to afford any evidence against them. At length, this busy magistrate obtained information, that a man, having the dress and appearance of the person who had wounded Hazelwood, had lodged on the evening before the rencontre at the Gordon Arms in Kippletringan. Thither Mr Glossin immediately went, for the purpose of interrogating our old acquaintance Mrs Mac-Candlish.

The reader may remember that Mr Glossin did not, according to this good woman's phrase, stand high in her books. She therefore attended his summons to the parlour slowly and reluctantly, and, on entering the room, paid her respects in the driest possible manner. The dialogue then proceeded as follows:

"A fine frosty morning, Mrs Mac-Candlish."

"Aye, sir; the morning's weel aneuch."

"Mrs Mac-Candlish, I wish to know if the justices are to dine here as usual after the business of the court on Tuesday?"

"I believe—I fancy sae, sir—as usual"—(about to leave the room).

"Stay a moment, Mrs Mac-Candlish. Why, you are in an unco hurry, my good friend—I have been thinking a club dining here once a month would be a very pleasant thing."

"Certainly, sir; a club of *respectable* gentlemen."

"True, true, I mean landed proprietors and gentlemen of weight in the country; and I should like to set such a thing agoing."

The short dry cough with which Mrs Mac-Candlish received this proposal, by no means indicated any dislike to the overture abstractedly considered, but only much doubt how far it would succeed under the auspices of the gentleman by whom it was proposed. It was not a cough negative, but a cough dubious, and as such Glossin felt it; but it was not his cue to take offence.

"Have there been brisk doings on the road, Mrs Mac-Candlish? plenty of company, I suppose?"

"Pretty weel, sir—But I believe I am wanted at the bar."

"No, no,—stop one moment, cannot you, to oblige an old customer?—Pray do you remember a remarkably tall young man, who lodged one night in your house last week?"

"Troth, sir, I canna weel say—I never take heed whether my company be lang or short, if they make a lang bill."

"And if they do not, you can do that for them, eh, Mrs Mac-Candlish?—ha, ha, ha!—But this young man that I enquire after had a dark frock, with metal buttons, light-brown hair unpowdered, blue eyes, and a straight nose, travelled on foot, had no servant or baggage—you surely can remember having seen such a traveller?"

"Indeed, sir, I canna charge my memory about the matter—there's mair to do in a house like this, I trow, than to look after passengers' hair, or their e'en, or noses either."

"Then, Mrs Mac-Candlish, I must tell you in plain terms, that this person is suspected of having been guilty of a crime, and it is in consequence of these suspicions that I, as a magistrate, require this information from you,—and if you refuse to answer my questions, I must put you upon your oath."

"Troth, sir, I am no free to swear—we aye gaed to the Antiburgher meeting—it's very true, in Baillie Mac-Candlish's time, (honest man) we keepit the kirk, whilk was most seemly in his station, as having office—but after his being called to a better place than Kippletringan, I hae gaen back to worthy Maister Mac-Grainer—and so ye see, sir, I am no clear to swear without speaking to the minister—especially against ony sackless puir young thing that's ganging through the country stranger and freendless like."

"I shall relieve your scruples, perhaps, without troubling Mr Mac-Grainer, when I tell you that this fellow whom I enquire after is the man who shot your young friend Charles Hazelwood."

"Gudeness! wha could hae thought the like o' that o' him?—na, if it had been for debt, or e'en for a bit tuilzie wi' the gauger, the deil o' Nelly Mac-Candlish's tongue suld ever hae wranged him. But if he really shot young Hazelwood—But I canna think it, Mr Glossin; this will be some o' your skits now—I canna think it o' sae douce a lad;—na, na, this is just some o' your auld skits.—Ye'll be for having a horning or a caption after him?"

"I see you have no confidence in me, Mrs Mac-Candlish; but look at these declarations, signed by the persons who saw the crime committed, and judge yourself if the description of the ruffian be not that of your guest."

He put the papers into her hands, which she perused very carefully, often taking off her spectacles to cast her eyes up to Heaven, or perhaps to wipe a tear from them, for young Hazelwood was an especial favourite with the good dame. "Aweel, aweel!" said she, when she had concluded her examination, "since it's e'en sae, I gie him up, the villain—But O, we are erring mortals!—I never saw a face I liked better, or a lad that was mair douce and canny—I thought he had been some gentleman under trouble.—But I gie him up, the villain!—to shoot Charlie Hazelwood—and before the young ladies, poor innocent things!—I gie him up."

"So you admit, then, that such a person lodged here the night before this vile business."

"Troth did he, sir, and a' the house were ta'en wi' him, he was sick a frank pleasant young man. It was na for his spending I am sure, for he just had a mutton-chop, and a mug of ale, and may be a glass or twa o' wine—and I asked him to drink tea wi' mysell, and did na put that into the bill; and he took nae supper, for he said he was defeat wi' travel a' the night afore—I dare say now it had been on some hellicat errand or other."

"Did you by any chance learn his name?"

"I wot weel did I—for he said it was likely that an auld woman like a gypsy wife might be asking for him—Aye, aye! tell me your company, and I'll tell you wha ye are! O the villain!—Aweel, sir, when he gaed away in the morning he paid his bill very honestly, and gae something to the chamber-maid, nae doubt, for Grizy has naething frae me, bye twa pair o' new shoon ilka year, and may be a bit compliment at Hansel Monanday"—— Here Glossin found it necessary to interfere, and bring the good woman back to the point.

"Ow than, he just said, if there comes such a person to enquire after Mr Brown, you will say I am gone to look at the skaters on Loch Creeran, as you call it, and I will be back here to dinner—But he never came back—though I expected him sae faithfully, that I gae a look to making the friar's chicken mysell, and to the crappit-heads too, and that's what I dinna do for ordinary, Mr Glossin—But little did I think what skating wark he was ganging about—to shoot Mr Charles, the innocent lamb!"

Mr Glossin, having, like a prudent examinator, suffered his witness to give vent to all her surprise and indignation, now began to enquire whether the suspected person had left any property or papers about the inn.

"Troth, he put a parcel—a sma' parcel under my charge, and he gae me some siller, and desired me to get him half-a-dozen o' ruffled sarks, and Peg Pasley's in hands wi' them e'en now—they may serve him to gang up the Lawn-market in, the scoundrel!" Mr Glossin then demanded to see the packet, but here mine hostess demurred.

"She didna ken—she wad not say but justice should take its course—but when a thing was trusted to ane in her way, doubtless they were responsible—but she suld cry in Deacon Bearcliff, and if Mr Glossin liked to tak an inventar o' the property, and gie her a receipt before the Deacon—or, what she wad like muckle better, an it could be sealed up and left in Deacon Bearcliff's hands, it wad mak her mind easy—She was for naething but justice on a' sides."

Mrs Mac-Candlish's natural sagacity and acquired suspicion being inflexible, Glossin sent for Deacon Bearcliff, to speak "anent the villain that had shot Mr Charles Hazelwood." The Deacon accordingly made his appearance, with his wig awry, owing to the hurry with which, at this summons of the Justice, he had exchanged it for the Kilmarnock-cap in which he usually attended his customers. Mrs Mac-Candlish then produced the parcel deposited with her by Brown, in which was found the gypsy's purse. Upon perceiving the value of the miscellaneous contents, Mrs Mac-Candlish internally congratulated herself upon the precautions she had taken before delivering them up to Glossin, while he, with an appearance of disinterested candour, was the first to propose they should be properly inventoried and deposited with Deacon Bearcliff, until they should be sent to the Crown office. "He did not," he observed, "like to be personally responsible for articles which seemed of considerable value, and had doubtless been acquired by the most nefarious practices."

He then examined the paper in which the purse had been wrapt up. It was the back of a letter addressed to V. Brown, Esquire, but the rest of the address was torn away. The landlady, now as eager to throw light upon the criminal's escape as she had formerly been desirous of withholding it—for the miscellaneous contents of the purse argued strongly to her mind that all was not right—Mrs Mac-Candlish, I say, now gave Glossin to understand, that her postillion and ostler had both seen the stranger upon the ice that day when young Hazelwood was wounded.

Our readers' old acquaintance, Jock Jabos, was first summoned, and admitted frankly, that he had seen and conversed upon the ice that morning with a stranger, who, he understood, had lodged at the Gordon Arms the night before.

"What turn did your conversation take?" said Glossin.

"Turn?—ow, we turned nae gate at a', but just keepit straught forward upon the ice."

"Well, but what did ye speak about?"

"Ow, he just asked questions like ony ither stranger."

"But about what?"

"Ow, just about the folk that was playing at the curling, and about auld Jock Stevenson that was at the cock, and about the leddies, and sic like."

"What ladies? and what did he ask about them, Jock?"

"It was Miss Jowlia Mannering and Miss Lucy Bertram, that ye ken fu' weel yoursell, Mr Glossin—they were walking wi' the young Laird of Hazelwood upon the ice."

"And what did you tell him about them?"

"Tut, we just said that was Miss Lucy Bertram of Ellangowan, that should ance have had a great estate in the country—and that was Miss Jowlia Mannering, that was to be married to young Hazelwood—See as she was hinging on his arm—we just spoke about our country clashes like—he was a very frank man."

"Well, and what did he say in answer?"

"Ow, he just stared at the young leddies very keen like, and asked if it was for certain that the marriage was to be between Miss Mannering and young Hazelwood—and I answered him that it was for positive and undoubted certain, as I had an undoubted right to say sae—for my third cousin, Jean Claverse, (she's a relation o' your ain, Mr Glossin, you wad ken Jean lang syne?) she's sib to the housekeeper at Woodbourne, and she's tauld me mair nor ance that there was naething mair likely."

"And what did the stranger say when you told him all this?"

"Say? naething at a'—he just stared at them as they're walking round the loch upon the ice, as if he could have eaten them, and he never took his e'e aff them or said another word, though there was the finest fun amang the curlers ever was seen—and he turned round and gaed aff the loch by the kirk stile through Woodbourne fir-plantings, and we saw nae mair o' him."

"Only think," said Mrs Mac-Candlish, "what a hard heart he maun hae had, to think o' hurting the poor young gentleman before the leddy he was to be married to!"

"O, Mrs Mac-Candlish," said Glossin, "there's been mony cases such as that on the record—doubtless he was seeking revenge where it would be deepest and sweetest."

"God pity us!" said Deacon Bearcliff, "we're puir creatures when left to oursells!—Aye, he forgot wha said, 'Vengeance is mine, and I will repay it.'"

"Weel, aweel, sirs," said Jabos, whose hard-headed and uncultivated shrewdness seemed sometimes to start the game when others beat the bush—"Weel, weel, ye may be a' mista'en yet—I'll never believe that a man would lay a plan to shoot another wi' his ain gun. Lord help ye, I was the keeper's assistant down at the Isle mysell, and I'll uphad it, the biggest man in Scotland shouldna take a gun frae me or I had weized the slugs through him, though I'm but sic a little feckless body, fit for naething but the outside o' a saddle and the fore-end o' a poschay—na, na, nae living man wald venture on that. I'll wad my best buckskins, and they were new coft at Kirkcudbright fair, it's been a chance job after a'. But if ye hae naething mair to say to me, I am thinking I maun gang to see my beasts fed."—And he departed accordingly.

The ostler, who had accompanied him, gave evidence to the same purpose. He and Mrs Mac-Candlish were then re-interrogated, whether Brown had no arms with him on that unhappy morning. "None," they said, "but an ordinary bit cutlass or hanger by his side."

"Now," said the Deacon, taking Glossin by the button, (for, in considering this intricate subject, he had forgot Glossin's new accession of rank)—"this is but doubtfu' after a', Maister Gibbert—for it was not sae dooms likely that he would go down into battle wi' sick sma' means."

Glossin extricated himself from the Deacon's grasp, and from the discussion, though not with rudeness; for it was his present interest to buy golden opinions from all sorts of people. He enquired the price of tea and sugar, and spoke of providing himself for the year; he gave

Mrs Mac-Candlish directions to have a handsome entertainment in readiness for a party of five friends, whom he intended to invite to dine with him at the Gordon Arms next Saturday week; and, lastly, he gave a half-crown to Jock Jabos, whom the ostler had deputed to hold his steed.

"Weel," said the Deacon to Mrs Mac-Candlish, as he accepted her offer of a glass of bitters at the bar, "the deil's no sae ill as he's ca'd. It's pleasant to see a gentleman pay the regard to the business o' the county that Mr Glossin does."

"Nae question, Deacon," answered the landlady; "and yet I wonder our gentry leave their ain wark to the like o' him.—But as lang as siller's current, Deacon, folk manna look ower nicely at what king's head's on't."

"I doubt Glossin will prove but *shand* after a', mistress," said Jabos, as he passed through the little lobby beside the bar; "but this is a gude half-crown ony way."

Chapter Twelve

> A man that apprehends death to be no more dreadful
> but as a drunken sleep; careless, reckless, and fear-
> less of what's past, present, or to come; insensible of
> mortality, and desperately mortal.
>
> *Measure for Measure*

GLOSSIN had made careful minutes of the information derived from these examinations. They threw little light upon the story, so far as he understood its purport; but the better informed reader has received, through means of this investigation, an account of Brown's proceedings, between the moment when we left him upon his walk to Kippletringan, and the time when, stung by jealousy, he so rashly and unhappily presented himself before Julia Mannering, and well nigh brought to a fatal termination the quarrel which his appearance occasioned.

Glossin rode slowly back to Ellangowan, pondering on what he had heard, and more and more convinced that the active and successful prosecution of this mysterious business was an opportunity of ingratiating himself with Hazelwood and Mannering, to be on no account neglected. Perhaps, also, he felt his professional acuteness interested in bringing it to a successful close. It was, therefore, with great pleasure that on his return to his house from Kippletringan, he heard his servants announce hastily, "that Mac-Guffog, the thief-taker, and twa or three concurrents, had a man in hands in the kitchen waiting for his honour."

He instantly jumped from horseback, and hasted into the house. "Send my clerk here directly, ye'll find him copying the survey of the estate in the little green parlour. Set things to rights in my study, and wheel the great leather chair up to the writing-table—set a stool for Mr Scrow.—Scrow, (to the clerk, as he entered the presence-chamber,) hand down Sir George Mackenzie on Crimes; open it at the section *Vis Publica et Privata*, and fold down a leaf at the passage 'anent the bearing of unlawful weapons.' Now lend me a hand off with my mickle coat, and hang it up in the lobby, and bid them bring up the prisoner—I trow I will sort him—But stay, first send up Mac-Guffog. —Now, Mac-Guffog, where did ye find this chield?"

Mac-Guffog, a stout bandy-legged fellow, with a neck like a bull, a face like a fire-brand, and a most portentous squint of the left eye, began, after various contortions by way of courtesy to the Justice, to tell his story, ekeing it out by sundry sly nods and knowing winks, which appeared to bespeak an intimate correspondence of ideas between the narrator and his principal auditor. "Your honour sees I went down to yon place that your honour spoke of, that's kept by her that your honour kens of, by the sea side.—So says she, what are you wanting here? ye'll be come wi' a broom in your pocket frae Ellangowan?—So says I, deil a broom will come frae there awa', for ye ken, says I, his honour Ellangowan himsell in former times"——

"Well, well, no occasion to be particular, tell the essential."

"Weel, so we sat niffering about some brandy that I said I wanted, till he came in."

"Who?"

"He!" pointing with his thumb inverted to the kitchen, where the prisoner was in custody. "So he had his griego wrapped close round him, and I judged he was not dry-handed—so I thought it was best to speak proper, and so he believed I was a Manks man, and I kept aye between her and him, for fear she had whistled. And then we began to drink about, and then I betted he wad not drink out a quartern of Hollands without drawing breath—and then he tried it—and just then Slounging Jock and Dick Spur'em came in, and we clinked the darbies on him, took him quiet as a lamb—And now he's had his bit sleep out, and is as fresh as a May gowan, to answer what your honour likes to speer." This narrative, delivered with a wonderful quantity of gesture and grimace, received at the conclusion the thanks and praises which the narrator expected.

"Had he no arms?" asked the Justice.

"Aye, aye, they are never without barkers and slashers."

"Any papers?"

"This bundle," delivering a dirty pocket-book.

"Go down stairs, then, Mac-Guffog, and be in waiting." The officer left the room.

The clink of irons was immediately afterwards heard upon the stair, and in two or three minutes a man was introduced, hand-cuffed and fettered. He was thick, brawny, and muscular, and although his shagged and grizzled hair marked an age somewhat advanced, and his stature was rather low, he appeared, nevertheless, a person few would have chosen to cope with in personal conflict. His coarse and savage features were still flushed, and his eye still reeled under the influence of the strong potation which had proved the immediate cause of his seizure. But the sleep, though short, which Mac-Guffog had allowed him, and still more a sense of the peril of his situation, had restored to him the full use of his faculties. The worthy judge, and the no less estimable captive, looked at each other steadily for a long time without speaking. Glossin apparently recognised his prisoner, but seemed at a loss how to proceed with his investigation. At length he broke silence. "Soh, Captain—this is you?—you have been a stranger on this coast for some years."

"Stranger?" replied the other, "strange enough, I think—for hold me der deyvil, if I been ever here before."

"That won't pass, Mr Captain."

"That must pass, Mr Justice—sapperment!"

"And how will you be pleased to call yourself, then, for the present," said Glossin, "just until I shall bring some other folks to refresh your memory, as to who you are, or at least who you have been?"

"What bin I?—donner and blitzen! I bin Jans Jansen, from Cuxhaven—what sall Ich bin?"

Glossin took from a case which was in the apartment, a pair of small pocket pistols, which he loaded with ostentatious care. "You may retire," said he to his clerk, "and carry the people with you, Scrow—but wait in the lobby within call."

The clerk would have offered some remonstrances to his principal on the danger of remaining alone with such a desperate character, although iron'd past the possibility of active exertion, but Glossin waved him off impatiently. When he had left the room, the Justice took two short turns through the apartment, then drew his chair opposite to the prisoner, so as to confront him fully, placed the pistols before him in readiness, and said in a steady voice, "You are Dirk Hattaraick of Flushing, are you not?"

The prisoner turned his eye intuitively to the door, as if he apprehended some one was listening. Glossin rose, opened the door, so that from the chair in which his prisoner sate he might satisfy himself there was no eve's-dropper within hearing, then shut it, resumed his seat, and repeated his question. "You are Dirk Hattaraick, formerly of the Yungfrau Haagenslaapen, are you not?"

"Tausend deyvil!—and you know that, why ask me?"

"Because I am surprised to see you in the very last place where you ought to be, if you regard your safety."

"Der deyvil!—no man regards his own safety that speaks so to me!"

"What? unarmed, and in irons!—well said, Captain! But, Captain, bullying won't do—you'll hardly get out of this country without accounting for a little accident that happened at Warroch Point a few years ago."

Hattaraick's looks grew black as midnight.

"For my part," continued Glossin, "I have no particular wish to be hard upon an old acquaintance—But I must do my duty—I shall send you off to Edinburgh in a post-chaise and four this very day."

"Poz donner! you would not do that—why you had the matter of half a cargo value in bills on Vanbeest and Verbruggen."

"It's so long since, Captain Hattaraick, that I really forget how I was recompensed for my trouble."

"Your trouble?—your silence, you mean."

"It was an affair in the course of business—and I have retired from business for some time."

"Aye, but I have a notion that I could make you go steady about, and try the old course again. Why, man, hold me der deyvil, but I meant to visit you, and tell you something that concerns you."

"Of the boy?" said Glossin eagerly.

"Yaw, Mynheer."

"He does not live, does he?"

"As lifelich as you or I."

"Good God!—But in India?"

"No, tausend deyvils, here! on this dirty coast of yours."

"But, Hattaraick, this,—that is if it be true, which I do not believe, —this will ruin us both, for he cannot but remember your neat job—and for me—it will be productive of the worst consequences! It will ruin us both, I tell you."

"I tell you it will ruin none but you—for I am done up already, and if I must strap for it, all shall out."

"Zounds, what brought you back to this coast like a madman?"

"Why, all the gelt was gone, and the house was shaking, and I thought the job was clayed over."

"Stay, what can be done?—I dare not discharge—but might you not be rescued in the way—aye sure—a word to Lieutenant Brown,—and I would send the people with you by the coast-road."

"No, no! that won't do—Brown's dead—shot—laid in the locker, man—the devil has the picking of him."

"Dead?—Shot?—at Woodbourne, I suppose?"

"Yaw, Mynheer."

Glossin paused—the sweat broke upon his brow with the agony of his feelings, while the hard-featured miscreant who sat opposite, coolly rolled his tobacco in his cheek, and squirted the juice into the fire-grate. "It would be ruin," said Glossin to himself, "absolute ruin, if the heir should re-appear—and then what might be the consequence of conniving with these men?—yet there is so little time to take measures—Hark you, Hattaraick; I can't set you at liberty—but I can put you where you may set yourself at liberty—I always like to assist an old friend. I shall confine you in the old castle for to-night, and give these people double allowance of grog. Mac-Guffog will fall in the trap in which he caught you. The stancheons on the window of the strong room, as they call it, are wasted to pieces, and it is not above twelve feet from the level of the ground without, and the snow lies thick."

"But the darbies," said Hattaraick, looking upon his fetters.

"Hark ye," said Glossin, going to a tool chest, and taking out a small file, "there's a friend for you, and you know the road to the sea by the stairs." Hattaraick shook his chains in exstacy, as if he were already at liberty, and strove to extend his fettered hand towards his protector. Glossin laid his finger upon his lips with a cautious glance at the door, and then proceeded in his instructions. "When you escape, better go to the Kaim of Derncleugh."

"Donner! that howff is blown."

"The devil!—well then, you may steal my skiff that lies on the beach there, and away. But you must remain snug at the Point of Warroch till I come to see you."

"The Point of Warroch?" said Hattaraick, his countenance again falling, "What, in the cave I suppose?—I would rather it were any where else;—es spuckt da!—they say for certain that he walks—But, donner and blitzen! I never shunned him alive, and I won't shun him dead—Strafe mich helle! it shall never be said Dirk Hattaraick feared either dog or devil!—So I wait there till I see you?"

"Aye, aye," answered Glossin, "and now I must call in the men."

"I can make nothing of Captain Jansen, as he calls himself, Mac-Guffog, and it's now too late to bundle him off to the county jail. Is there not a strong room up yonder in the old castle?"

"Aye is there, sir; my uncle, the constable, ance kept a man there for three days in auld Ellangowan's time. But there was an unco dust about it—it was tried in the inner-house afore the fifteen."

"I know all that, but this person will not stay there very long—it's only a makeshift for a night. There is a small room through which it opens, you may light a fire for yourselves there, and I'll send you plenty to make you comfortable. But be sure you lock the door upon the prisoner; and, hark ye, let him have a fire in the strong room too, the season requires it. Perhaps he'll make a clean breast to-morrow."

With these instructions, and with a large allowance of food and liquor, the Justice dismissed his party to keep guard for the night in the old castle, under the full hope and belief that they would neither spend the night in watching nor prayer.

There was little fear that Glossin himself should that night sleep over-sound. His situation was perilous in the extreme, for the schemes of a life of villainy seemed at once to be crumbling around and above him. He laid himself to rest, and tossed upon his pillow for a long time in vain. At length he fell asleep, but it was only to dream of his patron,—now, as he had last seen him, with the paleness of death upon his features, then again transformed into all the vigour and comeliness of youth, approaching to expel him from the mansion-house of his fathers. Then he dreamed, that after wandering long over a wild heath, he came at length to an inn, from which sounded the voice of revelry, and that when he entered, the first person he met was Frank Kennedy, all smashed and gory, as he had lain on the beach at Warroch Point, but with a reeking punch-bowl in his hand. Then the scene changed to a dungeon, where he heard Dirk Hattaraick, whom he imagined to be under sentence of death, confessing his crimes to a clergyman.—"After the bloody deed was done," said the penitent, "we retreated into a cave close beside, the secret of which was known but to one man in the country; we were debating what to do with the child, and we thought of giving it up to the gypsies, when we heard the cries of the pursuers hallooing to each other. One man alone came straight to our cave, and it was that man who knew the secret—but we made him our friend at the expence of half the value of the goods saved. By his advice we carried off the child to Holland in our consort, which came the following night to take us from the coast. That man was"——

"No, I deny it!—it was not I," said Glossin; and, struggling in his agony to express his denial more distinctly, he awoke.

It was, however, conscience, that had prepared this mental phantasmagoria. The truth was, that, knowing much better than any other person the haunts of the smugglers, he had, while the others were searching in different directions, gone straight to the cave, even before he had learned the murder of Kennedy, whom he expected to find their prisoner. He came upon them with some idea of mediation, but found them in the midst of their guilty terrors, while the rage, which had hurried them into murder, began, with all but Hattaraick, to sink into remorse and fear. Glossin was then indigent and greatly in debt, but he was already possessed of Mr Bertram's ear, and, aware of the facility of his disposition, he saw no difficulty in enriching himself at his expence, provided the heir-male were removed, in which case the estate became the unlimited property of the weak and prodigal father. Stimulated by present gain and the prospect of contingent advantage, he accepted the bribe which the smugglers offered in their terror, and connived at, or even encouraged, their intention of carrying away the child of his benefactor, who, if left behind, was old enough to have described the scene of blood which he had witnessed. The only palliative that the ingenuity of Glossin could offer to his conscience was, that the temptation was great, and came suddenly upon him, embracing as it were the very advantages upon which his mind had so long rested, and promising to relieve him from distresses which must have otherwise speedily overwhelmed him. Besides, he endeavoured to think that self-preservation rendered his conduct necessary. He was, in some degree, in the power of the robbers, and pleaded hard with his conscience, that, had he declined their offers, the assistance which he could have called for, though not distant, might not have arrived in time to save him from men, who, on less provocation, had just committed murder.

Galled with the anxious forebodings of a guilty conscience, Glossin now arose, and looked out upon the night. The scene, which we have already described in the beginning of our first volume, was now covered with snow, and the brilliant, though waste, whiteness of the land, gave to the sea by contrast a dark and livid tinge. A landscape covered with snow, though abstractedly it may be called beautiful, has, both from the association of cold and barrenness, and from its comparative infrequency, a wild, strange, and desolate appearance. Objects, well known to us in their common state, have either disappeared, or are so strangely varied and disguised, that we seem gazing on an unknown world. But it was not with such reflections, that the mind of this bad man was occupied. His eye was upon the gigantic and gloomy outlines of the old castle, where, in a flanking tower of enormous size and thickness, glimmered two lights, one from the window of the strong room, where Hattaraick was confined, the other from that of the adjacent apartment occupied by his keepers. "Has he made his escape, or will he be able to do so?—Have those watched, who never watched before, in order to complete my ruin?—If morning finds him there, he must be committed to prison; Mac-Morlan or some other person will take the matter up—he will be detected—convicted—and will tell all in revenge!"——

While these racking thoughts glided rapidly through Glossin's mind, he observed one of the lights obscured, as by an opake body placed at the window. What a moment of interest!—"He has got clear of his irons!—he is working at the stancheons of the window—they are surely quite decayed, they must give way—O God! they have fallen outward, I heard them clink among the stones!—the noise cannot fail to wake them—furies seize his Dutch awkwardness!—The light burns free again—they have torn him from the window, and are binding him in the room!—No! he had only retired an instant on the alarm of the falling bars—he is at the window again—the light is quite obscured now—he is getting out!"——

A heavy sound, as of a body dropped from a height among the snow, announced that Hattaraick had completed his escape, and shortly after Glossin beheld a dark figure, like a shadow, steal along the whitened beach, and reach the spot where the skiff lay. New cause for fear! "His single strength will be unable to float her," said Glossin to himself; "I must go to the rascal's assistance.—But no! he has got her off, and now, thank God, her sail is spreading itself against the moon—aye, he has got the breeze now—would to heaven it were a tempest to sink him to the bottom!"—After this last cordial wish, he continued watching the progress of the boat as it stood away towards the Point of Warroch, until he could no longer distinguish the dusky sail from the gloomy waves over which it glided. Satisfied then that the immediate danger was averted, he retired with somewhat more composure to his guilty pillow.

Chapter Thirteen

Why dost not comfort me, and help me out
From this unhallowed and blood-stain'd hole?
Titus Andronicus

ON THE NEXT morning, great was the alarm and confusion of the officers, when they discovered the escape of their prisoner. Mac-Guffog appeared before Glossin with a head perturbed with brandy and fear, and incurred a most severe reprimand for neglect of duty. The resentment of the Justice appeared only to be suspended by his anxiety to recover possession of the prisoner, and the thief-takers, glad to escape from his awful and incensed presence, were sent off in every direction (except the right one) to recover their prey, if possible. Glossin particularly recommended a careful search at the Kaim of Derncleugh, which was occasionally occupied under night by vagrants of different descriptions. Having thus dispersed his myrmidons in various directions, he himself hastened by devious paths through the Wood of Warroch, to his appointed interview with Hattaraick, from whom he hoped to learn, at more leisure than their last night's conference admitted, the circumstances attending the return of the heir of Ellangowan to his native country.

With manœuvres like those of a fox when he doubles to avoid the pack, Glossin strove to approach the place of appointment in a manner which should leave upon the snow no distinct track of his course. "Would to Heaven it would snow," said he, looking upward, "and hide these foot-prints. Should one of the officers light upon them, he would run the scent up like a blood-hound, and surprise us.—I must get down upon the sea-beach, and contrive to creep along beneath the rocks."

And, accordingly, he descended from the cliffs with some difficulty, and scrambled along between the rocks and the advancing tide, now looking up to see if his motions were watched from the rocks above him; now casting a jealous glance to mark if any boat appeared upon the sea, from which his course might be descried.

But even the feelings of selfish apprehension were for a time superseded, as Glossin passed the spot where Kennedy's body had been found. It was marked by the fragment of rock which had been precipitated from the cliff above, either with the body or after it. Its mass was now encrusted with small shell-fish, and tasselled with tangle and sea-weed; but still its shape and substance were different from those of the other rocks which lay scattered around. His voluntary walks, it will readily be believed, had never led to this spot; so that finding himself now there for the first time after the terrible catastrophe, the scene at once recurred to his mind with all its accompaniments of horror. He remembered how, like a guilty thing, gliding from the neighbouring place of concealment, he had mingled with eagerness, yet with caution, among the terrified group who surrounded the corpse, dreading lest any one should ask from whence he came. He remembered, too, with what conscious fear he had avoided gazing upon that ghastly spectacle. The wild scream of his patron, "My bairn! my bairn!" again rang in his ears. "Good God!" he exclaimed, "and is all I have gained worth the agony of that moment, and the thousand anxious fears and horrors which have since embittered my life!—O how I wish that I lay where that wretched man lies, and that he stood here in life and health!—But these regrets are all too late."

Stifling, therefore, his feelings, he crept forward to the cave, which was so near the spot where the body was found, that the smugglers might have heard from their hiding-place the various conjectures of the bye-standers concerning the fate of their victim. But nothing could be more completely concealed than the entrance to their asylum. The opening, not larger than that of a fox-earth, lay in the face of the cliff directly behind a large black rock, or rather upright stone, which served at once to conceal it from strangers, and as a mark to point out its situation to those who used it as a place of retreat. The space between the stone and the cliff was exceedingly narrow, and being heaped with sand and other rubbish, the most minute search would not have discovered the mouth of the cavern, without removing those substances which the tide had heaped before it. For the purpose of farther concealment, it was usual with the contraband traders who used this haunt, after they had entered, to stuff the mouth with withered sea-weed, loosely piled together as if drifted there by the waves. Dirk Hattaraick had not forgotten this precaution.

Glossin, though a bold and hardy man, felt his heart throb, and his knees knock together, when he prepared to enter this den of secret iniquity, in order to hold conference with a felon, whom he justly accounted one of the most desperate and depraved of men. "But he has no interest to injure me," was his consolatory reflection. He examined his pocket-pistols, however, before removing the weeds and entering the cavern, which he did upon hands and knees. The passage, at first very low and narrow, just admitting entrance to a man in a creeping posture, expanded after a few yards into a high arched vault of considerable width. The bottom, ascending gradually, was strewed with the purest sand. Ere Glossin had got upon his feet, the hoarse yet suppressed voice of Hattaraick growled through the recesses of the cave.

"Hagel and donner!—be'st du?"

"Are you in the dark?"

"Dark? der deyvil! aye; where should I have a glim?"

"Stay, I have brought light;" and Glossin accordingly produced a tinder-box, and lighted a small lanthorn.

"You must kindle some fire too, for hold mich der deyvil, Ich bin ganz gefrorne!"

"It is a cold place to be sure," said Glossin, gathering some decayed staves of barrels and pieces of wood, which had perhaps lain in the cavern since Dirk Hattaraick was there last.

"Cold? Snow-wasser and hagel! it's perdition—I could only keep myself alive by rambling up and down this d—d vault, and thinking about the merry rouses we have had in it."

The flame now began to blaze brightly, and Hattaraick hung his bronzed visage, and expanded his hard and sinewy hands over it, with an avidity resembling that of famine to which food is exposed. The light shewed his savage and stern features, and the smoke, which in his agony of cold he seemed to endure almost to suffocation, after curling round his head, rose to the dim and rugged roof of the cave, through which it escaped by some secret rents or clefts in the rock; the same doubtless that afforded air to the cavern when the tide was in, at which time the aperture to the sea was filled with water.

"And now I have brought you some breakfast," said Glossin, producing some cold meat and a flask of spirits. The latter Hattaraick eagerly seized upon, and applied to his mouth; and, after a hearty draught, he exclaimed with great rapture, "Das schmeckt!—That is good—that warms the liver!"—Then broke into the fragment of a High-Dutch song,

> "Saufen bier, und brante-wein,
> Schmeissen alle die fenstern ein;
> Ich ben liederlich,
> Du bist liederlich,
> Sind wir nicht liederlich leute a?"

"Well said, my hearty Captain!" cried Glossin, endeavouring to catch the tone of revelry,—

> "Gin by pailfuls, wine in rivers,
> Dash the window-glass to shivers!
> For three wild lads were we, brave boys,
> And three wild lads were we;
> Thou on the land, and I on the sand,
> And Jack on the gallows-tree!—

"That's it, my bully-boy! Why, you're alive again now!—And now let us talk about our business."

"*Your* business, if you please," said Hattaraick; "hagel and donner! —mine was done when I got out of the bilboes."

"Have patience, my good friend;—I'll convince you our interests are just the same."

Hattaraick gave a short dry cough, and Glossin after a pause proceeded.

"How came you to let the boy escape?"

"Why, fluch and blitzen! he was no charge of mine. Lieutenant Brown gave him to his cousin that's in the Middleburgh house of Vanbeest and Verbruggen, and told him some goose's gazette about his being taken in a skirmish with the land-sharks—he gave him for a foot-boy. Me let him escape?—the bastard kinchin should have walked the plank ere I troubled myself about him."

"Well, and was he bred a foot-boy then?"

"Nein, nein; the kinchin got about the old man's heart, and he gave him his own name, and bred him up in the office, and then sent him to India—I believe he would have packed him back here, but his nephew told him it would do up the free trade for many a day, if the youngster got back to Scotland."

"Do you think he knows much of his own origin now?"

"Deyvil! how should I tell what he knows now? But he remembered something of it long. When he was but ten years old, he persuaded another Satan's limb of an English bastard like himself to steal my lugger's kahn—boat—what do you call it—to return to his country, as he called it—fire him! Before we could overtake them, they had the skiff out of channel as far as the Deurloo—the boat might have been lost."

"I wish to Heaven she had—with him in her!"

"Why, I was so angry myself, that, sapperment! I did give him a tip over the side—but split him—the comical little devil swam like a duck; so I made him swim astern for a mile to teach him manners, and then took him in when he was sinking.—By the knocking Nicholas! he'll plague you, now he's come over the herring-pond! When he was so high, he had the spirit of thunder and lightning."

"How did he get back from India?"

"Why, how should I know?—the house there was done up, and that gave us a shake at Middleburgh, I think—so they sent me again to see what could be done among my old acquaintances here—for we held old stories were done and forgotten. So I had got a pretty trade again on foot within the last two or three trips; but that stupid houndsfoot schelm, Brown, has knocked it on the head again, I suppose, with getting himself shot by the colonel-man."

"Why were not you with them?"

"Why, you see, sapperment! I fear nothing—but it was too far within land, and I might have been scented."

"True. But to return to this youngster"——

"Aye, aye, donner and blitzen! *he's* your affair."

"—How do you know that he really is in this country?"

"Why, Gabriel saw him up among the hills."

"Gabriel? who is he?"

"A fellow from the gypsies, that, about eighteen years since, was pressed on board that d—d fellow Pritchard's sloop of war—It was he came off and gave us warning that the Shark was coming round upon us the day Kennedy was done; and he told us how Kennedy had given the information—the gypsies and Kennedy had some quarrel besides. He went to the East Indies on the same ship with your younker, and, sapperment! knew him well, though the other did not remember him. Gab kept out of his eye though, as he had served the States against England, and was a deserter to boot; and he sent us word directly, that we might know of his being here—though it does not concern us a rope's end."

"So he really is in this country then, Hattaraick, between friend and friend?"

"Wetter and donner, ya! What do you take me for?"

"A blood-thirsty, fearless miscreant!" thought Glossin internally, but said aloud, "And which of your people was it that shot young Hazelwood?"

"Sturm-wetter! do ye think we were mad?—none of *us*, man—Gott! the country was too hot for the trade already with that d—d frolic of Brown."

"Why, I am told it was Brown shot Hazelwood?"

"Not our lieutenant, I promise you; for he was laid six feet deep at Derncleugh the day before the thing happened.—Tausend deyvils, man! do ye think that he could rise out of the earth to shoot another man?"

A light here began to break upon Glossin's confusion of ideas. "Did you not say that the younker, as you call him, goes by the name of Brown?"

"Of Brown? ya—Vanbeest Brown; old Vanbeest Brown of our Vanbeest and Verbruggen gave him his own name—he did."

"Then," said Glossin, rubbing his hands, "it is he, by Heaven, who has committed this crime!"

"And what have we to do with that?" answered Hattaraick.

Glossin paused, and, fertile in expedients, hastily ran over his project in his own mind, and then drew near the smuggler with a confidential air. "You know, my dear Hattaraick, it is our principal business to get rid of this young man?"

"Umh!" answered Dirk Hattaraick.

"Not," continued Glossin—"not that I would wish any personal harm to him—if—if—if we can do without. Now, he is liable to be seized upon by justice, both as bearing the same name with your lieutenant, who was engaged in that affair at Woodbourne, and for firing on young Hazelwood with intent to kill or wound."

"Eye, eye—but what good will that do you? he'll be loose again so soon as he shews himself to carry other colours."

"True, my dear Dirk, well noticed, my friend Hattaraick! But there is ground enough for a temporary imprisonment till he fetch his proofs from England or elsewhere, my good friend. I understand law, Captain Hattaraick, and I'll take it upon me, simple Gilbert Glossin of Ellangowan, justice of peace for the county of ——, to refuse his bail, if he should offer the best in the country, until he is brought up for second examination—now where d'ye think I'll incarcerate him?"

"Hagel and wetter! what do I care?"

"Stay, my friend—you do care a great deal. Do you know your

goods, that were seized and carried to Woodbourne, are now lying in the custom-house at Portanferry? (a small fishing town)—Now I will commit this younker"——

"When you have caught him?"

"Aye, aye, when I have caught him, I shall not be long about that—I will commit him to the Workhouse, or Bridewell, which you know is beside the Custom-house."

"Ya, the Rasp-house; I know it very well."

"I will take care that the red-coats are dispersed through the country; you land at night with the crew of your lugger, recover your own goods, and carry the younker Brown with you back to Flushing. Won't that do?"

"Aye, or—to America?"

"Aye, aye, my friend."

"Or—to Jericho?"

"Psha! Wherever you have a mind."

"Aye, or—pitch him overboard?"

"Nay, I advise no violence."

"Nein, nein—you leave that to me. Sturm-wetter! I know you of old. But, hark ye, what am I, Dirk Hattaraick, to be the better of this?"

"Why, is it not your interest as well as mine?—besides I set you free this morning."

"*You* set me free!—Donner and deyvil! I set myself free—besides it was all in the way of your profession, and happened a long time ago."

"Pshaw! pshaw! don't let us jest; I am not against making a handsome compliment—but it's your affair as well as mine."

"What do ye talk of *my* affair? is it not you that keep the younker's whole estate from him? Dirk Hattaraick never touched a stiver of his rents."

"Hush—hush—I tell you it shall be a joint business."

"Why, will ye give me half the kitt?"

"What, half the estate?—d'ye mean we should set up house together at Ellangowan, and take the barony, rig-about?"

"Sturm-wetter, no! but you might give me half the value—half the gelt. Live with you? nein—I would have a lust-haus of mine own on the Middleburgh dyke, and a blumen-garten like a burgo-master's."

"Aye, and a wooden lion at the door, and a painted centinel in the garden, with a pipe in his mouth!—But hark ye, Hattaraick; what will all the tulips, and flower gardens, and pleasure-houses in the Netherlands do for you, if you are hanged here in Scotland?"

Hattaraick's countenance fell. "Der deyvil! hanged?"

"Aye, hanged! mein heer Captain.—The devil can scarce save Dirk Hattaraick from being hanged for a murderer and kidnapper, if the younker of Ellangowan should settle in this country, and if the gallant Captain chances to be caught there re-establishing his fair trade! And I won't say, but as peace is now so much talked of, their High Mightinesses may not hand him over to oblige their new allies, even if he remained in fader-land."

"Poz hagel blitzen and donner! I—I doubt you say true."

"Not," said Glossin, perceiving he had made the desired impression, "not that I am against being civil;" and he slid into Hattaraick's passive hand a bank-note of some value.

"Is this all?" said the smuggler; "you had the price of half a cargo for winking at our job, and made us do your business too."

"But, my good friend, you forget—in this case you will recover all your own goods."

"Aye, at the risk of our own necks—we could do that without you."

"I doubt that, Captain Hattaraick, because you would probably find a dozen red-coats at the custom-house. Come, come, I will be as liberal as I can, but you should have a conscience."

"Now strafe mich der teyfel!—this provokes me more than all the rest!—You rob and you murder, and you want me to rob and murder, and play the silver-cooper, or kidnapper, as you call it, a dozen times over, and then, hagel and wind-sturm! you speak to me of conscience! —Can you think of no fairer way of getting rid of this unlucky lad?"

"No, mein heer; but as I commit him to your charge"——

"To *my* charge—to the charge of brandy and gunpowder! and—well, if it must be, it must—but you have a good guess what's like to come of it."

"O, my dear friend, I trust no degree of severity will be necessary."

"Severity!" said the fellow, with a kind of groan, "I wish you had had my dreams when I first came to this dog-hole, and tried to sleep among the dry sea-weed.—First there was that d—d fellow there with his broken back, sprawling as he did when I hurled the rock over a-top on un—ha, ha! you would have sworn he was lying on the floor where you stand, wallowing like a crushed frog;—and then"——

"Nay, my friend, what signifies going over this nonsense?—if you are turned chicken-hearted, why the game's up, that's all—the game's up with us both."

"Chicken-hearted?—No. I have not lived so long upon the account to start at last, neither for deyvil nor Dutchman."

"Well, then take another schnaps—the cold's at your heart still.—And now tell me, are any of your old crew with you?"

"Nein—all dead, hanged, drowned, and damned. Brown was the last—all dead but Gypsey Gab, and he would go off the country again for a spill of money—or he'll be quiet for his own sake—or old Meg, his aunt, will keep him quiet for her's."

"Which Meg?"

"Meg Merrilies, the old devil's limb of a gypsey witch."

"Is she still alive?"

"Ya."

"And in this country?"

"And in this country. She was at the Kaim of Derncleugh, at Vanbeest Brown's last wake, as they call it, the other night, with two of my people, and some of her own blasted gypsies."

"That's another breaker a' head, Captain! Will she not squeak, think ye?"

"Not she—she won't start—she swore by the salmon, if we did the kinchin no harm, she would never tell how the gauger got it. Why, man, though I gave her a wipe with my hanger in the heat of the matter, and cut her arm, and though she was so long after in trouble about it up at your borough-town there, der deyvil! old Meg was as true as steel."

"Why, that's true as you say. And yet if she could be carried over to Zealand, or Hamburgh, or—or——any where else, you know,—it were as well."

Hattaraick jumped upright upon his feet, and looked at Glossin from head to heel.—"I don't see the goat's foot," he said, "and yet he must be the very deyvil!—But Meg Merrilies is closer yet with the Kobold than you are—aye, and I had never such weather as after having drawn her blood.—Nein, nein—I'll meddle with her no more—she's a witch of the fiend—a real deyvil's-kind—but that's her affair. Donner and wetter! I'll neither make nor meddle—that's her word—but for the rest—why, if I thought the trade would not suffer, I would soon rid you of the younker, if you send me word when he's under embargo."

In brief and under tones the two worthy associates concerted their enterprize, and agreed at which of his haunts Hattaraick should be heard of. The stay of his lugger on the coast was not difficult, as there was no king's vessel there at the time.

Chapter Fourteen

> You are one of those that will not serve God if the
> devil bids you—Because we come to do you service,
> you think we are ruffians.
>
> *Othello*

WHEN GLOSSIN returned home, he found, among other letters and papers to him, one of considerable importance. It was signed by Mr

Protocol, an attorney in Edinburgh, and, addressing him as the agent for Godfrey Bertram, Esq. late of Ellangowan, and for his representatives, acquainted him with the sudden death of Mrs Margaret Bertram of Singleside, requesting him to inform his clients thereof, in case they judged it proper to have any person present for their interest, at opening the repositories of the deceased. Mr Glossin perceived at once that the letter-writer was unacquainted with the breach which had taken place between him and his late patron. The estate of the deceased lady should by rights, as he well knew, descend to Lucy Bertram; but it was a thousand to one that the caprice of the old lady might have altered its destination. After running over contingencies and probabilities in his fertile mind, to ascertain what sort of personal advantage might accrue to him from this incident, he could not perceive any mode of availing himself of it, except in as far as it might go to assist his plan of recovering, or rather creating, a character, the want of which he had already experienced, and was likely to feel yet more deeply. "I must place myself," thought he, "on strong ground, that, if anything goes wrong with Dirk Hattaraick's project, I may have prepossessions in my favour at least."—Besides, to do Glossin justice, bad as he was, he might feel some desire to compensate to Miss Bertram in a small degree, and in a case in which his own interest did not interfere with hers, the infinite mischief which he had occasioned to her family. He therefore resolved early the next morning to ride over to Woodbourne.

It was not without hesitation that he took this step, having the natural reluctance to face Colonel Mannering, which fraud and villainy have to encounter honour and probity. But he had great confidence in his own *sçavoir faire.* His talents were natural, acute, and by no means confined to the line of his profession. He had at different times resided a good deal in England, and his address was free both from country rusticity and professional pedantry; so that he had considerable powers both of address and persuasion, joined to an unshaken effrontery, which he affected to disguise under plainness of manner. Confident, therefore, in himself, he appeared at Woodbourne, about ten in the morning, and was admitted as a gentleman come to wait upon Miss Bertram.

He did not announce himself until he was at the door of the breakfast parlour, when the servant, by his desire, said aloud, "Mr Glossin, to wait upon Miss Bertram."—Lucy, remembering the last scene of her father's existence, turned as pale as death, and had well nigh fallen from her chair. Julia Mannering flew to her assistance, and they left the room together. There remained Colonel Mannering, Charles Hazelwood, with his arm in a sling, and the Dominie, whose gaunt visage and wall-eyes assumed a most hostile aspect upon recognising Glossin.

That honest gentleman, though somewhat abashed by the effect of his first introduction, advanced with confidence, and hoped he did not intrude upon the ladies. Colonel Mannering, in a very upright and stately manner, observed, that he did not know to what he was to impute the honour of a visit from Mr Glossin.

"Hem! hem! I took the liberty to wait upon Miss Bertram, Colonel Mannering, on account of a matter of business."

"If it can be communicated to Mr Mac-Morlan, her agent, I believe it will be more agreeable to Miss Bertram."

"I beg pardon, Colonel Mannering;—you are a man of the world—there are some cases in which it is most prudent for all parties to treat with principals."

"Then, if Mr Glossin will take the trouble to state his object in a letter, I will answer that Miss Bertram pays proper attention to it."

"Certainly—but there are cases in which a *viva voce* conference—I perceive—I know Colonel Mannering has adopted some prejudices which may make my visit appear intrusive; but I submit to his good sense, whether he ought to exclude me from a hearing without knowing the purpose of my visit, or of how much consequence it may be to the young lady whom he honours with his protection."

"Certainly, sir, I have not the least intention to do so. I will learn Miss Bertram's pleasure upon the subject, and acquaint Mr Glossin, if he can spare time to wait for her answer." So saying, he left the room.

Glossin had still remained standing in the midst of the apartment. Colonel Mannering made not the slightest motion to invite him to sit down, and indeed remained standing himself during their short interview. When he left the room, however, Glossin seized upon a chair, and threw himself into it with an air between embarrassment and effrontery. He felt the silence of his companions disconcerting and oppressive, and resolved to interrupt it.

"A fine day, Mr Sampson."

The Dominie answered with something between an acquiescent grunt and an indignant groan.

"You never come down to see your old acquaintances on the Ellangowan property, Mr Sampson—You would find most of the old stagers still stationary there. I have too much respect for the late family to disturb old residenters, even under pretence of improvement—besides it's not my way—I don't like it—I believe, Mr Sampson, Scripture particularly condemns those who oppress the poor, and remove land-marks."

"Or who devour the substance of orphans," subjoined the Dominie. "Anathema Maranatha!" So saying, he rose, shouldered the folio which he had been perusing, faced to the right about, and marched out of the room with the strides of a grenadier.

Mr Glossin, no way disconcerted, or at least feeling it necessary not to appear so, turned to young Hazelwood, who was apparently busy with the newspaper. "Any news, sir?"—Hazelwood raised his eyes, looked at him, and pushed the paper towards him, as if to a stranger in a coffee-house, then rose, and was about to leave the room. "I beg pardon, Mr Hazelwood—but I can't help wishing you joy of getting so easily over that infernal accident."—This was answered by a sort of inclination of the head as slight and stiff as could well be imagined. Yet it encouraged our man of law to proceed. "I can promise you, Mr Hazelwood, few people have taken the interest in that matter which I have, both for the sake of the country, and on account of my particular respect for your family, which has so high a stake in it—indeed, so very high a stake, that, as Mr Featherhead is turning old now, and as there's a talk since his last stroke, of his taking the Chiltern Hundreds, it might be worth your while to look about you.—I speak as a friend, Mr Hazelwood, and as one who understands the roll; and if in going over it together"——

"I beg pardon, sir, but I have no views in which your assistance could be useful."

"O very well—perhaps you are right—it's quite time enough, and I love to see a young gentleman cautious. But I was talking of your wound—I think I have got a clue to that business—I think I have—and if I do not bring the fellow to condign punishment"——

"I beg your pardon, sir, once more—but your zeal outruns my wishes. I have every reason to think the wound was accidental—certainly it was not premeditated. Against ingratitude and premeditated treachery, should you find any one guilty of them, my resentment will be as warm as your own."

Another rebuff, thought Glossin; I must try him upon the other tack.—"Right, sir; very nobly said! I would have no more mercy on an ungrateful man than I would on a woodcock—And now we talk of sport, (this was a sort of diverting of the conversation which Glossin had learned from his former patron) I see you often carry a gun, and I hope you will be soon able to take the fields again. I observe you confine yourself always to your own side of the Hazelshaws-burn. I hope, my dear sir, you will make no scruple of following your game to the Ellangowan bank: I believe it is rather the best exposure of the two for woodcocks, although both are capital."

As this offer only excited a cold and constrained bow, Glossin was obliged to remain silent, and was presently afterwards somewhat relieved by the entrance of Colonel Mannering.

"I have detained you some time, I fear, sir," said he, addressing Glossin; "I wished to prevail upon Miss Bertram to see you, as, in my opinion, her objections ought to give way to the necessity of hearing in her own person what may be of importance that she should know. But I find that circumstances of recent occurrence, and not easily to be forgotten, have rendered her so utterly repugnant to a personal interview with Mr Glossin, that it would be cruelty to insist upon it: and she has deputed me to receive his command, or proposal, or, in short, whatever he may wish to say to her."

"Hem, hem! I am sorry, sir—I am very sorry, Colonel Mannering, that Miss Bertram should suppose—that any prejudice, in short—or idea that any thing on my part"——

"Sir, where no accusation is made, excuses or explanations are unnecessary. Have you any objection to communicate to me, as Miss Bertram's temporary guardian, the circumstances which you conceive interest her?"

"None, Colonel Mannering; she could not chuse a more respectable friend, or one with whom I, in particular, would more anxiously wish to communicate frankly."

"Have the goodness to speak to the point, sir, if you please."

"Why, sir, it is not so easy all at once—but Mr Hazelwood need not leave the room,—I mean so well, sir, to Miss Bertram, that I could wish the whole world to hear my part of the conference."

"My friend Mr Hazelwood will not probably be anxious, Mr Glossin, to listen to what cannot concern him—and now when he has left us alone, let me pray you to be short and explicit in what you have to say. I am a soldier, sir, a little impatient of forms and introductions." So saying, he drew himself up in his chair, and waited for Mr Glossin's communication.

"Be pleased to look at that letter."

The Colonel read it, and returned it, after pencilling the name of the writer in his memorandum-book. "This, sir, does not seem to require much discussion. I will see that Miss Bertram's interest is attended to."

"But, sir,—but, Colonel Mannering, there is another matter which no one can explain but myself. This lady—this Mrs Margaret Bertram, to my certain knowledge, made a general settlement of her affairs in Miss Lucy Bertram's favour while she lived with my old friend, Mr Bertram, at Ellangowan. The Dominie—that was the name by which my deceased friend always called that very respectable man Mr Sampson—he and I witnessed the deed. And she had full power at that time to make such a settlement, for she was in fee of the estate of Singleside even then, although it was life-rented by an elder sister. It was a whimsical settlement of old Singleside's, sir; he pitted the two cats his daughters against each other, ha, ha!"

"Well, sir,—but to the purpose. You say that this lady had power to settle her estate on Miss Bertram, and that she did so?"

"Even so, Colonel.—I think I should understand the law—I have followed it for many years, and though I have given it up to retire upon a handsome competence, I did not throw away the knowledge which is better than house and land, and that I take to be the knowledge of the law, which, as our common rhyme says,

> Is most excellent
> To win the land that's gone and spent.

No, no, I love the smack of the whip—I have a little, a very little law yet, at the service of my friends."

Glossin ran on in this manner, thinking he had made a favourable impression on Mannering. The Colonel indeed reflected that this might be a most important crisis for Miss Bertram's interest, and resolved that his strong inclination to throw Glossin out at window, or at door, should not interfere with it. He put a strong curb on his temper, and resolved to listen with patience at least, if without complacence. He therefore let Mr Glossin get to the end of his self-congratulations, and then asked him if he knew where the deed was?

"I know—that is, I think—I believe I can recover it—In such cases custodiers have sometimes made a charge."

"We won't differ as to that, sir," said the Colonel, taking out his pocket-book.

"But, my dear sir, you take me so very short—I said *some persons might* make such a claim—I mean for payment of the expences of the deed, trouble in the affair, &c.—but I, for my own part, only wish Miss Bertram and her friends to be satisfied that I am acting towards her with honour. There's the paper, sir! It would have been a satisfaction to me to have delivered it into Miss Bertram's own hand, and to have wished her joy of the prospects which it opens. But since her prejudices on the subject are invincible, it only remains for me to transmit her my best wishes through you, Colonel Mannering, and to express that I shall willingly give my testimony in support of that deed when I shall be called upon. I have the honour to wish you a good morning, sir."

This parting speech was so well got up, and had so much the tone of conscious integrity unjustly suspected, that even Colonel Mannering was staggered in his bad opinion. He followed him two or three steps, and took leave of him with more politeness (though still cold and formal) than he had paid during his visit. Glossin left the house, half pleased with the impression he had made, half mortified by the stern caution and proud reluctance with which he had been admitted. "Colonel Mannering might have had more politeness," he said to himself —"it is not every man that can bring a good chance of 400*l.* a-year to a pennyless girl. Singleside must be up to 400*l.* a-year now—there's Reilagganbeg, Gillifidget, Loverless, Lyalone, and the Spinster's Knowe—good 400*l.* a-year. Some people might have made their own of it in my place—and yet, to own the truth, after much consideration, I don't see how that is possible."

Glossin was no sooner mounted and gone, than the Colonel dispatched a groom for Mr Mac-Morlan, and, putting the deed into his hand, requested to know if it was likely to be available to his friend Lucy Bertram. Mac-Morlan perused it with eyes that sparkled with delight, snapped his fingers repeatedly, and at length exclaimed, "Available?—it's as tight as a glove—naebody could make better wark than Glossin, when he did na let down a steek on purpose—But (his countenance falling) the auld b——, that I should say so, might alter at pleasure."

"How shall we know that?"

"Somebody maun attend on Miss Bertram's part, when the repositories of the deceased are opened."

"Can you go?"

"I fear not—I must attend a jury trial before our court."

"Then I will go myself—I'll set out to-morrow. Sampson shall go with me—he is a witness to this settlement. But I shall want a legal adviser?"

"The gentleman that was lately sheriff of this county is high in reputation; I will give you a card of introduction."

"What I like about you, Mr Mac-Morlan," said the Colonel, "is, that you always come straight to the point. Let me have it instantly—shall we tell Miss Lucy her chance of becoming an heiress?"

"Surely, because you must have some powers from her which I will instantly draw out. Besides, I will be caution for her prudence, and that she will consider it only in the light of a chance."

Mac-Morlan judged well. It could not be discerned from Miss Bertram's manner, that she founded any exulting expectations upon the prospect thus unexpectedly opening before her. She did indeed, in the course of the evening, ask Mr Mac-Morlan, as if by accident, what might be the annual income of the Hazelwood property; but shall we therefore aver for certain that she was considering whether an heiress of four hundred a-year might be a suitable match for the young Laird?

Chapter Fifteen

> Give me a cup of sack to make mine eyes look red—
> For I must speak in passion, and I will do it in King
> Cambyses' vein.
>
> *Henry IV. Part I*

MANNERING, with Sampson for his companion, lost no time in his journey to Edinburgh. They travelled in the Colonel's post-chariot, who, knowing his companion's habits of abstraction, did not chuse to give him out of his own sight, far less to trust him upon horseback, when, in all probability, a knavish stable-boy might with little address have contrived to mount him with his face to the tail. Accordingly, with the aid of his valet, who attended on horseback, he contrived to bring Mr Sampson safe to an inn in Edinburgh,—for hotels in these days were there none,—without any other accident than arose from his straying twice upon the road. Upon one occasion he was recovered by Barnes, who understood his humour, when, after engaging in close colloquy with the schoolmaster of Moffat, respecting a disputed quantity in Horace's 7th Ode, Book II., the dispute led on to another controversy, concerning the exact meaning of the word *Malobathro*, in that lyric effusion. His other escapade was made for the purpose of visiting the field of Rullion-green, which was dear to his presbyterian predilections. Having got out of the carriage for an instant, he saw the sepulchral monument of the slain at the distance of about a mile, and was arrested by Barnes in his progress toward it up the Pentland-hills, having on both occasions forgot his friend, patron, and fellow-traveller, as completely, as if he had been in the East Indies. On being reminded that Colonel Mannering was waiting for him, he uttered his usual ejaculation of "Prodigious!—I was oblivious," and then strode back to his post. Barnes was surprised at his master's patience on both occasions, knowing by experience how little he brooked neglect or delay; but the Dominie was in every respect a privileged person. His patron and he were never for a moment in each other's way, and it seemed obvious that they were formed to be companions through life. If Mannering wanted a particular book, the Dominie could bring it; if he wished to have accompts summed, or checked, his assistance was equally ready; if he desired to recall a particular passage in the classics, he could have recourse to the Dominie as to a dictionary; and all the while this walking statue was neither presuming when noticed, nor sulky when left to himself. To a proud, shy, reserved man, and such in many respects was Mannering, this sort of living catalogue, and animated automaton, had all the advantages of a literary dumb-waiter.

So soon as they arrived in Edinburgh, and were established at the George inn near Bristo-port, (I love to be particular) the Colonel desired the waiter to procure him a guide to Mr Pleydell's, the advocate, for whom he had a letter of introduction from Mr Mac-Morlan. He then commanded Barnes to have an eye to the Dominie, and walked forth with a cadie, who was to usher him to the man of law.

The period was near the end of the American war. The desire of room, of air, and of decent accommodation, had not as yet made very much progress in the capital of Scotland. Some efforts had been made upon the south side of the town towards building houses *within themselves*, as they are emphatically termed; and the New Town on the north, since so much extended, was then just commenced. But the great bulk of the better classes, and particularly those connected with the law, still lived in flats, or stories, of the dungeons of the Old Town. The manners also of some of the veterans of the law had not admitted innovation. One or two eminent lawyers still saw their clients in taverns, as was the general custom fifty years before; and although their habits were already considered as old-fashioned by the younger barristers, yet the custom of mixing wine and revelry with serious business, was still maintained by those senior counsellors who loved the old road, either because it was such, or because they had got too well used to it to travel any other. Among these praisers of the past time, who with ostentatious obstinacy affected the manners of a former generation, was this same Paulus Pleydell, Esq. otherwise a good scholar, an excellent lawyer, and a worthy man.

Under the guidance of his trusty attendant, Colonel Mannering, after threading a dark lane or two, reached the High-street, then clanging with the voices of oyster-women and the bells of pyemen, for it had, as the cadie assured him, just "chappit eight upon the Tron." It was long since Mannering had been in the street of a crowded metropolis, which, with its noise and clamour, its sounds of trade, of revelry, and of licence, its variety of lights, and the eternally changing bustle of its hundred groupes, offers, by night especially, a spectacle, which, though composed of the most vulgar materials when they are separately considered, has, when they are combined, a striking and powerful effect upon the imagination. The extraordinary height of the houses was marked by lights, which, glimmering irregularly along their front, ascended so high among the attics, that they seemed at length to twinkle in the middle sky. This coup d'œil, which still subsists in a certain degree, was then more striking, owing to the uninterrupted range of buildings on each side, which, broken only at the space where the North Bridge joins the main street, formed a superb and uniform Place, extending from the front of the Luckenbooths to the head of the Canongate, and corresponding in breadth and length to the uncommon height of the buildings on either side.

Mannering had not much time to look and to admire. His conductor hurried him across this striking scene, and suddenly dived with him into a very steep paved lane. Turning to the right, they entered a scale stair-case, as it is called, the state of which, so far as it could be judged of by one of his senses, annoyed Mannering's delicacy not a little. When they had ascended cautiously to a considerable height, they heard a heavy rap at a door, still two stories above them. The door opened, and immediately ensued the sharp and worrying bark of a dog, the squalling of a woman, the screams of an assaulted cat, and the hoarse voice of a man, who cried in a most imperative tone, "Will ye, Mustard! Will ye! down, sir, down!"

"Lord preserve us!" said the female voice, "an he had worried our cat, Mr Pleydell would ne'er hae forgien me!"

"Aweel, my doo, the cat's no a prin the waur—so he's no in, ye say?"

"Na, Mr Pleydell's ne'er in the house on Saturday."

"And the morn's Sabbath too," said the querist, "I dinna ken what will be done."

By this time Mannering appeared, and found a tall strong countryman, clad in a coat of pepper-and-salt-coloured mixture, with huge metal buttons, a glazed hat and boots, and a large horse-whip beneath his arm, in colloquy with a slip-shod damsel, who had in one hand the lock of the door, and in the other a pail of whiting, or *camstane*, as it is called, mixed with water—a circumstance which indicates Saturday night in Edinburgh.

"So Mr Pleydell is not at home, my good girl?" said Mannering.

"Aye sir, he's at hame, but he's no in the house: he's aye out on Saturday at e'en."

"But, my good girl, I am a stranger, and my business express—Will you tell me where I can find him?"

"His honour," said the cadie, "will be at Clerihugh's about this time—Hersell could hae tauld ye that, but she thought ye wanted to see his house."

"Well then, shew me to this tavern—I suppose he will see me, as I come on business of some consequence?"

"I dinna ken, sir," said the girl, "he does nae like to be disturbed on Saturdays wi' business—but he's aye civil to strangers."

"I'll gang to the tavern too," said our friend Dinmont, "for I am a stranger and on business e'en sic like."

"Na," said the hand-maiden, "an he see the gentleman, he'll see the simple body too—but, Lord's sake, dinna say it was me sent ye there."

"Atweel, I am a simple body that's true, hinny, but I am no come to steal ony o' his skill for naething," said the farmer in his honest pride, and strutted away down stairs, followed by Mannering and the cadie. Mannering could not help admiring the determined stride with which the stranger who preceded them divided the press, shouldering from him by the mere weight and impetus of his motion, both drunk and sober passengers. "He'll be a Teviotdale tup tat ane," said the cadie, "tat's for keeping ta crown o' ta causeway tat gate—he'll no gang far or he'll get somebody to bell ta cat wi' him."

His shrewd augury, however, was not fulfilled. Those who recoiled from the colossal weight of Dinmont, upon looking up at his size and strength, apparently judged him too heavy metal to be rashly encountered, and suffered him to pursue his course unchallenged. Following in the wake of this first-rate, Mannering proceeded till the farmer made a pause, and, looking back to the cadie, said, "I'm thinking this will be the close, friend?"

"Aye, aye," replied Donald, "tat's ta close."

Dinmont descended confidently, then turned into a dark alley—then up a dark stair—and then into an open door. While he was whistling shrilly for the waiter, as if he had been one of his collies, Mannering looked round him, and could hardly conceive how a gentleman of a liberal profession, and good society, should chuse such a scene for social indulgence. Besides the miserable entrance, the house itself seemed paltry and half ruinous. The passage in which they stood had a window to the close, which admitted a little light during the day-time, and a villainous compound of smells at all times, but more especially about this hour of the evening. Corresponding to this window was a borrowed light on the other side of the passage, looking into the kitchen, which had no direct communication with the free air, but received in the day-time, at second hand, such straggling and obscure light as found its way from the lane through the window opposite. At present the interior of the kitchen was visible by its own huge fires—a sort of Pandæmonium, where men and women, half undressed, were busied in baking, broiling, roasting oysters, and preparing devils on the gridiron; the mistress of the place, with her shoes slip-shod, and her hair straggling like that of Megæra from under a round-eared cap, toiling, scolding, receiving orders, giving them, and obeying them all at once, seemed the mistress enchantress of that gloomy and fiery region.

Loud and repeated bursts of laughter from different quarters of the house proved that her labours were acceptable, and not unrewarded by a generous public. With some difficulty a waiter was prevailed upon to show Colonel Mannering and Dinmont the room where their friend, learned in the law, held his hebdomadal carousals. The scene which it exhibited, and particularly the attitude of the counsellor himself, the principal figure therein, struck his two clients with astonishment.

Mr Pleydell was a lively sharp-looking gentleman, with a professional shrewdness in his eye, and, generally speaking, a professional formality in his manners. But this, like his three-tailed wig and black coat, he could slip off on a Saturday evening when surrounded by a party of jolly companions, and disposed for what he called his altitudes. Upon the present occasion, the revel had lasted since four o'clock, and, at length, under the direction of a venerable compotator, who had shared the sports and festivity of three generations, the frolicsome company had begun to practise the ancient and now forgotten pastime of *High Jinks*. This game was played in several different ways. Most frequently the dice were thrown by the company, and those upon whom the lot fell were obliged to assume and maintain, for a time, a certain fictitious character, or to repeat a certain number of fescennine verses in a particular order. If they departed from the character assigned, or if their memory proved treacherous in the repetition, they incurred forfeits, which were either compounded for by swallowing an additional bumper, or by paying a small sum towards the reckoning. At this sport the jovial company were closely set when Mannering entered the room.

Mr Counsellor Pleydell, such as we have described him, was enthroned, as a monarch, in an elbow-chair placed on the dining-table, his scratch wig on one side, his head crowned with a bottle-slider, his eye leering with an expression betwixt fun and drunkenness, while his court around him resounded with such crambo scraps of verse as these:

> Where is Gerunto now? and what's become of him?
> Gerunto's dead because he could not swim, &c. &c.

Such, O Themis, were anciently the sports of thy Scottish children! Dinmont was first in the room. He stood aghast a moment—and then exclaimed, "It's him, sure enough—Deil o' the like o' that I ever saw!"

At the sound of "Mr Dinmont and Colonel Mannering wanting to speak to you, sir," Pleydell turned his head, and blushed a little when he saw the very genteel figure of an English stranger. He was, however, of the opinion of Falstaff, "Out, ye villains, play out the play!" wisely judging it the better way to appear totally unconcerned. "What ho our guards!" exclaimed this second Justinian; "see ye not a stranger knight from foreign parts arrived at this our court of Holyrood,—with our bold yeoman Andrew Dinmont, who has succeeded to the keeping of our royal flocks within the forest of Jedwood, where, thanks to our royal care in the administration of justice, they feed as safe as if they were within the bounds of Fife? Where be our heralds, our pursuivants, our Lyon, our Marchmount, our Carrick, and our Snawdoun?—Let the strangers be placed at our board, and regaled as beseemeth their quality, and this our high holiday—to-morrow we will hear their tidings."

"So please you, my liege, to-morrow's Sunday," said one of the company.

"Sunday, is it? then will we give no offence to the Assembly of the Kirk—On Monday shall be their audience."

Mannering, who had stood at first uncertain whether to advance or retreat, now resolved to enter for a moment into the whim of the scene, though internally fretting at Mac-Morlan for sending him to consult with a crack-brained humourist. He therefore advanced, and with three profound congees craved permission to lay his credentials at the feet of the Scottish monarch, in order to be perused at his best leisure. The gravity with which he accommodated himself to the humour of the moment, and the deep and humble inclination with which he at first declined, and then accepted, a seat presented by the master of ceremonies, procured him three rounds of applause.

"Deil hae me, if they are na a' mad thegither!" said Dinmont, occupying with less ceremony a seat at the bottom of the table, "or else they hae ta'en Yule before it comes, and are ganging a guisarding."

A large glass of claret was offered to Mannering, who drank it to the health of the reigning monarch. "You are, I presume to guess," said the monarch, "that celebrated Sir Miles Mannering, so renowned in the French wars, and may well pronounce to us if the wines of Gascony lose their flavour in our more northern realm."

Mannering, agreeably flattered by this allusion to the fame of his celebrated ancestor, replied, by professing himself only a distant relation of the preux chevalier, and added, "that in his opinion the wine was superlatively good."

"It's ower cauld for my stomach," said Dinmont, setting down the glass, (empty however.)

"We will correct that quality," answered King Paulus, the first of the name; "we have not forgotten that the moist and humid air of our valley of Liddle inclines to stronger potations.—Seneschal, let our faithful yeoman have a cup of brandy; it will be more germain to the matter."

"And now," said Mannering, "since we have unwarily intruded upon your majesty at a moment of mirthful retirement, be pleased to say when you will indulge a stranger with an audience on those affairs of weight which have brought him to your northern capital."

The monarch opened Mac-Morlan's letter, and running it hastily over, exclaimed, with his natural voice and manner, "Lucy Bertram of Ellangowan, poor dear lassie!"

"A forfeit! a forfeit!" exclaimed a dozen voices, "his majesty has forgot his kingly character."

"Not a whit! not a whit!" replied the king, "I'll be judged by this courteous knight. May not a monarch love a maid of low degree? Is not King Cophetua and the Beggar-maid, an adjudged case in point?"

"Professional! professional!—another forfeit," exclaimed the tumultuary nobility.

"Had not our royal predecessors," continued the monarch, exalting his sovereign voice to drown these disaffected clamours,—"Had they not their Jean Logies, their Bessie Carmichaels, their Oliphants, their Sandilands, and their Weirs, and shall it be denied to us even to name a maiden whom we delight to honour? Nay, then, sink state and perish sovereignty! for, like a second Charles V., we will abdicate, and seek in the private shade of life those pleasures which are denied to a throne."

So saying, he flung away his crown, sprung from an exalted station with more agility than could have been expected, ordered lights and a wash-hand bason and towel, with a cup of green tea, into another room, and made a sign to Mannering to accompany him. In less than two minutes he washed his face and hands, settled his wig in the glass, and, to Mannering's great surprise, looked perfectly a different man from the childish Bacchanal he had been a moment before.

"There are folks," he said, "Mr Mannering, before whom one should take care how they play the fool—because they have either too much malice, or too little wit, as the poet says. The best compliment I can pay Colonel Mannering, is to shew I am not ashamed to expose myself before him—and truly I think it is a compliment I have not spared to-night upon your good-nature—But what's that great staring fellow wanting?"

Dinmont, who had pushed after Mannering into the room, began with a scrape with his foot and a scratch of his head in unison. "I am Dand Dinmont, sir, of the Charlieshope—the Liddesdale lad—ye'll mind me?—it was for me ye won yon grand plea."

"What plea, you loggerhead? d'ye think I can remember all the fools that come to plague me?"

"Lord, sir, it was the grand plea about the grazing o' the Langtae-head!"

"Well, curse thee, never mind; give me the memorial, and come to me on Monday at ten."

"But, sir, I hae na got ony distinct memorial."

"No memorial, man?"

"Na, sir, nae memorial! for your honour said before, Mr Pleydell, ye'll mind, that ye liked best to hear us hill-folk tell their ain tale by word o' mouth."

"Beshrew my tongue, that said so! it will cost my ears a dinning—well, say in two words what you've got to say—you see the gentleman waits."

"Ow, sir, if the gentleman likes he may play his ain spring first; it's a' ane to Dandie."

"No, you looby, cannot you conceive that your business can be nothing to him, but that he may not chuse to have these great ears of thine regaled with his matters?"

"Aweel, sir, just as you and he like—so ye see to my business. We're at the auld wark of the marches again, Jock o' Dawstone Cleugh and me. Ye see we march on the tap o' Touthop-rigg after ye pass the Pomaragrains; for the Pomaragrains, and Slackenspool, and Bloodylaws, they come in there, and they belang to the Peel; but after ye pass Pomaragrains at a mickle great saucer-headed cutlugged stane, that they ca' Charlies Chuckie, there Dawstone Cleugh and Charlieshope they march. Now, I say, the march rins on the tap o' the hill where the wind and water shears, but Jock o' Dawstone Cleugh again, he contravenes that, and says that it hauds down by the auld drove road that gaes awa' by the Knot of the Gate ower Keeldar-ward—And that makes an unco difference."

"And what difference does it make, friend? How many sheep will it feed?"

"Ow, no mony—it's lying high and exposed—it may feed a hog, or aiblins twa in a good year."

"And for this grazing, which may be worth about five shillings a year, you are willing to throw away a hundred pound or two?"

"Na, sir, it's no for the value of the grass—it's for justice."

"My good friend, justice, like charity, should begin at home—do you justice to your wife and family—and think no more about the matter."

Dinmont still lingered, twisting his hat in his hand—"It's no for that, sir—but I would like ill to be bragged wi' him—he threeps he'll bring a score o' witnesses and mair—and I am sure there's as mony will swear for me as for him, folk that lived a' their days upon the Charlieshope, and wad na like to see the land lose its right."

"Zounds, man, if it be a point of honour, why don't your landlords take it up?"

"I dinna ken, sir, (scratching his head) there's been nae election-dust lately, and the lairds are unco neighbourly, and Jock and I canna get them to yoke thegither about it a' that we can say—but if ye thought we might keep up the rent"——

"No! no! that will never do—confound you, why don't ye take good cudgels and settle?"

"Odd, sir, we tried that three times already—that's twice on the land and ance at Lockerbye fair.—But I dinna ken—we're baith gay good at single-stick, and it could na weel be judged."

"Then take broad-swords, and be d—d to you, as your fathers did before you."

"Aweel, sir, if ye think it wad na be again the law, it's a' ane to Dandie."

"Hold! hold! we shall have another Lord Soulis' mistake—Prithee, man, comprehend me; I wish you to consider how very trifling and foolish a law-suit you wish to engage in."

"Aye, sir? So you winna take on wi' me, I'm doubting?"

"Me! not I—go home, go home, take a pint and agree." Dand looked but half contented, and still remained stationary. "Any thing more, my friend?"

"Only, sir, about the succession of this leddy that's dead, auld Miss Margaret Bertram o' Singleside."

"Aye, what about her?" said the counsellor, rather surprised.

"Ow, we have nae connexion at a' wi' the Bertrams—they were grand folk by the like o' us—But Jean Liltup, that was auld Singleside's housekeeper, and the mother of these twa young ladies that are gane—the last o' them's dead at a ripe age, I trow—Jean Liltup came out o' Liddle water, and she was as near our connexion as second cousin to my mother's half-sister—She drew up wi' Singleside, nae doubt, when she was his housekeeper, and it was a sair vex and grief to a' her kith and kin. But he acknowledged a marriage, and satisfied the kirk—and now I wad ken frae ye if we hae not some claim by law?"

"Not the shadow."

"Aweel, we're nae puirer—but she may hae thought on us if she was minded to make a testament.—Weel, sir, I've said my say—I'se e'en wish you good night, and"——putting his hand in his pocket.

"No, no, my friend; I never take fees on Saturday nights, or without a memorial—away with you, Dandie." And Dandie made his reverence, and departed accordingly.

Chapter Sixteen

But this poor farce has neither truth nor art,
To please the fancy or to touch the heart;
Dark but not awful, dismal but yet mean,
With anxious bustle, moves the cumbrous scene,
Presents no objects tender or profound,
But spreads its cold unmeaning gloom around.
Parish Register

"YOUR MAJESTY," said Mannering, laughing, "has solemnized your abdication by an act of mercy and charity—That fellow will scarce think of going to law."

"O, you are quite wrong—The only difference is, I have lost my client and my fee. He'll never rest till he finds somebody to encourage him to commit the folly he has predetermined—No! no! I have only shewn you another weakness of my character—I always speak truth of a Saturday night."

"And sometimes through the week I should think," said Mannering, continuing the same tone.

"Why, yes! as far as my vocation will permit. I am, as Hamlet says, indifferent honest, when my clients and their solicitors do not make me the medium of conveying their double-distilled lies to the bench. But *oportet vivere!* it is a sad necessity.—And now to our business. I am glad my old friend Mac-Morlan has sent you to me; he is an active, honest, and intelligent man, long sheriff-substitute of the county of —— under me, and still holds the office. He knows I have a regard for that unfortunate family of Ellangowan, and for poor Lucy. I have not seen her since she was twelve years old, and she was then a sweet pretty girl under the management of a very silly father. But my interest in her is of an early date. I was called upon, Mr Mannering, being then sheriff of that county, to investigate the particulars of a murder which had been committed near Ellangowan the day on which this poor child was born; and which, by a strange combination which I was unhappily unable to trace, involved the death or abstraction of her only brother, a boy of about five years old. No, Colonel, I shall never forget the misery of the house of Ellangowan—that morning—the father half-distracted—the mother dead in premature travail—the helpless infant, with scarce any one to attend to it, coming wawling and crying into this miserable world at such a moment of unutterable misery. We lawyers are not of iron, sir, or of brass, any more than you soldiers are of steel. We are conversant with the crimes and distresses of civil society, as you are with those that occur in a state of war, and to do our duty in either case a little apathy is perhaps necessary—But the devil take a soldier whose heart can be as hard as his sword, and his dam take a lawyer who bronzes his bosom instead of his forehead!—But come, I am losing my Saturday at e'en—Will you have the kindness to trust me with these papers which relate to Miss Bertram's business?—and stay —to-morrow you'll take a bachelor's dinner with an old lawyer,—I insist upon it, at three precisely—and come half an hour sooner.—The old lady is to be buried on Monday; it is the orphan's cause, and we'll borrow an hour from the Sunday to talk over this business—although I fear nothing can be done if she has altered her settlement—unless perhaps it occurs within the sixty days, and then if Miss Bertram can shew that she possesses the character of heir-at-law——

"But, hark! my lieges are impatient of their *interregnum*—I do not invite you to rejoin us, Colonel, it would be a trespass on your complaisance, unless you had begun the day with us, and gradually glided on from wisdom to mirth, and from mirth to—to—to—extravagance. —Good night—Harry, go home with Mr Mannering to his lodging—Colonel, I expect you at a little past two to-morrow."

The Colonel returned home, equally surprised at the childish frolics in which he found his learned counsel engaged, at the candour and sound sense which he had in a moment summoned up to meet the exigencies of his profession, and at the tone of feeling which he displayed when he spoke of the friendless orphan. "This is a gentle lawyer," he said; "I have no great opinion of the long robe in any country, but there are good men in all professions. What a pity that their habits of shirking, and tricking, and splitting hairs are inconsistent with the high point of honour and chivalrous zeal for their king and country, which after (rather combined with) moral and religious principle should form the moving spring of every principle as well as of ours."

Alas! my dear Colonel, whom I love so much that I have made thee stand godfather to this history, an honour to which many may doubt any other pretensions than my partiality—Were the learned advocate thinking on thee at this moment, when I rather think he is deeply engaged in his gambols at High Jinks, might he not with equal reason wonder that from India, believed to be the seat of European violence and military oppression, had arrived an officer of distinction, open to compassionate and liberal feelings? Alas! why should we go on in social life balancing the advantages and disadvantages of various occupations with such a partial balance. "Go to weigh equally, an you weigh equally a feather will turn the scale." Each profession hath virtues from which he who practises it dare not depart, and licences which he may use with less risk of censure than those of other vocations. The best is he who, adhering to the rules prescribed to him by his situation, adds the merit of resisting the temptations to which it throws him peculiarly open.

In the morning, while the Colonel and his most quiet and silent of all retainers, Dominie Sampson, were finishing the breakfast which Barnes had made and poured out, after the Dominie had scalded himself in the attempt, Mr Pleydell was suddenly ushered in. A nicely-dressed bob-wig, upon every hair of which a zealous and careful barber had bestowed its proper allowance of powder; a well-brushed black suit, with very clean shoes and gold buckles and stock-buckle; a manner rather reserved and formal than intrusive, but with all that, shewing only the formality of manner, by no means of awkwardness or intimidation; a countenance, the expressive and somewhat comic features of which were in complete repose,—all shewed a being perfectly different from the choice spirit of the evening before. A glance of shrewd and piercing fire in his eye was the only marked expression which recalled the man of "Saturday at e'en."

"I am come," said he with a very polite address, "to use my regal authority in your behalf in spirituals as well as temporals—can I accompany you to the presbyterian kirk, or the episcopal meeting-house?—*Tros Tyriusve*, a lawyer, you know, is of both religions, or rather I should say of both forms—or can I assist in passing the forenoon otherwise? You'll excuse my old-fashioned importunity—I was born in a time when a Scotchman was thought inhospitable if he left a guest alone a moment, except when he slept—but I trust you will tell me at once if I intrude."

"Not at all, my dear sir—I am delighted to put myself under your pilotage. I should wish much to hear some of your Scottish preachers whose talents have done such honour to your country—your Blair, your Robertson, or your Henry; and I embrace your kind offer with all my heart—Only," drawing the lawyer a little aside, and turning his eye towards Sampson, "my worthy friend there in the reverie is a little helpless and abstracted, and Barnes, who is his pilot in ordinary, cannot well assist him here, especially as he has expressed his determination of going to some of your darker and more remote places of worship."

The lawyer's eye glanced at him. "A curiosity worth preserving—and I'll find you a fit custodier.—Here you, sir, (to the waiter) go to Luckie Finlayson's in the Cowgate for Miles Macfin the cadie, he'll be there about this time, and tell him I wish to speak to him."

The person wanted soon arrived. "I will commit your friend to this man's charge," said Pleydell; "he'll attend him, or conduct him, wherever he chuses to go, with a happy indifference as to kirk or market, meeting or court of justice, or—any other place whatever—and bring him safe home at whatever hours you appoint; so that Mr Barnes there may be left to the freedom of his own will."

This was easily arranged, and the Colonel committed the Dominie to the charge of this man while they should remain in Edinburgh.

"And now, sir, if you please, we go to the Greyfriars church to hear our historian of Scotland, of the Continent, and of America."

They were disappointed—he did not preach that morning.—"Never mind," said the counsellor, "have a moment's patience, and we shall do very well."

The colleague of Dr R—— ascended the pulpit. His external appearance was not prepossessing. A remarkably fair complexion was strangely contrasted with a black wig without a grain of powder; a narrow chest and a stooping posture, hands which, placed like props on either side of the pulpit, seemed necessary rather to support the person than to assist the gesticulation of the preacher,—no gown, not even that of Geneva, a tumbled band, and a gesture which seemed scarce voluntary, were the first circumstances which struck a stranger. "The preacher seems a very ungainly person," whispered Mannering to his new friend.

"Never fear, he's the son of an excellent Scottish lawyer—he'll shew blood, I'se warrant him."

The learned counsel predicted truly. A lecture fraught with new, striking, and entertaining views of scripture history—a sermon in which the Calvinism of the Kirk of Scotland was ably supported, yet made the basis of a sound system of practical morals, which should neither shelter the sinner under the cloak of speculative faith or of peculiarity of opinion, nor leave him loose to the waves of unbelief and schism. Something there was of an antiquated turn of argument and metaphor, but it only served in our Mannering's opinion to give zest and peculiarity to the style of elocution. The sermon was not read—a scrap of paper containing the heads of the discourse was occasionally referred to, and the enunciation, which at first seemed imperfect and embarrassed, became, as the preacher warmed in his progress, animated and distinct; and although the sermon could not be quoted as a correct specimen of pulpit eloquence, yet Mannering had seldom heard so much learning, metaphysical acuteness, and energy of argument, brought into the service of Christianity.

"Such," he said, going out of the church, "must have been the preachers, to whose unfearing minds, and acute, though sometimes rudely exercised talents, we owe the Reformation."

"And yet that reverend gentleman," said Pleydell, "whom I love for his father's sake and his own, has nothing of the souring or pharisaical pride which has been imputed to some of the early fathers of the Calvinistic Kirk of Scotland. His colleague and he differ, and head different parties in the kirk, about particular points of church discipline; but without for a moment losing personal regard or respect for each other, or suffering malignity to interfere in an opposition steady, constant, and apparently conscientious on both sides."

"And you, Mr Pleydell, what do you think of their points of difference?"

"Why, I hope, Colonel, a plain man may go to heaven without thinking about them at all—besides, *entre nous*, I am a member of the suffering and episcopal church of Scotland—the shadow of a shade now, and fortunately so—but I love to pray where my fathers prayed before me, without thinking worse of the presbyterian forms, because they do not affect me with the same associations." And with this remark they parted until dinner-time.

From the awkward access to the lawyer's mansion, Mannering was induced to form very moderate expectations of the entertainment which he was to receive. The approach looked even more dismal by day-light than on the preceding evening. The houses on each side of the lane were so close, that the neighbours might have shaken hands with each other from the different sides, and occasionally the space between was traversed by wooden galleries, and thus entirely closed up. The scale-stair was not sweeter than it had been on the night before, and upon entering the house, Mannering was struck with the narrowness and meanness of the wainscotted passage. But the library, into which he was shewn by an elderly and respectable-looking man-servant, was a complete contrast to these unpromising appearances. It was a well-proportioned room, hung with a portrait or two of Scottish characters of eminence, by Jamieson, the Caledonian Vandyke, and surrounded with books, the best editions of the best authors. "These," said Mr Pleydell, "are my tools of trade; a lawyer without history or literature is a mechanic, a mere working mason; if he possess some knowledge of these, he may call himself an architect." But Mannering was chiefly delighted with the view from the windows, which commanded that incomparable prospect of the grounds between Edinburgh and the sea; the Firth of Forth, with its islands; the embayment which is terminated by the Law of North Berwick; and the varied shores of Fife to the northward, indenting with a hilly outline the clear blue horizon.

When Mr Pleydell had sufficiently enjoyed the surprise of his guest, he called his attention to Miss Bertram's affairs. "I was in hopes," he said, "though but faint, to have discovered some means of ascertaining her indefeasible right to this property of Singleside; but my researches have been in vain. The old lady was certainly absolute fiar, and might dispose of it in full right of property. All that we have to hope is, that the devil may not have tempted her to alter this very proper settlement. You must attend the old girl's funeral to-morrow, to which you will receive an invitation, for I have acquainted her agent with your being here on Miss Bertram's part, and I will meet you afterwards at the house she inhabited, and be present to see fair play at the opening of the settlements. The old cat had a little girl, the orphan of some relation, who lived with her as a kind of slavish companion. I hope she has had the conscience to make her independent, in consideration of the *peine forte et dure* to which she subjected her during her life-time."

Three gentlemen now appeared, and were introduced to the stranger. They were men of good sense, gaiety, and general information, so that the day passed very pleasantly over; and Colonel Mannering assisted, about eight o'clock at night, in discussing the landlord's bottle, which was, of course, a *magnum*. Upon his return to the inn, he found a card inviting him to the funeral of Miss Margaret Bertram, late of Singleside, which was to proceed from her own house to the place of interment in the Greyfriars church-yard, at one o'clock afternoon.

At the appointed hour Mannering went to a small house in the suburbs to the southward of the city, where he found the place of mourning, indicated, as usual in Scotland, by two rueful figures with long black cloaks, white crapes and hat-bands, holding in their hands poles, adorned with melancholy streamers of the same description. By two other mutes, who, from their visages, seemed suffering under the pressure of some strange calamity, he was ushered into the dining-parlour of the defunct, where the company were assembled for the funeral.

In Scotland is universally retained the custom, now disused in England, of inviting the relations of the deceased to the interment. Upon many occasions this has a singular and striking effect, but upon some it degenerates into mere empty form and grimace, in cases where the defunct has had the misfortune to live unbeloved and die unlamented. The English service for the dead, one of the most beautiful and impressive parts of the ritual of the church, would have, in such cases, the effect of fixing the attention, and uniting the thoughts and feelings of the audience present, in an exercise of devotion so peculiarly adapted to such an occasion. But according to the Scottish custom, if there be not real feeling among the assistants, there is nothing to supply the want, and exalt or rouse the attention; so that a sense of tedious form, and almost hypocritical restraint, is too apt to pervade the company assembled for the mournful solemnity. Mrs Margaret Bertram was unfortunately one of those whose good qualities had attached no general friendship. She had no near relations who might have mourned from natural affection, and therefore her funeral exhibited merely the exterior trappings of sorrow.

Mannering, therefore, stood among this lugubrious company of cousins in the third, fourth, fifth, and sixth degree, composing his countenance to the decent solemnity of all who were around him, and looking as much concerned upon Mrs Margaret Bertram's account, as if the deceased lady of Singleside had been his own sister or mother. After a deep and awful pause, the company began to talk aside —under their breaths, however, and as if in the chamber of a dying person. "Our poor friend," said one grave gentleman, scarcely opening his mouth, for fear of deranging the necessary solemnity of his features, and sliding his whisper from between his lips, which were as little unclosed as possible,—"Our poor friend has died well to pass in the warld."

"Nae doubt," answered the person addressed, with half-closed eyes; "poor Mrs Margaret was aye careful of the gear."

"Any news to-day, Colonel Mannering?" said one of the gentlemen, whom he had dined with the day before, but in a tone which might, for its impressive gravity, have communicated the death of his whole generation.

"Nothing particular, I believe, sir," said Mannering, in the cadence which was, he observed, appropriated to the house of mourning.

"I understand," continued the first speaker, emphatically, and with the air of one who is well informed; "I understand there *is* a settlement."

"And what does little Jenny Gibson get?"

"A hundred, and the auld repeater."

"That's but sma' gear, puir thing; she had a sair time o't with the auld leddy. But it's ill waiting for dead folk's shoon."

"I am afraid," said the politician, who was by Mannering, "we have not done with your old friend Tippoo Saib yet—I doubt he'll give the Company more plague; and I am told, but you'll know for certain, that East India Stock is not rising."

"I trust it will, sir, soon."

"Mrs Margaret," said another person, mingling in the conversation, "had some India bonds. I know that, for I drew the interest for her—it would be desirable now for the trustees and legatees to have the Colonel's advice about the time and mode of converting them into money—for my part I think—But there's Mr Mortcloke to tell us they are ganging to lift."

Mr Mortcloke the undertaker did accordingly, with a visage of professional length and most grievous solemnity, distribute among the pall-bearers little cards, assigning their respective situations in attendance upon the coffin. As this precedence is supposed to be regulated by propinquity to the defunct, the undertaker, however skilful a master of these lugubrious ceremonies, did not escape giving some offence. To be related to Mrs Bertram was to be of kin to the lands of Singleside, and was a propinquity of which each relative present at that moment was particularly jealous. Some murmurs there were upon the occasion, and our friend Dinmont gave more open offence, being unable either to repress his discontent, or to express it in the key properly modulated to the solemnity. "I think ye might hae at least gien me a leg o' her to carry," he exclaimed, in a voice considerably louder than propriety admitted; "God! an it had na been for the rigs o' land, I would hae got her a' to carry mysell, for as mony gentles as are here."

A score of frowning and reproving brows were bent upon the unappalled yeoman, who, having given vent to his displeasure, stalked sturdily down stairs with the rest of the company, totally disregarding the censures of those whom his remark had scandalized.

And then the funeral pomp set forth; saulies with their batons, and gumphions of tarnished white crape, in honour of the well-preserved maiden fame of Mrs Margaret Bertram. Six starved horses, themselves the very emblems of mortality, well cloaked and plumed, lugging along the hearse with its dismal emblazonry, creeped in slow state towards the place of interment, preceded by Jamie Duff, an idiot, who, with weepers and cravat made of white paper, attended upon every funeral, and followed by six mourning coaches, filled with the company. Many of these now gave more free loose to their tongues, and discussed with unrestrained earnestness the amount of the succession, and the probability of its destination. The principal expectants, however, kept a prudent silence, indeed ashamed to express hopes which might prove fallacious; and the agent, or man of business, who alone knew exactly how matters stood, maintained a countenance of mysterious importance, as if determined to preserve the full interest of anxiety and suspense.

At length they arrived at the church-yard gates, and from thence, amid the gaping of some dozen of idle women with infants in their arms, and accompanied by some twenty children who ran gambolling and screaming alongside of the sable procession, they finally arrived at the burial place of the Singleside family. This was a square enclosure, guarded on one side by a veteran angel, without a nose, and having only one wing, who had the merit of having maintained his post for a century, while his comrade cherub, who had stood centinel on the corresponding pedestal, lay a broken trunk among the hemlock, burdock and nettles, which grew in gigantic luxuriance around the walls of the mausoleum. A moss-grown and broken inscription informed the reader, that in the year 1650 Captain Andrew Bertram, first of Singleside, descended of the very ancient and honourable house of Ellangowan, had caused this monument to be erected for himself and his descendants. A reasonable number of scythes and hour-glasses, and death's heads, and cross bones, garnished the following sprig of sepulchral poetry to the memory of the founder of the mausoleum:

Nathaniel's heart, Bezaleel's hand,
If ever any had,
These boldly do I say had he,
Who lieth in this bed.

Here then, amid the deep black fat loam into which her ancestors were now resolved, they deposited the body of Mrs Margaret Bertram; and, like soldiers returning from a military funeral, the nearest relations who might be interested in the settlements of the lady, urged the dog-cattle of the hackney coaches to all the speed of which they were capable, in order to put an end to farther suspense on this interesting topic.

Chapter Seventeen

Die and endow a college or a cat.
POPE

THERE IS a fable told by Lucian, that while a troop of monkeys, well drilled by an intelligent manager, were performing a tragedy with great applause, the decorum of the whole scene was at once destroyed, and the natural passions of the actors called forth into very indecent and active emulation, by a wag who threw a handful of nuts upon the stage. In like manner, the approaching crisis stirred up among the expectants feelings of a nature very different from those, of which, under the superintendance of Mr Mortcloke, they had lately been endeavouring to imitate the expression. Those eyes which were lately devoutly cast up to heaven, or with greater humility bent solemnly upon earth, were now sharply and alertly darting their glances through shuttles, and trunks, and drawers, and cabinets, and all the odd corners of an old maiden lady's repositories. Nor was their search without interest, though they did not find the will of which they were in quest.

Here was a promissory note for 20l. by the minister of the non-juring chapel, interest marked paid up to Martinmas last, carefully folded up in a new set of words to the old tune of "Over the Water to

Charlie,"—there was a curious love correspondence between the deceased and a certain Lieutenant O'Kean of a marching regiment of foot; and tied up with the letters was a document, which at once explained to the relatives why a connection which boded them little good had been suddenly broken off, being the Lieutenant's bond for two hundred pounds, upon which *no* interest whatever appeared to have been paid. Other bills and bonds to a larger amount, and signed by better names (I mean commercially) than those of the worthy divine and gallant soldier, also occurred in the course of their researches, besides a hoard of coins of every size and denomination, and scraps of broken gold and silver, old ear-rings, hinges of cracked snuff-boxes, mountings of spectacles, &c. &c. &c. Still no will made its appearance, and Colonel Mannering began full well to hope that the settlement which he had obtained from Glossin contained the ultimate arrangement of the old lady's affairs. But his friend Pleydell, who now came into the room, cautioned him against entertaining this belief. "I know the gentleman," he said, "who is conducting the search, and I guess from his manner that he knows something more of the matter than any of us."

Meantime, while the search proceeds, let us take a brief glance at one or two of the company who seem most interested. Of Dinmont, who, with his huge hunting-whip under his arm, stood poking his large round face over the shoulder of the *homme d'affaires*, it is unnecessary to say any thing. That thin-looking oldish man, in a most correct and gentleman-like suit of mourning, is Mac-Casquil, formerly of Drumquag, who was ruined by having a legacy bequeathed to him of two shares in the Ayr bank. His hopes upon the present occasion are founded on a very distant relationship, upon his sitting in the same pew with the deceased every Sunday, and upon his playing at cribbage with her regularly on the Saturday evenings—taking great care never to come off a winner. That other coarse-looking man, wearing his own greasy hair tied in a leathern cue more greasy still, is a tobacconist, a relation of Mrs Bertram's mother, who, having a good stock in trade when the colonial war broke out, trebled the price of his commodity to all the world, Mrs Bertram alone excepted, whose tortoise-shell snuff-box was weekly filled with the best rappee at the old prices, because the maid brought it to the shop with Mrs Bertram's respects to *her cousin* Mr Quid. That young fellow who has not had the decency to put off his boots and buckskins, might have stood as forward as most of them in the graces of the old lady, who loved to look upon a comely young man. But it is thought he has forfeited the moment of fortune by sometimes neglecting her tea-table when solemnly invited; sometimes appearing there, when he had been dining with blither company; twice treading upon her cat's tail, and once affronting her parrot.

To Mannering, the most interesting of the group was the poor girl, who had been a sort of humble companion of the deceased, as a subject upon whom she could at all times expectorate her bad humour. She was for form's sake dragged into the room by the deceased's favourite female attendant, where, shrinking into a corner as soon as possible, she saw with wonder and affright the intrusive researches of the strangers amongst those recesses to which from childhood she had looked with awful veneration. This girl was regarded with an unfavourable eye by all the competitors, honest Dinmont only excepted; the rest conceived they should find in her a formidable competitor, whose claims might at least encumber and diminish their chance of succession. Yet she was the only person present who seemed really to feel sorrow for the deceased. Mrs Bertram had been her protectress, although from selfish motives, and her capricious tyranny was forgotten at the moment while the tears followed each other fast down the cheeks of her frightened and friendless dependant. "There's ower mickle saut water there, Drumquag," (said the tobacconist to the ex-proprietor) "to bode ither folk mickle gude. Folk seldom greet that gate but they ken what it's for." Mr MacCasquil only replied with a nod, feeling the propriety of asserting his gentry in presence of Mr Pleydell and Colonel Mannering.

"Very queer if there suld be nae will after a', friend," said Dinmont, who began to grow impatient, to the man of business.

"A moment's patience, if you please—she was a good and prudent woman, Mrs Margaret Bertram—a good and prudent and well-judging woman, and knew to chuse friends and depositaries—she will have put her last will and testament, or rather her *mortis causa* settlement as it relates to heritage, into the hands of some safe friend."

"I'll bet a rump and dozen," said Pleydell, whispering to the Colonel, "he has got it in his own pocket;"—then addressing the man of law, "Come, sir, we'll cut this short if you please—here is a settlement of the estate of Singleside, executed several years ago, in favour of Miss Lucy Bertram of Ellangowan"——The company stared fearfully wild. "You, I presume, Mr Protocol, can inform us if there is a later deed?"

"Please to favour me, Mr Pleydell;"—and so saying, he took the deed out of the learned counsel's hand, and glanced his eye over the contents.

"Too cool," said Pleydell, "too cool by half—he has another deed in his pocket still."

"Why does he not shew it then, and be d—d to him?" said the

military gentleman, whose patience began to wax threadbare.

"Why, how should I know?" answered the barrister,—"why does a cat not kill a mouse when she takes him?—the love of power and of teasing, I suppose.—Well, Mr Protocol, what say you to that deed?"

"Why, sir, the deed is a well drawn deed, properly authenticated and tested in forms of the statute."

"But recalled by another of posterior date in your possession?—eh!"

"Something of the sort I confess, Mr Pleydell,"—producing a bundle tied with tape, and sealed at each fold and ligature with black wax. "That deed, Mr Pleydell, which you produce and found upon, is dated 1st June, 17—, but this"—breaking the seals and unfolding the document slowly—"is dated the 20th—no, I see it is the 21st, of April of this present year, being ten years posterior."

"Marry, hang her, brock!" said the counsellor, borrowing an exclamation from Sir Toby Belch, "just the month in which Ellangowan's distresses became generally public. But let us hear what she has done."

Mr Protocol accordingly, having required silence, began to read the settlement aloud in a slow, steady, and business-like tone. The group around, in whose eyes hopes alternately awakened and faded, and who were straining their apprehensions to get at the drift of the testator's meaning through the mist of technical language in which the conveyancer had involved it, might have made a study for Hogarth.

The deed was of an unexpected nature. It set forth with conveying and disponing "all and whole the estate, lands of Singleside and others, with the lands of Loverless, Lyalone, Spinster's Knowe, Reilagganbeg, and Gillifidget, to and in favours of (here the reader softened his voice to a gentle and modest piano) Peter Protocol, Clerk to the Signet, having the fullest confidence in his capacity and integrity, (these are the very words which my worthy deceased friend insisted upon inserting). But in TRUST always, (here the reader recovered his voice and stile, and the visages of several of the hearers, which had attained a longitude that Mr Mortcloke might have envied, were perceptibly shortened) in TRUST always, and for the uses, ends, and purposes herein after-mentioned."

In these "uses, ends, and purposes," lay the cream of the affair. The first was introduced by a preamble setting forth, that the testatrix was lineally descended from the ancient house of Ellangowan, her respected great-grand-father, Andrew Bertram, first of Singleside, of happy memory, having been second son to Allan Bertram, fifteenth Baron of Ellangowan. It proceeded to state, that Henry Bertram, son and heir of Godfrey Bertram, now of Ellangowan, had been stolen from his parents in infancy, but that she, the testatrix, *was well assured that he was yet alive in foreign parts, and by the providence of heaven would be restored to the possessions of his ancestors*—in which case the said Peter Protocol was bound and obliged, like as he bound and obliged himself, by acceptance of these presents, to denude himself of the said lands of Singleside and others, and of all the other effects thereby conveyed (excepting always a proper gratification for his own trouble) to and in favour of the said Henry Bertram upon his return to his native country. And during the time of his residing in foreign parts, or in case of his never again returning to Scotland, Mr Peter Protocol, the trustee, was to distribute the rents of the land, and interest of the other funds, (deducing always a proper gratification for his trouble in the premises) in equal portions, among four charitable establishments pointed out in the will. The power of management, of letting leases, of raising and lending out money, in short, the full authority of a proprietor, was vested in this confidential trustee, and, in the event of his death, went to certain official persons named in the deed. There were only two legacies; one of a hundred pounds to a favourite waiting-maid, another of the like sum to Janet Gibson (whom the deed stated to have been supported by the charity of the testatrix) for the purpose of binding her apprentice to some honest trade.

A settlement in mortmain is in Scotland termed a *mortification*, and in one great borough (Aberdeen, if I remember rightly) there is a municipal officer who takes care of these public endowments, and is thence called the Master of Mortifications. One would almost presume, that the term had its origin in the effect which such settlements usually produce upon the kinsmen of those by whom they are executed. Heavy at least was the mortification which befell the audience, who, in the late Mrs Margaret Bertram's parlour, had listened to this unexpected destination of the lands of Singleside. There was a profound silence after the deed had been read over.

Mr Pleydell was the first to speak. He begged to look at the deed, and having satisfied himself that it was correctly drawn and executed, he returned it without any observation, only saying aside to Mannering, "Protocol is not worse than other people, I believe; but this old lady has determined that if he do not turn rogue it shall not be for want of temptation."

"I really think," said Mr Mac-Casquil of Drumquag, who, having gulped down one half of his vexation, determined to give vent to the rest, "I really think this is an extraordinary case! I should like now to know from Mr Protocol, who, being sole and unlimited trustee, must have been consulted upon this occasion; I should like, I say, to know, how Mrs Bertram could possibly believe in the existence of a boy, that a' the world kens was murdered many a year since?"

"Really, sir," said Mr Protocol, "I do not conceive it is possible for me to explain her motives more than she has done herself. Our excellent deceased friend was a good woman, sir—a pious woman—and might have grounds for confidence in the boy's safety whilk are not accessible to us, sir."

"Hout," said the tobacconist, "I ken very weel what were her grounds for confidence. There's Mrs Rebecca (the maid) sitting there, has tell'd me a hundred times in my ain shop, there was nae kenning how her lady wad settle her affairs, for an auld gypsey witch wife at Gilsland had possessed her with a notion, that the callant—Harry Bertram ca's she him?—would come alive again some day after a'—ye'll no deny that, Mrs Rebecca?—though I dare to say ye forgot to put your mistress in mind of what ye promised to do when I gied ye mony a half-crown—But ye'll no deny what I am saying now, lass?"

"I ken naething at a' about it," answered Rebecca doggedly, and looking straight forward with the firm countenance of one not disposed to be compelled to remember more than was agreeable to her.

"Weel said, Rebecca! ye're satisfied wi' your ain share ony way," rejoined the tobacconist.

The young buck of the second-head, for a buck of the first-head he was not, had hitherto sate slapping his boots with his switch-whip, and looking like a spoiled child that has lost its supper. His murmurs, however, were all vented inwardly, or at most in a soliloquy such as this—"I am sorry, by G—, I ever plagued myself about her—I came here, by G—, one night to drink tea, and I left King, and the duke's rider Will Hack. They were toasting a round of running horses, by G—; I might have got leave to wear the jacket as well as other folk, if I had carried it on with them—And she has not so much as left me that hundred!"

"We'll make the payment of the note quite agreeable," said Mr Protocol, who had no wish to increase at that moment the odium attached to his office—"And now, gentlemen, I fancy we have no more to wait for here, and—I shall put the settlement of my excellent and worthy friend on record to-morrow, that every gentleman may examine the contents, may have free access to take an extract—and ——" He proceeded to lock up the repositories of the deceased with more speed than he had opened them—"Mrs Rebecca, ye'll be so kind as to keep all right here until we can let the house—I had an offer this morning, if such a thing should be, and if I was to have any management"——

Our friend Dinmont, having had his hopes as well as another, had hitherto sate sulky enough in an arm-chair formerly appropriated to the deceased, and in which she would have been not a little scandalized to have seen this colossal specimen of the masculine sex lolling at length. His employment had been rolling up, into the form of a coiled snake, the long lash of his horse-whip, and then letting it uncoil itself into the middle of the floor.—The first words he said when he had digested the shock, contained a magnanimous declaration, which he probably was not conscious of having uttered aloud—"Weel—blood's thicker than water—she's welcome to the cheeses and the hams just the same." But when the trustee had made the above-mentioned motion for the mourners to depart, and talked of the house being immediately let, honest Dinmont got upon his feet, and stunned the company with this blunt question, "And what's to come o' this poor lassie than, Jenny Gibson? Sae mony o' us as thought oursells sib to the family when the gear was parting, we may do something for her amang us surely."

This proposal seemed to dispose most of the assembly instantly to evacuate the premises, although upon Mr Protocol's motion they had lingered as if around the grave of their disappointed hopes. Drumquag said, or rather muttered, something of having a family of his own, and took precedence, in virtue of his gentle blood, to depart as fast as possible. The tobacconist sturdily stood forward and scouted the motion—"A little huzzie like that was weel enough provided for already; and Mr Protocol at ony rate was the proper person to take direction of her, as he had charge of her legacy;" and after uttering such his opinion in a steady and decisive tone of voice, he also left the place. The buck made a stupid and brutal attempt at a jest upon Mrs Bertram's recommendation that the poor girl be taught some honest trade; but encountered a scowl from Colonel Mannering's darkening eye (to whom, in his ignorance of the tone of good society, he had looked for applause) that made him ache to the very back-bone. He shuffled down stairs therefore, as fast as possible.

Protocol, who was really a good sort of man, next expressed his intention to take a temporary charge of the young lady, under protest always, that his so doing should be considered as merely eleemosynary; when Dinmont at length got up, and having shaken his huge dreadnought great-coat, as a Newfoundland dog does his shaggy hide when he comes out of the water, ejaculated, "Weel, deil hae me then, if ye hae ony fash wi' her, Mr Protocol; if she likes to gae hame wi' me that is. Ye see, Ailie and me we're weel to pass, and we would like the lassies to hae a wee bit mair lair than oursells, and to be neighbour-like —that would we.—And ye see she canna miss but to ken manners, and the like o' reading books, and sewing seams—having lived sae lang wi' a grand lady like Lady Singleside. Or if she does na ken ony thing about it, I'm jealous that our bairns will like her a' the better; and I'll take care o' the bits o' claes, and what spending siller she maun hae, and the hunder pound may rin on in your hands, Mr Protocol, and I'll be adding something till't, till she'll may be get a Liddesdale joe that wants something to help to buy the hirsel.—What d'ye say to that, hinny? I'll take out a ticket for ye in the fly to Jeddart—odd, but ye maun take a poney after that o'er the Limestane-rig—deil a wheeled carriage ever gaed into Liddesdale:—and I'll be very glad if Mrs Rebecca comes wi' you, hinny, and stays a month or twa while you're stranger like."

While Mrs Rebecca was curtseying, and endeavouring to make the poor orphan girl curtsey instead of crying, and while Dandie, in his rough way, was encouraging them both, old Pleydell had recourse to his snuff-box.

"It's meat and drink to me, now, Colonel," he said, as he recovered himself, "to see a clown like this—I must gratify him his own way, must assist him to ruin himself—there's no help for it.—Here, you Liddesdale—Dandie—Charlieshope—what do they call you?"

The farmer turned, infinitely gratified even by this sort of notice, for in his heart, next to his own landlord, he honoured a lawyer in high practice.

"So you will not be advised against trying that question about your marches?"

"N—no! sir—naebody likes to lose their right, and to be laughed at down the hail water. But since your honour's no agreeable, and is may be a friend to the other side like, we maun try some other advocate."

"There—I told you so, Colonel Mannering!—Well, sir, if you must needs be a fool, the business is to give you the luxury of a law-suit at the least possible expence, and to bring you off conqueror if possible. Let Mr Protocol send me your papers, and I will advise him how to conduct your cause. I don't see, after all, why you should not have your law-suits too, and your feuds in the Court of Session, as well as your forefathers had their man-slaughters and fire-raisings."

"Very natural, to be sure, sir. We would just take the auld gate as readily, if it were no for the law. And as the law binds us, the law should loose us. Besides, a man's aye the better thought of in our country for having been afore the feifteen."

"Excellently argued, my friend! Away with you, and send your papers to me.—Come, Colonel, we have no more to do here."

"God, we'll ding Jock o' Dawstone Cleugh now after a'," said Dinmont, slapping his thigh in great exultation.

Chapter Eighteen

——I am going to the parliament;
You understand this bag: If you have any business
Depending there, be short, and let me hear it,
And pay your fees.

Little French Lawyer

"WILL YOU be able to carry this honest fellow's cause for him?" said Mannering.

"Why, I don't know; the battle is not to the strong, but he shall come off triumphant over Jock of Dawstone if we can make it out. I owe him something. It is the pest of our profession, that we seldom see the best side of human nature. People come to us with every selfish feeling, newly pointed and grinded; they turn down the very caulkers of their animosities and prejudice, as smiths do to horses' shoes in a white frost. Many a man has come to my garret yonder, that I have at first longed to pitch out at the window, and yet, at length, have discovered that he was only doing as I might have done in his case, being very angry, and, of course, very unreasonable. I have now satisfied myself, that if our profession sees more of human folly and human roguery than others, it is as affording the only channel through which they can vent themselves. In civilized society, law is the chimney through which all that smoke discharges itself that used to circulate through the whole house, and put every one's eyes out—no wonder, therefore, that the vent itself should sometimes get a little sooty.—But we will take care our Liddesdale-man's cause is well conducted and well argued, so all unnecessary expence will be saved—he shall have his pine-apple at wholesale price."

"Will you do me the pleasure," said Mannering as they parted, "to dine with me at my lodgings? my landlord says he has a bit of red-deer venison, and some excellent wine?"

"Venison—eh? But no! it's impossible—and I can't ask you home neither. Monday's a sacred day—so's Tuesday—and Wednesday, we are to be heard in the great teind case in presence—but stay—it's frosty weather, and if you don't leave town, and that venison would keep till Thursday"——

"You will dine with me that day?"

"Under certification."

"Well, then, I will indulge a thought I had of spending a week here; and if the venison will not keep, why we will see what else our landlord can do for us."

"O, the venison will keep," said Pleydell; "and now good bye—look at these two or three cards, and deliver them if you like the addresses. I wrote them for you this morning—farewell, my clerk has been waiting this hour to begin a d—d information."—And away walked Mr Pleydell with great activity, diving through closes and ascending covered stairs, in order to attain the High-Street by what, compared to the common route, was what the Streights of Magellan are to the more circuitous, but open passage by doubling Cape Horn.

Upon looking at the cards of introduction which Pleydell had thrust into his hand, Mannering was gratified with seeing that they were addressed to some of the first literary characters of Scotland. "To David Hume." "To John Home." "To Dr Ferguson." "To Dr Black." "To Lord Kaimes." "To Mr Hutton." "To John Clerk of Eldin." "To Adam Smith." "To Dr Robertson."

"Upon my word, my legal friend has a good selection of acquaintances—these are names pretty widely blown indeed—an Indian must rub up his faculties a little, and put his mind in order, before he enters this sort of society."

Mannering gladly availed himself of these introductions; and we regret deeply it is not in our power to give the reader an account of the pleasure and information which he received, in admission to a circle never closed against strangers of sense and information, and which has perhaps at no period been equalled, considering the depth and variety of talent which it embraced and concentrated. It is true he kept a journal of these golden days, but, as it afterwards passed through the hands of Mr Dominie Sampson, it is to be feared his indiscreet zeal mutilated Mannering's account of some of these philosophers, whose acute talents were more to be admired than their speculative opinions. One or two scraps I have been able to extract from some mutilated letters to Mr Mervyn, found in an old cabinet at Mervyn Hall, Llanbraithwaite; but as the room looked out upon the lake, they have suffered much from damp, and what is very provoking, I have not been able to assign to the fragments those names which are necessary to expound and to illustrate them. So that I hesitated for some time, whether or not I should insert them in this place. At length, upon the economical consideration that they will go far to complete this volume, without giving me any other trouble but that of a copyist, I will transfer two or three of these characters to this narrative.

Fragment First.

* * * You, my dear Mervyn, who are a worshipper of originality, should come a pilgrimage to Edinburgh on foot to see this remarkable man—that is, you should do so rather than not come at all. I found him with his family around him—a house full of boys and girls,

labouring at an abstracted proposition in mathematics, as if he had been in the solitude of the most quiet and secluded cell in our old college. The table at which he sate was covered with a miscellaneous collection of all sorts—pencils, paints, and crayons (he draws most beautifully), clay models half-finished or half-broken, books, letters, instruments, specimens of mineralogy, vials with chemical liquors for experiments, plans of battles ancient and modern, models of new mechanical engines, maps, and calculations of levels, sheets of music printed and written, in short an emblematical chaos of literature and science. Over all this miscellany two or three kittens, the *genii loci*, gambolled not only without rebuke, but apparently much to the amusement of the philosopher. His countenance is singularly expressive of sagacity and acuteness. Light eyes, deep sunk under a projecting brow, and shaded by thick eye lashes, emit an uncommon light when he is engaged in discussion. Frank, liberal, and communicative, his extensive information is at the service of every stranger who is introduced, and it is so general and miscellaneous that every one must find a subject of entertainment and information. He does not embarrass you with the manner I have sometimes remarked in men of genius, who expect to be incensed with praise, and yet affect to despise or disavow the tribute when it is offered. This gentleman seems frankly, and with good faith, to receive the homage willingly paid to him, and takes without affectation or assumption the conscious feeling of superiority *quæsitam meritis*.—Of his great discovery we have already had a happy illustration in the late naval success—Another generation may carry it farther—it has the great recommendation that it can serve no nation but ourselves, unless British tars and British oaks lose their superiority—I am told there is littleness of mind shown by some naval officers, who even go so far as to deny * * * * * * Columbus and the egg—if known before why was it not carried into execution? * * *

Fragment Second.

* * * at supper time: for such is the hour when this close imitator of the ancients holds his symposion. A man of his eccentric opinions in philosophy can scarcely be without peculiarities in private life, and accordingly he may be truly stiled an original. Our table was strewed with flowers, and garlands were hung upon the necks of the bottles of claret, which circulated freely to the memory of sages, dead and living, and to the prosperity of learning and literary institutions. Our entertainer was alternately eloquent and jocose, but equally original in his mirth as in his philosophy. The Quixotry which has introduced him to prick forth in defence of the battered standard of Aristotle, when

deserted by all the world besides, is gilded over and rendered respectable by such high feelings of honour and worth, that you cannot help respecting and loving the enthusiasm which abstractly is sufficiently ludicrous. It seems to be the soul of a knight errant which has, by strange transmigration, been put in possession of the pineal gland of a scholiast. To amuse me, he entered upon some of his favourite topics—the gradual degeneracy of the human race—the increase of luxury—the general introduction of wheel carriages (he always rides on horseback you must know) and sundry other consolatory topics.—He questioned me closely about sundry tribes in the East, which I endeavoured to answer with great caution, as I have no ambition to be quoted in a new edition of the Origin of * * * .

FRAGMENT THIRD.

* * * and possesses in reality that stern and self-relying cast of philosophy, which the other rather imitates than attains. A Roman soul, despising in the prosecution of his literary career the imperfections of a feeble frame, and the blandishments of indolence to which it so readily disposes us. He is generally known as the most chaste, clear, and luminous historian who has undertaken to guide us through the paths of antiquity; but he has also evinced, in the cause of his country, powers of satire worthy of Swift or Arbuthnot. He has adopted, for the sake of health, the severe diet of our Indian Bramins, and it may be reasonably hoped from his powers of perseverance, and the progress he has already made towards recovery, that his life may be long preserved to his country * * *

FRAGMENT FOURTH.

* * * Full of anecdote, which his acquaintance with the great men who flourished at the beginning of this reign has afforded him. He has also extensive information respecting the unfortunate war of 1745, and, as might be expected from his genius, he gives his stories with attention to the striking and picturesque points of the narrative. I saw him shed tears while he commemorated the gallantry, high principle, and personal worth of some of the unfortunate chiefs, against whom he had himself borne arms. He is proud of his family, for men of fortune and no fortune have alike family-pride in Scotland; and the manner in which his namesake the philosopher spells his name, joined to his preference of port to claret, are the only secular opinions on which they differ. I am told the philosopher offered (with philosophical indifference) to compound the first dispute, by throwing dice which should in future correspond to the orthography of the other. But the poet rejected this proposal, as altogether unequal, since, in the case of

his winning, his adversary only took his own proper name; whereas, if he the poet lost, he would be compelled to assume that of another man. * * * * * * why none of them are equal to his capital production. As far as I can judge, from hastily glancing at the others, he has injudiciously so managed the plot in each of them as to remind us of his *chef d'œuvre*, a sort of self-imitation which it is perhaps very difficult to avoid, but which is to a certainty destructive of the author's purpose * * *

There are several more of these fragments in my hands, but to detail them here would keep us too long from the proper business of our history, to which, with the reader's permission we now return.

Upon the Thursday appointed, Mr Pleydell made his appearance at the inn where Colonel Mannering lodged. The venison proved in high order, the claret excellent, and the learned counsel, a professed amateur in the affairs of the table, did distinguished honour to both. I am uncertain, however, if even the good cheer gave him more satisfaction than the presence of Dominie Sampson, from whom, in his own juridical style of wit, he contrived to extract great amusement, both for himself and one or two friends whom the Colonel regaled on the same occasion. The grave and laconic simplicity of Sampson's answers to the insidious questions of the barrister, placed the *bonhommie* of his character in a more luminous point of view than Mannering had yet seen it. Upon the same occasion he drew forth a strange quantity of miscellaneous and abstruse, though generally speaking, useless learning.—The lawyer afterwards compared his mind to the magazine of a pawnbroker, stowed with goods of every description, but so cumbrously piled together, and in such total disorganization, that the owner can never lay his hands upon any one article at the moment he has occasion for it.

As for the advocate himself, he afforded at least as much exercise to Sampson as he extracted amusement from him. When the man of law began to get into his altitudes, in particular when his wit, naturally shrewd and dry, became more lively and poignant, the Dominie looked upon him with that sort of surprise with which we can conceive honest Bruin might regard his future associate the monkey upon their being first introduced to each other. It was Mr Pleydell's delight to state in grave and serious argument some position which he knew the Dominie would be inclined to dispute. He then beheld with exquisite pleasure the internal labour with which the honest man arranged his ideas for reply, and tasked his inert and sluggish powers to bring up all the heavy artillery of his learning for demolishing the schismatic or heretical opinion which had been stated—when, behold, before the ordnance could be discharged, the foe had quitted the post, and appeared in a new position of annoyance on the Dominie's flank or rear. Often did he exclaim "prodigious!" when, marching up to the enemy in full confidence of victory, he found the field evacuated, and it may be supposed that it cost him no little labour to attempt a new formation. "He was like a native Indian army," the Colonel said, "formidable by numerical strength and size of ordnance, but liable to be thrown into irreparable confusion by a movement to take them in flank."—On the whole, however, the Dominie, though somewhat fatigued with these mental exertions, made at unusual speed and upon the pressure of the moment, reckoned this one of the white days of his life, and always mentioned Mr Pleydell as a very erudite and facetious person. By degrees the rest of the party dropped off, and left these three gentlemen together. Their conversation naturally turned to Mrs Bertram's settlements.

"Now what could drive it into the noddle of that old harridan," said Pleydell, "to disinherit poor Lucy Bertram, under pretence of settling her property on a boy who has been so long dead and gone?—I ask your pardon, Mr Sampson, I forgot what an affecting case this was for you—I remember taking your examination upon it—and I never had so much trouble to make any one speak three words consecutively. You may speak of your Pythagoreans, or your silent Bramins, Colonel, —go to—I tell you this learned gentleman beats them in taciturnity—but the words of the wise are precious, and not to be thrown away lightly."

"Of a surety," said the Dominie, taking his blue-checqued handkerchief from his eyes—"that was a bitter day with me indeed—Aye, and a day of grief hard to be borne—but he giveth strength who layeth on the load."

Colonel Mannering took this opportunity to request Mr Pleydell to inform him of the particulars attending the loss of the boy; and the counsellor, who was fond of talking upon subjects of criminal jurisprudence, especially when connected with his own experience, went through the circumstances at full length. "And what is your opinion upon the result of the whole?"

"O, that Kennedy was murdered—it's an old case which has occurred on that coast before now—the case of Smuggler *versus* Exciseman."

"What then is your conjecture concerning the fate of the child?"

"O, murdered too, doubtless. He was old enough to tell what he had seen, and these scoundrels would not scruple committing a second Bethlehem massacre if they thought their interest required it."

The Dominie groaned deeply, and ejaculated, "Enormous!"

"Yet there was mention of gypsies in the business too, counsellor, and from what that vulgar-looking fellow said after the funeral"——

"Mrs Margaret Bertram's idea that the child was alive was founded upon the report of a gypsey—I envy you the concatenation, Colonel—it is a shame to me not to have drawn the same conclusion. We'll follow this business up instantly—Here, hark ye, waiter, go down to Luckie Wood's in the Cowgate—ye'll find my clerk Driver; he'll be set down to High-Jinks by this time—(for we and our retainers, Colonel, are exceedingly regular in our irregularities)—tell him to come here instantly, and I will pay his forfeits."

"He won't appear in character, will he?"

"Ah! no more of that, Hal! an thou lovest me.—But we must have some news from the land of Egypt, if possible. O, if I had but hold of the slightest thread of this complicated skean, you should see how I would unravel it!—I would work the truth out of your Bohemian, as the French call them, better than a *Monitoire*, or a *Plainte de Tournelle*—I know how to manage a refractory witness."

While Mr Pleydell was thus vaunting his knowledge of his profession, the waiter re-entered with Mr Driver, his mouth still greasy with mutton pies, and the froth of the last draught of twopenny yet unsubsided on his upper lip, with such speed had he obeyed the commands of his principal.—"Driver, you must go instantly and find out the woman who was old Mrs Margaret Bertram's maid. Enquire for her everywhere, but if you find it necessary to have recourse to Protocol, Quid the tobacconist, or any of these folks, you will take care not to appear yourself, but send some woman of your acquaintance—I dare say you know enough that may be so condescending as to oblige you. When you have found her out, engage her to come to my chambers to-morrow at eight o'clock precisely."

"What shall I say to make her forthcoming?" asked the aid-de-camp.

"Any thing you chuse—is it my business to make lies for you, do you think?—but let her be *in presentia* by eight o'clock, as I have said before." The clerk grinned, made his reverence, and exit.

"That's a useful fellow," said the counsellor; "I don't believe his match ever carried a process. He'll write to my dictating three nights in the week without sleep, or, what's the same thing, he writes as well and correctly when he's asleep as when he's awake. Then he's such a steady fellow—some of them are always changing their ale-houses, so that they have twenty cadies sweating after them, like the bare-headed captains traversing the taverns of East-Cheap in search of Sir John Falstaff. But this is a steady fellow—he has his winter seat by the fire, and his summer seat by the window, in Luckie Wood's, betwixt which seats are his only migrations; there he's to be found at all times when he is off duty. It is my opinion he never puts off his clothes or goes to sleep—sheer ale supports him under every thing. It is meat, drink, and cloth, bed, board, and washing."

"And is he always fit for duty upon a sudden turn-out? I should distrust it, considering his quarters."

"O, drink never disturbs him, Colonel, he can write for hours after he cannot speak. I remember being called suddenly to draw an appeal case. I had been dining, and it was Saturday night, and I had ill will to begin to it—however, they got me down to Clerihugh's, and there we sate birling till I had a fair tappit hen under my belt, and then they persuaded me to draw the paper. Then we had to seek Driver, and it was all that two men could do to bear him in, for when found, he was, as it happened, both motionless and speechless. But no sooner was his pen put between his fingers, his paper stretched before him, and he heard my voice, than he began to write like a scrivener—and, excepting that we were obliged to have somebody to dip his pen in the ink, for he could not see the standish, I never saw a thing scrolled more handsomely."

"But how did your joint production look the next morning?" said the Colonel.

"Wheugh! capital—not three words required to be altered; it was sent off by that day's post.—But you'll come and breakfast with me to-morrow, and hear this woman's examination?"

"Why, your hour is rather early."

"Can't make it later. If I were not on the boards of the outer-house precisely as the nine-hours bell rings, there would be a report that I had got an apoplexy, and I should feel the effects of it all the rest of the session."

"Well, I will make an exertion to wait upon you."

Here the company broke up for the evening.

In the morning Colonel Mannering appeared at the counsellor's chambers, although cursing the raw air of a Scottish morning in December. Mr Pleydell had got Mrs Rebecca installed on one side of his fire, accommodated her with a cup of chocolate, and was already deeply engaged in conversation with her. "O, no, I assure you, Mrs Rebecca, there is no intention to challenge your mistress's will, and I give you my word of honour that your legacy is quite safe. You deserved it by your conduct to your mistress, and I wish it had been twice as much."

"Why, to be sure, sir, it's no right to mention what is said before ane—ye heard how that dirty body Quid cast up to me the bits o' compliments he gied me, and tell'd ower again ony loose cracks I might hae had wi' him; now if ane was talking loosely to your honour, there's nae saying what might come o't."

"I assure you, my good Rebecca, my character and your own age and appearance are your security, if you should talk as loosely as an amatory poet."

"Aweel, if your honour thinks I am safe—the story is just this.—Ye see, about a year ago, or no just sae lang, my leddy was advised to go to Gilsland for a while, for her spirits were distressing her sair. Ellangowan's troubles began to be spoken o' publicly, and sair vexed she was—for she was proud o' her family—for Ellangowan himsell and her, they sometimes 'greed, and sometimes no—but at last they did na 'gree at a' for twa or three years—for he was aye wanting to borrow siller, and that was what she could bide at no hand, and she was aye wanting it paid back again, and that the Laird he liked as little. So they were clean aff a' thegither.—And then some of the company at Gilsland tell'd her that the estate was to be sell'd; and you wad hae thought she had taen an ill will at Miss Lucy Bertram frae that moment, for mony a time she cried to me, "O, Becky, Becky, if that useless peenging thing of a lassie there, at Ellangowan, that canna keep her ne'er-do-weel of a father within bounds—if she had been but a lad-bairn, they could na hae sell'd the auld inheritance for that fool-body's debts,"—and she would rin on that way till I was just wearied to hear her.—And ae day at the spaw-well below the craig, she was seeing a very bonny family o' bairns—they belanged to ane Mac-Crossky—and she broke out—'Is not it an odd thing that ilka waf carle in the country has a son and heir, and that the house of Ellangowan is without male succession?' There was a gypsey wife stood ahint and heard her—a muckle stoor fearsome-looking wife she was as ever I set een on,—'Wha is it,' says she, 'that dare say the house of Ellangowan will perish without male succession?' My mistress just turned on her—she was a high-spirited woman, and aye ready wi' an answer to a' body. 'It's me that says it, says she, that may say it wi' a sad heart.' Wi' that the gypsy wife gripped till her hand, 'I ken you weel eneugh,' says she, 'though ye ken na me—But as sure as that sun's in heaven, and as sure as that water's rinning to the sea, and as sure as there's an e'e that sees, and an ear that hears us baith—Harry Bertram, that was thought to perish at Warroch Point, never did die there—he was to have a weary weird o't till his one-and-twentieth year, that was aye said o' him—but if ye live and I live, ye'll hear mair o' him this winter before the snaw lies twa days on the Dun of Singleside— I want nane o' your siller,' she said, 'to make ye think I am blearing your e'e—fare ye weel till after Martimas,' and there she left us standing."

"Was she a very tall woman?" interrupted Mannering.

"Had she black hair, and black eyes, and a cut above the brow?" added the lawyer.

"She was the tallest woman I ever saw, and her hair was as black as midnight, unless where it was grey, and she had a scar abune her brow, that ye might hae laid the lith of your finger in. Naebody that's seen her will ever forget her; and I am morally sure that it was on the ground o' what that gypsey-woman said that my mistress made her will, having ta'en a dislike at the young leddy of Ellangowan; and she liked her far waur after she was obliged to send her 20l.—for she said, Miss Bertram, no content wi' letting the Ellangowan property pass into strange hands, owing to her being a lass and no a lad, was coming, by her poverty, to be a burden and a disgrace to Singleside too.—But I hope my mistress's is a good will for a' that, for it would be hard on me to lose the wee bit legacy—I served for little fee and bountith, weel I wot."

The counsellor relieved her fears on this head, then enquired after Jenny Gibson, and understood she had accepted Mr Dinmont's offer; "and I have done sae mysell too, since he was sae discreet as to ask me," said Mrs Rebecca; "they are very decent folks the Dinmonts, though my lady did nae dow to hear mickle about the friends on that side the house. But she liked the Charlieshope hams, and the cheeses, and the moor-fowl, that they were aye sending, and the lamb's-wool hose and mittens—she liked them weel aneuch."

Mr Pleydell now dismissed Mrs Rebecca. When she was gone, "I think I know this gypsey woman," said the lawyer.

"I was just going to say the same," replied Mannering.

"And her name," said Pleydell——

"Is Meg Merrilies," answered the Colonel.

"Are you avised of that?" said the counsellor, looking at his military friend with a comic expression of surprise.

Mannering answered, that he had known such a woman when he was at Ellangowan twenty-five years since; and then made his learned friend acquainted with all the remarkable particulars of his first visit there.

Mr Pleydell listened with great attention, and then replied, "I congratulated myself upon having made the acquaintance of a profound theologian in your chaplain, but I really did not expect to find a pupil of Albumazar or Messahala in his patron.—I have a notion, however, this gypsy could tell us some more of the matter than she derives from astrology or second-sight—I had her through hands once, and could then make little of her, but I must write to Mac-Morlan to stir heaven and earth to find her out.—I will gladly come to —— shire myself to assist at her examination—I am still in the commission of the peace there, though I have ceased to be sheriff—I never had any thing more at heart in my life than tracing that murder, and the fate of the child. I must write to the Sheriff of Roxburghshire too, and to an active justice of peace in Cumberland."

"I hope when you come to the country you will make Woodbourne your head-quarters?"

"Certainly; I was afraid you were going to forbid me—but we must go to breakfast now, or I shall be too late."

On the following day the new friends parted, and the Colonel rejoined his family without any adventure worthy of being detailed in these chapters.

END OF VOLUME SECOND

GUY MANNERING

OR

THE ASTROLOGER

VOLUME III

Chapter One

> Can no rest find me, no private place secure me,
> But still my miseries like bloodhounds haunt me?
> Unfortunate young man, which way now guides thee,
> Guides thee from death? The country's laid around for thee—
>
> *Women Pleased*

OUR NARRATIVE now recalls us for a moment to the period when young Hazelwood received his wound. That accident had no sooner happened, than the consequences to Miss Mannering and to himself rushed upon Brown's mind. From the manner in which the muzzle of the piece was pointed when it went off, he had no great fear that the consequences could be fatal. But an arrest in a strange country, and while he was unprovided with any means of ascertaining his rank and character, was at least to be avoided. He therefore resolved to escape for the present to the neighbouring coast of England, and to remain concealed there, if possible, until he should receive letters from his regimental friends, and remittances from his agent; and then to resume his own character, and offer to young Hazelwood and his friends any explanation or satisfaction they might desire. With this purpose he walked stoutly forward, after leaving the spot where the accident had happened, and reached without adventure the village which we have called Portanferry, (but which the reader will in vain seek for under that name in the county map.) A large open boat was just about to leave the quay, bound for the little seaport of Allonby in Cumberland. In this vessel Brown embarked, and resolved to make that place his temporary abode, until he should receive letters and money from England.

In the course of their short voyage he entered into some conversation with the steersman, who was also owner of the boat, a jolly old man, who had occasionally been engaged in the smuggling trade, like most fishers on the coast. After talking about objects of less interest, Brown endeavoured to turn the discourse toward the Mannering family. The sailor had heard of the attack upon the house at Woodbourne, but disapproved of the smugglers' proceedings.

"Hands off is fair play; zounds, they'll bring the whole country doun upon them—na, na! when I was in that way I played at giff-gaff with the officers—here a cargo ta'en—vera weel, that was their luck; —there another carried clean through, that was mine—na, na! hawks should na pike out hawks' e'en."

"And this Colonel Mannering?"

"Troth, he's nae wise man neither to interfere—no that I blame him for saving the gaugers' lives—that was vera right; but it was na like a gentleman to be fighting about the poor folk's pocks o' tea and brandy kegs—however, he's a grand man and an officer man, and they do what they like wi' the like o' us."

"And his daughter," said Brown, with a throbbing heart, "is going to be married into a great family too as I have heard?"

"What, into the Hazelwoods'? na, na, that's but idle clashes—every sabbath-day, as regularly as it came round, did the young man ride hame wi' the daughter of the late Ellangowan—and my daughter Peggy's in service up at Woodbourne, and she says she's sure young Hazelwood thinks na mair of Miss Mannering than ye do."

Bitterly censuring his own precipitate adoption of a contrary belief, Brown yet heard with delight that the suspicion of Julia's fidelity, upon which he had so rashly acted, was probably void of foundation. How must he in the mean time be suffering in her opinion? or what could she suppose of conduct, which must have made him appear to her regardless alike of her peace of mind, and of the interests of their affection! The old man's connection with the family at Woodbourne seemed to offer a safe mode of communication, of which he determined to avail himself.

"Your daughter is a maid-servant at Woodbourne?—I knew Miss Mannering in India, and though I am at present in an inferior rank of life, I have great reason to hope she would interest herself in my favour. I had a quarrel unfortunately with her father, who was my commanding officer, and I am sure the young lady would endeavour to reconcile him to me. Perhaps your daughter could deliver a letter to her upon the subject, without making mischief between her father and her?" The old man readily answered for the letter being faithfully and secretly delivered, and, accordingly, so soon as they arrived at Allonby, Brown wrote to Miss Mannering, stating the utmost contrition for what had happened through his rashness, and conjuring her to let him have an opportunity of pleading his own cause and obtaining forgiveness for his indiscretion. He did not judge it safe to go into any detail concerning the circumstances by which he had been misled, and upon the whole endeavoured to express himself with such ambiguity, that, should the letter fall into wrong hands, it would be difficult either to understand its real purport, or to trace the writer. This letter the old man undertook faithfully to convey to his daughter at Woodbourne; and, as his trade would speedily again bring him or his boat to Allonby, he promised farther to take charge of any answer with which the young lady might entrust him.

And now our persecuted traveller landed at Allonby, and sought for such accommodations as might at once suit his temporary poverty, and his desire of remaining as much unobserved as possible. With this view he assumed the name and profession of his friend Dudley, having command enough of the pencil to verify his pretended character to his host of Allonby. His baggage he pretended to expect from Wigton, and, keeping himself as much within doors as possible, awaited the return of the letters which he had sent to his agent, to Delaserre, and to his Lieutenant-Colonel. From the first he requested a supply of money; he conjured Delaserre, if possible, to join him in Scotland; and from the Lieutenant-Colonel he required such testimony of his rank and conduct in the regiment, as should place his character as a gentleman and officer beyond the power of question. The inconvenience of being run short in his finances struck him so strongly, that he wrote to Dinmont upon that subject, requiring a small temporary loan, having no doubt that, being within sixty or seventy miles of his residence, he would receive a speedy as well as favourable answer to his request of pecuniary accommodation, which was owing, as he stated, to his having been robbed after their parting. And then, with impatience enough, though without serious apprehension, he waited the answers of these various letters.

It must be observed, in excuse of his correspondents, that the post was then much more tardy than since Mr Palmer's ingenious invention has taken place; and with respect to honest Dinmont in particular, as he rarely received above one letter a quarter, (unless during the time of his being engaged in a law-suit, when he regularly sent to his post-town,) his correspondence usually remained for a month or two sticking in the postmaster's window, among pamphlets, gingerbread, rolls, or ballads, according to the trade which the said postmaster exercised. Besides, there was then a custom, not yet wholly obsolete, of causing a letter, from one town to another, perhaps within the distance of thirty miles, perform a circuit of two hundred miles before delivery; which had the combined advantages of airing the epistle thoroughly, of adding some pence to the revenue of the post-office, and of exercising the patience of the correspondents. Owing to these circumstances, Brown remained several days in Allonby without answer, and his stock of money, though husbanded with the utmost economy, began to wear very low, when he received by the hands of a young fisherman the following letter:

"You have acted with the most cruel indiscretion, you have shewn how little I can trust to your declarations that my peace and happiness are dear to you, and your rashness has nearly occasioned the death of a young man of the highest worth and honour. Must I say more?—must I add, that I have been myself very ill in consequence of your violence, and its effects? and, alas! need I say still further, that I have thought anxiously upon them as they are likely to affect you, although you have given me such slight cause to do so? The C. is gone from home for several days; Mr H. is almost quite recovered, and I have reason to think that the blame is laid in a quarter different from that where it is deserved. Yet do not think of venturing here. Our fate has been crossed by accidents of a nature too violent and terrible to permit me to think of renewing a correspondence which has so often threatened the most dreadful catastrophe. Farewell, therefore, and believe that no one can wish your happiness more sincerely than

"J. M."

This letter contained the species of advice, which is frequently given for the precise purpose that it may lead to a directly opposite conduct from that which it recommends. At least so thought Brown, who immediately asked the young fisherman if he came from Portanferry.

"Aye; I am auld Willie Johnstone's son, and I got that letter frae my sister Peggy, whae's laundry-maid at Woodbourne."

"My good friend, when do you sail?"

"With the tide this evening."

"I'll return with you; but as I do not desire to go to Portanferry, I wish you could put me on the shore somewhere on the coast."

"We can easily do that," said the lad.

Although the price of provisions, &c. was then very moderate, the discharging his lodgings, and the expences of his living, together with that of a change of dress, which safety as well as decency rendered necessary, brought Brown's purse to a very low ebb. He left directions at the post-office that his letters should be forwarded to Kippletringan, whither he resolved to proceed and reclaim the treasure which he had deposited in the hands of Mrs Mac-Candlish. He also felt it would be his duty to assume his proper character so soon as he received the necessary evidence for supporting it, and, as an officer in the king's service, give and receive every explanation which might be necessary with young Hazelwood. "If he is not very wrong-headed indeed," he thought, "he must allow the manner in which I acted to have been the necessary consequence of his own overbearing conduct."

And now we must suppose him once more embarked on the Solway firth. The wind was adverse, attended by some rain, and they struggled against it without much assistance from the tide. The boat was heavily laden with goods, (part of which were probably contraband) and laboured deep in the sea. Brown, who had been bred a sailor, and was indeed skilled in most athletic exercises, gave his powerful and effectual assistance in rowing, or occasionally in steering the boat, and his advice in the management, which became the more delicate as the wind increased, and, being opposed to the very rapid tides of that coast, made the voyage perilous. At length, after spending the whole night upon the firth, they were at morning within sight of a beautiful bay upon the Scottish coast. The weather was now more mild. The snow, which had been for some time waning, had given way entirely under the fresh gale of the preceding night. The more distant hills, indeed, retained their snowy mantle, but all the open country was cleared, unless where a few white patches indicated that it had been drifted to an uncommon depth. Even under its wintry appearance, the shore was highly interesting. The line of sea-coast, with all its varied curves, indentures, and embayments, swept away from the sight on either hand, in that varied, intricate, yet graceful and easy line, which the eye loves so well to pursue. And it was no less relieved and varied in elevation than in outline, by the different forms of the shore; the beach in some places being edged by steep rocks, and in others rising smoothly from the sands in easy and swelling slopes. Buildings of different kinds caught and reflected the wintry sunbeams of a December morning, and the woods, though now leafless, gave relief and variety to the landscape. Brown felt that lively and awakening interest which taste and sensibility always derive from the beauties of nature, when opening suddenly to the eye, after the dulness and gloom of a night voyage. Perhaps,—for who can presume to analyse that inexplicable feeling which binds the person born of a mountainous country to his native hills?—perhaps some early associations, retaining their effect long after the cause was forgotten, mingled in the feelings of pleasure with which he regarded the scene before him.

"And what," said Brown to the boatman, "is the name of that fine cape, that stretches into the sea with its sloping banks and hillocks of wood, and forms the right side of the bay?"

"Warroch Point," said the lad.

"And that old castle, my friend, with the modern house situated just beneath it? It seems at this distance a very large building."

"That's the Auld Place, sir; and that's the New Place below it. We'll land you there if you like."

"I should like it of all things. I must visit that ruin before I continue my journey."

"Aye, it's a queer auld bit; and that highest tower is a good landmark as far as Ramsay-bay and the Point of Ayr—there was muckle fighting about it lang syne."

Brown would have enquired into farther particulars, but a fisherman is seldom an antiquary. His boatman's local knowledge was summed up in the information already given, that it was a grand landmark, and that there had been fighting about the "bit lang syne."

"I shall learn more of it," thought Brown, "when I get ashore."

The boat continued its course close under the point upon which the castle was situated, which frowned from the summit of its rocky scite upon the still agitated waves of the bay beneath. "I believe," said the steersman, "you'll get ashore here as dry as ony gate. There's a place where their berlins and gallies, as they ca'd them, used to lie in lang syne, but it's no used now, because it's ill carrying goods up the narrow stairs, or ower the rocks. Whiles of a moonlight night I have landed articles here though."

While he thus spoke, they pulled round a point of rock, and found a very small harbour, partly formed by nature, partly by the indefatigable labour of the ancient inhabitants of the castle, who, as the fisherman observed, had found it essential for the protection of their small craft, though it could not receive vessels of any burthen. The two points of rock which formed the entrance approached each other so nearly, that only one boat could conveniently enter at a time. On each side were still remaining two immense iron rings, deeply morticed into the solid rock. Through these, according to tradition, there was nightly drawn a huge chain, secured by an immense padlock, for the protection of the haven and the armada which it contained. A ledge of rock had, by the assistance of the chisel and pick-axe, been formed into a sort of quay. The rock was of extremely hard consistence, and the task so difficult, that, according to the fisherman, a labourer who wrought at the work might in the evening have carried home in his bonnet all the shivers which he had struck from the rock in the course of the day. This little quay communicated with a rude stair-case, already repeatedly mentioned, which descended from the old castle. There was also a communication between the beach and the quay by scrambling over the rocks.

"Ye had better land here," said the lad, "for the surf's running high at the Shellicoat-stane, and there will no be a dry thread amang us or we get the cargo out.—Na! na! (in answer to an offer of money) ye have wrought your passage, and wrought far better than ony o' us. Good day to you: I wuss ye weel."

So saying, he pushed off in order to land his cargo on the opposite side of the bay; and Brown, with a small bundle in his hand, containing the trifling stock of necessaries which he had been obliged to purchase at Allonby, was left on the rocks beneath the ruin.

And thus, unconscious as the most absolute stranger, and in circumstances, which, if not destitute, were for the present highly embarrassing; without the countenance of a friend within the circle of several hundred miles; accused of a heavy crime; and, what was as bad as all the rest, being nearly pennyless, did the harassed wanderer for the first time, after the interval of so many years, approach the remains of the castle, where his ancestors had exercised all but regal dominion.

Chapter Two

———Yes, ye moss-grown walls,
Ye towers defenceless, I revisit ye
Shame-stricken! Where are all your trophies now?
Your thronged courts, the revelry, the tumult,
That spoke the grandeur of my house, the homage
Of neighbouring Barons?—

Mysterious Mother

ENTERING the castle of Ellangowan by a postern door-way, which shewed symptoms of having been once secured with the most jealous care, Brown, (whom, since he has set foot upon the property of his fathers, we shall hereafter call by his father's name of Bertram) wandered from one ruined apartment to another, surprised at the massive strength of some parts of the building, the rude and impressive magnificence of others, and the great extent of the whole. In two of these rooms, close beside each other, he saw signs of recent habitation. In one small apartment were empty bottles, half-gnawed bones, and dried fragments of bread. In the vault which adjoined, and which was defended by a strong door, then left open, he observed a considerable quantity of straw, and in both were the reliques of recent fires. How little was it possible for Bertram to conceive, that such trivial circumstances were closely connected with incidents affecting his prosperity, his honour, perhaps his life!

After satisfying his curiosity by a hasty glance through the interior of the castle, Bertram now advanced through the great gate-way which opened to the land, and paused to look upon the noble landscape which it commanded. Having in vain endeavoured to guess the position of Woodbourne, and having nearly ascertained that of Kippletringan, he turned to take a parting look at the stately ruins which he had just traversed. He admired the massive and picturesque effect of the huge round towers, which, flanking the gateway, gave a double portion of depth and majesty to the high yet gloomy arch under which it opened. The carved stone escutcheon of the ancient family, bearing for their arms three wolves' heads, was hung diagonally beneath the helmet and crest, the latter being a wolf couchant pierced with an arrow. On either side stood as supporters, in full human size or larger, a salvage man *proper*, to use the language of heraldry, *wreathed and cinctured*, and holding in his hand an oak tree *eradicated*, that is, torn up by the roots.

"And the powerful barons who owned this blazonry," thought Bertram, pursuing the usual train of ideas which flows upon the mind at such scenes, "does their posterity continue to possess the lands which they had laboured to fortify so strongly? or are they wanderers, ignorant perhaps even of the fame or power of their forefathers, while their hereditary possessions are held by a race of strangers? Why is it," he thought, continuing to follow out the succession of ideas which the scene prompted—"Why is it that some scenes awaken thoughts, which belong as it were to dreams of early and shadowy recollection, such as my old Bramin Moonshie would have ascribed to a state of previous existence? Is it the visions of our sleep that float confusedly in our memory, and are recalled by the appearance of such real objects as in any respect correspond to the phantoms they presented to our imagination? How often we find ourselves in society which we have never before met, and yet feel impressed with a mysterious and ill-defined consciousness, that neither the scene, the speakers, nor the subject are entirely new; nay, feel as if we could anticipate that part of the conversation which has not yet taken place! It is even so with me while I gaze upon that ruin; nor can I divest myself of the idea, that these massive towers and that dark gateway, retiring through its deep vaulted and ribbed arches, and dimly lighted by the court-yard beyond, are not entirely strange to me. Can it be that they have been familiar to me in infancy, and that I am to seek in their vicinity those friends of whom my childhood has still a tender though faint remembrance, and whom I early exchanged for such severe task-masters? Yet Brown, who I think would not have deceived me, always told me I was brought off from the eastern coast, after a skirmish in which my father was killed; and I do remember enough of a horrid scene of violence to strengthen his account."

It happened that the spot upon which young Bertram chanced to station himself for the better viewing the castle, was nearly the same on which his father had died. It was marked by a large old oak tree, the only one on the esplanade, and which, having been used for executions by the barons of Ellangowan, was called the Justice-Tree. It chanced, and the coincidence was remarkable, that Glossin was this morning engaged with a person, whom he was in the habit of consulting in such matters, concerning some projected repairs, and a large addition to the house of Ellangowan, and that, having no great pleasure in remains so intimately connected with the grandeur of the former inhabitants, he had resolved to use the stones of the ruinous castle in his new edifice. Accordingly he came up the bank, followed by the land-surveyor mentioned upon a former occasion, who was also in the habit of acting as a sort of architect in case of necessity. In drawing the plans, &c. Glossin was in the custom of relying upon his own skill. Bertram's back was towards them as they came up the ascent, and he was quite shrouded by the branches of the large tree, so that Glossin was not aware of the presence of the stranger till he was close upon him.

"Yes, sir, as I have often said before to you, the old place is a perfect quarry of hewn stone, and it would be better for the estate if it were all down, since it is only a den for smugglers."

At this instant Bertram turned short round upon Glossin at the distance of two yards only—"Would you destroy the castle, sir?"

His face, person, and voice, were so exactly those of his father in his best days, that Glossin, hearing his exclamation, and seeing such a sudden apparition in the shape of his patron, and on nearly the very spot where he had expired, almost thought the grave had given up its dead!—He staggered back two or three paces, as if he had received a sudden and deadly wound. He instantly recovered however his presence of mind, stimulated by the thrilling reflection that it was no inhabitant of the other world which stood before him, but an injured man, whom the slightest want of dexterity on his part might lead to acquaintance with his rights, and the means of asserting them to his utter destruction. Yet his ideas were so much confused by the shock he had received, that his first question partook of the alarm.

"In the name of God, how came you here?"

"Here, sir? I landed a quarter of an hour since in the little harbour beneath the castle, and was employing a moment's leisure in viewing these fine ruins; I trust there is no intrusion?"

"Intrusion, sir?—no, sir," said Glossin, in some degree recovering his breath, and then whispered a few words into his companion's ear, who immediately left him and descended towards the house. "Intrusion, sir?—no, sir,—you or any gentleman are welcome to satisfy your curiosity."

"I thank you, sir. They call this the Old Place, I am informed?"

"Yes, sir; in distinction to the New Place, my house there below."

Glossin, it must be remarked, was, during the following dialogue, on the one hand eager to learn what local recollections young Bertram had retained of the scenes of his infancy, and, on the other, compelled to be extremely cautious in his replies, lest he should awaken or assist by some name, phrase, or anecdote, the slumbering train of association. He suffered, indeed, during the whole scene, the agonies which he so richly deserved; yet his pride and interest, like the fortitude of a North American Indian, manned him to sustain the tortures inflicted at once, by the contending stings of a guilty conscience, of hatred, of fear, and of suspicion.

"I wish to ask the name, sir, of the family to whom this stately ruin belongs?"

"It is my property, sir; my name is Glossin."

"Glossin—Glossin?" repeated Bertram, as if the answer was somewhat different from what he expected, "I beg your pardon, Mr Glossin, I am apt to be very absent.—May I ask if the castle has been long in your family?"

"It was built, I believe, long ago, by a family called Mac-Dingawaie," answered Glossin, suppressing for obvious reasons the more familiar sound of Bertram, which might have awakened the recollections which he was so anxious to lull to rest, and slurring with an evasive answer the question concerning the endurance of his own possession.

"And how do you read the half-defaced motto, sir, which is upon that scroll above the entablature with the arms?"

"I—I—I really do not exactly know," replied Glossin.

"I should be apt now to read it, *Our Right makes our Might*."

"I believe it is something of that kind."

"May I ask, sir, if it is your family motto?"

"N—n—no—no—not ours. That is, I believe, the motto of the former people—mine is—mine is—In fact I have had some correspondence with Mr Cumming of the Lion-office in Edinburgh, about mine. He writes me the Glossins anciently bore for a motto, 'He who takes it makes it.'"

"If there be any uncertainty, sir, and the case were mine, I would assume the old motto, which seems to me the better of the two."

Glossin, whose tongue by this time clove to the roof of his mouth, only answered by a nod.

"It is odd enough," said Bertram, fixing his eye upon the arms and gateway, and partly addressing Glossin, partly as it were thinking aloud—"it is odd the tricks which our memory plays us; the remnants of an old prophecy, or song, or rhyme, of some kind or other, return to my recollection upon hearing that motto—stay—it is a strange jangle of sounds:

> The dark shall be light,
> And the wrong made right,
> When Bertram's right and Bertram's might
> Shall meet on——

I cannot remember the last line—on some particular height—*height* is the rhyme, I am sure; but I cannot hit upon the preceding word."

"Confound your memory," thought Glossin, "you remember by far too much of it."

"There are other rhymes connected with these early recollections: Pray, sir, is there any song current in this part of the world, respecting a daughter of the King of the Isle of Man eloping with a Scottish knight?"

"I am the worst person in the world to consult upon legendary antiquities," answered Glossin.

"I could sing such a ballad," said Bertram, "from one end to another when I was a boy—you must know I left Scotland, which is my native country, very young, and those who brought me up discouraged all my attempts to preserve recollection of my native land, on account, I believe, of a boyish wish which I had to escape from their charge."

"Very natural," said Glossin, but speaking as if his utmost efforts were unable to unseal his lips beyond the width of a quarter of an inch, so that his whole utterance was a kind of compressed muttering, very different from the round bold bullying voice with which he usually spoke. Indeed his appearance and demeanour during all this conversation seemed to diminish even his strength and stature, so that he withered as it were into the shadow of himself, now advancing one foot, now the other, now stooping and wriggling his shoulders, now fumbling with the buttons of his waistcoat, now clasping his hands together,—in short, he was the picture of a mean-spirited shuffling rascal in the very agonies of detection.

To these appearances Bertram was totally inattentive, being

dragged on as it were by the current of his own associations. Indeed, although he addressed Glossin, he was not so much thinking of him, as arguing upon the embarrassing state of his own feelings and recollections. "Yes," he said, "I preserved my language among the sailors, most of whom spoke English, and when I could get into a corner by myself, I used to sing all that song over from beginning to end—I have forgot it all now—but I remember the tune well, though I cannot guess what should at present so strongly recall it to my memory."

He took his flageolet from his pocket, and played a simple melody. Apparently the tune awoke the corresponding associations of a damsel, who at a fine spring about half way down the descent, and which had once supplied the castle with water, was engaged in bleaching linen. She immediately took up the song:

> "Are these the links of Firth, she said,
> Or are they the crooks of Dee,
> Or the bonnie woods of Warroch-head
> That I so fain would see?"

"By heaven," said Bertram, "it is the very ballad! I must learn these words from the girl."

"Confusion!" thought Glossin, "if I cannot put a stop to this, all will be out. O the devil take all ballads, ballad-makers, and ballad-singers, and that d—d jade too, to set up her pipe!—You will have time enough for this upon some other occasion," he said aloud; "at present"—(for now he saw his emissary with two or three men coming up the bank,) "at present we must have some more serious conversation together."

"How do you mean, sir?" said Bertram, turning short upon him, and not liking the tone which he made use of.

"Why, sir, as to that—I believe your name is Brown?"

"And what of that, sir?"

Glossin looked over his shoulder to see how near his party had approached; they were coming fast on. "Vanbeest Brown? if I mistake not."

"And what of that, sir?" said Bertram with increasing astonishment and displeasure.

"Why, in that case," said Glossin, observing his friends had now gotten upon the level space close beside them—"in that case you are prisoner in the king's name"—At the same time he stretched his hand towards Bertram's collar, while two of the men who had come up seized upon his arms. He shook himself, however, free of their grasp by a violent effort, in which he pitched the most pertinacious down the bank, and, drawing his cutlass, stood on the defensive, while those who had felt his strength recoiled from his presence, and gazed at a safe distance. "Observe," he called out at the same time, "that I have no purpose to resist legal authority; satisfy me that you have a magistrate's warrant, and are authorised to make this arrest, and I will obey it quietly; but let no man who loves his life venture to approach me till I am satisfied for what crime and by whose authority I am apprehended."

Glossin then caused one of the officers shew a warrant for the apprehension of Vanbeest Brown, accused of the crime of wilfully and maliciously shooting at Charles Hazelwood, younger of Hazelwood, with an intent to kill, and also of other crimes and misdemeanours, and which appointed him, having been so apprehended, to be brought before the next magistrate for examination. The warrant being formal, and the fact such as he could not deny, Bertram threw down his weapon, and submitted himself to the officers, who, flying on him with eagerness corresponding to their former pusillanimity, were about to charge him with irons, alleging the strength and activity which he had displayed, as a justification of this severity. But Glossin was ashamed or afraid to permit this unnecessary insult, and directed the prisoner to be treated with all the decency, and even respect, that was consistent with safety. Afraid, however, to introduce him into his own house, where still further subjects of recollection might have been suggested, and anxious at the same time to cover his own proceedings by the sanction of another's authority, he ordered his carriage (for he had lately set up a carriage) to be got ready, and in the meantime directed refreshments to be given to the prisoner and the officers, who occupied one of the rooms in the old castle, until the means of conveyance should be provided.

Chapter Three

—— Bring in the evidence—
Thou robed man of justice, take thy place,
And thou, his yoke-fellow of equity,
Bench by his side—you are of the commission,
Sit you too.

King Lear

WHILE THE CARRIAGE was getting ready, Glossin had a letter to compose, about which he wasted no small time. It was to his neighbour, as he was fond of calling him, Sir Robert Hazelwood of Hazelwood, the head of an ancient and powerful interest in the country, which had in the decadence of the Ellangowan family gradually succeeded to much of their authority and influence. The present representative of the family was an elderly man, doatingly fond of his own family, which was limited to an only son and daughter, and stoically indifferent to the fate of all mankind besides. For the rest, he was honourable in his general dealings, because he was afraid to suffer the censure of the world, and just from a better motive. He was presumptuously over-conceited on the score of family pride and importance, a feeling considerably enhanced by his late succession to the title of a Nova Scotia Baronet; and he hated the memory of the Ellangowan family, though now a memory only, because a certain baron of that house was traditionally reported to have caused the founder of the Hazelwood family hold his stirrup until he mounted into his saddle. In his general deportment he was pompous and important, affecting a species of florid elocution, which often became ridiculous from his misarranging the triads and quaternions with which he loaded his sentences.

To this personage Glossin was now to write in such a conciliatory style as might be most acceptable to his vanity and family pride, and the following was the form of his card.

"Mr Gilbert Glossin" (he longed to add of Ellangowan, but prudence prevailed, and he suppressed that territorial designation) "Mr Gilbert Glossin has the honour to offer his most respectful compliments to Sir Robert Hazelwood, and to inform him, that he has this morning been fortunate enough to secure the person who wounded Mr C. Hazelwood. As Sir Robert Hazelwood may probably chuse to conduct the examination of this criminal himself, Mr G. Glossin will cause the man to be carried to the inn at Kippletringan, or to Hazelwood-house, as Sir Robert Hazelwood may be pleased to direct: And, with Sir Robert Hazelwood's permission, Mr G. Glossin will attend him at either of these places with the proofs and declarations which he has been so fortunate as to collect respecting this atrocious business."

"*Elln. Gn.*
"*Tuesday.*

Addressed,

"Sir Robert Hazelwood of Hazelwood, Bart.
"Hazelwood-House, &c. &c. &c."

This card he dispatched by a servant on horseback, and having given the man some time to get a-head, and desired him to ride fast, he ordered two officers of justice into the carriage with Bertram, and he himself, mounting his horse, accompanied them at a slow pace to the point where the roads to Kippletringan and Hazelwood-house separated, and there awaited the return of his messenger, in order that his farther route might be determined by the answer he should receive from the Baronet. In about half an hour his servant returned with the following answer, handsomely folded, and sealed with the Hazelwood arms, and having the Nova Scotia badge depending from the shield.

"Sir Robert Hazelwood of Hazelwood, returns Mr G. Glossin's compts., and thanks him for the trouble he has taken in a matter affecting the safety of Sir Robts. family. Sir R. H. requests Mr G. G. will have the goodness to bring the prisoner to Hazelwood-house for examination, with the other proofs or declarations which he mentions. And after the business is over, in case Mr G. G. is not otherwise engaged, Sir R. and Lady Hazelwood request his company to dinner."

"*Hazelwood-House*
"*Tuesday.*

Addressed,
"MR GILBERT GLOSSIN, &c."

"Soh!" thought Mr Glossin, "here is one finger in at least, and that I will make the means of introducing my whole hand. But I must first get clear of this wretched young fellow.—I think I can manage Sir Robert. He is dull and pompous, and will be alike disposed to listen to my suggestions upon the law of the case, and to assume the credit of acting upon them as his own proper motion. So I shall have the advantage of being the real magistrate, without the odium of responsibility."

As he cherished these hopes and expectations, the carriage approached Hazelwood-house, through a noble avenue of old oaks, which shrouded the ancient abbey-resembling building so called. It was a large edifice built at different periods, part having actually been a priory, upon the suppression of which, in the time of Queen Mary, the first of the family had obtained a gift of the house and surrounding lands from the crown. It was pleasantly situated in a large deer-park, on the banks of the river we have before mentioned. The scenery around was of a dark, solemn, and somewhat melancholy cast, according well with the architecture of the house. Every thing appeared to be kept in the highest possible order, and announced the opulence and rank of the proprietor.

As Mr Glossin's carriage stopped at the door of the hall, Sir Robert reconnoitred the new vehicle from the windows. According to his aristocratic feelings, there was a degree of presumption in this *novus homo*, this Mr G. Glossin, late writer in Kippletringan, presuming to set up such an accommodation at all; but his wrath was mitigated when he observed that the mantle upon the pannels only bore a plain cypher of G. G. This apparent modesty was indeed solely owing to the delay of Mr Cumming of the Lion Office, who, being at that time engaged in discovering and matriculating the arms of two commissaries from North America, three English-Irish peers, and two great Jamaica traders, had been more slow than usual in finding an escutcheon for the new Laird of Ellangowan. But his delay told to the advantage of Glossin in the opinion of the proud Baronet.

While the officers of justice detained their prisoner in a sort of steward's room, Mr Glossin was ushered into what was called the great oak-parlour, a long room pannelled with well-varnished wainscot, and adorned with the grim portraits of Sir Robert Hazelwood's ancestry. The visitor, who had no internal consciousness of worth to balance that of meanness of birth, felt his inferiority, and, by the depth of his bow and the obsequiousness of his demeanour, showed that the Laird of Ellangowan was sunk for the time in the old and submissive habits of the quondam retainer of the law. He would have persuaded himself, indeed, that he was only humouring the prejudices of the old Baronet, for the purpose of turning them to his own advantage. But his feelings were of a mingled nature, and he felt the influence of those very prejudices which he pretended to flatter. The Baronet received him with that condescending parade which was meant at once to assert his own vast superiority, and to shew the generosity and courtesy with which he could waive it, and descend to the level of ordinary conversation with ordinary men. He thanked Glossin for his attention to a matter in which "young Hazelwood" was so intimately concerned, and, pointing to his family pictures, observed with a gracious smile, "Indeed those venerable gentlemen, Mr Glossin, are as much obliged as I am in this case, for the labour, pains, care, and trouble which you have taken in their behalf; and I have no doubt, were they capable of expressing themselves, would join me, sir, in thanking you for the favour you have conferred upon the house of Hazelwood by taking care and trouble, sir, and interest, in behalf of the young gentleman who is to continue their name and family."

Thrice bowed Glossin, and each time more profoundly than before; once in honour of the knight who stood upright before him, once in respect to the quiet personages who patiently hung upon the wainscot, and a third time in deference to the young gentleman who was to carry on their name and family. *Roturier* as he was, Sir Robert was gratified by the homage which he rendered, and proceeded in a tone of gracious familiarity: "And now, Mr Glossin, my exceeding good friend, you must allow me to avail myself of your knowledge of law in our proceedings in this matter. I am not much in the habit of acting as a justice of peace; it suits better with other gentlemen, whose domestic and family affairs require less constant superintendance, attention, and management than mine."

Of course, whatever small assistance Mr Glossin could render was entirely at Sir Robert Hazelwood's service; but, as Sir Robert Hazelwood's name stood high on the list of the Faculty, the said Mr Glossin could not presume to hope it could be either necessary or useful.

"Why, my good sir, you will understand me to mean the practical knowledge of the ordinary details of justice-business. I was indeed educated to the bar, and might boast perhaps at one time, that I had made some progress in the speculative, and abstract, and abstruse doctrines of our municipal code; but there is in the present day so little opportunity of a man of family and fortune rising to that eminence at the bar, which is attained by adventurers who are as willing to plead for John a Nokes as for the first noble of the land, that I was really early disgusted with practice. The first case, indeed, which was laid on my table, quite sickened me; it respected a bargain, sir, of tallow, between a butcher and a candle-maker; and I found it was expected that I should grease my mouth, not only with their vulgar names, but with all the technical terms, and phrases, and peculiar language, of their dirty arts. Upon my honour, my good sir, I have never been able to bear the smell of a tallow-candle since."

Pitying, as seemed to be expected, the mean use to which the Baronet's faculties had been degraded on this melancholy occasion, Mr Glossin offered to officiate as clerk or assessor, or in any way in which he could be most useful. "And with a view to possessing you of the whole business, and in the first place, there will, I believe, be no difficulty in proving the main fact, that this was the person who fired the unhappy piece. Should he deny it, it can be proved by Mr Hazelwood, I presume?"

"Young Hazelwood is not at home to-day, Mr Glossin."

"But we can have the oath of the servant who attended him; indeed I hardly think the fact will be disputed. I am more apprehensive, that, from the too favourable and indulgent manner in which I have understood that Mr Hazelwood has been pleased to represent the business, the assault may be considered as accidental, and the injury as unintentional, so that the fellow may be immediately set at liberty, to do more mischief."

"I have not the honour to know the gentleman who now holds the office of King's Advocate," replied Sir Robert gravely; "but I presume, sir—nay, I am confident, that he will consider the mere fact of having wounded young Hazelwood of Hazelwood, even by inadvertency, to take the matter in its mildest and gentlest, and in its most favourable and improbable light, is a crime which will be too easily atoned by imprisonment, and is more deserving of deportation."

"Indeed, Sir Robert," said his assenting brother in justice, "I am entirely of your opinion; but, I don't know how it is, I have observed the Edinburgh gentlemen of the bar, and even the officers of the crown, pique themselves upon an indifferent administration of justice, without respect to rank and family, and I should fear"——

"How, sir? Without respect to rank and family?—will you tell me *that* doctrine can be held by men of birth and legal education?—no, sir—if a trifle stolen in the street is termed mere pickery, but is elevated into sacrilege if the crime be committed in a church, even so, according to the just gradations of society, the guilt of an injury is enhanced by the rank of the person to whom it is offered, done, or committed, sir."

Glossin bowed low to this declaration *ex cathedra*, but observed, that in case of the very worst, and of such unnatural doctrines being actually held as he had already hinted, "the law had another hold on Mr Vanbeest Brown."

"Vanbeest Brown? is that the fellow's name? Good God! that young Hazelwood of Hazelwood should have had his life endangered, the clavicle of his right shoulder considerably lacerated and dislodged, several large drops or slugs deposited in the acromion process, as the account of the family surgeon expressly bears, and all by an obscure wretch named Vanbeest Brown!"

"Why, really, Sir Robert, it is a thing which one can hardly bear to think of; but, begging ten thousand pardons for resuming what I was about to say, a person of the same name is, as appears from these papers (producing Dirk Hattaraick's pocket-book) mate to the smuggling vessel whose crew offered such violence at Woodbourne, and I have no doubt that this is the same individual; which, however, your acute discrimination will easily be able to ascertain."

"The same, my good sir, he must assuredly be—it would be injustice even to the meanest of the people to suppose there could be found among them *two* persons doomed to bear a name so shocking to one's ears as this of Vanbeest Brown."

"True, Sir Robert; most unquestionably; there cannot be a shadow of doubt of it—But you see farther, that this circumstance accounts for the man's desperate conduct. You, Sir Robert, will discover the motive for his crime—you, I say, will discover it without difficulty, on your giving your mind to the examination; for my part, I cannot help suspecting the moving spring to have been revenge for the gallantry with which Mr Hazelwood, with all the spirit of his renowned forefathers, defended the house at Woodbourne against this villain and his lawless companions."

"I will enquire into it, my good sir. Yet even now I venture to conjecture that I shall adopt the solution or explanation of this riddle, enigma, or mystery, which you have in some degree first started. Yes! revenge it must be—and, good Heaven! entertained by and against whom?—entertained, fostered, cherished, against young Hazelwood of Hazelwood, and in part carried into effect, executed, and implemented by the hand of Vanbeest Brown! These are dreadful days indeed, my worthy neighbour (this epithet indicated a rapid advance in the Baronet's good graces)—days when the bulwarks of society are shaken to their mighty base, and that rank which forms, as it were, its highest grace and ornament, is mingled and confused with the viler parts of the architecture. O, my good Mr Gilbert Glossin, in my time, sir, the use of swords and pistols, and such honourable arms, was reserved by the nobility and gentry to themselves, and the disputes of the vulgar were decided by the weapons which nature had given them, or by cudgels cut, broken, or hewed out of the next wood. But now, sir, the clouted shoe of the peasant galls the kibe of the courtier. The lower ranks have their quarrels, sir, and their points of honour and their revenges, which they must bring forsooth to fatal arbitrement. But well, well! it will last my time—let us have in this fellow, this Vanbeest Brown, and make an end of him at least for the present."

Chapter Four

—'Twas he
Gave heat unto the injury, which returned
Like a petar' ill lighted into the bosom
Of him gave fire to't. Yet I hope his hurt
Is not so dangerous but he may recover.

Fair Maid of the Inn

THE PRISONER was now presented before the two worshipful magistrates. Glossin, partly from some compunctious visitings, and partly out of his cautious resolution to suffer Sir Robert Hazelwood to be the ostensible manager of the whole examination, looked down upon the table, and busied himself with reading and arranging the papers respecting the business, only now and then throwing in a skilful catch-word as prompter, when he saw the principal and apparently most active magistrate stand in need of a hint. As for Sir Robert Hazelwood, he assumed on his part a happy mixture of the austerity of the justice, combined with the display of personal dignity appertaining to the baronet of ancient family.

"There, constables, let him stand there at the bottom of the table—

Be so good as look me in the face, sir, and raise your voice as you answer the questions which I am going to put to you."

"May I beg, in the first place, to know, sir, who it is that takes the trouble to interrogate me? for the honest gentlemen who have brought me here have not been pleased to furnish any information upon that point."

"And pray, sir, what has my name and quality to do with the questions I am about to ask you?"

"Nothing perhaps, sir; but it may considerably influence my disposition to answer them."

"Why, then, sir, you will please to be informed, that you are in presence of Sir Robert Hazelwood of Hazelwood, and another justice of peace for this county—that's all."

As this intimation produced a less stunning effect upon the prisoner than he had anticipated, Sir Robert proceeded in his investigation with an increasing dislike to the object of it.

"Is your name Vanbeest Brown, sir?"

"It is."

"So far well;—and how are we to design you farther, sir?"

"Captain in his majesty's —— regiment of horse."

The Baronet's ears received this intimation with astonishment; but he was refreshed in courage by an incredulous look from Glossin, and by hearing him gently utter a sort of interjectional whistle, in a note of surprise and contempt. "I believe, my friend, we shall find for you before we part a more humble title."

"If you do, sir, I will willingly submit to any punishment which such an imposture shall be thought to deserve."

"Well, sir, we shall see.—Do you know young Hazelwood of Hazelwood?"

"I never saw the gentleman who I am informed bears that name, excepting once, and I regret that it was under very unpleasant circumstances."

"You mean to acknowledge then, that you inflicted upon young Hazelwood of Hazelwood, that wound which endangered his life, considerably lacerated the clavicle of his right shoulder, and deposited, as the family surgeon declares, several large drops or slugs in the acromion process?"

"Why, sir, I can only say I am equally ignorant and sorry for the extent of the damage which the young gentleman has sustained. I met him in a narrow path, walking with two ladies and a servant; and before I could either pass them or address them, this young Hazelwood took his gun from his servant, presented it against my body, and commanded me in the most haughty tone to stand back. I was neither inclined to submit to his authority, nor to leave him in possession of the means to injure me, which he seemed disposed to use with such rashness. I therefore closed with him for the purpose of disarming him; and just as I had nearly effected my purpose, the piece went off accidentally, and to my regret then and since, inflicted upon the young gentleman a severer chastisement than I desired, though I am glad to understand it is like to prove no more than his unprovoked act fully merited."

"And so, sir," said the Baronet, every feature swoln with offended dignity,—"You, sir, admit, sir, that it was your purpose, sir, and your intention, sir, and the real jet and object of your assault, sir, to disarm young Hazelwood of Hazelwood of his gun, sir, or his fowling-piece, or his fuzee, or whatever you please to call it, sir, upon the king's highway, sir?—I think this will do, my worthy neighbour! I think he should stand committed?"

"You are by far the best judge, Sir Robert; but if I might presume to hint, there was something about these smugglers."

"Very true, good sir.—And besides, sir, you, Vanbeest Brown, who call yourself a captain in his majesty's service, are no better or worse than a rascally mate of a smuggler!"

"Really, sir, you are an old gentleman, and acting under some strange delusion, otherwise I should be very angry with you."

"Old gentleman, sir! strange delusion, sir! I protest and declare ——Why, sir, have you any papers or letters that can establish your pretended rank, estate, and commission?"

"None at present, sir; but in the return of a post or two"——

"And how do you, sir, if you are a captain in his majesty's service, chance to be travelling in Scotland without letters of introduction, credentials, baggage, or any thing belonging to your pretended rank, estate, and condition, as I said before?"

"Sir, I had the misfortune to be robbed of my clothes and baggage."

"Oho! then you are the gentleman who took a post-chaise from —— to Kippletringan, gave the boy the slip on the road, and sent two of your accomplices to beat the boy and bring away the baggage?"

"I was, sir, in a carriage as you describe, and lost my way endeavouring to find the road to Kippletringan. The landlady of the inn will inform you, that on my arrival there the next day, my first enquiries were after the boy."

"Then give me leave to ask where you spent the night—not in the snow, I presume? you do not suppose that will pass, or be taken, credited, and received?"

"I beg leave," said Bertram, his recollection turning to the gypsey female, and to the promise he had given her, "I beg leave to decline answering that question."

"I thought as much.—Were you not on that night in the ruins of Derncleugh?—in the ruins of Derncleugh, sir?"

"I have told you that I do not intend to answer that question."

"Well, sir, then you will stand committed, sir, and be sent to prison, sir, that's all, sir.—Have the goodness to look at these papers; are you the Vanbeest Brown there mentioned?"

It must be remarked, that Glossin had shuffled among the papers some writings which really did belong to Bertram, and which had been found by the officers in the old vault where his portmanteau was ransacked.

"Some of these papers," said Bertram, looking over them, "are mine, and were in my portfolio when it was stolen from the post-chaise. They are memoranda of little value, and, I see, have been carefully selected as affording no evidence of my rank or character, which many of the other papers would have established fully. They are mingled with ship accompts and other papers, belonging apparently to a person of the same name."

"And wilt thou attempt to persuade me, friend, that there are *two* persons in this country at the same time, of thy very uncommon and awkward sounding name?"

"I really do not see, sir, as there is an old Hazelwood and a young Hazelwood, why there should not be an old and young Vanbeest Brown. And, to speak seriously, I was educated in Holland, and I know that this name, however uncouth it may sound to British ears"——

Glossin, conscious that the prisoner was about to enter upon dangerous ground, now interfered, though the interruption was unnecessary, for the purpose of diverting the attention of Sir Robert Hazelwood, who was speechless and motionless with indignation at the presumptuous comparison implied in Bertram's last speech. In fact, the veins of his throat and of his temples swelled almost to bursting, and he sate with the indignant and disconcerted air of one who has received a mortal insult from a quarter, to which he holds it unmeet and indecorous to make any reply. While with a bent brow and an angry eye he was drawing in his breath slowly and majestically, and puffing it forth again with deep and solemn exertion, Glossin stepped in to his assistance. "I should think now, Sir Robert, with great submission, that this matter may be closed. One of the constables, besides the pregnant proof already produced, offers to make oath, that the sword of which the prisoner was this morning deprived (while using it, by the way, in resistance to a legal warrant) was a cutlass taken from him in the fray between the officers and smugglers, just previous to their attack upon Woodbourne. And yet," added he, "I would not have you form any rash construction upon that subject; perhaps the young man can explain how he came by that weapon."

"That question, sir, I shall also leave unanswered."

"There is yet another circumstance to be enquired into. This prisoner put into the hands of Mrs Mac-Candlish of Kippletringan, a parcel containing a variety of gold coins and valuable articles of different kinds. Perhaps, Sir Robert, you might think it right to ask, how he came by property of a description which seldom occurs?"

"You, sir, Mr Vanbeest Brown, sir, you hear the question, sir, which the gentleman asks you?"

"I have particular reasons for declining to answer that question."

"Then I am afraid, sir, our duty must lay us under the necessity to sign a warrant of committal."

"As you please, sir; take care, however, what you do. Observe that I inform you I am Captain in his Majesty's —— regiment, that I am just returned from India, therefore cannot possibly be connected with any of those contraband traders you talk of; that my Lieutenant-Colonel is presently at Nottingham, the Major, with the officers of my corps, at Kingston-upon-Thames; I offer before you both to submit to any degree of ignominy, if, within the return of the Kingston and Nottingham posts, I am not able to establish these points. Or you may write to the agent for the regiment, if you please——"

"This is all very well, sir," said Glossin, beginning to fear lest the firm expostulation of Bertram should make some impression on Sir Robert, who would almost have died of shame at committing such a solecism as sending a captain of horse to jail—"This is all very well, sir; but is there no one nearer whom you could refer to?"

"There are only two persons in this country who know any thing of me. One is a plain Liddesdale sheep farmer, called Dinmont of Charlieshope; but he knows nothing more of me than what I told him, and what I now tell you."

"Why, this is well enough, Sir Robert! I suppose he would bring this thick-skulled fellow to give his oath of credulity, Sir Robert, ha, ha, ha!"

"And who is your other witness, friend?" said the Baronet.

"A gentleman whom I have some reluctance to mention, because of certain private reasons; but under whose command I have served for some time in India, and who is too much a man of honour to refuse his testimony to my character as a soldier and a gentleman."

"And who is this doughty witness, pray, sir?—some half-pay quarter-master or serjeant, I suppose?"

"Colonel Guy Mannering, late of the —— regiment, in which, as I told you, I have a troop."

"Colonel Guy Mannering!" thought Glossin, "who the devil could have guessed this?"

"Colonel Guy Mannering?" echoed the Baronet, considerably shaken in his opinion, "My good sir,"—apart to Glossin, "the young man, though with a dreadfully plebeian name, and a good deal of modest assurance, has nevertheless something of the tone, and manners, and feeling, of a gentleman, of one at least who has lived in good society—they do give commissions very loosely, and carelessly, and inaccurately, in India—I think we had better pause till Colonel Mannering shall return; he is now, I believe, at Edinburgh."

"You are in every respect the best judge, Sir Robert," answered Glossin, "in every possible respect. I would only submit to you, that we are certainly hardly entitled to dismiss this man upon an assertion which cannot be satisfied by proof, and that we shall incur a heavy responsibility by detaining him in private custody, without committing him to a public jail. Undoubtedly, however, you are the best judge, Sir Robert;—but I would only say, for my own part, that I very lately incurred severe censure by detaining a person in a place as I thought perfectly secure, and under the custody of the proper officers. The man made his escape, and I have no doubt my character for attention and circumspection as a magistrate has in some degree suffered—I only hint this—I will join in any step you, Sir Robert, think most advisable." But Mr Glossin was well aware that such a hint was of power sufficient to guide the motions of his self-important, but not self-relying colleague. So that Sir Robert Hazelwood summed up the business in the following speech, which proceeded partly upon the supposition of the prisoner being really a gentleman, and partly upon the conviction that he was a villain and assassin.

"Sir, Mr Vanbeest Brown—I would call you Captain Brown if there was the least reason, or cause, or grounds to suppose that you are a captain, or had a troop in the very respectable corps you mention, or indeed in any other corps in his majesty's service, as to which circumstance I beg to be understood to give no positive, settled, or unalterable judgment, declaration, or opinion. I say therefore, sir, Mr Brown, we have determined considering the unpleasant predicament in which you now stand, having been robbed, as you say, an assertion as to which I suspend my opinion, and being possessed of much and valuable treasure, and of a brass-handled cutlass besides, as to your obtaining which you will favour us with no explanation—I say, sir, we have determined and resolved, and made up our minds, to commit you to jail, or rather to assign you an apartment therein, in order that you may be forthcoming upon Colonel Mannering's return from Edinburgh."

"With humble submission, Sir Robert," said Glossin, "may I enquire if it is your purpose to send this young gentleman to the county jail—for if that were not your settled intention, I would take the liberty to hint, that there would be less hardship in sending him to the little Bridewell at Portanferry, where he can be secured without public exposure; a circumstance, which, upon the mere chance of his story being really true, is much to be avoided?"

"Why there is a guard of soldiers at Portanferry, to be sure, for protection of the goods in the custom-house; and upon the whole, considering every thing, and that the place is comfortable for such a place, I say all things considered, we will commit this person, I would rather say authorize him to be detained, in the workhouse at Portanferry."

The warrant was made out accordingly, and Bertram was informed he was next morning to be removed to his place of confinement, as Sir Robert had determined he should not be taken there under cloud of night, for fear of rescue. He was, during the interval, to be detained at Hazelwood-house.

"It cannot be so hard as my imprisonment by the Looties in India," thought he, "nor can it last so long. But the deuce take the old formal dunderhead, and his more sly associate, who speaks always under his breath, they cannot understand a plain man's story when it is told them."

In the meanwhile Glossin took leave of the Baronet, with a thousand respectful bows and cringing apologies for not accepting his invitation to dinner, and ventured to hope he might be pardoned in paying his respects to him, Lady Hazelwood, and young Mr Hazelwood, upon some future occasion.

"Certainly, sir," said the Baronet very graciously. "I hope our family was never at any time deficient in civility to our neighbours; and when I ride that way, good Mr Glossin, I will convince you of this by calling at your house as familiarly as is consistent—that is, as can be hoped or expected."

"And now," said Glossin to himself, "to find Dirk Hattaraick and his people, to get the guard sent off the custom-house, and then for the grand cast of the dice. Every thing must depend upon speed.—How lucky that Mannering has betaken himself to Edinburgh! his knowledge of this young fellow is a most perilous addition to my dangers,"—here he suffered his horse to slacken his pace—"What if I should try to compound with the heir?—It's likely he might be brought to pay a round sum for restitution, and I could give up

Hattaraick—But no, no, no! there were too many eyes on me, Hattaraick himself, and the gypsey sailor, and that old hag—No, no! I must stick to my original plan." And with that he struck his spurs to his horse's flanks, and rode forward at a hard trot to put his machines in motion.

Chapter Five

A prison is a house of care,
A place where none can thrive,
A touchstone true to try a friend,
A grave for one alive.
Sometimes a place of right,
Sometimes a place of wrong,
Sometimes a place of rogues and thieves,
And honest men among.

Inscription on Edinburgh Tolbooth

EARLY on the following morning, the carriage which had brought Bertram to Hazelwood-house, was, with his two silent and surly attendants, appointed to convey him to his place of confinement at Portanferry. This building adjoined to the custom-house established at that little sea-port, and both were situated so close to the sea-beach, that it was necessary to defend the back part with a large and strong rampart, or bulwark of huge stones, disposed in a slope towards the surf, which often reached and broke upon them. The front was surrounded by a high wall, enclosing a small court-yard, within which the miserable inmates of the mansion were occasionally permitted to take exercise and air. The prison was used as a House of Correction, and occasionally as a chapel of ease to the county jail, which was old, and far from being conveniently situated with reference to the Kippletringan district of the county. Mac-Guffog, the officer by whom Bertram had at first been apprehended, and who was now in attendance upon him, was keeper of this palace of little-ease. He caused the carriage to be drawn close up to the outer gate, and got out himself to summon the warders. The noise of his rap alarmed some twenty or thirty ragged boys, who left off sailing their mimic sloops and frigates on the little pools of salt-water left by the receding tide, and hastily crowded round the carriage to see what luckless being was to be delivered to the prison-house out of "Glossin's braw new carriage." The door of the court-yard, after the heavy clashing of many chains and bars, was opened by Mrs Mac-Guffog, an awful spectacle, being a woman for strength and resolution capable of maintaining order among her riotous inmates, and of administering the discipline of the house, as it was called, during the absence of her husband, or when he chanced to have taken an over-dose of the creature. The growling voice of this amazon, which rivalled in harshness the crashing music of her own bolts and bars, soon dispersed in every direction the little varlets who had thronged around her threshold, and she next addressed her amiable help-mate.

"Be sharp, man, and get out the swell, can'st thou not?"

"Hold your tongue and be d—d, you ——," answered her loving husband, with two additional epithets of great energy, but which we beg to be excused from repeating. Then addressing Bertram—"Come, will you get out, my handy lad, or must we lend you a lift?"

Bertram came out of the carriage, and, collared by the constable as he put his foot upon the ground, was dragged, though he offered no resistance, across the threshold, amid the continued shouts of the little sans culottes, who looked on at such distance as their fear of Mrs Mac-Guffog permitted. The instant his foot had crossed the fatal threshold, the portress again dropped her chains, drew her bolts, and, turning with both hands an immense key, took it from the lock, and thrust it into a huge side-pocket of red cloth.

Bertram was now in the small court already mentioned. Two or three prisoners were sauntering along the pavement, and deriving, as it were, a feeling of refreshment from the momentary glimpse with which the opening door had extended their prospect to the other side of a dirty street. Nor can this be thought surprising, when it is considered, that unless upon such occasions their view was confined to the grated front of their prison, the high and sable walls of the court-yard, the heaven above them, and the pavement beneath their feet; a sameness of landscape, which, to use the poet's expression, "lay like a load on the wearied eye," and had fostered in some a callous and dull misanthropy, in others that sickness of the heart which induces him who is immured already in a living grave, to wish for a sepulchre yet more calm and sequestered.

Mac-Guffog, when they entered the court-yard, suffered Bertram to pause for a minute, and look upon his companions in affliction. When he had cast his eye around on faces in which guilt, and despondence, and low excess, had fixed their stigma; upon the spendthrift, and the swindler, and the thief, the bankrupt debtor, the "moping idiot, and the madman gay," whom a paltry spirit of economy assigned to share this dismal habitation, he felt his heart recoil with inexpressible loathing from enduring the contamination of their society even for a moment.

"I hope, sir," he said to the keeper, "you intend to assign me a place of confinement apart?"

"And what should I be the better of that?"

"Why, sir, I can but be detained here a day or two, and it would be very disagreeable to me to mix in the sort of company this place affords."

"And what do I care for that?"

"Why, then, sir, to speak to your feelings, I shall be willing to make a handsome compliment for this indulgence."

"Aye, but when, Captain? when and how? that's the question, or rather the twa questions."

"When I am delivered, and get my remittances from England."

Mac-Guffog shook his head incredulously.

"Why, friend, you do not pretend to believe that I am really a malefactor?"

"Why, I no ken," said the fellow; "but if ye *are* on the account, ye're nae sharp ane, that's the day-light o't."

"And why do you say I am no sharp one?"

"Why, wha but a curd-brained callant wad hae let them keep up the siller that ye left at the Gordon Arms? B—st me, but I wad have had it out o' their very wames! ye had nae right to be strippit o' your money and sent to jail without a mark to pay your fees; they might have keepit the rest o' the articles for evidence. But why, for a blind bottle-head, did not ye ask the guineas? and I kept winking and nodding a' the time, and the whoreson chield wad never ance look my way!"

"Well, sir, if I have a title to have that property delivered up to me, I shall apply for it, and there is a great deal more than enough to pay any demand you can set up."

"I dinna ken a bit about that; ye may be here lang eneugh. And then the giving credit maun be considered in the fees. But, however, as ye *do* seem to be a chap by common, though my wife says I lose by my good nature, if ye gie me an order for my fees upon that money—I dare say Glossin will make it forthcoming—I ken something about an escape from Ellangowan—aye, aye, he'll be glad to carry me through, and be neighbour-like."

"Well, sir, if I am not furnished in a day or two otherwise, you shall have such an order."

"Weel, weel, then ye shall be put up like a prince; but mark ye me, friend, that we may have nae colly shangie afterhend, these are the fees that I always charge a swell that must have his lib-ken to himsell —Thirty shillings a-week for lodgings, and a guinea for garnish; half-a-guinea a-week for a single bed,—and I dinna get the whole of it, for I must gie half-a-crown out of it to Donald Laider that's in for sheep-stealing, that should sleep with you by rule, and he'll expect clean strae, and maybe some whisky beside. So I make little upon that."

"Well, sir, go on."

"Then for meat and liquor, ye may have the best, and I never charge abune twenty per cent. over tavern price for pleasing a gentleman in that way—and that's little eneugh for sending in and sending out, and wearing the lassie's shoon out. And then if you're dowie, I will sit wi' you a gliff in the evening myself, man, and help you out wi' your bottle. —I have drank mony a glass wi' Glossin, man, that did you up, though he's a justice now.—And then I'se warrant ye'll be for fire thir cauld nights, or if ye want candle, that's an expensive article, for it's against the rules.—And now I have tauld ye the head articles of the charge, and I dinna think there's mickle mair, though there will aye be some odd expence ower and abune."

"Well, sir, I must trust to your conscience, if ever you happened to hear of such a thing—I cannot help myself."

"Na, na, sir, I'll no permit you to be saying that—I'm forcing naething upon ye;—an ye dinna like the price, ye needna take the article —I force no man; I was only explaining what civility was; but if ye like to take the common run of the house it's a' ane to me—I'll be saved trouble, that's a'."

"Nay, my friend, I have, as I suppose you may easily guess, no inclination to dispute your terms upon such a penalty. Come, show me where I am to be, for I would fain be alone for a little while."

"Aye, aye, come along then, Captain," said the fellow, with a contortion of visage which he intended to be a smile; "and I'll tell you now,—to show you that I have a conscience, as ye ca't, d—n me if I charge ye abune sixpence a day for the freedom o' the court, and ye may walk in it very near three hours a day, and play at pitch and toss, and hand-ba', and what not."

With this gracious promise he ushered Bertram into the house, and shewed him up a steep and narrow stone stair-case, at the top of which was a strong door, clenched with iron and studded with nails. Beyond this door was a narrow passage or gallery, having three cells on each side, wretched vaults, with iron bed-frames and straw mattresses. But at the farther end was a small apartment of rather a more decent appearance, that is, having less the air of a place of confinement, since, unless for the large lock and chain upon the door, and the crossed and ponderous stauncheons upon the window, it rather resembled "the worst inn's worst room." It was designed as a sort of infirmary for prisoners whose state of health required some indulgence; and, in fact, Donald Laider, Bertram's destined chum, had been just dragged out of one of the two beds which it contained, to try whether clean straw and whisky might not have a better chance to cure his intermitting fever. This process of ejection had been carried into force by Mrs Mac-Guffog while her husband parleyed with Bertram in the court-yard, that good lady having a distinct presentiment of the manner in which the treaty must necessarily terminate. Apparently the expulsion had not taken place without some application of the strong hand, for one of the bed-posts of a sort of tent bed was broken down, so that the tester and curtains hung forward into the middle of the narrow chamber, like the banner of a chieftain, half sinking amid the confusion of a combat.

"Never mind that being out o' sorts, captain," said Mrs Mac-Guffog, who now followed them into the room; then, turning her back to the prisoner, with as much delicacy as the action admitted she whipped from her leg her ferret garter, and applied it to splicing and fastening the broken bed-post—then used more pins than her apparel could well spare to fasten up the bed-curtains in festoons,—then shook the bed-clothes into something like form—then flung over all a tattered patch-work quilt, and pronounced that things were now "something purpose-like." "And there is your bed, captain," pointing to a massy four-posted hulk, which, owing to the inequality of the floor that had sunk considerably, (the house, though new, having been built by contract) stood upon three legs, and held the fourth aloft as if pawing the air, and in the attitude of advancing like an elephant passant upon the pannel of a coach—"There's your bed and the blankets; but if ye want sheets, or bowster, or pillow, or ony sort o' napery for the table, or for your hands, ye'll hae to speak to me about it, for that's out o' the gudeman's line, (Mac-Guffog had by this time left the room, to avoid, probably, any appeal which might be made to him upon this new exaction) and he never engages for ony thing like that."

"In God's name," said Bertram, "let me have what is decent, and make any charge you please."

"Aweel, aweel, that's sune settled; we'll no excise you neither, though we live sae near to the custom-house. And I maun see to get ye some fire and some dinner too, I'se warrant; but your dinner will be but a puir ane the day, no expecting company that wad be nice and fashious."—So saying, and in all haste, Mrs Mac-Guffog fetched a skuttle of live coals, and having replenished "the rusty grate, unconscious of a fire" for months before, she proceeded with unwashed hands to arrange the stipulated bed-linen, (alas, how different from Ailie Dinmont's!) and, muttering to herself as she discharged her task, seemed, in inveterate spleen of temper, to grudge even those accommodations for which she was to receive payment. At length, however, she departed, grumbling between her teeth, that "she wad rather lock up a hail ward than be fiked about thae niff-naffy gentles that gae sae mickle fash wi' their fancies."

When she was gone, Bertram found himself reduced to the alternative of pacing his little apartment for exercise, or gazing out upon the sea in such proportions as could be seen from the narrow panes of his window, obscured by dirt and by close iron-bars, or reading over the records of brutal wit and blackguardism which despair had scrawled upon the half-whitened walls. The sounds were as uncomfortable as the objects of sight; the sullen dash of the tide, which was now retreating, and the occasional opening and shutting of a door, with all its accompaniments of jarring bolts and creaking hinges, mingling occasionally with the dull monotony of the retiring ocean. Sometimes, too, he could hear the hoarse growl of the keeper, or the shriller strain of his help-mate, almost always in the tone of discontent, anger, or insolence. At other times the large mastiff, chained in the court-yard, answered with furious bark the insults of the idle loiterers who made a sport of incensing him.

At length the tedium of this weary space was broken by the entrance of a dirty-looking serving-wench, who made some preparations for dinner by laying a half-dirty cloth upon a whole-dirty deal table. A knife and fork, which had not been worn out by overcleaning, flanked a cracked delf plate; a nearly empty mustard-pot, placed on one side of the table, balanced a salt-cellar, containing an article of a greyish or rather blackish mixture, upon the other, both of stone-ware, and bearing too obvious marks of recent service. Shortly after, the same Hebe brought up a plate of beef collops, done in the frying-pan, with a huge allowance of grease, floating in an ocean of lukewarm water; and having added a coarse loaf to these savoury viands, she requested to know what liquors the gentleman chose to order. The appearance of this fare was not very inviting: but Bertram endeavoured to mend his commons by ordering wine, which he found tolerably good, and, with the assistance of some indifferent cheese, made his dinner chiefly upon the brown loaf. When his meal was over, the girl presented her master's compliments, and, if agreeable to the gentleman, he would help him to spend the evening. Bertram desired to be excused, and begged, instead of this gracious society, that he might be furnished with paper, pen, ink, and candles. The light appeared in the shape of one long broken tallow-candle, inclining over a tin candlestick coated with grease: as for the writing materials, the prisoner was informed he might have them the next day if he chose to send out to buy them. Bertram next desired the maid to procure him a book, and enforced his request with a shilling; in consequence of which, after long absence, she re-appeared with two odd volumes of the Newgate

Kalendar which she had borrowed from Sam Silverquill, an idle apprentice, who was laid up under charge of forgery. Having laid the books on the table she retired, and left Bertram to studies which were not ill adapted to his present melancholy situation.

Chapter Six

But if thou should'st be dragg'd in scorn
To yonder ignominious tree,
Thou shalt not want one faithful friend
To share the cruel fates' decree.
SHENSTONE

PLUNGED into the gloomy reflections which were naturally excited by his dismal reading, and disconsolate situation, Bertram, for the first time in his life, felt himself affected with a disposition to low spirits. "I have been in worse situations than this too," he said;—"more dangerous, for here is no danger; more dismal in prospect, for my present confinement must necessarily be short; more intolerable for the time, for here at least I have fire, food, and shelter. Yet, with reading these bloody tales of crime and misery, in a place so corresponding to the ideas which they excite, and in listening to these sad sounds, I feel a stronger disposition to melancholy than in my life I ever experienced. But I will not give way to it, though—begone, thou record of guilt and infamy!" said he, flinging the book upon the spare bed; "a Scottish jail shall not break, on the very first day, the spirits which have resisted climate, and want, and penury, and disease, and imprisonment in a foreign land. I have fought many a hard battle with Dame Fortune, and she shall not beat me now if I can help it."

Then bending his mind to a strong effort, he endeavoured to view his situation in the most favourable light. Delaserre must soon be in Scotland; the certificates from his commanding officer must soon arrive; nay, if Mannering were first applied to, who could say but the effect might be a reconciliation between them? He had often observed, and now remembered, that when his former colonel took the part of any one, it was never by halves, and that he seemed to love those persons most who had lain under obligation to him. This therefore, a favour which could be asked with honour and granted with readiness, might be the means of reconciling them to each other. From this his feelings naturally turned towards Julia, and without very nicely measuring the distance between a soldier of fortune, who expected that her father's attestation would deliver him from confinement, and the heiress of that father's wealth and expectations, he was building the gayest castle in the clouds, and varnishing it with all the tints of a summer-evening sky, when his labour was interrupted by a loud knocking at the outer gate, answered by the furious barking of the half-starved mastiff, which was quartered in the court-yard as an addition to the garrison. After much scrupulous precaution the gate was opened, and some person admitted. The house door was next unbarred, unlocked, and unchained, a dog's feet pattered up stairs in great haste, and the animal was heard scratching and whining at the door of the room. Next a heavy step was heard lumbering up, and Mac-Guffog's voice in his character of pilot—"This way, this way; take care of the step;—that's the room."—Bertram's door was then unbolted, and, to his great surprise and joy, his terrier, Wasp, rushed into the room, and almost devoured him with caresses, followed by the massy form of his friend from Charlieshope.

"Eh whow! Eh whow!" ejaculated the honest farmer, as he looked round upon his friend's miserable apartment and wretched accommodation—"What's this o't? what's this o't?"

"Just a trick of fortune, my good friend," said Bertram, rising and shaking him heartily by the hand, "that's all."

"But what will be done about it?—or what *can* be done about it?—it is for debt, or what is it for?"

"Why, it is not for debt; and if you have time to sit down, I'll tell you all I know of the matter."

"If I hae time?—ou, what the deevil am I come here for, man, but just ance errand to see about it? but ye'll no be the waur o' something to eat, I trow;—it's getting late at e'en—I tell'd the folk at the change where I put up Dumple, to send ower my supper here, and the chield Mac-Guffog is agreeable to let it in—I hae settled a' that—and now let's hear your story—whisht, Wasp, man!—wow but he's glad to see you, poor thing!"

Bertram's story, as he confined it to the business of Hazelwood, and the confusion made between his own name and one of the smugglers, who had been active in the assault of Woodbourne, was soon told. Dinmont listened very attentively. "Aweel," said he, "this suld be nae sick dooms-desperate business surely—the lad's doing weel again that was hurt, and what signifies twa or three draps of lead in his shouther? if ye had putten out his e'e it would hae been another case. But eh, as I wuss auld Shirra Pleydell was to the fore here!—odd, he was the man for sorting them, and the queerest rough-spoken deevil too that ye ever heard!"

"But now tell me, my excellent friend, how did you find out I was here?"

"Odd, lad, queerly enough; but I'll tell ye that after we are done wi' our supper, for it will may be no be sae weel to speak about it while that lang-lugged limmer o' a lass is ganging flisking in and out o' the room."

Bertram's curiosity was in some degree put to rest by the appearance of the supper which his friend had ordered, which, although homely enough, had the appetizing cleanliness in which Mrs MacGuffog's cookery was so eminently deficient. Dinmont also, premising he had ridden the whole day since breakfast time, without tasting any thing "to speak of," which qualifying phrase related to about three pounds of cold roast mutton which he had discussed at his mid-day stage,—Dinmont, I say, fell stoutly upon the good cheer, and, like one of Homer's heroes, said little, either good or bad, till the rage of thirst and hunger was appeased. At length, after a draught of home-brewed ale, he began by observing, "Aweel, aweel, that hen," looking upon the lamentable reliques of what had been once a large fowl, "was na a bad ane to be bred at a town-end, though it's no like our barn-door chuckies at Charlieshope—and I am glad to see that this vexing job has no ta'en awa' your appetite, Captain."

"Why, really, my dinner was not so excellent, Mr Dinmont, as to spoil my supper."

"I dare say no, I dare say no:—But now, hinny, that ye hae brought us the brandy and the mug wi' the het water, and the sugar, and a' right, ye may steek the door, ye see, for we wad hae some o' our ain cracks." The damsel accordingly retired, and shut the door of the apartment, to which she added the precaution of drawing a large bolt on the outside.

So soon as she was gone Dandie reconnoitred the premises, listened at the key-hole as if he had been listening for the blowing of an otter, and having satisfied himself that there were no eves-droppers, returned to the table, and making himself what he called a gay stiff cheerer, poked the fire, and began his story in an under tone of gravity and importance not very usual with him.

"Ye see, Captain, I had been in Edinbro' for twa three days, looking after the burial of a friend that we hae lost, and may be I suld hae had something for my ride; but there's disappointments in a' things, and wha can help the like o' that? and I had a wee bit law business besides, but that's neither here nor there. In short, I had got my matters settled, and hame I came; and the morn awa to the moors to see what the herds had been about, and I thought I might as weel gie a look to the Touthope-head, where Jock o' Dawstone and me has the outcast about a march—Weel, just as I was coming upon the bit, I saw a man afore me that I kend was nane o' our herds, and it's a wild bit to meet ony other body, so when I came up to him it was Tod Gabriel the fox-hunter. So I says to him, rather surprised like, 'What are ye doing up amang the craws here, without your hounds, man? are ye seeking the fox without the dogs?' So he said, 'Na, gudeman, but I wanted to see yoursel.'

"'Aye,' said I, 'and ye'll be wanting eilding now, or something to pitt ower the winter?'

"'Na, na,' quo' he, 'it's no that I'm seeking; but ye tak an unco interest in that Captain Brown that was staying wi' you, d'ye no?'

"'Troth do I, Gabriel,' says I; 'and what about him, lad?'

"Says he, 'There's mair tak an interest in him than you, and some that I am bound to obey, and it's no just on my ain will that I'm here to tell you something about him that will na please you.'

"'Faith, naething will please me,' quo' I, 'that's no pleasing to him.'

"'And than,' quo' he, 'ye'll be ill sorted to hear that he's like to be in prison at Portanferry, if he does na tak a' the better care o' himsell, for there's been warrants out to tak him as soon as he comes ower the water frae Allonby, and ane o' them was executed yesterday morning. And now, gudeman, an ever ye wish him weel, ye maun ride down to Portanferry, and let nae grass grow at the nag's heels; and ye maun stay beside him night and day, for a day or twa, for he'll want friends that hae baith heart and hand; and if ye neglect this ye'll never rue it but ance, for it will be for a' your life.'

"'But, safe us, man,' quo' I, 'how did ye learn a' this? it's an unco way between this and Portanferry.'

"'Never ye mind that,' quo' he, 'they that brought me the news rade night and day, and ye maun be aff instantly if ye wad do ony gude—and sae I hae naething mair to tell ye.'—So he sat himsell doun and hirselled doun into the glen, where it wad hae been ill following him wi' the beast, and I came back to Charlieshope to tell the gudewife, for I was uncertain what to do—it wad look unco-like, I thought, just to be sent out on a hunt-the-gowk errand wi' a land-louper like that. But, Lord! as the gudewife set up her throat about it, and said what a shame it wad be if ye was to come to ony wrang an I could help ye; and then in came your letter that confirmed it. So I took to the kist, and out wi' the pickle notes in case they should be needed, and a' the bairns ran to saddle Dumple. By great luck I had ta'en the other beast to Edinbro', sae Dumple was as fresh as a rose. Sae aff I set, and Wasp wi' me, for ye wad really hae thought he kenn'd where I was gaun, puir beast,—and here I am after a trot o' sixty mile or near bye."

In this strange story Bertram obviously saw, supposing the warning to be true, some intimation of danger more violent and imminent than could be likely to arise from a few days imprisonment. At the same time it was equally evident that some unseen friend was working in his behalf. "Did you not say," he asked Dinmont, "that this man Gabriel was of gypsey blood?"

"It was aye judged sae," said Dinmont, "and I think this maks it likely; for they aye ken where the gangs o' ilk ither are to be found, and they can gar news flee like a foot-ba' through the kintra an' they like. An' I forgot to tell ye, there's been an unco enquiry after the auld wife that we saw in Bewcastle; the sheriff's had folk ower the Limestane Edge after her, and down the Hermitage and Liddle, and a' gates, and a reward offered for her to appear, o' fifty pund sterling, nae less; and Justice Forster, he's had out warrants, as I am tauld, in Cumberland, and an unco ranging and ripeing they have had a' gates seeking for her; but she'll no be ta'en wi' them unless she likes, for a' that."

"And how comes that?" said Bertram.

"Ou, I dinna ken; I dare say it's nonsense, but they say she has gathered the fern-seed, and can gang ony gate she likes, like Jock the Giant-killer in the ballads, wi' his coat o' darkness and his shoon o' swiftness. Ony way she's a kind o' queen amang the gypsies; she is mair than a hunder year auld, folk say, and minds the coming in o' the moss-troopers in the troublesome times when the Stuarts were put awa. Sae if she canna hide hersell, they can hide her weel aneugh, ye needna doubt that. Odd, an' I had kenn'd it had been Meg Merrilies yon night at Tib Mumps's, I wad taen care how I crossed her."

Bertram listened with great attention to this account, which tallied so well in many points with what he had himself seen of this gypsey sybil. After a moment's consideration, he concluded it would be no breach of faith to mention what he had seen at Derncleugh to a person who held Meg in such reverence as Dinmont obviously did. He told his story accordingly, interrupted by ejaculations such as, "Weel, the like o' that now!" or "Na, deil an' that's no something now!"

When our Liddesdale friend had heard the whole to an end, he shook his great black head—"Weel; I'll aye uphaud there's baith gude and ill amang the gypsies, and if they deal wi' the enemy it's their ain business and no ours.—I ken what the streeking the corpse wad be weel aneugh. Thae smuggler deevils, when ony o' them's killed in a fray, they'll send for a wife like Meg far eneugh to dress the corpse; odd, it's a' the burial they ever think o'! and than to be put into the ground without ony decency, just like dogs. But they stick to it, that they'll be streekit, and hae an auld wife when they're dying to rhyme ower auld ballads, and charms, as they ca' them, rather than they'll hae a minister to come and pray wi' them—that's an auld threep o' their's; and I am thinking the man that died will hae been ane o' the folk that was shot when they burned Woodbourne."

"But, my good friend, Woodbourne is not burned."

"Weel, the better for them that bides in't. Odd, we had it up the water wi' us, that there was na a stane on the tap o' anither. But there was fighting, ony way; I dare to say, it would be fine fun! And, as I said, ye may take it on trust, that that's been ane o' the men killed there, and that it's been the gypsies that took your pockmanky when they fand the chaise sticking in the snaw—they wadna pass the like o' that—it wad just come to their hand like the boul o' a pint stoup."

"But if this woman is a sovereign among them, why was she not able to afford me open protection, and to get me back my property?"

"O, wha kens? she has mickle to say wi' them, but whiles they'll tak their ain way for a' that, when they're under temptation. And then there's the smugglers that they're aye leagued wi', she maybe couldna manage them sae weel—they're aye banded thegither—I've heard, the gypsies ken whan the smugglers will come aff, and where they're to land, better than the very merchants that deal wi' them. And than, to the boot o' that, she's whiles crack-brained, and has a bee in her head; they say that whether her spaeings and fortune-tellings be true or no, for certain she believes in them a' hersell, and is aye guiding hersell by some queer prophecy or anither. So she disna aye gang the straight road to the well.—But deil o' sic a story as yours, wi' glamour and dead folk and losing ane's gate, I ever heard out of the tale-books!—But whisht! I hear the keeper coming"——

Mac-Guffog accordingly interrupted their discourse by the harsh harmony of his bolts and bars, and showed his bloated visage at the opening door. "Come, Mr Dinmont, we have put off locking up for an hour to oblige ye; ye must go to your quarters."

"Quarters, man? I intend to sleep here the night. There's a spare bed in the captain's room."

"It's impossible!" answered the keeper.

"But I say it *is* possible, and that I winna stir—and there's a dram to you."

Mac-Guffog drank off the spirits, and resumed his objection. "But it's against rule, sir; you have committed nae malefaction."

"I'll break your head if ye say ony mair about it, and that will be malefaction aneugh to entitle me to ae night's lodging wi' you, ony way."

"But I tell ye, Mr Dinmont," reiterated the keeper, "it's against rule, and I would lose my post."

"Weel, Mac-Guffog, I hae just twa things to say. Ye ken wha I am weel aneugh, and that I wadna loose a prisoner."

"And how do I ken that?"

"Weel, if ye dinna ken that, ye ken you're whiles obliged to be up our water in the way o' your business. Now, if ye let me stay here quietly the night wi' the captain, I'se pay ye double fees for the room; and if ye say no, ye shall hae the best sark-fu' o' sair banes that ever ye had in your life, the first time ye set a foot bye Liddell-mote!"

"Aweel, aweel, gudeman," said Mac-Guffog, "a willfu' man maun hae his way; but if I am challenged for it by the justices, I ken wha sall bear the wyte;"—and having sealed this observation with a deep oath or two, he retired to bed, after carefully securing all the doors of the Bridewell. The bell from the town steeple tolled nine, just as this ceremony was concluded.

"Although it's but early hours," said the farmer, who had observed that his friend looked somewhat pale and fatigued, "I think we had better lie down, captain, if ye're no agreeable to another cheerer. But troth, ye're nae glass-breaker; and neither am I, unless it be a screed wi' the neighbours, or when I'm on a ramble."

Bertram readily assented to the motion of his faithful friend, but on looking at the bed, felt repugnance to trust himself undressed even to Mrs Mac-Guffog's clean sheets.

"I'm muckle o' your opinion, captain. Odd, this bed looks as if a' the colliers in Sanquhar had been in't thegither. But it winna win through my muckle coat." So saying, he flung himself upon the frail bed with a force that made all its timbers crack, and in a few moments gave audible signal that he was fast asleep. Bertram slipped off his coat and boots, and occupied the other dormitory. The strangeness of his destiny, and the mysteries which seemed to thicken around him, while he seemed alike to be persecuted and protected by secret enemies and friends, arising out of a class of people with whom he had no previous connection, for some time occupied his mind. Fatigue, however, gradually composed his mind, and in a short time he was as fast asleep as his companion. And in this comfortable state of oblivion we must leave them, until we acquaint our reader with some other circumstances which occurred about the same period.

Chapter Seven

———Say from whence
You owe this strange intelligence? or why
Upon this blasted heath you stop our way
With such prophetic greeting?—
Speak, I charge you.

Macbeth

UPON THE EVENING of the day when Bertram's examination had taken place, Colonel Mannering arrived at Woodbourne from Edinburgh. He found his family in their usual state, which probably, so far as Julia was concerned, would not have been the case, had she learned the news of Bertram's arrest. But as, during the Colonel's absence, the two young ladies lived much retired, this circumstance fortunately had not reached Woodbourne. A letter had already made Miss Bertram acquainted with the downfall of the expectations which had been formed upon the bequest of her kinswoman. Whatever hopes that news might have dispelled, the disappointment did not prevent her from joining her friend in affording a cheerful reception to the Colonel, to whom she thus endeavoured to express the deep sense she entertained of his paternal kindness. She touched on her regret, that at such a season of the year he should have made, upon her account, a journey so fruitless.

"That it was fruitless to you, my dear," said the Colonel, "I do most deeply regret; but for my own share, I have made some valuable acquaintances, and have spent the time I have been absent in Edinburgh with peculiar satisfaction; so on that score, there is nothing to be regretted. Even our friend the Dominie is returned thrice the man he was, from having sharpened his wits in controversy with the geniuses of the Northern Metropolis."

"Of a surety," said the Dominie with great complacency, "I did wrestle, and was not overcome, though my adversary was cunning in his art."

"I presume," said Miss Mannering, "the contest was somewhat fatiguing, Mr Sampson?"

"Very much, young leddy—howbeit I girded up my loins and strove against him."

"I can bear witness," said the Colonel, "I never saw an affair better contested. The enemy was like the Mahratta cavalry; he assailed on all sides, and presented no fair mark for artillery; but Mr Sampson stood to his guns notwithstanding, and fired away, now upon the enemy, and now upon the dust which he had raised. But we must not fight our battles over again to-night—to-morrow we shall have the whole at breakfast."

Upon the next day at breakfast, however, the Dominie did not make his appearance. He had walked out, a servant said, early in the morning. It was so common for him to forget his meals, that his absence never deranged the family. The housekeeper, a decent old-fashioned presbyterian matron, having, as such, the highest respect for Sampson's theological acquisitions, had it in charge upon these occasions to take care that he was no sufferer by his absence of mind, and therefore usually waylaid him upon his return, to remind him of his sublunary wants, and to minister for their relief. It seldom, however, happened that he was absent from two meals together, as was the case in the present instance. We must explain the cause of this unusual occurrence.

The conversation which Mr Pleydell had held with Mannering upon the subject of the loss of Harry Bertram, had awakened all the painful sensations which that event had inflicted upon Sampson. The affectionate heart of the poor Dominie had always reproached him, as if his negligence in leaving the child in the care of Frank Kennedy had been the proximate cause of the murder of the one, the loss of the other, the death of Mrs Bertram, and the ruin of the family of his patron. It was a subject which he never spoke upon, if indeed his mode of conversation could be called speaking at any time; but which was often present to his imagination. The sort of hope so strongly affirmed and asserted in Mrs Margaret Bertram's last settlement, had excited a corresponding feeling in the Dominie's bosom, which was exasperated into a sort of sickening anxiety, by the discredit with which Pleydell had treated it. "Assuredly," thought Sampson to himself, "he is a man of erudition, and well skilled in the weighty matters of the law; but he is also a man of humorous levity and inconstancy of speech; and wherefore should he pronounce *ex cathedra*, as it were, on the hope expressed by worthy Madam Margaret of Singleside?" All this, I say, the Dominie *thought* to himself; for had he uttered half the sentence, his jaws would have ached for a month under the unusual fatigue of such a continued exertion. The result of these cogitations was a resolution to go and visit the scene of the tragedy at Warroch Point, where he had not been for many years—not, indeed, since the fatal accident had happened. The walk was a long one, for the Point of Warroch lay on the farther side of the Ellangowan property, which was interposed between it and Woodbourne. Besides, the Dominie went astray more than once, and met with brooks swoln into torrents by the melting of the snow, where he, honest man, had only the summer-recollection of little trickling rills.

At length, however, he reached the woods which he had made the object of his walk, and traversed them with care, muddling his disturbed brains with vain efforts to recall every circumstance of the catastrophe. It will readily be supposed that the influence of local situation and association was inadequate to produce conclusions different from those which he had formed under the immediate pressure of the occurrences themselves. With "many a weary sigh, therefore, and many a groan," the poor Dominie returned from his hopeless pilgrimage, and wearily plodded his way towards Woodbourne, debating at times in his altered mind a question which was forced upon him by the cravings of an appetite rather of the keenest, namely, whether he had breakfasted that morning or no?—It was in this twilight humour, now thinking of the loss of the child, then involuntarily compelled to meditate upon the somewhat incongruous subject of hung-beef, rolls and butter, that his route, which was different from that which he had taken in the morning, conducted him past the small ruined tower, or rather vestige of a tower, called by the country people the Kaim of Derncleugh.

The reader may recollect the description of this ruin in the sixth chapter of our second volume, as the vault in which young Bertram, under the auspices of Meg Merrilies, witnessed the death of Hattaraick's lieutenant. The tradition of the country added ghostly terrors to the natural awe inspired by the situation of this place, which terrors the gypsies who so long inhabited the vicinity had probably invented, or at least propagated, for their own advantage. It was said that, during the times of Galwegian independence, one Hanlon Mac-Dingawaie, brother to the reigning chief, Knarth Mac-Dingawaie, murdered his brother and sovereign in order to usurp the principality from his infant nephew, and that being pursued for vengeance by the faithful allies and retainers of the house, who espoused the cause of the lawful heir, he was compelled to retreat, with a few followers whom he had involved in his crime, to this impregnable tower called the Kaim of Derncleugh, where he defended himself until nearly reduced by famine, when, setting fire to the place, he and the small remaining garrison desperately perished by their own swords rather than fall into the hands of their exasperated enemies. This tragedy, which, considering the wild times wherein it was placed, might have some foundation in truth, was larded with many legends of superstition and diablerie, so that most of the peasants of the neighbourhood, if benighted, would rather have chosen to make a considerable circuit than pass these haunted walls. The lights, often seen around the tower when used as the rendezvous of the lawless characters by whom it was occasionally frequented, were accounted for, under authority of these tales of witchery, in a manner at once convenient for the private parties concerned, and satisfactory to the public.

Now it must be confessed, that our friend Sampson, though a profound scholar and mathematician, had not travelled so far in philosophy as to doubt the reality of witchcraft or apparitions. Born indeed at a time when a doubt in the existence of witches was interpreted to be a justification of their infernal practices, a belief in such legends had been impressed upon him as an article indivisible from his religious faith, and perhaps it would have been equally difficult to induce him to doubt the one as the other. With these feelings, and in a thick misty day, which was already drawing to its close, Dominie Sampson did not pass the Kaim of Derncleugh without some feelings of tacit horror.

What then was his astonishment, when, on passing the door—that door which was supposed to have been put on by one of the latter lairds of Ellangowan to prevent presumptuous strangers from incurring the dangers of the haunted vault—that very door supposed to be always locked, and the key of which was popularly said to be deposited with the presbytery—that very door opened suddenly, and the figure of Meg Merrilies, well known, though not seen for many a revolving year, was placed at once before the eyes of the startled Dominie! She stood immediately before him in the foot-path, confronting him so absolutely, that he could not avoid her except by fairly turning back, which manhood prevented him from thinking of.

"I kenn'd ye wad be here," she said with her harsh and hollow voice: "I ken wha ye seek; but ye maun do my bidding."

"Get thee behind me!" said the alarmed Dominie—"Avoid ye!—*Conjuro te, scelestissima—nequissima—spurcissima—iniquissima—atque miserrima—conjuro te!!!*"——

Meg stood her ground against this tremendous volley of superlatives, which Sampson hawked up from the pit of his stomach, and hurled at her in thunder. "Is the carl daft," she said, "wi' his glamour?"

"*Conjuro*," continued the Dominie, "*adjuro*, *contestor*, *atque viriliter impero tibi!*"——

"What, in the name of Sathan, are ye feared for, wi' your fremit gibberish, that would make a dog sick? Listen, ye stickit stibbler, to what I tell ye, or ye sall rue it while there's a limb o' ye hings to anither!—Tell Colonel Mannering that I ken he's seeking me. He kens, and I ken, that the blood will be wiped out, and the lost will be found,

And Bertram's right and Bertram's might
Shall meet on Ellangowan height.

There's a line to him—I was ganging to send it in another way.—I canna write mysell—but I hae them that will baith write and read, and ride and rin for me. Tell him the time's coming now, and the weird's dree'd and the wheel's turning. Bid him look at the stars as he has looked at them before—will ye mind a' this?"

"Assuredly," said the Dominie, "I am dubi-ous—for, woman, I am perturbed at thy words—and my flesh quakes to hear thee."

"They'll do you nae ill though, and maybe mickle guid."

"Avoid ye! I desire nae good that comes by unlawfu' means."

"Fule-body that thou art," said Meg, stepping up to him with a frown of indignation that made her dark eyes flash like lamps from under her bent brows, "Fule-body! if I meant ye wrang, could na I clod ye ower that craig, and wad man ken how ye came by your end mair than Frank Kennedy? Hear ye that, ye worricow?"

"In the name of all that is good," said the Dominie, recoiling and pointing his long pewter-headed walking cane like a javelin at the supposed sorceress, "in the name of all that is good, bide off hands! I will not be handled—woman, stand off upon thine own proper peril! —desist, I say—I am strong—lo, I will resist!"—Here his speech was cut short, for Meg, armed with supernatural strength (as the Dominie asserted) broke in upon his guard, put by a thrust which he made at her with his cane, and lifted him into the vault, "as easily," said he, "as I could sway a Kitchen's atlas."

"Sit doun there," she said, pushing the half-throttled preacher with some violence against a broken chair, "sit down there, and gather your wind and your senses, ye black barrow-tram o' the kirk that ye are—are ye fow or fasting?"

"Fasting—from all but sin," answered the Dominie, who, recovering his voice, and finding his exorcisms only served to exasperate the intractable sorceress, thought it best to affect complaisance and submission, inwardly conning over, however, the wholesome conjurations which he durst no longer utter aloud. But as the Dominie's brain was by no means equal to carry on two trains of ideas at the same time, a word or two of his mental exercise sometimes escaped, and mingled with his uttered speech in a manner ludicrous enough, especially as the poor man shrunk himself together after every escape of the kind, from terror of the effect it might produce upon the irritable feelings of the witch.

Meg, in the meanwhile, went to a great black cauldron that was boiling on a fire on the floor, and, lifting the lid, an odour was diffused through the vault, which, if the vapours of a witch's cauldron could in aught be trusted, promised better things than the hell-broth which such vessels are usually supposed to contain. It was in fact the savour of a goodly stew, composed of fowls, hares, partridges, and moor-game, boiled in a large mess with potatoes, onions and leeks, and, from the size of the cauldron, appeared to be prepared for half a dozen of people at least. "So ye hae eat naething a' day?" said Meg, heaving a large portion of this mess into a brown dish, and strewing it savourily with salt and pepper.

"Nothing," answered the Dominie—"*scelestissima!*—that is—gudewife."

"Hae then," said she, placing the dish before him, "there's what will warm your heart."

"I do not hunger—*malefica*—that is to say—Mrs Merrilies," for he said in himself, 'the savour is sweet, but it hath been cooked by a Canidia or an Ericthoe.'

"If ye dinna eat instantly, and put some saul in ye, by the bread and the salt, I'll put it doun your throat wi' the cutty spoon, scauding as it is, and whether ye will or no. Gape, sinner, and swallow!"

Sampson, afraid of eye of newt, and toe of frog, tigers' chaudrons, and so forth, had determined not to venture; but the smell of the stew was fast melting his obstinacy, which flowed from his chops as it were in streams of water, when the witch's threats decided him to feed. Hunger and fear are excellent casuists.

"Saul," said Hunger, "feasted with the witch of Endor."—"And," quoth Fear, "the salt which she sprinkled upon the food sheweth plainly it is not a necromantic banquet, in which that seasoning never occurs." "And besides," says Hunger, after the first spoonful, "it is savoury and refreshing viands."

"So ye like the meat?" said the hostess.

"Yea," answered the Dominie, "and I give thee thanks—*sceleratissima!*—which means—Mrs Margaret."

"Aweel, eat your fill; but an ye kenn'd how it was gotten, ye may be wadna like it sae weel."

Sampson's spoon dropped, in the act of conveying its load to his mouth. "There's been mony a moonlight watch to bring a' that trade thegither—the folk that are to eat that dinner thought little o' your game-laws."

"Is that all?" thought Sampson, resuming his spoon, and shovelling away manfully; "I will not lack my food upon that argument."

"Now ye maun tak a dram."

"I will," quoth Sampson—"*conjuro te*—that is, I thank ye heartily," for he thought to himself, in for a penny in for a pound, and he fairly drank the witch's health in a cupfull of brandy. When he had put this cope-stone upon Meg's good cheer, he felt, as he said, "mightily elevated, and afraid of no evil which could befall."

"Will ye remember my errand now?" said Meg Merrilies; "I ken by the cast o' your e'e that ye're anither man than when ye came in."

"I will, Mrs Margaret," repeated Sampson stoutly; "I will deliver unto him the sealed billet, and add what you please to send by word of mouth."

"Then I'll make it short," says Meg; "tell him to look at the stars without fail this night, and to do what I desire him in that letter, as he would wish

> That Bertram's right and Bertram's might
> Should meet on Ellangowan height.

I have seen him twice when he saw na me; I ken whan he was in this country first, and I ken what's brought him back again. Up, and to the gate! ye're ower lang here—follow me."

Sampson followed the sybil accordingly, who guided him about a quarter of a mile through the woods, by a shorter cut than he could have found for himself; they then entered upon the common, Meg still marching before him at a great pace, until she gained the top of a small hillock which overhung the road.

"Here," she said, "stand still here. Look how the setting sun breaks through yon cloud that's been darkening the lift a' day. See where the first stream o' light fa's—it's on Donagild's round tower—the auldest tower in the castle of Ellangowan—that's no for naething—See as it's glooming to seaward abune yon sloop in the bay—that's no for naething neither.—Here I stood on this very spot," said she, drawing herself up so as not to lose one hair's-breadth of her uncommon height, and stretching out her long sinewy arm, and clenched hand, "Here I stood, when I tauld the last Laird of Ellangowan what was coming on his house—And did that fa' to the ground?—na—it hit even ower sair!—And here, where I brake the wand of peace ower him—here I stand again—to bid God bless and prosper the just heir of Ellangowan, that will sune be brought to his ain; and the best laird he shall be that Ellangowan has seen for three hundred years.—I'll no live to see it, may be; but there will be mony a blithe e'e see it though mine be closed. And now, Abel Sampson, as ever ye lo'ed the house, away wi' my message to the English Colonel, as life and death were upon your haste!"

So saying, she turned suddenly from the astounded Dominie, and regained with swift and long strides the shelter of the wood from which she had issued, at the point where it most encroached upon the common. Sampson gazed after her for a moment in utter astonishment, and then obeyed her directions, hurrying to Woodbourne at a pace very unusual for him, exclaiming three times, "Prodigious! prodigious! pro-di-gi-ous!"

Chapter Eight

——It is not madness
That I have utter'd; bring me to the test,
And I the matter will re-word; which madness
Would gambol from.

Hamlet

AS MR SAMPSON crossed the hall with a bewildered look, the good housekeeper, who was on the watch for his return, sallied forth upon him—"What's this o't now, Mr Sampson, this is waur than ever—ye'll really do yoursell some injury wi' these lang fasts—naething sae hurtful to the stomach, Mr Sampson—if you would but put some peppermint draps in your pocket, or let Barnes cut you a sandwich."

"Avoid thee!" quoth the Dominie, his mind running still upon his interview with Meg Merrilies, and making for the dining parlour.

"Na, ye need na gang in there, the cloth's been removed an hour ago, and the Colonel's at his wine; but just step into my room, I have a nice steak that the cook will do in a moment."

"*Exorcizo te!*" said Sampson,—"that is, I have dined."

"Dined! it's impossible—wha can ye hae dined wi', you that gangs out nae gate?"

"With Beelzebub, I believe," said the minister.

"Na, than he's bewitched for certain," said the housekeeper, letting go her hold; "he's bewitched, or he's daft, and ony way the Colonel maun just guide him his ain gate—Waes me! Hech, sirs! It's a sair thing to see learning bring folk to this!" and with this compassionate ejaculation, she retreated into her own premises.

The object of her commiseration had by this time entered the dining parlour, where his appearance gave great surprise. He was mud up to the shoulders, and the natural paleness of his hue was twice as cadaverous as usual, through terror, fatigue, and perturbation of mind. "What on earth is the meaning of this, Mr Sampson?" said Mannering, who observed Miss Bertram looking much alarmed for her simple but attached friend.

"*Exorcizo,*"—said the Dominie.

"How sir?"

"I crave pardon, honourable sir! but my wits"——

"Are gone a wool-gathering, I think—pray, Mr Sampson, collect yourself, and let me know the meaning of all this."

Sampson was about to reply, but finding his Latin formula of exorcism still came most readily to his tongue, he prudently desisted from the attempt, and put the scrap of paper which he had received from the gypsey into Mannering's hand, who broke the seal and read it with surprise. "This seems to be some jest," he said, "and a very dull one."

"It came from no jesting person," said Mr Sampson.

"From whom then did it come?"

The Dominie, who often displayed some delicacy of recollection in cases where Miss Bertram had an interest, remembered the painful circumstances connected with Meg Merrilies, looked at the young ladies, and remained silent. "We will join you at the tea-table in an instant, Julia; I see that Mr Sampson wishes to speak to me alone.—And now they are gone, what, in Heaven's name, is the meaning of this?"

"It may be a message frae Heaven," said the Dominie, "but it came by Beelzebub's postmistress. It was that witch, Meg Merrilies, who suld hae been burned wi' a tar-barrel twenty years since, for a harlot, thief, witch, and gypsey."

"Are you sure it was she?" said the Colonel with great interest.

"Sure, honoured sir? the like o' Meg Merrilies is no to be seen in any land."

The Colonel paced the room rapidly, cogitating with himself. "To send out to apprehend her—but it is too distant to send to Mac-Morlan, and Sir Robert Hazelwood is a pompous coxcomb; besides the chance of not finding her upon the spot, and the humour of silence that seized her before and may return;—no, I will not, to save being thought a fool, neglect the course she points out. Many of her class set out by being impostors, and end by being enthusiasts, or hold a kind of darkling conduct between both lines, unconscious almost when they are cheating themselves or imposing on others.—Well, my course is a plain one at any rate; and if my efforts are fruitless, it shall not be owing to over-jealousy of my own character for wisdom."

With this he rung the bell, and ordering Barnes into his private sitting-room, gave him some orders, with the result of which the reader may be made hereafter acquainted. We must now take up another thread, which is also to be woven into the adventures of this remarkable day.

Charles Hazelwood had not ventured to make a visit at Woodbourne during the absence of the Colonel. Indeed, Mannering's whole behaviour had impressed upon him an opinion that this would be disagreeable; and such was the ascendence which the successful soldier and accomplished gentleman had attained over his conduct, that in no respect would he have ventured to offend him. He saw, or thought he saw, in Colonel Mannering's general conduct, an approbation of his attachment to Miss Bertram. But then he saw still more plainly the impropriety of any attempt at a private correspondence, of which his parents could not be supposed to approve, and he respected this barrier interposed betwixt them, both on Mannering's own account, and as he was the liberal and zealous protector of Miss Bertram. "No," said he to himself, "I will not endanger the comfort of my Lucy's present retreat until I can offer her a home of her own."

With this valorous resolution, which he maintained, although his horse, from constant habit, turned his head down the avenue of Woodbourne, and although he himself passed the lodge twice every day, he withstood a strong inclination to ride down, just to ask how the young ladies were, and whether he could be of any service to them during Colonel Mannering's absence. But upon the second occasion, he felt the temptation so severe, that he resolved not to expose himself to it a third time; and, contenting himself with sending hopes and enquiries, and so forth, to Woodbourne, he resolved to make a visit long promised to a family at some distance, and to return in such time as to be one of the earliest among Mannering's visitors, who should congratulate his safe return from his distant and hazardous expedition to Edinburgh. Accordingly, he made out his visit, and having arranged matters so as to be informed within a few hours after Colonel Mannering reached Woodbourne, he fixed to take leave of the friends with whom he had spent the intervening time, with the intention of dining at Woodbourne, where he was in a great measure domesticated; and this (for he thought much more deeply on the subject than was necessary) would, he flattered himself, appear a simple, natural, and easy mode of conducting himself.

Fate, however, of which lovers make so many complaints, was, in this case, unfavourable to Charles Hazelwood. His horse's shoes required an alteration, in consequence of the fresh weather having decidedly commenced. The lady of the house, where he was a visitor, chose to indulge in her own room till a very late breakfast hour. His friend also insisted on showing him a litter of puppies, which his favourite pointer bitch had produced that morning. The colours had occasioned some doubts about the paternity, a weighty question of legitimacy, to the decision of which Hazelwood's opinion was called in as arbiter between his friend and his groom, and which inferred in its consequences, which of the litter should be drowned, which saved. Besides, the Laird himself delayed our young lover's departure for a considerable time, endeavouring, with long and superfluous rhetoric, to insinuate to Sir Robert Hazelwood, through the medium of his son, his own particular ideas respecting the line of a meditated turnpike road. It is greatly to the shame of our young lover's apprehension, that after the tenth reiterated account of the matter, he could not see the advantage to be obtained by the proposed road passing over the Langhirst, Windy-knowe, the Goodhouse-park, Kailzie-croft, and then crossing the river at Simon's pool, and so by the old road to Kippletringan; and the less eligible line pointed out by the English surveyor, which would go clear through the Mains inclosures at Hazelwood, and cut within a mile, or nearly so, of the house itself, destroying the privacy and pleasure, as his informer contended, of the ground.

In short, the adviser (whose actual interest was to have the bridge built as near as possible to a farm of his own) failed in every effort to attract young Hazelwood's attention, until he mentioned by chance, that the proposed line was favoured by that "fellow Glossin," who pretended to take a lead in the country. On a sudden young Hazelwood became attentive and interested; and having satisfied himself which was the line that Glossin patronized, assured his friend it should not be his fault if his father did not countenance any other instead of that. But these various interruptions consumed the morning. Hazelwood got on horseback at least three hours later than he intended, and, cursing fine ladies, pointers, puppies, and turnpike acts of parliament, saw himself detained beyond the time when he could, with propriety, intrude upon the family at Woodbourne.

He had passed, therefore, the turn of the road which led to that mansion, only edified by the distant appearance of the blue smoke, curling against the pale sky of the winter evening, when he thought he beheld the Dominie taking a foot-path for the house through the woods. He called after him, but in vain; for that honest gentleman, never the most susceptible of extraneous impressions, had just that moment parted from Meg Merrilies, and was too deeply wrapt up in pondering upon her vaticinations, to make any answer to Hazelwood's call. He was, therefore, obliged to let him proceed without enquiry after the health of the young ladies, or any other fishing question, to which he might, by good chance, have had an answer returned wherein Miss Bertram's name might have been mentioned. All cause for haste was therefore now over, and slacking the reins upon his horse's neck, he permitted him to ascend at his own leisure the steep sandy track between two high banks, which, ascending to a considerable height, commanded, at length, an extensive view of the neighbouring country. Hazelwood was, however, so far from eagerly looking forward to this prospect, though it had the recommendation, that great part of the land was his father's, and must necessarily be his own, that his head still turned towards the chimneys of Woodbourne, although at every step his horse made the difficulty of turning his eyes in that direction become greater. From the reverie in which he was sunk, he was suddenly roused by a voice too harsh to be called female, yet too shrill for a man:—"What's kept ye on the road sae lang? maun ither folk do your wark?"

He looked up; the spokes-woman was very tall, had a voluminous handkerchief rolled round her head, her grizzled hair flowing in elf-locks from beneath it, a long red cloak, and a staff in her hand, headed with a sort of spear point—it was, in short, Meg Merrilies. Hazelwood had never seen this remarkable figure before; he drew up his reins in astonishment at her appearance, and made a full stop. "I think," continued she, "they that hae ta'en interest wi' the house of Ellangowan suld sleep nane this night; three men hae been seeking ye, and you are ganging hame to sleep in your bed—d'ye think if the lad-bairn fa's the sister will do weel? na, na!"

"I don't understand you, good woman," said Hazelwood: "If you mean Miss——I mean any of the late Ellangowan family, tell me what I can do for them."

"Of the late Ellangowan family?" she answered with great vehemence, "Of the *late* Ellangowan family! and when was there ever, or when will there ever be a family of Ellangowan, but bearing the gallant name of the bauld Bertrams?"

"But what do you mean, good woman?"

"I am nae good woman—a' the county kens I am bad eneugh, and may be sorry eneugh that I am nae better. But I can do what good women canna, and darena do. I can do what would freeze the blood o' them that is bred in biggit wa's for naething but to bind bairns' heads, and to hap them in the cradle. Hear me—the guard's drawn aff the custom-house at Portanferry, and it's brought up to Hazelwood-house by your father's orders, because he thinks his house is to be attacked the night by the smugglers;—there's naebody means to touch his house; he's gude blood and gentle blood—I say little o' him but there's naebody thinks him worth meddling wi'. Send the horse-men back to their post, cannily and quietly—see an' they winna hae wark the night—aye will they—the guns will flash and the swords will glitter in the braw moon."

"Good God! what do you mean? your words and manner would persuade me you are mad, and yet there is a strange combination in what you say."

"I am not mad! I have been imprisoned for mad—scourged for mad —banished for mad—but mad I am not. Hear ye, Charles Hazelwood of Hazelwood; d'ye bear malice against him that wounded you?"

"No, dame, God forbid; my arm is quite well, and I have always said the shot was discharged by accident. I should be glad to tell the young man so."

"Then do what I bid ye, and ye'll do him mair gude than ever he did you ill; for if he was left to his ill-wishers he would be a bloody corpse ere morn, or a banished man—but there's ane abune a'.—Do as I bid you, send back the soldiers. There's nae mair fear o' Hazelwood-house than there's o' Cruffell-fell." And she vanished with her usual celerity of pace.

It would seem that the appearance of this female, and the mixture of frenzy and enthusiasm in her address, seldom failed to produce the strongest impression upon those whom she addressed. Her words, though wild, were too plain and intelligible for actual madness, and yet too vehement and extravagant for sober-minded communication. She seemed acting under the influence of imagination rather strongly excited than deranged; and it is wonderful how palpably the difference, in such cases, is impressed upon the mind of the auditor. This may account for the attention with which her strange and mysterious hints were heard and acted upon. It is certain, at least, that young Hazelwood was strongly impressed by her sudden appearance and imperative tone. He rode to Hazelwood at a brisk pace. It had been dark for some time before he reached the house, and on his arrival there, he saw a confirmation of what the sybil had hinted.

Thirty dragoon horses stood under a shade near the offices, with their bridles linked together. Three or four soldiers attended as a guard, while others stumped up and down with their long broad swords and heavy boots in front of the house. Hazelwood asked a non-commissioned officer from whence they came? "From Portanferry."

"Had they left any guard there?"

"No; they had been drawn off by order of Sir Robert Hazelwood for defence of his house, against an attack which was threatened by the smugglers."

Charles Hazelwood instantly went in quest of his father, and, having paid his respects to him upon his return, requested to know upon what account he had thought it necessary to send for a military escort. Sir Robert assured his son in reply, that from the information, intelligence, and tidings, which had been communicated to, and laid before him, he had the deepest reason to believe, credit, and be convinced, that a riotous assault would that night be attempted and perpetrated against Hazelwood-house, by a set of smugglers, gypsies, and other desperadoes. "And what, my dear sir, should direct the fury of such persons against ours rather than any other house in the country?"

"I should rather think, suppose, and be of opinion, sir," answered Sir Robert, "with deference to your wisdom and experience, that upon these occasions and times, the vengeance of such persons is directed or levelled against the most important and distinguished in point of rank, talent, birth, and situation, who have checked, interfered with, and discountenance their unlawful and illegal and criminal actions or deeds."

Young Hazelwood, who knew his father's foible, answered, that the cause of his surprise did not lie where Sir Robert apprehended, but that he only wondered they should think of attacking a house where there were many servants, and where a signal to the neighbouring tenants could call in such strong assistance; and added, that he doubted much whether the reputation of the family would not in some degree suffer from calling soldiers from their duty on the custom-house, to protect them, as if they were not sufficiently strong to defend themselves upon any ordinary occasion. He even hinted, that in case their house's enemies and maligners should observe that this precaution had been taken unnecessarily, there would be no end of their sarcasms.

Sir Robert Hazelwood was rather puzzled at this intimation, for, like most dull men, he heartily hated and feared ridicule. He gathered himself up, and looked with a sort of pompous embarrassment, as if he wished to be thought to despise the opinion of the public, which in reality he dreaded.

"I really should have thought," he said, "that the injury which had already been aimed at my house in your person, being the next heir and representative of the Hazelwood family, failing me—I should have thought and opined, I say, that this would have justified me sufficiently in the eyes of the most respectable and greatest part of the people, for taking such precautions as are calculated to prevent and impede a repetition of outrage."

"Really, sir, I must remind you of what I have often said before, that I am positive the discharge of the piece was accidental."

"Sir, it was not accidental; but you will still be wiser than your elders."

"Really, sir, in what so intimately concerns myself"——

"Sir, it does not concern you but in a very secondary degree—that is, it does not concern you, as a giddy young fellow, who takes pleasure in contradicting his father; but it concerns the country, sir; and the county, sir; and the public, sir; and the kingdom of Scotland, in so far as the interests of the Hazelwood family, sir, are committed, and interested, and pitted and put in peril, in, by, and through you, sir. And the fellow is in safe custody, and Mr Glossin thinks"——

"Mr Glossin, sir?"

"Yes, sir, the gentleman who has purchased Ellangowan—you know who I mean, I suppose?"

"Yes, sir; but I should hardly have expected to hear you quote such authority. Why, this fellow—all the world knows him to be sordid, mean, tricking, and suspect him to be worse. And you yourself, my dear sir, when did you call such a person a gentleman in your life before?"

"Why, Charles, I did not mean gentleman in the precise sense and meaning, and restricted and proper use, to which, no doubt, it ought legitimately to be confined; but I meant to use it relatively, as marking something of that state to which he has elevated and raised himself—as designing, in short, a decent and wealthy and estimable sort of person."

"Allow me to ask, sir, if it was by this man's orders that the guard was drawn from Portanferry?"

"Sir, I do apprehend that Mr Glossin would not presume to give orders, or even an opinion, unless asked, in a matter in which Hazelwood-house and the house of Hazelwood—meaning by the one this mansion-house of my family, and by the other typically, metaphorically, and parabolically, the family itself—I say then where the house of Hazelwood, or Hazelwood-house, were so immediately concerned."

"I presume, however, sir, he approved of the proposal?"

"Sir, I thought it decent and right and proper to consult him as the nearest magistrate, as soon as reports of the intended outrage reached my ears; and although he declined, out of deference and respect, as became our relative situations, to concur in the order, yet he did entirely approve of my arrangement."

"Do but think, however, my dear sir, upon the consequences of keeping these men here. I protest to you, that being in some degree the original cause of all this confusion, I intend to ride down to Portanferry myself this very night, and I beg you will permit a part at least of the soldiers to accompany me."

"You, go down to Portanferry indeed?—without my licence, or rather against the same? I protest to you, Mr Charles Hazelwood, your conduct this day is inexplicable, and undutiful, and impertinent, and unbeseeming"——

At this moment a horse's feet were heard coming very fast up the avenue. In a few minutes the door opened, and Mr Mac-Morlan presented himself. "I am under great concern to intrude, Sir Robert, but"——

"Give me leave, Mr Mac-Morlan,—this is no intrusion, sir; for your situation as sheriff-substitute calling upon you to attend to the peace of the county, (and, doubtless, feeling yourself particularly called upon to protect Hazelwood-house,) you have an acknowledged, and admitted, and undeniable right, sir, to enter the house of the first gentleman in Scotland, uninvited—always presuming you to be called there by the duty of your office."

"It is indeed the duty of my office," said Mac-Morlan, who waited with impatience an opportunity to speak, "that makes me an intruder."

"No intrusion!" reiterated the Baronet, gracefully waving his wand.

"But permit me to say, Sir Robert, I do not come with the purpose of remaining here, but to recall these soldiers to Portanferry, and to assure you that I will answer for the safety of your house."

"To withdraw the guard from Hazelwood-house?—and *you* will be answerable for the safety of it! And, pray, who are you, sir, that I should take your security, and caution, and pledge, official or personal, for the safety of Hazelwood-house?—I think, sir, and believe, sir, and opine, sir, that if any one of these family pictures were damaged, or destroyed, or injured, it would be difficult for me to make up the loss upon the guarantee which *you* so obliging offer me."

"In that case I shall be sorry for it, Sir Robert; but I presume I may escape the pain of feeling my conduct the cause of such irreparable loss, as I can assure you there will be no attempt upon Hazelwood-house whatever, and I have received information which induces me to suspect that the rumour was put afloat merely in order to occasion the removal of the soldiers from Portanferry. And under this strong belief and conviction I must exert my authority to order the whole, or greater part of them, back again. I regret much, that by my accidental absence a good deal of delay has already taken place, and we shall not now reach Portanferry until it is late."

As Mr Mac-Morlan was the superior magistrate, and expressed himself peremptory in the purpose of acting as such, the Baronet, though highly offended, could only say, "Very well, sir, it is very well. Nay, sir, take them all with you—I am far from desiring any to be left here, sir. We, sir, can protect ourselves, sir. But you will have the goodness to observe, sir, that you are acting on your own proper risque, sir, and peril, sir, and responsibility, sir, if any thing shall happen or befall to Hazelwood-house, sir, or the inhabitants, sir, or to the furniture and paintings, sir."

"I am acting to the best of my judgement and information, Sir Robert, and I must pray of you to believe so, and to pardon me accordingly. I beg you to observe it is no time for ceremony—it is already very late, and"——

But Sir Robert, without deigning to listen to his apologies, immediately employed himself in arming and arraying his domestics. Charles Hazelwood longed to accompany the party, which was about to depart for Portanferry, and which was now drawn up and mounted by direction and under guidance of Mr Mac-Morlan, as the civil magistrate. But it would have given pain and offence to his father to have left him at a moment when he conceived himself beset with enemies. Young Hazelwood therefore gazed from a window with suppressed regret and displeasure, until he heard the officer give the word of command —"From the right to the front, by files, ma–a–arch. Leading file, to the right wheel—Trot."—The whole party then getting into a sharp and uniform pace, were soon lost among the trees, and the noise of their hoofs died speedily away in the distance.

Chapter Nine

Wi' coulters and wi' forehammers
We garr'd the bars bang merrily,
Until we came to the inner prison,
Where Willie o' Kinmont he did lie.
Old Border Ballad

WE RETURN to Portanferry, and to Bertram and his honest-hearted friend, most innocent inhabitants of a place built for the guilty. The slumbers of the farmer were as sound as it was possible. But Bertram's first heavy sleep passed away long before midnight, nor could he again recover that state of oblivion. Added to the uncertain and uncomfortable state of his mind, his body felt feverish and oppressed. This was chiefly owing to the close and confined air of the small apartment in which they slept. After enduring for some time the broiling and suffocating feeling attendant upon such an atmosphere, he rose to endeavour to open the window of the apartment, and thus to procure a change of air. Alas! the first trial reminded him that he was in jail, and that the building being contrived for security, not comfort, the means of procuring fresh air were not left at the disposal of the wretched inhabitants. Disappointed in this attempt, he stood by the unmanageable window for some time. Little Wasp, though oppressed with the fatigue of his journey on the preceding day, crept out of bed after his master, and stood by him rubbing his shaggy coat against his legs, and expressing, by a murmuring sound, the delight which he felt at being restored to him. Thus accompanied, and waiting until the feverish feeling which at present agitated his blood should subside into a desire for warmth and slumber, Bertram remained for some time looking out upon the sea. The tide was now nearly full, and dashed hoarse and near below the base of the building. Now and then a large wave reached even the barrier or bulwark which defended the foundation of the house, and was flung upon it with greater force and noise than those which only broke upon the sand. Far at distance, under the indistinct light of a hazy and often over-clouded moon, the ocean rolled its multitudinous complication of waves, crossing, bursting against, and mingling with each other.

"A wild and dim spectacle," said Bertram to himself, "like those crossing tides of fate which have tossed me about the world from my infancy upwards. When will this uncertainty cease, and how soon shall I be permitted to look out for a tranquil home, where I may cultivate in quiet, and without dread and perplexity, those arts of peace from which my cares have been hitherto so forcibly diverted! The ear of

Fancy, it is said, can discover the voice of sea-nymphs and tritons amid the bursting murmurs of the ocean; would that I could do so, and that some syren or Proteus would arise from these billows to unriddle for me the strange maze of fate in which I am so deeply entangled!—Happy friend!" he said, looking at the bed where Dinmont had deposited his bulky person, "thy cares are few and confined to the narrow round of a healthy and thriving occupation! Thou canst lay them aside at pleasure, and enjoy the deep repose of body and mind which wholesome labour has prepared for thee!"

At this moment his reflections were broken by little Wasp, who, attempting to spring up against the window, began to yelp and bark most furiously. The sounds reached Dinmont's ears, but without dissipating the illusion which had transported him from this wretched apartment to the free air of his own green hills. "Hoy, Yarrow, man—far yaud—far yaud," he muttered between his teeth, imagining, doubtless, that he was calling to his sheep-dog. The continued barking of the terrier within was next answered by the angry challenge of the mastiff in the court-yard, which had for a long time been silent, excepting only an occasional short and deep note, uttered when the moon shone suddenly from among the clouds. Now, his clamour was continued and furious, and seemed to be excited by some disturbance, distinct from the barking of Wasp, which had first given him the alarm, and which with much trouble his master had contrived to still into an angry note of low growling. At last Bertram, whose attention was now fully awakened, conceived that he saw a boat upon the sea, and heard in good earnest the sound of oars and of human voices, mingling with the dash of the billows. "Some benighted fishermen," thought he, "or perhaps some of the desperate traders from the Isle of Man. They are very hardy, however, to approach so near to the custom-house, where there must be centinels.—It is a large boat, like a long-boat, and full of people; perhaps it belongs to the revenue service." Bertram was confirmed in this last opinion, by observing that the boat made for a little quay which ran into the sea behind the custom-house, and, jumping ashore one after another, the crew, to the number of twenty hands, glided secretly up a small lane which divided the custom-house from the Bridewell, and disappeared from his sight, leaving only two persons to take care of their boat.

The dash of these men's oars at first, and latterly the suppressed sounds of their voices, had excited the wrath of the wakeful centinel in the court-yard, who now exalted his deep voice into such a horrid and continuous din, that it awaked his brute master, as savage a ban-dog as himself. His cry from a window, of "How now, Tearum—what's the matter, sir?—down, d—n ye, down!" produced no abatement of Tearum's vociferation, which in part prevented his master from hearing the sounds of alarm which his ferocious vigilance was in the act of challenging. But the mate of the two-legged Cerberus was gifted with sharper ears than her husband. She also was now at the window; "B—t ye, gae down and let loose the dog," she said, "they're sporting the door of the custom-house, and the auld sap at Hazelwood-house has ordered off the guard. But ye hae nae mair heart than a cat." And down the Amazon sallied to perform the task herself, while her help-mate, more jealous of insurrection within doors, than of storm from without, went from cell to cell to see that the inhabitants of each were carefully secured.

These latter sounds with which we have made the reader acquainted, had their origin in front of the house, and were consequently imperfectly heard by Bertram, whose apartment, as we have already noticed, looked from the back part of the building upon the sea. He heard, however, a stir and tumult in the house, which seemed unaccording to the stern seclusion of a prison at the hour of midnight, and could not but suppose that something extraordinary was about to take place. In this belief he shook Dinmont by the shoulder—"Eh!—Aye!—Oh!—Ailie, woman, it's no time to get up yet," groaned the sleeping man of the mountains. More roughly shaken, however, he gathered himself up, shook his ears, and asked, "In the name of Providence, what's the matter?"

"That I can't tell you," replied Bertram; "but either the place is on fire, or some extraordinary thing is about to happen. Do you hear what a noise there is of clashing doors within the house, and of hoarse voices, murmurs, and distant shouts on the outside? Upon my word, I believe something very extraordinary is about to happen—Get up for the love of Heaven, and let us be on our guard."

Dinmont rose at the idea of danger, as intrepid and undismayed as one of his ancestors when the beacon-light was kindled. "Odd, Captain, this is a queer place! they winna let ye out in the day, and they winna let ye sleep in the night. Deil, but it wad break my heart in a fortnight. But, Lordsake, what a racket they're making now!—Odd, I wish we had some light.—Wasp—Wasp, whisht, hinny—whisht, my bonnie man, and let's hear what they're doing—deil's in ye, will ye whisht?"—They sought in vain among the embers the means of lighting their candle, and the noise without still continued. Dinmont in his turn had recourse to the window—"Lordsake, Captain! come here.—Odd, they'll hae broken the Custom-House."

Bertram hastened to the window, and plainly saw a miscellaneous crowd of smugglers, and blackguards of different descriptions, some carrying lighted torches, others bearing packages and barrels down the lane to the boat that was lying at the quay, to which two or three other fisher-boats were now brought round. They were loading each of these in their turn, and one or two had already put off to seaward. "This speaks for itself," said Bertram; "but I fear something worse has happened. Do you feel a strong smell of smoke, or is it my fancy?"

"Fancy?" answered Dinmont, "there's a reek like a killogie. Odd, if they burn the Custom-House, it will catch here, and we'll lunt like a tar-barrel a' thegither.—Eh! it wad be fearsome to be burned alive for naething, like as if ane had been a warlock! Mac-Guffog, hear ye!"—roaring at the top of his voice, "an ye wad ever hae a haill bane in your skin, let's out, man! let's out!"

The fire began now to rise high, and thick clouds of smoke rolled past the window, at which Bertram and Dinmont were stationed. Sometimes, as the wind pleased, the dim shroud of vapour hid every thing from their sight; sometimes a red glare illuminated both land and sea, and shone full on the stern and fierce figures, who, wild with ferocious activity, were engaged in loading the boats. The fire was at length triumphant, and spouted in jets of flame out at each window of the burning building, while huge flakes of burning materials came driving on the wind against the adjoining prison, and rolling a dark canopy of smoke over all the neighbourhood. The shouts of a furious mob resounded far and wide, for the smugglers, in their triumph, were joined by all the rabble of the little town and neighbourhood, now aroused, and in complete agitation, notwithstanding the lateness of the hour.

Bertram began to be seriously uneasy for their fate. There was no stir in the house; it seemed as if the jailor had deserted his charge, and left the prison with its wretched inhabitants to the mercy of the conflagration which was spreading towards them. In the mean time a new and fierce attack was heard upon the outer gate of the correction-house, which, battered with sledge-hammers and crows, was soon forced. The keeper and his wife had fled; their servants readily surrendered the keys. The liberated prisoners, celebrating their deliverance with the wildest yells of joy, mingled among the mob which had given them freedom. In the midst of the confusion which ensued, three or four of the principal smugglers hurried to the apartment of Bertram with lighted torches, and armed with cutlasses and pistols.—"Der deyvil," said their leader, "here's our mark!" and two of them seized on Bertram; but one whispered in his ear, "Make no resistance till you are in the street." The same individual found an instant to say to Dinmont—"Follow your friend, and help when you see the time come."

In the hurry of the moment Dinmont obeyed and followed close the two smugglers, who dragged Bertram along the passage, down stairs, through the court-yard, now illuminated by the glare of the fire, and into the narrow street to which the gate opened, and where, in the confusion, the gang were necessarily in some degree separated from each other. A rapid noise, as if of a body of horse advancing, seemed to add to the confusion. "Hagel and wetter, what is that?" said the leader; "keep together, kinder, look to the prisoner."—But in spite of his charge, those two who held Bertram were the last of his party.

The sounds and signs of violence were heard in front. The press became furiously agitated, while some endeavoured to defend themselves, others to escape; shots were fired, and the glittering broadswords began to appear flashing above the heads of the rioters. "Now," said the warning voice, "shake off that fellow, and follow me."

Bertram, exerting his strength suddenly and effectually, easily burst from the grasp of the man who held his collar on the right side. The fellow attempted to draw a pistol, but was prostrated by a blow of Dinmont's fist, which an ox could hardly have received without the same humiliation. "Follow me quick," said the friendly partizan, and dived through a very narrow and dirty lane which led from the street.

No pursuit took place. The attention of the smugglers was otherwise and very disagreeably engaged by the sudden appearance of Mac-Morlan and the party of horse. This indeed would have happened in time sufficient to have prevented the attempt, had not the magistrate received upon the road some false information, which led him to think that the smugglers were to be landed at the Bay of Ellangowan. Nearly two hours were lost in consequence of this false intelligence, which it may be no lack of charity to suppose that Glossin, so deeply interested in the issue of that night's daring attempt, had contrived to throw in Mac-Morlan's way, availing himself of the knowledge that the soldiers had left Hazelwood-house, which would soon reach an ear so anxious as his.

In the mean time Bertram followed his guide, and was in his turn followed by Dinmont. The shouts of the mob, the trampling of the horses, the dropping pistol-shots, sunk more and more faintly upon their ears; when at the end of this lane they found a post-chaise with four horses. "Are you here, in God's name?" said the guide to the postillion who drove the leaders.

"Aye, troth am I, and I wish I were ony gate else."

"Open the carriage then—you gentlemen get into it—in a short time you'll be in a place of safety—and (to Bertram) remember your promise to the gypsey wife!"

Bertram, determined to be passive in the hands of a person who had just rendered him such a distinguished piece of service, got into the chaise as directed. Dinmont followed; Wasp, who had kept close by them, sprung in at the same time, and the carriage drove off very fast. "Haud a care o' me," said Dinmont, "but this is the queerest thing yet!—Odd, I trust they'll no coup us—and than what's to come o' Dumple?—I would rather be on his back than in the Dewke's coach, God bless him."

Bertram observed, that they could not go at that rapid rate to any very great distance without changing horses, and that they might insist upon remaining till day-light at the first inn they stopped at, or at least upon being made acquainted with the purpose and termination of their journey, and Mr Dinmont might there give directions about his faithful horse.—"Aweel, aweel, e'en sae be it for Dandie.—Odd, if we were ance out o' this trindling kist o' a thing, I am thinking they wad find it hard wark to gar us gang ony gate but where we liked oursells."

While he thus spoke, the carriage making a sudden turn, showed them, through the left window, the village now distant, but still widely beaconed by the fire, which, having reached a storehouse in which spirits were deposited, now rose high into the air, a wavering column of brilliant light. They had not long time to admire this spectacle, for another turn upon the road carried them into a close lane between plantations, through which the chaise proceeded in nearly total darkness, but with unabated speed.

Chapter Ten

The night drave on wi' sangs and clatter,
And aye the ale was growing better.
Tam o' Shanter

WE MUST now return to Woodbourne, which it may be remembered we left just after the Colonel had given some directions to his confidential servant. When he returned, his absence of mind, and an unusual expression of thought and anxiety upon his features, struck the ladies whom he joined in the drawing-room. Mannering was not, however, a man to be questioned, even by those whom he most loved, upon the cause of the mental agitation which these signs expressed. The hour of tea arrived, and the party were partaking of that refreshment in silence, when a carriage drove up to the door, and the bell announced the arrival of a visitor. "Surely," said Mannering, "it is too soon by some hours."—

There was a short pause, when Barnes, opening the door of the saloon, announced Mr Pleydell. In marched the lawyer, whose well-brushed black coat, and well-powdered wig, together with his point ruffles, brown silk stockings, highly-varnished shoes, and gold buckles, exhibited the pains which the old gentleman had taken to prepare his person for the ladies' society. He was welcomed by Mannering with a hearty shake by the hand. "The very man I wished to see at this moment!"

"Yes, I told you I would take the first opportunity, so I have ventured to leave the court for a week in session time—no common sacrifice—but I had a notion I could be useful, and I was to attend a proof here about the same time.—But will you not introduce me to the young ladies?—Ah! there is one I should have known at once from her family likeness! Miss Lucy Bertram, my love, I am most happy to see you."—And he folded her in his arms, and gave her a hearty kiss on each side of the face, to which Lucy submitted in blushing resignation. —"*On n'arrête pas dans si beau chemin*," continued the gay old gentleman, and, as the Colonel presented him to Julia, took the same liberty with that fair lady's cheek. Julia laughed, coloured, and disengaged herself. "I beg a thousand pardons," said the lawyer, with a bow which was not at all professionally awkward; "age and old fashions give privileges, and I can hardly say whether I am most sorry just now at being too well entitled to claim them at all, or happy in having such an opportunity to exercise them so agreeably."

"Upon my word, sir," said Miss Mannering, laughing, "if you make such flattering apologies, we shall begin to doubt whether we can admit you to shelter yourself under your alleged qualifications."

"I can assure you, Julia," said the Colonel, "you are perfectly right, our friend the counsellor is a dangerous person; the last time I had the pleasure of seeing him, he was closetted with a fair lady who had granted him a *tête-à-tête* at eight in the morning."

"Aye, but, Colonel, you should add, I was more indebted to my chocolate than my charms for so distinguished a favour, from a person of such propriety of demeanour as Mrs Rebecca."

"And that should remind me, Mr Pleydell," said Julia, "to offer you tea—that is, supposing you have dined."

"Any thing, Miss Mannering, from your hands—yes, I have dined —that is to say, as people dine at a Scotch inn."

"And that is indifferently enough," said the Colonel, with his hand upon the bell-handle; "give me leave to order something."

"Why, to say truth, I had rather not; I have been enquiring into that matter, for you must know I stopped an instant below to pull off my boot-hose, 'a world too wide for my shrunk shanks,'" glancing down with some complacency upon limbs which looked very well for his time of life, "and I had some conversation with your Barnes, and a very intelligent old lady whom I presume to be the housekeeper, and it was settled among us—*tota re perspecta*—I beg Miss Mannering's pardon for my Latin—that the said old lady should add to your light family-supper the more substantial refreshment of a brace of wild-ducks. I told her (always under deep submission) my poor thoughts about the sauce, and, if you please, I would rather wait till they are ready before eating any thing solid."

"And we will anticipate our usual hour of supper," said the Colonel.

"With all my heart," said Pleydell, "providing I don't lose the ladies' company a moment the sooner. I am of counsel with my old friend B——; I love the *cœna*, the supper of the ancients, the pleasant meal and social glass that washes out of one's mind the cobwebs that business or gloom have been spinning in our brains all day."

The vivacity of Mr Pleydell's look and manner, and the quietness with which he put himself at home upon the subject of his little epicurean comforts, amused the ladies, but particularly Miss Mannering, who immediately gave the counsellor a great deal of flattering attention; and more pretty things were said upon both sides during the service of the tea-table than we have leisure to repeat.

So soon as this was over, Mannering led the counsellor by the arm into a small study which opened from the saloon, and where, according to the custom of the family, there were always lights and a good fire in the evening.

"I see," said Mr Pleydell, "you have got something to tell me about the Ellangowan business—Is it terrestrial or celestial? What says my military Albumazar? Have you calculated the course of futurity? have you consulted your Ephemerides, your Almochoden, your Almuten?"

"No, truly, counsellor, you are the only Ptolemy I intend to resort to upon the present occasion—a second Prospero, I have broke my staff, and drowned my book far beyond plummet depth. But I have great news notwithstanding. Meg Merrilies, our Egyptian sybil, has appeared to the Dominie this very day, and, as I conjecture, has frightened him not a little."

"Indeed?"

"Aye, and she has done me the honour to open a correspondence with me, supposing me to be as deep in astrological mysteries as when we first met; here is her scroll, delivered to me by the Dominie."

Pleydell put on his spectacles. "A vile greasy scrawl, indeed—and the letters are uncial or semiuncial, as somebody calls your large text hand, and in size and perpendicularity resemble the ribs of a roasted pig—I can hardly make it out."

"Read aloud," said Mannering.

"I will try:——'*You are a good seeker, but a bad finder; you set yoursell to prop a falling house, but had a gay guess it would rise again. Lend your hand to the wark that's near, as ye lent your e'e to the weird that was far. Have a carriage this night by ten o'clock, at the end of the crooked dykes at Portanferry, and let it bring the folk to Woodbourne that shall ask them, if they be there* IN GOD'S NAME.'—Stay, here follows some poetry—

> *'Dark shall be light,*
> *And wrong done to right,*
> *When Bertram's right and Bertram's might*
> *Shall meet on Ellangowan's height.'*

A most mystic epistle truly, and closes in a vein of poetry worthy of the Cumæan sybil—And what have you done?"

"Why, I was loth to risk any opportunity of throwing light on this business. The woman is perhaps crazed, and these effusions may arise only from visions of her imagination;—but you were of opinion that she knew more of that strange story than she ever told."

"And so you sent a carriage to the place named?"

"You'll laugh at me if I own I did."

"Who—I? no, truly, I think it was the wisest thing you could do."

"Yes, and the worst is paying the chaise-hire—I sent a post-chaise and four from Kippletringan, with instructions corresponding to the memorandum—the horses will have a long and cold station upon the out-post to-night if our intelligence be false."

"O, but I think it will prove otherwise. This woman has played a part till she believes it; or, if she be a thorough-paced impostor, without a single grain of self-delusion to qualify her knavery, still she may think herself bound to act in character—this I know, that I could get nothing out of her by the common modes of interrogation, and the wisest thing we can do is to give her an opportunity of making the discovery her own way. And now have you more to say, or shall we go to the ladies?"

"Why, my mind is uncommonly agitated, and—but I really have no more to say—only I shall count the minutes till the carriage returns; but you cannot be expected to be so anxious."

"Why, no—use is all in all—I am much interested certainly, but I think I shall be able to survive the interval, if the ladies will afford us some music."

"And with the assistance of the wild-ducks by and bye?"

"True, Colonel; a lawyer's anxiety about the fate of the most interesting cause has seldom spoiled either his sleep or digestion—and yet I shall be very eager to hear the rattle of these wheels on their return, notwithstanding."

So saying, he rose and led the way into the next room, where Miss Mannering, at his request, took her seat at the harpsichord. Lucy Bertram, who sung her native melodies very sweetly, was accompanied by her friend upon the instrument, and Julia afterwards performed some of Corelli's sonatas with great brilliancy. The old lawyer, scraping a little upon the violoncello, and being a member of the gentlemen's concert in Edinburgh, was so greatly delighted with this mode of spending the evening, that I doubt if he once thought of the wild-ducks until Barnes informed the company supper was ready.

"Tell Mrs Allan to have something in readiness," said the Colonel —"I expect—that is, I hope—perhaps some person may be here to-night; and let the men sit up, and do not lock the upper gate on the lawn until I desire you."

"Yes, sir."

"Lord, sir," said Julia, "whom can you possibly expect to-night?"

"Why, some persons, strangers to me, talked of calling in the evening about business—it is quite uncertain."

"Well, we shall not pardon them disturbing our party, unless they bring as much good humour, and as susceptible a heart, as my friend and admirer, for so he has dubbed himself, Mr Pleydell."

"Ah, Miss Julia," said Pleydell, offering his arm with an air of gallantry to conduct her into the eating room, "the time has been—when I returned from Utrecht in the year 1738"——

"Pray don't talk of it—we like you much better as you are—Utrecht, in heaven's name!—I dare say you have spent all the intervening years in getting rid of the effects of your Dutch education."

"O, forgive me, Miss Mannering; the Dutch are a more accomplished people in point of gallantry than their volatile neighbours are willing to admit. They are constant as clock-work in their attentions."

"I should tire of that."

"Imperturbable in their good temper."

"Worse and worse."

"And then, although for six times three hundred and sixty-five days, your swain has placed the capuchin round your neck, and the stove under your feet, and driven your little cabriole upon the ice in winter, and through the dust in summer, you may dismiss him at once, without reason or apology, upon the two thousand one hundred and ninetieth day, which, according to my hasty calculation, and without reckoning leap-years, will complete the cycle of the supposed adoration, and that without your amiable feelings having the slightest occasion to be alarmed for the consequences to Mynheer's bosom."

"Well, that last is truly a Dutch recommendation, Mr Pleydell—glasses and hearts would lose all their merit in the world, if it were not for their fragility."

"Why, as to that, Miss Mannering, it is as difficult to find a heart that will break, as a glass that will not; and for that reason I would press the value of mine own—Were it not that I see Mr Sampson's eyes have been closed, and his hands clasped for some time, attending the end of our conference to begin the grace—and to say truth, the appearance of the wild-ducks is very appetizing."

So saying, the worthy counsellor sat himself to table, and laid aside his gallantry for a while, to do honour to the good things placed before him. Nothing further is recorded of him for some time, excepting an observation that the ducks were roasted to a single turn, and that Mrs Allan's sauce was beyond praise.

"I see," said Miss Mannering, "I have a formidable rival in Mr Pleydell's favour, even on the very first night of his avowed admiration."

"Pardon me, my dear young lady—your acknowledged rigour alone has induced me to commit the solecism of eating a good supper in your presence—but how shall I support your frowns without reinforcing my strength?—Upon the same principle, and no other, I will ask permission to drink wine with you."

"This is the fashion of Utrecht also, I suppose, Mr Pleydell?"

"Forgive me, madam; the French themselves, the patterns of all that is gallant, term their tavern-keepers *restaurateurs*, alluding, doubtless, to the relief they afford disconsolate lovers, when bowed down to earth by their mistresses' rigour. My own case requires so much relief, that I must trouble you for that other wing, Mr Sampson, without prejudice to my afterwards applying to Miss Bertram for a tart —be pleased to tear the wing, sir, instead of cutting it off—Mr Barnes will assist you, Mr Sampson—thank you, sir—and, Mr Barnes, a glass of ale if you please."

While the old gentleman, pleased with Miss Mannering's liveliness and attention, rattled away for her amusement and his own, the impatience of Colonel Mannering began to exceed all bounds. He declined sitting down at table, under pretence that he never eat supper; and traversed the parlour, in which they were, with hasty and impatient steps, now throwing up the window to gaze out upon the dark lawn, now listening for the remote sound of the carriage advancing up the avenue. At length, in a feeling of uncontroulable impatience, he left the room, took his hat and cloak, and pursued his walk up the avenue, as if his doing so would have hastened the approach of those whom he desired to see. "I really wish," said Miss Bertram, "Colonel Mannering would not venture out after night-fall. You must have heard, Mr Pleydell, what a cruel fright we had."

"O, with the smugglers;—they are old friends of mine. I was the means of bringing some of them to justice a long time since."

"And then the alarm that we had immediately afterwards from the vengeance of one of these wretches."

"When young Hazelwood was hurt—I heard of that too."

"Imagine, my dear Mr Pleydell, how much Miss Mannering and I were alarmed, when a ruffian, equally dreadful for his great strength, and the sternness of his features, rushed out upon us!"

"You must know, Mr Pleydell," said Julia, unable to suppress her resentment at this undesigned aspersion of her admirer, "that young Hazelwood is so handsome in the eyes of the young ladies of this country, that they think every person shocking who comes near him."

"Oho!" thought Pleydell, who was by profession an observer of tones and gestures, "there's something wrong here between my young friends.—Well, Miss Mannering, I have not seen young Hazelwood since he was a boy, so the ladies may be perfectly right; but I can assure you, in spite of your scorn, that if you want to see handsome men you must go to Holland; the prettiest fellow I ever saw was a Dutchman, in spite of his being called Vanbost, or Vanbuster, or some such barbarous name. He won't be quite so handsome now, to be sure."

It was now Julia's turn to look a little out of countenance, but at that instant the Colonel entered the room. "I can hear nothing of them yet," he said; "still, however, we will not separate—Where is Dominie Sampson?"

"Here, honoured sir."

"What is that book you hold in your hand, Mr Sampson?"

"It's even the learned De Lyra, sir—I would crave his honour Mr Pleydell's judgment, alway with his best leisure, to expound a disputed passage."

"I am not in the vein, Mr Sampson," answered Pleydell; "here's metal more attractive.—I do not despair to engage these two young ladies in a glee or a catch, wherein I, even I myself, will adventure myself for the bass part—Hang De Lyra, man; keep him for a fitter season."

The disappointed Dominie shut his ponderous tome, much marvelling in his mind how a person, possessed of the lawyer's erudition, could give his mind to these frivolous toys. But the counsellor, indifferent to the high character which he was trifling away, filled himself a large glass of Burgundy, and after preluding a little with a voice somewhat the worse for the wear, gave the ladies a courageous invitation to join in "We be three poor Mariners," and accomplished his own part therein with great eclat.

"Are you not withering your roses with sitting up so late, my young ladies?" said the Colonel.

"Not a bit, sir," answered Julia; "your friend Mr Pleydell threatens to become a pupil of Mr Sampson's to-morrow, so we must make the most of our conquest to-night."

This led to another musical trial of skill, and that to lively conversation. At length, when the solitary sound of one o'clock had long since resounded on the ebon ear of night, and the next signal of the advance of time was close approaching, Mannering, whose impatience had long subsided into disappointment and despair, looked his watch, and said, "We must now give them up"——When at that instant—But what then befell will require a separate chapter.

Chapter Eleven

Justice. This does indeed confirm each circumstance
The gypsey told! ———
No orphan, nor without a friend art thou—
I am thy father, *here's* thy mother, *there*
Thy uncle—This thy first cousin, and these
Are all thy near relations!

The Critic

AS MANNERING replaced his watch, he heard a distant and hollow sound—"It is a carriage for certain—no, it is but the sound of the wind among the leafless trees. Do come to the window, Mr Pleydell." The counsellor, who with his large silk handkerchief in his hand was expatiating away to Julia upon some subject he thought interesting, obeyed however the summons, first throwing the handkerchief round his neck by way of precaution against the cold air. The sound of wheels became now very perceptible, and Pleydell, as if he had reserved all his curiosity till that moment, ran out to the hall. The Colonel rung for Barnes to desire that the persons who came in the carriage might be shown into a separate room, being altogether uncertain whom it might contain. It stopped however at the door, before his purpose could be fully explained. A moment after Mr Pleydell called out, "Here is our Liddesdale friend, I protest, with a strapping young fellow of the same calibre." His voice arrested Dinmont, who recognised him with equal surprise and pleasure. "Odd, if it's your honour, we'll be a' as right and tight as thack and rape can make us."

But while the farmer stopped to make his bow, Bertram, dizzied with the sudden glare of light, and bewildered with the whole circumstances of his situation, almost unconsciously entered the open door of the parlour, and confronted the Colonel, who was just advancing towards it. The strong light of the apartment left no doubt of his identity, and he himself was equally confounded with the appearance of those to whom he so unexpectedly presented himself, as they were by the sight of so utterly unlooked-for an object. It must be remembered that each individual present had their own peculiar reasons for looking with terror upon what seemed at first sight a spectral apparition. Mannering saw before him the man whom he supposed he had killed in India; Julia beheld her lover in a most peculiar and hazardous situation; and Lucy Bertram at once knew the person who had fired upon young Hazelwood. Bertram, who interpreted the fixed and motionless astonishment of the Colonel into displeasure at his intrusion, hastened to say that it was involuntary, since he had been hurried hither without even knowing whither he was to be transported.

"Mr Brown, I believe!" said Colonel Mannering.

"Yes, sir, the same you knew in India; and who ventures to hope, that what you did there know of him is not such as should prevent his requesting you would favour him with your attestation to his character, as a gentleman and man of honour."

"Mr Brown—I have been rarely—never—so much surprised—certainly, sir, in what passed between us, you have a right to command my testimony."

At this critical moment entered the counsellor and Dinmont. The former beheld, to his astonishment, the Colonel but just recovering from his first surprise, Lucy Bertram ready to faint with terror, and Miss Mannering in an agony of doubt and apprehension, which she in vain endeavoured to disguise or suppress. "What is the meaning of all this?" said he; "has this young fellow brought the Gorgon's head in his hand?—let me look at him.—By heaven!" he muttered to himself, "the very image of old Ellangowan—the witch has kept her word." Then instantly passing to Miss Bertram, "Look at that man, Lucy, my dear; have you never seen any one like him?"

Lucy had only ventured one glance at this object of terror, which, from his remarkable height and appearance, at once recognised the supposed assassin of young Hazelwood, and excluded, of course, the more favourable association of ideas which might have occurred on a closer view. "Don't ask me about him, sir; send him away, for heaven's sake! we shall be murdered!"

"Murdered!—where's the poker?"—said the advocate in some alarm; "but nonsense, we are three men besides the servants, and there is honest Liddesdale worth half-a-dozen to boot—we have the *major vis* upon our side—however—here, my friend Dandie—Davie—what do they call you?—keep between that tall fellow and us for the protection of the ladies."

"Lord! Mr Pleydell, that's Captain Brown; d'ye no ken the Captain?"

"Nay, if he's a friend of your's we may be safe enough; but keep near him."

All this passed with such rapidity, that it was over before the Dominie had recovered himself from a fit of absence, shut the book which he had been studying in a corner, and, advancing to obtain a sight of the strangers, exclaimed at once upon beholding Bertram, "If the grave can give up the dead, that is my dear and honoured master!"

"We're right after all, by heaven! I was sure I was right," said the lawyer; "he is the very image of his father.—Come, Colonel, what do you think of, that you do not bid your guest welcome? I think—I believe—I trust we're right—never saw such a likeness—but patience—Dominie, say not a word—sit down, young gentleman."

"I beg pardon, sir; if I am, as I understand, in Colonel Mannering's house, I should wish first to know if my accidental appearance here gives offence, or if I am welcome?"

Mannering instantly made an effort.—"Welcome? most certainly, especially if you can point out how I can serve you. I believe I may have some wrongs to repair towards you—I have often suspected so; but your sudden and unexpected appearance, connected with painful recollections, prevented my saying at first, as I now say, that whatever has procured me the honour of this visit, it is an acceptable one."

Bertram bowed with an air of distant, yet civil acknowledgment, to the grave courtesy of Mannering.

"Julia, my love, you had better retire. Mr Brown, you will excuse my daughter; there are circumstances which I perceive rush upon her recollection."

Miss Mannering rose and retired accordingly; yet, as she passed Bertram, could not suppress the words, "Infatuated! a second time!" but so pronounced as to be heard by him alone. Miss Bertram accompanied her friend, much surprised, but without venturing a second glance at the object of her terror. Some mistake she saw there was, and was unwilling to increase it by denouncing the stranger as an assassin. He was known, she observed, to the Colonel, and received as a gentleman; certainly he either was not the person, or Hazelwood was right in supposing the shot accidental.

The remaining part of the company would have formed no bad group for a skilful painter. Each was too much embarrassed with his own sensations to observe those of the others. Bertram most unexpectedly found himself in the house of one whom he was alternately disposed to dislike as his personal enemy, or to respect as the father of Julia; Mannering was struggling between his high sense of courtesy and hospitality, his joy at finding himself relieved from the guilt of having shed life in a private quarrel, and the former feelings of dislike and prejudice, which revived in his haughty mind at the sight of the object against whom he had entertained them; Sampson, supporting his shaking limbs by leaning on the back of a chair, fixed his staring eyes upon Bertram, with an expression of nervous anxiety which convulsed his whole visage; Dinmont, clothed in his loose shaggy great-coat, and resembling a huge bear erect upon his hinder legs, stared on the whole scene with great round eyes that witnessed his amazement.

The counsellor alone was in his element, shrewd, prompt, and active; he already calculated the prospect of brilliant success in a strange, eventful, and mysterious law-suit, and no young monarch, flushed with hopes, and at the head of a gallant army, could experience more glee when taking the field on his first campaign. He bustled about with great energy, and took the arrangement of the whole explanation upon himself. "Come, come, gentlemen, sit down; this is all in my province; you must let me arrange it for you. Sit down, my dear Colonel, and let me manage—Sit down, Mr Brown, *aut quocunque alio nomine vocaris*—Dominie, take your seat—draw in your chair, honest Liddesdale."

"I dinna ken, Mr Pleydell," said Dinmont, looking at his dreadnought coat, and then at the handsome furniture of the room, "I had maybe better gang some gate else and leave ye till your cracks—I am no just that weel put on."

The Colonel, who by this time recognized Dandie, immediately went up and bid him heartily welcome; assuring him, that from what he had seen of him in Edinburgh, he was sure his rough coat and thick-soled boots would honour a royal drawing-room.

"Na, na, Colonel, we're just plain up-the-country folk; but nae doubt I would fain hear o' ony pleasure that was gaun to happen the Captain, and I am sure a' will gae right if Mr Pleydell will tak his bit job in hand."

"You're right, Dandie—spoke like a hieland oracle—and now be silent.—Well, you are all seated at last; take a glass of wine till I begin my catechism methodically. And now," turning to Bertram, "my dear boy, do you know who or what you are?"

In spite of his perplexity, the catechumen could not help laughing at this commencement of his interrogation, and answered, "Indeed, sir, I thought I did; but I own late circumstances have made me somewhat uncertain."

"Then tell us what you formerly thought yourself."

"Why, I was in the habit of thinking and calling myself Vanbeest Brown, who served as a cadet or volunteer under Colonel Mannering, when he commanded the —— regiment, in which capacity I was not unknown to him."

"There," said the Colonel, "I can assure Mr Brown of his identity; and add what his modesty may have forgotten, that he was distinguished as a young man of talent and spirit."

"So much the better, my dear sir; but that is to general character—Mr Brown must tell us where he was born."

"In Scotland, I believe, but the place uncertain."

"Where educated?"

"In Holland, certainly."

"Do you remember nothing of your early life before you left Scotland?"

"Very imperfectly; yet I have a strong recollection, perhaps more deeply impressed upon me by subsequent hard usage, that I was during my early childhood the object of much solicitude and affection. I have an indistinct remembrance of a good-looking man whom I used to call papa, and of a lady who was infirm in health, and who, I think, must have been my mother; but it is an imperfect and confused recollection—I remember too a tall thin man in black, who used to teach me my letters and walk out with me—and I think the very last time"——

Here the Dominie could contain no longer. While every succeeding word served to prove that the child of his benefactor stood before him, he had struggled with the utmost difficulty to suppress his emotions; but, when the juvenile recollections of Bertram turned towards his tutor and his precepts, he was compelled to give way to his feelings. He rose hastily from his chair, and with clasped hands, trembling limbs, and streaming eyes, called out aloud, "Harry Bertram!—look at me—was I not that man?"

"Yes," said Bertram, starting from his seat as if a sudden light had burst in upon his mind, "Yes—that was my name!—and that is the voice and the figure of my kind old master!"

The Dominie threw himself into his arms, pressed him a thousand times to his bosom in convulsions of transport, which shook his whole frame, sobbed hysterically, and, at length, in the emphatic language of scripture, lifted up his voice and wept aloud. Colonel Mannering had recourse to his handkerchief; Pleydell made wry faces, and wiped the glasses of his spectacles; and honest Dinmont, after two loud blubbering explosions, exclaimed, "Deil's in the man, he's garr'd me do that I hae na done since my auld mither died."

"Come, come," said the counsellor at last, "silence in the court—we have a clever party to contend with—we must lose no time in gathering our information—for any thing I know there may be something to be done before day-break."

"I will order a horse to be saddled, if you please," said the Colonel.

"No, no, time enough—time enough—but come, Dominie, I have allowed you a competent space to express your feelings. I must circumduce the term—you must let me proceed in my examination."

The Dominie was habitually obedient to any one who chose to impose commands upon him; he sunk back into his chair, spread his chequed handkerchief over his face, to serve, I suppose, for the Grecian painter's veil, and, from the action of his folded hands, appeared for a time engaged in the act of mental thanksgiving. He then raised his eyes over the screen, as if to be assured that the pleasing apparition had not melted into air—then again sunk them to resume his internal act of devotion, untill he felt himself compelled to give attention to the counsellor, from the interest which his questions excited.

"And now," said Mr Pleydell, after several minute enquiries concerning his recollections of early events—"And now, Mr Bertram, for I think we ought in future to call you by your own proper name, will you have the goodness to let us know every particular which you can recollect concerning the mode of your leaving Scotland?"

"Indeed, sir, to say the truth, though the terrible outlines of that day are strongly impressed upon my memory, yet somehow the very terror which fixed them there has in a great measure confounded and confused the details. I recollect, however, that I was walking somewhere or other—in a wood, I think"——

"O yes, it was in Warroch-wood, my dear," said the Dominie.

"Hush, Mr Sampson," said the lawyer.

"Yes, it was in a wood—and some one was with me—this kind-hearted gentleman, I think."

"O, ay, ay, Harry, Lord bless thee—it was even I myself."

"Be silent, Dominie, and don't interrupt the evidence," said Pleydell;—"And so, sir?" to Bertram.

"And so, sir, like one of the changes of a dream, I thought I was on horseback before my guide."

"No, no," exclaimed Sampson, "never did I put mine own limbs, not to say thine, into such peril."

"On my word this is intolerable!—Look ye, Dominie, if you speak another word till I give you leave, I will read three sentences out of the Black Acts, whisk my cane round my head three times, undo all the magic of this night's work, and conjure Harry Bertram back again into Vanbeest Brown."

"Honoured and worthy sir, I humbly crave pardon—it was but *verbum volans.*"

"Well, *nolens volens*, you must hold your tongue."

"Pray, be silent, Mr Sampson," said the Colonel; "it is of great consequence to your recovered friend, that you permit Mr Pleydell to proceed in his enquiries."

"I am mute," said the rebuked Dominie.

"On a sudden," continued Bertram, "two or three men sprung out upon us, and we were pulled from horseback. I have little recollection of any thing else, but that I tried to escape in the midst of a desperate scuffle, and fell into the arms of a very tall woman who started from the bushes, and protected me for some time—the rest is all confusion and dread—a dim recollection of a sea-beach, and a cave, and of some strong potion which lulled me to sleep for a length of time. In short, it is all a blank in my memory, until I found myself first an ill-used and half-starved cabin-boy aboard a sloop, and then a school-boy in Holland under the protection of an old merchant, who had taken some fancy for me."

"And what account did your guardian give you of your parentage?"

"A very brief one, and a charge to enquire no farther. I was given to understand that my father was concerned in the smuggling trade carried on on the eastern coast of Scotland, and was killed in a skirmish with the revenue officers; and that his correspondents in Holland had a vessel on the coast at the time, part of the crew of which were engaged in the affair, and brought me off after it was over, from a motive of compassion, as I was left destitute by my father's death. As I grew older there was much of this story which seemed inconsistent with my own recollections, but what could I do? I had no means of ascertaining my doubts, nor a single friend with whom I could communicate or canvass them. The rest of my story is known to Colonel Mannering; I went out to India to be a clerk in a Dutch house; their affairs fell into confusion—I betook myself to the military profession, and, I trust, as yet I have not disgraced it."

"Thou art a fine young fellow, I'll be bound for thee," said Pleydell, "and since you have wanted a father so long, I wish from my heart I could claim the paternity myself. But this affair of young Hazelwood"——

"Was merely accidental," said Bertram; "I was travelling in Scotland for pleasure, and after a week's residence with my friend Mr Dinmont, with whom I had the good fortune to form an accidental acquaintance"——

"It was my gude fortune that," said Dinmont; "odd, my brains wad hae been knockit out by twa blackguards, if it hadna been for his four quarters."

"Shortly after we parted at the town of ——, I lost my baggage by thieves, and it was while residing at Kippletringan I accidentally met the young gentleman. As I was approaching to pay my respects to Miss

Mannering, whom I had known in India, Mr Hazelwood, conceiving my appearance none of the most respectable, commanded me rather haughtily to stand back, and so gave occasion to the fray in which I had the misfortune to be the accidental means of wounding him.—And now, sir, I have answered all your questions."

"No, no, not quite all," said Pleydell, winking sagaciously; "there are some interrogatories which I shall delay till to-morrow, for it is time, I believe, to close the sederunt for this night, or rather morning."

"Well then, sir, to vary the phrase, I have answered all the questions which you have chosen to ask to-night—Will you be so good as to tell me who you are that take such interest in my affairs, and who you take me to be, since my arrival has occasioned such commotion?"

"Why, sir, for myself, I am Paulus Pleydell, an advocate at the Scottish bar; and for you, it is not easy to say distinctly who you are at present; but I trust in a short time to hail you by the title of Henry Bertram, Esquire, representative of one of the oldest families in Scotland, and heir of tailzie and provision to the estate of Ellangowan—Aye," continued he, shutting his eyes and speaking to himself, "we must pass over his father, and serve him heir to his grand-father Lewis, the entailer—the only wise man of his family that I ever heard of."

They had now risen to retire to their apartments for the night, when Colonel Mannering walked up to Bertram, as he stood astonished at the counsellor's words. "I give you joy," he said, "of the prospects which fate has opened before you. I was an early friend of your father, and chanced to be in the house of Ellangowan as unexpectedly as you are now in mine, upon the very night on which you were born. I little knew this circumstance when—but I trust unkindness will be forgotten between us. Believe me, your appearance here, as Mr Brown, alive and well, has relieved me from most painful sensations, and your right to the name of an old friend renders your presence, as Mr Bertram, doubly welcome."

"And my parents?" said Bertram.

"Are both no more—and the family property has been sold, but I trust may be recovered. Whatever is wanted to make your right effectual, I shall be most happy to supply."

"Nay, you may leave all that to me," said the counsellor; "'tis my vocation, Hal—I shall make money of it."

"I am sure it's no for the like o' me," observed Dinmont, "to speak to you gentle-folks; but if siller would help on the Captain's plea, and, odd, they say nae plea gangs on without it"——

"Except on Saturday night," said Pleydell.

"Aye, but when your honour wadna take your fee you wadna hae the cause neither, sae I'll ne'er fash ye on Saturday at e'en again—but I was saying there's some siller in this spleuchan that's like the Captain's ain, for we've aye counted it such, baith Ailie and me."

"No, no, Liddesdale—no occasion, no occasion whatever—keep thy cash to stock thy farm."

"To stock my farm? Mr Pleydell, your honour kens mony things, but ye dinna ken the farm o' Charlieshope—it's sae weel stocked already, that we sell may be sax hundred pounds off it ilka year, flesh and fell thegither—na, na."

"Can't ye take another then?"

"I dinna ken—the Dewke's no that fond o' led farms, and he canna bide to put awa the auld tenantry; and than I wadna like mysell to gang about whistling and raising the rent on my neighbours."

"What, not upon thy neighbour at Dawstone—Devilstone—how d'ye call the place?"

"What, on Jock o' Dawstone? hout na—he's a camsteary chield, and fasheous about marches, and we've had some bits o' splores thegither; but deil o' me if I wad wrang Jock o' Dawstone neither."

"Thou'rt an honest fellow," said the lawyer; "get thee to bed. Thou wilt sleep sounder, I warrant thee, than many a man that throws off an embroidered coat, and puts on a laced night-cap.—Colonel, I see you are busy with our *Enfant trouvé*. But Barnes must give me a summons of wakening at seven to-morrow morning, for my servant's a sleepy-headed fellow; and I dare say Driver's had Clarence's fate, drowned by this time in a butt of your ale, for Mrs Allan promised to make him comfortable, and she'll soon discover what he expects from that engagement. Good night, Colonel—good night, Dominie Sampson—good night, Dinmont the downright—good night, last of all, to the new-found representative of the Bertrams, and the Mac-Dingawaies, the Knarths, the Arths, the Godfreys, the Dennis's, and the Rolands, and, last and dearest title, heir of tailzie and provision of the lands and barony of Ellangowan, under the settlement of Lewis Bertram, Esquire, whose representative you are."

And so saying, the old gentleman took his candle and left the room; and the company dispersed after the Dominie had once more hugged and embraced his "little Harry Bertram," as he continued to call the young soldier of six foot high.

Chapter Twelve

——My imagination
Carries no favour in it but Bertram's;
I am undone; there is no living, none,
If Bertram be away.——

All's well that ends well

AT THE HOUR which he had appointed in the preceding evening, the indefatigable lawyer was seated by a good fire, and a pair of wax candles, with a velvet cap upon his head, and a quilted silk night-gown on his person, busy arranging his memoranda of proofs and indications concerning the murder of Francis Kennedy. An express had also been dispatched to Mr Mac-Morlan, requesting his attendance at Woodbourne as soon as possible, upon business of importance. Dinmont, fatigued with the events of the evening before, and finding the accommodations of Woodbourne much preferable to those of MacGuffog, was in no hurry to rise. The impatience of Bertram might have put him earlier in motion, but Colonel Mannering had intimated an intention to visit him in his apartment in the morning, and he did not chuse to leave it. Before this interview he had dressed himself, Barnes having, by his master's order, supplied him with every accommodation of linen, &c. and now anxiously waited the promised visit of his landlord.

In a short time a gentle tap announced the Colonel, with whom Bertram held a long and satisfactory conversation. Each, however, concealed from the other one circumstance. Mannering could not bring himself to acknowledge the astrological prediction; and Bertram was, for motives which may be easily conceived, silent respecting his love for Julia. In other respects, their intercourse was frank and grateful to both, and had latterly, upon the Colonel's part, even an approach to cordiality. Bertram carefully measured his own conduct by that of his host, and seemed rather to receive his offered kindness with gratitude and pleasure, than to press for it with solicitation.

Miss Bertram was in the breakfast parlour when Sampson shuffled in, his face all radiant with smiles; a circumstance so uncommon, that Lucy's first idea was, that somebody had been bantering him with an imposition which had thrown him into this extacy. Having sate for some time, rolling his eyes and gaping with his mouth like the great wooden head at Merlin's exhibition, he at length began—"And what do you think of him, Miss Lucy?"

"Think of whom, Mr Sampson?"

"Of Har—no—of him that you know about?"

"That I know about?"

"Yes, the stranger, you know, that came last evening in the post vehicle—he who shot young Hazelwood—ha, ha, ho!"

"Indeed, Mr Sampson, you have chosen a strange subject for mirth —I think nothing about the man, only I hope the outrage was accidental, and that we need not fear a repetition of it."

"Accidental! ho, ho, ha!"

"Really, Mr Sampson," said Lucy, somewhat piqued, "you are unusually gay this morning."

"Yes, of a surety I am! ho, ho, ha! face-ti-ous—ha, ha, ho!"

"So unusually facetious, my dear sir, that I would wish rather to know the meaning of your mirth, than to be amused with its effects only."

"You shall know it, Miss Lucy—Do you remember your brother?"

"Good God! how can you ask me?—no one knows better than you he was lost the very day I was born."

"Very true, very true," answered the Dominie, saddening at the recollection, "I was strangely oblivious—aye, aye—ower true—But you remember your worthy father?"

"How should you doubt it, Mr Sampson? it's not so many weeks since"——

"True, true—aye, ower true—I will be facetious no more under these remembrances—but look at that young man!"—

Bertram at this instant entered the room. "Yes, look at him well—he is thy father's living image; and as God has deprived ye of your dear parents—O my children, love one another!"

"It is indeed my father's face and form," said Lucy, turning very pale; Bertram ran to support her—the Dominie to fetch water to throw upon her face—(which in his haste he took from the boiling tea-urn) when fortunately her colour returning rapidly, saved her from the application of his ill-judged remedy. "I conjure you to tell me, Mr Sampson," she said, in an interrupted yet solemn voice, "is this my brother?"

"It is—it is!—Miss Lucy, it is little Harry Bertram, as sure as God's sun is in that Heaven!"

"And this is my sister?" said Bertram, giving way to all that family affection which had so long slumbered in his bosom for want of an object to expand itself upon.

"It is—it is!—it is Miss Lucy Bertram, whom by my poor aid you will find perfect in the tongues of France, and Italy, and even of Spain—in reading and writing her vernacular tongue, and in arithmetic and book-keeping by double and single entry—I say nothing of her talents of shaping, and hemming, and governing a household, which, to give every one their due, she acquired not from me, but from the housekeeper—nor do I take merit for her performance upon stringed instruments, whereunto the instructions of an honourable young lady of virtue and modesty, and very facetious withal—Miss Julia Mannering—hath not meanly contributed—*Suum cuique tribuito.*"

"You then," said Bertram to his sister, "are all that remains to me! —Last night—but more fully this morning, Colonel Mannering gave me an account of our family misfortunes, though without saying I should find you here."

"That," said Lucy, "he left to this gentleman to tell you, one of the kindest and most faithful of friends, who soothed my father's long sickness, witnessed his dying moments, and amid the heaviest clouds of fortune would not desert his orphan."

"God bless him for it!" said Bertram, shaking the Dominie's hand, "he deserves the love with which I have always regarded even the shadow of his memory which my childhood retained."

"And God bless you both, my dear children," said Sampson; "if it had not been for your sake, I would have been contented (had Heaven's pleasure so been) to lay my head upon the turf beside my patron."

"But, I trust," said Bertram, "I am encouraged to hope, we shall all see better days. All our wrongs shall be redressed, since Heaven has sent me means and friends to assert my right."

"Friends indeed!" echoed the Dominie, "and sent, as you truly say, by HIM, to whom I early taught you to look up as the source of all that is good. There is the great Colonel Mannering from the Eastern Indies, who is a man of great erudition considering his imperfect opportunities; and there is, moreover, the great advocate Mr Pleydell, who is also a man of great erudition, but who descendeth to trifles unbeseeming thereof; and there is Mr Andrew Dinmont, whom I do not understand to have possession of much erudition, but who, like the patriarchs of old, is cunning in that which belongeth to flocks and herds—Lastly, there is even I myself, whose opportunities of collecting erudition, as they have been greater than those of the aforesaid valuable persons, have not, if it becomes me so to speak, been pretermitted by me in as far as my poor faculties have enabled me to profit by them—Of a surety, little Harry, we must speedily resume our studies. I will begin from the foundation—Yes, I will reform your education upward from the true knowledge of English grammar, even to that of the Hebrew or Chaldaic tongue."

The reader may observe, that, upon this occasion, Sampson was infinitely more profuse of words than he had hitherto exhibited himself. The reason was, that in recovering his pupil his mind went instantly back to their original connection, and he had, in his confusion of ideas, the strongest desire in the world to resume spelling-lessons and half-text with young Bertram. This was the more ridiculous, as towards Lucy he assumed no such powers of tuition. But she had grown up under his eye, and had been gradually emancipated by increase in years and knowledge from his government, whereas his first ideas went to take up little Harry pretty nearly where he had left him. From the same feelings of reviving authority, he indulged himself in what was to him a profusion of language; and as people seldom speak more than usual without exposing themselves, he gave those whom he addressed plainly to understand, that while he deferred implicitly to the opinions and commands, if they chose to impose them, of almost every one whom he met with, it was under an internal conviction, that in the article of eru-di-ti-on, as he usually divided and pronounced the word, he was himself infinitely superior to them all put together. At present, however, this intimation fell upon heedless ears, for the brother and sister were too deeply engaged in asking and receiving intelligence concerning their former fortunes to attend to it.

When Colonel Mannering left Bertram, he went to Julia's dressing-room, and dismissed her attendant. "My dear sir," she said as he entered, "you have forgot our vigils last night, and have hardly allowed me to comb my hair, although you must be sensible how it stood on end at the various wonders which took place."

"It is with the inside of your head that I have some business at present, Julia; I will return the outside to the care of your Mrs Mincing in a few minutes."

"Lord, papa, think how entangled all my ideas are, and you propose to comb them out in a few minutes! If Mincing was to do so in her department, she would tear half the hair out of my head."

"Well then, tell me where the entanglement lies, which I will try to extricate with due gentleness?"

"O, every where—the whole is a wild dream."

"Well then, I will try to unriddle it."—He gave a brief sketch of the fate and prospects of Bertram, to which Julia listened with an interest which she in vain endeavoured to disguise—"Well, are your ideas on the subject more luminous?"

"More confused than ever, my dear sir—Here is this young man comes home from India, after he had been supposed dead, like Aboulfouaris the great voyager to his sister Canzade and his brother Hour. I am wrong in the story, I believe—Canzade was his wife—but Lucy may represent the one, and the Dominie the other. And then this lively crack-brained Scotch lawyer appears like a pantomime at the end of a tragedy—And then how delightful it will be if Lucy gets back their fortune!"

"Now I think," said the Colonel, "that the most mysterious part of the business is, that Miss Julia Mannering, who must have known her father's anxiety about the fate of this young man Brown, or Bertram, as we must now call him, meets him when Hazelwood's accident took place, and never once mentioned to her father a word of the matter, but suffered the search to proceed against this young gentleman as a suspicious character and assassin."

Julia, much of whose courage had been hastily assumed to meet the interview with her father, was now unable to rally herself; she hung down her head in silence, after in vain attempting to utter a denial that she recollected Brown when they met.

"No answer!—Well, Julia, allow me to ask you, Is this the only time you have seen Brown since his return from India?—Still no answer. I must then naturally suppose that it is *not* the first time—Still no reply. Julia Mannering, will you have the kindness to answer me? Was it this young man who came under your window and conversed with you during your residence at Mervyn-Hall? Julia—I command—I entreat you to be candid."

Miss Mannering raised her head. "I have been, sir—I believe I am still very foolish—and it is perhaps more hard upon me that I must meet this gentleman, who has been, though not the cause entirely, yet the accomplice of my folly, in your presence."—Here she made a full stop.

"I am to understand, then, that this *was* the author of the serenade?"

There was something in this allusive change of epithet that gave Julia a little more courage—"He was indeed, sir; and if I am very wrong, as I have often thought, I have some apology."

"And what is that?" answered the Colonel, speaking quick and somewhat harshly.

"I will not venture to name it, sir—but"—She opened a small cabinet, and put some letters into his hands; "I will give you these that you may see how this intimacy began, and by whom it was encouraged."

Mannering took the packet to the window—his pride forbade a more distant retreat—he glanced at some passages of the letters with an unsteady eye and an agitated mind—his stoicism, however, came in time to his aid; that philosophy, which, rooted in pride, yet frequently bears the fruits of virtue. He returned towards his daughter with as firm an air as his feelings permitted him to assume.

"There is great apology for you, Julia, as far as I can judge from a glance at these letters—you have obeyed, at least you have not disobeyed, one parent. Let us adopt a Scotch proverb the Dominie quoted to your amusement the other day—'Let bygones be bygones.'—I will never upbraid you with want of confidence—do you judge of my intentions by my actions, of which hitherto you have surely had no reason to complain. Keep these letters—they were never intended for my eye, and I would not willingly read more of them than I have done, at your desire and for your exculpation.—And now, are we friends? Or rather do you understand me?"

"O my dear, generous father," said Julia, throwing herself into his arms, "why have I ever for an instant misunderstood you?"

"No more of that, Julia; he that is too proud to vindicate the affection and confidence which he conceives should be given without solicitation, must meet much and perhaps deserved disappointment. It is enough one—dearest—and most regretted member of my family has gone to the grave without knowing me; let me not lose the confidence of a child, who ought to love me if she really loves herself."

"O no danger—no fear—let me but have your approbation and my own, and there is no rule you can prescribe so severe that I will not follow."

"Well, my love," kissing her forehead, "I trust we will not call upon you for any thing too heroic. With respect to this young gentleman's addresses," he continued after a pause, "I expect in the first place that all clandestine correspondence—which no young woman can entertain for a moment without lessening herself in her own eyes, and in those of her lover—I request, I say, that clandestine correspondence of every kind may be given up, and that you will refer Mr Bertram to me for the reason. You will naturally wish to know what is to be the issue of such a reference. In the first place, I desire time to observe this young gentleman's character more closely than circumstances, and perhaps my own prejudices, have permitted formerly—I should also be glad to see his birth established. Not that I am anxious about his getting the estate of Ellangowan, though such a subject is held in absolute indifference no where except in a novel. But certainly Henry Bertram, heir of Ellangowan, whether possessed of the property of his fathers or no, is a very different sound from Vanbeest Brown, the son of nobody at all. His fathers, Mr Pleydell tells me, are distinguished in history as following the banners of their native princes, while our own fought at Cressy and Poictiers. In short, I neither give nor withhold my approbation, but I expect you will redeem past errors; and as you can now unfortunately only have recourse to *one* parent, that you will shew the duty of a child, by reposing that confidence in me, which I will say my inclination to make you happy renders a filial debt upon your part."

The first part of this speech affected Julia a good deal; the comparative merit of the ancestors of the Bertrams and Mannerings excited a secret smile, but the conclusion was such as to affect a heart peculiarly open to the feelings of generosity. "No, my dear sir," she said, extending her hand, "receive my faith, that from this moment you shall be the first person consulted respecting what shall pass in future between Brown—I mean Bertram—and me; and that no engagement will be undertaken by me, excepting what you shall immediately know and approve of. May I ask—if Mr Bertram is to continue a guest at Woodbourne?"

"Certainly, while his affairs render it advisable."

"Then, sir, you must be sensible, considering what is already past, that he will expect some reason for my withdrawing—I believe I must say the encouragement, which he may think I have given."

"I expect, Julia, he will respect my roof, and entertain some sense perhaps of the services I am about to render him, and so will not insist upon any course of conduct of which I might have reason to complain; and I expect of you, that you will make him sensible of what is due to both."

"Then, sir, I understand you, and you shall be implicitly obeyed."

"Thank you, my love; my anxiety (kissing her) is on your account. —Now wipe these witnesses from your eyes, and so to breakfast."

Chapter Thirteen

> And, Sheriff, I will engage my word to you,
> That I will by to-morrow dinner time,
> Send him to answer thee, or any man,
> For any thing he shall be charged withal.
>
> *First Part of Henry IV*

When the several bye-plays, as they may be termed, had taken place among the individuals of the Woodbourne family, as we have intimated in the preceding chapter, the breakfast party at length assembled. There was an obvious air of constraint on the greater part of the assistants. Julia dared not raise her voice in asking Bertram if he chose another cup of tea. Bertram felt embarrassed while eating his toast and butter under the eye of Mannering. Lucy, her affection for her recovered brother indulged to the uttermost, began to think of the quarrel betwixt him and Hazelwood. The Colonel felt the painful anxiety natural to a proud mind, when it deems its slightest action subject for a moment to the watchful construction of others. The lawyer, while sedulously buttering his roll, had an aspect of unwonted gravity, arising, perhaps, from the severity of his morning studies. As for the Dominie, his state of mind was ecstatic!—He looked at Bertram—he looked at Miss Lucy—he whimpered—he sniggled—he grinned—he committed all manner of solecisms in point of form—poured the whole cream (no unlucky mistake) upon his own plate of porridge, which was his usual breakfast—threw the slops of what he called his "crowning dish of tea" into the sugar-dish instead of the slop-bason, and concluded with spilling the scalding liquid upon old Plato, the Colonel's favourite spaniel, who received the libation with a howl that did little honour to his philosophy.

The Colonel's equanimity was rather shaken by this last blunder. "Upon my word, my good friend, Mr Sampson, you forget the difference between Plato and Zenocrates."

"The former was chief of the Academics, the latter of the Stoics," said the Dominie, with some scorn of the supposition.

"Yes, my dear sir, but it was Zenocrates, not Plato, who denied that pain was an evil."

"I should have thought," said Pleydell, "that very respectable quadruped, who is just now limping out of the room upon three of his four legs, was rather of the Cynic school."

"Very well hit off——But here comes our answer from Mr Mac-Morlan."

It was unfavourable. Mrs Mac-Morlan sent her respectful compliments, and her husband had been, and was, detained, by some alarming disturbances which had taken place the preceding night at Portanferry, and the necessary investigation which they had occasioned.

"What's to be done now, counsellor?" said the Colonel to Pleydell.

"Why, I wish we could have seen Mac-Morlan, who's a sensible fellow himself, and would besides have acted under my advice. But there is little harm. Our friend here must be made *sui juris*—he is at present an escaped prisoner; the law has an awkward claim upon him; he must be placed *rectus in curia*, that is the first object. For which purpose, Colonel, I will accompany you in your carriage down to Hazelwood-house. The distance is not far; we will offer our bail; and I am confident I can easily shew Mr——I beg his pardon—Sir Robert Hazelwood, the necessity of receiving it."

"With all my heart," said the Colonel; and, ringing the bell, gave the necessary orders. "And what is next to be done?"

"We must get hold of Mac-Morlan, and look out for more proof."

"Proof! the thing is as clear as day-light—here's Mr Sampson and Miss Bertram, and you yourself, at once recognise the young gentleman as his father's image; and he himself recollects all the very peculiar circumstances preceding his leaving this country—What else is necessary to conviction?"

"To moral conviction nothing more perhaps—but for legal proof a great deal. Mr Bertram's recollections are his own recollections merely, and therefore not evidence in his own favour; Miss Bertram, the learned Mr Sampson, and I, can only say what every one who knew the late Ellangowan will readily agree in, that this gentleman is his very picture—But that will not make him Ellangowan's son and give him the estate."

"And what will do so?"

"Why, we must have a distinct probation.—There's these gypsies, but then, alas! they are almost infamous in the eye of law—scarce capable of bearing evidence, and Meg Merrilies utterly so, by the various accounts which she formerly gave of the matter, and her impudent denial of all knowledge of the fact when I examined her respecting it."

"What must be done then?"

"We must try what proof can be got at in Holland, among the persons by whom our young friend was educated.—But then the fear of being called in question for the murder may make them silent; or if they speak, they are either foreigners or outlawed smugglers.—In short, I see doubts."

"Under favour, most learned and honoured sir," said the Dominie, "I trust HE who hath restored little Harry Bertram to his friends, will not leave his own work imperfect."

"I trust so too, Mr Sampson; but we must use means; and I am afraid we shall have more difficulty in procuring them than I at first thought.—But faint heart never won fair lady—and, by the way, (apart to Miss Mannering, while Bertram was engaged with his sister) there's a vindication of Holland for you! what smart fellows do you think Leyden and Utrecht must send forth, when such a very genteel and handsome young man comes from the paltry schools of Middleburgh?"

"Of a verity," said the Dominie, jealous of the reputation of the Dutch seminary, "Of a verity, Mr Pleydell, but I make it known to you that I myself laid the foundation of his education."

"True, my dear Dominie, that accounts for his proficiency in the graces without question—but here comes your carriage, Colonel. Adieu, young folks: Miss Julia, keep your heart till I come back again—let there be nothing done to prejudice my right, whilst I am *non valens agere.*"

Their reception at Hazelwood-house was more cold and formal than usual, for in general the Baronet expressed great respect for

Colonel Mannering, and Mr Pleydell was an old friend. But now he seemed dry and embarrassed in his manner. "He would willingly," he said, "receive bail, notwithstanding that the offence had been directly perpetrated, committed, and done against young Hazelwood of Hazelwood; but the young man had given himself a fictitious description, and was altogether that sort of person, who should not be liberated, discharged, or set loose upon society; and therefore"——

"I hope, Sir Robert Hazelwood," said the Colonel, "you do not mean to doubt my word when I assure you that he served under me as cadet in India?"

"By no means or account whatsoever. But you call him a cadet; now he says, avers, and upholds, that he was a captain, or held a troop in your regiment."

"He was promoted since I gave up the command."

"But you must have heard of it?"

"No. I returned on account of family circumstances from India, and have not since been solicitous to hear particular news from the regiment; the name of Brown too is so common, that I might have seen his promotion in the gazette without noticing it. But a day or two will bring letters from his commanding officer."

"But I am told and informed, Mr Pleydell, that he does not mean to abide by this name of Brown, but is to set up a claim to the estate of Ellangowan, under the name of Bertram."

"Ay, who says that?" said the counsellor.

"Or, if he prefers such a claim, whoever says so, does that give a right to keep him in prison?"

"Hush, Colonel," said the lawyer, "I am sure you would not, any more than I, countenance him, if he prove an impostor—And, among friends, who informed you of this, Sir Robert?"

"Why a person, Mr Pleydell, who is peculiarly interested in investigating, sifting, and clearing out this business to the bottom—you will excuse my being more particular."

"O, certainly—well, and he says?"——

"That it is whispered about among tinkers, gypsies, and other idle persons, that there is such a plan as I mention to you, and that this young man, who is a bastard or natural son of the late Ellangowan, is pitched upon as the impostor from his strong family likeness."

"And was there such a natural son, Sir Robert?"

"O, certainly, to my own positive knowledge. Ellangowan had him placed as cabin-boy or powder-monkey on board an armed sloop or yacht belonging to the revenue, through the interest of the late Commissioner Bertram, a kinsman of Ellangowan."

"Well, Sir Robert," said the lawyer, taking the word out of the mouth of the impatient soldier—"you have told me news; I will investigate them, and if I find them true, certainly Colonel Mannering and I will not countenance this young man. In the meanwhile, as we are willing to make him forthcoming, to answer all complaints against him, I do assure you, you will act most illegally, and incur heavy responsibility, if you refuse our bail."

"Why, Mr Pleydell, as you must know best, and as you promise to give up this young man"——

"If he proves an impostor."

"Aye, certainly; under that condition I will receive your bail, though I must say, an obliging, well-disposed, and civil neighbour of mine, who was himself bred to the law, gave me a hint or caution this morning against doing so. It was from him I learned that this youth was liberated and abroad, or rather had broken prison.—But where shall we find one to draw the bail-bond?"

"Here," said the counsellor, applying himself to the bell, "send up my clerk, Mr Driver—it will not do my character harm if I dictate the needful myself." It was written accordingly and signed, and the Justice having subscribed a regular warrant for Bertram *alias* Brown's discharge, the visitors took their leave.

Each threw himself into his own corner of the post-chariot, and said nothing for some time. The Colonel first broke silence: "So you intend to give up this poor young fellow at the first brush?"

"Who, I?—I will not give up one hair of his head, though I should follow them to the court of last resort in his behalf—but what signified mooting points and shewing one's hand to that old ass? Much better he should report to his prompter, Glossin, that we are indifferent or lukewarm in the matter. Besides, I wished to have a peep at the enemies' game."

"Indeed!—Then I see there are stratagems in law as well as war. Well, and how do you like their line of battle?"

"Ingenious, but I think desperate—they are finessing too much, a common fault on such occasions."

During this discourse the carriage rolled rapidly towards Woodbourne without any thing occurring worthy of the reader's notice, excepting a meeting with young Hazelwood, to whom the Colonel told the extraordinary history of Bertram's re-appearance, which he heard with high delight, and then rode on before to pay Miss Bertram his compliments on an event so happy and so unexpected.

We return to the party at Woodbourne. After the departure of Mannering, the conversation related chiefly to the fortunes of the Ellangowan family, their domains, and their former power. "It was then under the towers of my fathers," said Bertram, "that I landed some days since, in circumstances much resembling those of a vagabond. Its mouldering turrets and darksome arches even then awakened thoughts of the deepest interest, and recollections which I was unable to decypher. I will now visit them again with other feelings, and I trust other hopes."

"O do not go there now," said his sister. "The house of our ancestors is at present the habitation of a wretch as insidious as dangerous, whose arts and villainy accomplished the ruin and broke the heart of our unhappy father."

"You increase my anxiety to confront this miscreant, even in the den he has constructed for himself—I think I have seen him."

"But you must consider," said Julia, "that you are now left under Lucy's guard and mine, and are responsible to us for all your motions —consider I have not been a lawyer's mistress twelve hours for nothing, and I assure you it would be madness to attempt to go to Ellangowan just now.—The utmost to which I can consent is, that we shall walk in a body to the head of the avenue, and from that perhaps we may indulge you with our company as far as a rising ground in the common, whence your eyes may be blessed with a distant prospect of these gloomy towers which struck so strongly your sympathetic imagination."

The party was speedily agreed upon; and the ladies, having taken their cloaks, followed the route proposed under the escort of Captain Bertram. It was a pleasant winter morning, and the cool breeze served only to freshen, not to chill, the fair walkers. A secret though unacknowledged bond of kindness combined the two ladies, and Bertram, now hearing the interesting accounts of his own family, now communicating his adventures in Europe and in India, repaid the pleasure which he received. Lucy felt proud of her new brother, as well from the bold and manly turn of his sentiments, as from the dangers he had encountered, and the spirit with which he had surmounted them. And Julia, while she pondered on her father's words, could not help entertaining no slight hopes, that the independent spirit which had seemed to her father presumption in the humble and plebeian Brown, would have the grace of courage, noble bearing, and high blood, in the far-descended heir of Ellangowan.

They reached at length the little eminence or knoll upon the highest part of the common, called Gibbie's-know—a spot repeatedly mentioned in this history, being on the skirts of the Ellangowan estate. It commanded a fair variety of hill and vale, bordered with natural woods, which at this season relieved the general colour of the landscape with a dark purple hue; and in other places the prospect was more formally intersected by lines of plantation, where the Scotch firs displayed their variety of dusky green. At the distance of two or three miles lay the bay of Ellangowan, its waves rippling under the influence of the western breeze. The towers of the ruined castle, seen high over every object in their neighbourhood, received a brighter colouring from the wintry sun. "There," said Lucy Bertram, pointing them out in the distance, "there is the seat of our ancestors. God knows, my dear brother, I do not covet in your behalf the extensive power which the lords of these ruins are said to have possessed so long, and sometimes used so ill. But, O that I might see you in possession of such reliques of their fortune as should give you an honourable independence, and enable you to stretch your hand out for the protection of the old and destitute dependants of the family, whom my father's death"——

"True, my dearest Lucy; and I trust, with the assistance of Heaven, which has so far guided us, and with that of these good friends, whom their own generous hearts have interested in my behalf, such a consummation of my hard adventures is now not unlikely.—But as a soldier, I must look with some interest upon that 'worm-eaten hold of ragged stone,' and if this fellow, who is now in possession, displaces a pebble of it"——

He was here interrupted by Dinmont, who came hastily after them up the road unseen till he was near the party:—"Captain, Captain! ye're wanted—Ye're wanted by her ye ken o'."

And immediately Meg Merrilies, as if emerging out of the earth, ascended from the hollow way, and stood before them.

"I sought ye at the house," she said, "and found but him, (pointing to Dinmont;) but ye are right, and I am wrang. It is *here* we should meet, on this very spot. Remember your promise, and follow me."

Chapter Fourteen

To hail the king in seemly sort
 The ladie was full fain;
But King Arthur, all sore amazed,
 No answer made again.
"What wight art thou," the ladie said,
 "That wilt not speak to me?
Sir, I may chance to ease thy pain,
 Though I be foul to see."

The Marriage of Sir Gawaine

THE FAIRY BRIDE of Sir Gawaine, while under the influence of the spell of her wicked step-mother, was more decrepid probably, and what is commonly called more ugly, than Meg Merrilies; but I doubt if she possessed that wild sublimity which an excited imagination communicated to features, marked and expressive in their own peculiar character, and to the gestures of a form, which, her sex considered, might be termed gigantic. Accordingly, the knights of the Round Table did not recoil with more terror from the apparition of the loathly lady placed between "an oak and a green holleye," than Lucy Bertram and Julia Mannering did from the appearance of this Galwegian sybil upon the common of Ellangowan.

"For God's sake," said Julia, pulling out her purse, "give that dreadful woman something, and bid her go away."

"I cannot," said Bertram, "I must not offend her."

"What keeps you here?" said Meg, exalting the harsh and rough tones of her hollow voice, "Why do you not follow?—Must your fate call you twice?—Do you remember your oath?—were it at kirk or market, wedding or burial,"—and she held high her skinny forefinger in a menacing attitude.

Bertram turned to his terrified companions. "Excuse me for a moment, I am engaged by a promise to follow this woman."

"Good heavens! engaged to a mad woman!" said Julia.

"Or to a gypsey, who has her band in the wood ready to murder you," said Lucy.

"That was not spoke like a bairn of Ellangowan," said Meg, frowning upon Miss Bertram. "It is the ill-doers are ill-dreaders."

"In short, I must go," said Bertram, "it is absolutely necessary—Wait for me five minutes on this spot."

"Five minutes?" said the gypsey, "five hours will not bring you here again."

"Do you hear that?" said Julia, "for heaven's sake do not go!"

"I must, I must—Mr Dinmont will protect you back to the house."

"No," said Meg, "he must gang wi' you, it is for that he is here. He maun take part wi' hand and heart, and weel his part it is, for redding him might hae cost you dear."

"Troth, Luckie, it's very true; and ere I turn back frae the Captain's side, I'll show that I hae na forgotten it."

"O, yes," exclaimed both the ladies at once, "let him go with you, if go you must, on this strange summons."

"Indeed I must, but you see I am safely guarded—Adieu for a short time, go home as fast as you can."

He pressed his sister's hand, and took a yet more affectionate farewell of Julia with his eyes. Almost stupified with surprise and fear, the young ladies watched with their eyes the course of Bertram, his companion, and their extraordinary guide. Her tall figure moved across the wintry heath with steps so swift, so long, and so steady, that she appeared rather to glide than to walk. Bertram and Dinmont, both tall men, apparently scarce equalled her in height, owing to her longer dress and high head-gear. She proceeded straight across the common, without turning aside to the winding path, by which passengers avoided the inequalities and little rills that traversed it in different directions. Thus the diminishing figures often disappeared from the eye, as they dived into such broken ground, and again ascended to sight when they were past the hollow. There was something frightful and unearthly, as it were, in the rapid and undeviating course which she pursued, undeterred by any of the impediments which usually incline a traveller from the direct path. Her way was as straight, and nearly as swift, as that of a bird through the air. At length they reached those thickets of natural wood which extended from the skirts of the common towards the glades and brook of Derncleugh, and were there lost to the view.

"This is very extraordinary," said Lucy after a pause, and turning round to her companion, "What can he have to do with that old hag?"

"It is very frightful," answered Julia, "and almost reminds me of the tales of sorceresses, witches, and evil genii, which I heard in India. They believe there in a fascination of the eye, by which those who possess it controul the will and dictate the motions of their victims. What can your brother have in common with that fearful woman, that he should leave us, and obviously against his will, to attend to her commands?"

"At least," said Lucy, "we may hold him safe from harm, for she would never have summoned that faithful creature Dinmont, of whose courage and steadiness Henry said so much, to attend upon an expedition where she projected evil to the person of his friend. And now let us retire to the house till the Colonel returns—perhaps Bertram may be back first; at any rate the Colonel will judge what is to be done."

Leaning then upon each other's arms, but yet occasionally stumbling between fear and the disorder of their nerves, they at length reached the head of the avenue, when they heard the tread of a horse behind. They started, for their ears were awake to every sound, and beheld to their great pleasure young Hazelwood. "The Colonel will be here immediately," he said, "I galloped on before to pay my respects to Miss Bertram, with the sincerest congratulations upon the joyful event which has taken place in her family. I long to be introduced to Captain Bertram, and to thank him for the well-deserved lesson he gave to my rashness and indiscretion."

"He has left us just now," said Lucy, "and in a manner that has frightened us very much."

Just at that moment the Colonel's carriage drove up, and upon observing the ladies, stopped, while Mannering and his learned counsel alighted and joined them. They instantly communicated the new cause of alarm.

"Meg Merrilies again!" said the Colonel; "She certainly is a most mysterious and unaccountable personage; but I think she must have something to impart to Bertram, to which she does not mean we should be privy."

"The devil take the bedlamite old woman," said the counsellor; "will she not let things take their course, *prout de lege*, but must she always be pulling her own oar in her own way?—Then I fear from the direction they took they are going upon the Ellangowan estate—that rascal Glossin has shewn us what ruffians he has in his disposal. I wish honest Liddesdale may be guard sufficient."

"If you please," said Hazelwood, "I would be most happy to ride in the direction which they have taken. I am so well known in the country, that I scarce think any outrage will be offered in my presence, and I will keep at such a cautious distance as not to appear to watch Meg, or interrupt any communication which she may make."

"Upon my word, to be a sprig, whom I remember with a whey face and a satchel not so very many years ago, I think young Hazelwood grows a fine fellow. I am more afraid of a new attempt at legal oppression than at open violence, and from that this young man's presence would deter both Glossin and his understrappers. Hie away then, my boy—peer out, peer out—you'll find them somewhere about Derncleugh, or very probably in Warroch-wood."

Hazelwood turned his horse. "Come back to us to dinner, Hazelwood," cried the Colonel. He bowed, spurred his horse, and galloped off.

We now return to Bertram and Dinmont, who continued to follow their mysterious guide through the woods and dingles, between the open common and the ruined hamlet of Derncleugh. As she led the way, she never looked back upon her followers, unless to chide them for loitering, though the sweat, in spite of the season, poured from their brows. At other times she spoke to herself in such broken expressions as these—"It is to rebuild the auld house—it is to lay the corner stone—and did I not warn him?—I tauld him I was born to do it, if my father's head had been the stepping-stone, let alone his.—I was doomed—still I kept my purpose in the cage and in the stock—I was banished—I kept it in an unco land;—I was scourged—I was branded—it lay deeper than scourge or red iron could reach—And now the hour is come."

"Captain," said Dinmont, in a half whisper, "I wish she binna uncanny—her words dinna seem to come in God's name, or like other folk's. Odd, they threep in our country that there are sic things."

"Don't be afraid, my friend."

"Fear'd! fient a haet care I, be she witch or devil; it's a' ane to Dandie Dinmont."

"Hald your peace, gudeman," said Meg, looking sternly over her shoulder; "is this a time or a place for you to speak, think ye?"

"But, my good friend," said Bertram, "I have no doubt in your good faith and kindness, which I have experienced; but you should have some confidence in me—I wish to know where you are leading me."

"There's but ae answer to that, Henry Bertram.—I swore my tongue should never tell, but I never said my finger should never shew. Go on and meet your fortune—or turn back and lose it—that's a' I hae to say."

"Go on then," answered Bertram, "I will ask no more questions."

They descended into the glen about the same place where Meg had formerly parted from Bertram. She paused an instant beneath the tall rock where he had witnessed the burial of a dead body, and stamped upon the ground, which, notwithstanding all the care that had been taken, shewed vestiges of having been recently moved. "Here rests ane," she said, "he'll maybe hae neighbours sune."

She then moved up the brook until she came to the ruined hamlet, where, pausing with a look of peculiar and softened interest before one of the gables which was still standing, she said in a tone less abrupt, though as solemn as before, "Do you see that blacked and broken end of a sheeling?—there my kettle boiled for forty years—there I bore twelve buirdly sons and daughters—where are they now? —where are the leaves that were on that auld ash-tree at Martinmas—the west wind has made it bare—and I'm stripped too.—Do you see that saugh tree?—it's but a blackened rotten stump now—I've sate under it mony a bonny simmer afternoon when it hung its gay garlands ower the poppling water.—I've sate there, and," elevating her voice, "I've held you on my knee, Henry Bertram, and sung ye sangs of the auld barons and their bloody wars—It will ne'er be green again, and Meg Merrilies will never sing blithe sangs mair. But ye'll no forget her, and ye'll gar big up the auld wa's for her sake?—and let somebody live there that's ower guid to fear them of another warld—For if ever the dead came back amang the living, I'll be seen in this glen mony a night after these crazed banes are in the mould."

The mixture of insanity and wild pathos with which she spoke these last words, with her right arm bare and extended, her left bent and shrouded beneath the dark red drapery of her mantle, might have been a study worthy of our Siddons herself. "And now," she said, resuming at once the short, stern, and hasty tone which was most ordinary to her—"let us to the wark—let us to the wark."

She then led the way to the promontory on which the Kaim of Derncleugh was situated, produced a large key from her pocket, and unlocked the door. The interior of this place was in better order than formerly. "I have made things decent," she said; "I may be streekit here or night.—There will be few, few at Meg's like wake, for mony of our folk will blame what I hae done, and am to do!"

She then pointed to a table, upon which was some cold meat, arranged with more attention to neatness than could have been expected from Meg's habits. "Eat," she said; "ye'll need it this night yet."

Bertram, in complaisance, eat a morsel or two; and Dinmont, whose appetite was unabated either by wonder or apprehension, made his usual figure as a trencher-man. She then offered each a single glass of spirits, which Bertram drank diluted, and his companion plain.

"Will ye taste naething yoursell, Luckie?" said Dinmont.

"I will not need it," replied their mysterious hostess. "And now," said she, "ye must hae arms—ye maunna gang on dry-handed—but use them not rashly—take captive, but save life—let the law hae its ain—he maun speak or he die."

"Who is to be taken?—who is to speak?" said Bertram in astonishment, receiving a pair of pistols which she offered him, and which, upon examining, he found were loaded and locked.

"The flints are gude," she said, "and the powder dry—I ken that wark weel."

Then without answering his questions, she armed Dinmont also with a large pistol, and desired them to chuse sticks for themselves out of a parcel of very suspicious-looking bludgeons, which she brought from a corner. They then left the hut together, and in doing so, Bertram took an opportunity to whisper Dinmont, "There's something inexplicable in all this—But we need not use these arms unless we see necessary and lawful occasion—take care to do as you see me do."

Dinmont gave a sagacious nod; and they continued to follow over wet and dry, through bog and fallow, the footsteps of their conductress. She guided them to the woods of Warroch by the same track which the late Ellangowan had used when riding to Derncleugh in quest of his child, on the memorable evening of Kennedy's murder.

When Meg Merrilies had attained these groves, through which the wintry sea-wind was now whistling hoarse and shrill, she seemed to pause a moment as if to recollect the way. "He maun go the precise track," she said, and continued to go forwards, but rather in a zigzag and involved course than by her former steady and direct line of motion. At length she guided them through the mazes of the wood to a little open glade of about a quarter of an acre, surrounded by trees and bushes, which made a wild and irregular boundary. Even in winter it was a sheltered and snugly sequestered spot; but when arrayed in the verdure of spring, the earth sending forth all its wild flowers, the shrubs spreading their waste of blossom around it, and the weeping birches which towered over the underwood, drooping their long and leafy fibres to intercept the sun, it must have seemed a place for a youthful poet to study his earliest sonnet, or a pair of lovers to exchange their first mutual confession of affection. Apparently it now awakened very different recollections. Bertram's brow, when he had looked around the spot, became gloomy and embarrassed. Meg, after muttering to herself, "This is the very bit," looked at him with a ghastly side-glance,—"D'ye mind it?"

"Yes!" answered Bertram, "imperfectly I do."

"Aye!" pursued his guide, "On this very spot the man fell from his horse—I was behind that bourtree bush at the very moment—sair, sair he strave, and sair he cried for mercy—but he was in the hands of them that never kenn'd the word!—Now will I shew you the further track—the last time ye travelled it was in these arms."

She led them accordingly by a long and winding passage almost overgrown with brushwood, until, without any very perceptible descent, they suddenly found themselves by the sea-side. Meg then walked very fast on between the surf and the rocks, until they came to a remarkable fragment of rock detached from the rest. "Here," she said in a low, and scarce audible whisper, "the corpse was found."

"And the cave," said Bertram in the same tone, "is close beside it—are you guiding us there?"

"Yes. Bend up both your hearts—follow me as I creep in—I have placed the fire-wood so as to screen you—Bide behind it for a gliff till I say, *The hour and the man are baith come;* then rin in on him, take his arms, and bind him till the blood burst frae his finger-nails."

"I will—if he is the man I suppose—Jansen!"

"Aye, Jansen, Hattaraick, and twenty mair names are his."

"Dinmont, you must stand by me now," said Bertram.

"Ye need na doubt that—but I wish I could mind a bit prayer or I creep after the witch into that hole that she's opening—It wad be a sair thing to leave the blessed sun, and the free air, and gang and be killed, like a tod that's run to earth, in a dungeon like that. But, as I said, deil hae me if I baulk you." This was uttered in the lowest tone of voice possible. The entrance was now open. Meg crept in upon her hands and knees, Bertram followed, and Dinmont, after giving a rueful glance toward the day-light, whose blessings he was abandoning, brought up the rear.

Chapter Fifteen

—Die, prophet! in thy speech;
For this, among the rest, was I ordained.
Henry VI. Part III

THE PROGRESS of the Borderer, who, as we have said, was the last of the party, was fearfully arrested by a hand, which caught hold of his leg as he dragged his long limbs after him in silence and perturbation through the low and narrow entrance of the subterranean passage. The steel heart of the bold yeoman had well nigh given way, and he suppressed with difficulty a shout, which, in the defenceless posture and situation which they then occupied, might have cost all their lives. He contented himself, however, with extricating his foot from the grasp of this unexpected follower. "Be still," said a voice behind him, releasing him; "I am a friend—Charles Hazelwood."

These words were uttered in a very low voice, but they produced sound enough to startle Meg Merrilies, who led the van, and who, having already gained the place where the cavern expanded, had risen upon her feet. She began, as if to confound any listening ear, to growl, to mutter, and to sing aloud, and at the same time to make a bustle among some brushwood which was now heaped in the cave.

"Here—beldam—Deyvil's-kind," growled the harsh voice of Dirk Hattaraick from the inside of his den, "what makest thou there?"

"Laying the roughies to keep the cauld wind frae you, ye desperate do-nae-good—Ye're e'en ower weel off, and wots na; it will be otherwise soon."

"Have ye brought me the brandy, and any news of my people?"

"There's the bottle for ye. Your people—dispersed—broken—gone—or cut to ribbands by the red-coats."

"Der Deyvil!—this coast is fatal to me."

"Ye may hae mair reason to say sae."

While this dialogue went forward, Bertram and Dinmont had both gained the interior of the cave, and assumed an erect posture. The only light which illuminated its rugged and sable precincts was a quantity of wood burned to charcoal in an iron grate, such as they use in spearing salmon by night. On these red embers Hattaraick from time to time threw a handful of twigs or splintered wood; but these, even when they blazed up, afforded a light much disproportioned to the extent of the cavern; and, as its principal inhabitant lay upon the side of the grate most remote from the entrance, it was not easy for him to discover distinctly objects which lay in that direction. The intruders, therefore, whose number was now augmented unexpectedly to three, stood behind the loosely piled brushwood with little risk of discovery. Dinmont had the sense to keep back Hazelwood with one hand till he whispered to Bertram, "A friend—young Hazelwood."

It was no time for following up the introduction, and they all stood as still as the rocks around them, obscured behind the pile of brushwood, which had been probably placed there to break the cold wind from the sea, without totally intercepting the supply of air. The branches were laid so loosely above each other, that, looking through them towards the light of the fire-grate, they could easily discern what passed in its vicinity, although a much stronger degree of illumination than it afforded, would not have enabled the personages placed near the bottom of the cave to have descried them in the position which they occupied.

The scene, independent of the peculiar moral interest and personal danger which attended it, had, from the effect of the light and shade upon the uncommon objects which it exhibited, an appearance emphatically dismal. The light in the fire-grate was the dark-red glare of charcoal in a state of ignition, relieved from time to time by a transient flame of a more vivid or a duskier light, as the fuel with which Dirk Hattaraick fed his fire was better or worse adapted for his purpose. Now a dark cloud of stifling smoke rose up to the roof of the cavern, and then lighted into a reluctant and sullen blaze, which climbed wavering up the pillar of smoke, and was suddenly rendered brighter and more lively by some drier fuel, or perhaps some splintered fir-timber, which at once converted the smoke into flame. By such fitful irradiation, they could see, more or less distinctly, the form of Hattaraick, whose savage and rugged cast of features, now rendered yet more ferocious by the circumstances of his situation and the deep gloom of his mind, assorted well with the rugged and broken vault, which rose in a rude arch over and around him. The form of Meg Merrilies, which stalked about him, sometimes in the light, sometimes partially obscured in the smoke or darkness, contrasted strongly with the sitting figure of Hattaraick as he bent over the flame, and from his stationary posture was constantly visible to the spectator, while that of the female flitted around, appearing or disappearing like a spectre.

Bertram felt his blood boil at the sight of Hattaraick. He remembered him well under the name of Jansen, which the smuggler had adopted after the death of Kennedy, and he remembered, also, that this Jansen, and his mate Brown, had been the brutal tyrants of his infancy. Bertram knew farther, from piecing his own imperfect recollections with the narratives of Mannering and Pleydell, that this man was the prime agent in the act of violence which first tore him from his family and country, and had exposed him to so many distresses and dangers. A thousand exasperating reflections rose within his bosom; and he could hardly refrain from rushing upon Hattaraick and blowing his brains out. At the same time this would have been no safe adventure. The flame, as it arose and fell, while it displayed the strong, muscular, and broad-chested frame of the ruffian, glanced also upon two brace of pistols in his belt, and upon the hilt of his cutlass: it was not to be doubted that his desperation was commensurate with his personal strength and means of resistance. Both, indeed, were inadequate to encounter the combined power of two such men as Bertram himself and his friend Dinmont, without reckoning their unexpected assistant Hazelwood, who was unarmed, and of a slighter make; but Bertram felt there would be neither sense nor valour in anticipating the hangman's office, and he considered the importance of making Hattaraick prisoner alive. He therefore repressed his indignation, and awaited what should pass between the ruffian and his gypsey guide.

"And how are ye now?" said the harsh and discordant tone of his attendant: "Said I not it would come upon you—aye, and in this very cave, where ye harboured after the deed?"

"Wetter and sturm, ye hag! keep your deyvil's mattins till they're wanted. Have ye seen Glossin?"

"No: ye've missed your blow, ye blood-spiller! and ye have nothing to expect from the tempter."

"Hagel! if I had him but by the throat!—and what am I to do then?"

"Do?" answered the gypsey, "Die like a man, or be hanged like a dog!"

"Hanged, ye hag of Satan!—the hemp's not sown that shall hang me."

"It's sown, and it's grown, and it's heckled, and it's twisted. Did I not tell ye when ye wad take away the boy Harry Bertram, in spite of my prayers,—did I not say he wad come back when he had dree'd his weird in foreign land till his twenty-first year?—Did I not say the auld fire would burn to a spark, but wad kindle again?"

"Well, mother, you did say so; and, donner and blitzen! I believe you spoke the truth—that younker of Ellangowan has been a rock ahead to me all my life! and now, with Glossin's cursed contrivance, my crew have been cut off, my boats destroyed, and I dare say the lugger's taken—there were not men enough to work her, far less to fight—a dredge-boat might have taken her. And what will the owners say?—

Hagel and sturm! I shall never dare go back again to Flushing."

"You'll never need."

"What are ye doing there, and what makes ye say that?"

During this dialogue, Meg was heaping some flax loosely together. Before answer to his question, she dropped a fire-brand upon the flax, which apparently had been previously steeped in some spirituous liquor, for it instantly caught fire, and rose in a vivid pyramid of the most brilliant light up to the very top of the vault. As it ascended Meg answered the ruffian's question in a firm and steady voice:—"*Because the Hour's come, and the Man.*"

At the appointed signal, Bertram and Dinmont sprung over the brushwood, and rushed upon Hattaraick. Hazelwood, unacquainted with their plan of assault, was an instant behind them. The ruffian, who instantly saw he was betrayed, turned his first vengeance on Meg Merrilies, at whom he discharged a pistol. She fell, with a piercing and dreadful cry, between the shriek of pain and the sound of laughter, when at its highest and most suffocating height. "I kenn'd it would be this way," she said.

Bertram, in his haste, slipped his foot upon the uneven rock which floored the cave; a fortunate stumble, for Hattaraick's second bullet whistled over him with so cool and steady an aim, that had he been standing upright, it must have lodged in his brain. Ere Hattaraick could draw another pistol, Dinmont closed with him, and endeavoured by main force to pinion down his arms. Such, however, was the wretch's personal strength, joined to the efforts of his despair, that, in spite of the gigantic force with which the Borderer grappled him, he dragged Dinmont through the blazing flax, and had well nigh succeeded in drawing a third pistol, which might have proved fatal to the honest farmer, had not Bertram, as well as Hazelwood, come to his assistance, when, by main force, and no ordinary exertion of it, they threw him on the ground, disarmed him, and bound him. This scuffle, though it takes up some time in the narrative, passed in less than a single minute. When he was fairly mastered, after one or two desperate and almost convulsionary struggles, Hattaraick lay perfectly still and silent. "He's gaun to die game ony how," said Dinmont; "weel, I like him na the waur o' that."

This observation honest Dandie made while he was shaking the blazing flax from his rough coat and his shaggy black hair, some of which had been singed in the scuffle. "He is quiet now," said Bertram; "stay by him, and do not permit him to stir till I see whether the poor woman be alive or dead." With Hazelwood's assistance he raised Meg Merrilies.

"I kenn'd it would be thus; and it's e'en thus that it should be."

The ball had penetrated in the breast below the throat. It did not bleed much externally, but Bertram, accustomed to see gun-shot wounds, thought it the more alarming. "Good God! what shall we do for this poor woman?" said he to Hazelwood, the circumstances superseding the necessity of previous explanation or introduction to each other.

"My horse stands tied above in the wood," said Hazelwood, "I have been watching you this two hours—I will ride off for some assistants that may be trusted. Meanwhile you had better defend the mouth of the cavern against every one until I return." He hastened away. Bertram, after binding Meg Merrilies' wound as well as he could, took station near the mouth of the cave with a cocked pistol in his hand; Dinmont continued to watch Hattaraick. There was a dead silence in the cavern, only interrupted by the low and suppressed moaning of the wounded female, and by the hard breathing of the prisoner.

Chapter Sixteen

For, though seduced and led astray,
Thou'st travelled far and wandered long,
Thy God hath seen thee all the way,
And all the turns that led thee wrong.
The Hall of Justice

AFTER the space of about three quarters of an hour, which the uncertainty and danger of their situation made seem almost thrice as long, the voice of young Hazelwood was heard without. "Here I am, with a sufficient party."

"Come in then," answered Bertram, not a little pleased to find his guard relieved. Hazelwood then entered, followed by two or three countrymen, one of whom acted as a peace-officer. They lifted Hattaraick up, and carried him in their arms as far as the entrance of the vault was high enough to permit them; then laid him on his back, and dragged him along as well as they could, for no persuasion would induce him to assist the transportation by any exertions of his own. He lay as silent and inactive in their hands as a dead corpse, in no way either opposing or aiding their operations. When he was dragged into day-light, and placed erect upon his feet among three or four assistants, who had remained without the cave, he seemed stupified and dazzled by the sudden change from the darkness of his cavern. While others were superintending the removal of Meg Merrilies, those who remained with Hattaraick attempted to make him sit down upon a fragment of rock which lay close upon the high-water-mark. A strong shuddering convulsed his iron frame for an instant, as he resisted their purpose. "Not there—Hagel!—you would not make me sit *there?*"

These were the only words he spoke; but their import, and the deep tone of horror in which they were uttered, served to show what was passing in his mind.

When Meg Merrilies had also been removed from the cavern, with all the care for her safety that circumstances admitted, they consulted where she should be carried. Hazelwood had sent for a surgeon, and proposed that she should be lifted in the mean time to the nearest cottage. But the patient exclaimed with great earnestness, "Na—na—na! To the Kaim o' Derncleugh—the Kaim o' Derncleugh—the spirit will not free itself o' the flesh but there."

"You must indulge her, I believe," said Bertram; "her troubled imagination will otherwise aggravate the fever of the wound."

They bore her accordingly to the vault. Upon the way her mind seemed to run more upon the scene which had just passed, than on her own approaching death.—"There were three of them set upon him—I brought the twasome—but wha was the third?—It would be *himsell* returned to work his ain vengeance."

It was evident that the unexpected appearance of Hazelwood, whose person the outrage of Hattaraick left her no time to recognize, had produced a strong effect on her imagination. She often recurred to it. Hazelwood accounted for it to Bertram, by saying, that he had kept them in view for some time by the direction of Mannering; that, observing them disappear into the cave, he had crept after them, meaning to announce himself and his errand, when his hand in the darkness encountering the leg of Dinmont, had nearly produced a catastrophe, which indeed nothing but the presence of mind and fortitude of the bold yeoman could have averted.

When the gypsey arrived at the hut, she produced the key; and when they entered, and were about to deposit her upon the bed, she said, in an anxious tone, "Na! na!—not that way—not that way—the head to the east;" and appeared gratified when they reversed her posture accordingly.

"Is there no clergyman near," said Bertram, "to assist this unhappy woman's devotions?"

A gentleman, the minister of the parish, who had been Charles Hazelwood's tutor, had, with others, caught the alarm, that the murderer of Kennedy was taken on the spot where the deed had been done so many years before, and that a woman was mortally wounded. From curiosity, or rather from the feeling that his duty called him to scenes of distress, this gentleman had come to the Kaim of Derncleugh, and now presented himself. The surgeon arrived at the same time, and was about to probe the wound. But Meg resisted the assistance of either. "It's nae what man can do that will heal me or save me. —Let me speak what I have to say, and then ye may wark your will. I'se be nae hindrance.—But where's Henry Bertram?"—The assistants, to whom this name had been long a stranger, gazed upon each other. —"Yes!" she said in a stronger and harsher tone, "I said *Henry Bertram of Ellangowan.* Stand from the light and let me look upon him."

All eyes were turned towards Bertram, who approached the wretched couch. The wounded woman took hold of his hand. "Look at him," she said, "all that ever saw his father or his grandfather, and bear witness if he is not their living image."—A murmur went through the crowd—the resemblance was too striking to be denied. "And now hear me—and let that man," pointing to Hattaraick, who was seated with his keepers on a sea-chest at some distance—"let him deny what I say if he can. That is Henry Bertram, son to Godfrey Bertram, umquhile of Ellangowan; that is the child that Dirk Hattaraick carried off from Warroch woods the day that he murdered the gauger. I was there like a wandering spirit—for I longed to see that wood or we left the country. I saved the bairn's life, and sair, sair I prigged and prayed they would leave him wi' me—But they bore him away, and he's been lang ower the sea, and now he's come for his ain, and what should withstand him?—I swore to keep the secret till he was ane-and-twenty—I kenn'd he behoved to dree his weird till that day came—I keepit that oath—But I swore another to mysell, that if I lived to see the day o' his return, I would set him in his father's seat if every step was on a dead man. I have keepit that oath. I will be ae step mysell—He (pointing to Hattaraick) will soon be another, and there will be ane mair yet."

The clergyman now interposing, remarked it was a pity this deposition was not regularly taken and written down, and the surgeon urged the necessity of examining the wound, previously to exhausting her by questions. When she saw them removing Hattaraick, in order to clear the room and leave the surgeon to his operations, she called out aloud, raising herself at the same time upon the couch, "Dirk Hattaraick, you and I will never meet again until we are before the judgment seat—Will ye own to what I have said?" He turned his hardened brow upon her, with a look of dumb and inflexible defiance. "Dirk Hattaraick, dare ye deny, with my blood upon your hands, one word of what my dying breath is uttering?"—He looked at her with the same expression of hardihood and dogged stubbornness, and moved his lips, but uttered no sound. "Then fareweel!" she said, "and God forgive you! Your hand has sealed my evidence.—When I was in life, I was the mad randy gypsey, that had been scourged, and banished, and branded, that had begged from door to door, and been hounded like a stray tyke from parish to parish—wha would hae minded her word?—But now I am a dying woman, and my words will not fall to the ground, any more than the earth will cover my blood!"

She here paused, and all left the hut except the surgeon and two or three women. After a very short examination, he shook his head, and resigned his post by the dying woman's side to the clergyman.

A chaise returning empty to Kippletringan had been stopped on the high road by a constable, who foresaw it would be necessary to convey Hattaraick to jail. The driver, understanding what was going on at Derncleugh, left his horses to the care of a blackguard boy, confiding, it is to be supposed, rather in their years and discretion than in his, and set off full speed to see, as he expressed himself, "whaten a sort o' fun was ganging on." He arrived just as the group of tenants and peasants, whose numbers increased every moment, satiated with gazing upon the rugged features of Hattaraick, had turned their attention towards Bertram. Almost all of them, especially the aged men who had seen old Ellangowan in his better days, felt and acknowledged the justice of Meg Merrilies' appeal. But the Scotch are a cautious people; they remembered there was another in possession of the estate, and they as yet only expressed their feelings in low whispers to each other. Our friend Jock Jabos, the postillion, forced his way into the middle of the circle; but no sooner cast his eyes upon Bertram, than he started back in amazement with a solemn exclamation, "As sure as there's breath in man, it's auld Ellangowan arisen from the dead!"

This public declaration of an unprejudiced witness, was just the spark wanted to give fire to the popular feeling, which burst forth in three distinct shouts:—"Bertram for ever!"—"Long life to the heir of Ellangowan!"—"God send him his ain, and to live amang us as his forebears did of yore!"

"I hae been seventy years on the land," said one.

"I and mine hae been seventy and seventy to that," said another; "I have a right to ken the glance of a Bertram."

"I and mine hae been three hundred years here," said another old man, "and I sall sell my last cow, but I'll see the young laird in his right."

The women, ever delighted with the marvellous, and not least so when a handsome young man is the subject of the tale, added their shrill acclamations to the general all-hail. "Blessings on him—he's the very picture o' his father!—the Bertrams were aye the wale o' the country side!"

"Eh! that his puir mother, that died in grief and doubt about him, had but lived to see this day!" exclaimed some voices.

"But we'll help him to his ain, kimmers," cried others; "and ere that

Glossin sall keep the Place of Ellangowan, we'll howk him out o't wi' our nails!"

Others crowded around Dinmont, who was nothing loth to tell what he knew of his friend, and to boast the honour which he had in contributing to the discovery. As he was known to several persons present, his testimony afforded an additional motive to the general enthusiasm. In short, it was one of those moments of feeling, when the frost of the Scottish melts like a snow-wreath, and the dissolving torrent carries dam and dyke before it.

The sudden shouts interrupted the devotions of the clergyman; and Meg, who was in one of those dozing fits of stupefaction that precede the close of existence, suddenly started—"Dinna ye hear?—dinna ye hear?—he's owned!—he's owned!—I lived but for this.—I am a sinful woman—But if my curse brought it down, my blessing has ta'en it off! And now I wad hae liked to hae said mair. But it winna be.—Stay"—she continued, stretching her head towards the gleam of light that shot through the narrow slit which served for a window, "Is he not there?—stand out o' the light, and let me look upon him ance mair. But the darkness is in my ain een," she added, sinking back, after an earnest gaze upon vacuity—"it's a' ended now!

Pass breath,
Come death!"

And, sinking back upon her couch of straw, she expired without a groan. The clergyman and the surgeon carefully noted down all that she had said, now deeply regretting they had not examined her more minutely, but both remaining morally convinced of the truth of her disclosure.

Hazelwood was the first to compliment Bertram upon the near prospect of his being restored to his name and rank in society. The people around, who now learned from Jabos that Bertram was the person who had wounded him, were struck with his generosity, and added his name to Bertram's in their exulting acclamations.

Some, however, demanded of the postillion how he had not recognised Bertram when he saw him some time before at Kippletringan? to which he gave the very natural answer,—"Hout, what was I thinking about Ellangowan than?—It was the cry that was rising e'en now that the young laird was found, that put me on finding out the likeness—There was nae missing ance ane was set to look for't."

The obduracy of Hattaraick during the latter part of this scene was in some slight degree shaken. He was observed to twinkle with his eye-lids—to attempt to raise his bound hands for the purpose of pulling his hat over his brow—to look angrily and impatiently to the road, as if anxious for the vehicle which was to remove him from the spot. At length Mr Hazelwood, apprehensive that the popular ferment might take a direction towards him, directed he should be taken to the post-chaise, and so removed to the town of Kippletringan to be at Mr Mac-Morlan's disposal; at the same time he sent an express to warn that gentleman of what had happened. "And now," he said to Bertram, "I would be happy if you would accompany me to Hazelwood-house; but as that might not be so agreeable just now as I trust it will be in a day or two, you must allow me to return with you to Woodbourne. But you are on foot"—"O if the young laird would take my horse!"—"Or mine"—"Or mine"—said half a dozen voices—"Or mine; he can trot ten mile an hour without whip or spur, and he's the young laird's frae this moment, if he likes to take him for a herezeld, as they ca'd it lang syne."—Bertram readily accepted the horse as a loan, and poured forth his thanks to the assembled crowd for their good wishes, which they repaid with shouts and vows of attachment.

While the happy owner of the galloway was directing one lad to "gae down for the new saddle;" another "just to rin the beast ower wi' a dry wisp o' strae;" a third "to hie down and borrow Dan Dunkieson's plated stirrups," and expressing to his regret "there was na time to gie the naig a feed, that the young laird might ken his mettle," Bertram, taking the clergyman by the arm, walked into the vault, and shut the door immediately after them. He gazed in silence for some minutes upon the body of Meg Merrilies, as it lay before him, with the features sharpened by death, yet still retaining the stern and energetic character, which had maintained in life her superiority as the wild chieftainess of the lawless people amongst whom she was born. The young soldier dried the tears which involuntarily rose upon viewing this wreck, which might be said to have died a victim to her fidelity to his family. He then took the clergyman's hand, and asked solemnly—I hope he will not suffer for his simplicity in the opinion of my readers—if she appeared able to give that attention to the devotions which befitted a departing person?

"My dear sir," said the good minister, "I trust this poor woman had remaining sense to feel and join in the import of my prayers. But let us humbly hope we are judged of by our opportunities of religious and moral instruction. In some degree she might be considered as an uninstructed heathen, even in the bosom of a Christian country; and let us remember that the errors and vices of an ignorant life were balanced by instances of disinterested attachment, amounting almost to heroism. To HIM who can alone weigh our crimes and errors against our efforts towards virtue, we consign her with fear, but not without hope."

"May I request," said Bertram, "that you see every decent solemnity attended to in behalf of this poor woman? I have some property belonging to her in my hand—at all events I will be answerable for the expence—you will hear of me at Woodbourne."

Dinmont, who had been furnished with a horse by one of his acquaintances, now loudly called all was ready for their return; and Bertram and Hazelwood, after a strict exhortation to the crowd, which was now increased to several hundreds, to preserve good order in their rejoicing, as the least ungoverned zeal might be turned to the disadvantage of the young Laird, as they termed him, took their leaves amid the shouts of the multitude.

As they rode past the ruined cottages at Derncleugh, Dinmont said, "I am sure when ye come to your ain, Captain, ye'll no forget to bigg a bit cot-house there? Deil be in me but I wad do't mysell, an it were na in better hands.—I wadna like to live in't though, after what she said—Odd, I wad pit in auld Elspeth the bedral's widow—the like o' them's used wi' graves and ghaists and thae things."

A short but brisk ride brought them to Woodbourne. The news of their exploit had already flown far and wide, and the whole inhabitants met them on the lawn with shouts of congratulation. "That you have seen me alive," said Bertram to Lucy, who first ran up to him, though Julia's eyes even anticipated hers, "you must thank these kind friends."

With a blush expressing at once pleasure, gratitude, and bashfulness, Lucy curtsied to Hazelwood, but to Dinmont she frankly extended her hand. The honest farmer, in the extravagance of his joy, carried his freedom farther than the hint warranted, for he imprinted his thanks on the lady's lips, and then was instantly shocked at the rudeness of his conduct. "Lord sake, Madam, I ask your pardon," he said; "I forgot but ye had been a bairn o' my ain—the Captain's sae hamely, he gars ane forget himsell."

Old Pleydell now advanced: "Nay, if fees like these are going," he said——

"Stop, stop, Mr Pleydell," said Julia, "you had your fees beforehand—remember last night."

"Why, I do confess a retainer," said the barrister; "but if I don't deserve double fees from both Lucy and you when I conclude my examination of Dirk Hattaraick to-morrow—Gad I will so supple him!—You shall see, Colonel, and you, my saucy misses, though you shall not see, you shall hear."

"Aye, that's if we chuse to listen, Counsellor."

"And you think it's two to one you won't chuse that?—But you have curiosity that teaches you the use of your ears now and then."

"I declare, Counsellor, three such saucy bachelors as you would teach us the use of our fingers now and then."

"Reserve them for the harpsichord, my love. Better for all parties."

While this idle chat ran on, Colonel Mannering introduced to Bertram a plain good-looking man, in a grey coat and waistcoat, buckskin breeches, and boots. "This, my dear sir, is Mr Mac-Morlan."

"To whom," said Bertram, embracing him cordially, "my sister was indebted for a home, when deserted by all her natural friends and relations."

The Dominie then pressed forward, grinned, chuckled, made a diabolical sound in attempting to whistle, and finally, unable to stifle his emotions, ran away to empty the fullness of his heart at his eyes.

We will not attempt to describe the expansion of heart and glee of that happy evening.

Chapter Seventeen

——How like a hateful ape,
Detected grinning 'midst his pilfer'd hoard,
A cunning man appears, whose secret frauds
Are opened to the day—

Count Basil

THERE was a great movement at Woodbourne early on the following morning, to attend the examination at Kippletringan. Mr Pleydell, from the investigation which he had formerly bestowed on the dark affair of Kennedy's death, as well as from the general deference due to his professional abilities, was requested by Mr Mac-Morlan, Sir Robert Hazelwood, and another justice of peace who attended, to take the situation of chairman, and the lead in the examination. Colonel Mannering was invited to sit down with them. The examination being previous to trial, was private in other respects. The Counsellor resumed and re-interrogated former evidence. He then examined the clergyman and surgeon respecting the dying declaration of Meg Merrilies. They stated, that she distinctly, positively, and repeatedly, declared herself an eye-witness of Kennedy's death by the hands of Hattaraick, and two or three of his crew; that her presence was accidental; that she believed their resentment at meeting him, when they were in the act of losing their vessel, through means of his information, led to the commission of the crime; that she said there was one witness of the murder, but who refused to participate in it, still alive,—her nephew, Gabriel Faa; and that she had hinted at another person, who was an accessory after, not before, the fact; but her strength there failed her. They did not forget to mention her declaration, that she had saved the child, and that he was torn from her by the smugglers, for the purpose of carrying him to Holland.—All these particulars were carefully reduced to writing.

Dirk Hattaraick was then brought in, heavily ironed; for he had been strictly secured and guarded, owing to his former escape. He was asked his name; he made no answer:—His profession; he was silent:—Several other questions were put; to none of which he returned any reply. Pleydell wiped the glass of his spectacles, and considered the prisoner very attentively. "A very truculent-looking fellow," he whispered to Mannering; "but, as Dogberry says, I'll go cunningly to work with him.—Here, call in Soles—Soles the shoemaker.—Soles, do you remember measuring some foot-steps imprinted in the mud at the Wood of Warroch, upon —— November, 17—?" Soles remembered the circumstances perfectly. "Look at that paper—is that your note of the measurement?"—Soles verified the memorandum—"Now there stands a pair of shoes on that table—measure them, and see if they correspond with any of the marks you have noted there." The shoemaker obeyed, and declared, "that they answered exactly to the largest of the foot-prints."

"We will prove," said the Counsellor, aside to Mannering, "that these shoes, which were found in the ruins at Derncleugh, belonged to Brown, the fellow whom you shot on the lawn at Woodbourne.—Now, Soles, measure that prisoner's feet very accurately."

Mannering observed Hattaraick strictly, and could notice a visible tremor. "Do these measurements correspond with any of the foot prints?"

The man looked at the note, then at his foot-rule and measure—then verified his former measurement by a second. "They correspond," he said, "within a hair-breadth, to a foot-mark broader and shorter than the former."

Hattaraick's genius here deserted him—"Der deyvil," he broke out, "how could there be a foot-mark on the ground, when it was a frost as hard as the heart of a Memel log?"

"In the evening, I grant you, Captain Hattaraick, but not in the forenoon—will you favour me with information where you were upon the day you remember so exactly?"

Hattaraick saw his blunder, and again screwed up his hard features for obstinate silence—"Put down his observation, however," said Pleydell to the clerk.

At this moment the door opened, and, much to the surprise of most present, Mr Gilbert Glossin made his appearance. That worthy gentleman had, by dint of worming and eves-dropping, ascertained that he was not named in Meg Merrilies' dying declaration, a circumstance owing certainly not to her favourable disposition towards him, but to the delay of taking her regular examination, and to the rapid approach of death. He therefore supposed himself safe from all evidence but such as might arise from Hattaraick's confession; to prevent which he resolved to push a bold face, and join his brethren of the bench during his examination. "I shall be able," he thought, "to make the rascal sensible his safety lies in keeping his own council and mine; and my presence, besides, will be a proof of confidence and innocence. If I must lose the estate I must—but I trust better things."

He entered with a profound salutation to Sir Robert Hazelwood. Sir Robert, who had rather begun to suspect that his plebeian neighbour had made a cat's paw of him, inclined his head stiffly, took snuff, and looked another way—"Mr Corsand, your most humble servant."

"Your humble servant, Mr Glossin," answered Mr Corsand drily, composing his countenance *regis ad exemplar*, that is to say, after the fashion of the Baronet. "Mac-Morlan, my worthy friend—how d'ye do—always upon your duty?"

"Umph," said honest Mac-Morlan, with little respect either to the compliment or salutation. "Colonel Mannering (a low bow slightly returned) and Mr Pleydell, (another low bow) I dared not have hoped for the benefit of your assistance to poor country gentlemen at this period of the session."

Pleydell took snuff, and eyed him with a glance equally shrewd and sarcastic—"I'll teach him," said he, aside to Mac-Morlan, "the value of the old admonition, *Ne accesseris in consilium antequam voceris.*"

"But perhaps I intrude, gentlemen?—is this an open meeting?"

"For my part," said Mr Pleydell, "far from considering your attendance as intrusion, Mr Glossin, I was never so pleased in my life to meet with you, especially as I think we should have had occasion to request the favour of your company in the course of the day."

"Well then, gentlemen," said Glossin, drawing his chair to the table, and beginning to bustle about among the papers, "where are we?—how far have we got?—where are the declarations?"

"Clerk—give me all these papers," said Mr Pleydell; "I have an odd way of arranging my documents, Mr Glossin, another person touching them puts me out—but I shall have occasion for your assistance by and bye."

Glossin, thus reduced to inactivity, stole one glance at Dirk Hattaraick, but could read nothing in his dark scowl save malignity and hatred to all around. "But, gentlemen," said Glossin, "is it quite right to keep this poor man so heavily ironed, when he is taken up merely for examination?"

This was hoisting a kind of friendly signal to the prisoner. "He has escaped once before," said Mac-Morlan drily, and Glossin was silenced.

Bertram was now introduced, and, to Glossin's confusion, was greeted in the most friendly manner even by Sir Robert Hazelwood himself. He told his recollections of infancy with that candour and caution of expression which afforded the best warrant for his good faith. "This seems to be rather a civil than a criminal question," said Glossin, rising; "and as you cannot be ignorant, gentlemen, of the effect which this young person's pretended parentage may have on my fortune, I would rather beg leave to retire."

"No, my good sir," said Mr Pleydell, "we can by no means spare you —but why do you call this young man's claims pretended?—I don't mean to fish for your defences against them, if you have any, but"——

"Mr Pleydell, I think I can explain the matter at once.—This young fellow, whom I take to be a natural son of the late Ellangowan, has gone about this country for some weeks under different names, caballing with a wretched old mad woman, who, I understand, was shot in a late scuffle, and with other tinkers, gypsies, and persons of that description, stirring up the tenants against their landlords, which, as Sir Robert Hazelwood of Hazelwood knows"——

"Not to interrupt you, Mr Glossin," said Pleydell, "I ask who you say this young man is?"

"Why, I say, and I believe this gentleman (looking to Hattaraick) knows, that he is a natural son of the late Ellangowan, by a girl called Janet Lightoheel, who was afterwards married to Hewit the shipwright, that lived on the shore of Annan. His name is Godfrey Bertram Hewit, by which he was entered on board the Royal Caroline excise yacht."

"Aye?" said Pleydell, "that is a very likely story!—but, not to pause upon some difference of eye, complexion, and so forth—be pleased to step forward, sir."——A good-looking young seaman came forward. ——"Here's the real Simon Pure—here's Godfrey Bertram Hewit, arrived last night from Antigua *via* Liverpool, mate of a West Indian, and in a fair way of doing well in the world, although he came somewhat irregularly into it."

Some conversation past between the other justices and this young man, while Pleydell lifted from among the papers on the table Hattaraick's old pocket-book. A peculiar glance of the smuggler's eye induced the shrewd lawyer to think there was something here of interest. He therefore continued the examination of the papers, laying the book on the table, but instantly perceived that the prisoner's interest in the research had cooled. "It must be in the book still, whatever it is," thought Pleydell; and again applied himself to the pocket-book, until he discovered, on a narrow scrutiny, a slit between the pasteboard and leather, out of which he drew three small slips of paper. Pleydell now turning to Glossin, requested the favour that he would tell them if he had assisted at the search for the body of Kennedy, and the child of his patron, upon the day when they disappeared.

"I did not—that is—I did," answered the conscience-struck Glossin.

"It is remarkable though, that, connected as you then were with the Ellangowan family, I don't recollect your being examined, or even appearing before me, while that investigation was proceeding?"

"I was called to London on most important business the morning after that sad affair."

"Clerk," said Pleydell, "minute down that reply.—I presume the business, Mr Glossin, was to negociate these three bills drawn by you on Messrs Vanbeest and Verbruggen, and accepted by one Dirk Hattaraick in their name on the very day of the murder." Glossin's countenance fell. "This piece of real evidence makes good the account given of your conduct upon this occasion by a man called Gabriel Faa, whom we have now in custody, and who witnessed the whole transaction between you and that worthy prisoner—Have you any explanation to give?"

"Mr Pleydell," said Glossin with great composure, "I presume, if you were my counsel, you would not advise me to answer upon the spur of the moment to a charge which the basest of mankind seem ready to establish by perjury."

"My advice would be regulated by my opinion of your innocence or guilt. In your case I believe you take the wisest course; but you are aware you must stand committed?"

"What, sir? Upon a charge of murder?"

"No; only as art and part of kidnapping the child."

"That is a bailable offence."

"Pardon me," said Pleydell, "it is *plagium*, and *plagium* is felony."

"Forgive me, Mr Pleydell; there is only one case upon record, Torrence and Waldie. They were, you remember, resurrection-women, who had promised to procure a child's body for some young surgeons. Being upon honour to their employers, rather than disappoint the evening lecture of the students, they stole a live child, murdered it, and sold the body for three shillings and sixpence. They were hanged, but for the murder, not the *plagium*. Your civil law has carried you a little too far."

"Well, sir, but in the meantime we must commit you to the county jail, in case this young man repeats the same story.—Officers, remove Mr Glossin and Hattaraick, and guard them in different apartments."

Gabriel, the gypsey, was then introduced, and gave a distinct account of his deserting from Captain Pritchard's vessel and joining the smugglers in the action, and how Dirk Hattaraick set fire to his ship when he found her disabled, and under cover of the smoke escaped with his crew, and as much goods as they could save, into the cavern, where they proposed to lie till night-fall. Hattaraick himself, his mate Vanbeest Brown, and three others, of whom the declarant was one, went into the neighbouring woods to communicate with some of their friends in the neighbourhood. They fell in with Kennedy unexpectedly, and Hattaraick and Brown, aware that he was the occasion of their disasters, resolved to murder him. He dissented, he said, and endeavoured to prevent them; and he told the particulars of the murder distinctly, and that they resolved to throw him over the crag, as the best way of concealing the mode of his death, and dragged him away for that purpose. He added, that his aunt Meg Merrilies saved the child, and that he himself assisted in doing so. He stated, that they regained the cavern by different routes, and Dirk Hattaraick was giving an account how he had pushed a huge crag over above Kennedy, as he lay groaning on the beach, when Glossin suddenly appeared among them. To the whole transaction by which Hattaraick purchased his secrecy he was witness. Respecting young Bertram he could give a distinct account till he went to India, after which he had lost sight of him until he unexpectedly saw him in Liddesdale. He stated, that he instantly sent notice to his aunt, Meg Merrilies, as well as to Hattaraick, who he knew was then upon the coast, but that he had incurred his aunt's highest displeasure upon the latter account. He concluded, that his aunt had immediately declared that she would do all in her power to help young Ellangowan to his right, even if it should be by informing against Dirk Hattaraick, and that many of her people assisted her besides himself, from a belief that she was gifted with supernatural inspirations. With the same purpose, he understood, his aunt had given to Bertram the treasure of the tribe, of which she had the custody. Three or four gypsies mingled in the crowd when the Custom-House was attacked, for the purpose of liberating Bertram, which he had himself effected. He said, that in obeying Meg's dictates they did not pretend to estimate their propriety or rationality, the respect in which she was held by her tribe precluding all such subjects of speculation. Upon farther interrogation he added, that his aunt had always said that Harry Bertram carried that around his neck which would ascertain his birth. It was a spell, she said, that an Oxford scholar had made for him, and she possessed the smugglers with an opinion, that to deprive him of it would occasion the loss of the vessel.

Bertram here produced a small velvet bag, which he said he had worn round his neck from his earliest infancy, and which he had preserved, first, from superstitious reverence, and, latterly, from the hope it might serve one day to aid in the discovery of his birth. The bag being opened, was found to contain a blue silk case, from which was drawn a scheme of nativity. Upon inspecting this paper, Colonel Mannering instantly admitted it was of his own composition, and afforded the strongest and most satisfactory evidence that the possessor of it must necessarily be the young heir of Ellangowan, by avowing his having first appeared in this country in the character of an astrologer.

"And now," said Pleydell, "make out warrants of commitment for Hattaraick and Glossin until liberated in due course of law. I am sorry for Glossin."

"Now, I think," said Mannering, "he's incomparably the least deserving of pity of the two. The other's a bold fellow, though as hard as flint."

"Very natural, Colonel, that you should be interested in the ruffian and I in the knave—that's all professional taste—but I can tell you Glossin would have been a pretty lawyer, had he not had such a turn to the roguish part of the profession."

"Scandal would say, he might not ultimately be the worse lawyer for that."

"Scandal would tell a lie, then, as she usually does. Law's like laudanum; it's much more easy to use it as a quack does, than to learn to apply it like a physician."

Chapter Eighteen

Unfit to live or die—O marble heart!
After him, fellows, drag him to the block.
Measure for Measure

THE JAIL at the county town of the shire of —— was one of those old-fashioned dungeons which disgraced Scotland until of late years. When the prisoners and their guard arrived there, Hattaraick, whose violence and strength were well known, was secured in what was called the condemned ward. This was a large apartment near the top of the prison. A round bar of iron, about the thickness of a man's arm above the elbow, crossed the apartment horizontally at the height of about six inches from the floor, and was built into the wall at either end. Hattaraick's ancles were secured within shackles, which were connected at the distance of about four feet, with a large iron ring which travelled upon the bar we have described. Thus a prisoner might shuffle along the length of the bar from one side to another, but could not stir farther from it in any other direction than the length of his fetters admitted. When his feet had been thus secured, the keeper removed his hand-cuffs, and left his person at liberty in other respects.

Hattaraick had not been long in this place of confinement, before Glossin arrived at the same prison-house. In respect to his comparative rank and education, he was not ironed, but placed in a decent apartment, under the inspection of Mac-Guffog, who, since the destruction of the bridewell of Portanferry by the mob, had acted here as an under turnkey. When Glossin was inclosed within this room, and had solitude and leisure to calculate all the chances against him and in his favour, he could not prevail upon himself to consider the game as desperate. "The estate is lost," he said; "that must go—and between Pleydell and Mac-Morlan they'll cut down my claim on it to a trifle. My character—but if I get off with life and liberty, I'll get money yet, and varnish that over again. Let me see:—This Bertram was a child at the time—his evidence must be imperfect—the other fellow is a deserter, a gypsey, and an outlaw—Meg Merrilies, d—n her, is dead. —These infernal bills!—Hattaraick brought them with him, I suppose, to have the means of threatening me, or extorting money from me.—I must endeavour to see the rascal;—must get him to stand steady;—must get him to put some other colour upon the business."

His mind teeming with schemes of future deceit to cover former villainy, he spent the time in arranging and combining them until the hour of supper. Mac-Guffog attended upon this occasion. After giving him a glass of wine, and sounding him with one or two cajoling speeches, Glossin made it his request he would help him to an interview with Dirk Hattaraick. "Impossible! utterly impossible! it's contrary to the most express orders of Mr Mac-Morlan, and the captain (so the head jailor of a county jail is called in Scotland) would never forgie me."

"But why should he know of it?" said Glossin, slipping a couple of guineas into Mac-Guffog's hand.

The turnkey weighed the gold, and looked sharp at Glossin. "Eye, eye, Mr Glossin, ye ken the ways o' this place—Look ye, at locking up hour, I'll return and bring ye up stairs to him—But ye must stay a' night in his cell, for I must carry the keys to the captain for the night, and I cannot let you out again until morning—then I'll visit the wards half an hour earlier, and ye may get out, and be snug in your ain berth when the captain gangs his rounds."

When the hour of ten had pealed from the neighbouring steeple, Mac-Guffog came prepared with a small dark lantern. He said softly to Glossin, "Slip your shoes off and follow me." When Glossin was out of the door, Mac-Guffog, as if in the execution of his ordinary duty, and speaking to a prisoner within, called aloud, "Good-night to you, sir," and locked the door, clattering the bolts with much ostentatious noise. He then guided Glossin up a steep and narrow stair, at the top of which was the door of the condemned ward; he unbarred and unlocked it, and, giving Glossin the lantern, made a sign to him to enter, and locked the door behind him with the same affected accuracy.

In the large dark cell into which he was thus introduced, Glossin's feeble light for some time enabled him to discover nothing. At length he could dimly distinguish a pallet bed stretched on the floor beside the great iron bar which traversed the room, and on that pallet reposed the figure of a man. Glossin approached him. "Dirk Hattaraick!"

"Donner and hagel!" said the prisoner, sitting up, and clashing his fetters as he rose, "then my dream is true. Begone, and leave me to myself—it will be your best."

"What! my good friend, will you allow the prospect of a few weeks confinement to depress your spirit?"

"Yes—when I am only to be released by a halter!—Let me alone—go about your business, and turn the lamp from my face!"

"Psha! my dear Dirk, don't be afraid—I have a glorious plan to make all right."

"To the bottomless pit with your plans! you have planned me out of ship, cargo, and life, and I dreamt this moment that Meg Merrilies dragged you here by the hair, and gave me the long clasped knife she used to wear—you don't know what she said. Sturm wetter! it will be your wisdom not to tempt me!"

"But, Hattaraick, my good friend, do but rise and speak to me."

"I will not!—you have caused all the mischief; you would not let Meg keep the boy; she would have returned him after he had forgot all."

"Hattaraick, you're turned a driveller!"

"Wetter! will you deny that all that cursed attempt at Portanferry, which lost both sloop and crew, was your device for your own job?"

"But the goods"——

"Curse the goods! we could have got plenty more; but, der deyvil! to lose the ship and the fine fellows, and my own life, for a cursed coward villain, that always works his own mischief with other people's hands! Speak no more to me—I'm dangerous."

"But, Hattaraick, hear but a few words."

"Hagel! nein."

"Only one sentence."

"Tausend curses—nein!"

"At least get up, for an obstinate Dutch brute," said Glossin, losing his temper, and pushing Hattaraick with his foot.

"Donner and blitzen!" said Hattaraick, springing up and grappling with him; "you *will* have it then?"

Glossin struggled and resisted, but so ineffectually under his surprise at the fury of the assault, that he fell under Hattaraick, the back part of his neck coming full upon the iron bar with stunning violence. The death-grapple continued. The room immediately below the condemned ward, being that of Glossin, was, of course, empty; but the inmates of the second apartment beneath felt the shock of Glossin's heavy fall, and heard a noise as of struggling and groans. But all sounds of horror were too congenial to this place to excite much curiosity or interest.

In the morning, faithful to his promise, Mac-Guffog came—"Mr Glossin," said he, in a whispering voice.

"Call louder," answered Dirk Hattaraick.

"Mr Glossin, for God's sake come away!"

"He'll hardly do that without help," said Hattaraick.

"What are you chattering there for, Mac-Guffog," called out the captain from below.

"Come away, Mr Glossin, for God's sake!" repeated the turnkey.

At this moment the jailor made his appearance with a light. Great was his surprise and even horror to observe Glossin's body lying doubled across the iron bar, in a posture that excluded all idea of his being alive. Hattaraick was quietly stretched upon his pallet within a yard of his victim. On lifting Glossin, it was found he had been dead for some hours. His body bore uncommon marks of violence. The spine where it joins the scull had received severe injury by his first fall. There were distinct marks of strangulation about the throat, which corresponded with the blackened state of the face. The head was turned backward over the shoulder, as if the neck had been wrung round with the most desperate violence. So that it would seem that his inveterate antagonist had fixed a fatal gripe upon the wretch's throat, and never quitted it while life lasted. The lantern, crushed and broken to pieces, lay beneath the body.

Mac-Morlan was in the town, and came instantly to examine the corpse. "What brought Glossin here?" said he to Hattaraick.

"The devil!" answered the ruffian.

"And what did you do to him?"

"Sent him to hell before me!" replied the miscreant.

"Wretch, have you crowned a life spent without the practice of a single virtue with the murder of your miserable accomplice?"

"Virtue? donner! I was always faithful to my ship-owners—always accounted for cargo to the last stiver. Hark ye! let me have pen and ink, and I'll write an account of the whole to our house; and leave me alone a couple of hours, will ye—and let them take away that piece of carrion, donner!"

Mac-Morlan deemed it the best way to humour the savage; he was furnished with writing materials and left alone. When they again opened the door, it was found that this determined villain had anticipated justice. He had adjusted a cord taken from the truckle bed, and attached it to a bone, the relique of his yesterday's dinner, which he had contrived to drive firmly into the wall at a height as great as he could reach, standing upon the bar. Having fastened the noose, he had the resolution to drop his body as if to fall on his knees, and to retain that posture until resolution was no longer necessary. The letter he had written to his owners, though chiefly upon the business of their trade, contained many allusions to the younker of Ellangowan, as he called him, and afforded absolute confirmation of all Meg Merrilies and her nephew had told.

To dismiss the catastrophe of these two wretched men, I shall only add, that Mac-Guffog was turned out of office, notwithstanding his protestation, which he offered to attest by oath, that he had locked Glossin safely in his own room upon the night preceding his being found dead in Dirk Hattaraick's cell. His declaration, however, found faith with the worthy Mr Skreigh, and other lovers of the marvellous, who still hold that the Enemy of Mankind brought these two wretches together upon that night, that they might fill up the cup of their guilt by murder and suicide.

Chapter Nineteen

To sum the whole—the close of all.
DEAN SWIFT

AS GLOSSIN died without heirs and without payment of the price, the estate of Ellangowan was again thrown upon the hands of Mr Godfrey Bertram's creditors, the right of many of whom was however defeasible, in case Henry Bertram should establish his character of heir of entail. This young gentleman threw his affairs into the hands of Mr Pleydell and Mr Mac-Morlan, with one single proviso, that, though he should be obliged again to go to India, every debt, justly and honourably due by his father, should be made good to the claimant. Mannering, who heard this declaration, grasped him kindly by the hand, and from that moment might be dated a thorough understanding between them.

The hoards of Miss Margaret Bertram, and the liberal assistance of the Colonel, easily enabled the heir to make provision for payment of the just creditors, while the ingenuity and research of his law friends detected, especially in the accounts of Glossin, so many overcharges as greatly diminished the total amount. In these circumstances the creditors did not hesitate to recognise Bertram's right, and to surrender to him the house of his ancestors. All the party rushed from Woodbourne to take possession, amid the shouts of the tenantry and the neighbourhood; and so keen was Colonel Mannering to superintend certain operations which he had recommended to Bertram, that, upon his invitation, he removed with his family for a few weeks from Woodbourne to Ellangowan, although at present containing much less and much inferior accommodation.

The poor Dominie's brain was almost turned with joy. He posted up stairs, taking three steps at once, to a little shabby attic, his cell and dormitory in former days, and which possession of his much superior apartment at Woodbourne had never banished from his memory. Here one sad thought suddenly struck the honest man—the books!—no three rooms in Ellangowan were capable to contain them. While this qualifying reflection was passing through his mind, he was suddenly summoned by Mannering to assist in calculating some proportions relating to a large and splendid house, which was to be built on the scite of the New Place of Ellangowan, in a style corresponding to the magnificence of the ruins in its vicinity. Amid the various rooms, the Dominie observed, that one of the largest was entitled THE LIBRARY; and snug and close beside was a well-proportioned chamber, entitled, MR SAMPSON'S APARTMENT.—"Prodigious, prodigious, prodigious!" shouted the enraptured Dominie.

Mr Pleydell had left the party for some time; but he returned, according to promise, during the Christmas recess of the courts. He drove up to Ellangowan when all the family were abroad but the Colonel, who was busy with plans of buildings and pleasure-grounds, in which he was well skilled, and took great delight.

"Ah ha!" said the Counsellor, "so here you are! Where are the ladies? where is the fair Julia?"—

"Walked out with young Hazelwood, Bertram, and Captain Delaserre, a friend of his, who is with us just now. They are gone to plan out a cottage at Derncleugh.—Well, have you carried through your law-business?"

"With a wet finger; got our youngster's special service retoured into Chancery. We had him served heir before the macers."

"Macers? who are they?"

"Why, it is a kind of judicial Saturnalia. You must know, that one of the requisites to be a macer, or officer in attendance upon our supreme court, is, that they shall be men of no knowledge."

"Very well!"

"Now, our Scottish legislature, for the joke's sake, I suppose, has constituted those men of no knowledge into a peculiar court for trying questions of relationship and descent, such as this business of Bertram, which often involve the most nice and complicated questions of evidence."

"The devil they do? I should think that rather inconvenient."

"O, we have a practical remedy for the theoretical absurdity. One or two of the judges act upon such occasions as prompters and assessors to their own door-keepers. But you know what Cujacius says, '*Multa sunt in moribus dissentanea, multa sine ratione*.' However, this Saturnalian court has done our business; and a glorious batch of claret we had afterwards at Walker's. Mac-Morlan will stare when he sees the bill."

"Never fear," said the Colonel, "we'll face the shock, and entertain the country at my friend Mrs Mac-Candlish's to boot."

"And chuse Jock Jabos for your master of horse?"

"Perhaps I may."

"And where is Dandie, the redoubted Lord of Liddesdale?"

"Retired to his mountains; but he has promised Julia to make a descent in summer, with the goodwife, as he calls her, and I don't know how many children."

"O, the curlie-headed varlets! I must come to play at Blind Harry and Hy Spy with them.—But what is all this?" taking up the plans;—"tower in the centre to be in imitation of the Eagle Tower at Caernarvon—*corps de logis*—the devil!—wings—wings? why, the house will take the estate of Ellangowan on its back, and fly away with it!"

"Why then, we must ballast it with a few bags of Sicca rupees."

"Aha! sits the wind there? Then I suppose the young dog carries off my mistress Julia?"

"Even so, counsellor."

"These rascals, the *post-nati*, get the better of us of the old school at every turn. But she must convey and make over her interest in me to Lucy."

"To tell you the truth, I am afraid your flank will be turned there too."

"Indeed!"

"Here has been Sir Robert Hazelwood upon a visit to Bertram, thinking, and deeming, and opining"——

"O Lord! spare me the worthy Baronet's triads!"

"Well, sir; he conceived that as the property of Singleside lay like a wedge between two farms of his, and was four or five miles separated from Ellangowan, something like a sale, or exchange, or arrangement, might take place, to the mutual convenience of both parties."

"Well, and Bertram"——

"Replied, that he considered the original settlement of Mrs Margaret Bertram, as the arrangement most proper in the circumstances of the family, and that therefore the estate of Singleside was the property of his sister Lucy."

"The rascal!" said Pleydell, wiping his spectacles, "he'll steal my heart as well as my mistress—*Et puis?*"

"And then, Sir Robert retired after many gracious speeches; but last week he again took the field in force, with his coach and six horses, his laced scarlet waistcoat, and best bob-wig—all very grand, as the good-boy books say."

"And what was his overture?"

"Why, he talked with great form of an attachment on the part of Charles Hazelwood to Miss Bertram."

"Aye; he respected the little god Cupid when he saw him perched on the Dun of Singleside. And is poor Lucy to keep house along with that old fool and his wife, who is just the knight himself in petticoats?"

"No—we parried that. Singleside-house is to be repaired for the young people, and to be called hereafter Mount Hazelwood."

"And do you propose to continue at Woodbourne?"

"Only till we carry these plans into effect—see, here's the plan of my Bungalow, with all convenience for being separate and sulky when I chuse."

"And, being next door to the old castle, you may repair Donagild's tower for the nocturnal contemplation of the celestial bodies?"

"No, no, my dear counsellor! Here ends THE ASTROLOGER."

THE END

HISTORICAL NOTE

Chronology. The narrative of *Guy Mannering* consists of two distinct chronological sequences. The first, comprising ten chapters and filling half the original first volume, begins with the young Mannering lost on his northern tour in 'November, 17—'. It describes his overnight stay at Ellangowan and construction of a birth-chart the following morning, picks up later with the circumstances which lead to Godfrey Bertram's ejection of the Derncleugh gypsies, and ends with the mysterious disappearance of Harry Bertram and its inconclusive investigation. The second sequence, which fills the rest of the novel, effectively begins with Colonel Mannering's arrival at the Gordon Arms in November 'nearly seventeen years' (59.26) after this traumatic event. The whole action in this much larger sequence takes place in a relatively narrow space between November and December. The recurrence of events according to a seasonal pattern, combined with an absence of any specific internal dating by year or even decade, has encouraged some commentators to view the novel's temporal setting as almost deliberately hazy; those who mention a possible time frame generally place the main action (wrongly) in the late 1770s.[1]

Scott's 'tale of private life'[2] is singularly devoid of the concrete historical details found in *Waverley* (1814), and lacks too the connection with a public incident (the feared invasion of 1794) evident in its immediate successor, *The Antiquary* (1816). Allusion to broader political events, nevertheless, provides a useful marker in each sequence. Godfrey Bertram's appointment as a Justice of the Peace is made possible by the fall of the ruling administration 'about four years' (31.18) after the opening events in the story. Probably no specific occasion is intended, though in general outline this fits the circumstances of the mid-1760s, when ministries and their nominal leaders were frequently changing. Near the beginning of the second sequence, Mrs Mac-Candlish blames 'this weary American war' (67.41) for the shortage of capital in Scotland, an allusion which is later supported by the placing of Mannering's Edinburgh visit 'near the end of the American war' (201.6). Notwithstanding Cornwallis's surrender at Yorktown in October 1781, the American War of Independence only came fully to a conclusion with the Treaty of Versailles on 3 September 1783, which brought peace with France and Spain as well as recognition of American independence, though provisional articles of peace between Britain and the United States had been signed earlier on 30 November 1782.

A number of elements in the second sequence apply equally well to 1781 or 1782, and it is not impossible that Scott shifted between the two during the course of writing. Mannering arrives back in the district of Kippletringan on a Saturday evening. Mrs Mac-Candlish, while attending to him and on hearing that the Bertrams will not be arriving that evening, remarks 'the morn's the term—the very last day they can bide in the house—a' thing's to be roupit' (62.9–10). The term-day referred to is clearly Martinmas, 11 November, and if 11 November is to be a Sunday then the year according to the calendar must be 1781, the only year during the American war when 11 November fell on a Sunday. However, a number of elements in the Edinburgh scenes point more clearly to 1782. Mention by one of the funeral mourners of the continuing threat posed to East India stock by 'Tippoo Saib' (215.34) arguably applies better to 1782, when Tipu succeeded his father Haidar Ali as ruler in Mysore. A firmer indication still is found in the first of the four 'Fragments' describing Edinburgh illuminati, hitherto omitted from printed editions, where 'the late naval success' (227.25) is cited in illustration of the value of John Clerk of Eldin's 'great discovery'. This alludes to Sir George Romney's victory over the French off Dominica on 12 April 1782, which Clerk believed to have derived from knowledge of his own *Essay on Naval Tactics*, circulated in manuscript before being privately printed in 1782. Scott was no doubt intimate with these circumstances through his friendship with William Clerk, the tactician's son, and is hardly likely to have been imprecise over the date of a sea battle in which his own eldest brother, Robert, had taken part (Robert's verses written on the eve of the engagement, along with the exact date of the victory, were included by Scott in his Ashestiel 'Memoirs').[3] 1782 as the date for the Edinburgh scenes also fits marginally better with Scott's comment in the 'Advertisement' to *The Antiquary* that *Guy Mannering*, as the second of a trilogy on Scottish 'manners', embraced the period of 'our own youth'.

The larger chronological patterning of *Guy* is also shaped to a significant degree by Mannering's astrological prophecy. Crises are predicted for Bertram (involving death or captivity) in his fifth, tenth and twenty-first years, the last of these coinciding with a similarly calculated crisis facing Mannering's fiancée Sophia, then eighteen, in her thirty-ninth year. The first prediction is matched by the disappearance (by kidnapping) of Bertram on his fifth birthday (see 46.21, 72.36). This occurs a 'few days after' (46.18; compare 58.3) the expulsion of the gypsies from Derncleugh, which itself can be placed on Martinmas (11 November), one of the Scottish term-days, when leases expired and removals took place (see 41.35). The second crisis arrives through Bertram's attempt to escape from the Netherlands by boat, when 'but ten years old' (189.4), leading to his near death by drowning when recaptured. The third crisis (though readers might be tempted to associate it with the final dramatic confrontation in Hattaraick's cave) is fulfilled in India through Bertram's wounding in a duel with Mannering and seizure by native insurgents. The brief capture of Sophia Mannering, and her death from ill-health resulting from the shock 'eight months after this incident' (71.33), explains the coincidence of birth-charts noted at the beginning. The turbulence surrounding these events matches well with Mannering reaching the end of his military career in the early 1780s, a period marked by numerous engagements between

Haidar Ali and British forces under Sir Eyre Coote. Mannering's return with his daughter Julia shortly after his wife's death, followed by Bertram's release and the recall of his regiment, could then all conceivably take place in time for the resumption of events in Scotland late in either 1781 or 1782.

Mannering's entry into the Gordon Arms on a Saturday evening in November (Ch. 11) provides a firm marker against which the somewhat compressed events of the second sequence can be measured. Although Scott's motto from *The Winter's Tale* mentions a gap of sixteen years, an intervening space of seventeen years is clearly signalled more than once, as when Mrs Mac-Candlish corrects Deacon Bearcliff's loose 'twenty years': 'it's no abune seventeen at the outside in this very month' (62.35–36).[4] The sale of Ellangowan has been held over to Monday (12 November), 'the first free day', as Mrs Mac-Candlish explains to Mannering, the actual term day (as noted, Martinmas, 11 November) falling on the Sunday (see 67.37–39).[5] Mrs Mac-Candlish is also characteristically accurate when placing the Bertram tragedy 'in the middle of November, 17—' (67.31), though this manuscript wording (restored in the present edition) was altered by the first edition to read 'about the beginning of November, 17—'. In this alteration one can sense a conflict of priorities which remains for much of the rest of the narrative: between a quasi-mythical sense of recurring dates, revisitation, and seasonal patterning on the one hand, and a more practical need to find space for multifarious and interlocking narrative strands in a narrow span between 12 November and 31 December.

The following chart offers a brief version of Scott's chronology in the second narrative sequence, adopting the 1781 calendar for specific dates.

Late November. The sale of Ellangowan is postponed for a fortnight, i.e. from 12 to 26 November. Mannering, breaking a short tour, makes for Westmoreland on 22 November (see 81.38), interrupts Julia and Bertram's courtship, but misses the auction. Bertram walks north, arriving at Tib Mumps's about 26 or 27 November (Dinmont here mentions the elder Bertram's death 'about a fortnight since' (121.13)). He then stays at Charlieshope for a week (133.35, 140.12).

First week in December. Mannering and Julia take up residence at Woodbourne 'in the beginning of the month of December' (105.35), most obviously Saturday 1 December. The smugglers' attack on Woodbourne takes place on Tuesday morning (162.35), which would accord with 4 December, even if the earlier part of Julia's letter communicating this indicates a more established domestic scene. Meanwhile Bertram leaves the Dinmonts (4 December), and witnesses the wounded smuggler's death that night. He spends the night of 5–6 December at Mrs Mac-Candlish's, and has his scuffle with Hazelwood on 6 December. This is broadly compatible with Julia's mention of 'two or three days' (166.28) having elapsed since the smugglers' attack.

Second and third weeks. Next week (see 173.26) Glossin interrogates Mrs Mac-Candlish, plots with Hattaraick Bertram's re-kidnapping, and visits Woodbourne with news of Lucy's expectations. Mannering sets off for Edinburgh the following morning, takes up his lodgings on Saturday (15 December), finding Pleydell at High Jinks late that evening. He dines with Pleydell on Sunday, attends the funeral on Monday, entertains Pleydell on Thursday, is present at Mrs Rebecca's interview early on Friday ('cursing the raw air of a Scottish morning in December' (232.34–35)), and sets off home on Saturday (22 December), having spent a full week in the metropolis.

Fourth week. Recrossing the Solway Firth from Allonby, Bertram surveys the Galloway coastline in the early sun-light of a 'December morning' (241.36), but is arrested by Glossin almost immediately on entering Ellangowan Castle. After a brief exchange of letters between Glossin and Sir Robert Hazelwood, both dated 'Tuesday', he is taken to Hazelwood-house for interrogation, and is kept there overnight (see 262.17) before being transported to the prison in Portanferry early next morning. Mannering arrives back from Edinburgh on the same evening Bertram is examined (see 274.39–40), identifying the day as Tuesday 25 December if the preceding chronology is carried through. The 'remarkable day' (283.21) that follows involves Scott weaving together multiple threads in his story. Early in the morning, having himself returned from Edinburgh, Dinmont meets Gabriel, who informs him of Bertram's arrest and likely imprisonment (see 271.13–16). Dinmont then rides to Portanferry, arriving by supper-time and settling down to sleep in Bertram's cell just after nine (274.8). Meg's strategy is set into place through two confrontations that day: the first with Dominie Sampson, who is given the letter instructing Mannering to have a carriage waiting at Portanferry; and the second with young Hazelwood, who is warned that the movement of the soldiers from the custom-house to Hazelwood-house is part of a ruse. Pleydell meanwhile arrives at Woodbourne at tea-time, having 'ventured to leave the court for a week in session time' (297.7). The attack on Portanferry takes place at midnight (293.17), with the smugglers finally dispersing as a result of the (further delayed) arrival of Mac-Morlan with the guard. Bertram and Dinmont arrive by carriage at Woodbourne some time after one o'clock on the following morning. The dramatic events of the third key day (27 December) begin with Meg's sudden appearance at Gibbie's-know: this is followed by her retracing with Bertram and Dinmont of the terrain of the original kidnapping, the dramatic confrontation in Hattaraick's cave, Meg's dying testimony, and Bertram's acclamation by the Ellangowan tenantry. Glossin is arrested on the following day, and his assassination by Hattaraick and the latter's suicide take place on their first night together in the county jail.

The novel's conclusion is bundled together with accelerating speed and diminishing plausibility. Pleydell, after leaving for 'some time'

(353.31), returns 'during the Christmas recess of the courts' (i.e. 24 December to 1 January), having set in motion Bertram's recognition as legal heir of entail. Even before this, Pleydell's movements indicate that the time-scale has broken down: his earlier visit to Woodbourne, during session time, could only have taken place at least a week before 24 December (see above). Notwithstanding such inconsistencies, the sheer verve of Scott's narrative means there is little sense of entanglement. The action proceeds with the speed of a well-constructed play, even if, realistically, the events it describes must have taken longer. One overriding aim evidently is to finish before the new year, with the implication of a fresh beginning for Scottish provincial society. Scott's alleged description of the novel as 'the work of six weeks at a Christmas'[6] could equally well be applied to the hectic events in its main narrative sequence.

Topography. The main events in *Guy Mannering* take place in the south-west of Scotland, along the north coast of the Solway Firth. The novel also includes significant sequences involving two other Scottish locations: Liddesdale in southern Roxburghshire, in the West Border country, where the young Bertram stays for a week; and the Edinburgh Old Town, as experienced by Colonel Mannering for an equivalent length of time.

The action in the first narrative sequence is chiefly confined to Ellangowan (Old and New Places), the nearby gypsy encampment at Derncleugh, and Warroch Point (which stands at the other side of the bay from Ellangowan Castle). In the second sequence this locale is broadened through the introduction of significant scenes in the village or town of Kippletringan, two other country residences (Woodbourne and Hazelwood-house), and the 'small fishing town' (191.2) of Portanferry. All the names involved are fictitious (it is remarked (237.27) of Portanferry at one point that the reader 'will in vain seek for [it] under that name in the county map'), and as such encourage the view that Scott has created a largely ideal landscape. Several actual place names, mentioned as being in the vicinity, nevertheless offer tempting geographical pointers. The young Mannering, at the start of the novel, has evidently set out from Dumfries (at 64.40 Jock Jabos recalls that his horse 'belanged to the George at Dumfries'); and the monastic ruins he visits, though Scott places them in Dumfriesshire, are more obviously explained in terms of sites over the river Nith in the eastern part of the Stewartry of Kirkcudbright (the county which, along with Wigtownshire, forms Galloway). Immediately previous to the events leading to the kidnapping of Bertram, Kennedy the Supervisor has ridden out along the Solway to Wigtown to alert a King's vessel in the bay there, directing it further up the Firth (46.34, 63.3). Jock Jabos owns new boots bought at Kirkcudbright Fair, and talks also of having worked as an assistant keeper at 'the Isle', which is probably St Mary's Isle, a peninsula just south of Kirkcudbright (177.22–28). Godfrey Bertram's illegitimate son is brought up in the family of a shipwright living 'on the shore of Annan' (13.29, 345.26)—that is, conveniently to the east of

Dumfries. While on a few occasions Scott seems to be keeping his options open with regard to a possible Dumfriesshire setting (at 88.27–28 Mervyn, for example, talks about the prospect of Mannering visiting him from 'Galloway or Dumfries-shire'), a number of key local characters are clearly identified as natives of Galloway: Dominie Sampson is a 'Galloway Phœbus' (85.11), Glossin a 'Galwegian John o' the Scales' (82.15), and Meg 'this Galwegian sybil' (325.6). Scott also refers to Dumfriesshire by name several times, whereas the county in which Ellangowan and Kippletringan are set is left unspecified as 'the county of ——' (170.39, 190.39, 209.24). There are two references to the 'borough-town' (46.43, 193.16), which again is not named, though it is tempting to think of Kirkcudbright; and the 'bridewell' at Portanferry is described as being more conveniently situated for 'the Kippletringan district of the county' (262.28–29) than the county jail itself (though the latter is fittingly used for Hattaraick and Glossin (see 348.30)). Dinmont rides 'sixty mile or near bye' (271.39–40) from Liddesdale to aid the imprisoned Bertram in Portanferry: a distance which, at least if covered directly, would take him past Dumfries but not as far as Kirkcudbright. Notwithstanding a number of uncertainties, themselves perhaps partly the product of Scott's not wishing to be tied down, the weight of evidence argues for a largely imaginary setting somewhere along the coastline of east Kirkcudbrightshire.

In the later nineteenth century, nevertheless, it was argued with growing conviction that Scott's Galwegian localities were actually based on the short stretch of terrain covered by the coastal road between Gatehouse of Fleet and Creetown to the west.[7] Much of the impetus came from Galloway itself, and as such was arguably not disinterested, considering the sizeable tourist trade that developed as a result. Such claims also necessarily hinge, to some degree, on the uncertain issue of whether Scott did indeed visit the region. Even so, and bearing in mind the lukewarm stance adopted to the idea of a correlation with 'Galwegian localities' by Scott himself in his Magnum 'Additional Note', several of the alleged resemblances are striking. Similarities between the Gordon Arms and the Murray Arms (named after James Murray of Broughton, the developer of Gatehouse), and the presence in both communities of a Masonic lodge, lends some support to the view that Kippletringan is based on Gatehouse of Fleet; though, if this is the case, Scott blotted out the cotton mills, tanneries, and other works, that had made Gatehouse a significant industrial centre by the end of the eighteenth century. The scenery around the Fleet estuary, which incorporates the ruins of Cardoness Castle as well as the Ardwall estate, was well-known in Scott's time for its picturesque qualities, and there are certain parallels between it and the landscape surveyed first by night and then in day-time by Mannering when a guest at Ellangowan.[8] In a Magnum note Scott later likened the ruined Old Place at Ellangowan to 'the noble remains of Caerlaverock castle, six or seven miles from Dumfries',[9] though this 15th-century fortification (actually 9 miles SSE of Dumfries) bears little resemblance in its setting to Scott's original description. Proponents of the 'Galwegian' setting usually point either to

Barholm Castle (occupied by a branch of the McCulloch family) or Carsluith Castle (home to the Browns, who emigrated to India in 1748), both close to the Gatehouse-Creetown coastal road and overlooking the Solway, or argue for an amalgam of each. Portanferry in this scenario is based on Creetown, originally known as 'the Ferry' or 'Ferrytown of Cree', whose population had grown to nearly a thousand at the end of the eighteenth century, but which was not significant enough to contain a custom-house or small prison/workhouse. Derncleugh ('dark gorge') can be associated with the wooded Kirkdale Glen just to the west of Barholm, which leads up to Cairnholy (two prehistoric cairns); or, alternatively, to the Cleugh of Carsluith (the Ordnance Survey map marks a nearby 'Hazelwood' and 'Gypsy Well', though whether these predate the novel or not is a moot point). Dirk Hattaraick's cave is located at Ravenshall Point (Warroch Point?) just below Barholm Castle (it appears on the Ordnance Survey map as 'Meg Merrilees or Dirk Hatteraick's Cave'), and intrepid explorers who have been able to enter it describe a narrow entrance, with the cave expanding inside, and stone boxes cut along the wall (though one candidly acknowledges that, unlike in the novel, it is visible from the foot of the cliffs and well above sea-level).[10] Those intent on finding a parallel for every location liken Woodbourne to Cassencarrie house, just south of Creetown (in the novel it is 'within three miles' (100.3) of Ellangowan); and Hazelwood-house, with less probability still, is associated with Ardwall (itself, possibly through family connection, the true imaginative seed for Scott's enterprise).[11] These and other possible overlaps and echoes are discussed in greater detail in the Explanatory Notes.

The account of Liddesdale, centred on Dandie Dinmont's farm at Charlieshope, originates from first-hand knowledge gained by Scott during his Border 'raids' into the district in search of ballads, which began in Autumn 1792 and continued for seven years. Dandie and Bertram first meet in a 'small public-house' in Cumberland, whose landlady is named as Tib Mumps, and which Scott later identified in a Magnum note as being based on Mumps's Hall near Gilsland in the far east of the county. Gilsland in Scott's time included the spa establishment where in 1797 he had met and courted his future wife, Charlotte Carpenter, and it features again (with some accuracy) later in the novel when it transpires that Meg Merrilies had met Margaret Bertram 'at the spaw-well below the craig' (233.23). The landlady of the historical Mumps's Ha' (i.e. Beggar's Hotel) is thought to have been Meg Carrick (or Teasdale), who is buried in the churchyard at nearby Over-Denton; and subsequent reports suggest that until 1831 the inn remained much as it is described in the novel.[12] Bertram, not implausibly, has stumbled on it having decided to make a detour to visit the Roman Wall, on his journey from the Lake District into Scotland; Dinmont is on his return home from a tour of fairs in 'Galloway and Dumfries-shire', and has apparently been at a cattle-market near Carlisle earlier in the day (see 121.4–6). Directly north-west of Mumps's Ha' is 'the Waste of Cumberland' (124.9), a barren stretch of land (long associated with robbers) running up to the Border with Scotland, and which is also referred to in the course of the story (apparently synonymously) as 'the Waste', 'Bewcastle moss', and 'Bewcastle'.[13] Dinmont mentions two possible routes to Liddesdale, 'ower Willie's brae' or 'through Conscouthart-moss' (a place name found in the ballad 'Hobbie Noble'), incautiously mentioning to Tib his choice of the latter (122.25–26, 38). After his rescue by Bertram, and having proceeded on Dumple further through the moss, the two travellers meet firmer ground with the Maiden-way, the remains of a Roman road which supposedly ran into Scotland roughly parallel with the boundaries of Cumberland and Northumberland. The novel is not explicit about where they cross the Border, but the 'pretty little river winding its way through a pastoral country' (127.29–30), and which they eventually cross, is most obviously the Liddel.

By Scott's death, Charlieshope had been linked with a number of actual Border farms. Robert Shortreed, who had accompanied Scott on his 'raids', considered three possible prototypes when later recalling events: Thorlieshope, in upper Liddesdale; Hyndlee, some 24 km SW of Jedburgh and strictly speaking not part of the Liddesdale region; and Twislehope, in the upper reaches of Hermitage Water. Thorlieshope, a long-established settlement comparable in size to the 'farm-steading' described by Scott, could have been reached from Bewcastle much as indicated by Dinmont's journey (though it actually overlooks the Liddel from its *east* bank). Other possible parallels can be found in the old Peel-tower that once stood there, matching that inhabited by Dandie's ancestor, and in the close proximity of Dawston Burn (apparently with an adjoining settlement in the later eighteenth century, and the most obvious source of the novel's Jock o' Dawstone, with whom Dandie endlessly quarrels over marches).[14] If Charlieshope is identifiable with Thorlieshope, however, it seems strange that Dinmont should earlier have suggested to Bertram that he might stay overnight at Riccarton on his way over from Mumps's Ha', since Riccarton Mill, which provided the services of an inn in the later eighteenth century (and was used by Scott himself when visiting Liddesdale), is only about 3 km south further down Liddel Water than Thorlieshope. Shortreed for his part could 'not remember o' our being at Thorlieshope at all'. Of Hyndlee Shortreed likewise remarked that Scott only ever saw it when 'passing along the road', and the idea of this farm representing a topographical source only really developed as an offshoot of the association of Dinmont with its tenant, James Davidson, and his breed of Mustard and Pepper terriers (see also below). Twislehope at the time of Scott's 'raids' was occupied by Thomas Elliot, one of several Elliots who farmed in the Hermitage part of the Liddesdale region, and who had been among Scott's earliest contacts there. In this case Shortreed is less negative in his response, at least with regard to the setting: 'there's much o the kind o' scenery described—the deep & wild craggy dells & ravines—on the Farm of Twizelhope which it has always struck me was the Charlieshope of the Novel.'[15] Such a location would also make more sense of a stop at either Riccarton or 'the Rone' (120.31), the latter near the junction of Hermitage and Liddel waters; though the crossing of only one river, a mile before reaching Charlieshope, is hard to reconcile with Twislehope's far westerly situation. Very probably, as in the case of Heugh-foot in his later story, *The Black Dwarf* (1816), Scott constructed an imaginary location incorporating a number of elements from his early recollections. As in the later story, too, he also gives a strong sense of Liddesdale as it stood in relation to other parts of Scotland.

Mannering in travelling to Edinburgh goes through Moffat, skirts the Pentland Hills, and lodges 'at the George inn near Bristo-port' (201.1–2) on arrival. The Bristo Port was the main entry into Edinburgh from the south, and the nearby George Inn functioned as a starting-point for the Dumfries and Ayr coaches, in addition to those setting off for London by the Carlisle route. Scott's parenthesised remark that 'I love to be particular' (201.2) sets the tone for the following Edinburgh scenes, which feed on his own youthful memories, just as they also attempt to emulate the first-hand particularities found in the comparable visit paid by Matthew Bramble in Smollett's *The Expedition of Humphry Clinker* (1771). A particularly fine sense is given of the bustling life in the main area of the High Street, which then (as Scott explains) gave the impression of forming a self-contained square. Counsellor Pleydell's apartments are in a tenement building located in one of the Closes entered from the north side of the High Street, opposite St Giles Cathedral, which housed at this period many leading lawyers who operated in Parliament House. Clerihugh's, where Pleydell is eventually found at High Jinks, was actually situated down one of these Closes (Writers' Court, now demolished), and served as a popular meeting place for the magistrates and members of the Town Council in the later eighteenth century. References to other locations, nearly all within the crowded space of the Old Town, abound in the ensuing incidents: the taverns in the busy commercial Cowgate, parallel with the High Street; the Canongate, running down to Holyrood Palace, and at that time effectively separated from the High Street by Netherbow Port; Greyfriars Church, south of the Cowgate, where Mannering hears a sermon on Sunday, and witnesses Margaret Bertram's funeral the following day, after a procession from her 'small house in the suburbs to the southward of the city' (214.22–23). Apart from individual residential squares built to 'the south side of the town' (201.10), with their Georgian terraced houses, there is no evidence in the text of the rapid expansion to the north which was to transform the living style of the aristocracy and middle ranks in Edinburgh. The North Bridge (201.42) has already opened up the area beyond the drained North Loch, but the New Town itself, 'since so much extended, was then just commenced' (201.12). From his old-style apartment dwelling, looking down towards Leith, Pleydell thus enjoys a fairly uninterrupted view of 'the grounds between Edinburgh and the sea' (213.35–36).

Observed in a bleak December, the Edinburgh scenes show a community whose concentrated energies stand on the brink of sudden expansion. In this respect the three locales depicted—the moribund Ellangowan estate soon to find its saviour through restoration, Charlieshope adumbrating a burgeoning agricultural prosperity, the nation's capital facing imminent cultural transformation—are all interlinked in Scott's larger thematic scheme.

Character prototypes. Though it contains no historical characters, *Guy Mannering* has generated as much commentary about possible prototypes as any of the Waverley novels. Mostly the focus of attention has been placed on the striking 'secondary' characters created by Scott: notably, Meg Merrilies, Dandie Dinmont, Counsellor Pleydell; and (to a slightly lesser degree) Dominie Sampson and Dirk Hattaraick.

Meg Merrilies is most commonly associated with Jean Gordon (1670?–1746?), a leading member of the gypsy settlement at Kirk Yetholm, near the border of Roxburghshire with Northumberland. This identification was actively encouraged by Scott himself through his (anonymous) contribution to the article, 'Notices concerning the Scottish Gypsies', which appeared in the first issue of *Blackwood's Edinburgh Magazine* in April 1817: 'My father remembered old Jean Gordon of Yetholm, who had great sway among her tribe. She was quite a Meg Merrilies, and possessed the savage virtue of fidelity in the same perfection.'[16] Scott supplied a number of illustrative anecdotes, one concerning the tenant of Lochside farm who was granted shelter at night by Jean and protected by her from the rapacity of the rest of the gang (in circumstances closely matching Bertram's overnight stay in the Kaim of Derncleugh, though the connection is not directly made), and another about his own grandfather (Robert Scott) stumbling on a moorland gypsy feast at which Jean was probably present. The same article also includes an account of Madge Gordon, Jean's grand-daughter, provided by another contributor. This stresses a number of physical resemblances, and ends by suggesting that Scott's creation is an amalgam of the two Yetholm gypsies: 'If Jean Gordon was the prototype of the *character* of Meg Merrilies, I imagine Madge must have sat to the unknown author as the representative of her *person*.'[17] Both these sequences were included in the Magnum Introduction (1829) to *Guy*, where, in introducing the latter, Scott also claimed a personal connection with Madge Gordon: 'my memory is haunted by a solemn remembrance of a woman of more than female height, dressed in a long red cloak'.[18] Perhaps this second 'source' needs to be viewed with a degree of scepticism, however, if only in view of the apparent absence of any earlier mention (in 1826, writing to J. W. Croker, Scott still refers singly to 'poor Jean Gordon, the prototype of Meg Merrilees').[19]

There is also evidence that a significant part of Scott's knowledge about the Roxburghshire gypsies came to him as a result of his long acquaintance with William Smith, Provost of Kelso, whose 'Account of the Gypsies of Kirk Yetholm in 1815' matches Scott's depiction of Derncleugh in a number of ways. The suggestion of an oriental element in Meg's dress and demeanour, on the other hand, was no doubt informed by the growing contemporary debate over the origin of the gypsies, and in particular claims for an Indian source, as originally propounded by the German scholar Heinrich Grellmann in his *Dissertation on the Gipsies* (1783; translated 1787), and further explored by officers of the East India Company, including acquaintances of Scott in Edinburgh. The 'Indian' explanation is evident in the *Blackwood's* article of April 1817, and is accepted virtually as a certainty in John Hoyland's *Historical Survey of the Gypsies* (1816), which incorporated William Smith's account as well as a briefer report by Scott himself as sheriff of Selkirkshire.[20] An alternative local source for Meg—in the shape of Flora, one of the wives of the Galwegian gypsy 'king' Billy Marshall—was proposed in another *Blackwood's* article, in August 1817, probably contributed by James Murray McCulloch, Scott's brother-in-law (see Introduction, xv, and EEWN 2, 363). It is by no means improbable that Scott had heard through his connections of the redoubtable exploits of the long-lived Billy Marshall (d. 1792), including reports of his co-operation with smugglers; and proponents of a Galloway link have claimed a number of overlaps between Marshall's gang and the Derncleugh gypsies.[21] A full account of the 'Gallovidian Gipsies' was later sent to Scott by Joseph Train in May 1829, and passed fairly unmediated into the Magnum 'Additional Note'; Scott diplomatically declaring himself there 'content that Meg should be considered as a representative of her sect and class in general—Flora, as well as others'.[22]

Dandie Dinmont in Scott's lifetime was most commonly associated with James Davidson (1764–1820), tenant in Hyndlee, mainly as a result of Davidson's breeding of terriers all with the names of Mustard and Pepper, an activity which preceded the novel. A letter of Scott's to Daniel Terry, on 18 April 1816, written after attending a Circuit Court at Jedburgh, makes it clear however that he cannot have been an original model:

> there I was introduced to a man I never saw in my life before, namely, the proprietor of all the Pepper and Mustard family, —in other words, the genuine Dandie Dinmont. Dandie is himself modest, and says, "he b'lives it's only the dougs that is in the buik, and no himsel'." . . . In truth, I knew nothing of the man, except his odd humour of having only two names for twenty dogs. But there are lines of general resemblance among all these hillmen, which there is no missing; and Jamie Davidson of Hyndlea certainly looks Dandie Dinmont remarkably well.[23]

In a Magnum note, again recalling Davidson's good-humoured acknowledgement that 'the Sheriff had not written about him mair than about other folk, but only about his dogs', Scott stated categorically 'that the character of Dandie Dinmont was drawn from no individual'.[24] The popularity of the character nevertheless helped generate a number of real-life farming alternatives, among them: Archibald Park (1770–1820), described by Scott as 'five parts Dandie Dinmont with one part of civilisation',[25] after the loss of his Selkirkshire farm in 1815; John Thorburn of Juniper Bank, near Walkerburn (east of Innerleithen), a sportsman whose domestic life apparently resembled Dandie's, and who reportedly appeared before 'the feifteen' in the Court of Session; and James and Catherine Laidlaw, of Blackhouse, Yarrow, the parents of William Laidlaw, said by Lockhart jointly to represent the originals of Dandie and his wife Ailie. Robert Shortreed strongly favoured William Elliot of Milburnholm, near Hermitage Castle, recounting to his son, Andrew, how he had quizzed a not too resistant Scott on that score. Later Andrew Shortreed, working as a copyist at Abbotsford in May 1827, eagerly recorded what he took to be unequivocal proof:

> I have now got complete confirmation (was any needed?) of my fathers opinion about the original of Dandy Dinmont Jamie Davidson was certainly not the man—who was as certainly our friend Willie o' Milburnholm Mr Laidlaw once spoke to Sir Walter of the various persons to whom the character had been given— & Sir W said that he wondered Willie o' Millburn had never been spoken of for both in manner & figure he was liker Dandy than any of the others.[26]

Elliot, who had greeted Scott on the first day of his first Liddesdale visit, no doubt left an indelible impression as a robust and archetypal Border figure; he also appears to have been of a litigious disposition. Nonetheless the weight of evidence suggests that Dandie, like his home Charlieshope, is largely a generic creation.

Paulus Pleydell has been associated with two specific Scottish lawyers who flourished in the later eighteenth century: Andrew Crosbie (1735–85), and Adam Rolland (1734–1819). Andrew Crosbie was a native of Dumfries, gained a reputation in Parliament House as the leading pleader of his day, and lived during the height of his career off the High Street in Advocate's Close (where a plaque announcing the 'Residence of Andrew Crosbie, the jovial Counsellor Pleydell' is found today). Adam Rolland, a native of Fife, was called to the Bar in the same year as Crosbie (1757), but dealt almost exclusively in written pleas, gaining a reputation as an authority on legal matters. In a *Journal* entry for 19 June 1830, Scott records seeing 'with pleasure the painting by Raeburn of my old friend Samuel [*sic*] Roland Esq. who was in the external circumstances but not in frolick or fancy my prototype for Paul Pleydell'.[27] Not improbably though Scott's thoughts then were swayed by his need to get on with the sitter's nephew, Adam Rolland (1763–1837), a Principal Clerk of Session and Director of the Bank of Scotland. Henry Cockburn in *Memorials of His Time* (1856), commenting on the senior Rolland's death in 1819, offers a delightfully facetious portrait of an over-dressed ('a stain would kill him'), punctilious, woman-shy ('shuddered at the vicinity of a petticoat'), narrow-minded pedant, who had advised him at the start of his legal studies that 'philosophy is the vice of the age' (in fact, more Sir Robert Hazelwood than Pleydell).[28] Crosbie's intellectual verve (he was one of the few Scots to stand up to Samuel Johnson on his visit to Edinburgh in 1773) and his well-known tavern-haunting both make him a much better match for Scott's dashing figure, and he was clearly well-remembered as a brilliant if slightly wayward son in Parliament House (where his portrait hung) in Scott's day. His death in financial ruin as a result of drink and ill-judged speculation, reportedly in the attic of a splendid house he had built in the New Town, hardly fits on the other hand with the 'philosophical' lawyer whose apartments so confidently overlook the Forth in Scott's novel.

Suggested prototypes for Dominie Sampson include James Sanson (d. 1795), a minister of the Church of Scotland, who worked as a tutor because of his narrow circumstances; and George Thomson (1792–1838), tutor to Scott's children between 1812 and 1820, and also licensed as a preacher, though he was never inducted to a charge. In the case of Sanson the name is perhaps the most appealing link, there being no direct record of Scott's ever knowing him (though there is evidence that he worked for a while in the family of Scott's uncle, Thomas Scott, in Roxburghshire). Thomson, who had a wooden leg owing to a childhood accident, was something of a familiar at Abbotsford, where he sat at table and read grace, and there are fairly numerous references in Scott's letters to his eccentricities. Both were genuinely scholarly men, however, who faced their difficulties with courage, and it seems unlikely that Scott would create a caricature figure directly from either. Even less likely is the claim that the Dominie was based on John Leyden (1775–1811), Scott's early collaborator, though the idea that Scott was the originator of a caricature idea of Leyden as 'autodidact zany' still persists today. At first sight there might seem tempting parallels in Scott's obituary comments on Leyden, first published in the *Edinburgh Annual Register* for 1811 (but probably written by Scott in 1813):

> The late worthy and learned Professor Andrew Dalzell used to describe, with some humour, the astonishment and amusement excited in his class when John Leyden first stood up to recite his Greek exercise. The rustic, yet undaunted manner, the humble dress, the high, harsh tone of his voice, joined to the broad provincial accent of Teviotdale, discomposed, on the first occasion, the gravity of the professor, and totally routed that of his students.[29]

In the equivalent-seeming passage in *Guy*, where Sampson suffers 'the ridicule of all his school-companions' (11.19), it is his physical characteristics which make him the object of mirth, whereas in the case of Leyden social class is plainly the issue. A more fitting source for Sampson's pedantry and awkwardness might even have come from the direction of Galloway, a possibility apparently not hitherto acknowledged. In his *Scottish Gallovidian Encyclopedia* (1824), John Mactaggart (himself a humbly-born autodidact, and apparently oblivious to the existence of *Guy*) tells a story about Robert Heron's unwillingness to leave his books for dinner which reads like a carbon copy of the Dominie's similar self-absorption in his library (see note to 110.3). Scott had known Heron, and was aware of the tragic circumstance of his death as an impoverished author in 1807, albeit later calling him (at least in terms of literary value) 'a mere sot & beast'.[30]

One indisputable Galloway original is the smuggling skipper Jack Yawkins, whose entries into the Solway with his lugger and unloading of tea and spirits in the region of Kirkcudbright and Creetown are mentioned in several surviving Customs records,[31] and whose exploits were clearly legion in Galloway at the time. An account of 'the Dutch skipper Yawkins whose smuggling adventures on the Coast of Galloway and Ayrshire are yet well remembered' was sent by Joseph Train to Scott in May 1829, and duly went into the Magnum 'Additional Note', albeit with a garbling of some of the place names which suggests that Scott then (or a coadjutor) had little knowledge of the landing-points being described.[32] Possible etymological and historical origins for surnames such as Hattaraick, Dinmont, and Pleydell will be found at relevant points in the Explanatory Notes, which as a group also bear witness to the amazing range of allusion and polyphonic variety to be found in Scott's second novel.

NOTES

1 See e.g. Edgar Johnson, *Sir Walter Scott: The Great Unknown*, 2 vols (London, 1970), 1.536, also David Brown, *Walter Scott and the Historical Imagination* (London, 1979), 34, 212 (note 9).

2 Scott's own description of his nearly-completed novel, in a letter to J. B. S. Morritt, 19 January 1815 (*Letters*, 4.13). For standard abbreviations in references, see 372–73.

3 In *Scott on Himself*, ed. David Hewitt (Edinburgh, 1981), 8–9. The reference to Rodney's victory was first used as a means of dating the later plot of the novel by Jane Millgate, in her '*Guy Mannering* in Edinburgh: The Evidence of the Manuscript', *The Library*, 32 (1977), 244–45.

4 This also tallies with Lucy Bertram's age, which is twice given as seventeen (see 74.40, 84.11).

5 The post-manuscript addition in which Mrs Mac-Candlish offers this explanation presumably came as the result of a last-minute awareness that business could not be conducted on the Sabbath: otherwise the elder Bertram's death would have occurred on the exact anniversary of his ejection of the gypsies, which was probably Scott's original intention. See also Note on the Text, xlii, and EEWN 2, 383–84.

6 As reported by J. G. Lockhart, in *Life*, 3.321.

7 See e.g. P. H. M'Kerlie, *Galloway in Ancient and Modern Times* (Edinburgh and London, 1891), 310: 'In fact, all along the road and coast in that part the scene is laid.' The resemblances are elaborated in Andrew M'Cormick, *The Tinkler-Gypsies of Galloway* (Dumfries, 1906), especially 115–25. Another account is given in Rev. C. H. Dick's *Highways and Byways of Galloway and Carrick* (1916; reprinted Wigtown, 1994), 143–48, where it is again stated that 'The coast between Gatehouse and Creetown is the country of *Guy Mannering*' (143). Indicative of the tourist interest generated is H. Drummond Gauld's 'In the Land of *Guy Mannering*. The Cruives of the Cree', *SMT Magazine*, 9:6 (Dec. 1932), 25–30. SMT is an acronym for Scottish Motor Traction. An Ellangowan Hotel is still to be found in Creetown.

8 Robert Heron described the view as seen in Autumn 1792 in the following terms: 'Within the bounds of one landscape, the eye beholds the river Fleet discharging itself into the Firth; the house of *Bardarroch*, of *Ardwell*, of *Cally*, the beautiful and populous village of *Gatehouse*, and the ancient castle of *Cardiness*, with a large extent of adjacent country, either cultivated, and thick-set with farm-houses, with abundance of wood interspersed, or —towards the extremities of the prospect—wildly picturesque' (*Observations made in a Journey through the Western Counties of Scotland in the Autumn of MDCCXCII*, 2nd edn, 2 vols (Perth, 1799), 2.212). This invites

comparison with the prospect from Ellangowan, especially as viewed in day-time by Mannering (21.43–22.28).

9 Magnum, 3.41n. Scott expressed a desire to 'see Carlaverock' when proposing a visit to his friend Charles Kirkpatrick Sharpe on 18 June 1812 (*Letters*, 3.131). Sharpe resided at Hoddam Castle, between Ecclefechan and Lockerbie in SE Dumfriesshire.

10 Dick, 146 ('If Scott had seen this cave, he certainly did not attempt to describe it'). Another cave with the reputation of being 'Dirk Hatteraick's Cave' (and so marked on Ordnance Survey maps) is found just below Torrs Point on the east bank of Kirkcudbright Bay.

11 For Scott's family connection with the McCullochs of Ardwall, see Introduction, xiv, and EEWN 2, 362.

12 Scott's extensive note, headed 'Mumps's Ha'', is in Magnum, 3.228–30. For a useful account of Scott's 1797 visit, and the condition of the village and spa at that time, see F. B. Whitehead and P. J. Yarrow, 'Sir Walter Scott and Gilsland', *Durham University Journal*, 80 (1987), 3–7. The landlady of Mumps's Ha' is named as Meg Carrick or Teasdale in W. S. Crockett, *The Scott Originals* (Edinburgh, 1915), 50, 115; and as Margaret Teasdale in Rev. W. G. Bird, *Gilsland and Neighbourhood. Description and History*, 5th edn (Rothbury, 1926), 17–18. Denton Church is now unused, and a recent search among the surrounding graves failed to reveal either name.

13 In his Magnum note on Mumps's Ha' Scott uses yet another descriptive term, in describing 'a barren and lonely district, without either road or pathway, emphatically called the Waste of Bewcastle' (3.228). On John Thomson's map of the 'Southern Part of Roxburghshire' (1822) 'Bewcastle' and 'The Waste' (the latter positioned slightly higher than the former) are both shown running up to the southern bank of Kershope Water, where it forms the boundary between England and Scotland.

14 'Dawstane' appears as a settlement, just above Saughtree at the head of Liddesdale, on Matthew Stobie's 'Map of Roxburghshire and Tiviotdale' (1770).

15 For Shortreed's responses, as recorded by his son Andrew, see 'Conversations with my Father on the Subject of his tours with Sir Walter Scott in Liddisdale', National Library of Scotland (NLS), MS 8993, ff. 111–12. Shortreed also describes how, at one point, Scott had ridden six miles to Twislehope just to verify the 'lilt' of a ballad (f. 101).

16 *Blackwood's Edinburgh Magazine*, 1 (April 1817), 54. Passages contributed by Scott to the article are identifiable through his surviving holograph manuscript (NLS, MS 23057).

17 *Blackwood's Edinburgh Magazine*, 1.57. According to Thomas Pringle, the section on Madge Gordon was supplied by 'my early & intimate friend the Revd. Robert Story, now minister of Roseneath in Dunbartonshire', whose father had been the parish schoolmaster at Yetholm (letter to Scott, 23 October 1829 (NLS, MS 3910, f. 264r)).

18 Magnum, 3.xxvi.

19 *Letters*, 9.474.

20 Scott had recommended William Smith as the best authority on the Yetholm gypsies when asked to respond to a questionnaire concerning the

gypsies circularised among the Scottish sheriffs in September 1815. Smith's response is given in full in John A. Fairley, *Bailie Smith of Kelso's Account of the Gypsies of Kirk Yetholm* (Hawick, 1907). Scott's briefer answer appears in John Hoyland, *A Historical Survey of the Customs, Habits and Present State of the Gypsies* (York, 1816), 93–95. For a fuller account of the arguments in favour of an Indian origin for the gypsies, and the possible influence of this theory on Scott's novel, see Peter Garside, 'Meg Merrilies and India', in *Scott in Carnival*, ed. J. H. Alexander and David Hewitt (Aberdeen, 1993), 154–71.

21 See especially M'Cormick, *Tinkler-Gypsies of Galloway*, *passim*.

22 Magnum 4.377. Train's account is in NLS, MS 874, ff. 134–38 (sent as part of a letter to Scott, 16 May 1829).

23 *Letters*, 4.216–17.

24 Magnum, 3.241n–42n.

25 *Letters*, 4.129. Park (a brother of Mungo Park, the explorer) and other contenders to be the 'original' of Dinmont are described in Robert Chambers's *Illustrations of the Author of Waverley*, 2nd edn (Edinburgh, 1825), and in Crockett, *Scott Originals*, themselves the two main secondary sources for information concerning possible prototypes for Scott's characters in *Guy Mannering*.

26 NLS, MS 8993, f. 136. For Shortreed's earlier 'Conversations' (1824) with his son on this topic, including an account of Scott's first meeting with William Elliot, see ff. 94–96. Robert Shortreed also offers a solution to the apparent anomaly of Scott including the Mustard and Pepper dogs in *Guy* previous to meeting their owner, by suggesting that John Wilson (1785–1854) had earlier visited Hyndlee and told Scott about them (see f. 112).

27 *Journal*, 599.

28 Henry Cockburn, *Memorials of His Time* (Edinburgh, 1856), 360–63.

29 *Prose Works*, 4.144. Scott refers in a letter to Archibald Constable, of 25 June 1813, to having completed this memoir (*Letters*, 3.291). The term 'autodidact zany' is taken from John Sutherland's *The Life of Walter Scott* (Oxford, 1995), 78, where Scott is attacked for having originated a caricature version of Leyden later completed by Lockhart.

30 John Mactaggart, *The Scottish Gallovidian Encyclopedia* (London, 1824), 260; *Letters*, 3.396.

31 Transcripts of reports in 1787 and 1789 relating to incursions by Yawkins are given in Frances Williams, *Dumfries & Galloway's Smuggling Story* (Kidderminster, 1993), 104–05.

32 Train's account appears in his two letters, 12 and 16 May 1829, NLS, MS 874, ff. 126–30, 132–33. In the Magnum Note (4.374–76) Raeberry becomes Rueberry, and Train's 'the entrance of the Dee and the Cree' (f. 132r) is presented as if one location rather than as alternatives. Reference to Scott's holograph 'Additional Note', consisting of four large folio sheets found at the end of Vol. 3 of the Interleaved Set (ISet), and taken directly from Train's materials, indicates that the mis-spelling of Raeberry is probably a mistake by an intermediary in reading Scott's hand, while the confusion over the Dee and the Cree stems at least in part from Scott's misinterpretation of Train's sentence structure.

EXPLANATORY NOTES

In these notes a comprehensive attempt is made to identify Scott's sources, and all quotations, references, historical events, and historical personages, to explain proverbs, and to translate difficult or obscure language. (Phrases are explained in the notes while single words are treated in the glossary.) The notes are brief; they offer information rather than critical comment or exposition. When a quotation has not been recognised this is stated: any new information from readers will be welcomed. References are to first editions, standard editions, or to the editions Scott himself used. Books in the Abbotsford Library are identified, where significant, by reference to the appropriate page of the *Catalogue of the Library at Abbotsford.* When quotations reproduce their sources accurately, the reference is given without comment. Verbal differences in the source are indicated by a prefatory 'see', while a general rather than a verbal indebtedness is indicated by 'compare'. Biblical references are to the Authorised Version. Plays by Shakespeare are cited without authorial ascription, and references are to *William Shakespeare: The Complete Works*, edited by Peter Alexander (London and Glasgow, 1951, frequently reprinted). Manuscripts referred to with the prefix MS/MSS are in the National Library of Scotland.

The following publications are distinguished by abbreviations:

CLA [J. G. Cochrane], *Catalogue of the Library at Abbotsford* (Edinburgh, 1838).

Child Francis James Child, *The English and Scottish Popular Ballads*, 5 vols (Boston and New York, 1882–98).

Christian Astrology William Lilly, *Christian Astrology* (London, 1647): *CLA*, 148.

Grose Francis Grose, *A Classical Dictionary of the Vulgar Tongue* (London, 1785): see *CLA*, 156.

ISet the Interleaved Set, *Novels and Tales of the Author of Waverley*, 12 vols (Edinburgh, 1822): vols 2 and 3, MSS 23002–03.

Journal *The Journal of Sir Walter Scott*, ed. W. E. K. Anderson (Oxford, 1972).

Kinsley *The Poems and Songs of Robert Burns*, ed. James Kinsley, 3 vols (Oxford, 1968).

Letters *The Letters of Sir Walter Scott*, ed. H. J. C. Grierson and others, 12 vols (London, 1932–37).

Life J. G. Lockhart, *Memoirs of the Life of Sir Walter Scott, Bart.*, 7 vols (Edinburgh, 1837–38).

Magnum Walter Scott, *Waverley Novels*, 48 vols (Edinburgh, 1829–33).

Minstrelsy Walter Scott, *Minstrelsy of the Scottish Border*, ed. T. F. Henderson, 4 vols (Edinburgh, 1902).

ODEP *The Oxford Dictionary of English Proverbs*, 3rd edn, rev. F. P. Wilson (Oxford, 1970).

OED *The Oxford English Dictionary*, 12 vols (Oxford, 1933).

Percy *Reliques of Ancient English Poetry*, [ed. Thomas Percy], 3 vols (London, 1765): see *CLA*, 172.

Poetical Works *The Poetical Works of Sir Walter Scott, Bart.*, ed. J. G. Lockhart, 12 vols (Edinburgh, 1833–34).

Prose Works *The Prose Works of Sir Walter Scott, Bart.*, 28 vols (Edinburgh, 1834–36).

Ramsay Allan Ramsay, *A Collection of Scots Proverbs* (1737), in *The Works of Allan Ramsay*, 6 vols, Vol. 5, ed. Alexander M. Kinghorn and Alexander Law (Edinburgh and London: Scottish Text Society, 1972), 59–133.

Ray J[ohn] Ray, A *Compleat Collection of English Proverbs*, 3rd edn (London, 1737): *CLA*, 169.

Information derived from the notes of the late Dr J. C. Corson is indicated by '(Corson)'. In legal matters the notes (MS 23071, loose slips; MS 23096, notebook) of the late Lord Normand '(Normand)' have been useful. The following editions of *Guy Mannering* have proved most helpful: The Border Edition, with notes by Andrew Lang, 24 vols (London, 1901), Vol. 2; ed. A. D. Innes (Oxford, 1910); ed. R. F. Winch (London, 1913). Useful information has also been found in J. H. Boardman, *Notes on Scott's Guy Mannering* (London, 1922).

title-page *Waverley* was Scott's first novel, published anonymously in 1814.

epigraph see Walter Scott, *The Lay of the Last Minstrel* (1805), Canto 6, stanza 5 (*Poetical Works*, 6.190).

3 motto Samuel Johnson, *The Idler*, no. 49 (Saturday, 24 March 1759); *The Works of Samuel Johnson*, Vol. 2, ed. W. J. Bate and others (New Haven and London, 1963), 154.

3.19 monastic ruins . . . county of Dumfries likely to have been in Scott's mind are Lincluden College, 2 km N of Dumfries, originally a Benedictine nunnery, founded *c.* 1160; Dundrennan Abbey, 10 km E of Kirkcudbright, a Cistercian foundation of 1142, mentioned in several other of his works, but actually in the Stewartry of Kirkcudbright; and Sweetheart Abbey (founded 1273), 10 km S of Dumfries, to which Scott himself paid a visit in 1807, and also in Kirkcudbrightshire.

4.6 village of Kippletringan probably fictitious, though some commentators have claimed that Gatehouse of Fleet is the prototype (see Historical Note, 361). The name itself is close to that of Killantringan, a small settlement 2 km N of Portpatrick (Wigtownshire), where there is also a Killantringan Bay.

4.10 cross interrogatories the term *interrogatories* was commonly used in Scottish legal proceedings to describe questions put to witnesses; 'cross interrogatories' are questions to be put to witnesses called for the other party. 'Leading' questions, such as those directed at Mannering here, are permissible in cross examination (i.e. through cross interrogatories) but not when examining one's own witnesses.

4.12 Abbey o' Halycross probably fictitious, but perhaps echoing Sweetheart Abbey (see note to 3.19).

4.13–14 house o' Pouderloupat probably fictitious.

4.19 a gay bit a considerable distance.

4.22 there awa thereabout.

4.38 North-Britain i.e. Scotland; a term commonly used after the Union with England in 1707.

5.7–8 bog-blitter, or bull-of-the-bog common Scots terms for the bittern, a wading bird of the heron species, noted for its booming cry.

5.33 three points of admiration three exclamation marks, with *admiration* being used in its old sense of 'wonder' or 'astonishment'. Compare Scott's journal entry for 12 April 1826: 'I have finishd my task this morning at half past eleven, easily and early and I think not amiss. I hope J.B. will make some great points of admiration!!!' (*Journal*, 129).

5.35 the Whaap 'The Hope, often pronounced Whaap, is the sheltered part or hollow of the hill' (Magnum, 3.7n).
5.35 Ballenloan not identified, probably fictitious.
5.40 Drumshourloch fair not identified, though there is a Drummuckloch (presently a farm) 3 km SW of Gatehouse of Fleet. Fairs at which livestock were exchanged were a common feature of life in SW Scotland, one of the most prominent in Galloway being held at Keltonhill near Castle Douglas.
6.2 I'se warrant I'll bet, I'll be sure.
6.2 gentle or semple well-born or commoner.
6.15 canny moment moment of childbirth.
6.36–37 rood of the simple masonry *rood* here apparently denotes a linear measurement (commonly 18 feet: 5.4 metres) commonly used when building stone walls in the 18th century.
7.2–3 Ellangowan Auld Place probably fictitious, though Scott in the Magnum noted a physical likeness to Caerlaverock Castle in Dumfriesshire, while other commentators have claimed connections with a number of castles in the Stewartry of Kirkcudbright (see Historical Note, 361–62). There is a Killiegowan Wood 1 km NW of Gatehouse of Fleet.
7 motto *1 Henry IV*, 3.1.98–100.
7.25 feras consumere nati *Latin* born to consume wild game. An adaptation from Horace's 'fruges consumere nati' ('born to consume the fruits of the earth') in *Epistles*, 1.2.27. It was originally used by Henry Fielding in relation to the sporting squires of England, in his novel *Tom Jones* (1749), Bk 3, Ch. 2.
7.38 Galwegian independence Galloway, the district comprising Wigtownshire and the Stewartry of Kirkcudbright in SW Scotland, anciently formed part of the Celtic kingdom of Cumbria or Strathclyde. In the early 12th century Fergus, Lord of Galloway, claimed independence from the Scottish crown, and a kind of semi-autonomy was maintained for more than 100 years.
7.39–40 Godfreys, and Gilberts, and Dennis's, and Rolands Norman family names familiar among the Crusaders.
7.41 Arths, and Knarths, and Donagilds, and Hanlons apparently representing names of old Celtic families.
8.2 Mac-Dingawaie evidently Scott's humorous invention based on the Scots verb *ding*, 'to beat, strike'.
8.13 Vicar of Bray Bray is a small parish on the Thames in Berkshire; and in the 16th century its vicar, Simon Aleyn, is supposed to have survived in office by changing between Catholic and Protestant religions during the reigns of four monarchs. In the well-known song of that name, the time-serving vicar adheres to the same principle 'to live and die the Vicar of Bray' through political changes from the Stuart Charles II to the Hanoverian George I.
8.16 tempore Caroli primi in the time of Charles the First, i.e. Charles I (reigned 1625–49).
8.17 Sir Robert Douglas, in his Scottish Baronage Sir Robert Douglas of Glenbervie (1694–1770), Scottish genealogist, was the compiler of *The Peerage of Scotland* (1764) and *The Baronage of Scotland; containing an historical account of the Gentry of that Kingdom* (1798). Scott's account of the Ellangowan 'entry' offers a fair parody of Douglas's style and royalist sympathies.
8.19–20 Marquis of Montrose James Graham (1612–50), first Marquis and fifth Earl of Montrose, leader of the Royalist campaign in Scotland, which after a succession of victories ended with defeat at Philiphaugh in 1645.
8.22–23 sequestrated as a malignant by the parliament deprived of the revenues of his estates by the Scottish Parliament subject to the payment of heavy fines. The term *malignant*, as employed here, denotes Catholics and Episcopalians considered by the Presbyterian party as standing outside the pale of the true Church. No Scottish parliament sat in 1642, and Scott is perhaps

thinking of the English Parliament and the outbreak of the Civil War. The Scottish Parliament, however, had a standing committee called the Conservators of Peace, which was active in suppressing episcopacy.
8.23 resolutioner the name given to a new party which emerged in 1650–51 (not as Scott states 1648), whose aim was to reconcile the Royalists with the more moderate Presbyterians, and with the purpose of raising an army for the invasion of England in support of Charles II. It is unlikely that Ellangowan, already a royalist, would ever have been described as a resolutioner; and Scott may have confused the *resolutioners* with the *engagers*, who, under the Duke of Hamilton, actively supported the king in 1648.
8.27 council of state a commission set up in 1654 to manage Scottish affairs during the Cromwellian occupation of Scotland.
8.35 the Highland host Highland regiments were quartered in the West of Scotland in 1678, during the Royalist administration of the Duke of Lauderdale, in an effort to disarm and intimidate the Presbyterian Covenanters, or, as some people believed, to incite them into open rebellion; they were authorised to take free quarters and horses as needed, and were indemnified from legal action.
8.38 Argyle's rebellion an abortive Scottish rising in 1685, against the now openly Roman Catholic James VII and II. It was headed by Archibald Campbell, ninth Earl of Argyll, and was meant to coincide with Monmouth's Protestant rebellion in England.
8.39 Dunnottar Castle 2 km S of Stonehaven, in Kincardineshire, in NE Scotland.
8.39–40 the Mearns a traditional name for an area of Kincardineshire, S of Aberdeen.
8.41 Whigs' Vault between May and July 1685 Dunnottar Castle was used as a state prison for over 160 Covenanters, who were confined in a cellar still called the Whigs' Vault. A group of some 25 escaped through a window and crept along the edge of the cliff; but two died in the attempt, and most of the others were recaptured. A tombstone in Dunnottar churchyard, which Scott visited in 1796, commemorates those who died at Dunnottar, including 'two who perished comeing doune the rock one whose name was James Watson the other not known'.
8.42 appriser in Scots law roughly equivalent to the holder of a mortgage in England, as Scott implies. *Apprising* was a procedure whereby a creditor could have the lands of his debtor sold to satisfy the debt (or transferred to him if no purchaser came forward). Whereas in English law the mortgager had immediate power of sale, in Scots law the debtor had a right of redemption within seven years. The Act 1672, c. 45 introduced the process of adjudication for debt whereby, in place of apprising, the creditor had to raise an action in the Court of Session and, if successful, have a proportion of the debtor's land adjudged to him to settle the debt.
9.1 came me cranking in see *1 Henry IV*, 3.1.99, where, in examining a map which divides the kingdom into three, Hotspur objects to the incursions into his own part made by the winding course of the River Trent.
9.6 the Rev. Aaron Macbriar Scott also gives the name Macbriar to one of the leading Covenanting preachers in *The Tale of Old Mortality* (1816).
9.9 Laird of Lagg, Theophilus Oglethorpe, and Sir James Turner Sir Robert Grierson (1655?–1733), Laird of Lagg, gained notoriety for persecuting the Covenanters in SW Scotland, and is supposedly the model for Sir Robert Redgauntlet (of 'Wandering Willie's Tale') in Scott's *Redgauntlet* (1824). Sir Theophilus Oglethorpe (1650–1702) commanded the advance guard against the Covenanters at Bothwell Bridge, 1679, and rose to the rank of brigadier-general under James VII and II. Sir James Turner (1651–86?) accompanied

Charles II to the Battle of Worcester, 1651, and after the Restoration of the monarchy in 1660 commanded forces in SW Scotland against the Covenanters, briefly falling captive to them; he is probably a prototype of Sir Dugald Dalgetty in Scott's *A Legend of the Wars of Montrose* (1819): see EEWN 7b, 220.

9.11 **Clavers at Killie-krankie . . . Dunkeld** the Jacobite army led by John Graham of Claverhouse (*c.* 1649–89), first Viscount Dundee, gained a crushing victory over government forces at Killiecrankie in 1689, though at the cost of its leader's life. Dunkeld, also in Perthshire, was the scene of a defeat of the Jacobites, less than a month later.

9.12 **Cameronian with a silver button** the Cameronians, followers of the doctrines of Richard Cameron (d. 1680), a noted member of the Reformed Presbyterian Church, formed a regiment serving the government side on the accession of William III in 1689, and distinguished themselves by their defence at Dunkeld (see note above). The superstition that a person in league with the devil can only be shot by a gun containing a silver button or bullet, is more commonly associated with the career and death of Claverhouse; it is referred to explicitly in *The Tale of Old Mortality* (EEWN 4b, 142.17–20).

9.20 **went out with Lord Kenmore** i.e. joined arms against the Hanoverian government in 1715. William Gordon, sixth Viscount Kenmure, headed the Jacobite rising among certain members of the country gentry in SW Scotland, eventually combining with a similar revolt by the Earl of Derwentwater in Northumberland. He was executed in 1716 on Tower Hill in London and forfeited his title.

9.22 **Earl of Mar** John Erskine (1675–1732), sixth Earl of Mar, leader of the Scottish Jacobites in 1715, who fled to France after the indecisive Battle of Sheriffmuir.

9.23 **Scylla and Charybdis** a sea-monster (later rationalised into a rock) and a whirlpool, situated in the Straits of Messina, between Sicily and Italy, and equally threatening to ancient mariners who must pass between them (see Homer, *Odyssey*, 12.73).

9.23 **a word to the wise** proverbial: *ODEP*, 914. Originally from the Latin 'verbum sapienti sat est' ('a hint is sufficient to any intelligent person'). The hint is evidently to the twin perils represented by Scylla and Charybdis.

9.27 **as a mouse . . . firlot** not found as a proverb; but Scott uses the expression at least twice in his correspondence with reference to conditions at Abbotsford (see *Letters*, 5.224, 9.380). A *firlot* (8 gallons or 36 litres) is a Scottish dry measure used for corn etc.

9.28–29 **narrow house of three stories** Scott's description of the New Place at Ellangowan matches in some respects the Georgian house at Ardwall built by David McCulloch in 1762 (see Introduction, xiv, and EEWN 2, 363). In a letter of 26 November 1816 to Joanna Baillie, detailing his plans for variety at Abbotsford, Scott expresses a desire to rise above 'the cut-lugged bandbox with four rooms on a floor and two stories rising regularly above each other' (*Letters*, 4.301).

9.30 **cross lights** lights whose rays cross each other.

9.34 **took some land into his own hand** undertook the farming of land previously let out.

9.35–36 **Highland cattle and Cheviot sheep** 'Cheviot sheep', a hardy breed from the eastern Borders and so named after the range of hills separating England and Scotland, were gradually replacing the older and less profitable 'blackface' breed in the 18th century. Highland cattle refers to the 'black cattle' bred in the West Highlands and sold in southern markets. Lewis Bertram's activities in the latter respect reflect those of Scott's grandfather, Robert Scott, as described by Scott in his Ashestiel 'Memoirs': 'He was one of the first who was active in the cattle trade afterwards carried to such extent between the Highlands of Scotland and the feeding counties in England, and by his droving transactions acquired a considerable sum of money' (*Scott on Himself*, ed. David Hewitt (Edinburgh, 1981), 4).

9.36–37 held necessity at the staff's end proverbial: see *ODEP*, 769.

9.41–42 the article of Ellangowan's gentry compare *The Merry Wives of Windsor*, 2.1.45–46 ('the article of thy gentry').

10.10 man of business Scottish term for a family solicitor or law agent.

10.12–13 moveable bonds became hereditable *moveable bonds*, which are written obligations to pay money, were replaced by *heritable bonds*, which are secured on landed property, so that in the event of a failure to pay the creditor has possession of the land without needing to go through the process of adjudication (see note to 8.42).

10.15 charged to make payment legally compelled to pay (a *charge* is a writ ordering the debtor to pay his debt).

10.22 division of a common under the Act 1695, c. 69 commons could be divided and sold. Such lands often involved traditional rights such as pasturing animals, cutting peat, etc., hence the unpopularity of such procedures.

10.23 black-fishing salmon were termed *black fish* just after the spawning season, when fishing was illegal; though *black-fishing* is sometimes used more broadly to describe the poaching of salmon at night, by means of torches.

10.33 nae nice body not a fussy or fastidious person.

11.10 Dominie Sampson *Dominie* in Scots can mean a schoolmaster or a clergyman, though the immediate context indicates that schoolmaster is intended here. For possible prototypes of this character, see Historical Note, 368.

11.21 the yards the enclosed grounds outside a school or college, with specific reference here to those at Glasgow College. Compare *Rob Roy* (1818): 'I wandered from one quadrangle of old-fashioned buildings to another, and from thence to the College-yards, or walking-ground' (2.242.14–17). At Edinburgh High School, Scott felt that he had 'made a brighter figure in the *yards* than in the *class*': see 'Memoirs', in *Scott on Himself*, ed. David Hewitt (Edinburgh, 1981), 21.

11.36–38 torn cloak and tattered shoe . . . from Juvenal's time downward the Roman poet Juvenal (in Satire 3) actually refers to poor people in general. Among the trappings of poverty which make them objects of ridicule are mentioned 'scissa lacerna' (3.148: a torn cloak) and 'rupta calceus alter/ pelle' (3.149–50: one shoe with torn leather).

12.4 probationer of divinity one who has graduated and been licensed by a presbytery or synod of the Church of Scotland to preach under supervision; normally, on the way to becoming ordained as a parish minister.

12.12 stickit minister one who has failed to find a position in the Church of Scotland after studying for it.

12.19 Sampson's Riddle the original Samson's Riddle is in Judges 14.14 ('Out of the eater came forth meat, and out of the strong came forth sweetness').

12.20 student of humanity i.e. studying Latin as a subject (though a pun stemming from the wider connotation of 'humanity' is apparently also intended).

12.21 college gates Samson carried off the gates at Gaza when surrounded by his enemies (see Judges 16.3).

12.34 snuff candles trim the wick, remove the used part of the wick to enable the candle to burn more brightly.

13 motto Samuel Butler, *Hudibras* (1663), 2.3.685–90.

13.11 Chaldeans, learned Genethliacs both terms are archaic synonyms for 'astrologer'. The Chaldeans, from ancient Babylonia, were famous for being soothsayers; *genethliac* stems from a Greek noun meaning 'time of birth'. Butler's line echoes Aulus Gellius, *Noctes Atticae*, 14.1.1, where he mentions 'istos

qui sese "Chaldaeos" seu "genethliacos" appellant' ('those who call themselves Chaldeans or nativity-casters').
13.26 **kirk dues** the father of an illegitimate child had a duty to contribute to the lying-in expenses of the mother, as well as for the its later support; this was regulated by the parish where the mother was settled, the Kirk Session having a general jurisdiction over the morals of its parishioners.
13.26–27 **it was put till her ere she had a sark ower her head** perhaps meaning the baby was presented to the mother (i.e. shown to her by the midwife) before she was dressed in a shift, a reference to the speed of delivery.
13.29 **Annan** town at the mouth of the River Annan, *c.* 25 km SE of Dumfries, on the north bank of the Solway Firth.
13.33–34 **Board of Excise . . . commissionership** members of the Excise Board for Scotland were called commissioners, and were elected by those with a vote in county elections.
13.37 **Laird of Balruddery** fictitious character; though there is Balruddery, Angus, near Dundee.
13.37–38 **out with Kenmore** as a participant in the 1715 Jacobite rising in favour of the exiled Stuart monarchy; see also note to 9.20.
13.38 **never took the oaths** i.e. the oaths of allegiance (to the Hanoverian crown) and of abjuration (of the Pretender).
13.39 **off the roll** non-jurors, that is Episcopalians refusing to take the oath of allegiance to the monarchy, were excluded from the electoral roll. See also note to 28.5.
13.41 **Sir Thomas Kittlecourt** burlesque name, implying a willingness to flatter the powers that be; *kittle* in Scots means 'tickle'.
14.7–10 **Canny moment . . . mass** this verse, along with the two stanzas at 14.41–15.4, is apparently Scott's own composition (but see also note to 14.38–39).
14.11 **Meg Merrilies, the gypsie** for possible historical prototypes of this character, see Historical Note, 365–66. Compare also Meg's entry here and the appearance of the gypsy (also accompanied by song) at an early point in M. G. Lewis's novel, *The Monk* (1796).
14.29 **snakes of the gorgon** the heads of the three Gorgon sisters, in Classical mythology, had serpents in place of hair.
14.37 **gyre carlings** supernatural female beings, witches.
14.38–39 **Saint Colme's charm** St Columba (d. 597) established a monastery at Iona, from which missionaries began the evangelisation of Scotland. He is traditionally associated with the performance of miracles. The second quatrain of the verse which follows closely matches a traditional charm meant to protect the household, as cited in George Sinclair's *Satans Invisible World Discovered* (Edinburgh, 1685), 217: 'Who fains the house the night,/ They that fains it ilk a night:/ Saint *Bryde* and her Brat,/ Saint *Colme* and his Hat,/ Saint *Michael* and his Spear,/ keep this house from the Wear'. Citations in the present notes from this work relate to the copy in the Abbotsford Library (*CLA*, 142).
14.41 **Trefoil, vervain, John's-wort, dill** *Trefoil* is a plant with clover-like leaves and yellow flowers, found in grassy places; *vervain* is a perennial purple-flowering plant, once much used in medicines and also mixed in love potions; leaves and flowers of *St John's Wort*, a yellow-flowered plant of the genus Hypericum, are a traditional herbal remedy; *dill* is an annual herb whose fruit and seeds are still widely used as flavouring in cooking.
14.44 **St Andrew's day** 30 November; St Andrew is the patron saint of Scotland.
15.1 **Saint Bride and her brat** St Bride (or St Brigit) was an Irish saint, with a reputation for purity and innocence. The word *brat* has been interpreted variously as denoting a cloak (from the Gaelic word for an apron) or alternat-

ively a child, but the former seems more probable in view of the legend that St Brigit spread her cloak across the sky.

15.2 **Saint Colme and his hat** St Columba is not commonly associated with either a 'hat' (the manuscript reading) or a 'cat' (the Ed1 reading). 'Hat', however, matches the earlier version of this quatrain found in George Sinclair's *Satans Invisible World Discovered* (1685), *CLA*, 142: see note to 14.38–39.

15.3 **Saint Michael and his spear** the archangel St Michael is often represented with a spear in one hand and a banner in the other.

15.16 **gae them leg-bail** ran off, decamped.

15.18 **black be his cast** bad fortune to him.

15.19 **drap's bluid** blood relation.

15.22–23 **if the red cock craw not** i.e. whether fire does not burst out.

15.28 **Fire-raising** the technical term in Scots law equivalent to arson: it was a capital offence.

15.37 **the trysting-tree** a trysting place was a location, usually a well-known landmark, employed as a rendezvous and used for undertaking oaths and obligations.

15.41 **student from Oxford** compare James Hogg's *The Private Memoirs and Confessions of a Justified Sinner*, where Robert Wringhim tells the occupants at an inn that he is a student of theology at Oxford: 'they had some crude conceptions that nothing was taught at Oxford but the *black arts*, which ridiculous idea prevailed all over the south of Scotland' (1st edn (London, 1824), 353).

16.2 **Triplicities** in astrology a combination of three of the twelve signs of the zodiac, each related to one of the four elements.

16.2 **Pythagoras** Greek philosopher and mathematician, born at Samos *c.* 580 BC. The most important ideas associated with him were connected with number and music. Having demonstrated intervals of the scale could be described in simple ratios, he tried to apply these to calculate the distances between the planets. For Pythagoras number was the building block of the universe.

16.2 **Hippocrates** celebrated physician, born in the island of Cos *c.* 460 BC, who taught in Athens and is credited with numerous medical treatises (his name survives in the 'Hippocratic oath' taken by modern physicians). In attempting to relate the four elements to the four humours of the body, he is supposed to have laid the ground for medical astrology.

16.2 **Diocles** Greek philosopher and pioneer in medicine of the 4th century BC, second only to Hippocrates in reputation and ability according to tradition.

16.3 **Avicenna** alternative name for the celebrated Arabian philosopher, physician and astronomer, Ibn Sina (980–1037). His *Canon of Medicine* was the fundamental text for medical studies in the late Middle Ages, and he was also a pioneer in the fields of optics and mechanics.

16.3 **ab hora questionis** *Latin* from the hour of the investigation or enquiry. Having offered to calculate the natal chart in order to describe the temperament and future prospects of the child, and citing his first four authorities, Mannering turns to the option of treating the chart as a horary (i.e. pertaining to an hour) question. Horary astrology is a form of divination, capable of responding to very specific questions. The astrologer makes a note of the time a question is asked, and then draws a chart in the same way as for a birth but interprets it through a complicated set of rules to reach an answer. William Lilly (see note to 20.6) is the father of horary practice in English.

16.3 **Haly** Albohazen Haly, author of *Preclarissimus in Judiciis Astrorum* (Venice, 1503): probably an alternative name for Ali Ibn Abi Al-Rijal, 11th century Arabian astrologer.

16.3 **Messahala** Masha'allah (died *c.* 815), astronomer of the Islamic school, whose *Book of Eclipses* contained an astrological history, pointing to the correspondence between historical periods and the intervals between planetary conjunctions; materials attributed to him were first translated into Latin in the 12th century, and continued to be influential among astrologers in the Renaissance period.

16.4 Ganivetus Jean Ganivet (fl. 1431–34), medical astrologer, whose *Amicus Medicorum* appeared in several editions in the 15th and 16th centuries.

16.4 Guido Bonatus Guido Bonatti, Italian astronomer of the 13th century, a significant figure in the transition between Arabian astronomy and later European horary astrology. His 146 aphorisms were translated by Henry Coley and published in William Lilly's *Anima Astrologiae* (1676).

16.8–9 bites and bams, since denominated hoaxes and quizzes Scott is here contrasting two modish slang words of his period with two equivalents belonging to the mid-18th century. See glossary for specific words.

16.16 Prodigious! see note to 41.23.

16.27 Sir Isaac Newton (1642–1727), the English natural philosopher, whose scientific discoveries included the law of gravitation, and who also made advances in the construction of the telescope; he was appointed Master of the Mint, 1699, and elected President of the Royal Society in 1703.

16.30 oracular jaws compare *Hamlet*, 1.4.50, and George Crabbe, *The Parish Register* (1807), 1.682.

16.34–35 grave and sonorous authorities the list of names which follows, apart from differences in spelling and the omission of one name, matches William Lilly's prefatory 'To the Reader' in his *Christian Astrology* (London, 1647): 'yet have I conferred my owne notes with Dariot, Bonatus, Ptolomey, Haly, Etzler, Dietericus, Naibod, Hasfurtus, Zael, Tanstettor, Agrippa, Ferriers, Duret, Maginus, Origanus, Argol' ([ii]). Specific works by the above are also cited in the bibliography ('A Catalogue of most Astrological Authors now extant, where printed, and in what yeer') at the end of *Christian Astrology*, [833–44]. A first edition of Lilly's *Christian Astrology* is in the Abbotsford Library (*CLA*, 148), and citations in the present notes have been taken from that copy. With the exception of Ptolemy, and to a lesser extent Agrippa, little is now known about these authorities, who are perhaps meant here to read like an arbitrary and empty, if impressive-sounding, succession of names. For Lilly, see note to 20.6.

16.35 Dariot Claude Dariot (1533–94), author of several astrological treatises published in Latin in the 16th century, including *Ad Astrorum Judicia Facilis Introductio* (Lyons, 1557). An English translation, *Judgment of the Stars* (London, 1598), is listed by William Lilly under Claudius Dariot in the bibliography at the end of *Christian Astrology*, [835].

16.35 Bonatus see note to 16.4.

16.35 Ptolemy (*c.* 100–170) celebrated astronomer of Alexandria, who established the science on a geometrical basis, with the earth at the centre of the heavenly bodies.

16.35 Haly see note to16.3.

16.35 Etzler August Etzler, 17th-century German medical astrologer, whose works include *Isagoge physico-magico-medica* (Strasbourg, 1631), listed by Lilly under Augustus Etzlerus in *Christian Astrology*, [836].

16.36 Dieterick Helvig Dieterich (1601–55), author of several works of astronomy, including *Elogium Planetarum Coelestium et Terrestrium Macrocosmi et Microcosmi* (Strasbourg, 1627). Lilly lists this under Helvicus Dietericus, in *Christian Astrology*, [835].

16.36 Naibod Valentin Naibod (d. 1593), author of *Enarratio Elementorum Astrologiae* (Cologne, 1560) and other works of astrology. Lilly lists two titles as by Valentinus Naibod in *Christian Astrology*, [840].

16.36 Hasfurt Johann Virdung von Hasfurt (*c.* 1465–*c.* 1535), German astrologer. Lilly lists (under Joannes Hasfurtus) his *De Medendis Morbis ex Corporum Coelestium Positione lib. 3* (Venice, 1584), in *Christian Astrology*, [837].

16.36 Zael not identified, but possibly a corruption of Sahl Ibn Bishr. *Liber Novem Judicum in Judiciis Astrorum* (1509) is a compilation of Zael, Messahala [Masha'allah], Ptolemy, and others.

16.36 Tanstetter Georg Tannstetter von Thannau (1482–1535), author of several treatises in Latin, including *Artificium de applicatione astrologie ad medicina* (Strasbourg, 1531). Lilly lists under Collimitius Tanstettter his *Canones Astronomici* (Strasbourg, 1531), in *Christian Astrology*, [843].

16.36 Agrippa Henricus Cornelius Agrippa von Nettesheim (1486–1535), German scholar and occult philosopher, who studied throughout Europe and for a while in London. His key work, *De Occulta Philosophia Libri Tres*, deals with astrology in some depth, but largely in the service of magic rather than as a means of reading fate. The Abbotsford Library (*CLA*, 148) contains two English translations of Agrippa: *Of the Vanitie and Uncertaintie of Artes and Sciences. Englished by James Sandford* (1575), and *Three Books of Occult Philosophy. Translated by J. F.* (1651).

16.36 Duretus Noel Duret (*c.* 1590–*c.* 1650), French astrologer. Lilly lists, under Natalis Duret, his *Novae Ephemerides* (Paris, 1647), in *Christian Astrology*, [836].

16.37 Maginus Giovanni Antonio Magini (1555–1617), author of *Ephemerides Coelestium Motuum . . . Ab anno 1581 usque annum 1620* (Venice, 1582) and *Primum Mobile . . .* (Venice, 1609). Lilly cites 5 Latin titles under Johannes Maginus in *Christian Astrology*, [840]. Prophecies by Magini also appeared in English versions, e.g. *A Strange and Wonderfull Prognostication* (London, 1624).

16.37 Origan David Origanus (1558–1628), author of *Ephemerides Novae Annorum XXXVI* (1599) and similar works. Lilly lists his *Ephemerides* (Frankfurt, 1609), in *Christian Astrology*, [840].

16.37 Argol Andreas Argoli (1570–1657), author of various astronomical almanacs. Lilly lists as by Andreas Argolus his *Primum Mobile de Directionibus* (Romae, 1610), *Ephemerides* (Padua, 1639), and *Pandosion Sphericum* (Padua, 1644), in *Christian Astrology*, [834].

16.40 Communis error *Latin* a common mistake.

17.3 Abusus non tollit usum *Latin* the abuse does not take away the utility (i.e. the legitimate use of a thing). Scott's own translation is also accurate.

17.5–6 woodcock caught in his own springe proverbial: see *ODEP*, 768; see also *Hamlet*, 1.3.115 and 5.2.298.

17.12–13 hard terms of art difficult technical expressions.

17.16–17 sextile, quartile, trine . . . cusps, hours astrological terms, relating to the division of the celestial sphere into twelve sections called houses, each appropriated to one of the twelve signs of the zodiac. A *cusp* is the entry to a house. According to position planets were said to be in conjunction or opposition: *sextile* means making an angle of 60°, *quartile* of 90°, *trine* of 120°. In traditional astrology sextiles, trines and some conjunctions are benign; quartiles ('squares') and oppositions tend to be malign. 'Hours' refers to planetary hours: the idea that each hour has a planetary ruler, which is significant in horary astrology.

17.18 Almuten, Almochoden archaic astrological terms, used respectively for the ruling planet in a birth chart and of a planet which by virtue of its position is regarded as the 'giver or sustainer of life'. '*Almuten*, of any house is that Planet which hath most dignitie in the Signe ascending or descending upon the Cuspe of any house, whereon or from whence you require your judgment' (*Christian Astrology*, 49).

17.18 Anahibazon, Catahibazon archaic terms for the Moon's North and South Node, a point made by the intersection of the Moon's orbit with the ecliptic; also known as the Dragon's Head and the Dragon's Tail. 'The Dragons Head we sometimes call Anabibazon [and] The Dragons Taile . . . Catabibazon' (*Christian Astrology*, 49).

17.21 the pelting of this pitiless storm *King Lear*, 3.4.29.

17.26 groaning malt 'ale brewed for the purpose of being drunk after the lady or goodwife's safe delivery' (Magnum, 3.29n). Compare 'Trial between Mr Annesley and the E. of Anglesey', in *The Gentleman's Magazine*, where a witness is reported as stating: 'That Ld *Altham* (in 1715) said he must come and drink some groaning Drink, for, that his Wife was in Labour' (14, (1744), 27). For the Annesley case, see Introduction, xv, and EEWN 2, 366.

18.11–12 Ware hawk! Douse the glim! Beware of danger! Put out the light! Grose glosses 'ware hawk' as 'the word to look sharp, a bye word when a bailiff passes' (under *Hawk*).

18.34–19.8 For fable . . . that's fair from S. T. Coleridge's translation of Friedrich Schiller's *Piccolomini*, 2.4. Scott in the manuscript, instead of transcribing this passage, gives the instruction: 'A book is herewith sent. Copy from p. 82 top of page'. This matches the pagination of *The Piccolomini; or the First Part of Wallenstein. A Drama in Five Acts* (London, 1800): *CLA*, 212.

19.7 Jupiter chief of the Roman gods: also the largest and, next to Venus (see note below), the brightest of the planets.

19.8 Venus Roman goddess of love, and the planet of that name.

19.11 Heydon and Chambers Sir Christopher Heydon (d. 1623), whose *Defence of Judiciall Astrologie* (1602) was in answer to an attack on astrology in 1601 by John Chamber (1564–1604), Canon of Windsor.

19 motto Friedrich Schiller, *The Death of Wallenstein*, trans. S. T. Coleridge (1800), 5.3.21–24: *CLA*, 212.

20.6 William Lilly English astrologer (1602–81), author of a series of almanacs and prophecies, beginning during the English Civil War, when he was consulted by both parties. His *Christian Astrology* (1647) was a leading authority on horary astrology.

20.6–7 a curious fancy . . . nativity Lilly's *Christian Astrology* (1647) includes a whole section, with its own title-page, called 'An Easie and plaine Method Teaching how to judge Nativities'. In the manuscript Scott writes in a smaller hand and in a different pen stroke for this quotation, which gives the impression that he has consulted Lilly directly.

20.10 secundum artem *Latin* according to the rules of the art.

20.13–14 twelve houses see note to 17.16–17.

20.14 Ephemeris a generic term for an almanac or table showing the predicted daily position of the heavenly bodies for a given period. The ephemeris tells the astrologer where the planets are at noon or midnight. He then 'rectifies' (i.e. adjusts) their positions to the time of birth by working out how far they travel per hour and subtracting or adding the movement to the positions in the book.

20.17 judicial astrology the art of judging the influence of the planets and stars on human affairs (as distinct from 'natural astrology').

20.18 one significator 'The *significator* is no more than the Planet which ruleth the house that signifies the thing demanded' (*Christian Astrology*, 123). Scott at this point appears to be combining elements of horary and natal astrology.

20.19–20 Mars . . . death traditionally in astrology the planet Mars (its meanings derived from the god of war) in the 12th house represents secret enemies, kidnapping, imprisonment, but not of itself alone 'sudden and violent death'. Lilly describes the 'Twelfth House' as 'the house of Sorrow, Anguish of Mind, Affliction, Labour, Poverty, Imprisonment, private Enemies, Impostors' (*Christian Astrology*, 559).

21.10 Bacon Francis Bacon (1561–1626), English lawyer, moralist and natural philosopher, whose his views on astrology are found in *De Augmentis Scientiarum* (1623), where he argues for its purification, rather than complete rejection, to form an 'atrologia sana'. The context makes it clear that this is not Roger Bacon (1214?–94), who wrote on astrology.

21.10 Sir Thomas Browne the physician and author (1605–82), whose works include *Religio Medici* (1642) and *Pseudoxia Epidemica* (1646). A believer in alchemy and witchcraft, Browne in the latter treatise acknowledged the possibility of malign forces in astrological interpretation.

21.20 like Prospero in *The Tempest*: see 5.1.50–51 ('this rough magic I here abjure').

23.10 under Deane Richard Deane (1610–53), English admiral and general at sea. He fought on the Parliament side during the Civil War, and acted as commander-in-chief of the army in occupied Scotland, where he was instrumental in the pacification of the Highlands in 1652. He was killed in action against the Dutch fleet in 1653.

23.10 long civil war hostilities continued in Scotland for several years after the effectual ending of the Civil War in England with the execution of Charles I in 1649.

23.28 spun a thread Meg Merrilies's action here is reminiscent of the Carrick witch Elcine De Aggart, in the poem of that name by Joseph Train, where she sits on a promontory with a ball of yarn while determining the fate of ships from the Spanish Armada as they sail in the Clyde: see *Strains of the Mountain Muse* (Edinburgh, 1814), 109–12 (*CLA*, 165). Scott picked out this poem for special mention when writing to Train on 28 July 1814 (*Letters*, 3.476).

25.4 Donner and blitzen! *German* Thunder and lightning!

25.17 shark alongside according to Grose, *shark* is a slang term for 'a custom house officer, or tide waiter'.

25.19–20 Cut ben whids, and stow them—a gentry cove of the ken 'Meaning,—Stop your uncivil language—that is a gentleman from the house below' (Magnum, 3.44n). Although Scott says that Meg is using 'the canting language of her tribe', the terms used derive more obviously from thieves' cant or slang, as found in Francis Grose's *A Classical Dictionary of the Vulgar Tongue* (1785). Grose differs slightly from Scott by defining 'To cut bene whiddes' as 'to give good words' (under To *Cut Bene*), and by translating 'stow your whidds and plant'em, for the cove of the ken can cant'em' as 'you have said enough, the man of the house understands you' (under *Stow*). For another likely source, see notes to 149.5 and 149.18.

25.26 Captain Dirk Hattaraick the surname was evidently taken from George Sinclair's *Satans Invisible World Discovered* (Edinburgh, 1685), which includes a section 'Anent *Hattaraik* an old Warlock' (Relation XVII; 122–25). By Sinclair's account, 'This mans name was Sandie Hunter, who called himself Sandie Hamilton, and it seems was called Hattaraik by the Devil, and by others, as a Nick-name' (122). Scott reiterated this in his *Letters on Demonology and Witchcraft*, when introducing his own more sceptical account of this alleged Scottish wizard: 'Alexander Hunter . . . generally known by the nickname of Hatteraick, which it had pleased the devil to confer upon him' (2nd edn (London, 1831), 291). Quotations from Sinclair's *Satans Invisible World Discovered* are taken from the copy in the Abbotsford Library (*CLA*, 142). For a probable prototype in Yawkins, a Dutch smuggler, see Historical Note, 368.

25.26–27 Yungfrau Haagenslaapen *German literally* young woman who sleeps in a grove or wood; equivalent to 'Miss Tramp'.

25.30 Tausend donner *German* thousand thunders.

25.31 Douglas, in the Isle of Man Douglas, the chief town and port of the Isle of Man, is situated some 80 km SW of the Galloway coastline. The island's fiscal rights were purchased by the government in 1765, in an effort to stop contraband trade, but its use as a staging-post for smuggling goods into Scotland continued for several decades. Thomas Scott, Scott's brother, was stationed in the Isle of Man 1808–10.

25.32 **Mechlin lace** Mechelen (*French*, Malines), in north Belgium, was celebrated in the 17th and 18th centuries for its fine lace, frequently mentioned in contemporary accounts of clothing.

26 **motto** see *Richard II*, 3.1.22–27.

26.26 **Manks** variant form of Manx, a term applied to the inhabitants of the Isle of Man.

26.27 **top-gallant sails, royals, and skyscrapers** sails above the top mast and below the royal mast; small sails hoisted above the top-gallant sails; triangular sails above the royals.

26.35 **Like orient pearls at random strung** Sir William Jones (1746–94), 'A Persian Song of Hafiz', line 51. This poem was anthologised in Scott's *English Minstrelsy*, 2 vols (Edinburgh, 1810), 1.256–59.

26.40 **in ballast** i.e. in the capacity of ballast.

27.2 **Ramsay** Ramsey, a port on the Isle of Man, 20 km N of Douglas (see note to 25.31), and a centre for smuggling vessels in the 18th century.

27.10 **short-dated bill** note promising to pay cash after a short lapse of time.

27.13 **Gudgeonford** apparently a fictitious name: a *gudgeon* is an easily caught small carp-like freshwater fish, and also slang for an easily cheated person.

27.14 **kain hens** *kain* or *cane* was payment of poultry or eggs to landlords in kind as part of rent. As a duty, it goes back to Celtic laws in Scotland.

27.34–35 **justice of peace** the office of Justice of the Peace was created in Scotland by the Act 1587, c. 17, though it has never attained the importance that it enjoys in England. For the attempts of Rev. M'Naught to operate as a J. P. in Gatehouse of Fleet, see Introduction, xv, EEWN 2, 364–65.

27.42 **commission** i.e. commission of the peace: the official list of those named as justices in a county.

27.43 **plough-gate** an amount of land capable of being cultivated by one plough: variable, according to location and conditions, though in Scott's period it was equated with 40 Scots acres.

27.43 **quarter sessions** held in Scotland by the justices of the peace four times a year at the county town.

28.2 **sit in my skirts** *proverbial* hinder severely or press hard upon someone (Ray, 210; *ODEP*, 738).

28.5 **roll of freeholders** freeholders, i.e. those holding land directly from the Crown, were the electors in the counties in Scotland, if they held land of a certain value. The sheriff of the county had the duty of keeping the roll of names, and it was generally revised at the Michaelmas head-court of the sheriffdom or at the election meeting. In the present instance it appears that a political faction has ensured that the person elected to preside at the election meeting has caused Godfrey Bertram to be left off the roll.

28.7 **David Mac-Guffog, the constable** 'David M'Guffog, Constable in Gatehouse' is prominent in the written libels presented against Rev. M'Naught, Minister of Girthon (see also note to 28.12). Scott's written defence, when the case appeared before the General Assembly in May 1793, singled out M'Guffog as an unreliable witness. Constables (also called 'peace-officers') were appointed in the counties by justices of the peace, and in the Royal Burghs by the magistrates. For further details of M'Naught's trial, and the derivation of other names in the novel from the case, see Introduction, xv, EEWN 2, 364–65.

28.8 **a nose o' wax** a pliable or easily moulded character.

28.12 keepit...castle an unlawful form of detention, since after committal a prisoner should have been sent directly to the county jail. One of the charges made against Rev. M'Naught (see note to 28.7) was that he had abused his position as justice of the peace by committing 'persons not to a jail, where alone they could be committed, if they ought to have been made prisoners, but into the hands of the Constable to be by him detained' (MS 1627, 'Libel before the Presbytery of Kirkcudbright', 10).

28.15 sick and sicklike similar, alike, much of a muchness.

28.15 seat in the Kirk of Kilmagirdle gentry had traditional rights to seats in churches, jealously guarded as displaying status. Kilmagirdle, though a fictitious name, bears a similarity to Kirkmabreck, the parish incorporating Creetown and Carsluith in the Stewartry of Kirkcudbright and several of the locations traditionally associated with *Guy Mannering* (see Historical Note, 362). The original kirk of Kirkmabreck is now a ruin in open country.

28.17 Mac-Crosskie of Creochstone apparently fictitious names; the upwardly-mobile Mac-Crosskies appear again at 233.25.

28.23 trustees i.e. those responsible for a local road (as defined by the Act 1686, c. 13).

28.23 the cloven foot i.e. the presence of the devil.

28.36–37 Ilay and Cantire Islay, an island of the Inner Hebrides, off the coast of Argyllshire; Kintyre, a narrow peninsula at the south of the same county.

29.3 John Hay also the name of a keen angler, known to Scott, who worked as a pressman for James Ballantyne & Co. He died at Kelso, 29 June 1855, aged 79, and was proud of having been mentioned in *Guy Mannering*. (Corson)

29.4 Hempseed ford presumably fictitious.

29.30 Apollyon's quiver Apollyon, 'the angel of the bottomless pit', is named in Revelation 9.11. John Bunyan describes the struggle of Christian against Apollyon and his darts in *The Pilgrim's Progress* (1678).

29.38 jesting with edge-tools proverbial (Ray, 124; *ODEP*, 411).

30 motto see *As You Like It*, 2.7.153–57.

30.32 blessings on his dainty face compare 'blessings on your frosty pow': Robert Burns, 'John Anderson my Jo', line 7 (Kinsley, no. 302).

31.21 change of ministry i.e. change of the governing party or administration. Ministries were constantly changing at this period, with the Earl of Bute, George Grenville, the Marquis of Rockingham, and Duke of Grafton all acting as nominal heads of government between 1760 and 1770; but Scott is perhaps thinking particularly of Grenville's succession to Bute as Prime Minister in 1763, or of the formation of a government by William Pitt the Elder (created Earl of Chatham) in 1766, supported by the general election of 1768.

31.34 Gilbert Glossin the name Glossin, apart from more general association with varnish and veneer, might also contain an allusion to the medieval Roman lawyers who wrote 'glosses' on the text of Justinian's *Corpus iuris civilis* (see note to 204.39), and whose interventions were later disparaged as a disfigurement of the pure Roman law. For commentary on this name, and the way it might contrast with the more Classical values suggested by that of Paulus Pleydell, see John W. Cairns, 'The Noose Hidden under the Flowers: Marriage and Law in *Saint Ronan's Well*', *Legal History*, 16:3 (Dec. 1995), 252.

32.2 splitting and subdividing making additional voters from the rights of a landed estate. There were several ways of doing this, all demanding an accurate knowledge of feudal law, the general principle being that anyone claiming a vote must have completed a feudal title in property or superiority and be in possession of a forty shillings land held of the Crown. *Splitting* is achieved through a separation of the rights of the land into the superiority and the feu right, while *subdividing* refers to the division of an estate into separate parcels to create votes.

32.10–11 clerk of the peace officer who prepares indictments and keeps a record of proceedings at sessions of the peace.

32.16 malice prepense malice premeditated or planned beforehand; wrong or injury purposely done.

32.17 Fools should not have chapping sticks proverbial (Ramsay, 78; Ray, 286; *ODEP*, 278). Scott alludes to this proverb in a letter to his son, Walter, of 17 June 1826: 'Power—military power especially, is one of those *Chapping* sticks as our proverb calls them which should not be in the hands of knaves or fools' (*Letters*, 10.63).

32.43–33.1 New brooms . . . sweep clean proverbial (Ray, 140; *ODEP*, 564).

33.8 pickers and stealers *Hamlet*, 3.2.327.

33.10 Duke Humphrey Humphrey Plantagenet, Duke of Gloucester (1391–1447), 'the Good Duke Humphrey', youngest son of Henry IV. In 2 *Henry VI*, 2.1 he orders a person faking lameness to be whipped by a beadle.

33.12 black-fishers see note to 10.23.

33.12–13 pigeon-shooters pigeon keeping was encouraged by the Scottish Parliament and their shooting made illegal by Acts 1567 c. 17 and 1597 c. 37; these were not formally repealed until 1906.

33.18 his own lachesse apart from its usual connotation of slackness or laziness, *lachesse* is a term in English law meaning negligent delay in asserting a right.

33.22 long-remembered beggar Oliver Goldsmith, *The Deserted Village* (1770), line 151.

33.36 Captain Ward a broadside ballad describing the adventures of a pirate famous in the early 17th century. It was published by the Bannatyne Club in 1848 as one of *Two Bannatyne Garlands from Abbotsford*, with a Preface dated Abbotsford, 16 September 1831. In an Introductory Notice there, Scott acknowledges 'an attachment to an old favourite', recalling how children would sing the ballad when *guisarding* in Scotland and *mumming* in England.

33.36 Bold Admiral Benbow sea ballad, also found as 'The Death of Admiral Benbow', which raucously describes how Vice-Admiral Benbow (1653–1702) fought on in an engagement with the French in spite of being deserted by his captains and after his leg was shattered by chain-shot. This was based on an actual event in 1701–02.

34.3 a gowpen (handful) more usually, a *gowpen* means two hands full; as much as can be held in both hands held together.

34.14–15 mirk Monanday i.e. Black Monday. In Scotland the expression traditionally describes 29 March 1652, when a total eclipse of the sun took place, the day being considered one of supernatural darkness. In English tradition Black Monday is supposedly Easter Monday, 14 April 1360, when Edward III was besieging Paris, and the day was so dark and cold that many men and horses died.

35 motto John Fletcher, *The Beggar's Bush* (1622), 2.1.1–5.

35.14–15 one of the Scottish monarchs probably James V (1512–42), who in 1540 signed a writ in favour of Johnnie Faa, leader of the Egyptians (i.e. gypsies), instructing sheriffs and others in authority to help him carry out justice upon his people according to the laws of Egypt: see Anne Gordon, *Hearts Upon the Highway: Gypsies in South-East Scotland* (Galashiels, [1980?]), 9.

35.15–16 subsequent law see note to 35.23.

35.23 Egyptians once a common name for the gypsies, and the etymological origin of the term, based on the (mistaken) belief that they came from

Egypt. The Scottish statutes against rogues and vagabonds always specifically mention 'Egyptians'. An Act 1609, c. 20 followed a Privy Council order of 1603 to all Egyptians to quit Scotland on penalty of death, and made it a capital offence to be 'called, known, repute and holden Egyptians'. The Act 1661, c. 338 gave justices of the peace the duty to enforce the laws against gypsies—hence Ellangowan's ensuing actions.

35.23 **mingled race** Scott's words at this point are close to his slightly later response, as Sheriff of Selkirkshire, to a questionnaire on the gypsies, as reproduced in John Hoyland, *A Historical Survey of the Customs, Habits and Present State of the Gypsies* (York, 1816): 'I do not conceive them to be the proper Oriental Egyptian race, at least they are much intermingled with our own national outlaws and vagabonds' (95).

35.31 **Fletcher of Saltoun** Andrew Fletcher (1653–1716), Scottish patriot and political writer; he sat for many years as a representative of East Lothian in the Scottish Parliament, where he vehemently opposed the proposed Union with England of 1707.

35.33–36.14 **There are . . . fighting together** this long passage is from the second of *Two Discourses Concerning the Affairs of Scotland; written in the year 1698*: see *Andrew Fletcher of Saltoun: Selected Political Writings and Speeches*, ed. David Daiches (Edinburgh, 1979), 55. In the manuscript the transcription is in another hand, probably that of Scott's wife. A 1737 edition of Fletcher's *Political Works* is listed in *CLA*, 16.

35.34 **church boxes** boxes containing charity funds collected at church.

36.38 **farmer's ha'** principal room of a farm-house, used by family, servants and workers. The reference is apparently to Charles Keith's 'Farmer's Ha'' (1774; revised and expanded, 1776), a poem which describes the social life of the farm circle. See *Longer Scottish Poems*, Vol. 2, ed. Thomas Crawford, David Hewitt, and Alexander Law (Edinburgh, 1987), 185–90.

37.1 **Parias of Scotland** a *pariah* is a member of an extensive low caste in southern India, once especially numerous in Madras; the term was also applied more broadly to anyone of low Hindu caste, and by Europeans to one of no caste, an outcast. Some contemporary commentators claimed a specific connection with the gypsies. According to Heinrich Grellmann, one of the earliest proponents of an Indian origin for the gypsies, 'the Gipsies are of the lowest class of Indians, namely, *Parias*': *Dissertation on the Gipsies* (London, 1787), 168. In 'Notices Concerning the Scottish Gypsies' (partly by Scott) in *Blackwood's Edinburgh Magazine*, the gypsies are more broadly described as 'the *Parias* of Europe' (1:1 (April 1817), 58).

37.14 **city of refuge** biblical phrase, describing a walled town set apart for the protection of those who had accidentally committed manslaughter (see Joshua Ch. 20).

37.31–32 **broken victuals** fragments of food left over after a meal, leftovers.

37.35 **Derncleugh** fictitious name, meaning a hidden or dark gorge in Scots. Scott, however, might have had partly in mind the settlement of gypsies at Kirk Yetholm in Roxburghshire (for a contemporary account, by an associate of Scott's, see John A. Fairley, *Bailie Smith of Kelso's Account of the Gypsies of Kirk Yetholm in 1815* (Hawick, 1907)). See also Historical Note, 362, for some claimed Galwegian topographical equivalents.

37.36 **exceeding good friends** see *Hamlet*, 2.2.223 ('My excellent good friends'), and compare *2 Henry IV*, 5.1.47–48 ('The knave is mine honest friend').

38.1 **keep his own fish-guts for his own sea-mews** *proverbial* keep his own fish-guts for his own seagulls, i.e. look after the interests of those nearest home. See Ramsay, 95 and *ODEP*, 418.

38.7 quarter sessions court of review and appeal held quarterly by the justices of the peace.
38.19 conservator of the peace based on the Latin 'custos pacis', and used of the precursors of (and here as an alternative term for) the justices of the peace.
38.28 halcyon days times of calm and happiness.
38.31 l'un vaut bien l'autre *French* the one is quite as good as the other, i.e. there is nothing to choose between them.
38.33–34 spring-guns, stamps, and man-traps mechanical devices laid by landowners in their grounds as a deterrent against poachers. It was judged illegal by Scots common law to set spring guns and man traps against poachers.
38.35 nota bene *Latin* note well, take careful note (commonly abbreviated as NB).
39.9–10 pointed by the ground-officer the *poinding* (seizing) of stray cattle was recognised by the early common law of Scotland and confirmed by the Act known as the Winter Herding Act of 1686 (James VII, c. 11). The poinded animals could be detained till the landlord was compensated for any damage done. The *ground-officer*, a servant of the owner, had charge of the lands of an estate.
39.11 turnpike acts more than 350 local Turnpike Acts were passed between 1750 and 1844, establishing the system of turnpike roads, maintained by tolls, in Scotland. Provisions for *poinding* (see note above) animals straying on roads were usually included in these acts.
39.15 with scruple scrupulously, with an element of caution. Compare Edward Gibbon in *The Decline and Fall of the Roman Empire* (1766–88): 'At first, the experiment was made with caution and scruple' (Ch. 49).
39.16–17 hen-roosts . . . linen stolen compare Joseph Addison's account of gypsies in *The Spectator*, no. 130 (Monday, July 30, 1711): 'If a stray Piece of Linen hangs upon an Hedge, says Sir Roger [de Coverley], they are sure to have it . . . if a Man prosecutes them with Severity, his Hen-roost is sure to pay for it'.
39.17 bleaching ground area of ground for bleaching linen on.
39.24 impress service at D—— a reference to enforced service in the Navy.
39.29 city of refuge see note to 37.14.
40 motto see John Leyden, *Scenes of Infancy* (1803), Part 4, stanza 9 (*CLA*, 193). The lines are not consecutive, Scott omitting several without indication.
40.13 Maroon war freed or escaped slaves (*maroons*), living in the hills and mountains of the West Indies and South America, kept up an irregular war with the British in the late 17th and early 18th centuries.
40.17 fifth revolving birth-day compare Richard Brinsley Sheridan, *The Critic* (1779): 'You know my friend, scarce two revolving suns,/ And three revolving moons, have closed their course' (2.2.26–27).
40.37 battle o' the Bloody Bay apparently fictitious.
40.38 good for naething proverbial: see *ODEP*, 319.
40.40 sovereign as a febrifuge powerful as a remedy to ward off fever.
40.42 crisis was over *crisis* is used here in the medical sense, as the turning point of a disease for better or worse.
41.11 Adam Smith the Scottish moral philosopher and economist (1723–90), author of *The Wealth of Nations* (1776). His kidnapping by gypsies when three years old is described in Dugald Stewart's biography of him prefixed to *Essays on Philosophical Subjects by the late Adam Smith LL.D* (London, 1795): 'He had been carried by his mother to Strathenry on a visit to his uncle . . . and was one day amusing himself alone at the door of the house, when he was stolen by a party of that set of vagrants who are known in Scotland by the name of tinkers. Luckily he was soon missed by his uncle, who hearing that some vag-

rants had passed, pursued them, with what assistance he could find, till he overtook them in Leslie wood; and was the happy instrument of preserving to the world a genius, which was destined, not only to extend the boundaries of science, but to enlighten and reform the commercial policy of Europe' (p. x).

41.23 Prodi-gi-ous the first visually emphatic use of what effectively becomes Sampson's catchword for the rest of the novel. Corson suggests that Scott may have recalled the incident where Edwards reminded Johnson: 'Sir, I remember you would not let us say *prodigious* at College' (James Boswell, *Life of Johnson*, ed. G. B. Hill, rev. L. F. Powell, 6 vols (Oxford 1934–50), 3.303).

41.29 Ne moveas Camerinam *Latin* 'do not move Camerina', i.e. do not stir up uncalled for difficulty (originally a Greek proverb, with the import of 'let sleeping dogs lie'). The citizens of Camerina, in Sicily, drained a swamp in spite of a warning from Apollo not to disturb it, and as a result an enemy army was able to capture the city by marching over dry land.

41.32 chalked by the ground-officer the practice of chalking a tenant's door as notice to quit was common in the 18th century. In country areas this was done by the landlord's ground-officer (see note to 39.9–10).

41.35 term-day . . . Martinmas Martinmas, 11 November, is one of the four Scottish term-days, when rent became due and leases began and ended. For tenancies the crucial terms were Whitsunday (15 May) and Martinmas.

41.40–41 still practised . . . remote parts of Scotland most notoriously during the Highland Clearances, as when in June 1814 the Duchess of Sutherland's factor, Patrick Sellar, evicted 27 sub-tenants at Strathnaver and burned their cottages. For further information on this incident, and its possible influence on the novel, see Elaine Jordan, 'The Management of Scott's Novels', in *Europe and Its Others*, ed. Francis Barker *et al.*, 2 vols (Colchester, 1985), 1.146–61.

42.2 Tartars nomadic people living in Central Asia.

42.4 quorum . . . custos rotulorum *Latin literally* 'of whom' and 'keeper of the rolls'. Here 'of the quorum' alludes to Ellangowan's role as a justice of the peace, the term being loosely used to refer to those nominated to perform a particular function, here to sit as a JP in the county. In England, *quorum* had a more technical meaning, referring to those justices of the peace who have certain superior powers. The 'custos rotulorum' is the officer in charge of the rolls of the sessions of the peace and of the commission of the peace. The terms feature playfully in *The Merry Wives of Windsor*, 1.1.4–7.

42.8 supervisor, or riding-officer Scott's terms are not strictly synonymous: a *riding officer* was a mounted customs officer, whose function was to patrol approximately ten miles of coastline in search of smugglers; a *supervisor* or *surveyor* generally oversaw the work of subordinate excisemen or *gaugers* in Scotland.

43.5 tarrying no farther question see *2 Henry IV*, 1.1.48 ('Staying no longer question'). A Magnum footnote remarks 'This anecdote is a literal fact' (3.77n). For what is almost certainly Scott's root story, involving the gypsy leader Will Faa and one Dr Walker, see John A. Fairley, *Bailie Smith of Kelso's Account of the Gypsies of Kirk Yetholm in 1815* (Hawick, 1907), [6].

43.12 Calotte Jacques Callot (1592–1635), French graphic artist, whose series of four etchings, *Les Bohémiens* (*c.* 1621) were known to Scott (see *Letters*, 3.122) and are evidently in mind here. The first of a pair entitled 'Journeyings', which depicts a travelling group in procession, is especially close to Scott's description. See Howard Daniel, *Callot's Etchings* (New York, 1974), xix, plates 149–52. There is a French legend that Callot had briefly lived with gypsies as a child.

44.5 Dukit Park a name given in Scotland to a park containing a dovecote.

44.28 Margaret of Anjou (1430–82), wife of Henry VI, and one of the leaders of the Lancastrian armies during the Wars of the Roses. Scott is perhaps thinking of *3 Henry VI*, 5.5, where she witnesses the murder of her son, Prince Edward, after the Battle of Tewkesbury in 1471; though her 'malediction' is more fully expressed in *Richard III*, 1.3, where Richard (one of the assassins) is her main target.

45 motto Robert Burns, 'The Author's Earnest Cry and Prayer, to the Right Honorable and Honorable, the Scotch Representatives in the House of Commons' (1784–85), lines 37–42 (Kinsley, no. 81).

45.32–33 seriously incline *Othello*, 1.3.145–46 ('This to hear/ Would Desdemona seriously incline').

45.36–37 wrong side of the blanket proverbial expression implying illegitimate birth: *ODEP*, 924.

45.38 Glengabble evidently a burlesque name.

45.40 Harrigate Harrogate, in Yorkshire, a popular spa resort.

46.13 broad arrow mark placed on Government stores and impounded goods.

46.24 quarter sessions see note to 38.7.

46.25 dies inceptus *Latin literally* day begun. In Roman and Scots law, the expression *dies inceptus pro completo habetur* has the meaning 'a day that has commenced will be held to be completed'. Ellangowan therefore uses the maxim quite wrongly: it has the opposite meaning to that he attributes to it.

46.30 Whitsunday . . . Martinmas two of the Scottish term-days, Whitsunday (15 May) and Martinmas (11 November): see also note to 41.35.

46.34 Wigton Wigtown is a town in Galloway, commanding Wigtown Bay, to the W of Gatehouse of Fleet and 12 km S of Newton Stewart.

46.41 Collector Snail a burlesque name, but the title is correct: a collector was a senior customs officer in overall charge of an outport and directly responsible to the Commissioners of Excise. A David Staig was Collector at Dumfries from the 1780s: see Frances Wilkins, *Dumfries & Galloway's Smuggling Story* (Kidderminster, 1993), 78.

46.42 meddling and making a once familiar combination of words, with *making* in the sense of 'interfering'; see also note to 123.37.

46.43 frae the Borough-town possibly a reference to Kirkcudbright, a Royal Burgh from 1455; see also Historical Note, 360–61.

47.8–9 at an orra time occasionally, now and then.

47.13 head and pinners a lace head-dress, with two flaps pinned on and hanging down, sometimes fastened in front; worn by women, especially those of rank, in the 17th and 18th centuries.

47.16 in a low on fire, alight.

47.34 at long bowls i.e. shooting at long range: *long-bowls* was a game similar to ninepins, in which heavy bullets were thrown from the hand.

47.36 Nantz brandy (a term derived from Nantes, on the Loire in France).

47.40 hark to Ranger a call of attention, as in hunting; *Ranger* was a term applied to a forest officer or gamekeeper, or, alternatively, to a hunting-dog.

48.14 Point of Warroch fictitious name; though the physical description (already given) in some ways matches Ravenshall Point, approximately halfway along the coast between Gatehouse of Fleet and Creetown: see Historical Note, 362.

48.18 French article i.e. brandy.

48.26 playing Punch i.e. mimicking the character of Mr Punch in the Punch and Judy puppet play.

48.32–33 the tune of "the deil's awa wi' the exciseman" 'The De'il's awa wi' th' Exciseman' is a song by Robert Burns first published in 1792; the accompanying air, which may be English, was first published in 1719. See Kinsley, no. 386 and 3.1408.

50.5 the humbled cow a *humble* cow is a polled cow, a cow without horns.

51.1 Would to God I had died for him! see 2 Samuel 18.33: 'would God I had died for thee, O Absalom, my son, my son!'
53 motto *2 Henry VI*, 3.2.168–73.
53.9 Sheriff-depute the sheriff in Scotland is the chief officer of a shire or county, responsible for peace and order as well as having a judicial function. At this period hereditary sheriffs had been replaced by sheriffs-depute appointed by the Crown. Often they did not reside within their sheriffdoms, and sheriffs-substitute were often appointed who did much of the routine legal work (see note to 68.7). In the 18th century the sheriff-depute or his substitutes had the duty of investigating crimes.
53.19 procès verbal *French* written report; a legal term for an account of official proceedings.
53.20 precognition a technical term in Scots law, as Scott indicates, referring to an examination of witnesses or suspected persons, by the sheriff-depute or sheriff-substitute, finally reduced to writing and signed. The taking of precognitions by the sheriff was a vital start to the investigation of a crime in Scotland.
54.6 couteau de chasse *French* hunting-knife.
56.5 press of sail as much sail as the state of the wind will permit a ship to carry.
56.22 Hamburgh colours the German port of Hamburg was then a free city; it thus offered a suitable 'flag of convenience'.
56.41 William Pritchard a namesake of William Prichard, master of the *Antelope* in which Gulliver was wrecked off Lilliput: see Swift's *Gulliver's Travels* (1726), Part 1, Ch. 1.
58.12–13 damnum minatum . . . malum secutum *Latin*, and correctly translated by Scott, though *malum secutum* means more plainly 'an evil having followed'. The phrases *damnum minatum* and *malum secutum* are used by George Sinclair in his *Satans Invisible World Discovered* (Edinburgh, 1685), 123–24 (*CLA*, 142), when recounting a threat (and its fulfilment) made by the Scottish warlock, Alexander Hunter, named by Satan as Hattaraik (see note to 25.26). The terms also feature in Scott's own account of the anecdote in *Letters on Demonology and Witchcraft*, 2nd edn (London, 1831), 292–93.
58.21 no canny unnatural, supernatural.
59 motto *The Winter's Tale*, 4.1.1–7.
59.33 Gordon Arms for a possible prototype in the Murray Arms, Gatehouse of Fleet, see Historical Note, 361.
59.41 clerk and precentor the parish clerk was clerk to the kirk session, the lowest court in the Presbyterian system; a precentor led the singing of a Presbyterian congregation.
60.2–3 Bearcliff another name which might derive from the case of the Rev. M'Naught: see note to 28.7.
60.26–27 Hazelwoods of Hazelwood evidently a fictitious appellation (but see Historical Note, 362, for a possible geographical origin).
60.31 King of Man the Isle of Man was Celtic before Norse incursions began *c.* 800, the island then becoming a Norwegian dependency until 1266, when it was ceded to Scotland. The Kingship of the Isle of Man was disputed between several contenders in the 12th century, during the late Norwegian period.
60.32–33 Blithe Bertram . . . her hame actually a variation of the opening lines of the ballad 'Willie's Ladye': see *Minstrelsy*, 3.215.
60.38 Mr Skreigh Scott's name for his 'clerk and precentor' (see note to 59.41) has a facetious edge: *skreigh* is Scots for 'screech, shriek'.
60.42 pit mirk as dark as a pit, pitch black.
61.1 haud to the right side Scott tells of a similar bridge in a note near the

beginning of 'The Highland Widow': 'In one of the most beautiful districts of the Highlands was, not many years since, a bridge bearing this startling caution, "Keep to the right side, the left being dangerous"' (*Chronicles of the Canongate*, EEWN 20, 69n). See also editor's note to 31.14 in *The Antiquary*, EEWN 3, 463–64.

61.22-25 To every guest . . . good night see George Crabbe, *The Borough* (1810), Letter XI ('Inns'), lines 49–52.

62.20 entered into possession i.e. taken over the estate and its rents to enforce payment of their debt, a remedy open to creditors in Scots law.

62.27 for fear the heir-male since the Ellangowan estate was settled on the heirs male, according to the law of entailment it could not be sold to satisfy debts if Godfrey Bertram had a son or remoter descendant through the male line; any purchaser also ran the risk of annulment of the sale if a male heir was discovered.

63.13 unco wark wi' great affection for.

63.38 Thou shalt not suffer a witch to live Exodus 22.18.

64.13 the Evil One the devil.

64.40 George at Dumfries then the leading inn of the town, in the High Street.

65.16–17 the Enemy of Mankind the devil.

66.5 conveyed to Fairy-land as in the ballad 'The Young Tamlane': see *Minstrelsy*, 2.300–407, including Scott's long Introduction on 'Popular Superstition'. This traditional theme was also used in James Hogg's contemporary poem 'Kilmeny' (1813).

66.25 East Indies i.e. India. The name is used because of the association of India with the East India Company, a trading company which owned and ruled large parts of India. Its military and civil officers regularly made large fortunes.

66.27–28 Cuddiebum . . . Chingalore bear a similarity to two engagements in the Indian Mysore wars, at Cuddalore (1783) and Sholingar (1781), but are here perhaps distorted by the speaker (*Cuddiebum* in Scots suggests 'donkey's bottom').

66.28 Mahratta (or Maratha) the name of an alliance of Hindu states in central and south-western parts of India; the First Anglo-Maratha War ended with the treaty of Salbai (17 May 1782).

66.28–29 Ram Jolli Bundleman a garbled name, comparable to the military engagements at 66.27–28.

67 motto see Ben Jonson, *The New Inn* (1629), 4.4.48–57.

67.25 got up grew up, got older.

67.26 house and hauld house and home, every refuge.

67.38 the first free day i.e. the first day after Sunday (a non-business day). Only limited types of legal business (such as criminal warrants) can be conducted on Sunday.

67.41–42 weary American war the American War of Independence lasted from 1775 to 1783, with peace terms between Britain and the United States being provisionally signed on 30 November 1782 and formally ratified by the treaty of Versailles on 3 September 1783; the events described apparently occur during November 1781 or 1782, a time of economic depression: see also Historical Note, 356.

68.7 sheriff substitute the appointee of the sheriff-depute (see note to 53.9), normally responsible for day-to-day legal business in a county. For three-fourths of Scott's term of office as Sheriff of Selkirkshire, Scott's friend Charles Erskine, writer in Melrose, was his substitute (commission dated 14 March 1800). According to John Chisholm, 'Erskine . . . sat in Sir Walter's mental studio for the portrait of the Sheriff-Substitute in *Guy Mannering*': *Sir Walter Scott as a Judge: His Decisions in the Sheriff Court of Selkirk* (Edinburgh, 1918),

8. Mr Mac-Morlan, the holder of this post in the novel, is first mentioned by name at 68.14.

68.8 Court of Session the supreme Court in Scotland for civil matters, under whose authority a sale of this kind would have been held.

68.10 sheriff depute (that's his principal like) in spite of the apparent contradiction, Mrs Mac-Candlish shows accurate knowledge. She uses the term *sheriff depute*, which was the correct designation, and gives also the correct relationship between the sheriff substitute and sheriff depute in her parenthetical explanation; see also note to 53.9.

68.31 Arthur Mervyn the name matches that of the eponymous hero of *Arthur Mervyn* (1798–1800; London, 1803), by the American writer Charles Brockden Brown. The 1821 edition is listed in *CLA*, 114.

68.32 Llanbraithwaite echoes Braithwaite, between Bassenthwaite Lake and Derwent Water, in the Lake District.

68.38–39 Skiddaw . . . Crossfell two notable peaks: the first in the Lake District, N of Keswick, the second one of the highest in the Pennine Chain.

69.15 Lombard Street a street principally given over to bankers, extending from the Mansion House to Gracechurch Street in the City of London.

69.21 span-counter with moidores *span-counter* is a game with counters, in which the player tries to pitch his own counter within a hand's length of his opponent's; a *moidore* is a Portuguese gold coin, current in England in the early 18th century, the term being later used to describe the sum of 27s (£1.35), the approximate value of the coin. Compare *2 Henry VI*, 4.2.152–53 ('boys went to span-counter for French crowns').

69.22 thread-papers of bank-notes see Richard Brinsley Sheridan, *The Rivals* (1775), 1.1.49: 'all her thread-papers are made of bank-notes'. Compare Scott's letter to Charles Kirkpatrick Sharpe on 29 August 1824 (concerning the banker's wife, Mrs Coutts): 'she can make thread papers of bank notes' (*Letters*, 12.454).

71.19 Looties a name, given in India, to a body of native irregular troops whose main object was plunder. The term appears in slightly different form in Robert Orme's *A History of the Military Transactions of the British Nation in Indostan*, a favourite of Scott's as a young man, in its account of Robert Clive's Bengal campaign in 1757: 'a body of their *Louchees*, or plunderers, who are armed with clubs, passed into the company's territory about noon' (2nd edn, 2 vols (London, 1775–78), 2.129: *CLA*, 253).

72.3 day fatality a fixed and unalterable course of events which must occur on a certain day. John Aubrey's *Miscellanies, Upon the Following Subjects* (2nd edn, London 1721) begins with a Section headed 'Day-Fatality: or, Some Observations of Days Lucky and Unlucky' (*CLA*, 149).

72.22–23 retaining . . . a large proportion of the price in the case of an entailed property, such as the Ellangowan estate, it was normal procedure for the purchaser to retain part of the price to set against the possibility of the missing heir's return.

73 motto see Thomas Otway, *Venice Preserv'd; or, a Plot Discover'd* (1682), 1.1.

75.43–76.1 Lady Jean Devorgoil Scott here appears to associate a commanding woman from SW Scotland with Devorgilla, wife of the hapless Scottish monarch John de Balliol (*c.* 1250–1315), and founder of Sweetheart Abbey (see note to 3.19); the name also reappears in Scott's play *The Doom of Devorgoil*, first written 1817–18, published 1830.

76.28 Avoid ye! *avoid* is here used in the now obsolete sense of to expel or drive out a person from a place. Compare *Marmion* (1808), Canto 6, stanza 32: 'Avoid thee, Fiend!' (*Poetical Works*, 7.350).

76.43 friendless, houseless, pennyless see Matthew 25.35–38.

78 motto Edward Young, *The Complaint: or Night Thoughts* (1742–45), 'Night the First', lines 54–57.
78.14–17 Our hopes ... surely ours see Edward Young's *Night Thoughts*, 'Night the First', lines 61–64.
78.28 wand of the prophet i.e. Moses's rod, as in Exodus 17.6 ('and thou shalt smite the rock, and there shall come water out of it, that the people may drink').
79.17–18 memorable case of Homer's birth-place a number of Greek cities (traditionally seven) are supposed to have claimed the honour of being Homer's birthplace. There is an anecdote about Scott as a boy precociously (mis-)reciting the lines 'Seven *Roman* cities strove for Homer dead, / Through which the living Homer begged his bread' (see *Life*, 1.89).
80.38–39 rocked ... declining age see Alexander Pope, *Epistle to Dr Arbuthnot* (1735), line 409.
81.10 Masons' Lodge at Kippletringan a number of towns in Dumfriesshire and Galloway have Masonic lodges dating from the late 18th century. Robert Heron, on his visit in 1792, noted the presence of one in Gatehouse of Fleet: 'Here is a mason-lodge, too—for free-masonry is a hobby-horse with some of these people,—to which no fewer than seventy members belong' (*Observations Made in a Journey through the Western Counties of Scotland*, 2nd edn, 2 vols (Perth, 1799), 2.221: *CLA*, 10). *Pigot and Co's New Commercial Directory of Scotland for 1825–26* (London and Manchester, n.d.) lists the Mason's Arms (a public house which still stands next to the Murray Arms in Gatehouse), and states also that there is a 'masonic lodge' in the town (446, 447). For a more general commentary on claimed similarities between Kippletringan and Gatehouse, see Historical Note, 361.
81.22 the upset price the lowest sum for which the estate could be sold.
82.1–2 power of attorney legal document giving power for one person to act for another (an English rather than Scottish legal term).
82 motto 'The Heir of Linne', Part 1, lines 29–36, from Percy 2.310–11 (Child, 267). In the ballad the Heir of Linne is defrauded by his steward, John o' the Scales, who buys his estate for less than a third of its value.
82.11 gods pennie small sum of money paid as a token deposit on making a bargain.
82.17 telling ... gold see 'The Heir of Linne', Part 2, line 109 (see also note to 82 motto, above).
83.15–20 Ruth ... thee and me see Ruth 1.16–17.
83.37 book-keeping by double entry and the Italian method see note to 313.42.
84.9 squire of dames one who devotes himself to the service of ladies. The expression is found in a number of literary sources, notably Edmund Spenser (*c.* 1552–99): 'Call me the *Squyre of Dames*, that me beseemeth well' (*The Faerie Queene*, 3.7.51).
85.10 neque semper arcum tendit Apollo *Latin* Apollo does not always draw his bow tight (i.e. is not always at full stretch): Horace (65–8 BC), *Odes*, 2.10.19–20.
85.11 Galloway Phœbus jocular sobriquet combining Phoebus Apollo, the Greek god of music and poetry, and the south-west area of Scotland where the novel is apparently set.
85.18 sits the wind in that quarter? proverbial: see *ODEP*, 893, and *Much Ado About Nothing*, 2.3.91.
86.19 varium et mutabile *Latin* alluding to Virgil's 'Varium et mutabile semper Femina' ('Woman is always inconstant and fickle'), in *Aeneid*, 4.569–70.
86.39 peculium term of Roman law, referring to a fund given to a slave or

son; also used, more loosely, for pocket money.
87 motto see John Gay, *The Beggar's Opera* (1728), 1.8.1–2, 5–6 (Air VII).
87.15 a secretis *Latin* in secret; as a confidant.
87.33 any one but a quaker the *Quakers* (a term first used derogatorily) were members of a religious society (the Society of Friends) founded by George Fox in 1648–50; they are noted for their pacifist principles.
87.40 Lancaster or Carlisle county towns of Lancashire and Cumberland, in NW England; assizes, presided over by judges of the High Court, were held periodically in each county.
88.5–6 twelve judges of England, with the chancellor to boot in effect, the superior judicial establishment of England. Four judges sat in each of the Courts of Common Pleas, King's Bench, and Exchequer; while the Chancellor headed the Court of Chancery and also presided in the House of Lords.
88.35 in rerum natura *Latin literally* in the nature of things; i.e. extant in actual nature, 'alive'.
88.40 Downright Dunstable Dunstable, a town in Bedfordshire, is proverbial for its straightforwardness (see Ray, 233; *ODEP*, 209). Scott used the same nickname for his English friend, J. B. S. Morritt, in a letter to Joanna Baillie of 17 March 1817 (see *Letters*, 4.409); this encourages the view that Morritt, one of the few to be privy to the authorship of the novel, was a prototype for Arthur Mervyn.
89.24–25 This is no 'Much ado about nothing' not only a pun on Shakespeare's title, but also implicitly an allusion to the balcony incident in the play and the plot of mistaken identity (see Act 2, Scene 2).
89.29 Spanish rendezvous after the manner of the stereotypical Spanish lovers with serenade and balcony setting.
89.35 twelve-oared barge used as the second boat of a man-of-war.
90.32 walking gentlemen of all descriptions the 1780s saw an acceleration of the fashion for visiting the Lake District. According to James Clarke, the 'romantic situation' around Keswick 'has induced several of the nobility and gentry ... to purchase lands in the neighbourhood: it likewise draws, every summer, vast numbers from all parts of the kingdom to visit many natural curiosities in its neighbourhood': *A Survey of the Lakes of Cumberland, Westmorland and Lancashire* (London, 1787), 69 (see *CLA*, 232).
90.33–34 rave, and recite, and madden see Alexander Pope, *Epistle to Dr Arbuthnot* (1735), line 6: 'They rave, recite, and madden round the land'.
91.5–6 stinted nor staid paused nor halted: a common ballad phrase.
91 motto not identified: possibly by Scott (or a near-contemporary), in imitation of Alexander Pope.
91.28 Paesiello's sonatas Giovanni Paesiello (1740–1816) was a prolific composer of operas and other compositions, noted by contemporaries for their clarity and simplicity.
92.5–6 gauzy frippery of a French translation probably referring to *The Arabian Nights' Entertainments*, which was first translated by Antoine Galland (1646–1715), and on whose French English versions during the 18th century were based. Galland's *Mille et Une Nuits*, which appeared between 1704 and 1717, was very elegant, but inaccurate and incomplete.
92.29–30 in the trade of war has oft slain men see *Othello*, 1.2.1.
93.14 sounding cataracts see William Wordsworth, 'Tintern Abbey' (1798), lines 76–77 ('The sounding cataract/ Haunted me like a passion').
93.17–18 Salvator ... Claude Salvator Rosa (1615–73), Italian painter; and Claude Geleé, known as Claude Lorraine (1600–82), French painter living in Italy. Both were celebrated in 18th-century Britain for their landscapes: Rosa for his 'wild' sublimity, Claude for his Classical pastorals and incandescent use of light.

93.32 good lack *exclamation* alack!

93.39–40 turnips ... lucerne ... timothy grass all indicative of agricultural improvement in the 18th century. Lucerne is a variety of clover, used as fodder; timothy grass (*phelum pratense*) is the American name for a native British grass re-introduced into England for cultivation *c.* 1750.

94.31–32 scene in the Merchant of Venice at the beginning of Act 5, Scene 1 (involving Lorenzo and Jessica).

95 motto see *Much Ado About Nothing*, 4.1.306.

96.9–12 With prospects ... would make George Crabbe, *Tales* (1812), Tale XI ('Edward Shore'), lines 35–38.

97.6 Poictiers town in France, near which the Black Prince defeated and captured King John II of France, in the battle of that name in 1356, during the Hundred Years' War.

97.6 Agincourt site in northern France of the famous battle, won by Henry V in 1415.

98.38 left the army Julia is wrong: Brown (Bertram) has not resigned his commission, but is on leave.

100.30 a's and aa's, and i's and ee's representing Mannering's view of the different vowel sounds of English and Scottish speech.

101.11 the Residence name for the place of work and home of a high official of the East India Company.

101.27 coup de main *French* stroke, sudden overpowering attack.

101.27 keen encounter of our wits as in *Richard III*, 1.2.115 (Richard to Lady Anne: 'To leave this keen encounter of our wits').

101.35–36 Rosencrantz and Guildenstern two courtiers in *Hamlet*.

102 motto Thomas Warton (1728–90), 'Ode on the Approach of Summer', lines 295–300.

102.7 Tusculane a term originating from the Roman orator Cicero's country villa at Tusculum, *c.* 15 km SE of Rome, mentioned by him in his works as a place of repose.

102.9 Woodbourne probably fictitious. Scott had already used the name in *Rokeby* (1813), Canto 1, stanza 20: 'Sweet Woodburne's cottages and trees' (*Poetical Works*, 9.56). There is a Woodburn, probably visited by Scott as a young man, in N. Northumberland (see *Letters*, 4.271).

102.20–21 set up the staff of his rest proverbial expression denoting the taking up of a fixed and settled abode: see *ODEP*, 717.

102.28–29 some of the creditors ... purchase-money see note to 72.22–23.

105.9 outward man compare *Hamlet*, 2.2.6–7 ('Sith nor th'exterior nor the inward man/ Resembles that it was').

105.16–17 by the aid of use, cleaved to their mould see *Macbeth*, 1.3.144–46.

105.27–28 Afrite in the tale of the Caliph Vathek *Afrite* in Arabian mythology is a powerful evil demon; Caliph Vathek is the central character in William Beckford's *Vathek, An Arabian Tale* (1786), where an Afrite-like Indian ogre lures the Caliph onto the road to damnation. Scott is perhaps here alluding specifically to the scene in which the ogre surprises the company by laughing 'immoderately': see *Vathek*, ed. Roger Lonsdale (Oxford, 1970), 16. The running-titles of the 1st (1786) edition of *Vathek* read 'A History of the Caliph Vathek'. An Afrite of an unreliable disposition likewise appears in 'The Adventures of Aboulfouaris' (from *The Arabian Nights' Entertainments*) in Henry Weber's *Tales of the East*, 3 vols (Edinburgh, 1812), 2.486–96 (*CLA*, 43); this tale is elsewhere alluded to in *Guy Mannering* (see note to 315.40).

106 motto James Boswell, *The Life of Samuel Johnson* (1791), at 3 April 1776: 'His present appearance put me in mind of my uncle, Dr Boswell's description of him, "A robust genius, born to grapple with whole libraries"' (see James Boswell, *Life of Johnson*, ed. G. B. Hill, rev. L. F. Powell, 6 vols (Oxford, 1934–50), 3.7). According to Boswell's Journal, 27 August 1769, his uncle had described Johnson as 'a Herculean genius, just born to grapple with whole libraries': see *Boswell in Search of a Wife, 1766–69*, ed. Frank Brady and Frederick A. Pottle (London, 1957), 280.

106.21 Why tarry the wheels of their chariot? see Judges 5.28.

107.27–28 extraordinary countenance Julia is making a pun on the meaning of *countenance* as both 'face' and 'favour'. Countenance in the latter meaning is biblical: see e.g. Numbers 6.26 ('The Lord lift up his countenance upon thee, and give thee peace').

107.34 chewing the cud proverbial: see *ODEP*, 118, and *As You Like It*, 4.3.100 ('Chewing the food of sweet and bitter fancy').

108.13 sacrificed to the graces the expression 'sacrifice to the graces' is used by Lord Chesterfield, 9 March 1748, in his *Letters to his Son* (1774).

109.30 modern poet George Crabbe, in *The Library* (1808), lines 145–50.

110.3 half way up the library steps compare the anecdote about Sir Isaac Newton (see note to 16.27), told by Scott in his 'Life of Swift' (1814): 'The Dean used also to tell of Sir Isaac, that his servant having called him one day to dinner, and returning, after waiting some time, to call him a second time, found him mounted on a ladder placed against the shelves of his library, a book in his left hand, and his head reclined upon his right, sunk in such a fit of abstraction, that he was obliged, after calling him once or twice, actually to jog him, before he could awake his attention' (*The Works of Jonathan Swift*, ed. Scott, 2nd edn, 1824, 1.331n.). A similar story is told about Robert Heron, the humbly-born Galwegian historian: 'When the house-maid would have wanted him to come to dinner, in vain might she have stood at a distance and called on *Mr. Heron*; he heard her not, being so deeply absorbed with his books' (John Mactaggart, *The Scottish Gallovidian Encyclopedia* (London, 1824), 260: *CLA*, 124). For Heron, see also Historical Note, 368.

110.11–12 How happily . . . Thalaba went bye see Robert Southey, *Thalaba the Destroyer* (1801), 3.130.

110 motto George Crabbe, *Tales* (1812), Tale V ('The Patron'), lines 186–89.

111.22 Delaserre also the name of a young officer, the narrator's companion, in Henry Mackenzie's *The Lounger* (1785–87), nos 82–84 (Saturday 26 Aug. to Saturday 9 Sept. 1786).

111.40 a cock and a bottle meaning unclear; perhaps a variation (or mistake for) 'a cock and bull story', i.e. an incredible or exaggerated yarn.

112.15 money to pay the turnpike tolls were payable at intervals on turnpike roads either at turnpike gates or toll-houses: see also note to 39.11. More broadly, Brown (Bertram) is referring to the then common practice of purchasing commissions in the British army.

112.31 Whoy, ho Why, he: Scott had presented Cumbrian speech similarly in *Waverley*, Vol. 3, Ch. 13.

112.34 a-laking Scott uses *lake* here in its original Northern dialect meaning of 'playing'. The emergence of the more 'polite' meaning of 'lake', as a result of the fashion for visiting the Lake District, is wryly noted by James Clarke in a chapter on 'Keswick and Derwentwater': 'Since many of the curious have visited these lakes, *our native rusticks* have pretended to imitate them. Within these few years, not half a dozen persons in Keswick knew what the word *Lake* meant; it was either called *Daran* (that is, Derwent) or *Keswick water*, and had only two or three fishing boats upon it: now every cottager attempts to be polite, and to speak better language; and the name of *Daran* is not known, but the *Lake* only' (*A Survey of the Lakes of Cumberland, Westmorland and Lancashire* (London,

1787) p. 69: see *CLA*, 232). Clarke also gives a passage of dialogue in which a local mother asks her daughter, who has come home from an afternoon on 'the lake', 'What lake wast? Tennis, or Anthony Blindman [i.e. Blind Man's Buff]?' Scott's addition of 'on the mere' leaves no doubt of his own meaning.

112.35 make no sport... spoil none proverbial (see Ramsay, 84; *ODEP*, 501).

112.36 cross as poy-crust apparently proverbial, but not identified as such. Scott uses the expression when referring to the difficulties of the mail in a letter of 2 October 1817 to the Duke of Buccleuch: 'The posts which are as cross as pye-crust have occasiond some delay' (*Letters*, 4.535).

112.38 fourth Station on the Survey Thomas West's *Guide to the Lakes* (1778), which went through seven editions by the end of the century, described eight viewing stations on Derwentwater, four on Coniston Water, four on Bassenthwaite, and five on Windermere. P. Crossthwaite's *Map of Windermere* (1783) shows West's five stations at Windermere: a 1794 copy of the map is in *CLA*, 33.

113.23 ferme ornée *French literally* ornamented farm. The most celebrated example in England, effectively a landscape garden, was the poet William Shenstone's transformed grazing farm, the Leasowes, developed in the mid-18th century.

114.13 isle of Zealand province in the Netherlands, comprising the islands at the mouth of the Schelde.

114.19 celebrated pass in the Mysore country Mysore in SW India was an independent state until the defeat of Tipu Sultan (see note to 215.34) by the British in 1799. The Western and Eastern Ghauts, twin mountain ranges, run on either side of the Mysore plateau, with a few peaks reaching 3000 metres. No particular pass has been identified; but a journey up 'one of these perilous passes' is described by Scott in 'The Surgeon's Daughter', in *Chronicles of the Canongate*, EEWN 20, 268–70.

114.42 Is Saul... among the prophets? 1 Samuel 10.11–12.

115.7 the affair of Cuddyboram perhaps referring to the battle at Cuddalore (13 June 1783) during the Indian Mysore wars (see also note to 66.27–28).

115.17 Marybone the district of Mary-le-bone, then on the outskirts of London.

115.27 cabbined, cribbed, and confined *Macbeth*, 3.4.24.

117 motto see *The Winter's Tale*, 4.3.118–21.

117.14 Skiddaw and Saddleback two peaks in the Lake District, in Cumbria, *c.* 6 km N and NE of Keswick.

118.7 from want of thought see John Dryden, *Cymon and Iphigenia* (1700), line 85: 'He whistled as he went, for want of thought'. This line is quoted in *The Spectator*, no. 71, 22 May 1711.

118.17–19 Dr Johnson... post-chaise as reported of Samuel Johnson by James Boswell, 21 March 1776: 'In the afternoon, as we were driven rapidly along in the post-chaise, he said to me, "Life has not many things better than this"' (*Life of Johnson*, ed. G. B. Hill, rev. L. F. Powell, 6 vols (Oxford, 1934–1950), 2.453).

118.25 Roman Wall line of connected forts, running between the Tyne and Solway Firth, built in the 2nd century by the Roman emperor Hadrian (hence, commonly, Hadrian's Wall). It is likely that Brown (Bertram) scrambled over the wall somewhere near Birdoswald, near Gilsland and 20 km NE of Carlisle, one of the earliest points approaching from the west where the wall is still visible; see also Historical Note, 362.

118.36 Vauban and Coehorn celebrated military engineers of the 17th century. Sébastien le Prestre de Vauban (1633–1707) was employed to strengthen the fortifications of Dunkirk, Lille, Maestricht, Valenciennes, and Ghent, and wrote treatises on fortification. Baron Menno van Coehoorn (1641–1704), called the Dutch Vauban, was the author of a famous treatise on fortress construction, *Nieuwe Vestingbouw* (1685), and became Master General of the Artillery in 1695; the fortifications at Bergen op Zoom were considered his masterpiece.

119.12 cabaret drinking house, pot-house. Scott in a Magnum note (3.228–30) at this point identifies Mumps's Hall as the original. For further details, see Historical Note, 362.

119.14 jockey great-coat large overcoat of a kind apparently formerly worn by horse-dealers.

119.28 Mr Dinmont's for alleged prototypes of Dandie Dinmont, who shares his surname with a type of sheep and whose forename is a diminutive of Andrew, see Historical Note, 366–67.

119.34 store-farmer one who buys lean animals for fattening. In the Border region of Scotland a store-farm is often a farm in the hills, on which sheep are reared and grazed.

119.37 weel entered well trained. Compare Scott's letter to Maria Edgeworth, 2 January 1824, about his finding a puppy for a Dr King: 'I could have got one yesterday about two years old but then it had been *enterd* as it is called that is regularly trained to the destruction of vermin and when they have fairly adopted that profession they seldom make quiet companions' (*Letters*, 8.143).

119.42 Pepper . . . Mustard for the original owner of dogs with these names, James Davidson of Hyndlee, see Historical Note, 366.

120.6 The Deuke the Duke of Buccleuch, one of the largest landowners in southern Scotland.

120.7 Charlieshope for possible prototypes, see Historical Note, 363–64.

120.7 Dandie see note to 119.28.

120.8–9 Jamie Grieve in the Magnum text this supposedly fictitious name is replaced by that of Tam Hudson, with a footnote stating 'The real name of this veteran sportsman is now restored' (3.222n). Thomas Hutson was gamekeeper to the Duke of Buccleuch, and in 1805 was the complainer (plaintiff) in a case before Scott as Sheriff of Selkirkshire (see *Letters*, 1.254). For a possible original of Jamie Grieve, however, see note to 120.32.

120.10 again e'en towards or by evening.

120.17 museum at Keswick Keswick, at the northern end of Derwentwater in the Lake District, had at least two museums at this period, Hutton's and Crosthwaite's, both catering for visiting tourists. Crosthwaite's, the larger of the two, contained a collection of stuffed birds among other curiosities: see Norman Nicolson, *The Lakers: The First Tourists* (London, 1972), 106–07, 222–23.

120.24 proof of the matter . . . eating proverbial (see Ray, 149; *ODEP*, 650); 'pudding' rather than 'matter' is more usual.

120.31 Riccarton . . . a public Riccarton is an ancient settlement in upper Liddesdale, Roxburghshire, on the north bank of Liddel Water, *c.* 10 km NE of Newcastleton. For an account of its history, and operation as a thriving sheep farm in the 18th century, see Michael J. H. Robson, *A Break with the Past* (Newcastleton, 1991), 41–82. Riccarton Mill, nearby, provided the services of an inn or public house in the later 18th century, which Scott himself used when visiting Liddesdale with his friend Robert Shortreed (see e.g. Shortreed's reference to grazing their horses there, in MS 8993, f. 104).

120.32 Jock Grieve's at the Rone Roan is a settlement 2 km N of Newcastleton in Liddesdale. Early records refer to it as 'the Rone', in keeping with the custom of using the definite article as part of the name of a farm. In 1766 it was let to James Grieve (National Archives of Scotland, Buccleuch Muniments GD224/281/1), and was still rented by him in 1792 (GD224/528/1).

120.35–36 the Waste the Waste of Cumberland, a wild area of moor lying SE of Liddesdale, on the English side of the Border. See also Historical Note, 362–3.
120.39 the Liddel Liddel Water, river in Liddesdale, in SE Roxburghshire.
120.42–121.1 Sawney Culloch... Rowley Overdees... Jock Penny none of these have been identified.
121.1 Bewcastle in Cumbria, approximately 25 km NE of Carlisle; in medieval times an English fortress, now a small settlement. Also used (as here) in the sense of the surrounding 'waste' (see note to 120.35–36).
121.3 when the deil's blind proverbial: Ray, 55; *ODEP*, 181. Scott's usage here matches that in Dialogue 1 of Jonathan Swift's *A Compleat Collection of genteel and Ingenious Conversations* (1738): 'Ay, when the Devil is blind, and his Eyes are not sore yet' (*The Prose Works of Jonathan Swift*, ed. Herbert Davis, Vol. 4 (Oxford, 1957), 144).
121.4 maist feck the greatest part.
121.6 Staneshiebank fair cattle-market just north of Carlisle, on the River Eden. In the ballad 'Kinmont Willie', stanzas 26–28, the rescuers cross the Eden at 'the Staneshaw-bank' (see *Minstrelsy*, 2.63).
121.22–23 quits a' scores pays all debts, settles all disputes.
121.31 writer chields lawyer chaps, solicitors.
122.24 Tib Mumps for the origin of this character, and her inn, see Historical Note, 362.
122.26 Conscouthart-moss Conscouthart-green features in the ballad 'Hobbie Noble' (stanza 17); Scott locates it in the Waste of Bewcastle (see *Minstrelsy*, 2.122).
123 motto *The Winter's Tale*, 4.3.27–28.
123.37 meddle not and make not proverbial, with *make* in the sense of 'interfere' (see Ray, 53, 202; *ODEP*, 522); compare uses at 145.29 and 193.27.
124.4 death pays a' scores proverbial (see *ODEP*, 174).
124.6 scouring the cramp-ring 'To scour the cramp-ring, is said metaphorically, for being thrown into fetters, or, generally, into prison' (Magnum, 3.233n). Grose has 'to scower the cramp ring, to wear bolts or fetters' (under *Scower*).
124.9 Waste of Cumberland see note to 120.35–36.
124.31 bye-law of the corporation of Newcastle typical of bylaws made in Newcastle upon Tyne against the inhabitants of the English border dales such as Tynedale and Redesdale is that of the Merchant Adventurers' Company in 1544, stating that 'No fre brother of this Fellysshype shall, from hensfourthe, take non apprentice, to serve in this Fellysshype of none suche as is or shalbe borne or brought up in Tyndall, Ryddisdall or anye other suche lycke places; in payne of £20'. See Madeline Hope Dodds, *A History of Northumberland*, Vol. 15 (Newcastle upon Tyne, 1940), 156.
124.33 Give a dog... hang him proverbial (Ramsay, 78; *ODEP*, 302).
126.15 en croupe *French* behind.
126.26 Withershins-latch not located, and possibly fictitious. In the Introduction to John Leyden's 'The Cout of Keeldar', included in *Minstrelsy of the Scottish Border*, it is stated of the Kielder Stone ('on the confines of Jed Forest, and Northumberland') that 'it is held unlucky to ride thrice *withershins* around it'. *Withershins* is there glossed as 'a direction contrary to the course of the sun' (*Minstrelsy*, 4.260); *latch* is Scots for mire, or patch of bog.
127.6 Maiden-way an old road said to have run northward through Bewcastle Waste (see note to 121.1) parallel with the present boundary between Cumberland and Northumberland, and entering into Scotland in the upper reaches of Kershope Burn.

127.13–14 Staneshiebank fair see note to 121.6.
127.25 hum-dudgeon an alternative form of *hum durgeon*, which is glossed by Grose as 'an imaginary illness': used here, evidently, in the sense of 'unnecessary fuss'.
128.2 farm-steading of Charlieshope *farm-steading* here signifies the farm buildings and farm house; *hope* in place names in Liddesdale usually means the remote upper part of a river valley. For possible prototypes of Charlieshope, see Historical Note, 363–64.
128.8 ben the house towards (or through into) the inner apartment of the house.
128 motto John Armstrong, *The Art of Preserving Health: A Poem* (1744), Book 3 ('Exercise'), lines 77–79, 81.
129.13 Lowrie Lowther's not identified, and presumably fictitious.
130.6 gory locks *Macbeth*, 3.4.51.
130.28 four-hours scones taken as a snack between dinner and supper, about four o'clock.
130.42–43 behave themselves "distinctly" i.e. behave in a distinct way, such as might differentiate them from other children.
131.7 Bristol hearth-rug before the Industrial Revolution, carpet making was an important industry in the region of Bristol in SW England.
131.30–31 served as a "shoeing-horn" . . . cup of ale i.e. provided an excuse for another drink (a *shoeing-horn*, literally, is a piece of horn used to aid putting on a shoe). Compare *Gammer Gurton's Needle* (1575), 1.1.24: 'Shall serve for a shoeing-horn to draw on two pots of ale'.
131.36–37 raw wound and his bloody coxcomb see *Henry V*, 5.1.39.
132 motto James Thomson, *The Seasons* (1726–30), 'Autumn', lines 470–74.
132.35–36 the rogues . . . quicksilver see 2 *Henry IV*, 2.4.219.
133.14 Withershins-latch see note to 126.26.
133.20 Christenbury Craig Christianbury Crags, in Cumbria, are on the western verge of Bewcastle Fells, *c.* 12 km SE of Newcastleton.
133.21–22 a screed o' drink i.e. a bout of drinking. Scott sometimes uses *screed* alone: 'Our Ettrick Foresters . . . are sometimes terrible fellows for a screed, and temptations occur frequently where there is plenty both of whiskey and idle time to drink it' (*Letters*, 4.419). Compare Dandie at 274.13.
133.25 Tam o' Todshaw see note to 139.16.
133.30 fiend a bit the devil a bit! not the least!
134.3 Otterscope-scaurs not located, and possibly fictitious; *scaur*, as found in place names, means a precipitous bank or a steep eroded cliff.
134.24 Pychely Hunt the Pytchley Hunt, in Northamptonshire, was renowned for its pack of hounds.
135.1–2 Mongrel . . . low degree see Oliver Goldsmith, 'An Elegy on the Death of a Mad Dog' (1766), lines 15–16 ('mongrel, puppy, whelp and hound/ And curs of low degree').
135.10–11 strained at the slips compare *Henry V*, 3.1.31–32 ('I see you stand like greyhounds in the slips/ Straining upon the start').
135.33 Nabob of Arcot the Indian ruler (*nawab*) of a state in SE India situated between the Eastern Ghauts and the Coromandel Coast (and later included in the Presidency of Madras). After the famous defence of Arcot in 1751 under Robert Clive (1725–1774), the nabobs were allies and effectively puppets of the British: the Nawab Mahomed Ali Wallajah (1717–95) would have been the ruler at the time of the main events in the story.
136 motto 'Johnie Armstrang', stanza 3 (see *Minstrelsy*, 1.352).
136.18 waster apparently synonymous with *leister*, which is offered as an alternative in a Magnum footnote, with the following commentary: 'The long

spear is used for striking; but there is a shorter, which is cast from the hand, and with which an experienced sportsman hits the fish with singular dexterity' (Magnum, 3.259n). For accounts of Scott leistering at night in the River Tweed with friends, see James Hogg's *Memoirs of the Author's Life and Familiar Anecdotes of Sir Walter Scott*, ed. Douglas S. Mack (Edinburgh and London, 1972), 140–41, and James Skene, *Memories of Sir Walter Scott*, ed. Basil Thomson (London, 1909), 29–30.

136.18 **mouth of the Esk** the River Esk flows into the Solway Firth, near Gretna close to the Border with England.

137.8 **water-kelpy** water demon, usually in the form of a horse, said to haunt rivers and fords, and lure the unwary to their deaths.

137.17 **Pandæmonium** the name used in John Milton's *Paradise Lost* for the capital of Hell; a place of confusion and uproar.

138.30 **savoury mess** compare Genesis 27.4 and 27.31; and John Milton, 'L'Allegro' (*c.* 1631), lines 84–85.

138.31 **Johnnie Armstrong** Border freebooter and castle-rustler, executed by James V near Langholm in 1529, and the hero of several Border ballads. In Scott's version of the ballad 'Johnie Armstrang', the eponymous hero is described as having 'venison in great plentie' and a 'gallant cumpanie' (see *Minstrelsy*, 1.352).

138.40 **deserved his paiks** merited a beating-up or suitable thrashing.

139.13 **Armstrongs and Elliots** two leading clan names in Liddesdale during the 'riding' days in the 16th century.

139.16 **Tam o' Todshaw, Will o' the Flat, Hobbie o' Sorbietrees** while intended to be characteristic, all three names evidently relate to real locations: Sorbietrees and Flatt are settlements on the east bank of Liddel Water, between Newcastleton and Kershopefoot; a 'Todshaw' (fox wood) belonged to Todscleughside, a farm bordering Riccarton (see note to 120.31) and eventually absorbed into it.

139.20–21 **Tod Gabbie** nickname originating from hunting the fox (*tod*). According to James Skene the original, albeit called 'Tod Willie', was discovered during an excursion with Scott into 'the wilds glens of Roxburghshire': 'He was one of those vermin-destroyers who gain a subsistence among the farmers in Scotland by relieving them of foxes, polecats, and such like depredators' (*Memories of Sir Walter Scott*, ed. Basil Thomson (London, 1909), 34).

139.37 **Venus speedily routed Bacchus** i.e. the power of love overcame that of drink: Venus is the Roman goddess of love, Bacchus the god of wine and revelry.

140.37–38 **the Castletown** the settlement of (old) Castleton, 3.5 km NE of Newcastleton, once an important focal point in Liddesdale.

141.3 **the old song** the traditional song 'I'll make ye be fain to follow', in which 'a sodger' courts 'a bonie young lass'. Robert Chambers gives the line quoted by Scott as 'Wi' part o' my supper, and part o' my bed' (*Scottish Songs*, 2 vols (Edinburgh, 1829), 1.279). See also *Songs from David Herd's Manuscript*, ed. Hans Hecht (Edinburgh, 1904), where the second line of the third and final quatrain reads: 'A part of my supper, a part o' my bed' (148).

141.13 **Lay of the Last Minstrel** Scott's long poem, set on the Borders in the 16th century, and first published (under his name) in 1805.

141.25 **Highland fairs** either referring to fairs in Galloway and Dumfriesshire and the Border hill country, from which Dinmont has recently returned (see 121.4–6), or to the fairs in Northern Scotland (such as Crieff, Falkirk, and Doune) where lowlanders came to buy cattle from the Highlands.

141.38 **buy yoursells up a step** gain promotion by purchasing a commission (see also note to 112.15).

141.39–40 **bit scrape o' your pen** indicating a memorandum

acknowledging the debt, a promissory note.
142 motto Joanna Baillie (1762–1851), *Ethwald; a Tragedy*, Part Second, 2.2.
142.36 sevenfold shield of Ajax shield belonging to Ajax, one of the Greek warriors who fought at Troy: its exceptional thickness, based on seven layers of ox-hide, is described in Homer's *Iliad*, 7.219–20.
143.16 ignis fatuus *Latin literally* a foolish fire. A phosphorescent light caused by marsh gas; in popular superstition called a 'Will o' the Wisp' and similar names.
144.33 her song evidently Scott's own composition, though an affinity between what follows and 'A Lyke-Wake Dirge' (a Catholic ballad of Northern origin communicated to Scott from the papers of the antiquary Joseph Ritson) was later noted by J. G. Lockhart (see *Minstrelsy*, 3.163–72, 168).
145.10–14 He cannot pass . . . the door a Magnum note, headed 'Gipsy Superstitions', comments: 'The popular idea, that the protracted struggle between life and death is painfully prolonged by keeping the door of the apartment shut, was received as certain by the superstitious eld of Scotland' (3.283). Scott also discusses the open door as a feature of 'the lykewake, or watching a dead body' in his Introduction to the ballad 'Young Benjie' (see *Minstrelsy*, 3.10–11).
145.29 Make not, meddle not see 123.37 (and note).
145.30 redding strake blow from a combatant, frequently the lot of one who tries to separate those who fight.
145.30 fair-strae death death from natural causes.
146.20 with salt sprinkled upon it compare Scott's comment apropos 'A Lyke-Wake Dirge': 'The word *sleet*, in the chorus, seems to be corrupted from *selt* or salt; a quantity of which, in compliance with a popular superstition, is frequently placed on the breast of a corpse' (*Minstrelsy*, 3.163).
146.26 cold drops burst out Brown's (Bertram's) reaction closely matches that of the similarly-beleaguered hero in Tobias Smollett's *The Adventures of Ferdinand Count Fathom* (1753), Ch. 21. In his 'Life' of Smollett, Scott praised Smollett's description in the following terms: 'The horrible adventure in the hut of the robbers, is a tale of natural terror which rises into the sublime; and, though often imitated, has never yet been surpassed, or perhaps equalled' (*Prose Works*, 3.137).
146.42–43 Lady Macbeth . . . . father see *Macbeth*, 2.2.12–13 ('Had he not resembled/ My father as he slept, I had done't').
148 motto Joanna Baillie (1762–1851), *Orra: A Tragedy*, 3.1. The quoted passage is a stanza of a song ('The Chough and the Crow') performed by outlaws, which Scott in 1811 told the authoress had caused him to cancel a similar song of his own, later rewritten for *Rokeby* (1813): see *Letters*, 3.35, 61, 199. Baillie's song was later included, on Scott's recommendation, in Daniel Terry's hugely popular dramatisation (1816) of *Guy Mannering* (see *Letters*, 4.170).
148.29 milling in the darkmans 'Murder by night' (Magnum, 3.286n).
148.30 lap and pannel 'Liquor and food' (Magnum 3.286n). *Lap*, defined in *OED* as slang for 'drink, liquor in general', is glossed by Grose more specifically as 'butter milk, or whey'; while 'pannel' is perhaps a variant of (or mistake for) *pannam* ('bread' in Grose). See also note to 149.18.
148.31 Johnnie Faa the name Faw or Faa was the oldest belonging to gypsies in Scotland, dating back to the early 16th century (see Anne Gordon, *Hearts upon the Highway. Gypsies in South-East Scotland* (Galashiels, [1980?]), 9, and note to 35.14–15 above). Johnnie Faa is also the celebrated if historically indistinct hero of the ballad 'The Gypsy Laddie' (Child, 200). In Scott's time the Faas were one of the most prominent gypsy or tinker families on the Borders, those based at Kirk Yetholm, Roxburghshire, taking the title of Kings.

148.31 the upright man 'an upright man signifies the chief, or principal of a crew [gang] . . . He often travels in company with thirty or forty, males and females, . . .over whom he presides arbitrarily' (Grose, under *Upright Men*).
148.32–33 altered from the good auld rules Meg Merrilies's reproach to the gypsies seems to owe something to Scott's recollection of Jean Gordon's shame at her sons for robbing their benefactor (see Magnum Introduction, 3.xx).
148.33 scour the cramp-ring see note to 124.6.
148.34 trine to the cheat 'Get imprisoned and hanged' (Magnum, 3.286n), but more probably meaning 'go to the gallows' (see Glossary).
149.2 Bing out and tour 'Go out and watch' (Magnum, 3.287n). Grose glosses *touting* as from 'tuare, to look about'. See also note to 149.18.
149.5 the great fight between our folk and Patrico Salmon's for Scott's account of two such bloody skirmishes between rival groups of gypsies, see 'Notices Concerning the Scottish Gypsies', *Blackwood's Edinburgh Magazine*, 1:1 (April 1817), 51. See also Anne Gordon, *Hearts upon the Highway* (Galashiels, [1980?]), 19–20, for details of a battle at Hawick in 1772 or 1773 between the Kennedys and Taits in which Jean Gordon took an active part. An account of a fight involving Billy Marshall's gang and 'a powerful body of tinkers from Argyle or Dumbarton' appeared in *Blackwood's Edinburgh Magazine*, 1:5 (August 1817), 464. Patrico Salmon is perhaps a composite name originating from an end note to Richard Brome's play *A Jovial Crew; or, the Merry Beggars* (1641), in *Ancient British Drama*, 3 vols (London, 1810), 3.216: *CLA*, 43. An 'Explanation of the cant terms used in this play' glosses a number of words, including *salmon* ('or rather *salomon*, the Beggars Oath'), and describes, more extensively, *Patrico* as 'amongst beggars . . . their priest; every hedge being his parish; every wandering harlot and rogue his parishioners'. For Scott's editorial input into this revision of the 1780 edition of Dodsley's *Old Plays*, from which the 'Explanation' of cant terms derives, see Bill Ruddick, 'Scott on the Drama: A Series of Ascriptions', *The Scott Newsletter*, no. 14 (Spring, 1989), 2–6. The name 'Patrico' also features in John Fletcher's play, *The Beggar's Bush* (see above 35, motto).
149.18 canting language several of the cant terms found in this sequence are glossed in the 'Explanation' attached to Richard Brome's *A Jovial Crew; or, the Merry Beggars* (1641), in *Ancient British Drama* (1810), as described in the previous note. These include: *Darkman* ('the night'); *Lap* ('porridge'); *Strummel* ('straw'); *Bing awast* ('get you hence'); and *Toure* ('see, look out'). See also note to 25.19–20.
149.21 have his gruel receive his punishment, get killed.
149.34 bought so many brooms 'Got so many warrants out' (Magnum, 3.288n).
149.38 sing out peach, turn informer.
151.41 japanned with turf i.e. blackened with smoke (from peat fires) in a way similar to *japanned* ('lacquered') furniture.
154.29 depositary equivalent to the Latin *depositarius*, a person with whom anything is left for safe-keeping: a technical legal term, appropriately spelt this way.
155 motto *A Midsummer Night's Dream*, 3.2.202–08.
156.21 Bingo Grose glosses *Bingo* as a cant term for 'brandy or other spiritous liquor'. It also features as a dog's name in a folk-song, sung at the Theatre Royal *c.* 1780, with a spelling chorus: 'A farmer's dog jump'd over the stile, and I think his name was Bingo': see *The Oxford Dictionary of Nursery Rhymes*, ed. Iona and Peter Opie (Oxford, 1951), 155.
157.4 Cicipici a mock name for an Italian teacher.
157.12 La Pique's steps apparently involving a burlesque name for a

French dance master. A real Monsieur Charles Le Picq nevertheless had a dancing school in Edinburgh during the later 18th century (see *The Book of the Old Edinburgh Club*, 19 (1933), 62; and *Redgauntlet*, EEWN 17, 9.38 and note).
158.35 Mess Baartraam Julia Mannering's mimicry reflects Mannering's view of the difference between Scottish and English speech at 100.30 (see note).
159.40 Mahratta's turban the *mahratta* or *maratha*, a Hindu people, lived mainly in the central and south-west part of India, and formed a powerful military confederacy in the 18th century (see note to 66.28).
160.35 Hyder-Ally Haidar Ali (*c.* 1722–82), Indian general and ruler of Mysore. In 1780 he invaded the presidency of Madras, threatening the annihilation of British power in India, before being defeated in a series of engagements during the following year.
161.22 eastern genie *genie* is properly a form of the Arabian word 'jinnee', one of the sprites or goblins of Mahommedan mythology, although through the influence of the word 'genius' it has often had the connotation of a guiding spirit.
162 motto see *The Merry Devil of Edmonton* (1608), 5.2.48–54.
162.20 Salvator see note to 93.17–18.
162.32 Mars Roman god of war, and the planet of that name (see also note to 20.19–20).
163.27 voluntary explosion *voluntary* here in the sense of 'independent, spontaneous, not prompted by another': compare 'voluntary excursion' at 40.23.
166.5 Ophir in the Old Testament, the place from which ships were sent to bring gold to King Solomon (1 Kings 9.28).
166.8–9 pinchbeck gilt cheap jewellery covered with an overlay resembling gold in appearance, made from an alloy of copper and zinc, and named after its inventor, the clock-maker Christopher Pinchbeck (1670?–1732).
166.16 Thomas Aquinas Italian philosopher and Dominican monk (*c.* 1225–74), leading figure in scholasticism, whose works embodied the world view taught in the universities until the 17th century.
166.17 venerable Chrysostom Saint John Chrysostom (*c.* 347–407), called 'golden-mouthed' because of his great eloquence, became Patriarch of Constantinople in 397, but after attempting to reform the city was later driven into exile. He wrote a large number of scriptural homilies, plus treatises, and collections of the text of his works were published in France (1609–37) and by Sir Henry Savile in England (1610–13).
166 motto *King John*, 4.3.116.
167.13–14 curlers . . . ice referring to the game of *curling*, popular at this time in Scotland, in which large rounded stones are propelled on the ice towards a mark.
170 motto *King Lear*, 4.6.150–54.
172.18 escape from Coventry i.e. from social ostracism: a reversal of the common proverbial expression, 'to send (a person) to Coventry' (see *ODEP*, 149), meaning to exclude from society.
172.23–24 sheriff-substitute . . . belonged see note to 53.9.
172.43 high in her books high in her favour, amongst her list of friends.
173.19 cough negative . . . cough dubious compare Touchstone's speeches in *As You Like It*, 5.4.65–97.
173.42–43 Antiburgher meeting the *Antiburghers* were a Presbyterian sect, who split from other seceders from the Church of Scotland in 1747, on the grounds that taking the Burgess oath expressed approval of the established religion; Mrs Mac-Candlish here conveniently interprets the principle as prohibiting her from taking an oath before a civil magistrate.

174.1 keepit the kirk i.e. attended the established Church of Scotland (see also note above).

174.16 a horning or a caption *Scots law* 'letters of horning' were directions to messengers at arms (officers appointed to execute the orders of the Court of Session) to charge the person to whom the letters are directed to pay a debt or perform some other duty on pain of being declared a rebel. A *caption* was a warrant to arrest or apprehend a person for non-payment of debt. In reality, the acquisition of letters of horning became a procedural step towards procuring letters of caption which allowed the arrest of a debtor. Mrs Mac-Candlish obviously cannot believe Glossin would seek anyone other than for debt.

174.42–43 tell me your company . . . wha ye are proverbial (see Ray, 114; *ODEP*, 807).

175.3–4 Hansel Monanday the first Monday of the year, when a small gift of money (*hansel* or *handsel*) was put into the hand.

175.7–8 Loch Creeran probably fictitious; but 'Loch Cree', 8 km N of Newton Stewart and actually a widening of the River Cree, was much larger before alterations to the river *c.* 1798 and had a reputation as a beauty spot: see Rev. C. H. Dick, *Highways and Byways of Galloway and Carrick* (1916; reprinted Wigtown, 1994), 156.

175.10 friar's chicken Edward Topham describes this as 'Chicken cut into small pieces, and boiled with parsley, cinnamon, and eggs, in strong beef soup': *Letters from Edinburgh; Written in the Years 1774 and 1775* (London, 1776), 161 (*CLA*, 9).

175.10 crappit-heads haddock-heads stuffed with the roe, oatmeal, onions and pepper.

175.21 up the Lawn-market i.e. to his execution. The Lawnmarket, a street in Edinburgh, is part of the route along which condemned prisoners passed on their way from the Tolbooth (the city prison in the 18th century) to the Grassmarket, the place of execution.

175.35 Kilmarnock-cap knitted conical skull-cap worn by indoor working men; named after Kilmarnock, a town in Ayrshire, noted for its weaving.

175.43 the Crown office the office of the Crown Agent in Scotland, an appointee of the Lord Advocate, whose duties are to decide on and prepare for criminal prosecution. Sending property to the Crown Office after inventory was proper procedure.

177.16–17 Vengeance . . . repay it see Romans 12.19.

177.19–20 start the game . . . beat the bush variation of the proverb 'Ane beats the bush, and anither grips the game' (Ramsay, 67; see also Ray, 143 and *ODEP*, 37).

177.22 down at the Isle probably a reference to St Mary's Isle, a small peninsula 2 km S of Kirkcudbright.

177.27 Kirkcudbright fair Kirkcudbright is a royal burgh, and the capital of the Stewartry of Kirkcudbright, at the mouth of Kirkcudbright Bay and some 12 km SE of Gatehouse of Fleet; two annual fairs were held there, on 12 August or the following Friday, and 29 September or the Friday after.

177.42 buy golden opinions . . . people see *Macbeth*, 1.7.32–33.

178.7 the deil's no sae ill as he's ca'd proverbial (see *ODEP*, 182).

178 motto see *Measure for Measure*, 4.2.135–38.

179.6 Sir George Mackenzie (1636–91) King's Advocate during the later Stuart period; he wrote several legal and historical works, including *The Laws and Customs of Scotland in Matters Criminal* (1678).

179.7 Vis Publica et Privata *Latin* oppression, public and private. Scott refers to Mackenzie's *Laws and Customs* (see note above), of which Title 32 of Book I is 'Bearing of unlawful weapons'; and Title 34 is 'Robbery, Oppression, *vis publica & privata*'.

179.9 mickle coat overcoat.
180.22 sapperment corruption of the German *sakrament*, meaning 'sacrament': an oath used by a German speaker.
180.26 Cuxhaven port on the southern side of the River Elbe, at its entrance into the North Sea; an outport for Hamburg, it is now part of Germany.
180.27 sall Ich bin *German* shall I be.
180.39 Flushing (Vlissengen) port at the north entrance to the Wester-schelde, in the Netherlands.
181.15 Poz donner! *German* God's thunder!
181.39 clayed over covered up and concealed.
181.43 laid in the locker i.e. dead: a nautical expression from *locker*, a chest for keeping rigging etc.
182.7–8 absolute ruin, if the heir should re-appear in this event the sale of Ellangowan would be ruled invalid and overturned. Glossin would lose the title and not get back any money he might have paid because the sale was by public roup (auction). At a public roup there is no 'warrandice', i.e. there is no guarantee that a good title will be given. See also note to 62.27.
182.25 Kaim of Derncleugh a *kaim* in Scots means a long narrow steep-sided mound or ridge, but Scott's usage indicates that he is referring to a building rather than just a situation (compare 'the promontory on which the Kaim of Derncleugh was situated' at 329.2–3). For the probably fictitious name of Derncleugh, see note to 37.35.
182.33 es spuckt da *German* it is haunted there.
182.34 Strafe mich helle! *German* punish me hell!
182.40–41 constable . . . three days recalling the incident already mentioned by Godfrey Bertram at 28.12 (see note). This would constitute private imprisonment, and so represent an illegal act.
182.42 inner-house afore the fifteen before the Inner House of the Court of Session in Edinburgh. At this period, the Court was organised into Outer and Inner Houses. In the Outer House each judge (except the Lord President) presided separately as a judge of first instance; and although much routine litigation did not progress beyond the Outer House, cases could be remitted to the Inner House for final decision, or to seek rulings on particular legal issues. In the Inner House all 15 judges sat together. The Act 1701, c 6 lays down penalties for 'wrongous imprisonment' which must be sued for before the Court of Session.
183.9 in watching nor prayer see Mark 13.33, 14.38.
185 motto *Titus Andronicus*, 2.3. 209–10.
186.29 like a guilty thing *Hamlet*, 1.1.148–49: 'And then it started like a guilty thing/ Upon a fearful summons' (Horatio on the ghost).
187.27 Hagel and donner!—be'st du? *German* Hail and thunder! is it you?
187.32–33 hold mich der deyvil, Ich bin ganz gefrorne! *German* devil fetch me! I am completely frozen.
187.37 Snow-wasser and hagel! *German* snow-water and hail!
188.9 Das schmeckt! *German* that tastes good!
188.11 High-Dutch i.e. German: as opposed to Low Dutch (correctly Low German), the language spoken in the low-lying lands on the North Sea coast from which modern Dutch developed.
188.12–16 Saufen bier . . . leute a? these lines are in the style of a popular German drinking song. Roughly translated it means: We swill beer, and spirits;/ We smash all the windows;/ I am immoral and debauched,/ You are immoral and debauched,/ Are we not immoral people?
188.19–20 Gin by the pailfuls . . . shivers these first two lines effectively follow the song in German preceding; for the following four lines see next note.

188.21–24 three wild lads . . . gallows-tree these final four lines parallel a song near the beginning of George Peele's *The Old Wives Tale* (1595), lines 26–29: 'Three merie men, and three merrie men,/ And three merrie men be wee./ I in the wood, and thou on the ground,/ And Jacke sleepes in the tree.' The title of the song, which is found in varied forms in several early Jacobean dramas, is mentioned by Sir Toby Belch in *Twelfth Night*, 2.3.74.
188.27 hagel and donner! *German* hail and thunder!
188.34 fluch and blitzen! *German* curse and lightning!
188.35 Middleburgh town in SW Netherlands, capital of the Dutch province of Zeeland, and an old commercial centre.
188.36 goose's gazette made-up story.
189.8 Deurloo a narrow arm on the Westerschelde, between Walcheren and Zeeuws Vlaanderen, in the Netherlands.
189.14 By the knocking Nicholas! the full meaning of this phrase has not been discovered. 'Nicholas's clerks' is a term for highwaymen, and the devil is often referred to as 'Old Nick'.
189.22–23 houndsfoot schelm *German* clumsy rascal.
189.40 served the States i.e. had enlisted in the (naval) forces of the United Provinces of the Netherlands. Britain declared war on the Netherlands on 20 November 1780, for aiding the Americans, and a naval battle took place on the Dogger Bank the following year.
190.3 Wetter and donner, ya! *German* foul weather and thunder, yes!
191.2 custom-house at Portanferry for a possible link between Portanferry and Creetown, 16 km W of Gatehouse of Fleet in Galloway, see Historical Note, 362. While a tidewaiter was stationed at Creetown in the later 18th century, it was not significant enough to warrant a custom-house. A 'Custom-house, with the necessary set of officers' was, on the other hand, observed in Kirkcudbright (another possible model) by Robert Heron on his 1792 tour of the region: *Observations Made in a Journey through the Western Counties of Scotland*, 2nd edn, 2 vols (Perth, 1799), 2.187: *CLA*, 10. The sound of the name echoes the small landing-station noted by James Boswell while visiting Iona with Samuel Johnson: 'The place which I went to see is about two miles from the village. They call it *Portawherry*, from the wherry in which Columba came' (*Journal of a Tour to the Hebrides with Samuel Johnson Ll.D*, 20 October [1773], ed. R. W. Chapman (Oxford, 1924), 388).
191.15 to Jericho part of a proverbial expression, 'to go to Jericho', meaning to go no-one knows where (see *ODEP*, 410).
191.33 the barony, rig-about in the feudal system a *barony* is an estate held by direct grant from the Crown. *Rig-about* refers to the 'runrig' system, a form of cultivation where the land was divided into strips to ensure a fair distribution of productive and less productive ground between tenants. *Rig-about* would involve the possession of alternate strips. In the 18th and early 19th centuries the runrig system was represented as the epitome of inefficient agriculture. In his diary entry of 4 August 1814 Scott remarks of the agriculture of the Shetlands: 'there are several obstacles to improvement, chiefly the undivided state of the properties, which lie *run-rig*' (*Life*, 3.143). In Scott's edition of *Memorie of the Somervilles* (1815), a footnote to 'rune rig' reads: 'That is, lying by alternate ridges, a very inconvenient state of property' (2.115n).
191.35–36 lust-haus . . . blumen-garten in German literally pleasure-house and flower garden. Glossin's answer to Hattaraick's ambition compares interestingly with Scott's later comments on 'the paltry imitations of the Dutch, who clipped yews into monsters of every species and description, and relieved them with the painted wooden figures which are seen much in the attitude of their owners, silent and snugly smoking at the end of the paltry walk of every *Lust-huys*' ('On Landscape Gardening' (1828), in *Prose Works*, 21.87). A *lust-*

huis in Dutch describes a villa or country seat, while in German *lusthaus* referred to a summer-house or garden house (in the grounds of an estate etc.).

191.43 murderer and kidnapper the stealing of children, known in Scots law as *plagium*, was by itself a crime punishable by death.

192.3 as peace is now so much talked of the treaty of Versailles, 3 September 1783, brought peace with France and Spain and recognition of American independence; hostilities between the Netherlands and Britain (see note to 189.40), though not part of this treaty, were brought to a close by a separate truce. See also Historical Note, 356.

192.3–4 High Mightinesses members of the States-General, the Dutch legislative assembly: a literal translation of *Hoogmogendheiden*.

192.6 Poz hagel blitzen and donner! *German* God's hail, lightning, and thunder!

192.18 strafe mich der teyfel *German* may the devil punish me.

192.20 silver-cooper from the Low German/Dutch *zielverkoper* (soul-seller), used for kidnapper and in relation to the press gang.

192.37 upon the account an old phrase for living as a pirate or sailing on a piratical expedition.

193.12 swore by the salmon *salmon*, or salamon, according to Grose, is 'the beggars sacrament or oath'; see also note to 149.5.

193.22 goat's foot referring to the devil's cloven hoof.

193.24 Kobold a goblin or underground spirit in German folklore.

193.27 make nor meddle proverbial expression, which, as Hattaraick notes, is a favourite with Meg Merrilies: see note to 123.37.

193.30 under embargo under seizure (as if he were contraband goods).

193 motto see *Othello*, 1.1.109–11.

194.1 Protocol, an attorney in Edinburgh a protocol book was a book kept by a notary in which he was supposed to keep copies of documents that he drew up to be preserved as a record. Hence the special appropriateness of the name, given this lawyer's punctiliousness in keeping copies.

194.28 sçavoir faire *French* knowledge of what to do.

195.17 viva voce *Latin* by the living voice, by oral testimony.

195.42–43 Scripture . . . land-marks see Proverbs 22.16, 28: 'He that oppresseth the poor to increase his riches . . . shall surely come to want'; 'Remove not the ancient landmark, which thy fathers have set'. Landmarks are also similarly mentioned in Deuteronomy 19.14, Proverbs 23.10, and Job 24.2.

196.2 Anathema Maranatha! 1 Corinthians 16.22: 'If any man love not the Lord Jesus Christ, let him be Anathema Maranatha'. *Anathema* in Greek means 'a thing set apart', 'a thing accursed'; *Maranatha* is an Aramaic expression, borrowed into Greek, signifying something equivalent to 'Our Lord has come'. The appearance of the two together in 1 Corinthians has led to their misunderstanding as an intensified curse.

196.18 Chiltern Hundreds the name given to three manors ('hundreds') in Buckinghamshire, where the Sovereign formally appointed stewards to suppress robbers in the Chiltern Hills. The office became obsolete, though a nominal salary remained, and from 1750 a member of Parliament wishing to leave office during a Parliament applies for the Stewardship of the Chiltern Hundreds, which being an office of profit under the Crown necessitates resignation from Parliament. Mr Featherhead's 'taking the Chiltern Hundreds' would thus open up the possibility of Hazelwood obtaining the seat.

196.20 one who understands the roll i.e. the roll of electors, which Glossin not only understands but is adept in manipulating (see also notes to 28.5 and 32.2).

196.27 condign punishment compare *2 Henry VI*, 3.1.130 ('I never gave them condign punishment').

197.39 general settlement a *settlement* in Scots law is a document such as a will in which provision can be made for the future of an estate on death.

198.1–2 in fee . . . life-rented a person *in fee* of an estate, i.e. its feudal proprietor, can make a settlement (see above note) of the estate even though at the time it is *life-rented* by another (i.e. by one who has the right for life to the use of the property and the income arising from it, but without ownership). So Margaret Bertram could settle the estate of Singleside, as she is the owner, though her sister was in possession as life rentrix. See also note to 214.1–2.

198.12–13 Is most excellent . . . spent Glossin turns to his own advantage a proverbial rhyme (see *ODEP*, 389). Scott quoted the orthodox version in his Journal entry for 3 March 1826: 'When House and Land are gone and spent/ Then Learning is most excellent' (*Journal*, 103).

198.14 I love the smack of the whip contemporary phrase, indicating a relish for an old practice or occupation.

198.28 take me so very short i.e. interrupt me very quickly, not allowing a full explanation.

199.7 Reilagganbeg, Gillifidget, Loverless, Lyalone, and the Spinster's Knowe all apparently fictitious names. The last four suggests a process from flirtatiousness (a *gillie* in Scots is a flighty girl), through 'loverless' and 'lie alone' states, to death as a spinster.

199.24 a jury trial before our court referring to the Sheriff Court, where a jury would be used for certain criminal trials.

200 motto see *1 Henry IV*, 2.4.373–76.

200.13–14 hotels in these days were there none as noted by the English traveller, Edward Topham: 'I should hope, ere long, the pride or good sense of Scotland will so far prevail, as to establish an Hotel in some suitable part of the town' (*Letters from Edinburgh; written in the Years 1774 and 1775* (London, 1776), 23: *CLA*, 9). Hugo Arnot's *History of Edinburgh* (Edinburgh, 1788 edn; *CLA*, 14) similarly contrasts the position in 1763 compared with the present: 'In 1763—A stranger coming to Edinburgh was obliged to put up at a dirty uncomfortable inn, or to remove to private lodgings. There was no such place as an Hotel; the word indeed was not known, or only intelligible to French scholars' (658).

200.17 Moffat town 40 km NE of Dumfries, and a staging-post on the way to Edinburgh or Glasgow.

200.17–18 disputed quantity in Horace's 7th Ode, Book II probably concerning the pronunciation of the word *ciboria* (drinking cup) in 'Ciboria exple, funde capacibus' (*Odes*, 2.7.22). According to the disputants Horace had either i) transliterated the word wrongly from Greek into Latin and introduced a false quantity, or ii) unusually allowed a short syllable to appear in a line where a long syllable would be more regular.

200.19 Malobathro *Latin* the dative and ablative case singular of the word *malobathrum* (a product of the Indian tamala tree which could take the form of a spice or an oil or an ointment). The passage alluded to occurs at the end of the second stanza of Horace's Ode (*Odes*, 2.7.7–8): 'nitentis malobathro Syrio capillos' ('hair gleaming with Syrian malobathrum'), where 'hair-oil' is apparently meant. Possibly the controversy mentioned by Scott related to the nature or origin of Malobathrum as an ointment and plant, or, alternatively, he is misremembering a dispute about the word 'Syrio'.

200.21 Rullion-green battle-site on the eastern shoulder of the Pentland Hills, *c.* 15 km SW of Edinburgh, where Covenanters from SW Scotland were defeated in 1666 by the royalist General Dalzell.

200.23 sepulchral monument of the slain Ordnance Survey maps etc. show 'Martyrs Tomb' close to the battlefield at Rullion Green (see note above).

200.24 Pentland-hills a range of hills to the S and SW of Edinburgh.

201.2 George inn near Bristo-port the George Inn was a coaching inn in Bristo Street, close to Bristo Port, the main entry into the city of Edinburgh from the south. It was from the George Inn that the Flying Diligence at this time set off for London, by the Carlisle route, completing the journey in four days; and it was also the starting-point for the Ayr and Dumfries coaches. In the ISet Scott added the words 'then kept by old Cockburn', which was introduced into the Magnum text (4.77). This is a reference to John Cockburn, who became tenant of the hostelry in 1767, and under whose management it thrived as a busy coaching centre, until his retirement in 1779. By the end of the century it had begun to suffer from the rivalry of the more modern New Town hotels. For further details, see 'Some Inns of the Eighteenth Century', in *Book of the Old Edinburgh Club*, 14 (1925), 139–45; and Marie W. Stuart, *Old Edinburgh Taverns* (London, 1952), 122.

201.3 to Mr Pleydell's, the advocate in addition to the various suggested prototypes for this character discussed in Historical Note (367), the name suggests 'plead well'.

201.6 cadie messenger or errand-boy. Cadies formed organised corps in large towns such as Edinburgh. 'These are a Society of men who constantly attend the Cross in the High-street, and whose office it is to do any thing that any body can want, and discharge any kind of business. On this account it is necessary for them to make themselves acquainted with the residence and negotiation of all the inhabitants; and they are of great utility, as without them it would be very difficult to find any body, on account of the great height of the houses, and the number of families in every building. This Society is under particular regulations, and it requires some interest to become a member of it' (Edward Topham, *Letters from Edinburgh; written in the Years 1774 and 1775* (London, 1776), 87: *CLA*, 9).

201.7 near the end of the American war see note to 67.41–42, and Historical Note, 356.

201.10 south side of the town where the earliest Georgian residential squares in Edinburgh were built, notably Brown Square and George Square (where Scott's own family settled in 1774), previous to the more extensive New Town development to the north of the Old Town.

201.10 houses within themselves i.e. self-contained, after the manner of English houses, as opposed to the traditional tenement dwellings (with their shared staircases) of the Old Town of Edinburgh. Scott used a similar phrase ('house within itself'), when assessing the value of the two systems in his later 'General Account of Edinburgh' in *Provincial Antiquities and Picturesque Scenery of Scotland*, 2 vols (London, 1826), 1.74: also *Prose Works*, 7.231. See also note below.

201.11–12 New Town on the north the New Town of Edinburgh, an extensive Georgian development on land to the north of the drained North Loch, was based on the plan of the architect James Craig in 1767, though work was not feasible until the construction of the North Bridge, first built 1768–69, and completed in 1772. The foundation stone of the Register House, the first prominent public building, was laid at the east end of Princes Street on 27 June 1774 and the first phase of building ended in 1778. By 1781 St Andrew's Square had been completed, Princes Street was being developed, and other building was going on as far west as Hanover Street. Large stretches of land, however, still remained untouched.

201.14 flats, or stories, of the dungeons *dungeon* is used here in the sense of 'tower' or 'keep' in describing the high-rise tenement buildings of the Edinburgh Old Town; a *flat*, originally a term peculiar to Scotland, was an apartment comprising a single floor of a tenement building.

201.17 fifty years before by which is evidently meant 50 years before the situation being described; thus in the early 1730s.

201.22 praisers of the past 'laudator temporis acti' (Horace, *Ars Poetica*, 173).

201.24 Paulus Pleydell's Christian name echoes that of the great Roman lawyer, Iulius Paulus, active 181–235 under the Emperors from Commodus to Alexander, for long a member of the Imperial Council, and a voluminous writer on law. For his surname, see note to 201.3; and for suggested prototypes see Historical Note, 367.

201.29 the Tron the Tron Church, which stands on the south side of the High Street in Edinburgh opposite where the *tron*, or city weighing machine, was placed; the surrounding area was one of the busiest in Edinburgh.

201.39 coup d'œil *French* view or scene as it strikes the eye at a glance.

201.42 North Bridge the main thoroughfare between the old and new parts of Edinburgh, first built in 1768–69, with improvements making it safer for pedestrians in 1772. The North Bridge (originally Bridge Street) enters the High Street nearly opposite the Tron Church: see also notes to 201.29 and 201.11–12.

201.43 uniform Place the sense of a 'Place' (i.e. a square) between St Giles Cathedral and St Mary's Street is still to some extent intact, but now broken by the North Bridge and Cockburn Street on the north side, and the South Bridge on the south. The unusual length and breadth of the High Street, then a forum of public life, was commented on by numerous visitors to Edinburgh in the 18th century: see A. J. Youngson, *The Making of Classical Edinburgh 1750–1840* (Edinburgh, 1966; reissued 1993), 52–53. Scott makes the same point that the High Street then represented 'a Place [rather] than a street', in *Provincial Antiquities and Picturesque Scenery of Scotland*, 2 vols (London, 1826), 1.68: also *Prose Works*, 7.243.

201.43 Luckenbooths part of old Edinburgh named after the 'locked booths', i.e. small generally timber-fronted shops, found on the ground floor of a four-storey block of buildings which stood against the north side of St Giles Cathedral in the High Street, half closing off the High Street near its head. 'The *Luckenbooth* row, which contains the *Tolbooth*, or city prison, and the weighing-house .... stands in the middle of the High-street, and ... contributes to spoil as fine a street as most in Europe, being in some places eighty feet wide': Thomas Pennant, *A Tour of Scotland* (Chester, 1771), 49. An illustration showing the buildings as standing in the High Street *c.* 1750 is given in A. J. Youngson, *The Making of Classical Edinburgh 1750–1840* (Edinburgh, 1966; reissued 1993), 9; they were demolished in 1817.

202.1 the Canongate now a continuation of the High Street, running down to Holyroodhouse, though at this period the two streets were effectively separated by the Netherbow Port.

202.6 scale stair-case stairs which are straight (as opposed to a spiral staircase).

202.24–26 whiting, or camstane ... Saturday night in Edinburgh *camstane* refers to a form of limestone or white clayey substance used for whitening hearthstones and doorsteps; it would have been used in Edinburgh on Saturday in preparation for the Sabbath.

202.32 Clerihugh's tavern in the (now demolished) Writers' Court off the High Street, opposite St Giles Cathedral, and a favourite meeting-place of the magistrates and Town Council in the later 18th century. Clerihugh was the proprietor, the tavern's sign being The Star and Garter.

202.33 Hersell ... she this is the first indication that the *cadie*, who is here speaking of himself, is a Highlander: gender confusion when moving from Gaelic to English or Scots is a literary device for suggesting Highland speech and is found as early as Richard Holland's *The Buke of the Howlat* (*c.* 1450).

203.6 Teviotdale tup ram from Teviotdale (the valley of the River Teviot in Roxburghshire, but often used by Scott for the Scottish Borders generally).
203.8 bell ta cat proverbial expression, from the fable of the mice proposing to hang a bell round the cat's neck as a warning signal, but timorously failing in their plan since no mouse was prepared to carry out the deed (see Ramsay, 118; Ray, 85; *ODEP*, 44). The words had a special historical connotation for Scott: Archibald Douglas, Earl of Angus, supposedly earned the nickname of Bell-the-Cat by being prepared to take the lead in the assassination of James III's favourite, Cochran, in 1482 (see *Tales of a Grandfather*, in *Prose Works*, 22.320). In the present instance, in spite of the cadie's expectation, none of the Edinburgh citizens are willing or brave enough to intervene.
203.13 this first-rate likening Dinmont's progress to that of a battleship of the first class.
203.25 villainous compound of smells see *The Merry Wives of Windsor*, 3.5.82–83: 'the rankest compound of villainous smell that ever offended nostril'.
203.27 borrowed light opening which reflects light at second hand.
203.32 Pandæmonium see note to 137.17.
203.34 devils on the gridiron left-overs of poultry or game, strongly seasoned and then broiled over a fire.
203.35 Megæra one of the three Furies, who are usually represented with serpents twined in their hair.
203.43 learned in the law compare *2 Henry IV*, 1.2.127–28: 'my learned counsel in the laws'.
204.6 three-tailed wig wig having the hair gathered behind into three tails. Such appear to have been worn by advocates at least in the earlier 18th century, though today's wigs have only two tails. See *The Heart of Mid-Lothian* (1818), where Halkit, in relation to his advocate friend Hardie, speaks of 'the inspiring honours of a gown and three-tailed periwig' (1.46.10–11).
204.8 his altitudes compare Ben Jonson, *The New Inn* (1629), 1.5.17: 'Though I have talked somewhat above my share/ At large, and been i' the altitudes'.
204.13 High Jinks i.e. high pranks, a name given to various tricks performed at drinking-parties. It appears in the 4th stanza of 'Elegy on Maggy Johnston who died Anno 1711', by Allan Ramsay (1686–1758): 'Aften, in *Maggy's*, at Hy-jinks,/ We guzl'd Scuds,/ Till we cou'd scarce wi hale out Drinks/ Cast aff our Duds' (lines 21–24). The 1721 edition of Ramsay's *Poems* includes a note on 'Hy-jinks', detailing at some length the rules of a drinking game of forfeiture involving dice. See also note to 204.29.
204.17 fescennine verses originating from an early Italian form of verse, possibly named after the town of Fescennium in Etruria, and characterised by extempore dialogues in a jeering style.
204.25 scratch wig small, short wig (possibly derived from its allowing an opportunity for scratching the head).
204.27–28 crambo scraps of verse *crambo* is a game in which one player gives a word or line of verse to which each of the others has to find a rhyme.
204.29 Gerunto not identified; possibly a fictitious name for a Roman or African general. In an unpublished note in the ISet, Scott offered the following explanation for the kind of High Jinks being played: 'I believe this strange species of game or revel to be the same mentiond in old English plays and which was calld "Coming from Tripoli". When the supposed King was seated on his post of elevation the most active fellow in the party came into the presence leaping over as many chairs & stools as he could manage to spring over. He is announced as

A post—
King From whence? *Post*—From Tripoli My Leige

He then announces to the Mock Monarch the destruction of his army and fleet. This species of High Jinks was calld Gerunto from the name of the luckless general. I have seen many who have played at it. Among the rest an excellent friend and relation now no more (the late Mr Keith of Dunottar & Ravelston) gave me a ludicrous account of a country gentleman coming up to Edinburgh rather unexpectedly and finding his son whom he had hoped was diligently studying the law in silence and seclusion basely engaged in personating the King in a full drama of Gerunto. The Monarch somewhat surprized at first paid it off with assurance calling for a seat to his honourd father and refusing to accost him otherwise than in the Slang of the character. This incident in itself the more comick situation of the two suggested the scene in the text.' (ISet, interleaf facing 3.188). The expression to 'come from Tripoli', as mentioned by Scott in this note, in Jacobean drama usually means to caper and leap high: see e.g. John Fletcher, *Monsieur Thomas* (performed 1619), 4.2.68–69 ('Get up that window there, and presently / Like a most compleat Gentleman, come from *Tripoly*').

204.31 Themis Greek goddess of Justice.

204.37 Falstaff...play out the play see *1 Henry IV*, 2.4.467, where Falstaff resists interruption of his impersonation of the King and then Prince Hal with the words 'Out, ye rogue! Play out the play'.

204.39 Justinian Roman emperor of the 6th century, celebrated for his codification of Roman law, notably through the compilation between AD 529 and 534 of the *Corpus iuris civilis* ('The Body of the Civil Law'), including the *Digest*, a collection of extracts from writings of Roman lawyers, and the *Institutes*, an elementary textbook.

204.40 court of Holy-rood alluding to Holyroodhouse, the Scottish royal palace, situated at the foot of the Canongate in Edinburgh; it was originally built by James V, and Mary Queen of Scots held court there later in the 16th century. See also note to 202.1.

204.42 forest of Jedwood in medieval times a forest near Jedburgh in Roxburghshire, close to the Border with England.

205.1 Fife region of E Scotland, immediately to the north of the Firth of Forth; a relatively safe and settled area during the 16th century, where the royal-hunting palace at Falkland provided a home for both James IV and James V.

205.2–3 Lyon...Marchmount...Carrick...Snawdoun in Scotland, the chief heraldic authority is the Lord Lyon King of Arms, assisted from 1500 to 1866 by six Heralds and six Pursuivants: among the Heralds were Marchmount and Snawdoun (Snowdon), while Carrick was one of the Pursuivants.

205.8–9 Assembly of the Kirk the General Assembly of the Church of Scotland, its ruling body.

205.22 a guisarding i.e. masquerading in fantastic guise or dress, as was traditional in Scotland at New Year. In an 'Introductory Notice' (1831) to *Two Bannatyne Garlands from Abbotsford* (Edinburgh, 1848), Scott remembers how when he was a boy children would 'go from house to house disguised with shirts over their clothes, and fantastic vizards, which was termed in Scotland *guisarding*, and in England *mumming*' (5).

205.26 Gascony province in SW France, celebrated for its wines, and often in the control of the Kings of England during the Middle Ages.

205.30 preux chevalier *French* valiant knight.

205.36 valley of Liddle locating Dinmont more accurately, as a Liddesdale man, than Pleydell has done previously (see also note to 120.39 and Historical Note, 363–64).

205.37–38 more germain to the matter *Hamlet*, 5.2.155–56.

206.7 King Cophetua and the Beggar-maid Cophetua was a legendary king in Africa who disdained women until casting his eye on a beggar, Penelephon, and marrying her. The story is told in a ballad, 'King Cophetua and the Beggar-Maid', included in Percy, 1.166–71. Cophetua and his love are also alluded to by Shakespeare and other contemporary dramatists: see e.g. *Romeo and Juliet*, 2.1.14.
206.7 adjudged case in point precedent in the technical legal sense of a decision made by a court on the same point of law: hence the objection that Pleydell has adopted a professional manner.
206.12 their Jean Logies the first in a list of women who were mistresses of Scottish kings. In this instance, Scott appears to have in mind Margaret Logie who became the second wife of David II (though he later separated from her). In his later novel, *The Fair Maid of Perth* (1828), 'Catharine Logie' is mentioned as having been the mistress and wife of David II (see Magnum, 42.27, 59n; also EEWN 21, 14.8–10 and note).
206.12 Bessie Carmichael Elizabeth, daughter of Lord Carmichael, mistress of James V of Scotland.
206.12–13 Oliphants . . . Sandilands . . . Weirs all reputedly mistresses of James V. They appear together in a scurrilous contemporary four-line epigram headed 'On King James V his three Mistresses', in Allan Ramsay's *The Ever Green, Being a Collection of Scots Poems*, 2 vols (Edinburgh, 1724), *CLA*, 170: 'Saw not they Seid on *Sandylands*,/ Spend not thy Strength on *Weir*,/ And ryd not on the *Oliphant*,/ For hurting of thy Geir' (1.184).
206.14 whom we delight to honour echoing the biblical phrase (see Esther 6.6–11).
206.15 Charles V of Spain, who abdicated in 1556.
206.25–26 too much malice, or too little wit, as the poet says no specific reference has been identified.
206.37 Langtae-head not identified, probably fictitious.
207.6 play his ain spring first i.e. go ahead, tell his own story first; a *spring* is a lively dance-tune.
207.12 auld wark of the marches i.e. familiar business of (disputes about) borders. Boundaries in country areas were often imprecise and a source of contention, and Scott as Sheriff of Selkirkshire presided over several such disputes. In two cases of 1808 and 1814 he fixed the line of march after personally visiting the locations: see John Chisholm, *Sir Walter Scott as a Judge* (Edinburgh, 1918), nos 22 (126–27) and 73 (166).
207.12 Jock o' Dawstone Cleugh Dawston Burn runs into Liddel Water just below Saughtree, near the head of Liddesdale. On Matthew Stobie's 'Map of Roxburghshire and Tiviotdale', 1770, 'Dawstane' is also marked as a settlement, just to the N of Saughtree. See also Historical Note, 363.
207.13–15 Touthop-rigg . . . the Pomaragrains . . . Slackenspool . . . Bloodylaws . . . the Peel all apparently fictitious, though possibly echoing actual Border locations. Tudhope Hill overlooks the upper Hermitage part of Liddesdale, some 8 km NW of Hermitage castle. Bloodylaws, a farm on Oxnam Water, *c.* 8 km SE of Jedburgh, and overlooked by Bloodylaws Hill, is mentioned by Scott in relation to his ancestry on his mother's side in three letters of 1823–24 (see *Letters* 8.7, 221, 234). The Peel is 5 km NE of Saughtree, in upper Liddesdale, near the road running to Kielder, off the track from the former farm of Myredykes.
207.17 Charlies Chuckie humorously diminishing a mickle (large, big) stone to a riverside pebble (as used in a game similar to marbles).
207.18–19 where the wind and water shears on the ridge of a hill, on the highest ground.
207.20–21 auld drove road . . . Keeldar-ward such an old drove road,

used for driving cattle over the Border to southern markets, ran south from Hawick, through Note o' the Gate, Saughtree Fell, and then parallel with the North Tyne to Falstone. See K. J. Bonser, *The Drovers* (London, 1970), 152, map [150]. Note o' the Gate, by which way Scott entered on his Liddesdale raids, is 8 km NE of Saughtree. The drove road would later pass through Kielder, SE of Liddesdale just over the Border, on its way to Falstone in Northumberland.

207.34 bragged wi' him beaten or overcome by him.

208.4 Lockerbye fair Lockerbie in Annandale, Dumfriesshire, where regular markets for livestock were held: see *The Dumfries and Galloway Directory for the year 1835* (Dumfries, 1834).

208.10 another Lord Soulis' mistake i.e. of taking advice too literally. According to legend, the tyrannical William, Lord Soulis, of Hermitage Castle in Liddesdale, was boiled alive by his vassals, as a result of a too specific response to the King's irritated reaction to their complaints. See Scott's Introduction to John Leyden's ballad, 'Lord Soulis', in *Minstrelsy*, 4.224.

208.14 take a pint and agree proverbial: as in 'Take a Pint and gree, the Law's costly' (Ramsay, 109).

209 motto George Crabbe, 'The Parish Register' (1807), Part 3 ('Burials'), lines 272–73, 278–81.

209.19 my vocation see *1 Henry IV*, 1.2.101.

209.19 as Hamlet says to Ophelia, *Hamlet*, 3.1.122: 'I am myself indifferent honest'.

209.22 oportet vivere *Latin* one must live. An echo of Horace, *Epistles*, 1.10.12: 'Vivere naturae si convenienter oportet' ('If one must live in accordance with nature').

209.37 wawling and crying see *King Lear*, 4.6.180–81: 'the first time that we smell the air/ We wawl and cry'.

210.1–2 devil . . . and his dam 'the devil and his dam' is a proverbial expression (see *ODEP*, 179), the 'devil's dam' being applied opprobriously to a woman. Pleydell's words also echo Falstaff in *The Merry Wives of Windsor*, 4.5.97: 'The devil take one party and his dam the other!'

210.3 bronzes his bosom see Horace's 'aes triplex circa pectus erat' ('threefold bronze was around his heart') in *Odes*, 1.3.9–10.

210.6–7 bachelor's dinner . . . at three precisely previous to the social revolution caused by the New Town development, according to Henry Cockburn, the 'prevailing dinner hour was about three o'clock', this afterwards slipping by degrees to six or later: see *Memorials of His Time* (Edinburgh, 1856), 33–34.

210.9 borrow an hour compare *Macbeth*, 3.1.26–27: 'I must become a borrower of the night/ For a dark hour or twain'.

210.11 within the sixty days the law of deathbed in Scotland allowed heirs to land to have set aside any deed prejudicing them made by the deceased in the sixty days before death, if the deceased was already ill and had not subsequently attended church or the market.

210.24 long robe legal profession.

210.35 High Jinks see note to 204.13.

210.41 a feather will turn the scale 'turn the scale', said of an excess of weight on one side or other, is a standard phrase, as found in *The Merchant of Venice*, 4.1.325–26: 'if the scale do turn/ But in the estimation of a hair'. 'Feather' is also found as a variation of the more familiar 'straw' in the proverbial expression 'It is the last feather / straw that breaks the horse's back' (see *ODEP*, 443). Scott repeats his own formulation in *The Bride of Lammermoor*: 'Betwixt two scales equally loaded, a feather's weight will turn the scale' (EEWN 7a, 155.12–13).

211.15 choice spirit a Shakespearean phrase: see *1 Henry VI*, 5.3.3, and *Julius Caesar*, 3.1.164.

211.20–21 presbyterian kirk ... episcopal meeting-house Presbyterianism (first introduced in the 16th century) became the established religion in Scotland in 1690 under William III, and its status as such was confirmed by the Act of Union in 1707. Episcopal places of worship survived nevertheless in some Scottish towns. A new Episcopal chapel in Edinburgh, in the Cowgate, was begun in 1771 and opened for public worship in 1774. 'The New English Chapel is a neat, elegant building, but hardly large enough for the Members of the Church of England, who are constant inhabitants of this City': Edward Topham, *Letters from Edinburgh; written in the Years 1774 and 1775* (London, 1776), 193 (*CLA*, 9). See also note to 213.10–11.

211.21 Tros Tyriusve *Latin* Trojan or Tyrian. See Virgil, *Aeneid*, 1.574: 'Tros Tyriusque mihi nullo discrimine agetur' ('No difference will I make between Tyrian or Trojan'). The passage occurs when Dido, Queen of Carthage, is trying to persuade Aeneas and his band of Trojan exiles to stay in Carthage with her and her Tyrian people.

211.29 Blair Hugh Blair (1718–1800), Scottish divine and author, was licensed as a preacher in 1741, and appointed minister at the High Kirk (St Giles Cathedral), Edinburgh, in 1758; he became Regius Professor of Rhetoric at the University in 1762, and enjoyed a high literary reputation in England as well as Scotland, his *Sermons* (5 vols, 1777–1801) being regarded as a model of their kind.

211.30 Robertson William Robertson (1721–93), the celebrated historian, and Principal of Edinburgh University from 1762. Ordained a minister of the Church of Scotland at the age of 22, he took a prominent part in the General Assembly, becoming leader of the Moderate party there. From 1761 he was joint minister of Greyfriars Church, Edinburgh (see also notes to 212.6 and 212.11).

211.30 Henry Robert Henry (1718–90), author of a *History of Great Britain ... Written on a New Plan* (1771–93); he was also a Presbyterian minister, officiating at New Greyfriars, Edinburgh (1768) and at Old Greyfriars (1776–90).

211.39 Luckie Finlayson's in the Cowgate not identified. But compare Scott's letter to J. B. S. Morritt, in 1812, concerning a silver chamber-pot owned by Lady Holland and the debate as to who should clean it: 'Truly Lucky Finlaysons apostrophe was but a faint and fleeting ejaculation compared to this knotty and doughty altercation' (*Letters*, 3.113). *Luckie* was a name commonly given to hostesses of taverns, one of the more famous establishments being that of Lucky Middlemas in the Cowgate, a street (then busy and prosperous) running south of and parallel to the High Street.

211.39 Miles Macfin the cadie not identified, and perhaps fictitious. For *cadie*, see note to 201.6.

212.6 Greyfriars church south of the Cowgate, off Candlemaker Row. The original church was erected 1612–20 on a site formerly belonging to the monastery of Grey Friars. It was an important Presbyterian kirk, where the National Covenant of 1638 was signed, and with a cemetery in which are buried many persons of historical importance. New Greyfriars was added to the west end in 1721. Scott's father was an elder of the parish and is buried in the churchyard.

212.7 our historian of Scotland ... the Continent ... America alluding to three important historical works by William Robertson, namely: *The History of Scotland* (1759); *The History of the Reign of the Emperor Charles V* (1769); and *The History of America* (1777). See also note to 211.30.

212.11 colleague of Dr R—— John Erskine (1721–1803), minister at

New Greyfriars, Edinburgh, 1758–67; and from 1767 of Old Greyfriars, the latter jointly with William Robertson, the historian (see note to 211.30). See Sir Henry Moncrieff Wellwood, *Account of the Life and Writings of John Erskine, D.D.* (Edinburgh, 1818), 265: 'Two such men officiating together in the same congregation for six and twenty years, can scarcely be mentioned in the history of any other Church.' Scott later identified more fully 'the celebrated Dr Erskine, a distinguished clergyman, and a most excellent man' (Magnum, 4.98n).

212.17 that of Geneva a simple black gown worn by the strict Protestant community founded in Geneva by John Calvin (1509–1564), and introduced into Scotland by John Knox.

212.17 tumbled band *bands* (strips of white linen hanging from the collar in front) were part of clerical dress, and would normally have been worn by a Presbyterian clergyman along with the Geneva gown (see note above); *tumbled* is used here in the sense of 'tossed down, rumpled'.

212.21 Scottish lawyer John Erskine (1695–1768), admitted to the Faculty of Advocates 1718; Professor of Scots Law in the University of Edinburgh from 1737 to 1765, and author of *Principles of the Law of Scotland* (1754) and *Institute of the Law of Scotland* (1773), the latter published posthumously. Later identified by name, like his son, in the Magnum (4.98n).

212.25 Calvinism of the Kirk of Scotland the Church of Scotland is Calvinist because of its adherence to the model of church government, the theology and the religious practice associated with the Frenchman John Calvin (1509–64), the foremost theologian of the Reformation who established a theocracy in the city-state of Geneva from 1541. The Church of Scotland is Presbyterian in government (see note to 211.20–21), that is it is ruled by a hierarchy of church courts, kirk session, presbytery, synod, and the supreme body, the General Assembly. It follows Calvin in saying that the Bible contains all that is necessary to know God, in its extreme emphasis on the omnipotence of God and predestination (a position that was systematically eroded in the 18th century, particularly among the Moderate party in the Church), and in its belief in an unadorned, non-liturgical form of worship.

213.3 different parties in the kirk William Robertson was the leader of the Moderate party in the Church of Scotland, which was less firm on the doctrine of predestination (see note to 212.25) and more inclined in temporal matters to co-operate with the state, while Erskine on some issues leaned more to the Evangelical side. In the debate in the General Assembly on Catholic emancipation, for example, Erskine spoke against the measure with Robertson arguing eloquently on the other side: see Sir Henry Moncrieff Wellwood, *Account of the Life and Writings of John Erskine, D.D.* (Edinburgh, 1818), 292–93.

213.10 entre nous *French* between ourselves, confidentially.

213.10–11 a member of the suffering and episcopal church of Scotland Episcopal church government was abolished in Scotland and Presbyterianism established in its place in the Act of 1690, and confirmed by the Act of Union of 1707. All ministers were required to take the oaths of allegiance to the crown and abjuration of James VII and II and his descendants. Those Episcopalian ministers who refused to take the oaths (known as non-jurors) were ejected from their parishes and forbidden to conduct religious services in public. In the early 18th century many Episcopalians in Scotland were Jacobites (i.e. supporters of James VII and II and his descendants), and a new wave of oppressive legislation followed the failure of the 1745 rising. By an Act of Parliament of 1746, every Episcopal pastor in Scotland who failed to register his letters of orders, to take all the oaths required by law, and to pray for the House of Hanover, should for the first offence suffer six month's imprisonment; and for the second or any subsequent offence transportation, with life imprisonment the penalty if he should return from transportation. See also note to 211.20–21.

213.11 the shadow of a shade similar expressions occur occasionally in 17th and 18th-century poetry, but this appears to be the first appearance of what became a common phrase in 19th-century literature.

213.29 Jamieson, the Caledonian Vandyke George Jameson (*c.*1588–1644), painter, was apprenticed in Edinburgh, worked in Aberdeen, then returned to Edinburgh in the 1630s. He is the first Scottish portraitist of significance. Anthony Van Dyck (1599–1641), the Flemish painter, with whom he is likened here, lived in England from 1632 and produced numerous portraits of royalty and aristocrats. The accolade of Jameson being 'the Vandyck of Scotland' was originally granted by Horace Walpole, in his *Anecdotes of Painting in England* (1762).

213.34 view from the windows the view northward from Edinburgh in the direction of the Firth of Forth, then largely unaffected by the New Town development, was considered one of the most picturesque in Scotland. A similar scene is described by Scott in *Marmion* (1808), Canto 4, stanza 30 (*Poetical Works*, 7.219–20).

213.37 Law of North Berwick a prominent hill known as North Berwick Law, 1 km S of the town of North Berwick, near the entrance of the Firth of Forth.

214.1–2 absolute fiar *Scots law* unconditional owner of landed property who could freely dispose of it.

214.11 peine forte et dure *French* strong and hard punishment: a term in English (but not Scottish) law referring to the subjection of those charged with a felony to torture by increasing weights (not abolished until 1772). Compare Scott in a letter to Daniel Terry of 10 November 1814: 'The *peine forte et dure* is, you know, nothing in comparison to being obliged to grind verses' (*Letters*, 3.514).

214.20 Greyfriars church-yard see note to 212.6.

214.31–32 In Scotland . . . interment the custom of inviting all relations, contrasting with English practice, was noted by Edward Topham: 'instead of applying to an undertaker for a groupe of grim figures, and dismal faces, they send a card, as the French do, to all the persons of their acquaintance, desiring their attendance at the Funeral' (*Letters from Edinburgh; written in the Years 1774 and 1775* (London, 1776), 281: *CLA*, 9).

215.5 merely the exterior trappings compare *Hamlet*, 1.2.86: 'These but the trappings and the suits of woe'.

215.16 well to pass well off, prosperous.

215.32 ill waiting for dead folk's shoon proverbial (see Ramsay, 81; Ray, 95; *ODEP*, 171).

215.34 Tippoo Saib Tipu Sahib (*c.* 1750–99), Sultan of Mysore from the death of his father Haidar Ali in 1782 (see note to 160.35). He died of his wounds when his capital, Seringapatam (Shrirangapattana), was captured by the British.

215.36 East India Stock shares of the East India Company, the trading company which effectively ruled large parts of India in the later 18th century.

215.39 India bonds loans accepted by the East India Company at fixed interest, and thus unlike the East India Stock not subject to variation in price or interest.

216.26 Jamie Duff a 'singular mad man', according to Robert Chambers, who 'lived with his mother, in the upper flat of a house at the foot of the College Wynd, near the Cowgate' and died in 1788. 'His master-passion was a love of funerals. Scarcely one ceremony of this sort happened in Edinburgh during forty years, that was not graced with his presence. He walked, hat in hand, in advance of the *saulies*, with weepers and cravat; and it is said that he preserved a gravity in his countenance, perfectly appropriate to the occasion': *Traditions of Edinburgh*, 2 vols (Edinburgh, 1825), 2.64–70, *CLA*, 332. A portrait of 'Jamie Duff, an Idiot' appears in John Kay, *A Series of Original Portraits and Caricature Etchings*, Vol. 2, 1877, facing p. 17.

216.27 weepers and cravat *weepers* were bands of white linen or muslin worn on the sleeve as a sign of mourning; while a plain muslin or lawn cravat replaced shirt frills at such times. See Lou Taylor, *Mourning Dress: a Costume and Social History* (London, 1983), 108.

216.33 man of business see note to 10.10.

216.41 burial place of the Singleside family the description that follows is characteristic of the family tombs crowded into Greyfriars churchyard, many of the more ornate ones belonging to the 17th century. For an account see James Brown, *The Epitaphs and Monumental Inscriptions in Greyfriars Churchyard Edinburgh* (Edinburgh, 1867); this records a variety of 'sepulchral' verses found there, mostly Latin, some in English, but none matching Scott's lines at 217.11–14.

217.11 Nathaniel's heart, Bezaleel's hand alluding to two biblical figures. Nathaniel, a disciple of Jesus Christ, is described as 'an Israelite indeed, in whom is no guile' (John 1.47). Bezaleel, of the tribe of Judah, was a divinely-inspired craftsman 'filled . . . with the spirit of God, in wisdom, in understanding, and in knowledge, and in all manner of workmanship' (Exodus 35.31). The short verse beginning with this line has not been identified, and is possibly Scott's own composition (see note above).

217 motto Alexander Pope, *Epistle to Bathurst* (1733), line 98.

217.25 fable told by Lucian see the story in the Greek satirical writer Lucian's *Piscator*, Ch. 36, in which apes taught to dance by a king of Egypt are in this way thrown into disarray.

217.39–40 non-juring chapel place of worship ministered to by non-juring Episcopalian clergy, i.e. those who refused to take the oaths of allegiance to the Hanoverian monarchy and of abjuration of the Pretender; commonly attended by those with Jacobite sympathies: see also note to 213.10–11.

217.43–218.1 Over the Water to Charlie popular Jacobite song, expressing loyalty to the exiled Charles Edward Stuart (1720–88), grandson of James VII and II, and leader of the Jacobite rising in 1745–46. James Hogg describes it as 'A well known popular song and tune, describing the feelings of the Jacobite ladies of those days': see his *Jacobite Relics of Scotland*, 2 vols (Edinburgh, 1819–21), 2.76–77, 290. A version is also given in Robert Chambers, *Scottish Songs*, 2 vols (Edinburgh, 1829), 2.448–49.

218.23 homme d'affaires *French* man of business; also used of an agent, lawyer etc.

218.27 shares in the Ayr bank alluding to the spectacular crash of the banking-house of Douglas, Heron & Co., trading under the name of the Ayr Bank. The head office in Ayr (on the west coast of Scotland) opened in 1769, followed by branches in Edinburgh and Dumfries, but closure was forced in 1772 after the bank was unable to pay cash for notes, leading to liquidation in 1773. Losses exceeded £660,000, and liability on each share is said to have amounted to £2600.

218.34 the colonial war the war of American Independence (1775–83), during which the price of imported Virginian tobacco rose sharply.

218.38 Mr Quid a *quid* is a piece of tobacco held in the mouth and chewed.

219.29 mortis causa settlement until 1863 in Scots law a will or testament was ineffectual to dispose of heritage (landed property). This could only be done by a deed containing a conveyance of the heritage, which, if it was *mortis* *causa* (*Latin* in contemplation of death), could not take place till after the dispensee's death.

219.31 rump and dozen a rump of beef and a dozen bottles of wine: apparently a common wager in the 18th and early 19th centuries.

220.16 exclamation from Sir Toby Belch see *Twelfth Night*, 2.5.95.

220.24 a study for Hogarth William Hogarth (1697–1764), English painter and engraver, famous for his moralising genre scenes. Scott's prompting here was taken up by the Scottish genre painter David Wilkie (1785–1841), whose 'The Reading of a Will' (1819) was exhibited with an extract from the novel. Scott's own description is anticipated in Ch. 4 of Smollett's *Roderick Random* (1748): 'the will was produced in the midst of the expectants, whose looks and gestures formed a group that would have been very entertaining to an unconcerned spectator'.

220.29 Clerk to the Signet now more commonly Writer to the Signet: member of a prestigious body of lawyers in Scotland; roughly equivalent to an English solicitor or attorney.

221.22 settlement in mortmain . . . mortification 'settlement in mortmain' is an English legal term for property vested in a public body or corporation that cannot alienate it, so that it is said to be in *mortmain* (*French literally* dead hand). The term *mortification* in Scotland originally applied to lands bequeathed to the Church for religious purposes, but was extended to include public charitable benefactions.

221.25 Master of Mortifications the Master of Mortifications was for centuries one of the office-bearers of the Aberdeen Town Council, the *mortifications* (see note above) under its charge going back as far as 1449. In 1709 it was resolved that all the mortifications under the charge of the Council should be set out on 'broads' (wooden tablets), and these are still displayed in the vestibule of the Town House. See also David Marshall, *Sir Walter Scott and Scots Law* (Edinburgh and London, 1932), 73.

222.11 Gilsland village and spa on the border of Cumberland and Northumberland, 25 km NE of Carlisle. Gilsland had been a spa resort for about half a century when Scott first met his future wife there in 1797 (see also Historical Note, 362).

222.21 buck of the second-head . . . first-head *buck* (male deer) is slang for a dandy or fop. *First-head* and *second-head* are similarly derived from stag-hunting, the first describing a deer when the antlers are just developed (this term also being used figuratively of a man newly enobled or elevated in rank); the second referring to a stag not of the younger sort but between five and six years old.

222.27 toasting a round of running horses the old custom of proposing 'Rounds of toasts' at Edinburgh dinners, with diners being invited to propose matching pairs, is described by Henry Cockburn in the following terms: 'each gentleman named an absent lady, and each lady an absent gentleman, separately; or one person was required to give an absent lady, and another person was required to match a gentleman with that lady, and the pair named were toasted, generally with allusions and jokes about the fitness of the union' (*Memorials of His Time* (Edinburgh, 1856), 38). Cockburn also observes that Scott, when presiding at dinner, 'always insisted on rounds of ladies and gentlemen, and of authors and printers, poets and kings, in regular pairs' (40). Presumably the two jockeys mentioned in this passage are extending this principle to race-horses. Another possible explanation is that 'rounds' refers to the circuits or heats in a horse-race, and that the two jockeys named are drinking the health of horses they hope will win.

222.28 leave to wear the jacket permission to wear an owner's colours in a horse-race.

222.31 payment of the note i.e. of the promissory note given to Miss Bertram in return for a loan of £100.

222.34–35 put the settlement . . . on record to-morrow such a settlement was recorded in a register of transactions open to scrutiny. It was possible to get an 'extract' or official copy.

223.7–8 blood's thicker than water proverbial (Ramsay, 73; *ODEP*, 69).

223.36 dreadnought great-coat overcoat made of stout woollen cloth with thick long pile.

223.39 weel to pass well off, prosperous.

224.1 I'm jealous I suspect.

224.6 Jeddart variant form of Jedburgh, royal burgh and formerly county town of Roxburghshire, in the Scottish Borders.

224.7 Limestane-rig probably an alternative name for Limekiln Edge, an escarpment 12 km S of Hawick and 26 km SW of Jedburgh, on one of the routes into Liddesdale from the Scottish direction.

224.8 wheeled carriage . . . Liddesdale Liddesdale was virtually inaccessible to carriages until the building of roads began near the end of the 18th century. A Magnum note later stated that 'About thirty years ago, the author himself was the first person who ever drove a little open carriage into these wilds' (4.120n). See also J. G. Lockhart's account of Scott's Liddesdale 'raids' in the 1790s (*Life*, 1.195).

224.15–16 meat and drink . . . to see a clown see *As You Like It*, 5.1.10.

224.25 down the hail water down the whole riverside, throughout the valley or district.

224.37 the feifteen i.e. the Court of Session (the supreme court in Scotland for civil matters), which at this time had 15 judges (see also note to 182.42).

225 motto John Fletcher (and probably Philip Massinger), *The Little French Lawyer* (printed 1647), 2.1.75–77.

225.9 the battle is not to the strong see Ecclesiastes 9.11.

225.27 pine-apple at wholesale price not identified as an expression, but evidently indicating the acquisition of a luxury at a bargain price.

225.33 the great teind case in presence *teinds* ('tithes'), as the source of church ministers' stipends, were a great cause of litigation in the 18th century; 'in presence' means before the 15 judges of the Court of Session (see note to 182.42), who sat as Commissioners for Teinds every second Wednesday during session. No particular 'great teind case' has been identified.

226.3 information written argument on law presented to the court. In the 18th century written rather than oral pleading played the major role in litigation in the Court of Session.

226.6–7 Streights of Magellan . . . Cape Horn i.e. the 'short cut' passage between the island of Tierra del Fuego and the southern part of the mainland of South America, compared with the sea route round the southern point of Tierra del Fuego.

226.11 David Hume (1711–76), the celebrated Enlightenment philosopher and historian, whose works include *A Treatise of Human Nature* (1739–40) and *The History of England* (1754–62). After spells in Paris and London, he returned to settle in his native Edinburgh in 1768. Although the major part of *Guy Mannering* is imagined as taking place in 1781 or 1782, making Hume's inclusion here an anachronism, the list in which his name is included is intended to show the brilliance of Edinburgh in the Enlightenment.

226.11 John Home (1722–1808), clergyman and dramatist, best known for his tragedy *Douglas* (1756), which won great popularity in Edinburgh and London. Home resigned his ministry in 1757, and became Private Secretary to the Earl of Bute and tutor to the Prince of Wales, returning to settle in Edinburgh in 1779. See also note to 228.29 below.

226.11 Dr Ferguson Adam Ferguson (1723–1816), Professor of Moral Philosophy at Edinburgh, and author of *An Essay on the History of Civil Society* (1767)—a pioneering contribution to political thought—and other philosophical and historical works. See also note to 228.15 below.

226.11 Dr Black Joseph Black (1728–99), physician and chemist, Professor of Medicine and Chemistry at Edinburgh from 1766 to 1797, he discovered latent heat and carbon dioxide. He was also first physician to George III for Scotland, and a member of the Royal Society, Edinburgh.

226.12 Lord Kaimes Henry Home, Lord Kames (1696–1782), lawyer and philosopher; a leading figure in the Scottish Enlightenment, whose works include *Historical Law-Tracts* (1758), *Elements of Criticism* (1762), and *Sketches of the History of Man* (1774). Kames also took a great interest in agricultural improvement.

226.12 Mr Hutton James Hutton (1726–97), geologist, who moved back to his native Edinburgh in 1768; his *A Theory of the Earth*, expounded before the Royal Society of Edinburgh and first published in 1785, helped form the basis of modern geology in arguing that rocks had been laid down successively.

226.12 John Clerk of Eldin (1728–1812), author of *An Essay on Naval Tactics* (privately printed, 1782). The younger son of Sir John Clerk of Penicuick, the eminent Judge and antiquary, and himself a successful merchant in Edinburgh, Clerk bought Eldin, near Lasswade to the SE of Edinburgh, in about 1773. See also notes to 226.40–41 and 227.24.

226.13 Adam Smith (1723–90), the celebrated philosopher and economist, author of *Theory of Moral Sentiments* (1759) and *An Inquiry into the Nature and Causes of the Wealth of Nations* (1776), and Professor of Moral Philosophy at Glasgow 1752–64. His appointment as Commissioner of Customs brought him back to Edinburgh in 1778, where he died and was buried in the Canongate churchyard.

226.13 Dr Robertson William Robertson (1721–93), the celebrated historian, and Principal of Edinburgh University from 1762 till 1792. See also note to 211.30.

226.29 Lyanbrathwaite see note to 68.32.

226.40–41 this remarkable man John Clerk of Eldin (see note to 226.12). Scott was a close friend of Clerk's second son, William, and the account which follows is clearly based on his visits in the late 1780s and 1790s to the Clerk residences at Princes Street (Edinburgh) and Eldin, near Lasswade.

227.10 genii loci *Latin* presiding spirits of the place.

227.24 quæsitam meritis *Latin* sought after by merit.

227.24 his great discovery the naval tactic of dividing the line, as propounded in *An Essay on Naval Tactics* (1782; 1790). Scott in his *Life of Napoleon Buonaparte* (1827) later recalled as a boy seeing a demonstration: 'he can remember having been guilty of abstracting from the table some of the little cork models by which Mr Clerk exemplified his manœuvres; unchecked but by his good-humoured raillery, when he missed a supposed line-of-battle ship, and complained that the demonstration was crippled by its absence' (*Prose Works*, 12.101n).

227.25 the late naval success Sir George Rodney's victory over the French off Dominica on 12 April 1782. Clerk and his friends believed that Rodney's tactics derived from knowledge of his *Essay on Naval Tactics* (see note above; and Historical Note, 357). This was disputed at the time by naval personnel. Admiral Nelson's plan at Trafalgar is said to have been influenced by Clerk's theory, a circumstance tacitly alluded to in Mannering's anticipation that 'Another generation may carry it farther'.

227.30 Columbus and the egg alluding to a story about Christopher

Columbus's response to the claim that others would have discovered America if he had not done so. Columbus challenged the guests at a banquet to make an egg stand on end. All having failed, he flattened one end of the egg by tapping it against the table, so enabling it to stand up.

227.33–34 this close imitator of the ancients James Burnett, Lord Monboddo (1714–99), Scottish Judge and pioneer anthropologist, author of *Of the Origin and Progress of Language* (1773–92). In a Magnum note, relating to a later remark by Pleydell (see 298.9–10), Scott gave another account of the dinners given by Monboddo while residing in Edinburgh: 'Enthusiastically partial to classical habits, his entertainments were always given in the evening, when there was a circulation of excellent Bourdeaux, in flasks garlanded with roses, which were also strewed on the table after the manner of Horace. The best society, whether in respect of rank or literary distinction, was always to be found in St John's Street, Canongate' (Magnum, 4.267).

227.42 defence of the battered standard of Aristotle a reference to *Antient Metaphysics; or, the Science of Universals* (1779–99), Monboddo's second great work, which revealed his considerable powers as a Greek scholar and an accurate knowledge of ancient philosophy, including the ideas of Aristotle (384–322 BC).

228.5 the pineal gland is situated behind the third ventricle of the brain, and was considered by some natural philosophers as being the site of the soul.

228.6 favourite topics those were listed again by Scott in notes provided to J. W. Croker for his edition (1831) of James Boswell: 'He was a devout believer in the virtues of the heroic ages, and the deterioration of civilized mankind; a great contemner of luxuries, insomuch that he never used a wheel-carriage' (see *Life of Johnson*, ed. G. B. Hill, rev. L. F. Powell, 6 vols (Oxford, 1934–50), 2.74n).

228.11–12 no ambition to be quoted in a new edition i.e. of *Of the Origin and Progress of Language*, which attracted a good deal of attention (by no means all favourable), and went into a second edition in 1774. Monboddo's views, especially those on evolution and man's affinity with the ourang-outang, were considered highly eccentric by Samuel Johnson and others, and continued to be treated as a subject of ridicule in Scott's own period by writers such as Thomas Love Peacock.

228.15 Roman soul that of Adam Ferguson (see note to 226.11), the subject of this Fragment. Ferguson's many works, philosophical and historical, included a *History of the Progress and Termination of the Roman Republic* (1783). It was at Ferguson's residence of Sciennes Hill House (then outside Edinburgh) that Scott in 1787, according to his recollection, saw Robert Burns (see *Life*, 1.136–37).

228.21 powers of satire worthy of Swift or Arbuthnot as in *The History of the Proceedings in the Case of Margaret, commonly called Peg, only lawful sister of John Bull* (1761; *CLA*, 21), a satirical pamphlet on the refusal of the British parliament to sanction a Scottish militia, written in the Augustan satirical style of Jonathan Swift (1667–1745) and John Arbuthnot (1667–1735).

228.22 severe diet according to Scott's later essay on John Home, written for the *Quarterly Review* (1827), Ferguson 'recovered from a decided shock of paralysis in the sixtieth year of his life; from which period he became a strict Pythagorean in his diet, eating nothing but vegetables, and drinking only water or milk' (*Prose Works*, 19.332).

228.22 Indian Bramins the highest caste amongst the Hindus, and the guardians of priestly knowledge, whose diet is strictly vegetarian.

228.29 information respecting the unfortunate war of 1745 John Home, the subject of this Fragment, fought on the government side during the Jacobite uprising of 1745–46, and was taken prisoner at Falkirk, later making a daring escape from his captors. He subsequently published a *History of the Rebellion of 1745* (1802). Scott first met Home at Bath when a child, and was a frequent guest as a young man after Home had settled again close to Edinburgh (see *Life*, 1.22, 139). A full account of one of his dinner parties is given from an eye-witness account in Scott's 1827 review of Home's *Life and Works* (see *Prose Works*, 19.320–21). See also note to 226.11.

228.36 his namesake the philosopher the celebrated David Hume (see note to 226.11), a close friend.

228.39–40 throwing dice . . . orthography David Hume and John Home only dispute about how to spell their names (both are pronounced Hume). John Home's objection to the contest is apparently based on the claim that he has more to lose, since Home is the correct and traditional spelling of the name.

229.6 chef d'œuvre *French* masterpiece. Though he continued to write plays, along similar lines to his highly successful tragedy *Douglas* (1756), Home never managed to reproduce the success of this early work.

229.33 his altitudes see note to 204.8.

229.36 honest Bruin . . . monkey compare Scott's account of the relationship between Boswell and Johnson, in a letter to J. W. Croker of 1829: 'Like the jackanapes mounted on the bear's back, he contrived now and then to play the more powerful animal a trick by getting him into situations . . . merely to see how he would look' (*Letters*, 11.118). Bruin is a long-standing appellation for the Common or Brown Bear.

230.12–13 one of the white days of his life i.e. one of the most favourable and propitious.

230.23 Pythagoreans . . . Bramins the followers of Pythagoras, the Greek philosopher (6th century BC), were bound by strict vows and lived in an ascetic way; the Brahmins, not normally associated with silence, are the highest and priestly caste among the Hindus.

230.25 the words of the wise are precious proverbial (see Ray, 286; *ODEP*, 914).

230.29–30 he giveth strength, who layeth on the load not identified as a proverbial or biblical expression, but compare Psalm 55.22; Matthew 11.28.

230.43 Bethlehem massacre murder of the Innocents by Herod, as described in Matthew 2.16.

231.8 Luckie Wood's in the Cowgate Lucky Wood had an ale-house in the Canongate early in the 18th century, but an establishment of this name in the Cowgate has not been identified: see also note on Luckie Finlayson (211.39).

231.8 my clerk Driver not identified by name.

231.9 High-Jinks see note to 204.13.

231.13 Ah . . . lovest me *1 Henry IV*, 2.4.273.

231.14 the land of Egypt gypsy land: based on the misapprehension that the gypsies derived from Egypt.

231.16 Bohemian gypsy: stemming from the early association of the gypsies with Bohemia and eastern Europe.

231.17 Monitoire in old French law a writ by an ecclesiastical judge requiring all persons with evidence concerning a crime to come forward, under penalty of excommunication.

231.17 Plainte de Tournelle the *Tournelle* was a criminal court established as a branch of the Parlement de Paris; it sat in the small tower of St Louis, hence its name. A *plainte* is a declaration or complaint initiating prosecution.

231.34 in presentia *Latin* present in person, in presence: an action heard before the whole Court of Session in the Inner House was one 'in praesentia'.

231.41–42 bare-headed captains . . . East-Cheap see *2 Henry IV*, 2.4.345–46. Eastcheap, where Shakespeare's Falstaff inhabits the Boar's Head Tavern, was originally a market in the East End of London.

232.9–10 draw an appeal case *Scots law* to prepare a statement of facts and argument as part of the process of appeal from the Court of Session to the House of Lords in London.

232.11 Clerihugh's for this tavern, see note to 202.32.

232.12 tappit hen a decanter or mug, usually made of pewter, with a lid knob resembling the crest of a hen. Scott's Magnum note at this point states that it 'contained three quarts of claret' (4.137).

232.23 not three words required to be altered in a note headed 'Convivial Habits of the Scottish Bar', Scott later told an anecdote about a similar incident involving President Dundas of Arniston (see Magnum, 4.137–38).

232.27 the outer-house of the Court of Session, in Parliament Hall, where judges sat in rotation to deal with preliminary matters and certain other types of case. Pleydell is referring to the fact that he appears regularly in the Parliament Hall ready for the start of the business of the Court.

232.28 nine-hours bell apparently referring to the clock (removed in 1912) of St Giles Cathedral, close to the Edinburgh Law Courts in Parliament House, striking the hour at which the Court of Session meets.

233.16 Gilsland see note to 222.11.

233.24 spaw-well below the craig Gilsland Spa, about half a mile north of the village of Gilsland, is in a deep gorge of the river Irthing.

233.25 ane Mac-Crossky compare note to 28.17.

233.35–36 as sure as that water's rinning to the sea recalls the legal phrase, used to express perpetuity, 'as long as grass groweth upward or water runneth downward'. (Normand)

233.42 blearing your e'e i.e. deceiving or hoodwinking you.

234.30 Are you avised of that? *The Merry Wives of Windsor*, 1.4.91.

234.39 Albumazar Abu Ma'shar, Arabian astrologer of the 9th century. His *De magnis coniunctionibus* (translated from the Arabic by John of Seville) claimed to expose the effects of planetary combinations on the rise and fall of earthly dynasties, and exerted a great influence in the Middle Ages and later.

234.39 Messahala see note to 16.3.

235.4 Sheriff of Roxburghshire . . . justice of peace in Cumberland justices of the peace in England had powers equivalent to those of sheriffs in Scotland to conduct examinations of witnesses in investigations of crime.

237 motto John Fletcher, *Women Pleased* (*c.* 1620), 4.1.68–71.

237.27 Portanferry see note to 191.2

237.30 Allonby village on the coast of Cumbria, 35 km SW of Carlisle.

238.12–13 hawks should na pike out hawks' e'en proverbial (see *ODEP*, 359).

239.19 Wigton either Wigtown in Galloway (see note to 46.34), or, alternatively, Wigton in Cumbria 15 km SW of Carlisle (midway between Carlisle and Allonby).

239.36 Mr Palmer's ingenious invention John Palmer (1742–1818) helped establish in 1784–85 the mail coach service, which greatly increased the speed of distribution, and Post Office revenue.

239.39–40 his post-town i.e. Jedburgh (which Scott first wrote in the manuscript, before deleting it in favour of the present wording).

242.14 Ramsay-bay and the Point of Ayr Ramsey Bay is at the NE end of the Isle of Man, facing in the direction of the Solway Firth; the Point of Ayre is the northerly cape of Man, at the other end of Ramsey Bay from the town of Ramsey (see note to 27.2).

243.7 Shellicoat-stane the *shellicoat* is a marine demon, covered with barnacles and other shells, whose appearance is supposed to foretell death or disaster.

243 motto Horace Walpole, *The Mysterious Mother: A Tragedy* (1768), 2.1.

244.30 Bramin Moonshie a *moonshie* in India was an educated man often employed in business houses, government departments, or as a language tutor to Europeans; the *brahmins* are the highest caste amongst the Hindus.
245.11 Justice-Tree the power of capital punishment was once part of the juridical powers of a barony.
246.18–19 the fortitude of a North American Indian this reference to the physical fortitude of the American Indians is reminiscent of William Robertson's account of their methods of torture and tests of endurance in his *History of America* (1777).
246.43 Mr Cumming . . . Lion-office the Lyon Office was the herald's office, the Lord Lyon King of Arms (largely a sinecure by Scott's time) having the jurisdiction to grant arms in Scotland. James Cummyng was in office as Keeper of the Lyon Records at the time of the main events in the story: he was elected a member of the Royal Company of Scottish Archers, 22 June 1771; and a *Catalogue of Books, Manuscripts, Curiosities &c. belonging to . . . Mr James Cummyng* was published in Edinburgh, shortly after his death, in 1793.
247.5 tongue . . . clove to the roof of his mouth an Old Testament expression: as in Job 29.10, Psalm 137.6, Ezekiel 3.26, etc.
247.13–16 The dark . . . meet on probably by Scott (see also note below).
247.22–24 song . . . Scottish knight for one origin of this ballad, the 'extracts' from which are otherwise probably Scott's own composition, see note to 60.32–33.
248.14 links of Firth apparently referring to the sandy shoreline of the Solway Firth. One of the poems in Joseph Train's *Strains of the Mountain Muse* (Edinburgh, 1814; *CLA*, 165), is titled 'The Inks of Crie [*sic*]', and has the following footnote: 'The banks of Cree, from Newton Stewart to the sea, are called the Inks' (127n). In his *Scottish Gallovidian Encyclopedia* (London, 1824; *CLA*, 124), John Mactaggart considers *inks* and *links* to be equivalent words (280). For Scott's receipt of Train's volume of poems in July 1814, see Introduction, xiv, and EEWN 2, 361.
248.15 crooks of Dee the winding River Dee runs southwards into Kirkcudbright Bay on the north bank of Solway.
249 motto see *King Lear*, 3.6.35–39.
250.7 Nova Scotia Baronet this title was instituted in Scotland by Charles I with a view to colonising Nova Scotia in the New World. Baronetcies were conferred in return for a fee of £3000, and the newly-created baronet received a notional estate in Nova Scotia.
250.13 triads and quaternions the grouping together of things or words in three and fours (a familiar pattern in Hazelwood's ensuing speeches).
251.25 Hazelwood-house apparently a fictitious location; but, for possible links with the countryside near Gatehouse of Fleet, see Historical Note, 362.
251.28 Queen Mary Mary Queen of Scots (1542–87); during her reign much church property was appropriated by the laity, and was never recovered by the Church either before or after the Reformation of 1560.
251.38–39 novus homo *Latin* new man; upstart.
252.3 Mr Cumming of the Lion Office see note to 246.43.
253.6 high on the list of the Faculty i.e. as a member of the Faculty of Advocates of long standing.
253.15 John a Nokes a fictitious name used to denote one of the parties in a legal action (usually coupled with John-a-Stiles as the name of the other); here with the added connotation of 'any sort of person'.
253.40 King's Advocate alternative name for the Lord Advocate, the chief legal officer of the crown in Scotland, who is in charge of criminal prosecution.
254.15 ex cathedra *Latin literally* from the chair; from a position of authority.

254.17 the law had another hold see *The Merchant of Venice*, 4.1.342: 'The law hath yet another hold on you'.

255.4 first started apparently involving a hunting metaphor, with *start* meaning to force an animal (such as a hare) from its lair or resting-place.

255.18 clouted shoe of the peasant galls the kibe of the courtier compare *Hamlet*, 5.1.136–37: 'the toe of the peasant comes so near the heel of the courtier, he galls his kibe'.

255 motto John Fletcher (probably with Philip Massinger and others), *The Fair Maid of the Inn* (1625), 2.1.59–63.

255.31 compunctious visitings *Macbeth*, 1.5.42–43: 'That no compunctious visitings of nature/ Shake my fell purpose'.

261.21 Looties see note to 71.19.

262 motto not identified; the tag is absent in the manuscript. The Edinburgh tolbooth served as the city prison, previous to its demolition in 1817.

262.27 chapel of ease originally a meeting-place for parishioners living at a distance from the parish church; here, ironically, as an overflow prison.

263.1 an over-dose of the creature i.e. too much to drink. *Creature* in the sense of whisky or other liquors has been explained as a facetious adaptation of 1 Timothy 4.4 ('For every creature of God is good'). Compare Dryden, *Amphitryon*, 3.1.190: 'I find my master took too much of the creature last night, and is now angling for a quarrel'.

263.14 sans culottes *French literally* without breeches; a name given to republicans of the poorer classes during the French Revolution, here applied to local urchins.

263.27–28 lay like a load on the wearied eye see S. T. Coleridge, *The Ancient Mariner* (1798), line 251.

263.37 moping idiot, and the madman gay George Crabbe, *The Village* (1783), 1.239. In a letter dated 21 October [1812], Scott wrote to Crabbe describing how more than twenty years ago (as a boy at Kelso) he had memorised extracts from this section of the poem found in Dodsley's *Annual Register* (see *Letters*, 3.182).

264.13 on the account see note to 192.37.

264.28 by common out of the ordinary, unusual.

265.38 the worst inn's worst room Alexander Pope, *Epistle to Bathurst* (1733), line 299.

266.37–38 the rusty grate, unconscious of a fire Oliver Goldsmith, 'Description of an Author's Bedchamber' (1760), line 16.

267.26 Hebe in Greek mythology, daughter of Zeus and Hera and the handmaiden to the gods.

267.30–31 mend his commons improve his ordinary fare.

267.43–268.1 Newgate Kalendar a record of notorious crimes and criminals from 1700, *The Newgate Calendar* (named after Newgate prison in London) was first published in about 1773 in five volumes, with various other compilations in the same mould following in the next 50 years.

268 motto William Shenstone (1714–63), 'Jemmy Dawson', stanza 11. Shenstone's song, about a young woman's loyalty to a Manchester Jacobite put to death in 1746, was written close to the event and published in the poet's posthumous works. A version was also included in Percy, 1.306–09, where Scott is likely to have first seen it.

269.24 ance errand for the one purpose, on the single errand.

269.37 to the fore present, on the spot, within call.

270.10–11 like one of Homer's heroes there is frequent reference to eating and drinking in the Homeric epics, and talk and action are both suspended while this goes on.

270.39 Touthope-head compare Touthop-rigg at 207.13 (and see note to 207.13–15).
271.4–5 pitt ower get through, last out for.
271.13 ill sorted displeased, put out of sorts.
271.30 hunt-the-gowk errand fool's errand, April fool trick.
272.7 Bewcastle signifying Bewcastle Waste (see note to 121.1).
272.7 Limestane Edge see note to 224.7.
272.8 Hermitage and Liddle the two main rivers in Liddesdale.
272.10 Justice Forster Forster was a common name south of the Border, in Cumberland.
272.15 gathered the fern-seed the 'seed' (spores) of the fern was popularly supposed to make those who carried it invisible. Compare *1 Henry IV*, 2.1.84: 'we have the receipt of fern-seed, we walk invisible'.
272.15–16 Jock the Giant-killer the hero (more usually Jack) of the nursery tale, who had a coat which rendered him invisible, a cap of wisdom, shoes of swiftness, and a resistless sword.
272.19 moss-troopers in the troublesome times the *moss-troopers*, so called from their frequenting the moss country or wastes, were bands of lawless men on the Borders in the 17th century. Their activities were at a height during the Civil War period.
273.7 like the boul o' a pint stoup like the handle of a pint mug, i.e. most acceptably and opportunely. A proverbial expression (Ramsay, 74; *ODEP*, 136), used again by Scott in *The Bride of Lammermoor* (1819): see EEWN 7a, 94.37–38.
273.16 bee in her head proverbial expression, indicating crankiness or obsessiveness (see Ramsay, 81 and *ODEP*, 39).
273.19–20 the straight road to the well not identified as a proverbial expression.
274.2 sark-fu' o' sair banes proverbial (see *ODEP*, 724), meaning effectively a sore body.
274.3 Liddell-mote the Mote of Liddel, sometimes called Liddel Strength, a medieval fortress (of which only earthworks remain) near the confluence of Liddel Water and the Esk in northern Cumbria. Geographically, it might be said to mark the most southerly entrance into Liddesdale, especially for someone approaching from the north Solway coast.
274.4–5 a willfu' man maun hae his way proverbial: see *ODEP*, 890, where the first example given is from Scott's *Rob Roy* (1818), Ch. 28.
274.19 colliers in Sanquhar Sanquhar, in Upper Nithsdale, NE Dumfriesshire, was a mining centre in the 18th century.
274 motto *Macbeth*, 1.3.75–78.
275.19 Northern Metropolis name applied to Edinburgh after the Union with England in 1707.
275.25 girded up my loins echoing a common biblical phrase (see e.g. Job 38.3 and Jeremiah 1.17).
275.28 Mahratta cavalry for the *Mahratta*, see note to 66.28.
276.17–18 weighty matters of the law see Matthew 23.23.
276.19 ex cathedra see note to 254.15.
276.38–39 many a weary sigh . . . groan matching Alexander Pope's translation (1725–26) of Homer's *Odyssey*: 'With many a weary step, and many a groan,/ Up the high hill he heaves a huge round stone' (11.735–36). This description of the labour of Sisyphus is quoted in Samuel Johnson's 'Life of Pope' (1781), where Johnson offered a parody later quoted by Scott as a motto in *Quentin Durward* (1823) and *Castle Dangerous* (1831).
278.14 Avoid ye! withdraw! depart! See also note to 76.28.
278.15–16 Conjuro te . . . miserrima *Latin* I constrain you; most

accursed, iniquitous, base, wicked, and wretched woman.

278.21–22 Conjuro . . . impero tibi *Latin* I constrain, adjure, obtest and strongly command you.

279.9 Kitchen's atlas Thomas Kitchen (or Kitchin) was a well-known geographer and cartographer, whose maps date from the 1740s to the 1780s.

279.14 Fasting—from all but sin meaning fasting (abstaining from food and drink), but, because of the present company, not avoiding sin. Compare Cervantes' *Don Quixote*, Part 2 (1615), Ch. 73, in Motteux's free translation (1700–03), where the housekeeper says to Don Quixote: 'I am neither drunk nor mad, but fresh and fasting from every thing but sin'. These words are retained in Lockhart's revised version of Motteux: *The History of the Ingenious Gentleman, Don Quixote of La Mancha*, 5 vols (1822), 5.316.

279.36–37 scelestissima !—that is—gudewife most evil one!—that is—mistress [of the house]. The first of several instances where Sampson mistranslates his Latin into more conciliatory terms.

279.42 Canidia the witch of Horace's *Epodes*, 5.15–24, and *Satires*, 1.8, 2.1, and 2.8.

279.42 Ericthoe Thessalian enchantress mentioned by the Roman poet Lucan in his *Pharsalia*, 6.507.

279.43–280.1 by the bread and the salt an oath, from the old Eastern custom of eating bread and salt when pledges were made.

280.1 cutty spoon short-handled spoon, usually of horn.

280.3 eye of newt . . . chaudrons ingredients in the witches' cauldron in *Macbeth*, 4.1.14–33.

280.8 Saul . . . witch of Endor see 1 Samuel 28.20–25. 'Saul and the Witch of Endor' was also the subject of a celebrated painting by Salvator Rosa, the 17th-century Italian artist, which Scott greatly admired when viewing the original in the Louvre on his French tour of Summer 1815: see John Scott of Gala, *Journal of a Tour to Waterloo and Paris in Company with Walter Scott in 1815* (London, 1842), 159. Rosa's painting (more widely available in prints) was praised in some detail for its 'grandeur and sublimity' in Richard Payne Knight's influential *An Analytical Inquiry into the Principles of Taste* (London, 1805), 301–02, and it is possible that Scott was conscious of offering a more comic and grotesque version in his own figures. For Salvator Rosa, see note to 93.17–18.

280.9 salt which she sprinkled salt is traditionally considered to be a security against the devil.

280.26 in for a penny . . . pound proverbial (*ODEP*, 402).

280.31 ye're anither man *anither* (another) is used here in the sense of 'different in effect or character'; compare 1 Samuel 10.6 ('thou . . . shalt be turned into another man').

281.15 wand of peace also used of a silver-tipped baton carried by the king's messenger in Scotland as a symbol of his office, and broken by him (by way of protest) if he was resisted in the execution of his duty.

281 motto *Hamlet*, 3.4.141–44.

282.6 Exorcizo te *Latin literally* I exorcise you.

282.9 Beelzebub used as an alternative name for the devil, and described in Matthew 12.24 and Mark 3.22 as 'the prince of the devils'.

282.12 Waes me! alas!

282.25 gone a wool-gathering proverbial expression, indicating absent-mindedness (Ray, 216; *ODEP*, 905).

283.1 burned wi' a tar-barrel burning in a tar-barrel, i.e. a wooden barrel which had contained tar, was a punishment for witches. Compare Scott's ballad 'Christie's Will': 'I have tar-barrell'd mony a witch' (*Minstrelsy*, 4.72).

284.28–29 turnpike road see note to 39.11.

284.31–33 Lang-hirst . . . Simon's pool, and so by the old road to Kipple-

tringan the place names listed are apparently fictitious.
284.35 the Mains inclosures at Hazelwood the enclosures belonging to the home farm of the Hazelwood estate.
286.34 Cruffell-fell prominent hill (Criffel, 569m) SSW of Dumfries, dominating the Solway in that area.
290.34–35 from the right . . . wheel the soldiers are lined up shoulder to shoulder in two ranks of 15. The back rank is ordered to come forward to join the front; this starts on the right with each soldier from the back coming in to the left of the soldier in front of him, and takes place 'by files' (i.e. successively by file, each file being a pair of soldiers, one behind the other). The leading file, i.e. the soldier at the right of what is now a single rank, is told to wheel his horse to the right, and the rest follow and go off into the trees one behind the other.
291 motto 'Kinmont Willie', stanza 34 (see *Minstrelsy*, 2.64).
292.1 it is said . . . tritons *tritons* are fabulous sea deities; attendants to sea-god Poseidon (Greek) and Neptune (Roman); no specific literary reference here has been discovered.
292.3 syren or Proteus *sirens* are fabulous creatures in Classical mythology who possess the power of drawing people to destruction by their song and are omniscient; Proteus, in Homer's *Odyssey*, is a soothsayer who lives on the island of Pharos, off the coast of Egypt, and has the power of assuming different shapes in order to avoid being questioned.
292.15 far yaud far away. A call made to a sheep-dog to drive away sheep at a distance.
293.3 Cerberus monstrous dog, the watchdog of Hades.
293.31 his ancestors when the beacon-light was kindled fires placed at the top of hills were used anciently in the Borders to warn of incursions by English forces (see *The Lay of the Last Minstrel* (1805), Canto 3, stanzas 25–29: *Poetical Works*, 6.112–16, and 113n).
295.6 Hagel and wetter *German* hail and foul weather.
296.3 Haud a care take care, beware.
296.5 the Dewke's coach i.e. the Duke of Buccleuch's coach (see note to 120.6).
296 motto Robert Burns, 'Tam o' Shanter' (1790), lines 45–46 (Kinsley, no. 321).
296.40–297.1 point ruffles lace or cambric frills on a coat.
297.7 in session time i.e. during the sitting of the Court of Session: at this period, from 1 June to 31 July and from 1 November to the last day of February (with a break from 24 December to 1 January).
297.8–9 attend a proof attend the taking of evidence on oath. It was a common practice in procedure before the Court of Session in the 18th century for evidence to be taken not before the court itself, but by giving a commission for a witness elsewhere to be questioned by, say, the local sheriff.
297.14 On n'ârrete pas dans si beau chemin *French* one doesn't stop on such a good road (i.e. one young lady kissed won't suffice).
297.40 a world too wide for my shrunk shanks see *As You Like It*, 2.7.160–61 (Jaques on the sixth of the seven ages of man).
298.1 tota re perspecta *Latin* taking everything into consideration.
298.9–10 my old friend B—— James Burnett, Lord Monboddo (1714–99), the Scottish judge and philosopher. Following the ISet, the Magnum supplies the full surname in its text (as Burnet), and also supplies a Note headed 'Lord Monboddo' (4.256, 267). For an extract, describing Monboddo's supper parties in Edinburgh, see note to 227.33–34.
298.10 cœna *Latin* supper: the principal meal of the day for the Romans, normally eaten in the evening.
298.24 terrestial or celestial compare *The Merry Wives of Windsor*,

3.1.96–97 ('Give me thy hand, terrestrial . . . celestial').

298.25 Albumazar see note to 234.39.

298.26 Ephemerides astronomical almanac(s), showing the relative position of the planets each day: the plural (sometimes used as singular) of *ephemeris* (see note to 20.14).

298.26 Almochoden . . . Almuten for these astrological terms, see note to 17.18.

298.27 Ptolemy see note to 16.35.

298.28 Prospero . . . broke my staff see *The Tempest*, 5.1.54–57.

298.38 uncial or semiuncial large and medium sized letters (usually rounded and separate) in writing. These terms, as well as Pleydell's following epithet, are used by Roger North (1653–1734) in his *Life of the Right Honourable Francis North, Baron of Guilford, Lord Keeper of the Great Seal, under King Charles II. and King James II.*: 'He acquired a very small but legible Hand; for, where contracting is the main Business, it is not well to write, as the Fashion now is, uncial or semiuncial Letters, to look like Pigs Ribs' (ed. Montague North, London, 1742, 16). Scott's interest in this work is evident in *Letters*, 3.82, 8.66.

298.42 good seeker . . . bad finder variation of a familiar proverbial combination (see Ray, 7; *ODEP*, 711).

298.43 a gay guess a pretty good guess, a good inkling.

299.4 Stay, here follows some poetry compare *Twelfth Night*, 2.5.127: 'Soft! here follows prose' (Malvolio reading a letter).

299.10 Cumæan sybil prophetess who inhabited a grotto at Cumae, a Greek colony in southern Italy. Virgil introduces the Cumaean sibyl into *Aeneid*, Bk 6 (*passim*).

300.2 Corelli's sonatas Arcangelo Corelli (1653–1713), composer and one of the first virtuoso violinists, whose music includes five sets of chamber sonatas. In the Magnum text (4.259) Corelli is replaced by Scarlatti, probably referring to Domenico Scarlatti (1685–1757), who was famous for his keyboard sonatas.

300.3–4 the gentlemen's concert in Edinburgh referring to the Musical Society of Edinburgh, instituted in the year 1728, whose concerts from 1762 were held in the specially-built St Cecilia's Hall off the Cowgate. During the 1760s and 1770s, according to Henry Cockburn, it was 'our most selectly fashionable place of amusement': see *Memorials of His Time* (Edinburgh, 1856), 29. The best musicians, some brought over from Italy, performed work by contemporary composers. With the move of fashionable society to the New Town, however, and the opening of the Assembly Rooms in George Street in 1787, the Society lost much of its original glamour and was finally wound up in 1801.

300.20 Utrecht in the year 1738 during the early and mid-18th century, the Netherlands was a popular location for Scottish students of Roman law. James Boswell studied law at Utrecht between 1763–64, advised by Sir David Dalrymple that it offered advantages over Leiden for improving himself 'generally in culture and manners'. For further details and other cases, as well as statistical information about numbers of attendance (which began to tail off *c.* 1760), see Robert Feenstra, 'Scottish-Dutch Legal Relations in the Seventeenth and Eighteenth Centuries', in *Academic Relations between the Low Countries and the British Isles 1450–1700*, ed. H. De Ridder-Symoens and J. M. Fletcher (Gent, 1989), 25–45.

301.20 term their tavern-keepers restaurateurs *restaurateur* is French for a restaurant owner, but can also mean a 'restorer', hence Pleydell's pun.

302.25 De Lyra Nicholas De Lyra, French Franciscan (*c.* 1270–1340), author of Latin commentaries on the Bible, which were the standard authority in the late medieval and early modern periods; over 100 editions appeared between 1471 and 1600.

302.28 I am not in the vein *Richard III*, 4.2.122.

302.29 metal more attractive *Hamlet*, 3.2.106.

302.30 in a glee or a catch inviting them into a song for unaccompanied voices. According to Hugo Arnot, a 'catch-club' met after the concerts of the Musical Society of Edinburgh (see note to 300.3–4): 'Select pieces of vocal musick were performed, intermingled with Scots songs, duets, catches, and glees' (*History of Edinburgh*, 1788 edn, 381: *CLA*, 14).

302.39 We be three poor Mariners a song for treble, tenor and bass parts published as song no. 6 in Thomas Ravenscroft's *Deuteromelia: or the Second Part of Musicks Melodie, or melodius Musick* (London, 1609). The song also appears as no. 53 in *The Oxford Song Book*, collected and arranged by Thomas Wood (Oxford, 1927), 73–74.

303 motto see Richard Brinsley Sheridan, *The Critic* (1779), 3.1.71–72, 76–79.

303.34 thack and rape thatching and the straw rope with which it is secured, as in thatched houses: figuratively used to indicate that something is in a well-secured state.

304.25 Gorgon's head the head of Medusa, one of the three Gorgon sisters (see note to 14.29), which retained its petrifying powers after her slaying by Perseus.

304.39 major vis *Latin literally* the greater force; in Scots law, more commonly as *vis major*, usually signifying one person exerting unlawful force to compel another party to do something. Here used less technically by Pleydell.

306.16–17 aut quocunque alio nomine vocaris *Latin* or by whatever other name you are called. The phraseology recalls Classical escape clauses for ensuring that a god or goddess was correctly addressed. See, for example, Catullus, 34.21–22, 'quocumque tibi placet nomine' ('under whatever name pleases you').

306.22 no just that weel put on not quite properly dressed.

307.34 lifted up his voice and wept Genesis 29.11.

308.2–3 circumduce the term *Scots law* declare judicially the time elapsed for bringing forward evidence.

308.7 Grecian painter's veil possibly alluding to the story of the contest between Zeuxis and Parrhasius. The former painted some grapes so well that the birds flew at them; Parrhasius, on the other hand, won the contest by drawing a curtain with such accuracy that his rival asked for it to be drawn aside in order that the picture beneath might be revealed.

308.10 melted into air compare *The Tempest*, 4.1.148–50: 'These our actors . . . Are melted into air'.

308.37 Black Acts referring here it would seem to the laws of magic, rather than to the Acts of the Scottish Parliament (which in the 16th century were printed in black-letter type).

308.41 verbum volans *Latin* a fleeting word, a chance remark.

308.42 nolens volens *Latin* willing or unwilling; i.e. whether you like it or not.

309.39–40 his four quarters his four limbs (i.e. his total effort).

310.7 interrogatories *Scots law* questions (in strict theory written) put to witnesses: see also note to 4.10. In the 18th century witnesses who did not appear in Court were generally examined in this way before a Commissioner.

310.8 the sederunt the 'sitting of the Court' (as Pleydell playfully presents himself); properly *sederunt* in Scots law means the list of persons who take part as members of the Court.

310.17 heir of tailzie and provision the heir provided by the terms of the entail (see note below) as distinguished from the heir-at-law.

310.19–20 heir to his grand-father Lewis, the entailer any land owner could entail heritable property, specifying which descendants (usually heirs male) could inherit, and in so doing preventing heirs from disposing of either the whole or any part of it. By encumbering the estate with debt, Godfrey Bertram lost the right to the estate in favour of the next heir of entail, his son, which is why the latter is to be served (i.e. declared) heir to the estate of his grandfather, not his father.

310.37–38 'tis my vocation, Hal *1 Henry IV*, 1.2.101.

311.11 led farms farms on which the tenant did not reside. The Duke (of Buccleuch) preferred resident tenants because the 'person who resides upon a farm, is always doing something for his own convenience, that is connected with the improvement of it' (Buccleuch estate factor's report, 1791).

311.22 Enfant trouvé *French* recovered child, foundling.

311.22–23 summons of wakening in Scots law a means of reviving an action in court that was judged to have fallen asleep because there had been no judicial proceedings for a year and a day. Pleydell's habit of punning apparently never sleeps!

311.24 Clarence's fate drowning in a butt of malmsey wine (see *Richard III*, 1.4.268).

312 motto *All's Well that Ends Well*, 1.1.76–79.

312.38 Merlin's exhibition Merlin's Mechanical Museum was a celebrated collection of mechanical devices, invented by John Joseph Merlin, and exhibited at 11 Princes Street, Hanover Square, London, from the 1770s to its closure in 1808.

313.26 love ane another see John 13.34; 15.12, 17; 1 Thessalonians 4.9; 1 Peter 1.22.

313.42 book-keeping by double and single entry usually as a means of keeping creditor and debtor accounts. In the single-entry system each debit or credit is entered only once in the ledger, either as a debit or credit item; in the double-entry system, each item is entered twice in the ledger, once on the debit and once on the credit side.

314.5 Suum cuique tribuito *Latin* render each person their due. This precept, originally enunciated by the Roman jurist Ulpian (d. AD 228), appears in Justinian's *Institutes* and *Digest* (see note to 204.39), and became a central maxim in Scots law, which itself was derived from the Roman. James Boswell refers to 'the great rule of Courts, *Suum cuique tribuito*', under 31 August 1772, in his *Life of Johnson* (ed. G. B. Hill, rev. L. F. Powell, 6 vols (Oxford, 1934–50), 2.201).

314.41 Chaldaic tongue language of the Chaldeans, a group of five tribes who became dominant in Babylonia during the late 6th century BC; their idiom was supposed to occur with (and corrupt) the Hebrew of the Old Testament.

315.26 Mrs Mincing stereotypical name for a lady's attendant: there is a Mrs Mincing in William Congreve's *The Way of the World* (1700).

315.40 Aboulfouaris he and the others mentioned are characters in a Persian tale, which had recently been published in Henry Weber's edition of *Tales of the East*, 3 vols (Edinburgh, 1812), 2.469–96 (*CLA*, 43). Julia's qualifying remark is correct: Aboulfouaris, a great traveller, is married to Canzade, who is not his sister! In the culmination of the tale, Aboulfouaris returns after a long absence to find his brother Hour ruined through improvidence and Canzade on the point of consummating an arranged marriage to a rich young man.

317.3 Let bygones be bygones proverbial (Ramsay, 96; *ODEP*, 96).

317.39 Cressy and Poictiers two battles (fought in 1346 and 1356) in which the English defeated the French during the Hundred Years War.

318.22 wipe these witnesses from your eyes compare *Macbeth*, 2.2.47:

'wash this filthy witness from your hand'.

318 motto *1 Henry IV*, 2.4.496–99.

319.12 Zenocrates evidently a slip: either for Xenocrates, a successor of the Greek philosopher Plato; or (more probable in the light of following banter) for Zeno of Citium in Cyprus (fl. *c.* 300 BC), the founder of the Stoic school of philosophy: see also note below.

319.13 Academics . . . Stoics the members of Plato's school of philosophy at Athens were known as the *Academics*, the building where they met being called the Academia. The *Stoics*, founded in Athens by Zeno (see note above), believed that humankind should be independent of the vicissitudes of fortune, though in popular opinion stoicism became synonymous with endurance and the suppression of feeling.

319.19 the Cynic school a school of philosophy, founded in Athens in the 5th century BC, which later became known for its general contempt of worldly things. Pleydell is perhaps also playing on the origin of this name from the Greek word for 'dog' (*kuon*).

319.31 sui juris *Latin literally* of one's own right: a term of Roman law referring to those who are not under the authority of others and can make legally binding transactions.

319.33 rectus in curia *Latin literally* upright in court; one who stands at the bar of a court but against whom no charge is made.

320.12 infamous in the eye of the law those convicted of certain crimes were considered as being unsuitable to testify. Some individuals of bad character were also judged to be infamous and their evidence affected as to credibility.

320.28 faint heart . . . fair lady proverbial (Ramsay, 77; Ray, 104; *ODEP*, 238).

320.31 Leyden and Utrecht two notable Dutch university towns, both popular with Scottish students of Law in the earlier 18th century; see also note to 300.20.

320.32 Middleburgh Dutch commercial town (see note to 188.35).

320.40–41 non valens agere *Latin* (and *Scots law*) unable to act.

321.19 promotion in the gazette the Gazette was an official periodical containing such announcements as civil and military appointments.

322.6 refuse our bail since the assault was a bailable offence, it was the magistrate's duty to allow bail unless there was reason to fear the accused would corrupt witnesses or quit the country.

322.17–18 the needful what is necessary or requisite.

322.25 court of last resort i.e. the House of Lords, to which appeals could be taken from the Court of Session in civil matters.

322.26 mooting points i.e. debating hypothetical and disputable issues.

324.18–19 worm-eaten hold of ragged stone *2 Henry IV*, Induction, 35.

324 motto 'The Marriage of Sir Gawaine' (Child, 31), Part the First, lines 101–08, in Percy, 3.11–24.

325.4–5 loathly lady . . . green holleye in the ballad (see note above), the *loathly* ('hideous', 'loathsome') lady first appears before King Arthur 'Betweene an oke, and a greene holleye' (line 91). Sir Gawaine later offers to marry the lady, who is then transformed into a beautiful woman.

325.22 ill-doers are ill-dreaders proverbial (Ramsay, 91; *ODEP*, 398).

326.18 evil genii . . . in India more properly *djins* or *jinnees* (see note to 161.22).

327.9 prout de lege *Latin* according to law.

327.24 peer out, peer out see *The Merry Wives of Windsor*, 4.2.21.

328.3 fient a haet devil a bit! not a jot!

328.42 worthy of our Siddons herself the stage career of Sarah Siddons

(1755–1831) spanned from the 1770s to her retirement in 1812. She was renowned for a variety of Shakespearean female roles, and played Lady Macbeth in her farewell performance. Among numerous contemporary portrayals are her statue by Sir Francis Chantrey in Westminster Abbey and a picture of her as the 'Tragic Muse' by Sir Joshua Reynolds.

329.21 or he die before he dies.

329.24 loaded and locked loaded and fitted with a flint-lock ready for firing.

330.32 The hour and the man are baith come 'The hour's come, but not the man' is used as the motto to Ch. 4 of *The Heart of Mid-Lothian* (1818), and in a Magnum note to that novel Scott later attributed the words to a water demon shortly before the drowning of a man on horseback impelled by fate (Magnum, 11.210n). A version of the story referred to in Scott's note is in Katharine M. Briggs, *A Dictionary of British Folk-Tales*, 4 vols (London, 1970–71), Part B, 1.208–09, under the title 'The Doomed Rider'. There is perhaps also an echo of John 13.1 etc.: 'when Jesus knew that his hour was come'.

331 motto *3 Henry VI*, 5.6.57–58.

333.24 deyvil's mattins service of satanic worship carried out by witches; also used to describe an uproar, an unholy racket.

334.10 the Hour's come see note to 330.32.

335 motto George Crabbe, 'The Hall of Justice' (1807), Part the First, lines 105–08.

337.34 judgment seat see Romans 14.10; 2 Corinthians 5.10.

337.41 Your hand has sealed my evidence one of the exceptions to the rule that hearsay testimony cannot be accepted in court is the admissibility of the words of a dying person.

339.21–22 Pass... death! almost certainly Scott's own composition.

340.12 herezeld the best horse or other animal belonging to a tenant or vassal due on his death to the landlord or superior (a due long obsolete by this time, though sometimes found in land titles).

341.16 used wi' familiar with, used to.

342 motto Joanna Baillie, *Count Basil: A Tragedy* (1798), 5.3.

342.39 accessory after, not before, the fact i.e. the other person had assisted the perpetrators of the crime after they had committed it, but had neither planned nor participated in the actual crime.

343.9 as Dogberry says in *Much Ado About Nothing*, 4.2.23–24: 'A marvellous witty fellow, I assure you; but I will go about with him.'

343.22 measure that prisoner's feet a similar story, concerning the murderer of a girl in Galloway discovered through his footprint, is told by Scott to J. B. S. Morritt in a letter of 12 January 1813 (see *Letters*, 3.225–26). The circumstances of this case, tried at Dumfries in 1787, were later given in an article in *Chambers's Edinburgh Journal*, 1.41 (Saturday, 10 March 1832): William Richardson, the culprit, is said there to have committed his crime 'in a remote district in the Stewartry of Kirkcudbright'.

343.32 Memel log Memel is the German name for Klaipeda, a port in Lithuania on the Baltic coast; in Scott's time it exported lumber, hence Memel log.

344.11 cat's paw i.e. a dupe, the tool of another (from the fable of the monkey who used the paw of a cat to get chestnuts out of the fire).

344.15 regis ad exemplar *Latin* according to the king's example.

344.21–22 this period of the session see note to 297.7.

344.25 Ne accesseris in consilium antequam voceris *Latin* enter not into counsel till you are called.

345.26 shore of Annan see note to 13.29.

345.32 the real Simon Pure i.e. the real man, the authentic article. In

Susannah Centlivre's play, *A Bold Stroke for a Wife* (1718), Simon Pure is a Quaker from Pennsylvania, impersonated by a Colonel Feignwell who (in that guise) gains assent to marry Anne Lovely, an heiress, a plan interrupted by the appearance of 'the real Simon Pure'.

345.33 Antigua in the West Indies, one of the Leeward Islands; an exporter of sugar and rum to Britain in the 18th century.

345.34–35 came somewhat irregularly into it compare *King Lear*, 1.1.20: 'Though this knave came something saucily to the world'.

346.30 art and part technical term of Scots law meaning aiding or participating in a crime by giving advice or assistance. One who is guilty art and part is, in Scots law, as guilty as the actual perpetrator of the same crime. If Glossin is art and part guilty of *plagium* (see note below), and it is a capital offence, he is guilty of a capital offence and thus cannot get bail.

346.32 plagium is felony *plagium*, the offence of child-stealing or kidnapping, was punishable in Scots law by death; and as a capital offence it was not bailable. The term *felony*, though one of English law, was commonly used in Scots law in the 18th century to denote capital crimes.

346.34 Torrence and Waldie a case decided in 1752 and reported in John MacLaurin's *Arguments and Decisions in . . . Cases before the High Court of Justiciary* (Edinburgh, 1774), 152. It appears that the two women were convicted and hanged on a verdict that found them guilty of *plagium* and of delivering the dead boy to the surgeons. They were not found guilty of murdering him. Thus Glossin is not correct in his report.

348.11 warrants of commitment were used when a person after examination by the magistrate was committed to prison to await trial.

348 motto see *Measure for Measure*, 4.3.60–61.

348.35 bar of iron 'This mode of securing prisoners was universally practised in Scotland after condemnation. When a man received sentence of death, he was put upon *the Gad*, as it was called, that is, secured to the bar of iron in the manner mentioned in the text' (Magnum, 4.359n).

352.9 truckle bed a low bed running on truckles or castors, usually pushed under a larger bed when not in use.

352 motto Alexander Pope (in imitation of Jonathan Swift), 'The Happy Life of a Country Parson' (written *c.*1713), line 16.

352.33–39 Godfrey Bertram's creditors . . . claimant Glossin having died without paying for the estate, the creditors' only resource is the estate of Ellangowan, but there will be no legal duty on Henry Bertram to pay once he is proved the heir male. Bertram nevertheless honourably decides that the debts incurred by his father should be paid.

353.32 Christmas recess for the Court of Session, at this period, from 24 December to 1 January (see note to 297.7).

353.42 With a wet finger with little effort, easily or readily: a metaphor probably derived from spinning, in which the spinner constantly wetted the fore-finger with the mouth, though also applicable to turning the pages of a book.

353.42 special service *Scots law* the procedure for ascertaining and declaring who is the heir to a special estate.

353.42–43 retoured into Chancery . . . macers under Scots law it was necessary that someone in Bertram's situation should establish his identity, descent, and status as heir. The normal mode was by an inquest before the sheriff. The heir would purchase a brieve of inquest (that is a royal order commanding trial by jury to ascertain whether the claimant was in fact heir), which was then addressed to the sheriff of the county where the lands were. When the jury had determined the issue, the brieve was 'retoured' (returned) by the sheriff to Chancery (the office in the General Register House in Edinburgh in which is kept a record of all writs relative to crown lands, services of heirs etc.). Where there was a need for expedition, it was the practice for the brieve to be directed to the macers of the Court of Session given a special commission as sheriffs to deal with this particular brieve. The procedure was as Scott states. Macers were (and are) officers attending on the Court of Session (and some other courts) with a variety of functions, such as keeping silence in court and announcing the beginning of cases.

354.2 **judicial Saturnalia** the Saturnalia of Rome was a festival celebrated in December, during which greater license was allowed to slaves: similar in some respects to the topsy-turvy world of the modern Carnival.

354.4–7 **men of no knowledge . . . court** the procedure involving the Macers (see note to 353.42–43) was abolished only in 1821, and had a certain topicality in Scott's day.

354.14 **Cujacius** Latinised form of (Jacques) Cujas (1522–1590), celebrated French jurist who taught at Bourges (where several contemporary Scottish students learned their law).

354.14–16 **Multa sunt in moribus dissentanea, multa sine ratione** *Latin* in customs there are many things inconsistent and many devoid of reason.

354.17 **Walker's** probably referring to Charles Walker, a vintner and tavern keeper in Writers' Court.

354.26–27 **Blind Harry and Hy Spy** two children's games, the equivalent of blindman's buff and hide-and-seek.

354.28 **Eagle Tower at Caernarvon** one of the most imposing and elaborate towers at Caernarvon Castle, in North Wales; Edward II of England is said to have been born in this tower.

354.29 **corps de logis** *French* main building. Scott used the phrase twice in letters of 1814, in describing his residency at and plans for rebuilding Abbotsford (see *Letters*, 3.446, 514).

354.31 **Sicca rupees** newly coined rupees (Indian coins), of a higher value than those worn by use: between 1793 and 1836 applied specifically to rupees coined by the Government of Bengal, containing more silver than those of the East India Company.

354.35 **post-nati** *Latin* born after, i.e. the younger generation; also used in Scotland to describe those born after the Union of the Crowns in 1603.

354.39 **your flank will be turned** a military expression, referring to the strategy of getting round an enemy's side or wing to make an attack.

355.15 **good-boy books** referring to didactic stories designed for children, such as 'The History of Little Goody Two Shoes'.

GLOSSARY

This selective glossary defines single words; phrases are treated in the Explanatory Notes. It covers Scottish words, archaic and technical terms, and occurrences of familiar words in senses that are likely to be strange to the modern reader. For each word (or clearly distinguishable sense) glossed, up to four occurrences are normally noted; when a word occurs more than four times in the novel, only the first instance is normally given, followed by 'etc.'. Orthographical variants of single words are listed together, usually with the most common use first. Often the most economical and effective way of defining a word or expanding a definition is to refer the reader to the appropriate explanatory note.

'a he 148.22, 148.22
a' all 15.22 etc.
abune above 15.22 etc.
accompts accounts, financial reckonings 84.4, 200.35, 258.18
account for 192.37 and 264.13 see note to 192.37
acromion outer extremity of the shoulder blade 254.22, 256.37
ae one 15.23 etc.
aff off 15.18 etc.
afore before 10.26 etc.
Afrite see note to 105.27–28
afterhend afterwards 264.36
after-names surnames 139.10
again against 208.8
a' head, a-head *nautical* at the head, in front 193.10, 333.39
ahint behind 139.23, 233.28
aiblins perhaps 4.20, 207.26
aid-de-camp officer who assists a general in his military duties 32.35, 164.13, 231.31
aik oak 40.36
ails prevents 120.26
ain own 10.26 etc.
air-bell air-bubble 136.32
a-laking see note to 112.34
alane alone 46.39
alang along 63.14
almaist almost 65.38
aloe drug of nauseous odour and bitter taste, hence bitter experience or trial 69.34
altitudes lofty mood and ways 204.8, 229.33
alway at all times, on all occasions 302.26
amang among 34.14 etc.
an, an' if 14.35 etc.
an', an and 45.4 etc.
anathema curse 51.36; an accursed thing 196.2 (see note)
ance, anes once 13.23 etc.; for 269.24 see note
ane one 15.22 etc.; a person, somebody 15.13 etc.
anent concerning 8.33, 175.31, 179.7
anes see **ance**
aneugh, aneuch enough 28.14 etc.
anither another 273.2, 273.19, 278.25, 280.31 (see note)
a-noights *Cumbrian* at nights 112.35
Antiburgher see note to 173.42–43
appriser see note to 8.42
assessor assistant to a judge or magistrate 253.25, 354.13
assistants participants, those present 214.41, 318.33
atweel indeed, assuredly 202.43
auld old 4.11 etc.
avised informed, made aware 234.30
avoid expel, drive out 76.28 (see note) etc.
awa, awa' away 5.39 etc.; about, abouts 4.22, 139.24, 179.21
aweel well 14.34, etc.
awfu' awful 121.36
awmous alms, food or money given in charity to the poor 34.3, 152.37
aye, ay yes 14.37 etc.
aye always 6.23 etc.

Bacchanal a devotee of Bacchus (the Roman god of wine), drunken reveller 136.25, 206.23
bail-bond written undertaking by another person that the accused will appear to answer the charge under pain of forfeiture of the sum fixed as bail 322.15
bairn child 11.12 etc.
bairn-time brood of children, offspring of one mother 129.7
baith both 52.27 etc.
bam hoax, trick story 16.8 (see note to 16.8–9)
band for 212.17 see note
banditti bandits, brigands 35.31, 36.21, 37.35, 165.31
ban-dog a dog tied or chained on account of its ferocity or one posted to guard a house 292.41
bane bone 34.20, 274.2, 294.10, 328.38
bannock round flat cake of oat or barley meal baked on a girdle 131.13
banter delude, trick 312.35
barken dry up, harden 127.20
barker pistol 179.41
barley-meal meal made from barley 131.13
barn-door reared at the barn-door 270.15
barony lands held directly of the Crown 32.3 etc.
barrow-tram the shaft of a barrow, hence a raw-boned awkward-looking person 279.12
bauld bold, courageous 286.6
baulk *noun* unploughed ridge, uncultivated piece of land 40.20
baulk *verb* refuse 330.41
be by 120.18
bedlamite befitting an inmate of Bedlam, lunatic 327.8
bedral beadle, sexton 341.15
beef-ham beef cured like ham, by salting, smoking etc. 131.12
beetle beat, pound 131.41
behoof benefit 84.25
behoved, behooved was obliged, had to 133.22, 337.22
belang belong 64.40, 207.15, 233.25
beldam hag, witch 149.1, 331.23
ben *thieves' cant* good 25.19 (see note to 25.19–20)
ben see note to 128.8
benighted overtaken by the darkness of night 3.31, 277.27. 292.27
berling, berlin barge, galley 28.36, 242.25
bestad placed, situated 62.16
biddin stayed for 129.14
bide stay, remain 62.10, 330.31; endure, bear 233.14, 311.12; live 273.1; keep 279.3
bield shelter 44.18
big, bigg build 328.35, 341.12
biggit built 15.33, 286.11
bilboes iron leg-fetters 188.28
billet short letter, note 280.33
billies fellows 133.26
bin *German* am 180.26, 180.26, 180.27, 187.32
bing *thieves' cant* go 149.2 (see note)
binna be not 327.42
birk birch 15.21
birl drink, carouse 232.12
bit *goes with the following word* indicating smallness or familiarity 15.21 etc.; spot, place etc. 122.14 etc.; for 4.19 see note
bite imposition, deception 16.8 (see note to 16.8–9)
bitters alcoholic liquor impregnated with extracts of bitter substances, sometimes used medicinally 178.7
bittock a small bit 4.21
black-cock male of the black grouse 44.19 etc.
black-fishers, black-fishing for 10.23 and 33.12 see note to 10.23
blate modest, bashful 6.22
blawn blown 122.15
blazonry collection of heraldic devices, heraldry 244.21
blear blur, blind 233.42 (see note)
blind indistinct, obscure 117.15
blithe, blythe happy, merry 44.10 etc.
blitzen *German* lightning 25.4 etc.
blood-bay of reddish bay colour 64.40
blude, bluid blood 15.19 (see note), 121.19, 121.28
blumen-garten see note to 191.35–36
blunker cloth-printer 15.33
bob-wig wig with bottom turned up in curls 211.8, 355.14
boddle small copper coin worth twopence Scots (0.17p) 46.32, 77.33
body person 5.41 etc.
body-servant personal attendant 6.16

bog-blitter see note to 5.7–8
bogle ghost 7.3
bohemian see note to 231.16
boltsprit bowsprit, spar or boom running out of the bow of a vessel to which are attached the foremast stays 26.26
bongrace broad-brimmed hat fitted to shade the face 14.30
bonhommie *French* easy good nature 229.22
bonnie, bonny fine, dear, beautiful, pleasant 14.34 etc.
boot-hose boot-stocking 37.22, 297.40
borough-town burgh, town with special privileges conferred by charter 46.43, 193.16
bottle-head hammer head, stupid fellow 264.20
bottle-slider tray for a decanter 204.25
boul semi-circular handle 273.7 (see note)
bountith gratuity 234.15
bourtree elder-tree 330.18
bow boll, measure of capacity or weight for grain etc. (also used for valuing land according to the quantity produced) 27.17
bowls see note to 47.34
bowster bolster, long pillow 266.24
brae hillside, slope 61.2, 122.26
bragged see note to 207.34
brake broke 65.32, 281.15
Bramin for 228.22, 230.23 and 244.30 see note to 228.22
brander gridiron, open girdle 131.11
brat see note to 15.1
braw fine, splendid 44.21, 262.37, 286.20
brawly very well 61.3
bridewell kind of prison in which minor criminals and beggars were engaged in forced labour 33.32 etc.
brigg bridge 60.43
brindled spotted, streaked 40.3
broad church collection plate 34.26
brock badger 120.2, 140.9, 140.11; stinking person, one given to dirty tricks 220.15
brood breeding 133.27
broom warrant from a magistrate 149.34 (see note), 179.20, 179.21
brush encounter, meeting 322.23
buck dandy, fop 222.21, 222.21, 223.26
buckskins clothing (usually breeches) made from the skin of the buck 177.27, 218.39
buirdly well-built, sturdy 328.26
bull-of-the-bog see note to 5.7–8
bully-huff boaster and bully 149.11
bumper cup or glass of wine filled to the brim 204.20
burgo-master chief magistrate of a Dutch or Flemish town 191.36
by compared to 208.21; for 264.28 see note
bye besides 15.15, 175.2
bye-law regulation made by the members of a corporation 124.31
bye-names nicknames 139.18
bye-play action apart from the main action 318.29
bye-talk talk aside 15.31
ca' call 34.16 etc.
cabal plot, intrigue 32.35, 345.16
cabaret see note to 119.12
cabbined closed in, confined 115.27
cabriole light two-wheeled chaise driven by one horse 300.32
cachinnation loud or immoderate laughter 16.14
cadie for 201.6 etc. see note to 201.6
caird tinker or gypsy 36.21
cake-house house where cakes are sold 90.32
caliph title given in Muslim countries to the chief civil and religious ruler 105.28
callant lad, fellow 64.31, 120.36, 222.11, 264.16
Cameronian see note to 9.12
camlet a type of fabric originally thought to have been made of silk and camel's hair but afterwards made of wool and other materials 74.34
camstane see note to 202.24–26
camsteary perverse, fractious 311.16
Candlemas 2 February, a Scottish quarter-day 46.33
canna cannot 62.7 etc.
cannily carefully, steadily 129.15, 286.18
canny natural 58.21 (see note); lucky 63.25; shrewd, wise 122.23; quiet, cautious 124.5; pleasant, good 174.27; for 6.15 and 14.7 see note

to 6.15
cantle slice or portion 7.17, 9.2
canton one of the states which form the Swiss confederation 114.9
canty cheerful, pleasant 6.23
capriole leap or caper 129.43
caption see note to 174.16
captious disposed to find fault 75.2
capuchin female garment consisting of a cloak and hood 300.31
carbine fire-arm between the size of a pistol and a musket 164.27, 164.36
carle, carl fellow 27.42, 233.26, 278.19
carling see note to 14.37
ca't call it 265.25
catch song for three or more voices, with the second singer beginning the first line as the first goes to the second line (and so on with each successive singer) 302.30
catched caught 29.3
catechism series of questions and answers used for the purposes of instruction etc. 306.33
catechumen one undergoing instruction or being questioned 306.35
cauld cold 205.32, 265.8, 331.25
caulker the after part of a horseshoe turned down and sharpened to prevent slipping, especially on ice-covered roads 225.13
causeway cobbled street or roadway 127.7, 203.7
cess local tax or land-tax 28.28
chaise name applied to a variety of travelling carriages 60.15 etc.
Chaldaic language of the Chaldeans 314.41 (see note)
Chaldeans see note to 13.11
Chancery see note to 353.42–43
change, change-house wayside inn at which horses could be changed 127.5, 269.25
chapping stick instrument to strike with, weapon of offence 32.17
chappit struck 201.29
charge fill, render replete 173.34; load, lay weight on 249.16
chase *nautical* ship chased 47.33, 56.22
chaudrons entrails 280.3
cheat *thieves' cant* gallows 148.34 (see note)
cheerer glass of spirits and hot water 129.14, 131.31, 270.30, 274.12
chield fellow, man 63.6 etc.; for 121.31 see note
chirurgery surgery 130.5
chuckie pebble, stone 207.17 (see note)
chuckies chickens 270.16
ci-devant *French* former 112.42
cinctured girdled 244.19
circumduce see note to 308.2–3
claes clothes 224.2
clanjamfray mob, rabble 126.6
clash chatter, gossip 67.19, 176.35, 238.22
claught clutch, snatch 65.40
claver talk idly 122.20
clavicle collar-bone 254.21, 256.35
clayed see note to 181.39
clecking hatching 6.23
cleek salmon gaff or hook 138.5
clod throw forcibly 66.1, 278.42
close passageway, alley 203.15, 203.17, 203.24
clour blow, knock 126.3
clouted patched, repaired (possibly meaning strengthened with a thin metal plate or with flat-headed nails) 13.1, 255.18
cloy *thieves' cant* steal 148.32
cock circle at the end of the rink at which the stones are aimed in curling 176.24; for 15.22–23 and 111.40 see notes
cœna see note to 298.10
coft bought, purchased 177.27
collector for 46.41 and 48.19 see note to 46.41
collie sheep-dog 203.19
collie-shangie, colly shangie dispute, uproar 129.42, 264.36
collop thickish slice of meat 267.26
come-o'-will illegitimate child 13.32
comfortable sustaining, refreshing to the bodily organs 7.12, 59.39
commons for 267.31 see note to 267.30–31
composition agreement, compromise 125.31
compotator fellow-drinker 204.10
con turn over in the mind 129.39, 279.17
concatenation chain, linkage of ideas 26.34, 231.5
concurrent *Scots law* one who accompanies a sheriff's-officer as witness

or assistant 178.40
condign worthily deserved, fitting 196.27
confer compare, collate 50.43
confidant person entrusted with secrets or private matters 12.14, 111.22, 112.41
confidante female confidant 156.5
congee bow 205.14
conjunction *astrology* an apparent proximity of two heavenly bodies, 19.39, 20.27
conservator see note to 38.19
consort ship sailing in company with another 183.32
construe analyse or trace grammatically the structure of a sentence, especially in classical languages 85.8
conveyancer lawyer who prepares documents for the conveyance of property 220.23
cot-house, cottar house farm-worker's cottage 44.10, 341.13
cottar tenant or farm-worker who occupies a cottage 138.22
couchant *heraldry* lying down 244.16
couldna could not 273.12
coulter iron blade in the front of a plough 291.2
counsellor counselling lawyer, advocate 201.20 etc.
coup overturn 296.4
cove *thieves' cant* man, fellow 25.19 (see note to 25.19–20)
coxcomb simpleton, showy person 90.36, 112.25, 283.8; head 131.37
cozener cheat, impostor 17.1
crack talk, easy conversation 233.1, 270.23, 306.21
craig crag, cliff 52.32 etc.
crambo see note to 204.27–28
cramp-ring *thieves' cant* shackles, fetters 124.6 (see note), 148.33
crane-berries cranberries 37.28
cranking twisting, bending 7.15, 9.1
crappit-heads see note to 175.10
cravat article of dress worn around the neck by men 216.27
craw *noun* crow, rook 271.1
craw *verb* crow 15.23
crazy full of cracks or flaws 136.24
creature for 263.1 see note
creel deep wicker basket carried on the back 121.33
cribbed confined within narrow space or limits 115.27
crisis for 40.42 see note
crooks windings, curves 248.15
cross-grained of opposed nature or temperament, contrarious 8.24, 41.17
crowning completing, consummating 319.6
crows crow-bars 165.15, 294.31
cuddy donkey 15.21, 42.35
cue pigtail 218.32
cummerband waist-band, sash 159.10
curd-brained soft-headed 264.16
cur-dog low bred dog 5.24
curler, curling for 167.13, 167.42, 176.23, and 177.7 see note to 167.13–14
cusp see note to 17.16–17
cusser stallion 65.42
custodier custodian 198.25, 211.38
cut *thieves' cant* speak, say 25.19 (see note to 25.19–20), 149.42
cutlugged crop-eared 207.16
daft foolish, stupid, mad 33.30 etc.
dam mother 210.2 (see note to 210.1–2)
darbies *thieves' cant* fetters 179.35, 182.18
darena dare not 5.40, 286.10
darkmans *thieves' cant* night 148.29 (see note), 149.36
date time during which something lasts, period 30.7
day-dawing dawn, daybreak 15.23
deacon chief official of a trade or craft, formerly an *ex officio* member of a town council 28.17 etc.
dead-thraw death-throe, agony of death 52.22, 52.25, 147.23
deal made of planks of fir or pine 119.26, 267.20
deduce deduct, subtract 221.12
deevil devil 269.23, 269.38, 272.34
defeasible capable of being annulled or declared void 352.34
defeat exhausted, worn out 174.37
deil devil 48.32 etc.; never, not 15.12 etc.
delf glazed earthenware, after a style of pottery originally made at Delf, the Netherlands 267.22
demur delay, hesitation 4.41
depend hang down 251.4
depositary for 154.29 and 219.28 see

note to 154.29
der *German* the 180.20 etc.
descry detect, perceive 65.33, 186.18, 332.15
design describe, designate 256.19, 288.39
devils for 203.34 see note
devoted consigned to destruction, doomed 136.38
dewke, deuke duke 120.6 (see note), 139.19, 296.5, 311.11
deyvil devil 24.22 etc.; for 333.24 see note
deyvil's-kind off-spring of the devil 193.26, 331.23
didna didn't 175.23
dike see dyke
dill see note to 14.41
ding knock, strike 34.26; defeat 224.40
dingle wooded dell or hollow 40.19, 327.30
dinna don't 49.22 etc.
dirk short dagger usually worn in the belt 42.20
discreet civil, polite 234.19
disna doesn't 273.19
dispone *Scots law* make over, assign 220.26
dispositions arrangement of troops for a military operation 164.7
disprovided unprovided, unsupplied 154.37
distance outstrip 26.30
distinctly for 130.43 see note to 130.42–43
doating in dotage, weak minded 153.10
doddered decayed, having lost branches through age 132.28
dog-cattle contemptuous term for ill-nourished animals 217.19
dominie schoolmaster, clergyman 11.10 (see note) etc.
do-nae-good ne'er do well 331.26
donner *German* thunder 25.4 etc.
doo dove, pigeon 120.14; dear one 202.16
dooket dovecot 120.15
doomed sentenced to punishment 327.38
dooms very 177.38, 269.34
do't do it 341.13
double *nautical* sail or pass round the other side of a cape or point so that the ship is bent upon itself 48.3 etc.
double for 83.37 and 313.42 see note to 313.42
doubt fear, suspect 178.14, 208.13, 215.34
doubtfu' doubtful 177.37
douce quiet, respectable 174.14, 174.27
doun down 6.1 etc.
douse *thieves' cant* put out 18.12
dow list, care 234.21
dowie melancholy 265.5
dram small drink of liquor 120.33, 122.25, 273.30, 280.24
drap drop 15.19 (see note) etc.
drave drove 296.24
dreadnought for 223.36 and 306.19 see note to 223.36
dree endure, suffer 278.33, 333.35, 337.22
driveller one who talks in a babyish or idiotic way 149.37, 350.33
drub beat in a fight 26.30
drum beat, thump 34.27; expel publicly by beating a drum 63.19
dry-handed unarmed 179.29, 329.19
du *German* you 187.27, 188.15
dub pool 13.31
dud article of clothing 141.36, 148.32
dumb-waiter article of furniture for dispensing food at table without a waiter 200.41
dun hill, hill-fort 233.41, 355.20
dungeon for 201.14 see note
durst dare 21.16 etc.
d'ye do you 128.41 etc.
dyke, dike wall, embankment 28.22, 191.36, 299.2, 339.9
easel eastward 5.34, 6.8
ebon black, dark 303.5
eclaircissement mutual explanation of equivocal conduct 109.5
eclat brilliancy, dazzling effect 302.40
edge-tools implements with sharp cutting edges 29.38
edibles eatables, articles of food 131.17
e'e eye 177.5 etc.
e'en, een eyes 121.3 etc.
e'en[1] evening 6.17 etc.; for 120.10 see note
e'en[2] even 15.16 etc.
e'en now just now, at the present time 62.23 etc
effulgence splendid radiance 17.36

eik increase, supplement 32.5
eilding fuel 271.4
elbow-chair armchair 204.24
election-dust the commotion of an election 207.40
eleemosynary done as an act of charity 223.34
elf-lock tuft of curled, matted hair 14.28, 43.43, 285.34
else or 139.1
empressement *French* animated display of cordiality 106.29
endlang on end, continuously 65.7
endurance duration 246.33
eneugh enough 6.23 etc.
ensigncy rank or position of an ensign (commissioned officer of the lowest rank) in the army 112.17
entailer one who entails an estate 310.20 (see note to 310.19–20)
entered trained 119.37 (see note), 120.1, 125.42
Ephemeris, Ephemerides see notes to 20.14 and 298.26
eradicated *heraldry* having the roots exposed 244.19
erect *astrology* set up 19.17, 20.13
errand for 269.24 see note
escutcheon painted or sculptured shield on which a coat of arms is represented 244.14, 252.6
esplanade levelled space beneath a castle 21.42, 71.16, 245.10
ewer pitcher with a wide spout, used to bring water for washing the hands 130.38
examinator examiner 175.14
exorcizo for 282.6 and 282.22 see note to 282.6
expectorate discharge, spit forth 219.5
eye yes 147.27 etc.
fa' fall 281.7, 281.14, 285.42
fader-land fatherland, native country 192.5
faem foam 60.32
fain willingly, be glad to 171.27, 248.17, 265.22, 306.28; obliged 128.12; glad 324.31
fair-strae see note to 145.30
fair-trade euphemism for smuggling 45.20, 57.28
fambles *thieves' cant* hands 149.6
fand found 273.6
fash *verb* trouble annoy, bother 46.41, 311.1
fash *noun* annoyance, bother 223.38, 267.2
fashious, fasheous troublesome, annoying 266.36, 311.17
faste *French* pomp, ostentation 102.25
fathers early Christian writers of the post New Testament period 109.38
fauld fold, pen 28.22
fauld-dike wall built around a fold 28.25
fause false, faithless 6.12
fay fairy 18.35
feal loyal, faithful 47.23
feared, fear'd afraid 7.3, 278.23, 328.3
febrifuge remedy against fever 40.40 (see note)
feck see note to 121.4
feckless incompetent, stupid 149.7; feeble, unimportant 177.25
fee for 198.1 see note to 198.1–2
feifteen, fifteen for 182.42 and 224.37 see note to 182.42
fell[1] *noun* hill or waste land 120.37, 286.34
fell[2] *noun* hide, skin 311.9
fell *adjective* clever, doughty, adept 119.36, 139.5, 139.23
felony see note to 346.32
fern-seed see note to 272.15
ferret stout tape made of cotton etc. 266.13
fescennine see note to 204.17
fiar owner of the fee of a property rather than life-renter 214.2 (see note to 214.1–2)
fie doomed, grasped by peculiarly elated behaviour thought to evince death 47.42, 65.41
fiend, fient (the) devil 8.10 etc.; for 133.30 and 328.3 see notes
fike vex, trouble 267.1
finessing *whist* attempting to take a trick with a lower card than another held 322.32
finger-post guide post at the parting of roads 4.37
fire-brand piece of wood kindled at the fire 179.13, 334.5
fire-raising arson 15.28 (see note), 224.33
firlot see note to 9.27
first-head see note to 222.21
first-rate see note to 203.13

flageolet small flute, wind instrument 89.10 etc.
flat *thieves' cant* gull, foolish fellow 149.2
flat floor or storey in a house 201.14 (see note)
flee fly 52.34, 272.5
flick *thieves' cant* cut 150.5
flisk frisk, dart about 270.1
flit remove, shift 124.5
fly quick travelling carriage, stage-coach 224.6
folio book made from sheets of paper folded in half, i.e. a large book 156.29, 164.4, 166.9, 196.2
foot-ba' foot-ball 272.5
foot-boy boy attendant 188.38, 188.40
forbye besides, in addition to 15.12, 119.42
fore see note to 269.37
forehammer sledge-hammer 291.2
forgie forgive 63.21, 202.15, 349.32
for't for it 120.38, 126.27, 138.40, 339.38
fortalice small fort 132.32
foul a disease in the feet of sheep and cattle 61.9
foumart polecat, ferret, or weasel 120.9
four-hours see note to 130.28
fow full of food 279.13
fowk folk 15.36
fowling-piece light gun for shooting wild fowl 42.19 etc.
frae from 4.13 etc.
freend friend 4.16
freendless friendless 174.6
freestone fine grained sandstone or limestone suitable for cutting 21.37
free-traders smugglers 26.24, 29.25
fremit strange, foreign 278.23
frippery tawdry finery, frivolity 92.6
front frontage 23.4, 29.1
frummagem'd *thieves' cant* choked, strangled 149.7
fu' full 176.28, 274.2
fule-body, fool-body fool 233.22, 278.39, 278.41
furze gorse 38.24, 134.33
fuzee light musket 257.13
Gad God 341.37
gae[1] go 5.34 etc.
gae[2] gave 15.16 etc.
gaed went 64.37 etc.
gae-down drinking spree 120.10
gaen, ga'en gone 28.38, 129.13, 174.3
gait see gate
gall chafe, make sore by rubbing 255.18
galloway, gallaway small sturdy type of horse originally bred in Galloway 48.25 etc.
Galwegian belonging to the district of Galloway 7.38 (see note), 82.15, 277.14, 325.6
gane gone 62.24, 208.23
gang go 4.12 etc.
gangrel vagrant 15.20
gang-there-out vagrant, vagabond 5.41
gar make 63.19 etc.
garner granary 148.2
garnish *thieves' cant* money demanded from a new prisoner 264.38
gate, gait way 4.24 etc.
gauger exciseman 46.16 etc.
gaun going 50.26 etc.
gay considerable, good 4.19 (see note), 4.19, 126.3, 298.43 (see note); very 208.4
gear worldly possessions, property 15.36, 215.19, 215.31, 223.14
gelding castrated horse 9.10, 42.36
gelt *German* money 181.38, 191.35
Genethliac one who calculates nativities 13.11 (see note)
genie see notes to 161.22 and 326.18
genius guardian spirit 343.30
gentle well-born, person of gentle birth or rank 6.2 (see note) etc.
gentry quality or rank of gentleman 9.42, 219.23; for 25.19 see note to 25.19–20
germain pertinent 205.37
ghaist ghost 341.16
gie give 15.13 etc.
gi'en, gien given 152.37, 216.13
giff-gaff give and take 238.10
glaikit foolish, playful 139.19
glamour magic, enchantment 273.20, 278.19
glass-breaker hard drinker, tippler 274.13
glazed covered with a coating to resist the rain 202.22
glee musical composition for three or more voices (one voice to a part): in strict use without accompaniment 302.30

gliff short space of time 265.6, 330.31
gliffing moment, instant 122.25
glim *thieves' cant* light, candle or lantern 18.12, 187.29
glowr stare, scowl 44.14
going gait 127.11
goodman see **gudeman**
goodwife see **gudewife**
Gott *German* God 190.8
gotten got 13.20 etc.
gowan daisy 131.41, 179.36
gowd gold 153.22
gowk fool 271.30 (see note)
gowpen see note to 34.3
gratification recompense, return for a favour or service 221.7, 221.12
'gree agree 233.12, 233.13
greet weep, cry 45.2, 219.21
grenadier infantry soldier (originally applied to those who threw grenades, later to the first company of every battalion of foot) 9.29, 40.16, 196.4
grey-fowl female of the black grouse, or grouse when in winter plumage 120.14
griego coarse jacket with a hood, or a rough great-coat 179.28
grieve farm-bailiff, overseer 39.8
gripe grip, grasp 351.34
grippit gripped 66.1
grizzled greyed, streaked or flecked with grey 123.7, 180.6, 285.34
groaning for 17.26 see note
ground-officer one who has charge of the lands of an estate 39.9, 41.32
gruel see note to 149.21
gude, guid good 60.27 etc.
gudeman, goodman master, husband, proprietor or tenant of a small farm 27.17 etc.
gudewife, goodwife wife, female head of the household 63.22 etc.
guisarding see note to 205.22
gumphion funeral banner 216.22
gyre see note to 14.37
ha' hall, 34.21, 64.7; for 36.38 see note
habited dressed 64.8
hadden held 5.34, 63.1
hadna hadn't 309.39
hae have 4.11 etc.
haet see note to 328.3
hafflin half-grown 64.31
hagel *German* hail, hailstones 187.27 etc.
haik hack, horse let out for hire 64.39
haill, hail whole 24.16 etc.
hald hold 328.5
half-a-crown, half-crown coin worth 2s 6d (12.5p) 7.10 etc.
half-bred of mixed breed, underbred 124.22
half-pay on reduced pay because laid off or permanently retired 259.42
half-text size of handwriting half the size of large hand 315.4
hame home 44.21 etc.
hamely friendly, unaffected 341.30
hand to lead or assist with the hand 94.2
hand-ba' hand-ball 265.28
hand-barrow stretcher on which mendicants were carried from door to door 33.26
handy-dandy choose which you please 170.32
hanger short sword usually hung from the belt 54.7, 55.18, 177.34, 193.14
hank coil or skein of yarn of a definite length 24.16
hansel gift to mark some special occasion 15.13, 175.3 (see note)
hantle large number 7.3
hap cover 286.12
happen happen to, befall 306.28
hard-favoured of a hard and unpleasing appearance 24.31
hard-headed stubborn 129.41
haud hold 5.35 etc.; for 296.3 see note
hauld shelter, refuge 67.26 (see note)
hawk *thieves' cant* for 18.11 see note to 18.11–12
hawk *verb* bring up with a strong effort of clearing the throat 278. 18
head[1] head-dress 47.13 (see note)
head[2] portrait in which only head and shoulders are shown 69.30
heartsome cheerful, lively 62.40
hebdomadal weekly 203.43
hech sigh-like exclamation 282.12
heckle to dress flax or hemp so as to straighten out the fibres 333.33
hedge-ruffian ruffian living by the roadside 169.39
heer see **Mynheer**
heezie heave upwards 77.32
heir-at-law *Scots law* one who succeeds to the heritable property of a

deceased person 210.12
heir-male an heir who is male and who traces his rights through the male line 62.27 (see note), 72.21 121.25, 184.5
hellicat wild, romping 174.38
hen-hearted timorous, cowardly 149.24
herd shepherd 133.23, 270.38, 270.41
herezeld see note to 340.12
heritage *Scots law* property in the form of land and houses 219.30
herring-pond sea, ocean 189.15
hersell herself 131.41 etc.; for 202.33 see note
het hot 270.21
heugh steep bank 137.3
hie hasten 327.23, 340.18
hieland highland 306.31
High-Dutch see note to 188.11
high jinks, high-jinks for 204.13, 210.35, and 231.9 see note to 204.13
himsell himself 63.42 etc.
hing hang 44.20, 122.16, 176.34, 278.25
hinny, hinney honey, sweetheart, darling 126.4 etc.
hirsel *noun* flock of sheep, area of pasturage grazed by a flock 133.22, 224.5
hirsel *verb* slide, slither 271.27
hizzie, huzzie female animal 83.41; servant girl, young woman 223.22
ho *Cumbrian* he 112.31
hoax humorous or mischievous deception 16.9 (see note to 16.8–9)
Hollands grain spirit made in Holland 179.33
holleye holly 325.5
horning see note to 174.16
horn-spoon spoon made of horn 36.26
horse-couper horse-dealer 129.7
houdie midwife 6.17
hout, hout tout *used to express annoyance or dismissal of another opinion* hoot! tut-tut! 6.22 etc.
howbeit be that as it may, notwithstanding 275.25
howff meeting-place, resort 182.26
howk dig 339.1
howm stretch of low-lying grassland by the banks of a river 15.34
humbled see note to 50.5
hum-dudgeon see note to 127.25
hunder hundred 224.3, 272.18
hung-beef meat hung in the air to be cured by drying 277.3
hunt-the-gowk see note to 271.30
hyson type of green tea from China 25.31, 61.37
Ich *German* I 180.27, 187.32, 188.14
ilk each 133.14, 272.4
ilka each, every 34.22 etc.
impress device with a motto 26.14; for 39.24 see note
incense flatter 227.20
indefeasible absolutely vested and not subject to annulment by the occurrence of some future event 213.43
indicia *Latin* marks, signs 54.10
induct lead, conduct 7.11
infamous deprived of certain rights as a result of criminal reputation 320.12 (see note)
information for 226.3 see note
ingle-side fireside 67.20
inner-house see note to 182.42
in-shore towards the shore 56.27
insouciance *French* carelessness, unconcern 24.32
in't in it 273.1, 274.19, 341.14
interregnum *Latin* period without a ruler or monarch 210.13
interrogatories see notes to 4.10 and 310.7
inventar inventory 175.26
I'se I shall 6.2 etc.
ither other 176.21, 219.20, 272.4, 285.32
jacket garment worn by a jockey in horse-racing 222.28 (see note)
Jacobite supporter of the Stuart rather than the Hanoverian dynasty 13.37
jade derogatory term applied to a woman 248.22
jangle discordancy, mingled noise 247.11
japanned see note to 151.41
jaw-hole open entrance to a sewer 6.7, 6.32
jealous suspicious, apprehensive 105.23, 186.17, 293.9; for 224.1 see note
jet point, gist 257.11
jockey for 119.14 and 133.2 see note

to 119.14
jockies beggars, vagabonds 36.21
joe sweetheart 224.5
John's-wort see note to 14.41
jumpit jumped 129.15
kahn *German* rowing boat 189.6
kaim for 182.25 etc. see note to 182.25
kain see note to 27.14
keepit kept 13.39 etc.; for 174.1 see note
ken know 6.1 etc.
ken *thieves' cant* house 25.20 (see note to 25.19–20)
kenna know not 60.22
kend, kenn'd *past participle* known 64.4, 64.33, 139.18, 272.21
kenn'd, kend *past tense* knew 62.38 etc.
kettle pot for cooking and boiling water 52.7, 328.25; large pot of fish, as cooked on hunting expeditions etc. 138.27
kibe chapped or ulcerated chilblain 255.18
killogie kiln, furnace 34.19, 50.23, 294.6
Kilmarnock-cap see note to 175.35
kilt overturn, upset 34.26
kimmer female friend 338.43
kinchin *thieves' cant* child, kid 188.38, 188.41, 193.13
kinchin-mort *thieves' cant* beggar girl 148.27
kinder *German* children 295.7
kintra country 272.5
kipper cured salmon 29.3; male salmon during the spawning season 138.4
kirk church 13.26 etc.; for 174.1 see note
kirk-keeper one who attends church regularly 60.17
kist chest, box, trunk 129.22, 271.33, 296.13
kitt *thieves' cant* collection of personal effects, total possessions 191.31
kittle unreliable 120.40
knave-bairn male child 64.14, 121.29
knevel punch, pummel 129.17
knew knew how (to), understood the way (to) 219.28
knock beating 123.2
knockit knocked 309.39
knowe, know knoll, little hill 65.21 etc.
Kobold see note to 193.24
koind *Cumbrian* kind 118.11
lachesse see note to 33.18
lad-bairn male child 233.21, 285.41
lair learning, education 223.40
laird landlord of a landed estate, lord 6.16 etc.
lampit limpet 45.7
land-louper roving vagabond, thief 129.15, 271.30
land-shark one who preys on sailors when ashore, customs officer 188.37 (see also note to 25.17)
lang long 4.24 etc.
lang-lugged long-eared, eavesdropping 270.1
langsyne long ago 7.2
lanthorn lantern 187.31
lap *noun* see note to 148.30
lap *verb* wrap 145.1
lass girl, female 13.24 etc.
lassie young girl, female 206.2 etc.
latch mire, swampy place, or stream flowing through boggy ground 126.26 (see note), 126.43, 133.14
lea untilled ground usually covered in grass 40.19
led for 311.11 see note
leddy lady 6.18 etc.
lee lie, falsify 64.5
leg-bail see note to 15.16
legerdemain sleight of hand 36.37
levin lightning 144.43
Lexicon dictionary 11.24
lib-ken *thieves' cant* place to sleep in 264.37
lick wallop, hard blow 129.19
lifelich lifelike 181.28
life-rented see note to 198.1–2
lift *noun* sky 281.6
lift *verb* carry out (a corpse) for burial, start a funeral possession 215.43
ligature band, tie 220.10
light bright 55.42
like-wake, like wake vigil over a dead body, a wake 147.28, 329.6
limmer worthless creature, idle hussy 61.5, 270.1
links undulating open sandy ground near the shore 248.14
lippen trust, depend 122.34
lith end joint, tip 234.6
loan, loaning grassy track through

arable land or fields, open pathway 6.6, 6.13
loathly see note to 325.4–5
locked for 329.24 see note
locker see note to 181.43
lo'ed loved 281.20
loggerhead blockhead, stupid person 206.35
long-boat largest boat belonging to a sailing vessel 292.31
looby lout, clownish person 207.8
look look at, inspect 17.26, 303.7
loon fellow, young man, boy 6.12, 129.41
loop-hole narrow vertical opening cut into a wall or other defence 144.8, 164.21
loose set free 273.40
Looties for 71.19 and 261.21 see note to 71.19
lot object used for the purposes of divination 63.39
loup leap 59.12, 63.10, 149.27
low flame, fire 47.16 (see note), 55.42
lubberly loutish, clumsy, stupid 6.26
lucerne see note to 93.39–40
Luckenbooths see note to 201.43
luckie familar name for an elderly woman, more specifically for a midwife or the mistress of an ale-house 13.23 etc.; for 211.39 and 231.8 see notes
lucre gain, pecuniary advantage 83.8, 83.9
lug ear 129.17
lugger small sailing vessel 18.9 etc.
lunt burn, blaze 294.7
lust-haus see note to 191.35–36
macers for 353.43, 354.1, and 354.3 see note to 353.42–43
magnum bottle containing four pints (2.27 litres) of wine or spirits 214.17
main unmitigated, out and out 28.9
mains home farm, i.e. the principal farm of an estate 284.35 (see note)
main-sail principal sail of a ship 26.27, 48.5
main-yard beam on which the mainsail is extended 56.25
mair more 15.15 etc.
maist most 62.21 etc.
maister master 174.3, 177.37
majority rank of major 111.28
mak make 175.28, 272.3
make interfere 46.42 (see note), 123.37, 145.29, 193.27
malefica *Latin* evil doer 279.40
malignant for 8.23 and 8.25 see note to 8.22–23
Malobathro see note to 200.19
Manks from the Isle of Man 26.26 (see note), 179.30
manna, maunna mustn't 122.24, 178.12, 329.19
mantle *heraldry* ornamental surrounds of an escutcheon granted for achievement 252.1
maranatha see note to 196.2
march *noun* boundary 207.12 (see note) etc.
march *verb* border upon, adjoin 207.13, 207.18
mark coin worth 13*s.* 4*d* Scots, 1*s.* 1⅓*d.* (5½p) sterling 264.19
marl limy clay 55.10
maroon for 40.13 and 41.26 see note to 40.13
Martinmas, Martimas 11 November, a Scottish quarter-day 41.35 (see note) etc.
massy solid, weighty, bulky 73.13, 138.31, 266.19, 269.13
matriculate *heraldry* to record (arms) in an official register 252.4
mattins morning service 333.24 (see note)
maud checked plaid or wrap worn by shepherds 133.1
maun must 5.34 etc.
maunder grumble 112.36
maunna see **manna**
meeting-house dissenting place of worship 211.20 (see note to 211.20–21)
meikle see **mickle**
mein heer see **Mynheer**
memorial *Scots law* statement to an advocate setting out a legal problem for his opinion and advice 206.39 etc.
mendicant beggar 34.4, 38.2; begging, beggar-like 33.18, 148.13
mere lake 112.35
messan cur, mongrel 83.13
mickle, muckle, meikle big, large 6.13 etc; much 15.11 etc.; for 179.9 and 274.20 see note to 179.9
milch-cow cow giving milk or kept for milking 132.20
mill *thieves' cant* murder, kill 148.29

(see note)
mill-wear mill-weir, mill-dam 136.25
minatory threatening 38.29
mind remember 63.4 etc.
mirk dark, black 34.14, 60.42
misprision contempt, neglect 16.26
mista'en mistaken 177.20
mither mother 307.38
moidore see note to 69.21
moiety half, portion 8.36
mon *Cumbrian* man 112.31, 112.36
Monanday see notes to 34.14–15 and 175.3–4
monitoire see note to 231.17
mony many 4.12 etc.
moonshie see note to 244.30
moor-fowl red grouse 120.14, 234.23
moot discuss, dispute 322.26 (see note)
morally by virtue of evidence probable though not demonstrative 234.7, 339.26
morass bog, marsh 3.23 etc.
morn morrow, tomorrow 62.9 etc.
mortification see notes to 221.22 and 221.25
mortmain see note to 221.22
moss bog, moor 3.28 etc.
moss-trooper see note to 272.19
mote mound 274.3 (see note)
mould earth of the grave 328.38
moveable see note to 10.12–13
muckle see **mickle**
mullion vertical bar dividing the lights in a window 23.1
murther murder 57.35, 57.36
Muscovado raw or unrefined sugar 28.41
mutchkin measure equalling a quarter of a Scots pint or three-quarters of an imperial pint (0.43 litres) 45.3, 122.20
Mynheer, mein heer *Dutch* Sir 181.26 etc.
myrmidons contemptuous term for inferior officers of the law 185.40
mysell myself 7.4 etc.
na not 6.1 etc.; no 6.22 etc.
nabob one returned from India with a large fortune acquired there 81.32, 102.26; nawab, native Indian ruler 135.33 (see note)
nae no 10.33 etc.; not 40.35 etc.
naebody nobody, anybody 6.15 etc.
naething nothing 34.12 etc.
naig horse 340.20
nane none 15.36 etc.
Nantz brandy 47.36 (see note)
napery linen 266.25
nathless nevertheless 79.37
native *astrology* subject of a nativity or horoscope 20.21, 20.31
nativity birth considered astrologically, horoscope 16.1 etc.
needful see note to 322.17–18
needna needn't 6.22, 7.3, 265.16, 272.21
ne'er-do-weel good for nothing 233.20
neighbour-like friendly, sociable 223.40, 264.32
nein *German* no 188.41 etc.
nice particular, fastidious 10.33 (see note) etc.
niffer haggle, bargain 179.24
niff-naffy trifling, finicky 267.1
nine-hours see note to 232.28
no not 4.16 etc.
noa *Cumbrian* no 112.38, 112.38
non-juring see note to 217.39–40
nor than 120.13, 176.43
north-easter wind blowing from the north east 148.22
o' of 4.12 etc.
occasions affairs, business 49.4
odd God 208.3 etc.
odd-come-shortly some day or other in the near future 149.38
ofter more frequently, oftener 148.34
on't on it 68.23, 178.13
ony any 5.41 etc.
oop join, bind 24.17
or before 47.14 etc.
oracular of the nature of an oracle, portentous 16.30, 41.28
ordnance artillery, cannon 230.2, 230.8
orra for 47.9 and 133.22 see note to 47.8–9
ostler man who attends horses at an inn 61.10 etc.
o't of it 121.10 etc.
oursells ourselves 177.16, 223.13, 223.40, 296.14
out in arms against the Hanoverian government (here in 1715) 9.20, 13.37
outcast quarrel 270.39

outer-house see note to 232.27
ow, ou *exclamation* oh 5.33 etc.
ower over 13.20 etc.
pagoda temple 123.23
paiks see note to 138.40
palanquin covered litter 71.25
palfrey saddle-horse for ordinary riding 30.15, 126.8
Pandaemonium for 137.17 and 203.32 see note to 137.17
pannel see note to 148.30
pannier basket 148.32
papistrie papistry, popery 34.24
paria for 37.1 and 38.17 see note to 37.1
parridge porridge 15.22
partizan adherent, supporter 19.35, 31.31, 295.18
passant *heraldry* walking, looking to the right and with the right fore paw raised 266.23
patten wooden shoe, overshoe 68.24
peat-hag hole or pit left by an old peat working 129.16
peculium see note to 86.39
peenging whining, complaining 233.19
penny-stane round flat stone used in the game of quoits 64.29
periapt something worn about the person as a charm 29.29
petar' military explosive device used to blow in doors etc. 255.26
peter *thieves' cant* portmanteau, travelling-bag 150.5
phantasmagoria shifting series of phantasms or imaginary figures 183.37
pharisaical resembling the pharisees in assuming an outward show of spiritual pride and superiority 212.43
piano softened low tone 220.29
picker thief, especially of small things 33.8
pickery *Scots law* petty theft 254.10
pickle few 271.34
pike pick 238.13
pinchbeck see note to 166.8–9
pineal see note to 228.5
pinners two long flaps, one down either side of the face, of a woman's head-dress 47.13 (see note)
pirn weaver's spool for holding weft yarn in the shuttle 140.37
pit, pitt put 47.12, 341.15; for 271.4 see note to 271.4–5
pith strength, mettle 137.32
pitted opposed 288.25
plagium see note to 346.32
plaid long rectangle of twilled woollen cloth worn as an outer garment 133.2, 140.32
plaister plaster 127.20, 130.10
plash splash about 13.31
plough-gate see note to 27.43
pock bag, small sack 238.17
pockmanky portmanteau, travelling-bag 273.5
poind seize, impound 39.9 (see note to 39.9–10)
polyglot book in several languages, especially a bible 109.38
poppling bubbling, rippling 328.31
portfolio receptacle for keeping loose sheets of paper etc. 68.27 etc.
portmanteau travelling-bag, clothes bag 150.6, 150.16, 150.23, 258.11
poschay post-chaise 177.26
post travel with haste, especially with relays of horses 31.25, 31.30
post-cattle post-horses 61.2
post-chaise travelling carriage either hired from stage to stage or drawn by horses so hired 74.42 etc.
post-chariot light four-wheeled carriage having a driver's seat in front 200.7, 322.21
post-horse horse hired by the stage 33.29
postillion post boy, rider of one of the horses drawing a carriage when there is no driver on the box 62.7 etc.
post-nati see note to 354.35
post-town town having a head post-office 87.12, 239.40 (see note to 239.39–40)
potatoe-bogle scarecrow 41.22
pow head 11.13, 127.26
powder-monkey boy employed on a ship to carry gunpowder from the powder room to the guns 321.40
poy-crust *Cumbrian* pie crust 112.36
preceese precise 63.36
precentor official appointed to lead the singing in a church congregation 59.41 etc.
preceptor tutor 84.31, 86.9
precognition see note to 53.20
premises (the) aforesaid, what has

been previously mentioned 221.13
prepense see note to 32.16
press crowd, throng 203.4, 295.9
press-gang body of sailors empowered to force men into the navy 40.27
pretermit omit, neglect 314.36
prig plead 337.19
prime in prime order, excellently 134.2
prin pin 133.41, 202.16
probation trial, examination 320.11
probationer see note to 12.4
process legal action 231.37
proper *heraldry* represented in natural colouring 244.18
prosing dull, tedious 12.39
protegée *French* female under the protection and guidance of another person 85.20
public inn, hostelry 120.31 (see note)
puir poor 10.27 etc.
puncheon large cask for liquids 28.41
pund pounds 272.9
pu'pit pulpit 11.13
putten put 269.36
quartern quarter pint 179.32
quarters limbs 309.40 (see note to 309.39–40)
quartile see note to 17.16–17
quaternion four things grouped together 250.13 (see note)
quean impudent woman 122.32
quicksilver mercury 132.36
quiz practical joke, hoax 16.9 (see note to 16.8–9)
quo' said 271.6 etc.
quondam former 252.17
quorum see note to 42.4
rade rode 6.17, 271.24
rally assail with banter, make fun 94.1
rampauge rampage, rage furiously 65.41
randle-tree horizontal bar across a chimney for hanging pots, hence a thin pole-like person 141.30
randy rough, loud-mouthed, aggressive 63.17 etc.
range search widely 272.11
Ranger see note to 47.40
rape rope 65.33, 303.34 (see note)
rappee coarse snuff 218.36
rasp-house house of correction in Holland or Germany where prisoners were employed in rasping (i.e. filing, grating) wood 191.8
red-coat soldier of the British army 191.9, 192.16, 331.30
redd save, rescue 325.30
redding see note to 145.30
reek smoke 34.19 etc.
reif robbery 15.4
reise branch, twig 44.25
reist cure by drying or smoking 138.5
rencontre chance meeting, encounter 172.39
rent-roll register of rents and the income generated by them 7.36, 68.6
repeater clock or watch which strikes the last hour or quarter when required 215.30
residence for 101.11 see note
residenters residents, inhabitants 195.40
resolutioner see note to 8.23
restaurateur *French* keeper of a restaurant 301.20 (see note)
resurrection-women female corpse-stealers 346.34
retainer retaining fee 341.35
retour return, send in 353.42 (see note to 353.42–43)
riding-officer see note to 42.8
rifle-gun fire-arm with a spirally grooved bore 163.24
rig, rigg ridge, hill crest, extent of land 207.13, 216.15, 224.7
rig-about see note to 191.33
rin run 139.22 etc.
ripe search thoroughly 272.11
rive tear, wrench 34.20, 44.10
roll for 13.39, 28.5, and 196.20 see notes
roll-about podgy, roly-poly 140.22
rood measure of land, 1 rood = 0.12 hectares 28.26; for 6.36 see note to 6.36–37
roof-tree main beam or ridge-pole of a roof 44.11, 51.37
rotten rat 120.1
roturier *French* commoner 252.39
roughies withered boughs or splinters, especially ones used for a torch or fire 138.42, 331.25
round-eared having round ears or ear-like appendages 203.36
roup sale by public auction 121.17, 121.18
roupit sold by public auction 62.10, 67.39

rouse carousal, bout of drinking 187.39
rout snore 6.11
royals see note to 26.27
rubbit robbed 121.6
rubrick passage written in red or otherwise distinguished in lettering 38.34
ruckle rattle or gurgle in the throat 145.41
ruffled adorned with ruffles, frilly 175.19
running racing 222.27 (see note)
rupee monetary unit of India 354.31 (see note)
rush-light candle made by dipping a rush in tallow or other grease 6.27
rusty ill-tempered, cross 149.33
sack general name for a class of white wine from Spain and the Canaries 200.2
sackless innocent 174.5
sack-whey beverage made from white wine and milk used as a preventative against colds 98.32
sae so 15.34 etc.
safe save 66.30, 140.10, 271.22
saft wet, damp 126.27
sain bless 14.10
sair sorrowful, grievous 52.27 etc.; grievously 62.16 etc.; sore 121.4, 274.2, 281.15
salam oriental act of obeisance 100.14
salmon for 193.12 see note
salvage *heraldry* human figure naked or enveloped in foliage 244.18
samyn same 67.23
sang song 14.16 etc.
sap simpleton 293.6
sapperment *oath* sacrament; for 180.22, 189.11, 189.26, and 189.39 see note to 180.22
sárk woman's shift or chemise 13.26 (see note to 13.26–27); shirt 175.20, 274.2
Saturnalia, Saturnalian for 354.2 and 354.15 see note to 354.2
saturnine gloomy 16.15
saugh willow 122.15, 122.17, 122.18, 328.29
saul soul, spirit, mettle 279.43
saulies hired mourners at a funeral 216.21
saut salt 219.19
saw saying, maxim 30.26
sax six 311.8
saxpence sixpence 34.26, 122.20
scaff-raff riff-raff 133.15
scale, scale-stair for 202.6 and 213.23 see note to 202.6
scart scratch 127.26
scauding scalding 280.1
scaur see note to 134.3
sceleratissima *Latin* most accursed one 280.14
scelestissima see notes to 278.15–16 and 279.36
scented detected, caught the scent 149.3
schnaps type of Hollands gin, or a dram of the same 25.37, 192.39
scholiast ancient commentator on texts, (more loosely) medieval schoolman 228.6
scite site 242.22, 353.24
scour *thieves' cant* wear 124.6 (see note), 148.33
scout reject with scorn, deride 223.21
screed for 133.21 and 274.13 see note to 133.21–22
scruple for 39.15 see note
sea-mew seagull 38.1
sea-room space at sea in which a ship can be manoeuvred easily 48.12, 48.41
sea-ware seaweed washed up on the shore and suitable for manure 76.19
second-head see note to 222.21
secretary one entrusted or familiar with secret matters 90.13
sederunt see note to 310.8
seignories feudal territories 26.11
sell self 140.23
selled, sell'd sold 121.24, 121.25, 233.17, 233.22
semiuncial see note to 298.38
semple, simple commoner, low-born 6.2 (see note), 202.42, 202.43
seneschal steward 205.36
sequestered retired, secluded 22.17, 263.31, 330.5
sequestrated see note to 8.22–23
settlement for 197.39 etc. see note to 197.39
sextile see note to 17.16–17
shade shelter, protection from the elements 119.3, 119.5, 119.15, 287.7
shake-rag ragged, disreputable 141.25
shand counterfeit, base coin 178.14

shangie see collie-shangie
shark *thieves' cant* customs officer 25.17 (see note), 164.39
sharp *thieves' cant* acute, keen-witted 264.14, 264.15
shealing, sheeling hut or rude shelter 37.17 etc.
shear cleave, divide 207.19 (see note to 207.18–19)
shellicoat see note to 243.7
sheriff-depute, sheriff depute for 53.9, 68.10, and 72.41 see note to 53.9
sheriff-substitute, sheriff substitute for 68.7 etc. see note to 68.7
shirk evade 210.26
shirra sheriff 269.37
shoeing-horn see note to 131.30–31
shoon shoes 175.3, 215.32, 265.5, 272.16
short-dated see note to 27.10
shotted loaded with shot or ball as well as powder 56.32
shouther shoulder 269.36
shuttle small drawer or box in a chest 217.36
sib related by blood, kin 176.42, 223.13
sick, sic such 4.15 etc.; for 28.15 see note
sicken such 120.9, 120.10
sicklike suchlike, similar 28.15 (see note)
significator see note to 20.18
siller silver, money 28.14 etc.
silver-cooper see note to 192.20
simmer summer 328.30
single-stick fighting with a stick requiring only one hand 208.5
sizes assizes, county court 112.32
skean thread that is ravelled or tangled up 231.15
skiff small light boat 94.28 etc.
skit trick, hoax 174.14, 174.15
skyscrapers see note to 26.27
slack *noun* boggy hollow 126.11, 132.32
slack *verb* loosen, relax 285.20
slap gap, breach 6.35
slasher sword 179.41
sleepry inclined to sleep 13.21
slings *nautical* the middle part of the yard 48.5, 56.25
slip *noun* leash for a dog 135.11
slip *verb* release 135.4, 135.25
slounging lounging, skulking 179.34
sma' small 62.23 etc.
smack loud kiss 129.10
smaik rogue, rascal 141.27
snaw snow 233.41, 273.6
sniggle snigger, snicker 319.2
soi-disant self-styled 26.6
souchong fine variety of Chinese black tea 25.32
sound test, probe 349.27
soup sup, small amount 47.10
souple *adjective* supple, wily 64.39
souple *noun* stout stick 133.14
spae predict, foretell 15.39, 15.41, 149.1
spaeings prophecies 273.17
spae-wark prophesying 64.37
span-counter see note to 69.21
spavin disease of horses leading to lameness through leg tumours 64.41
spaw-well spa-well 233.24
speer, speir ask 6.1, 122.23, 122.24, 179.37
spill small gift, tip 192.43
spleuchan pouch 311.2
splore quarrel, commotion 311.17
sport force open 293.5
sprig specimen 217.9; stripling 327.19
spring lively tune accompanying a dance 207.6 (see note)
springe snare 17.6
spring-gun gun set to go off like a trap and used to deter trespassers 38.33, 98.24
sprug sparrow 65.27
spunk spark 61.11
sputter bustling confusion, explosive noise 6.37
squeak *thieves' cant* turn informer, squeal 193.10
squoire *Cumbrian* squire 112.32, 112.36
stage division of a journey 142.14; place at which rest or food are taken on a journey 270.10
stamp trap 38.33
stancheon, stauncheon stanchion, iron window-bar 182.14, 185.4, 265.37
standish inkstand 232.19
stane stone 66.1, 207.16, 273.2
start[1] discharge 47.36
start[2] desert, withdraw on a promise 149.41, 193.12

start[3] drive from its lair 255.4 (see note)
States States-General of the Netherlands, Dutch Parliament 189.40 (see note)
station for 112.38 see note
staved broken, burst 57.24
steek *noun* stitch in sewing or knitting 199.17
steek *verb* shut, make fast 270.22
steer, stir disturb, molest 15.36, 120.42
stell still for making whisky 45.5
stern-chaser gun belonging to stern of a ship 47.34
stibbler probationer in the Presbyterian church who has not been called to a regular charge 278.24
stickit halted in the chosen profession 12.12 (see note), 278.24
stir see **steer**
stirk young bullock 44.12
stirrup-cup, stirrup dram parting drink taken on horseback 122.25, 122.36
stirrup-iron metal portion of a stirrup 7.33
stiver small coin of little value from the Netherlands 191.28, 352.2
stock instrument of punishment, consisting of a heavy frame with holes for confining the ankles 327.38
stock-buckle buckle used to secure a neck-cloth or cravat 211.10
stocking livestock and farm implements 67.38, 121.17
stoor rough, grim 233.29
stoppit stopped 121.18
store-farmer for 119.34 and 128.26 see note to 119.34
stot stoat 120.2
stoup drinking-vessel 45.3, 273.7 (see note)
stow *thieves' cant* cease speaking 25.19 (see note to 25.19–20)
stown stolen 63.17
strae straw 264.42, 340.18
strait straighten, lay out 146.18
strammel *thieves' cant* straw 148.35
strap hang 181.36
straught straight 176.18
strave strove, struggled 330.19
streek, streak lay out 147.11, 272.33, 272.38, 329.5
striek stretch, pull 64.23
strippit stripped 264.18
stump walk heavily 287.9
sturm *German* storm 333.24, 334.1, 350.27
sturm-wetter, sturm wetter *German* storm weather 190.7, 191.19, 191.34, 350.27
subaltern commissioned army officer below the rank of captain 114.36
sugar-plum sweet made of boiled sugar 34.6
suld should 174.12 etc.
sum summarise, epitomise 352.29
sune soon 266.32, 281.17, 328.20
sunkets dainties, tit-bits 44.15
sunkie little seat 122.17, 122.18
superiorities the rights of the superior of a feudal estate 32.3 (see note to 32.2)
supervisor for 42.8 etc. see note to 42.8
supple soften, make compliant 341.37
supporters *heraldry* figures standing either side of a shield and supporting it 244.17
survey for 112.38 see note
swear difficult, unwilling 120.37
swell *slang* person of good social position, 'toff' 263.6
switch-whip slender riding-whip 222.22
sybil prophetess, female fortune-teller 23.20 etc.; for 299.10 see note
symposion *Greek* meeting over food or drink for intellectual conversation and discussion 227.34
syne ago 60.30 etc.
syren see note to 292.3
ta the 203.7, 203.7, 203.8, 203.16
tack *nautical* course of movement obliquely opposed to the direction of the wind 48.11, 56.28
ta'en taken 6.19 etc.
tailzie *Scots law* entail 310.17, 311.31
tait small tuft or bundle 140.35
tak take 175.26 etc.
talisman charm, object with magical powers 18.35, 92.4
tangle longer varieties of coarse seaweed 186.23
tap top 133.20, 207.13, 207.18, 273.2
tappit crested, tufted 232.12 (see note)
tarry wait for, stay for 43.5, 83.39; wait 80.10; linger, delay 106.21

tars sailors 227.27
tass cup, goblet 15.8
tat that 203.6, 203.7, 203.7, 203.16
tauld told 176.43 etc.
tausend *German* thousand 24.22 etc.
teind tithe 225.33 (see note)
tell'd told 64.13 etc.
tent care, attention 6.6
term-day see note to 41.35
testator one who has died leaving a will 220.22
testatrix female leaver of a will 220.38
tester canopy over a bed 266.7
tête-à-tête *French* private conversation between two persons 84.39, 297.28
thack thatch 44.10, 303.34 (see note)
thae those, these 121.31 etc.
than then 5.29 etc.
thegither together 205.20 etc.
themsells themselves 112.39
the-night tonight 61.39
therebye thereabouts 62.34
thewes muscles 133.5
thir these 265.8
thorough-paced accomplished, complete 299.23
thrapple throat, throttle 5.29
thread-papers strips of paper folded to make divisions for different skeins of thread 69.22
threep *noun* strongly held belief, superstition 272.40
threep *verb* argue, contend 207.34, 328.1
thrissle, thristle, thistle 15.20, 45.2
tiff small quantity of liquor 60.36
till to 13.26, 233.34, 306.21
till't to it 83.41, 224.4
timber unmusical, wooden 14.22
tippeny see two-penny
tod fox 44.19 etc.; for 139.20 and 270.42 see note to 139.20–21
tolbooth prison 15.14, 262.15
toom empty 45.3
top-gallant see note to 26.27
topknot knot or bow of ribbon worn on the top of the head 131.19
tould *Cumbrian* told 112.34
tour *thieves' cant* look about 149.2 (see note)
tow rope, cord 65.33
town a farm and the buildings immediately surrounding it 128.3
tract expanse of land 3.23, 124.9, 124.17; track 117.16
trafficking dealing, trading 29.28
travail labour and pain of child-birth 209.36
trefoil see note to 14.41
trench encroach, infringe 100.24
trencher plate 36.25, 119.26, 146.20
trencher-man hearty eater 329.14
triad group of three associated things 250.13 (see note), 354.43
trials series of examinations prescribed by a Presbytery for a candidate to become a preacher after he has completed theological training 105.20
trindling trundling, rolling 296.13
trine *astrology* see note to 17.16–17
trine *thieves' cant* go, step 148.34 (see note)
triplicities see note to 16.2
triton see note to 292.1
trocking dealing 63.43
tron see note to 201.29
troth *exclamation* truth 5.39 etc.
trow believe, think 14.37 etc.
truckle see note to 352.9
tryst meeting, rendezvous 9.36, 133.24
trysting-tree see note to 15.37
tuilzie quarrel, fight 174.11
tumbled for 212.17 see note
tumbler small cart 42.22
tup ram 203.6
turband turban, Indian head-dress 159.10
turnpike toll road 39.11, 112.15, 284.28, 285.5
twa two 6.18 etc.
twascore forty 60.28
twasome pair, couple 336.17
tweel strong twilled woollen cloth 140.36
two-penny, twopenny, tippeny weak ale or beer sold at two pence the Scots pint 6.18, 34.28, 60.6, 231.21
t'ye to you 122.20
tyke dog, cur 15.36, 140.8, 337.43
umquhile, umwhile sometime, formerly 16.28, 337.15
un him 112.38, 118.11, 192.32
unaccording not accordant, not in agreement or harmony 293.17
uncial see note to 298.38
unco very, remarkably 4.24, 207.41;

great, unusual 62.36 etc; strange 327.39
unco-like strange, unbefitting 271.29
unction appreciation, enjoyment 88.32
understrapper underling, subordinate 172.33, 327.23
unlawfu' unlawful 278.38
unmeaning vacant, expressionless 52.23, 209.7
unsurmountable incapable of being overcome, insurmountable 91.32
uphad, uphaud affirm, warrant 177.23, 272.31
up-putting lodging, accommodation 49.27
upright *thieves' cant* big, sturdy 148.31 (see note)
vaticinations prophecies 285.15
vera very 238.11, 238.16
vervain see note to 14.41
victual grain 27.17; for 37.32 see note to 37.31–32
violoncello bass violin 300.3
vulnerary having healing properties 130.8
wa' wall 47.7, 122.12, 286.11, 328.35
wad, wald would 10.26 etc.
wad wager, bet 177.26
wadded wed, married 13.28
wadna wouldn't 60.10 etc.
waesome woeful, sorrowful 121.37, 121.37
waf good-for-nothing, insignificant 233.26
wag shake 11.13
wald see wad
wale best, pick 338.39
walise valise, travelling case or portmanteau suitable for strapping to a saddle 122.5
wall-eye an eye in which the colour of the iris is pale or the white part unusually large 195.1
wame belly 264.18
wand stick or staff 78.28, 281.15 (see note), 289.34
ware[1] beware, look out 18.11 (see note to 18.11–12)
ware[2] spend, waste 141.37
wark work, fuss, business 175.12 etc.; for 63.13 and 207.12 see notes
warld world 121.36, 122.21, 215.17, 328.36
warlock wizard, male witch 64.22, 64.32, 294.9
warrant bet, be sure, guarantee 6.2 (see note) etc.
warse worse 65.22, 66.21, 83.13
waste for 120.36 etc. see note to 120.35–36
waster fishing spear with several prongs 136.18 (see note), 137.31, 137.31, 139.24
watch-light night light, slow-burning candle 90.1
water-kelpy see note to 137.8
water-spout violent fall of rain 125.5
waur worse 29.28 etc.
wean child 15.39
wear *nautical* come round by turning the head away from the wind 48.10
wear last, hold out 131.26
weary wearisome, dispiriting, hard to endure 4.24 etc.
wedder wether, castrated ram 131.6
weel well 6.14 etc.; for 223.39 see note
weel-faur'd well-favoured, handsome 64.33
weeper see note to 216.27
weir war 15.4
weird destiny, fate 233.39 etc.
weize aim, shoot 177.24
well-looked good-looking 128.17
wessel westward 6.6, 6.8
wetter *German* weather 190.3 (see note) etc.
wha who 14.36 etc.
whae's who is 240.32
whan when 273.14, 280.40
whaten what kind of, what sort of 338.12
whids *thieves' cant* words 25.19 (see note to 25.19–20)
whig move at a steady pace, jog along 129.15
whiles sometimes, from time to time 34.17 etc.
whilk which 174.1, 222.5
whin few 15.12, 47.8, 122.11, 133.25
whinger short sword 58.39
whisht hush! be quiet! 64.25 etc.
whistle turn informer 179.31
whiting white-wash 202.24 (see note to 202.24–26)
whittret weasel 126.6
whoy *Cumbrian* why 112.31
wi' with 5.30 etc.; for 207.34 see note
wicket small gate 6.38
wight person 324.34

willfu' wilful, stubborn 274.4
win get 24.18, 274.19
wind-sturm *German* whirlwind 192.21
wine-cooler container in which wine can be immersed in iced water 75.31
winna won't 208.13 etc.
winsome pleasant, charming 60.18
wis know, believe 82.13
wi't with it 24.18
withershins for 126.26 and 133.14 see note to 126.26
witter barb of a fishing spear 138.41
woo' wool 140.35, 141.33
woodie gallows rope 148.40
wool-gathering see note to 282.25
worm[1] extract the 'worm' or lytta from the tongue of a dog (supposed to be a safeguard against madness) 37.26
worm[2] pry, spy 343.41
worriecow, worricow hobgoblin, demon 14.37; person fearful in appearance 278.43
wot know 62.35, 331.26
wow wow! gee! 60.29, 129.7, 269.28
wraith spectral appearance of a living person 58.20
wrang wrong 63.22 etc.
wreathed *heraldry* encircled with a twisted band or wreath 244.19
writer lawyer, solicitor 31.34 etc.
wuss wish 243.10, 269.37
wyte blame 274.6
ya, yaw *German and Dutch* yes 181.26 etc.
yaffing barking, yelping 5.30
yard *nautical* long beam on a mast for spreading sails 48.5
yards for 11.21 see note
yaud see note to 292.15
yawl small sailing or rowing boat 48.19
ye you 4.11 etc.
year-aulds yearlings 5.40
yoke engage in dispute, join battle 207.42
yont yonder, over there 15.9
younker youngster 189.38 etc.
yoursell, yoursel yourself 47.5 etc.
Yule Christmastide 205.22
zounds *oath* by God's wounds 181.37, 207.38, 238.9

JONATHAN SWIFT

Gulliver's Travels

'I felt something alive moving on my left Leg . . . when bending my Eyes downwards as much as I could, I perceived it to be a human Creature not six Inches high'

Shipwrecked and cast adrift, Lemuel Gulliver wakes to find himself on Lilliput, an island inhabited by little people, whose height makes their quarrels over fashion and fame seem ridiculous. His subsequent encounters – with the crude giants of Brobdingnag, the philosophical Houyhnhnms and the brutish Yahoos – give Gulliver new, bitter insights into human behaviour. Swift's savage satire views mankind in a distorted hall of mirrors as a diminished, magnified and finally bestial species, presenting us with an uncompromising reflection of ourselves.

This text, based on the first edition of 1726, reproduces all its original illustrations and includes an introduction by Robert Demaria, Jr, which discusses the ways *Gulliver's Travels* has been interpreted since its first publication.

'A masterwork of irony . . . that contains both a dark and bitter meaning and a joyous, extraordinary creativity of imagination. That is why it has lived for so long' MALCOLM BRADBURY

Edited with an introduction and notes by
ROBERT DEMARIA, JR

DANIEL DEFOE

A Journal of the Plague Year

'It was a most surprising thing, to see those Streets, which were usually so thronged, now grown desolate'

In 1665 the Great Plague swept through London, claiming nearly 100,000 lives. In *A Journal*, written nearly sixty years later, Defoe vividly chronicled the progress of the epidemic. We follow his fictional narrator through a city transformed: the streets and alleyways deserted; the houses of death with crosses daubed on their doors; the dead-carts on their way to the pits. And he recounts the horrifying stories of the citizens he encounters, as fear, isolation and hysteria take hold. *A Journal* is both a fascinating historical document and a supreme work of imaginative reconstruction.

This edition, based on the original 1722 text, contains a new introduction, an appendix on the plague, a topographical index and maps of contemporary London, and includes Anthony Burgess's original introduction.

'The most reliable and comprehensive account of the Great Plague that we possess' ANTHONY BURGESS

'Within the texture of Defoe's prose London becomes a living and suffering being' PETER ACKROYD

Edited with an introduction and notes by CYNTHIA WALL

DANIEL DEFOE

Robinson Crusoe

'A raging wave, mountain-like, came rowling a-stern of us . . . we were all swallowed up in a moment'

The sole survivor of a shipwreck, Robinson Crusoe is washed up on a desert island. In his journal he chronicles his daily battle to stay alive, as he conquers isolation, fashions shelter and clothes, first encounters another human being and fights off cannibals and mutineers. With *Robinson Crusoe*, Defoe wrote what is regarded as the first English novel, and created one of the most popular and enduring myths in literature. Written in an age of exploration and enterprise, it has been variously interpreted as an embodiment of British imperialist values, as a portrayal of 'natural man' or as a moral fable. But above all it is a brilliant narrative, depicting Crusoe's transformation from terrified survivor to self-sufficient master of his island.

This edition contains a full chronology of Defoe's life and times, explanatory notes, glossary and a critical introduction discussing Robinson Crusoe as a pioneering work of modern psychological realism.

'*Robinson Crusoe* has a universal appeal, a story that goes right to the core of existence' SIMON ARMITAGE

Edited with an introduction and notes by JOHN RICHETTI

GEORGE ELIOT

Silas Marner

'God gave her to me because you turned your back upon her, and He looks upon her as mine: you've no right to her!'

Wrongly accused of theft and exiled from a religious community many years before, the embittered weaver Silas Marner lives alone in Raveloe, living only for work and his precious hoard of money. But when his money is stolen and an orphaned child finds her way into his house, Silas is given the chance to transform his life. His fate, and that of the little girl he adopts, is entwined with Godfrey Cass, son of the village Squire, who, like Silas, is trapped by his past. *Silas Marner*, George Eliot's favourite of her novels, combines humour, rich symbolism and pointed social criticism to create an unsentimental but affectionate portrait of rural life.

The text uses the Cabinet edition, revised by George Eliot in 1878. David Carroll's introduction is accompanied by the original Penguin Classics introduction by Q. D. Leavis.

Edited with an introduction by DAVID CARROLL

GEORGE ELIOT

Middlemarch

'People are almost always better than their neighbours think they are'

George Eliot's most ambitious novel is a masterly evocation of diverse lives and changing fortunes in a provincial community. Peopling its landscape are Dorothea Brooke, a young idealist whose search for intellectual fulfilment leads her into a disastrous marriage to the pedantic scholar Casaubon; the charming but tactless Dr Lydgate, whose pioneering medical methods, combined with an imprudent marriage to the spendthrift beauty Rosamond, threaten to undermine his career; and the religious hypocrite Bulstrode, hiding scandalous crimes from his past. As their stories entwine, George Eliot creates a richly nuanced and moving drama, hailed by Virginia Woolf as 'one of the few English novels written for grown-up people'.

This edition uses the text of the second edition of 1874. In her introduction, Rosemary Ashton, biographer of George Eliot, discusses themes of change in *Middlemarch*, and examines the novel as an imaginative embodiment of Eliot's humanist beliefs.

'The most profound, wise and absorbing of English novels ... and, above all, truthful and forgiving about human behaviour' HERMIONE LEE

Edited with an introduction and notes by ROSEMARY ASHTON

ANTHONY TROLLOPE

Phineas Redux

'He had given up everything in the world with the view of getting into office; and now that the opportunity had come . . . the prize was to elude his grasp!'

Phineas Finn is living quietly in Dublin, resigned to the fact that his political career is over and coming to terms with the death of his wife, when he receives an unexpected invitation to return to Parliament. He jumps at the chance and old romances and rivalries are revived. When his adversary Mr Bonteen is murdered suspicion immediately falls on Finn, and even the friends and lovers who formerly advanced him seem only to add to his shame. The fourth novel in the Palliser series, *Phineas Redux* stands alone as a compelling work of political intrigue, personal crisis and romantic jealousy.

In his introduction, Gregg A. Hecimovich relates the political and historical background of the time to the Phineas novels. This edition also contains a detailed chronology, further reading and notes.

'We have come to believe that his style of writing was certainly the best (and probably the only) way of constructing a political novel' ROY HATTERSLEY, *Guardian*

Edited with an introduction and notes by
GREGG A. HECIMOVICH